FUNDAMENTALS OF BIOLOGY

PARTS 1-3

PENNY REID

FUNDAMENTALS OF BIOLOGY

PARTS 1-3

PENNY REID

HTTP://WWW.PENNYREID.NINJA/NEWSLETTER/

Made in the United States of America

Print Edition

ISBN: 978-1-960342-64-5

DEDICATION

For all the science deniers. I honestly wouldn't have felt compelled to write this book without you.

CONTENT WARNINGS

If you are a science denier, you don't want to read this book. Even though it was written because you exist, you'll likely feel personally attacked and offended by it.

Other content that may be concerning includes: discussion of the manosphere, mRNA vaccines, billionaires, revenge, adoption, bankruptcy, cancer, fraud, violence/assault, racism, using food as a coping mechanism, and insomnia, sleepwalking, and other sleep disorders.

[PART 1]

INHERITANCE

[1]

THE COMPOSITION AND CHEMISTRY OF LIFE

Samantha

I opened the piece of mail in my hand and discovered it was a wedding invitation. To my own wedding.

Wait. Let me back up for a second.

It was just after midnight and I'd walked home from the lab, ducking under awnings and construction scaffolding and thinking that New York City must manufacture wind for the sole purpose of making my life difficult. Kaitlyn, my former roommate from undergrad and the only person who would pick up my call at this hour, kept me company as I dodged puddles. Collectively we were dissecting whether or not the TV show *Friends* had ever actually been funny.

"It's not that I think Chandler wasn't funny," Kaitlyn said, and I could hear the telltale babbling of her baby in the background as I unlocked the three dead bolts of my front door, "but he definitely pioneered the whole 'man-child who can't communicate with women' genre. And I resent him for that."

"Are you suggesting," I said, twisting my wrist, "that sitcoms bear some responsibility for Martin's emotional constipation?" Martin Sandeke was her husband and basically a bully to everyone but her as far as I was concerned.

She snorted. "Martin's emotional constipation was definitely present in utero. Don't slander Chandler Bing like that."

"You named your baby after a sitcom character, and you expect me to not make the connection."

3

Kaitlyn paused, possibly switching boobs, possibly weighing the threat of my mockery. "We named him Joey because it was the only name we both didn't hate. And Joey is short for Joseph, which is a perfectly reasonable name. If you don't like the name, that's on you, Sam. You never suggested anything better."

I had, in fact, suggested at least a dozen better names, including but not limited to: Bartholomew, Snape, and Dr. Indiana Jones. Kaitlyn had summarily rejected them all. I suspected that when the baby reached object permanence, he'd resent her for it.

"You could have named him after me. Samantha's a perfect name for any child if you say it with confidence."

The baby made a squelching sound like he'd inhaled a portion of his mother's areola. "Okay, 'Sam,' I have to finish feeding your godson. Text me if you get home alive."

"I'm already home, and"—I lowered my voice to a whisper—"you have to admit that the pivot scene was funny."

"That was one scene! One scene in a million seasons."

"Good night, mamma," I whispered.

"Good night, gorgeous friend," she whispered.

The call ended and I was left with the warmth of Kaitlyn's concern to guide me into the dark hallway. My calves were still burning from the four flights of stairs as I used my cell phone's flashlight and tiptoed to my shared bedroom.

Both bedrooms were silent, but I recalled something about my roommate Diya being on a long hospital shift. Kendra, who shared the other bedroom with Nakita, was probably sleeping at her boyfriend's studio apartment, which was even smaller than ours but had the benefit of being a five-minute walk from her job at the Lower East Side's only vegan barbeque restaurant.

My stomach rumbled, so I padded into the kitchen, poured myself a glass of water, and stared into the fridge with the vague, quixotic hope that some new form of nutrition would have materialized in the past twelve hours. It hadn't. But a bag of expired shredded cheese glared back at me from the top shelf, accusatory and possibly sentient.

Abandoning hope of finding sustenance in the fridge, I quickly scarfed down a protein bar and washed it down with a glass of water. After flossing and brushing and doing the bare minimum of my skincare routine, I finally made it to my room. I'd left the overhead light off, but the lamp atop my nightstand was on. A stack of mail sat on the center of my bed, presumably Kendra's passive-aggressive way of reminding me that I hadn't touched my basket of mail by the front door for the last two weeks.

That's when I spotted the envelope.

It was large, not quite cream colored, with elaborate calligraphy. There was gold foil. There was an actual wax seal. The front read, "Miss Samantha Jarlston" and had my address. I frowned, guessing it was an invitation to a wedding but wracking my brain trying to figure out who might be getting hitched. Slitting it open with the nearest sharp object, which happened to be my lab ID badge, inside I found the world's most excessive wedding invitation. The kind you had to hold with both hands, as substantive as an Amex Platinum card.

The honor of your presence
is requested
for the marriage of
Andreas Kristiansen
to
Samantha Jarlston
Saturday, June 19th, 7:00 PM
The Oslo Opera House
Oslo, Norway
Dinner & Dancing to Follow

I stared at it for a long, dumb second, then glanced around as if someone were filming my reaction. This was so random and weird.

I had not agreed to marry Andreas Kristiansen. I hadn't even spoken to him in over a decade. Actually, fifteen years and one month to be precise. The last time we saw each other, I'd been thirteen and numb. He'd been eleven, wearing an ill-fitting black suit, and crying into a bowl of fruit salad at my father's funeral.

This had to be a prank. Or maybe he was marrying someone with exactly my name? But then, why send me an invite? Or, more likely, this was a mind-game maneuver by the Kristiansen family to force me into a position where I would have to publicly acknowledge them or some such nonsense. I still received requests for interviews about the events surrounding my father's disgraceful downfall and death, even now, and even though I'd never given a single one.

The Kristiansens were shady as a forest, but they had more money than the devil. I wasn't stupid. As much as I wanted to see them all burn in hell, I wasn't going to cross them without equivalent financial backing, or rock-solid evidence, or both. Realistically, the closest I would ever get to revenge against that family would be to ignore their existence, let them think I might someday give an interview that would tank their company's stock, and live as well as possible.

Basically, I didn't want anything to do with them unless it meant reading their obituaries.

I tossed the invitation into the trash and, for the second time that night, reached for my phone. There was a text from Diya ("I'll be home in the morning") and a missed call from a New York City area code I didn't recognize. I ignored both and started to compose a ranting text message to Kaitlyn, only to stare at the screen for two minutes, and then delete it. There were limits to our friendship. She had a baby who she'd purposefully named Joey. Clearly, she was dealing with a lot right now. I didn't want to bother her with this nonsense.

Crawling under the covers fully clothed, I tried to sleep but my brain performed an elaborate postmortem on every interaction I'd ever had with Andreas Kristiansen.

Andreas was two years younger than me, and he was the kind of child prodigy that other prodigies resented on principle. He was fluent in three languages by eight—but, to be fair, his mother was Italian, his father Norwegian, and he spent summers in the USA—and the kid played chess like he'd been born with every possible opening, middle game, and ending hardcoded in his DNA.

His father, Oskar, had been my dad's business partner and, eventually, one of the people who'd bankrupted and then destroyed my family (according to my mother). I don't want to dwell on that part—if you spend fourteen years in therapy, you learn to summarize childhood trauma in one sentence or less—but suffice it to say, I had zero interest in sharing my last name with anyone in the Kristiansen bloodline. The invitation was absolute nonsense. Like, Mad Hatter nonsense.

Still, Andreas had always been . . . different. And not in a bad way. Not at all.

I'd spent my childhood summers at his family's Hamptons house, where the two older Kristiansen boys ignored me in favor of their wild-oats sowing. However, Andreas followed me around with the intensity of a golden retriever, always asking questions, always eager to play. He was sweet and curious, once getting so invested in building a blanket fort that he convinced their housekeeper to sew custom curtains for the windows. When he was nine, he found a dead baby bird in their garden and wept for a full hour, insisting on holding a proper funeral with eulogies and everything.

I was the officiant, naturally. Because I'm eloquent and look fabulous in robes.

He was lean and pale and had this thick, chaotic mop of dark hair that made him look like an extra from a Tim Burton movie. And, if you weren't used to it, his gaze was intense and intimidating. There was something about the color of his olive-green irises and the shape of his large eyes, something about how his lids naturally drooped when he was in a state of concentration, listening, or rest that made him appear both bored and belligerent, like he was just about to give you a judgmental, unimpressed slow blink.

Almost ten years ago, while doomscrolling, I'd stumbled across a news article about him. According to a reputable British newspaper, he'd become a six-foot-two chess demigod and the second youngest grand master in Europe's history. Also, he was a vegan at sixteen. Which, to be clear, is not an insult *at all*, but I was generally suspicious of anyone who forgoes cheese by choice. That's an inhuman amount of self-control.

There'd also been a relatively famous meme about him and his intimidating stare. It was a photo of a teenage Andreas looking at an opponent across a chessboard, and in bold white text outlined in black it read, "My mouth may not say it, but my face definitely will."

That was the last I'd heard of Andreas Kristiansen until, suddenly, out of absolutely nowhere, and after not hearing from him for years, he reached out to me last month.

I didn't hear from him personally. He reached out through his assistant. *But of course.*

I'd been ignoring the emails from his personal assistant since the first one arrived thirty days ago. They always contained the same message, just with slightly different wording.

Mr. Kristiansen requests a half hour of your time to discuss a private matter.

Mr. Kristiansen requests that I reach out to arrange a brief meeting.

Mr. Kristiansen is in town and would like to meet you for a half hour to discuss something urgent and sensitive in nature.

At first, I suspected that he wanted to make amends for our parents' war, but the more I thought about it, the less I cared. He might've been something like a best friend to me when we were younger, but he'd grown up as a Kristiansen. Since I had no power or means to annihilate them, my life was just fine without reopening that chapter. Better to pretend they—all of them—didn't exist.

Then, two weeks ago, I was leaving the building where my lab was housed, and a stranger approached me with a slim manila envelope and a practiced smile. He introduced himself as "the personal assistant to Mr. Kristiansen" and asked if I could open my calendar to schedule a mutually agreeable meeting time. I told him the only arrangement I was interested in was a restraining order, and then I walked directly to the nearest pizza shop and stress-ate two slices of mushroom, cheese, and extra pepperoni.

But now, side-eyeing the invitation in my trash can, I realized that the situation had mutated. What began as passive pursuit was now full-tilt campaign. The Kristiansens had upped the ante. There was a calligraphed RSVP card with gold leaf embossed detail. There were flight vouchers. There was a slip of paper printed with a New York City phone number, and underneath it, two sentences:

Samantha, please give me half an hour of your time. If you don't want to talk or see me again after that, then I'll leave you alone. —Andreas

I wanted to crumple the card, burn it, toss it out the window into the East River.

My phone vibrated with a new text, pulling me out of my violent musings.

Kaitlyn: Did you think of any other funny episodes or scenes?

I typed back: "Not yet. But if I'm kidnapped, it's the Norwegians. Will explain later."

I placed the phone on the nightstand, turned off the light, and rolled onto my back, letting the city's ambient glow seep through the window and bathe my face in blue. Outside, a siren wailed, insistent and urgent.

I lay there for a long time, thinking about the last time I held a wedding invitation in my hands. Grandpa's second marriage. The memory made my stomach hurt.

I wondered if there was any universe in which I could RSVP no to my own arranged marriage. Probably not since I hadn't even been proposed to.

Eventually, I got up, fished the card from the trash, and ran my thumb over the embossed letters. I didn't recognize the font, but I liked how it looped, the swirls, the softness. Then, I studied the note from Andreas, presumably in his own handwriting. His cursive was sharp and tidy. It was nice, but it was aggressive, like a handshake from a man who thinks handshakes are tests of strength.

And as I stared at the points and lines of the black ink script on the thick ecru card, I couldn't help but think, *What the hell kind of person does something like this?*

[2]

INTRODUCTION TO THE
CELL AND CELL MEMBRANE

Samantha

The sound that woke me was the ancient creak of our apartment's front door, followed by the telltale thud of a person surrendering their entire body weight onto the entryway rug. I groaned into my pillow and checked my phone: 5:33 AM. I'd fallen asleep a little after 2:00, which meant I was running a solid deficit on cognitive function and would need to supplement with at least two pharmaceutical-grade quad-shot Americanos.

There was a scrabble of keys, a sigh, and then the shuffle-shuffle of sneakers. Diya. Even before she creaked open our bedroom door, I could smell the ghost of antiseptic that always trailed her home from the ER.

"Samantha?" she whispered, voice raw from twelve hours of telling drunk NYU kids that their insides would stay inside if they'd simply stop doing shots for five goddamn minutes.

I rolled over, exposing my face to the icy air, and grunted. "In the flesh. What's up?"

Diya poked her head in. Even in the dark, I could see the reverse raccoon marks from her safety goggles. "Sorry I woke you," she said, genuine remorse in her tone. "I think I'm just so tired, I'm confused. I keep telling myself not to talk, and here I am, still talking."

"S'okay." I turned and buried my face into my pillow, letting it muffle my next words. "I should get up. I should get up. I should get up."

9

Motivated by the power of self-talk, I sat up in bed and cracked my eyes open.

Already removing her scrubs as she crossed the room, Diya tossed them into the laundry basket with one hand. She'd mastered the art of undressing without ever being technically naked; a hoodie materialized over her tank top before the scrubs even hit the basket. "You should go back to sleep. It's not even six."

"I'd have to fall asleep for that to work," I said, and then yawned. I knew myself and my terrible relationship with insomnia enough to know more sleep was now impossible. "I'll just get up and go to the lab early."

Diya grunted and plopped onto my desk chair. "Why am I sitting here?"

"You need a shower and you don't want to get in bed until you're clean," I filled in.

Diya let out a tragic sigh and blearily blinked around the room. "But the bathroom is so far away."

Her eyes drifted, but then she did a double take, frowning at something on my nightstand. I followed her line of sight and cringed. Our early-morning, sleep-deprived repartee would now be derailed by the bright, accusatory rectangle of the wedding invitation on my nightstand. I could see in the dance of her dark eyebrows on her forehead the train of her thoughts.

"What's that?" she asked, tilting her head. "Are you getting married?"

"It's junk mail." I snatched it from the nightstand and folded it in half. "You're hallucinating. Take a shower. Go to sleep. Dream of your mom's rogan josh."

"No, no. I know myself. I don't start hallucinating until I've been up for seventy-two hours. That was your name on there. Who is the guy? Is it the Stanford guy? I hate that guy. Or the one who did CrossFit? Please tell me it's the CrossFit guy, I miss his shirtless sleepovers. Oh! The lawyer guy, the one you went to law school with who keeps making us dinner. Or the rower? Eric? Is that his name?"

"None of those," I said, shoving the folded invite into my backpack on the floor next to my bed, where it could no longer radiate weirdness throughout my personal space. "Just an old family fri—" I stopped myself from saying *friend*. He might've been my friend when we were little, but we were strangers now. And, obviously, no one else in his family had ever been a friend to me. "Someone I used to know playing a joke."

Diya made a skeptical face but let it go. Apparently, she was too tired to chase the scent of gossip.

"I'm heading out early," I said, flipping back my covers. "Have a project due and the sequencer is actually free before eight."

She nodded, her head tilting back as she succumbed to a massive yawn.

Standing, I hunted around my room and threw on the least-wrinkled pair of jeans I could find, a Genetics Bowl Champion tee, and a cardigan that might've been trendy seven years ago but now existed solely to telegraph "harmless grad student" to the outside world. I finger-combed my hair into a haphazard bun and grabbed my bag. Leaving Diya to her dozing, I washed my face, brushed my teeth, and called it good.

After I put on my coat and slung the backpack over one shoulder, I caught my reflection in the mirror by the front door. When I was on the tennis team in undergrad, I'd been told a few times that I resembled a young Anna Kournikova, the infamous Russian tennis pro. This was back when I worked out daily, was outside in the sun often, and still dyed my hair blond. I definitely preferred the light brown of my hair color now. My thoughts must've still been preoccupied by that stupid fake wedding invitation because, in my quick assessment of my reflection, my brain told me I looked like someone who could plausibly be a mail-order bride, but only if the groom had specified "bargain bin, will not arrive as advertised."

The thought made me snicker.

Yes, yes. Make it all a joke. Everything is a joke. Life is so much nicer that way.

* * *

By 6:00 AM, the city was running on three-quarters power. I could actually enjoy a sidewalk without having to weave through a marathon of tourists and startup founders on electric scooters. The air was crisp, and even though I could see my breath, I left my hands exposed. The summer had been so hot, I was still enjoying the cooler temperatures of fall.

Central Grounds, my favorite coffee shop, operated on the theory that coffee should taste like coffee and be better than good. The line was mercifully nonexistent, and this small win buoyed my mood.

My barista—Kevin to his friends and regulars—smiled sympathetically when he saw me. "Rough night?"

"You have no idea," I said, rubbing at my temples. "Quad-shot Americano, please."

"On the house if you can recite the Krebs cycle backward."

I blinked. "You know I can."

"I know you can, but I want to see if you can do it before coffee."

"Fine," I said. "Malate, fumarate, succinate, succinyl-CoA, alpha-ketoglutarate, isocitrate, citrate, oxaloacetate." I stopped for a second. "Wait. I started with malate. That's not—"

"Impressive enough," he said, waving it off. "Nobody ever gets that far."

I grinned, because it felt good to be a monster at something.

He slid the coffee across the counter with a nod of respect. "Make good decisions."

"I shan't." I tipped him, grabbed the drink, and inhaled it.

Ah. Coffee.

I loved coffee so much. I'd always liked coffee, but now I loved coffee. It was likely the closest I would ever come to a committed relationship.

Armed with my favorite thing on earth, I beelined for my department building. The NYC campus was close to the university's research hospital, a collection of structures cobbled together by whatever real estate happened to be available during the dot-com crash. The genetics building, my home for the next indefinite period of time, was a neoclassical monstrosity complete with white columns made of cement and fairly decent scrollwork, considering the building was less than one hundred years old.

Gulping the last of my coffee, I would've been perfectly content to marinate in my own productivity until noon. But as I turned onto the sidewalk, an unusual sight pinged my situational awareness. A new stranger—a genuinely remarkable-looking fella—leaned against one of the entrance columns with an aura of extreme confidence. He wore an obscenely nice tan overcoat. The kind you see in European cologne ads, probably cashmere. It was unbuttoned and therefore open, revealing his all-black attire beneath. Black turtleneck, black pants, and black shoes shined to a mirror finish. Unlike mine, his hands were ensconced in leather gloves.

Currently, he checked his phone, then pocketed it and stared straight ahead. If this were an undergrad psych experiment where one rated an individual's attractiveness on a Likert scale, I'd have categorized him as "dangerous levels of hot." So, a 5.

The part of myself that was still somewhat aware of my outward appearance wished I'd brushed my hair this morning. Hell, I wished I'd done literally anything other than roll out of bed and slap on the first clean-ish T-shirt I found. But . . . whatever. Who cared if Mr. European Perfume Ad saw me looking like this. We'd probably never encounter each other again.

Squaring my shoulders, I adjusted my bag and told myself not to get distracted. I had things to do, data to analyze, coffee to drink. I was making for the door, eyes fixed on my phone screen as I pulled up my email, when he stepped directly into my path.

I glanced up. He looked at me. I took a step back. He kept looking at me.

So, the stepping in my path wasn't an accident. It was calculated. He'd measured the trajectory and plotted an intercept.

My heart, which had coasted along inertly for the better part of a year, spiked a little.

"Pardon me," he said.

Nice voice. Very nice. Low and smooth, with a faint European inflection that I couldn't pin down but absolutely believed got him laid on a regular basis.

I blinked at him, then did the New Yorker thing where you make yourself so unimpressed that it comes back around to seeming interested.

"Yes?"

"You're Samantha, yes?" He cocked his head, his green eyes sweeping over my face. The man's tone broadcasted interest, but his gaze seemed somehow both bored and intense.

I took another step back, scrutinizing him, and considered pretending I wasn't Samantha, but the way he'd pronounced my name, dragging the *a* out ever so slightly, made me want to engage rather than lie outright. "Depends. Who's asking?"

He smiled, and it was a micro-expressive thing, barely more than a twitch at the corners of his mouth. "Andreas Kristiansen. You got my note, yes?"

It took my tired brain a full second to realize that this wasn't just some random European thirst trap. This was *that* Andreas, the youngest Kristiansen, the boy—no, the man—who'd sent me a wedding invite and put himself as the groom. And when it did, my heart tripped all over itself and I stood paralyzed for several long seconds, chasing my breath.

I had no idea if he noticed or was bothered by my sleep-deprived gaping. Andreas simply stood there and returned my stare, giving me time to collect myself, as though he'd foreseen this reaction to his sudden appearance after fifteen years.

By the time I'd collected myself enough to respond, I was breathing hard and my heart had taken off at a gallop. I cycled through every available response and landed on the most mature by far. "I'm busy."

He didn't seem offended. Good for him.

"You remember me," he said, sounding certain and pleased, though his expression didn't change.

I didn't respond. I owed him nothing. Also, I didn't know what to say or why my body had suddenly divorced itself from my mind.

After studying me for another long moment, he gathered a deep breath and glanced over my shoulder. "It's urgent that we meet."

I spoke without thinking. "So, you show up at my job?"

His attention cut back to mine and he gave me another of his micro smiles.

"Despite the risk, I suspected waiting for you here would be more efficient than waiting for you to answer an email. Or a letter. Or a courier."

I laughed, once, because it was either that or throw my empty coffee cup at him. "I was hoping the next step would be a singing telegram. Or a skywriter." Again, I'd spoken on instinct, the sarcasm emerging without thought. His sudden presence had sent me into a panic and I didn't understand why.

Andreas's face flickered with what might have been amusement, hard to tell. "If there'd been time, I would've done that next."

I glared at him while also suddenly very aware of his proximity. He didn't smell like cologne, but there was a faint, unfamiliar trace of something herbal and clean. Like rosemary and ozone, like the air after a thunderstorm, if that's even possible.

Clinging to sarcasm like a shield, I made no attempt to hide the largeness or loudness of my sigh and took yet another step away, outside of the radius of his seductive olfactory assault. "What do you want?"

His gaze darted past me, scanning, then fixed on my face. "May I buy you a coffee? Or is that redundant?"

The fact that his voice was so incredibly alluring irritated me. I looked at my cup of coffee, which I'd just finished, then back at Andreas, intending to turn him down.

Thus, no one was more surprised than me when what came out was, "Fine."

"Thank you," he said, sounding sincerely grateful, gaze moving over my face like he was hungry for the sight of it. My eyes narrowed.

What are you doing, Samantha? This feels dangerous. Don't do it!

Clearing my throat, I added testily, "If you promise to leave me alone after, then fine. I shall go get a cup of coffee and listen to whatever you have to say."

If my glare bothered him, he didn't make any outward sign of it, instead saying, "There is a café just there. I believe they opened at six." He lifted his hand toward the corner across the street. "We can talk for a bit, and—"

"No." I turned and began marching toward the café he'd indicated, not waiting to see if he'd follow. "You said in your note a half hour would suffice. I'll give you a half hour. And that's it."

[3]

CELL INTERIOR AND FUNCTION

Samantha

We sat across from each other, a table's width and fifteen years of silence between us. I picked at the sleeve of my cardigan, which had sprouted a new hole at the elbow I hadn't noticed until now, and wished I'd insisted on meeting somewhere less . . . sterile.

Cafés were supposed to be neutral ground, but this one had only fake plants. Who can trust a café where every plant is fake? What else is fake? The beans? The tea leaves? The milk? Is the barista made of cake?

I'm just saying.

Andreas looked even more beautiful with prolonged exposure, in the uncanny way that only comes from a ruthless culling of childhood awkwardness. His features had all grown into themselves. The nose was still prominent, but now it belonged on a man instead of a scrawny middle school student. The jawline could cut diamonds, and the chocolate-brown hair, which had once lived in perpetual revolt, was mostly tamed and combed with a kind of clinical precision that made my scalp itch with sympathy. The only thing unchanged was his eyes. Large, round, olive green, and weirdly soulful for a twenty-six-year-old nepo baby.

When I initially spotted him earlier, I'd thought that his eyes were rather large, yet he must've been tired or bored or something similar because his eyelids were lowered, at half-mast. But now I recalled this quality to his gaze—the appearance of drooping eyelids, as though he were unimpressed with everything—was just part of his eyes' natural shape.

Presently, Andreas stared at me, silent and perfectly still, save for the gentle motion of one foot, which tapped against the marble tile in some intricate tempo I couldn't decipher.

I was immediately viscerally annoyed.

"So," I said, after exactly enough time had passed for the silence to become an entity with its own mortgage, "are you going to say something, or is this some kind of strategic interrogation?"

Andreas blinked, startled out of whatever he'd been thinking. "I haven't seen you in fifteen years. I'm curious."

"Curious?" I repeated, incredulous. "Did your family hope I'd be in a ditch somewhere? Preferably not breathing, I suppose."

His eyes narrowed slightly, but he didn't dignify that with a response, instead continuing to stare at me with a level of focus that left me unsettled. I wondered when and why his family had decided to use him to make contact. I wondered, not for the first time, why I'd agreed to this.

But I also wondered if he still wept for baby birds; I wondered if he still built pillow forts; and I wondered whose bed he slept in when he had nightmares.

Summers when we were young, he used to climb in my bed whenever he had a bad dream. This was almost every night. We'd stay together until early morning, then he'd leave silently so as not to be found out.

But that was a long time ago.

My attention wandered, eventually moving to the espresso machine behind the counter as I longed for the nutty, robust taste of the coffee I'd finished earlier. The server —an androgynous twentysomething with sleeve tattoos and a septum ring—caught my eye and smirked. Andreas had ordered us two cappuccinos when we'd entered. I raised my eyebrows at the server and didn't smile, in the universal expression for "please save me from this torture," and they nodded, presumably recognizing my desperation.

After too many seconds to count, during which Andreas continued to stare and I felt increasingly like something under a microscope, I snapped, "What is it?" If I didn't take control, Andreas was going to benzodiazepine me into a coma. "You asked for half an hour. That's two percent of my day if I round for scientific digits and don't count leap seconds. I need a return on my investment."

As though deciding something, he leaned forward, elbows on the table, hands folded with priestly solemnity. "I did not want to meet you in person like this, not in public. But you left me with no other choice."

"Why? What? Are you still mad at me for hiding that puzzle piece when we were little?" I looked him down, then up. "Are you going to throw a pie in my face? Is it humble? Will I be expected to eat it?"

"I want to marry you."

I choked so hard that I fleetingly worried I would aspirate on my own tongue. "Excuse me?" I finally croaked out.

He didn't blink. "The offer is sincere."

"I—" For the second time in less than twelve hours, I looked around to see if there was a hidden camera, but no one jumped out of the faux foliage. "Andreas, I haven't seen you since we were both preteens. You can't just—What is wrong with you?"

He seemed unbothered by the fact that he'd just detonated the world's most awkward and inappropriate proposal. "You asked what I wanted. I told you. I want to marry you."

Before I could formulate a reply, the server arrived with two cappuccinos, each topped with a foamy heart. I was ninety percent sure this was not a standard design, and ten percent sure the barista was flirting with Andreas.

Yes. Please. Take him off my hands.

But I only said, "Thank you."

After a brief exchange during which the server confirmed we were all set, they left. Andreas, meanwhile, didn't even nod or otherwise acknowledge the café employee. He simply kept looking at me.

I waited until the server was out of earshot before continuing. "Did your family put you up to this? Is this damage control for the sake of shareholders before something new about my father comes out?"

Andreas shook his head. "I don't associate with my family. I haven't since I turned eighteen."

"Then you're here on your own." I side-eyed him, deciding that if he said so, I would believe him. Maybe that made me stupid, but I didn't think so.

Andreas's childhood hadn't been easy, and I got a sense that it had continued to be difficult after I'd disappeared from his life.

Confirming my statement, he nodded. "This is something I want. They do not know I am here, and if they did, they definitely would not approve."

I stared at his beautiful face for several seconds, trying to wrap my mind around what he might be thinking with this random, out-of-the-blue proposal after fifteen years of no contact.

Eventually, I huffed. "Seriously, is this some kind of performance art? Do you need a green card? Is there a reality show I'm not aware of for world's most uncomfortable reunions? Why are you doing this to me?"

The faintest hint of a smile barely curved his lips. "You have not changed," he said, the words sounding tender.

My adrenaline spiked and I sipped the cappuccino just to have something to do. It was good. Not great, but a credible effort.

"Okay, so—why—" I floundered, unsure why I hadn't picked up my bag and coat and left already. Old time's sake, maybe? "Let's say, for the sake of argument, that I don't immediately tell you to get lost. Why would you want to marry me?"

Eyes narrowing, he tugged at the fingertips of his gloves—first the right, then the left—proceeding to pull the black leather from his hands, revealing long, thick fingers and finely formed knuckles, everything strong, veiny, smooth, and perfectly proportioned.

I squirmed, viscerally annoyed once more. Andreas had one of the finest sets of man-hands I'd ever seen in my life. *Infuriating.*

Rather than roll my eyes, I frowned. I definitely needed to get out more, go to a bar, find a nice set of hands for a night. At the very least, I needed some time off work and my dissertation when I wasn't exhausted, time to take care of my dearth in sexy-times business myself. Things must've been desperate if I was noticing my sworn enemy's hands.

He is not your enemy. He never has been.

That said, this—sitting across from him now—was *hard.* Just seeing him was difficult. Talking to him brought back too many memories.

My mother, when I was little, before she'd died, had said that Andreas preferred me over his own family and she'd always felt a little guilty at the end of every summer when we'd have to part—him for Norway, then almost immediately for school in Switzerland, and me for school in Connecticut. He'd cry like he'd never see me again and I'd feel melancholy for weeks.

At my father's funeral, Andreas had refused to let me go, requiring four grown men to untangle his arms from my body and forcibly carry him away. I would never forget his tearstained face and how his hands reached for me. At thirteen, I'd been in no state to console him, since my dad had—you know—just died right after declaring bankruptcy. I had no home, and my mother had been a shell, and every day was a struggle.

Over the years, every time I thought about reaching out to Andreas, some new hellish event stopped me: my mother's death, my grandparents' divorce, my grandmother's death.

When I looked Andreas up ten years ago, just before starting college, he was the best chess player in the world and seemed to be doing just fine. And so, I'd let go of my childhood friend once and for all. It had brought me closure. I'd never regretted it.

But looking at him now and his bonkers offer, maybe he hadn't let go of me . . . ?

That's nuts. It's been fifteen years.

Ignorant as to the direction of my thoughts, Andreas reached into the inner pocket of his coat and produced a document. He slid it across the table with the same gravity one uses to reveal a murder weapon in a game of Clue.

I glanced at it, then at him. "What is this?"

"Just read it."

Careful to avoid touching his perfect fingers, I picked up the page. It was a photocopy, not an original, and the English was so precisely translated that it felt unnatural. The letterhead said Genetix, Inc., and the footer was dated approximately one month ago. The rest was legalese, but the gist was unmistakable.

Upon my death, my shares in GENETIX INC. shall be transferred not to my biological children, but to my first grandchild, regardless of gender or national origin. The shares shall not be held in trust by any Kristiansen, Aaberg, or Loretto relation until such time as the grandchild reaches the age of majority.

I read it twice, noting that Aaberg was the maiden name of Oskar Kristiansen's first wife and Loretto was the surname of his second wife. Finished, I set the paper down.

"Whose will is this?" I asked, but I already knew.

"My father's," Andreas said.

I tried to swallow around the tightness in my throat. "Oskar is still alive?"

He nodded.

"That's a shame. Do your brothers know about this part of his will?"

"No."

Blinking against a sudden rush of tears, I huffed again, then snorted, hoping to dispel the stupid, tiresome liquid emotion. "What does any of this have to do with me or you wanting to marry me?"

I needed to get out of here. *Feelings* were clawing at my lungs, heart, and throat, which was not a sensation I enjoyed. Ever.

He met my gaze, unflinching. "Those shares should go to you. Or your mother."

I felt my throat tighten further. "My mother died when I was fourteen, Andreas. Bit late for inheritance games."

He tilted his head, and for a second, I thought he might say something normal, like "I'm sorry" or "That must have been hard."

Instead, he went for the jugular. "I believe my father—and, in part, my brothers —they are the reason your father died. I believe either my father or Tobias defrauded the company and framed your father for it. Henrik helped them cover it up. That stress led to your father's sudden death."

The words hung in the air like a chemical spill, but they also helped me, centered me. When the old familiar numbness threatened, I embraced it. Breathing deeply, I looked down at my hands, then at the table, then at the page of the will, then back at Andreas, who was the picture of unruffled patience.

I swallowed without difficulty. "You think I don't know that?" I sounded so detached, so calm. *What a relief.*

He frowned at my response, another micro expression. "Samantha, I need to make it right for you."

"And marrying me is your solution?" Admittedly, I was only half listening to his words now, and I was definitely not in a state of mind to scrutinize them.

He nodded, like he was agreeing to a flavor of yogurt, not a life-altering commitment. "My father is very sick. He will not have a chance to change this again. If we marry, the shares pass to our child. You will control them. Don't you see? It's built into the language. My father wants his future daughter-in-law to control the shares before the child comes of age, to ensure either me or my brothers only marry someone trustworthy, ideally someone we're in love with." Andreas paused here, dipping his head and watching me as though to gauge my reaction to his words.

When I continued meeting his searching stare blankly, he sighed and added, "No need for me to sign anything over since I am a Kristiansen. The shares, and the company, will be yours to control from the start."

We gazed at each other silently for so long that the little foam hearts floating above our coffees began to blur. I tried to imagine any scenario in which this was a normal, sane offer, and came up empty.

"You want to have a baby with me," I said, slow and deliberate, "so you can keep Genetix out of the hands of your brothers."

"Not for me." Andreas's tone sounded gentle, so at odds with his cold beauty. "For you. For your family. Your father built that company. The patents, the technology, those were his."

I pushed the photocopy back across the table and lied, "I don't care about Genetix. Or your father's dirty money. Or any of this."

The intensity of his already-intimidating stare multiplied. "If you walk away, the shares will eventually go to one of my half brothers. Henrik, or Tobias. They will not hesitate to get married and have a child in order to control the company, or try to. You remember what they were like. They have not changed."

I did remember. Henrik liked to punch Andreas and call it wrestling. Tobias once superglued my hair to a piano bench. I had not kept in touch. Thus, I didn't know what havoc they'd wreaked since growing to maturity. To label them both bullies would be a charitable understatement.

Andreas must have perceived my indecision, because he leaned forward, voice dipping low. "You deserve your father's company. Not them, not me, not my father. You're getting a PhD in genetics, just like your parents. There has to be a reason for that. I'm offering you a chance to take back what should be yours by birthright. Why say no?"

I shook my head, suddenly exhausted, and not just from lack of sleep.

Yes, I would do almost anything to screw over his family and I'd gladly watch them suffer, but I wasn't completely morally bankrupt. I wouldn't involve an innocent—my own child—as a means to an end. That was some next-level evil strategic bullshit.

"I'm not bringing a child into the world just to spite your family and take control of a company. I would never do that."

He reached across the table and placed his hand on mine, his big palm completely dwarfing my fingers, and I flinched at the feel of it, yet was unable to pull away. The contact was warm and electric. It paralyzed me. A tingling heat coursed up my arm and my breath turned to fire in my lungs. My body's unexpected reaction to his touch threatened to incinerate the blanket of numbness I'd been clinging to, and that was unacceptable.

"You don't ever have to see my family." He squeezed my fingers in a way that felt insistent and familiar. Comfortable and yet also alarming. "I would not let them near you. Trust me, Samantha."

"That's not the point," I croaked out, because—maybe it made me irrational—but I did trust Andreas. Careful to keep my voice just above a whisper, I said, "The mere idea of conceiving a child out of spite, especially with you, is loathsome"—I didn't miss how he winced, or how his eyes dropped to the table, but I wasn't finished—"to me. How could I do that? How could you even suggest it?"

His shoulders rose and fell, and his attention remained on the table as he added, "You don't have to see me after, if you prefer. We can arrange everything in writing."

Now I flinched, his words felt like a slap.

I found I had to swallow several times to gain control of my voice before I could trust myself to speak. "By 'after,' you mean after we are married and conceive a baby. Isn't that right? Are you telling me you want to have a child with me and then disappear from my life, from our baby's life?" While I spoke, I glanced at his hand covering mine, then at him, then back at his hand. I needed to pull away.

Any minute now.

Andreas's eyes cut to mine. He stared at me, giving none of his thoughts away. Or maybe he was giving his thoughts away. Perhaps he was broadcasting them loudly, but I couldn't read them, or him. I felt too many things I didn't usually allow myself to feel. And I was sleep-deprived. I couldn't think.

Finally, heart hammering, I pulled my hand back. I felt the loss of his touch and our contact in a way I dared not analyze.

"Exactly," I said, deciding to assume his silent stare meant that he would not, in fact, feel perfectly at peace with never knowing his own kid. Cupping my cappuccino, I didn't lift it for a sip. My hands felt unsteady. "I appreciate the offer to conspire to bring down your family, but no."

Face unreadable, his gaze shifted to some point over my shoulder. "This can be the beginning of the conversation. We don't have to decide anything right now."

Exhaling a humorless laugh, I set the cup down with a clatter and stood up, shoving my chair back with more force than necessary. It was well past time for me to leave.

"No. This isn't the beginning of anything."

He also stood. "Samantha—"

"You need to let it go." I looked around for my belongings, anywhere but at him, and wrapped my scarf around my neck even though my chest felt hot and achy.

"I cannot let you go, or let this go. The company should be yours."

I shrugged, still not looking at him. "Yeah, and people shouldn't be starving or unhoused in first world countries, marine animals shouldn't be choking on plastic, babies shouldn't be dying of preventable diseases, but neither you nor I can fix the inherent unfairness of life."

Andreas walked around the table and stood in front of me, his hands fisted at his sides. I could feel his restraint as though it were a tangible thing.

"Please, if I find another way, may I call you? May I—"

Yanking on my coat, I cut him off. "Sure. If you find a way that doesn't involve us getting married or having a baby together, be my guest."

"Wait." He grabbed and held my wrist, pausing until I—unenthusiastically—gave him my eyes. For once, his didn't look bored. They were wide and imploring. "If either Tobias or Henrik contact you, you must let me know. You have my number. Call me."

No. No way. I had no desire to relive this level of emotional upheaval. Not ever.

Disentangling myself from his grip, I shook my head again, firmer this time. "You won't be hearing from me."

"Sama—"

"Please. Leave me alone. Okay?" I hated that my voice wavered and cracked, but I seemed to no longer have control over my vocal cords.

Thankfully, Andreas made no move to grab me again. He didn't say another word. But I felt his eyes on me as I gathered my things, walked around him, and fled the café. My heart and lungs hurt, as if they were encased in rubber bands.

Feelings are THE WORST!

Outside, the cold felt bracing. I stood on the sidewalk, eyes stinging, lungs burning, and realized that I had never, in all my years of therapy, been this profoundly unsettled by a single conversation. I walked back to my department building. My hands shook, so I stuffed them in the pockets of my jacket. My stomach felt sour, and my mouth tasted bitter. And I had a headache.

I tried to convince myself sleep deprivation was the culprit, but even I didn't buy it.

[4]

METABOLISM OVERVIEW AND ENZYMES

Samantha

I spent the rest of the morning in a state of low-level dissociation, the kind where you run experiments and pipette reagents with the slow, sputtering detachment of a glitching DNA sequencer whose firmware is three updates behind. Perhaps it was my lack of sleep, but every time I thought about Andreas's offer to be my baby daddy, or his attempt at a hostile marriage takeover, or *him* in general, I spent no less than fifteen minutes staring into space and thinking about his face or his hands or his eyes, and reliving our moments together this morning before I caught myself.

Another side effect of Andreas's unexpected visit was the reemergence of my burning hatred for his family. I'd tried to forget, but the best I'd managed was letting go of my childhood in its entirety, like those years were a kite caught in a windstorm and the only way to be free was to let go of the string. For some reason, I couldn't seem to pick and choose which parts of my past to hold on to. At eighteen, I'd decided to throw it all away and start afresh.

But now here I was, marinating in the injustice of it all, how they'd stolen my father's company and ruined my family . . .

Then I'd blink and come back to myself in the present. Basically, I'd never been more grateful for the monotonous rituals of the lab.

My research project—my baby, my nemesis, the thing keeping me from sleeping, socializing, or remembering to send good friends happy birthday texts—

25

was bioremediation of ocean plastics via genetically modified microbes. If you find that impressive, don't. There are lots of scientists trying to do the exact same thing.

Basically, if I could convince the right microorganism to eat the right plastic, and not, say, eat the entire aquatic ecosystem along with it or excrete hazardous toxins as biowaste, we might be one step closer to saving the planet's oceans before they became one giant floating landfill. My day-to-day reality involved mutating a microbe that could, under strictly controlled conditions, dissolve polyethylene like it was fondue cheese. Getting it to do so in an actual marine environment, without triggering a new bubonic plague, was the tricky part.

Today I was running a third (or maybe fourth, I'd lost count) pass at sequencing some candidate plasmids to see if yesterday's late-night gamble with the CRISPR kit had stuck. It had, in that the bacteria were very much alive and very much eating the control plastics at an alarming rate. It hadn't, in that every organism that I'd genetically modified was now a different, nightmarishly resistant superbug that would likely haunt my dreams for the rest of the semester.

This was why our entire floor had security—badge access and state-of-the-art cameras—and even the offices were off-limits to anyone who didn't have a PhD in genetics, hope to have a PhD in genetics, collaborate with a PhD in genetics, or work for someone with a PhD in genetics.

I'd almost convinced myself that this latest failed attempt was merely another important datapoint in my research journey when a knock at the glass wall of my cubicle startled me into an upright posture.

Dr. James Nieminen stood there, perfect posture, perfect jawline, even his glasses were so clear and free of fingerprints I suspected he changed them out for a new pair daily. Unlike most of the assistant professors, who either dressed in "I'm hoping for tenure" cargo shorts or "I'm hip and relevant" hoodies, Nieminen wore business casual. He was the only person I knew who could make a button-down shirt look like a tactical garment.

I forced a polite, if not particularly sincere, smile.

"Hey, Sam," James said, lingering in the doorway. I didn't miss the way his gaze moved down to my chest, then up. "You got a second?"

"Sure," I said, even though I really didn't. And I didn't know what he hoped to get a glimpse of by checking out the vicinity of my boobs. I currently wore scrubs and a lab coat, having changed out of my T-shirt and jeans when I arrived. Perhaps this was just a habit for him with all women. He never did this to men.

Nieminen leaned against the doorframe, arms crossed, his stubby fingers gripping his elbows, and smiled the kind of smile you only saw on toothpaste commercials. "How's the ocean plastic project going?"

"Swimmingly," I deadpanned, then regretted the pun. "I'm making incremental progress. One day closer to creating an organism that will save the world, or at least delay the heat death of the oceans by a few fiscal quarters."

He laughed a little too loudly. "That's great, that's great. I always say, if the world doesn't appreciate the subtlety of your genetic engineering jokes, they deserve the microplastics." He laughed again, even louder.

I nodded, even though . . . *what did that even mean?*

James lingered, shifting his weight from one foot to the other. "So, hey, I was just wondering, are you going to the department holiday party this year?"

It was the beginning of November. "The one in, like, December?"

"Yeah! It's never too early to plan." He ran a hand through his dark hair, the movement calculated for maximum effect to show off his bulging biceps in his short-sleeve shirt, but my attention affixed to his hand. The palm was entirely too big for the size of his fingers. "Last year was such a blast. I thought maybe we could go together."

Blinking away from his disproportionate digits and up to his face, I floundered for an excuse.

I had nothing against James personally other than a mild sense of dislike. He was, objectively, smart and very good-looking, and he had the kind of research budget that made junior grad students swoon. But I'd never seen him be particularly kind to anyone unless he wanted something from them.

And, maybe this was me just being petty, but he'd interrupted my lab meeting last spring to debate the etymology of the word *pseudogene* in such a way that I'm pretty sure he expected me to remove my pants on the spot. The memory still left a bad taste in my mouth.

More importantly, James had a not-insignificant probability of being on my dissertation panel next year, and my entire academic future would be at his mercy for at least another twelve months.

Presently, I played it as cool as possible. "Oh, you know, I haven't really thought that far ahead. December feels very theoretical to me right now."

James grinned, undeterred. "I get that. You're very focused. It's what I admire about you. But you should come. Let loose a little. We'll go together." At the last minute, he lifted his hands. "Just as friends. No pressure."

No pressure, I repeated in my head, feeling as if I'd heard the phrase at least one million times in my life. "I'll think about it."

He took a step inside, lowering his voice like he was about to share state secrets. "You know, if you ever want to talk about your research, or anything really, my door is always open. Especially now that I finally got rid of my last postdoc.

She was a total drama queen, you know? But you're different than other women. You're very mature."

"Thanks," I said, deserving of an Olympic medal for not cringing.

Ladies, beware men who tell you things like, "You're different" or "You're very mature." If a man says you're different from or more mature than other women, then he's just insulted either all women or you. And neither makes him attractive.

He smiled again, showing all his teeth, and I wondered if he'd practiced that in the mirror. "Great! So, I'll see you around, Sam."

I nodded, saying nothing.

He left, and I exhaled a long-suffering sigh. Returning to my notes, I did my best to concentrate, but my frustrations about Andreas's visit and his evil family and the unfairness of my parents' fates were now intermingled with the aftertaste of James's cologne, which was some mix of spearmint and musk that *lingered*.

Actually, it loitered.

Less than five minutes passed before a familiar voice floated over the partition.

"Are you hiding from Dr. Nieminen?"

I spun in my chair to see Dmitry Bortnik, fellow grad student and unintentional expert in the art of the slow approach. Dmitry was a year ahead of me, a Russian expatriate with high cheekbones and the kind of unhurried confidence that made him the natural enemy of all horny straight-male assistant professors.

"Not hiding," I said. "Strategically waiting until he's distracted by someone else's pheromones."

Dmitry snorted, then ducked into my cubicle, balancing a mug of something black and tarry with long, elegant fingers. "He talks about you all the time, you know. In the grad student lounge. Says you have 'the most graceful pipetting hands' he's ever seen."

"Gross," I muttered, but I was also a tiny bit pleased. As a hand aficionado, I never turned down a compliment about my hands.

Okay. Fine. Yes. I have a hand kink. I admit it.

I'd always been a hand woman. Some women liked eyes, some butts, some biceps, still others forearms, smiles, thighs, or six-packs. Not me. I loved me some well-proportioned man-hands. The kind I could imagine on my body, the kind that could grab fistfuls of me without any part spilling over.

I also took ridiculously good care of my own hands and owned a paraffin wax machine because I couldn't afford manicures but refused to have dry cuticles.

Dmitry grinned. "He's not wrong, though. You have good hands. Very steady."

"Stop." I tried to play it off, waving his words away, but I blushed. Obviously,

I'd never told Dmitry about my hand fetish, so these compliments were hitting a bullseye he didn't know existed.

"Fine, fine." He perched on my desk, ignoring the pile of ungraded quizzes I'd been using as a coaster. "You look terrible, by the way. Trouble sleeping?"

I considered for a moment. My interaction with Andreas earlier today flashed through my mind. I knew Dmitry didn't mean to be offensive nor did I take his comment about me looking terrible that way. He was simply painfully direct and didn't have any interest in me as woman. Neither of us were interested in messing around with colleagues or orgasming where we ate.

Eventually, I nodded. "Something like that."

He raised his eyebrows, waiting for elaboration, but I was not about to unspool my entire morning with Andreas Kristiansen and his offer of transactional matrimony and baby making, or my body's completely bizzarro overreaction to seeing him again.

Instead, I focused on the safer, nerdier topics.

"Ever just . . . get the feeling your work is completely pointless?" I asked.

Dmitry sipped his coffee, then shrugged. "All the time. Especially when I see the latest paper from the MIT group. They are always three months ahead, no matter what I do."

"Those nerds." I punched the palm of my hand with a fist. "They clobber us in innovation, but we could totally take them in a fistfight."

He laughed, then softened. "If it makes you feel better, Nieminen will probably be suspended before your dissertation defense. I don't think he even understands what the postdocs do in his lab and I've heard murmurs from the grants oversight department that there's a problem with his expense reports."

"That does make me feel better, actually. Thanks." Perpetually turning down an assistant professor's romantic overtures was almost as dangerous as dating one. If Nieminen were suspended, then I'd breathe easier.

Dmitry's phone vibrated. He checked it, face going neutral. "My PI needs me. Don't let Nieminen bully you into going to the party. In fact, say you have a boyfriend. He might back off."

"Will you pretend to be my boyfriend, Dmitry?" I flapped my eyelashes at him.

"No," he said, and promptly disappeared, leaving behind a faint aroma of cigarette smoke.

I looked back at my notes, but the ability to focus had completely deserted me. Despite my best efforts, my brain continued replaying the morning's meeting with Andreas on a loop, refusing to let me rest.

Andreas Kristiansen wanted to marry me.

No. Correction, Andreas Kristiansen wanted to marry me and have a baby with me and then . . . ? He clearly had no idea and hadn't thought about what would happen next. The entire plan was so diabolically nonsensical. I would have to ask Kaitlyn if her uber-rich husband had ever proposed something as diabolically nonsensical. *Why are rich people so weird?*

Even worse, a not-insignificant, totally mortifying part of me—likely the part that hadn't gotten laid in over a year—was curious about what would happen if I said yes. Would we actually get married? Would he move in? Would we have to cohabitate and share a bathroom? Or would it be like a one-night stand, only with way more paperwork and the potential for a trust fund baby?

Even worser, that same part of me did not hate the idea of a one-night stand with Andreas. I was a living, breathing, straight woman after all.

Thankfully, a much larger part shied away from the idea like a teenage virgin faced with her first erection.

Andreas felt . . . scary. To me. His presence in my life felt volatile, like two bacteria competing with each other via pathogen signals. I wasn't afraid of Andreas. I knew he'd never hurt me on purpose and cared about me deeply, even now. But I also was afraid of Andreas, because he'd never hurt me on purpose and apparently cared about me deeply, even now. And how did any of that make sense?

Or maybe he doesn't care deeply about you at all. Maybe he cares about injustice, and this is all just about righting a wrong . . . ?

Ugh. I wished I'd gotten more sleep last night.

Regardless, I made a mental note to do an internet search for "Who is currently the best chess player in the world?" For now, I had to escape this lab before Nieminen returned with his weird tiny fingers, or before I fell asleep on my desk.

Grabbing my notes, I headed for the lockers, determined to spend the rest of the day doing something other than staring at my laptop. Maybe I'd go to the library and peruse the new fiction titles, pretending I had time to read them. Or maybe the bagel shop down the street. Or maybe a sensory deprivation tank, if I could sneak into the psychology building undetected.

Anything to stop thinking about the reprehensible Kristiansens.

And anything to avoid thinking about Andreas Kristiansen, and why I couldn't stop thinking about him.

* * *

I TOOK the long way home, which is to say, I walked an extra ten minutes in the opposite direction of my apartment, just for the pleasure of existing outside in the cold. The sun had started to set, painting the sky directly overhead in orange and pink. It had been too long since I'd been outside at this hour.

The wind was up, and the temperature had dropped ten degrees since I'd last stepped outside, but I kept my hands out of my pockets. My lungs felt clean, my brain less so, but at least this was an improvement over the emotional whiplash of the morning.

The usual route home took me past two coffee shops, a gym I'd never entered, a boarded-up candy store, and my favorite corner bodega. There was something almost poetic about the consistency of New York bodegas. They all had subtle differences, sure. But no matter the time, weather, or global mood, their neon signs always flickered in the window, and the same sullen old man always seemed to be running the register.

I told myself I'd walk right past, but a sign in the window caught my eye: "HÄAGEN-DAZS 2-FOR-1, ALL FLAVORS." I froze, then backtracked, because sometimes you had to let fate call the shots. I'd been attacked by the memories of my past this morning and now I deserved some sweet, creamy compensation.

Inside, I grabbed two pints of coffee ice cream (the only valid flavor, as far as I was concerned) and cruised through the aisles, just in case there were any new flavors of ramen.

When I stepped up to the counter, the sullen old man gave me his standard look of profound disappointment, then rang up my purchase without a word. I pulled out my credit card, mentally calculated the "I've been good, I deserve this" justification, and tapped.

Declined.

I blinked, then tried again. Still declined.

The sullen old man raised a single world-weary eyebrow. "You got another one?"

I did, but I knew better. The other card was for emergencies only, and if I started treating a Häagen-Dazs craving as an emergency, there was no coming back.

"Uh, hang on," I said, stalling while I fumbled for cash.

I found a five crumpled in my coat pocket, plus some dimes. I slid them across the counter, and the man made no comment, just handed me the bag and muttered, "Receipt?"

"No, thanks." I tucked the ice cream under my arm and hustled outside, cheeks burning in the cold and from embarrassment. Maybe I'd been pushing my luck with the recent takeout splurges, but it wasn't like I'd bought anything extravagant in the past month unless you counted genetic sequencing kits (I'd already maxed out the allowable number specified by my PhD's grant for the fiscal year, sadly) and the commemorative T-shirt from Kaitlyn's baby shower.

Outside, I did what any self-respecting grown woman would do. I sat on a stoop, opened the pint, and began eating the ice cream with the plastic spoon the bodega man had thrown in the bag. I didn't care if it was almost freezing outside. Ice cream, in my opinion, is an anytime food.

It was good, and I hated myself for needing it so badly.

After a few bites, I propped my phone on my knee and logged into my banking app, more out of morbid curiosity than anything else. The interface took an eternity to load, as if it knew what horrors awaited me.

Current balance: $303.46

Next, I checked my credit card. Maxed out, and—oh, great—a missed payment from last month.

I stared at the screen, then at my ice cream, then at the screen again. How had I let this happen? My cheeks burning hotter, I checked my savings account, just to see how close to the red zone I was. As it turns out, I was very close to the red zone. I'd have enough to cover rent and my next student loan payment, maybe, but not if I kept treating ice cream as therapy.

I scooped out another bite, letting the sweet bitterness of the coffee offset my quickly souring mood. If nothing else, the day had at least given me the clarity to see that I needed to change course, stat. No more takeout. No more fancy coffee. No more lunches out with colleagues.

I set the half-eaten pint on the step, wiped my hands on my jeans, and told myself it would be okay. I'd survived worse. I could definitely survive a few weeks or more of extreme austerity.

$$[\ 5\ ]$$

PHOTOSYNTHESIS

Samantha

week of silence and I'd almost convinced myself it had been a hallucination. The bizarre offer, his electric touch, even Andreas's beauty and the way he'd stared at me with those half-lidded olive-green eyes. I'd thrown myself into lab work with the zeal of a person determined to never contemplate babies, or the possibility that one of those babies could be weaponized in a transatlantic corporate pissing match, until I'd finished my PhD.

The problem with this plan was that my department's building was a concrete tomb, it's neoclassical façade an elaborate ruse. The only thing more mind-numbing than running the PCR machine on three hours of sleep was grading undergraduate lab reports for the world's most detail-oriented professor.

Which is where I found myself on a Thursday while trying not to entertain vengeful thoughts. I sat hunched over a battered wooden table in the windowless TA office, red pen poised to massacre the concept of "experimental design" as described by a flock of premeds who'd rather be anywhere but here. If you've never graded a report for a lab course, let me summarize: Never in the history of humanity have so many words been written, so little information conveyed, and so few clues given about what the actual assignment was.

I tried to channel my frustration into productivity. Every time I marked "vague, be specific," I imagined my pen was a tiny sword, stabbing a member of the

Kristiansen family (Andreas excluded). I made it through a half stack of blue books—my PI was old-school about lab reports, they all had to be hand-written, likely as a means to combat rampant AI usage—before my phone vibrated, jolting me out of my reverie.

The message was from building security. I squinted at the screen, then at my own handwriting in the margin of the lab report I'd been grading ("Explain how yeast actually works, Kelsey!"), then back at the phone.

"Please come to the lobby. You have a delivery."

I immediately assumed it was Kaitlyn. I'd texted her yesterday to turn down an invitation for dinner and offer to cook for us instead. When she'd pushed the issue, I told her about my vow to go cold turkey on ice cream and takeout, and this had triggered a predictable best friend meltdown in which she tried to Venmo me twice and threatened to order groceries to my door. It would be just like her to send something, possibly a three-tiered Edible Arrangement with "I'm proud of you, Samwise" spelled out in pineapple.

Kaitlyn called me Samwise, as in Samwise Gamgee, her favorite character from Tolkien's epic, *Lord of the Rings*. Strider had been my favorite, predictably. But I didn't mind the nickname because Samwise was a sexy badass and fantastic cook.

Bracing myself for embarrassment and pineapple, I headed down the hallway and toward the elevator, weaving past a pair of lost-looking students who were wearing identical university sweatshirts. The building's lobby was a relic of another era, all faux marble and bulletproof glass. The security desk sat next to a bronze bust of one of the genetics department's founders. Behind the desk, the security guard saw me and nodded toward the waiting area.

"Someone's here for you," he said. "Office is to your left."

I frowned. There was a second glass-enclosed space just off the lobby. I stepped inside, expecting to see a box of fruit.

Instead, standing in front of the window, with the posture of a man who could not believe he'd been made to wait for anything in his entire life, was Tobias Kristiansen.

If Andreas had inherited his mother's Roman goddess genes, Tobias was pure Norse, minus the Viking. He was taller than I remembered, and his suit was navy, tailored to within a micron of his existence. The effect was that of a man who wanted to dominate a boardroom but had never, ever laughed at a fart joke. His blond hair was aggressively parted and his skin was the color of mayonnaise, so pale it practically reflected the fluorescent lights. Despite all this, he was extremely and irritatingly handsome.

I didn't recognize him immediately. It had taken me two point two seconds. This was understandable since I hadn't seen Tobias since my dad's funeral, and even then, he'd stayed on the periphery, too busy being important to make eye contact with a grieving thirteen-year-old. But something in his face was familiar. Maybe it was the nose, objectively small compared to the rest of his features, or the unsettlingly pale blue eyes that tracked me across the room.

"Miss Jarlston," he said, tone modulated for maximum condescension and superiority.

I stopped in the doorway, pulse spiking while my extremities went cold. My first impulse was to turn on my heel and leave. But that would be cowardly, and instinct told me Tobias would almost certainly use it against me later. Instead, I shifted my weight, crossed my arms, and said, "I thought I smelled cabbage."

He smiled, the barest movement of lips. "Thank you for making time for me in your busy, important schedule."

I didn't say anything, because nothing I could say would be as potent as a well-timed silence.

Tobias gestured to the lone chair in the room. "Please, have a seat."

I stood, deliberately.

He shrugged, as if my disobedience was just as he expected. "How is grad school treating you?"

"You don't care, so why ask?"

Another smile, wider this time. "You always were a quick one, Sam."

I hated that he called me Sam. No one called me Sam except for my friends, and he was not in that category.

"How long is this going to take?" I asked, glancing at my phone screen before returning my glare to him. I could've finished grading those reports by now.

He appraised me, gaze moving from my clogs to my scrubs, my lab coat, and the ID badge around my neck, then back to my face. "Direct, smart, and beautiful. I like that. I can see why my little brother is so fixated."

I blanched, my stomach churning. "Excuse me?"

He waved a dismissive hand. "I'll get to the point. You and Andreas, you met."

I thought about denying it, but Andreas had sorta warned me that one of his brothers might contact me. I suspected Tobias kept tabs on Andreas and likely possessed proof that we'd met.

Thus, I shrugged. "So?"

"What did you two discuss?"

"He wanted to catch up," I said, infusing my technically true statement with boredom. "It's been over a decade."

Tobias's eyes narrowed. "You expect me to believe that he just wanted to catch up? Andreas doesn't have friends, Sam. He has adversaries and useful allies. Which are you?"

My jaw clenched. "I don't know what you're talking about."

He stepped closer, and even though there was a desk between us, the sense of threat was real. "See, here's the thing. Genetix is a major donor to your university. In fact, our family's foundation funds a sizable chunk of your department's budget. It would be a shame if something complicated that relationship."

I stared at him, but I plotted an escape route. Security was just outside the door. If I had to run out of here, I'd be fine. "Are you threatening me?"

He shrugged again. "Just letting you know how things work."

"Good. Because here's how they work for me." I put my hands on the back of the plastic chair, gripping it tight enough to make my knuckles go white. "I have no interest in your family—including your little brother—your company, or your money. Andreas sought me out, not the other way around. I told him to get lost. Therefore, I assume we're done."

Tobias administered a slow, appraising look. Then he reached into the inner pocket of his suit and pulled out a slim manila envelope. He set it on the desk with exaggerated care.

"Open it," he said.

I hesitated, then picked it up. Inside were glossy color prints, old-school-private-investigator-style. Obviously, I recognized myself immediately. The photos were in reverse chronological order: me walking out of the café, arms crossed, eyes narrowed; me sitting at a table with Andreas, looking at a piece of paper; me standing on the sidewalk just after Andreas had approached.

I set the photos down, face burning even though Andreas and I hadn't done anything to be embarrassed about. But still. It felt awful to know I'd been spied on and photographed.

"Cute," I said. "I didn't deny we met. What's your point?"

Tobias's voice was patient, almost gentle. "My brother is the best chess player in the world, but otherwise, he's an idiot. He thinks he can get away with . . . whatever this is." He tapped the photos, as if that explained everything. "But you are smarter than that. You know there are consequences to getting involved with my family again. For everyone."

I looked at the photos, then at him. "Why do you care who Andreas speaks to? Don't you have more important things to do than stalk your little brother's social life?"

He bristled. "I am invested in *my* family's company, and in keeping things stable until Father passes. We can't afford distractions."

I shrugged. "Then maybe you should talk to your brother about not ambushing people outside their jobs."

"Or maybe you should stop meeting with him, entertaining his schemes and giving him false hope, or else I will have no choice but to make you suffer," Tobias said, voice dropping to a low whisper.

There was a beat of silence.

I couldn't help it, I started to laugh. Not a big, hearty laugh, but a thin, incredulous one, because of course this family would bully me for absolutely no reason. That was their opening bid, that's all they ever did.

"I see. So, you do know what we discussed. Why pretend otherwise?" I said, going for broke, deciding I'd play around with him, just a little, just enough to irritate the man.

Tobias hesitated, then said, "Why don't you fill me in on what you think I know."

I leaned in, like I was going to spill my darkest secret. "You're right. I was the one to set up the meeting. Because—gosh, I don't know how to say this, and I can't believe you found out so quickly." I pressed my lips together and gave him my best big I'm-so-bashful eyes.

"What? What is it?" he demanded, leaning further over the desk.

"I'm in love with Andreas."

He reared back. "What?"

"I've had a crush on your brother since I was, like, eight. I have a shrine to him in my closet, always have. My prized possession is a paper cup he once used. Sometimes, as night, I press my lips to the rim of the cup and—"

He huffed impatiently, his eyes narrowing.

I wasn't finished. "—pretend we're kissing. So, I finally told him at the coffee shop. Andreas was nice about it and let me down gently. But still, one day, I'm determined that he will be mine."

Tobias looked furious, but also seemed caught off guard, his gaze flicking over me. "I know you are lying."

"How would you know? Did you record our conversation? If you did, you wouldn't be here." Irritating him—even in this small way—felt incredibly satisfying. Better than ten ice-cream pints. This moment and Tobias Kristiansen's frustrated glower would sustain me for months.

"Because Andreas would not have refused your overtures, nor would he have let you down gently." He studied me, suddenly looking tired, lips pressed into a thin line. "Obviously, I do not believe you. You are after something."

I spread my hands. "If I am, it's none of your business. But I suggest you talk to your brother, instead of me."

He glared, then pocketed the envelope. "Stay away from him."

I grinned, because irritating him was the only weapon I had. "Or what? You'll have me kicked out of grad school? Remove funding for the college? Have your goons follow me to my favorite bagel shop and buy out all the chive cream cheese before I can order?"

He shook his head, eyes skating over me, seeming genuinely perplexed. "I understand his preoccupation, now that I have seen you again. But you are more trouble than you are worth, Sam."

"Right back at you, *Toby*."

Tobias opened his mouth, likely to object to my usage of his childhood moniker, but just then, my phone buzzed again. I looked down, expecting another passive-aggressive message from Kaitlyn about accepting her food offerings, but it was from Dmitry.

Dmitry: Your plates are done. What do you want me to do with the samples? Also, Dr. Nieminen says hi.

I smiled grimly, then looked up at Tobias, who was still standing there, radiating contempt but also curiosity. The curiosity felt more dangerous.

"Sorry, gotta run," I said, lifting my phone. "Duty calls."

He straightened to his full height again, but not before muttering, "You would do well to remember my warning."

"You sound like a Disney villain. Get a better writer," I shot back, already halfway out the door.

I headed for the elevator, adrenaline pounding in my ears, and hit the up button twice just for the satisfaction of it. As the doors closed behind me, I replayed the entire encounter, and three statements stood out as particularly alarming.

I can see why my little brother is so fixated.

Because Andreas would not have refused your overtures, nor would he have let you down gently.

I understand his preoccupation.

"Damn it," I muttered, giving my head a shake and resolving to ignore Tobias's statements.

Tobias Kristiansen was just as diabolical as his father. Maybe he'd said those things to unsettle me and get under my skin. Or maybe they served some other evil, strategic purpose. Nothing that man said should be accepted as truth, I knew that. The only thing I could do was get on with my life.

Let go of the past. Let it all go.

Forget Tobias. Forget that psycho family.

But Andreas isn't a psycho.

My steps slowed and I felt my frown intensify as the image of adult Andreas sitting across from me in that café last week replayed again in my mind for the millionth time in seven days. I tried closing my eyes, but it was no use. He was still there, reaching across the table, staring at me, voice gentle.

Ugh. This is the worst.

Thank goodness I still had the other pint of ice cream in my freezer at home. I was going to need it.

[6]

CELLULAR RESPIRATION

Samantha

After the day I'd had—after Tobias and his glossy photos, the threat to my academic future, and the three-hour marathon of grading half-literate premed lab reports—I was so tired that the edges of the world looked sanded down.

Yet, I couldn't sleep. This was not unusual for me, but sleep had been markedly elusive for the last week. I simply lay there, arms at my sides, staring at the water stains above my bed, and tried not to think about Tobias's threats. And Andreas. Again.

And if I somehow succeeded at pushing thoughts of the Kristiansens from my mind, my dumb brain would then remind me that my grandma's savings account, the one I'd promised myself I would only ever touch in a real emergency, was now $708.63 lighter than it had been twelve hours ago.

Even with my Teaching Assistantship and work-study paycheck, even with the elaborate system of ramen rotation and energy-bar rationing, grad school in Manhattan was like feeding hundred-dollar bills into a paper shredder. The rent had cleared today, as it did every month, and I'd felt the click of it in my chest.

Grandma's money wasn't anywhere close to gone, but I hated using it. When I closed my eyes, I could see her writing a check in perfect, old-lady cursive, with tidy, sweeping loops. I never cashed her checks when she was alive, but in her will

41

she'd left all her savings to me, making me promise, on her actual deathbed, not to use the money for "anything stupid or self-destructive, like revenge."

I could take out more student loans, but I really, really, really didn't want to. I already had to pay back my law school loans. Becoming and being a PhD geneticist was a labor of love; no one in theoretical science and bench research was here for fame, fortune, or glory.

Maybe I should've just practiced law for a few years first, paid back the loans, made bank, and then returned to school. Too late now.

Shaking my head, I tried closing my eyes again. Somewhere in the apartment, a radiator shuddered, then spat out a series of hollow clanks that perfectly echoed the arrhythmia of my thoughts. I reached for my phone; the screen told me it was now just past 1:00 AM; I'd lain down at 10:30 PM. There were no new texts. I checked my email. A single line from my PI sent ten minutes ago: "Can you meet tomorrow at 11 to discuss sequencing results?" I marked it unread, like that would somehow keep the obligation at bay. But I'd be there, if only I could get some sleep.

Rolling onto my side, I stared at the prescription bottle on my nightstand. The sleeping pills were supposed to be for emergencies only, which my therapist had described as when my brain was actively hostile. I'd made it almost to Thanksgiving this year, seven months since I'd last taken one, which was a new record. But as the minutes slid by and my brain kept insisting I think about Andreas and money and my grandmother, I decided this insistence counted as hostility.

I popped the cap off the sleeping pills, shook one into my palm, and swallowed it dry. The bitterness spread across my tongue, a microsecond of revolt, and then nothing. Just the promise of oblivion.

To maximize my odds of making it to campus on time for the 11:00 AM meeting with my PI, I set three alarms—9:30, 10:00, and 10:30—in case the first two failed to breach the drug fog. I double-checked that I'd plugged in my phone. My sleep hygiene was a disaster, but at least my alarm game was strong.

I burrowed back under the covers and did the thing my therapist called "progressive relaxation." First, the toes. Then the calves. Then the quads. It was supposed to work like hypnosis, but mostly it made me hyper-aware that I hadn't shaved my legs in four weeks, and that my calves were now 80 percent tension, 20 percent bone.

Somewhere in the process, the pill hit. Not like a sledgehammer. More like the slow and quiet dying of a fire. The next thing I knew, I was in a dream.

It was a room that could have been any room, but the walls pulsed with a kind of warm glow, like I viewed it through stained glass. Sun through dust motes, the hum of an ancient fan, the thump of tennis shoes on hardwood. I was twelve, I knew that for sure, because I could see my own knees, sharp and unscarred, poking out from a pair of cutoff shorts that used to be my favorite.

Andreas was there. Not the current, Roman statue version, but the kid I remembered. Eleven years old, hair a dark riot, eyes enormous, always on the edge of either tears or laughter. He was stacking pillows on the floor with a focus so intense it looked like he was planning the Normandy invasion. A pillow fort. When he noticed me, he grinned, wide and guileless.

He said something, voice insistent, but the words were garbled.

I responded, and I could hear my own kid-voice, awkward and crackly, but again the words didn't make sense.

The pillows rearranged themselves until the structure wasn't just a fort; it was a labyrinth. We built it higher and wider than any pillow and blanket fort had a right to be, stealing every pillow, every chair, every bit of fabric. There was a sense of real urgency, like the whole world depended on our ability to barricade ourselves in.

At some point, the walls started to change. The colors got brighter, the edges sharper. Suddenly I was myself again, or at least the version of myself that existed now. Twenty-eight, five foot eight, long limbs, pale skin. Andreas was also older, though I hadn't seen it happen. One minute he was a kid, the next he was a giant in the six-thousand-dollar coat, arms longer and stronger, eyes the same improbable shade of green.

We were sitting inside the blanket fort, knees almost touching, and I could feel my face get hot with the knowledge of him. The knowledge that we'd once been children together, and now we were not.

He reached out, one big, careful hand, and cupped my cheek. His fingers were cool and dry, but his thumb was gentle as he brushed it along my jawline.

"I want to marry you," he said, voice echoing. It was what he'd said in the café, but this time the words were softer, like an apology or an incantation.

"Why?" dream-me asked, hoping for something I couldn't name.

"You deserve revenge," he said, his tone sounding like an out-of-tune piano. Or perhaps it was the words. All I knew was, he'd given me the wrong answer. This wasn't right. This wasn't how we were supposed to meet each other or be together.

I tried to pull away, but his grip was both light and inescapable.

"You don't want me. You just want to use me," I whispered.

His eyes were so open it hurt to look at them. "We will use each other."

I shook my head. This man wasn't Andreas. Andreas would never suggest something like this. He wasn't that kind of person.

I tried to move, tried to push myself backward through the pillow wall, but the fort had become a maze, and every time I thought I'd found the exit, he was already there, waiting for me with those hands and those eyes and his sad, perfect patience.

"Let me go," I pleaded.

He shook his head, slow and almost fondly. "I won't."

My hands were fists, my fingers fused together as one, and I couldn't look at him. "But you did."

He reached out again, fingers spreading, and he said, "Sam!" but his voice was wrong.

I opened my mouth to yell for help and he disappeared.

"Sam?"

I awoke to the sound of someone clapping. I stood in the middle of the kitchen, barefoot, one arm clutching my pillow like a flotation device. My hair was a nest, some of it in my face.

Diya hovered by the stove, her eyes wide and her lips parted.

"You okay?" Her tone sounded oddly soft and so totally at odds with the chaos of my dream that it made me want to burst into tears.

I looked around, tried to orient myself. The clock on the microwave read 5:06 AM. The only light was the under-cabinet LED.

"I—" My throat was dry. "How did I get here?"

Diya moved a step closer. "I was following you to make sure you didn't walk out the door. You went into the living room, then back to our room, then back here."

I sank to the floor, knees up, pillow still clutched tight. "Sorry. Sorry. I don't usually—that doesn't happen anymore." I wasn't awake yet, not fully. Between the dream and the sleeping pills, my brain felt impossibly foggy.

She sat down opposite me on the kitchen floor, cross-legged and wearing her favorite pair of tie-dyed pajama pants. "You were sleepwalking."

I repeated, "Sleepwalking."

"Have you ever done this before?"

Pushing my hair out of my face, I nodded. "I used to when I was a teenager, after my parents . . ." *After my parents died.*

Diya knew my parents had passed away before I turned eighteen, but that was all she knew. I wasn't a big fan of talking about my past. Better to focus on the present and future than dwell unnecessarily on old, unchangeable events.

I felt her study me for a long moment, then she asked, "Has something stressful happened recently?"

"No," I lied, staring at my bare feet. "Just the usual." I glanced at her.

She watched me, a doctor's gaze, patient but also methodical. "You know, sometimes these things start up again when there's a trigger. Even a small one."

"Yeah," I said, voice barely more than a whisper. "Makes sense."

Diya was silent for a bit, then leaned over and gently pried the pillow from my grip. "You ever try talking about it?"

"About what?"

She gave me a look like, *Seriously, dude?* "Whatever is making you sleepwalk through the apartment tonight."

I shook my head. "It's nothing. Just dreams."

"Bad dreams?"

I shrugged. "Not really. Just . . . weird. Nostalgic, I guess."

There was a pause, and then Diya handed my pillow back. "If you need to talk, just let me know."

"Noted." I hugged the pillow to my chest again, trying to will my heartbeat into something resembling normal.

Diya started to say something else, but then stopped herself. Instead, she stood, stretched, and flicked the light off.

"Good night, Sam," she said, and padded back to our room.

I stayed on the floor a few minutes longer, just breathing and trying not to cry. Eventually, I shuffled back to my own bed, still clutching the pillow, and lay there in the darkness, counting watermarks and waiting for the silence to take shape again.

* * *

I AWOKE with the 9:30 AM alarm and to the distant, muffled sound of my roommates' voices. The memory of my sleepwalking episode from last night kept me in bed even though I had to pee like a racehorse. Eventually, I flipped back the covers and ran to the bathroom, hoping I wouldn't have to stand outside the door doing the pee-pee dance for very long.

The fates favored me because the bathroom was empty. But after completing my business and as I washed my hands, I caught sight of my hair in the mirror over the sink. Sleep-matted and greasy at the roots, it was approaching "self-aware ecosystem" status.

When was the last time I showered? One of life's unanswerable questions.

Yanking my hair back in a high ponytail, I washed my face and brushed my teeth. Then, feeling moderately more human, I stumbled into the hallway. Blinking at the too-bright world, I stretched as I walked into the little kitchen, Diya's and Nakita's low, conspiratorial whispers ending abruptly at my entrance. They were both sitting at the tiny two-person rectangular table that doubled as extra counter space.

"Morning," I croaked, voice two registers below normal as I shuffled past.

Diya looked up from her mug, eyes doing a quick scan of my form. "Hey. You slept in."

Nakita, by contrast, didn't bother with the subtlety. "Why are you sleepwalking? Diya said you used to when you were a kid? Why? Because of your parents? Did something happen?"

I glanced at Diya. She'd lowered her forehead to her palm, her face turned to the side toward Nakita, presumably to give our roommate an intense stink eye while mouthing, *Shut up!*

And this, ladies and gentlemen, was one of the reasons why I didn't talk about myself, or my past, to anyone.

While wracking my fuzzy brain for a deflecting joke, I poured a glass of water and sipped it. "I sleepwalk when a storm's a comin'. Some people have knees that hurt when it rains, I sleepwalk."

Diya exchanged a look with Nakita. There was a silent communication there, a kind of backchannel that only develops between people who gossip both before and after breakfast.

"So," Diya said, "any plans for today?"

"Meeting with my PI at eleven. Then lab stuff," I said. "Might grade some reports. Why?"

She hesitated, then asked, "Do you have any days off planned? Maybe a weekend at your friend Kaitlyn's mansion in the Hamptons?"

Kaitlyn had invited me to her family's place in the Hamptons, right on the beach, it was true. But the house was a two-bedroom cottage, not a mansion. It had belonged to Kaitlyn's grandmother, who'd been a physicist in the 1930s and '40s. Kaitlyn's family tree was like a who's who for notable US scientists and politicians.

"Yeah," Nakita chimed in. "You should take some time off, you seem stressed."

I put my hand over my mouth and yawned, hard, then leaned against the wall for support. "Yeah, okay. I'll think about it. Are there any of my eggs left in the fridge?"

Diya set down her mug, her expression gentle. "You know, sleepwalking is super rare in adults. Like, one or two in a hundred."

"Guess I'm special." I tried to smile, frustrated that my roommates wouldn't take a hint and drop the subject.

Diya opened her mouth again, likely to press me further, but the apartment buzzer went off, sounding like an electrified goose. All three of us jumped.

"And now I'm fully awake." My hand flew to my heart and I closed my eyes, laughing.

Nakita, closest to the entry, stood. "I'll get it," she said, and vanished around the corner.

I bent and peered into the fridge, spotting two hard-boiled eggs in a glass dish. "Can I eat these?" I lifted the dish and gave it a little shake.

"Go ahead, I boiled them this morning." Diya took a sip from her mug, watching me over the rim.

In the background, I heard Nakita at the intercom. "Who is it?"

A voice crackled back, slightly distorted but still perfectly recognizable. "Andreas Kristiansen, here to see Samantha."

[7]

DNA, RNA, AND PROTEINS

Samantha

For a moment, the world went completely silent except for the slow metronome of my heart in my ears. There was no way it was him. Couldn't be. No way he'd show up at my apartment.

And yet, I'd heard his voice crackling through the old door speaker, *Andreas Kristiansen, here to see Samantha.*

Diya's eyes cut to mine, then away, then back again, a question behind them. Unable to spare a single synapse to regulate my facial expression, I simply stared at her in return, straining my ears.

Nakita, never one for subtlety, snorted. "Yeah, right. Get lost."

There was a beat of dead air, and then through the intercom, "Please tell Samantha that Andreas is here for her." He sounded irritated.

All at once, I was out of the kitchen, sprinting to the wall-mounted speaker. I pressed the button with a trembling thumb. "I'm here. Sorry. Andreas, I'm buzzing you in."

The response was a flat, "Thank you," with an intonation that made it sound suspiciously like, *Finally.*

Then *click*. Silence.

When I turned around, both Diya and Nakita were staring at me with curiosity, but Nakita's eyes also held disbelief. "Wait. You actually know someone named Andreas Kristiansen?"

I bit my lip. "Yeah. He's—" I tried to figure out how to explain him without triggering an avalanche of follow-up questions. "We go way back."

Diya, master of the understated eyebrow, let hers inch upward. "Should I recognize the name? And, by 'way back,' do you mean to the childhood you never talk about?"

I tried to smile and huff out a laugh. It came out more like a snort. "Yes. Childhood. Our parents were—uh—business partners." This was the biggest understatement since "the Titanic ran into a little trouble."

Nakita's brain appeared to be working at double speed now. "But—like—is it *that* Andreas Kristiansen?"

I played dumb and tried employing a non sequitur, which sometimes distracted her enough for me to plot an escape. "He's not a politician, if that's what you mean."

"Who is Andreas Kristiansen?" Diya glanced between Nakita and me.

Nakita shook her head vigorously, ponytail whipping, ignoring Diya. She reached out and gripped my upper arm. "No, no, I mean the chess guy. The prodigy? Best player in the world? The dude who destroys other grand masters in thirty seconds or less and then just walks off stage like, whatever. That's your Andreas?"

I tried not to grimace and failed. "I don't know. Who's to say. It's been a while since we—" The sound of heavy footsteps on the stairs cut me off.

The color drained from Nakita's face. "Holy shit. It's him, right? Is he coming up? Oh my God. You know Andreas Kristiansen! Why didn't you say anything? I would've put on pants!"

I wiped my palms down my thighs, a new burst of adrenaline making my hands sweat. "It's not a big deal. He's just a person. Also, you're literally wearing pants."

"I meant real pants, not pajama pants!" she hissed.

There was a knock on the door and all three of us flinched like house cats sprayed with water.

Diya, the only person in the apartment who could reliably do anything with grace, peered out the peephole and then looked back at me, her eyes three sizes bigger than normal. "You should get the door," she whispered, then to Nakita added, "Are all chess players so hot? Holy shit!"

I hesitated, then motioned for Nakita to stand to my left. "Back up," I whispered. Nakita nodded gravely, like this was the most important moment of her life.

With my heart banging against my ribs, I undid the chain and the three dead bolts, then turned the knob and swung the door open.

There he was, brooding in a black wool coat and a perfectly ironed dark green button-up, standing in my doorway, looking as though he'd just stepped out of a magazine cover. His hair was a little messier than last week, and his dark, thick eyebrows were drawn low over those absurdly intense eyes. He looked annoyed, but also a bit wary.

"Hello, Samantha," he said, voice low and—God help me—still unreasonably attractive.

I realized I was just standing there, holding the doorknob with both hands like an idiot. "Uh. Hi. Come in."

He did, brushing past me in a wave of cool air and rosemary-scented something, pausing at the entryway table. He sized up Diya and Nakita, then looked back at me as if waiting for an introduction.

Nakita, apparently unable to contain herself, blurted, "Oh my God, you're Andreas Kristiansen!"

His face did not move. "Yes."

I turned to Nakita and shot her the most vicious side-eye I could muster. "Can you not?"

She grinned, hands clasped under her chin now. "Sorry, but do you even know how much I am freaking out right now? My sister would lose her mind if she knew you were in our apartment. She literally talks about you every day. Like, every day."

Andreas looked at me, then at her. "Your sister plays chess?"

Nakita nodded. "She plays tournaments, women's chess."

This was news to me, but it tracked with everything I knew about Nakita's family.

Diya interjected, "What's 'women's chess'? Why isn't it just chess?"

Andreas held his gloved fingers out to Diya for a shake. "Andreas."

"Diya," she said, accepting the handshake.

"The short answer is, women's chess exists because men are horrible," Andreas answered her question, very matter-of-factly. "But it persists because not many girls and women play chess—for many reasons—and therefore women make more money in women's chess."

Diya made a choking sound, her eyes widening with surprise, presumably at his candor.

But Nakita only grinned wider. "My sister has a livestream account with a ton of followers. She sits in Central Park and challenges people to games in real time. If they win, she pays them fifty dollars."

"Does she ever have to pay out?" Diya asked.

"No, never." Nakita beamed. "But a lot of men get angry—I mean, absolutely furious—when they lose."

I was trying to keep up and abruptly realized the door was still open. I shut it and took the opportunity to shake out my hands, telling myself I had no reason to be so nervous.

"Ah, yes. I think I've seen her videos." Andreas nodded subtly. "She has a strong end game, but favors the Ruy Lopez."

Nakita gasped and inched forward like she might grab him. "Are you serious? We are such huge fans. She would absolutely die if she could play you. Or just meet you."

Andreas's expression remained unreadable, but he sounded thoughtful as he said, "I do not usually play strangers in parks."

Diya, who'd watched the interaction between Nakita and Andreas like a true spectator, gave him the once-over. "Do you play women?"

"Whenever my counterparts are willing, of course. But I am a man and therefore not allowed to play in women's chess tournaments."

Diya crossed her arms. "And do you always win when you play women?"

He stared at her for a beat, then said, "I generally win, no matter who I play."

I couldn't decide if he sounded arrogant or not, so I looked at Nakita to see if his words bothered her. She was still grinning at him like he'd invented cheese. Either she didn't notice his arrogance or wasn't bothered by it.

"But, yes. I have lost to a player before who happened to be a woman." Andreas, tone flat, began removing his gloves.

My heart spiked, pulse fluttering, and I grabbed his wrist to still his movements before he could reveal his ridiculously sexy hands. "Are you here to—why are you here? I mean, what do you want?"

"I want to talk to you," he said, voice low, communicating with a small incline of his head that he'd prefer to speak in private. Which, given the crowd, was fair.

And, just in case I hadn't understood his head tilt, he added, "Alone, if possible." His voice was a touch softer than before.

I glanced around the crowded entryway and then toward the small sitting area and even smaller kitchen. "Sure, we can . . ." I trailed off, searching for a more private venue than the kitchen table.

Diya saved me, gesturing down the hall. "Use our room," she said, the faintest smile ghosting her lips. "I'll keep Nakita occupied. Come on, Nakita, let's go see if my chai chia pudding recipe actually worked."

Nakita frowned for the first time since Andreas had walked in, shooting me a look that threatened, *We'll talk later!* and followed Diya toward the kitchen, her head turning back toward us with every few steps.

Andreas waited until they'd disappeared before facing me. "Lead the way."

And, with my heart in my throat, I did.

I realized as we walked down the hallway that I'd left a week's worth of dirty laundry in a mountainous heap in the middle of the floor last night, sorted and ready for the coin laundry down the street. I also realized that my desk probably looked like a tornado had passed through, if that tornado had a fondness for empty ramen bowls, highlighters, and sticky notes with things like "NIEMINEN IS A GNOME WITH TINY HANDS" written in all caps.

Preemptively mortified, I hurried ahead and started scooping up clothes, balling them into a nest and shoving them into my closet, which immediately caused a small avalanche of more items to tumble out.

Andreas watched the process in silence, hands still gloved and hanging at his sides. He looked slightly less out of place in my tiny room than he had in the entryway, but only slightly.

"You share this room," he observed.

Finally able to shut the closet door by pressing my back against it, I pointed at the cracked faux-leather desk chair. "You can sit. Sorry about . . . all of this." I waved my hand, taking in the entirety of my mess.

He walked to the chair, sat, then tugged at the leather around his wrists and at his fingertips. I tried not to watch, but it felt impossible. Cheeks flushing, I turned my back until I could be sure his gloves were off. Pretending to straighten my nightstand became clearing off my nightstand as I swiped the contents—including the sleeping pills but not the lamp—into the top drawer.

Crossing my arms, I twisted at the waist just in time to see him tuck his gloves into his coat pocket. Andreas then set his elbows on the chair arms. He may have appeared bored to someone who didn't grow up with him, but I recognized the calculating quality behind those droopy-lidded eyes.

"You have more roommates?" he asked, glancing at the closed door behind me.

"Three in total," I replied as I gathered a pile of textbooks from the floor at the foot of my bed and stacked them on the windowsill. "Diya and Nakita, both of whom you just met briefly, plus Kendra. I could've signed up for subsidized housing through the University, but this place is actually less expensive."

He frowned, as if I'd confessed to sleeping in a dumpster. "You feel safe? To share a room?"

I stared at him and his question, at a loss.

His face reassembled itself into something perfectly neutral, but he added, "You might recall, my brother Henrik and I shared a room, for a time."

"Ah, yes." Now his question made sense. "I remember. And, yes. Diya is great. I trust her."

Andreas's stare seemed to drill into mine, as though hoping to pull the truth out of me with the force of his attention alone. When I said nothing else, he glanced away, dusting the fabric of his black pants with the back of his fine fingers.

"So . . ." I glanced behind me to ensure I wouldn't be sitting on another pile of laundry; finding the space empty save for the mattress and covers, I sat on my bed. "What brings you to my humble abode?"

Andreas exhaled, the sound almost imperceptible, but enough for me to know he was still irritated. "I wanted to talk."

"We're talking now."

His eyes seemed to darken. "You didn't call."

I blinked. "When?"

The subtle shift in the line of his mouth told me he was already losing patience. "After Tobias visited you yesterday. I requested that you let me know if he or Henrik bothered you."

Oh. That.

I crossed my arms again, fighting against a strange sense of disappointment, and I felt my own temper begin to simmer. "I never agreed to your request."

"It would be wise to keep me apprised." His voice was ice-water calm, which only made his words sound condescending.

I didn't respond. Not for the first time this week, I reminded myself that we weren't anything to each other. I owed him nothing, not even an explanation. *And he owes me nothing.*

Andreas leaned back in the desk chair, studying me with a flat, cold intensity that reminded me of a microscope. "He will escalate. You know that, right?"

"If he does, I'll deal with it." I couldn't explain it, not even to myself, but I didn't want Andreas to be here because of Tobias, or Genetix, or any reason related to his family or mine. And the fact that *this*—Tobias's unwelcomed visit yesterday—was the purpose of Andreas's visit today, annoyed me.

He tapped his fingers on the arms of the chair, his gaze assessing, evaluating, calculating. "You should have called me."

I looked at the water stains on the ceiling, then at the closet door where I'd just shoved my laundry, then at him. "This is getting us nowhere. What exactly do you want, Andreas?"

He was silent for a long moment, his eyes flicking over my face, my arms, my posture, as if recalibrating some internal schema. Finally, he said, "I want to protect you."

Something about the way he said it made my pulse trip. Not in a romantic way. More like how you feel when a fire alarm goes off in the middle of an exam and you don't know if it's a drill or the real thing.

"Don't," I said, more softly than I meant. "If that's why you're here, you should leave."

Andreas's jaw flexed. "You should not have to deal with Tobias and his threats. I know he threatened you. I know—"

"If you felt that way, then you should've left me alone," I snapped, the words out before I could choke them back. "You're the reason I'm on his radar now."

Eyes narrowed, exhaling through his nose, he stood abruptly. The chair nearly toppled over, but he caught it, steadied it, and then turned to face me. "If you had answered my messages last month, all of this could have been avoided."

"If you'd left well enough alone, then Tobias wouldn't have shown up yesterday." I also stood, squaring my shoulders, not caring how angry I sounded. "Why would I trust you to protect me from a situation you created?"

Something like fury passed behind his features. "You really want Henrik or Tobias to inherit your father's company? Is that what you want?"

I said nothing, clenching my hands until my knuckles hurt. I couldn't bring myself to lie about this again like I'd done in the coffee shop, especially not after seeing Tobias yesterday.

"Answer me," he demanded.

"No," I whisper-shouted, having just enough wherewithal to keep my voice down so as not to give Nakita and Diya something new to gossip about. "No, I don't. I want revenge. I want them destitute and desperate. I want the company so badly, I can't sleep at night thinking about your evil father and all the ways I wish he would suffer. I hope your entire family—you excluded—dies in a fire. Happy?"

He didn't reply. Instead, he took a step back, his chin lifting as he stared at me and my ugly confessions.

I realized I'd gone too far, but the anger wouldn't stop choking me. I wanted to be finished with my past bitterness and resentment, but my true feelings had spiraled out, vengefulness saturating my words. I dropped my eyes and stared at the threadbare carpet, wishing I could go back to the version of myself that existed before my admission ten seconds ago, before seeing him last week, before all of it.

Why did he come here? Why can't he just leave me alone?

My heart ached, just like last week. And the rubber bands around my lungs returned, squeezing tight.

Rubbing my forehead, I heaved a sigh and it was just on the tip of my tongue to ask him to leave when he said, "I'm not only here because of Tobias."

I blinked, peeking at him, unsure what to do with that. "Oh?"

He hesitated, then moved closer. Not in a threatening way, just enough to bridge the gap between us. "I have found another way to ensure you inherit Genetix upon my father's death. And do not worry, it does not involve anything you might find revolting, like marrying me or having my child." For once, he'd allowed emotion to enter his voice, and it sounded like disdain.

I bit back a sarcastic response, instead grinding out, "Fine. What is it?"

He hesitated for a split second, then said, "I will adopt you."

I stared at him, waiting for him to say, *Just kidding*, or, *Got you!*

When he didn't, I blinked. Then blinked again. His passive stare—deadly serious, not even a hint of humor in it—told me what I could not accept from his words alone. I realized he meant it.

He meant it. *He's serious.*

"You have read the pertinent page of the will, it makes no mention of marriage or any other type of union, nor does it state that the grandchild needs to be biological." Andreas sounded as though he were explaining the rules to a card game and not outlining why it made sense for him to *adopt* me. "It merely states 'first grandchild.' When I adopt you, you will obviously be the first. You're two years older than me, which—given the situation—is somewhat amusing."

I stared at him, completely dumbstruck, my brain floundering. "But—but—"

I searched for the flaw, the trick, the punchline, and found none.

The side of his mouth hitched but his gaze was wholly and starkly devoid of humor as he asked, "So, what say you, Samantha? Will you consent to be my daughter?"

[8]

GENES AND HEREDITY

Samantha

The city felt several degrees colder than the week before, and I ducked my nose inside my thick scarf as I scuttled east on Seventy-Third, hands deep in my coat pockets and chin tucked low. A fierce wind funneled straight down the cross streets, whipping at my hair and occasionally flinging it across my face like I'd pissed off some minor weather deity.

It was seven o'clock in the evening, give or take a minute, and the sky was that weird color it gets just after dark in early winter, less blue, more like a violet bruise above the city skyline. Every inhale had that metallic cold-snap taste and my breath became clouds of white with every exhale.

I passed a mother in a Canada Goose parka dragging her son by the wrist while he mewled about not wanting to go to flute lessons. The doorman in front of Kaitlyn's building smiled at me, an avuncular twitch of the mouth that said, *You don't live here, but I recognize you.* I smiled back. He reminded me of my grandpa, and I briefly considered calling him.

But, no. My grandfather and I hadn't talked since he'd remarried and moved to Arizona.

Kaitlyn's apartment building was the kind of structure you saw in movies about people who never worried about health insurance or whether one ramen serving could be stretched into two full meals with enough broccoli. The lobby was marble, the elevator was wood-paneled, and the whole place had that subtle, permanent scent of new carpet mixed with whatever they used to clean glass.

If you let Andreas adopt you and you inherit Genetix, then you'd be able to afford an apartment in a building with a doorman, no problem. Maybe even the whole damn building.

I sighed.

As the elevator ferried me up, I tried, for maybe the thousandth time, to make a decision about Andreas's offer. It had been just two days, but it had felt like weeks since he'd stood in my tiny apartment and explained his plan.

Andreas, even as a child, had been the type to make amends for the sake of his own internal sense of righteousness. More and more, I was beginning to suspect that he'd only reached out to me in an attempt to correct a wrong between our respective families, settle a debt, make things right.

But for me . . . my intentions and motivations for considering his offer were much less virtuous.

Also, both my past and current feelings for Andreas Kristiansen didn't have much to do with correcting historical injustices. Mind you, none of my present feelings for (i.e., attraction to) Andreas were at all voluntary. A fact that didn't stop the attraction from existing. Even sleep-deprived, even discombobulated and emotional and blindsided, both times he'd popped up unannounced, I couldn't seem to stop checking him out.

How incredibly inconvenient.

But here's the thing about attraction: It always fades.

See, attraction is like a plant. If you water it too much, it dies. If you water it too little, it also dies. And that's the key to killing attraction. Over time, with either enough exposure or enough distance, it goes away. Thus, either I needed A LOT more exposure to Andreas—like, daily—or I needed to cut him out of my life.

I was currently leaning toward cutting him out. True, I'd asked Andreas for time to think about his plan. In reality, I hadn't stopped thinking about it for even a second.

I also hadn't told anyone. Not my therapist, not Diya, obviously not my grandfather, not even Kaitlyn. Which was why I was here now, in front of her apartment, steeling myself before the door.

I pressed the little call button and waited.

"Sam!" Kaitlyn's excited voice sounded from the speaker. They had an app on their phones, instead of a built-in intercom, that allowed them to interact with door-button pushers.

Despite my mood, I tried to sound chipper. "Hey, it's me."

The lock buzzed. I entered and let myself in to the warmth and soft golden light of the apartment. I used to love coming here just after Kaitlyn and Martin got married. The apartment belonged to them both, but the grand piano was entirely Kaitlyn's. She'd changed her major in college to music theory and now did what she loved, writing compositions for famous singers and collaborating with famous songwriters.

Kaitlyn's family had money, but not a Standard-Oil-before-the-trust-breakup amount. Her mother was a senator and her father was the dean of the School of Medicine at UCLA. So, well-off, but not tech-bro well-off. Martin's father was the absurdly wealthy one in their family tree, but both Martin and Kaitlyn had severed ties with the telecom giant years ago.

Still, every square foot of the apartment screamed antique and quality, and nothing looked cheap or temporary.

I hung my coat on the rack by the door, then called out, "Where are you?"

From somewhere deeper in the apartment, her voice called back, "Come in! I'm at the piano."

I padded down the hallway, past the powder room and the minimalist kitchen, and into the living room, where Kaitlyn sat perched on the piano bench with a mug in one hand and a pencil in the other. She seemed to be writing something in an open notebook set on the music stand. Her curly, dark brown hair was up in a bun and tonight she wore black leggings, a wildly oversized red turtleneck, and not a stitch of makeup.

She stood as I entered and set her mug down on the mission-style coffee table.

"Sam," she said, and her face lit up with real joy, her big smile showing off the subtle gap between her two front teeth. She never used my full name, unless it was in print or on a birthday cake. "Get over here, you gorgeous beast."

We hugged. She always went for a full-body embrace, even if one of us was holding something sharp or breakable. There was a long moment of pure, unspoken comfort. I tried to remember the last time I'd hugged anyone longer than five seconds.

It was the last time you saw Kaitlyn.

"Where's the baby?" I asked, pulling away.

"Martin is in the nursery rocking him. If he's still awake, you can go peek in before you leave, but he's been a monster all day and the last thing anyone needs is him catching a second wind." Kaitlyn grinned. "Sorry if I stink, I'm in feral momma mode and I have a deadline on this new song with Abram."

I looked her up and down, then gestured at myself: scrubby jeans, fraying cardigan, T-shirt I'd found at the bottom of my laundry. "If this is feral, I'm basically a trash panda in human skin."

She grinned, reaching for her mug again. "You say that, but you have no idea what feral is until the aroma of sour breast milk seasons all your clothes. Here, sit, I have a new tea I want you to try."

Kaitlyn motioned me toward the sofa, then disappeared into the kitchen to retrieve the tea. I glanced at the piano and noticed the book she'd placed on the bench—*The Queen's Gambit*.

Not subtle.

Last night, when I'd called to see if she had time for me to come over, I hadn't told her about Andreas's offers to marry me / impregnant me / adopt me, but I had told her that my old friend Andreas Kristiansen had reached out with a proposition, and I wanted to discuss it with her. Kaitlyn, being a nerd, already knew who he was in the chess world. She also already knew a bit about my history with him. I'd shared more of myself and my past with Kaitlyn than I had with any other (non-therapist) person in my life.

She returned with a new mug, handed it to me, and plopped onto the large leather couch, tucking her feet under her. "Tell me everything."

I took a sip. It tasted faintly of cardamom and something sweet. "Oh! It's good."

"I think so. That's fenugreek that you're tasting. It increases breast milk production."

I froze, cup halfway to my mouth.

She laughed. "It won't do anything to nonlactating humans, you goose."

Regardless, I set the mug on the coffee table and folded my hands.

"Okay, now tell me, what's going on with your old friend Andreas? What's this proposition? This is the youngest in that family that screwed over your family, right?"

I inhaled, exhaled, and prepared to sound ridiculous. "Yes, the Kristiansens are the family in question. And yes, the father—his name is Oskar—and potentially the oldest son—let's call him Satan, even though his Christian name is Tobias— framed my father for fraud."

I then went on to summarize how my father, while under an active criminal investigation, lost his shares in his own company, was voted out by the board, declared bankruptcy, and then died of a sudden and massive heart attack.

Kaitlyn listened patiently to the CliffsNotes version of a story she'd heard before, her features soft with compassion. "So, we hate everyone in this family but the youngest, Andreas. And wasn't teenage you in love with him? Or am I thinking of someone else?"

I felt my face heat up. "Not in love. More like . . . I don't know how to describe it." *Crap.*

This sometimes happened when I spoke to Kaitlyn or my therapist. They'd make an offhanded comment, or an assumption, and then things about myself—my past behavior and my past choices—would suddenly make sense.

The reason you can't stop thinking about Andreas and the reason why your body goes haywire whenever you see him now is probably because you had a serious crush on him back then, dummy.

"Okay, sure. He was something like my first love, but I was only thirteen, and he was eleven, so it doesn't count. We were too young for those kinds of feelings, or at least he was. In any case, it was one-sided."

Her eyes narrowed. "Sam. That would make him your *only* love."

"Whatever." I needed to stop explaining about the past since, back then, I hadn't been certain what I'd felt. They'd been emotions I didn't possess any context for at the time as an extremely sheltered thirteen-year-old. And did it matter? I'd been a kid. He'd been a kid. Kid-feelings fifteen years ago shouldn't matter to grown adults.

I pressed on. "Anyway, last week—"

"Wait." She reached forward. "Do you still have feelings for him?"

I flinched back. "What? No! Like I said, we were kids."

Her eyes narrowed and skated over me. "Are you sure? What did you feel when he contacted you?"

I rolled my eyes at myself. "Sure. Fine. Maybe I felt something like nostalgia. And I couldn't help but notice that he's extremely attractive. Thus, I find him attractive. You've seen his photo online, right? But I don't know him now. How could I have relevant, real feelings for someone I don't know?"

This last rhetorical question seemed to resonate with Kaitlyn because she nodded like my logic passed muster. "That makes sense. Then, proceed. What happened last week?"

"Last week, Andreas showed up at my job, then at my apartment on Friday."

Kaitlyn sat up straighter. "Wait, he's here? In the city? I thought you said he called you."

"No, I said he *contacted* me." I then proceeded to tell her, in the most objective language I could find, about my recent interactions with the Kristiansens and Andreas's offers: the meeting at the café, the sinister visit from Tobias, Andreas's second visit and his last-resort plan to adopt me, complete with all the legal logic and strategic implications.

I watched Kaitlyn's face run the full spectrum of disbelief, delight, then a little concern.

I concluded, "So, basically, if I allow him to adopt me, I will inherit controlling interest in Genetix. Unlike marriage, adoptions are extremely difficult to contest when it comes to inheritance, in part due to intestacy laws."

"Does that count? Isn't Oskar Kristiansen Norwegian?"

"Andreas has dual citizenship, but Oskar renounced his Norwegian citizenship. He's a naturalized US citizen and his personal holdings fall under US law. In the US, adoptions are extremely difficult to reverse, so there would be no going back. And it's not like this is unprecedented. Adult adoption is a common practice used by estate lawyers as a way to circumvent established legacy trusts and limits on inheritance eligibility."

"So, what's the problem?"

"I'm not sure." I rubbed my forehead. "If he adopts me, then—legally—it severs ties with my own biological family, but that doesn't matter. My grandfather and I don't keep in touch and I have no one else left."

She covered my hand with hers and gave it a squeeze. "But, what happens if Andreas adopts you? Is that it? Or does he want anything else? Or is it just, like, he adopts you secretly, you sign the paperwork, you both get on with your lives until Oskar kicks the bucket? And then—BAM! Reveal at the will reading."

"He didn't mention anything about the logistics or additional contact, so I have to assume we sign the paperwork and move on, go back to being strangers." I met her concerned gaze. "Listen, I realize it makes sense. This is my chance. I don't have anything to lose, but it *feels* like I do. It feels like the price is—I don't even know. My dignity? Life as I know it? The space-time continuum?"

Kaitlyn let out a slow whistle, the kind my grandmother would use when she decided to keep her thoughts—but not her judgy whistles—to herself. "This is a lot."

Before either of us could process further, the nursery door creaked, and Martin, six-foot-three former varsity rower, strode into the room. He wore an NYC Club Crew sweatshirt and gym shorts, despite the temperature.

"He's out," he said to his wife, crossing directly to her and bending down to give her a kiss, then staring at her.

After a beat, Kaitlyn frowned at her husband. "Say hi to Sam. Don't be rude."

Martin gave Kaitlyn a small smile, then straightened, his smile disappearing into the ether. "Sam," he said.

"Sandeke," I said with an equivalent amount of warmth.

We weren't frenemies, nor were we friends, nor were we enemies. More like, we tolerated each other's existence for the sake of our mutual adoration for Kaitlyn.

I turned my attention back to Kaitlyn, planning to ask her to help me make a pro / con list, when Martin unexpectedly said, "Andreas's strategy is solid."

I blinked, stunned, and croaked out, "You were listening?"

"Your voice carries. And don't worry. Obviously, I won't tell anyone." He sat down behind Kaitlyn, encouraging her to lean back against him. "You can seal and hide an adoption, but you can't do the same thing with a marriage. Adopting you is a much better strategy than getting married and trying to have a baby. Anything could happen in nine months. Likewise, a sudden marriage between two people who haven't seen each other in years, given your families' history, is suspect. Andreas's brothers would start to dig and discover the addendum to the will, then make their own plans, which would include interfering with yours. I doubt you want your child to be a perpetual target."

"Okay. Noted," I said, reluctantly grateful for his rational assessment of the situation. Martin Sandeke had no skin in the game, he certainly didn't care about me or Andreas. Thus, his impartiality was valuable. Not to mention the man was one of the most inherently shrewd businessmen I'd ever met. "But, to be clear, I have not agreed to be adopted. Yet."

Kaitlyn leaned over and stage-whispered, "But you want to."

I considered this, then hunched forward with the weight of it. "Maybe? I don't know. It would fantastic to screw them over, but also . . . really fucking weird to have Andreas as my adopted *father*." Just thinking about it gave me *Flowers in the Attic* heebie-jeebies, even though I knew it shouldn't. We weren't biologically related, and adult adoption for inheritance purposes wasn't unheard of.

Martin slid his arms around Kaitlyn, drawing her further back. "Let me ask you something, Sam. Do you trust Andreas?"

I didn't even have to think. "Yes."

Martin inspected me for a moment. "You don't trust many people. Why him?"

I picked up my tea. "When we were kids, he always kept my secrets, and I'm the holder of his. Even when it cost him. Even after my dad died, even after the two families went thermonuclear."

Kaitlyn snuggled back against her husband. "You know, Martin and you have that in common. He doesn't trust people, either."

I twisted my lips to the side. "Well, the trust is moot unless I can survive the psychological fallout of being the adopted daughter of my childhood . . ." I struggled for a moment on how to best describe Andreas, finally settling on, "My childhood best friend."

Martin lifted an eyebrow. "You went to law school, you know that's not how the law sees it. There was that famous case a few years ago about that man who adopted his girlfriend to avoid paying out in a civil suit. The primary use of adult adoption is inheritance. Many people adopt their significant other to get around legacy trust inheritance limitations or civil court rulings."

I lifted an eyebrow. "'Many people'?"

"Fine. Many rich people with sizable trust funds. Happy?"

I nodded. "Proceed."

"I'm just saying, an adult adoptee is not in the same category as a child adoptee. It's basically paperwork. Don't let the label psyche you out or keep you from taking what you want. Or, more accurately, taking what it sounds like you deserve."

I already knew and logically understood the difference between adult and childhood adoption. Logic wasn't the problem. *Feelings* were the problem.

Kaitlyn leaned back, her head on Martin's shoulder, and looked at him. "You think Sam deserves Genetix?"

He nodded. "I mean, yeah. After what they did to your family? Why are you hesitating? Just do it. If it were me, I'd jump at the chance to take Genetix from the Kristiansens."

Kaitlyn patted his hand. "I know you would, honey." Then to me she whispered, "He just wishes he had more targets for his revenge plots."

He glowered at his wife from behind her back while I fought a laugh.

"Anyway." Martin gave his attention back to me. "If you do go through with it, you'll need a cover story. Something to distract the rest of the Kristiansens from what's really happening. Your friend, Andreas, he needs to make it look like he's taking some sort of action on the will addendum. Otherwise, the brothers will sniff out the adoption eventually, even if the record is sealed."

I leaned forward, wondering if I should be taking notes. "Like what, exactly?"

Martin's eyes lifted up and to the left. "Like . . . once they discover the addendum to the will, Andreas should pretend to be trying to have a baby with someone. It doesn't have to be you, just someone believable. Or, at the very least, get engaged. That'll keep them distracted."

I blinked. "That's ridiculous. Didn't you just say getting married and having a baby is the weaker strategy? And who would sign up to pretend to be Andreas's fake—" I stopped myself before completing that sentence, because *plenty* of people would line up to be Andreas Kristiansen's fake fiancée.

Just the thought made my stomach sour.

Luckily, Kaitlyn chimed in, "No, actually, that's smart. It *is* the wrong strategy, but that doesn't mean they'll question it. If he makes it look like he's getting together with someone just to have a baby, just to meet the requirements of the will, nobody will suspect that you're already the first grandchild by adoption."

Martin nodded. "Exactly. Give the brothers a plausible red herring."

I squinted at them both. "Is this a normal thing? Am I the only one who thinks this is bonkers?"

Kaitlyn smiled. "Sam, you called me yesterday to say you needed to talk. I assumed it was because you'd finally set the lab on fire. But instead, you're about to execute a legendary revenge plot against the men who ruined your family and become the heiress of a multinational corporation. What is the actual downside? How could I not support this?"

My chest felt weirdly tight, like my heart was expanding but also getting ready to collapse under its own weight. "I haven't agreed to anything yet. I said I needed time to think."

Martin shook his head. "No. You've already made your decision, Sam. You just need to convince yourself you're okay with it."

I thought about that. About the way I kept recalling the words of the will addendum like a prayer; the way I'd memorized the addendum after only reading it twice, every legalese loophole; how I'd researched sealed adoptions using a public library computer browser yesterday morning. I thought about the way I'd spent my entire life pretending I didn't care about what the Kristiansens did, when in fact I'd been quietly dreaming of this exact moment for fifteen years.

"Yeah," I admitted, voice soft. "I want it. I want to make them suffer and lose everything, I want to take back my father's company. I think I'd do almost anything. Even this."

Martin nodded, the movement slow and deliberate. "From my own personal experience, here's what I can tell you. It'll be worth it, so long as you don't lose something—or someone—more important to you in the process."

I looked from him to Kaitlyn, then back at him. "You mean, like how you almost lost Kaitlyn when you went after your own dad?"

He shrugged, like this was old news. "Sometimes you don't know what your priorities are until you're forced to choose."

"And you ultimately chose Kaitlyn over justice," I supplied.

He nodded, looking not at all regretful.

Kaitlyn squeezed his hand. "Let's be honest when among friends. You're both talking about revenge, Sam. Maybe it's also justice, but for you, it's definitely the latter."

"You're right." I shook my head and looked up to the ceiling. "Thank you. For not thinking I'm completely foolish, or irrational."

Martin stretched his legs out on the large leather sofa. "I know you graduated from law school and passed the bar, but if you need a lawyer to draw up an adoption contract with Andreas, let me know. You can use someone from our legal department."

My eyes widened with surprise at his offer. He was correct. I'd graduated from law school and passed the bar, but that was four years ago, a career path abandoned after I realized how much I disliked confrontation and pointless arguments. The only thing I enjoyed about law was the research aspect, and those jobs were being replaced by AI.

"Hey. Thanks, Martin. That's . . . nice of you."

His expression flattened. "You act like I'm never nice to you."

I didn't respond to that, saying instead, "I guess I didn't realize that all it would take for us to truly get along was a little revenge bonding."

He scoffed, but he also sorta smiled.

Kaitlyn, her eyelids drooping tiredly, spoke around a yawn. "I'm not a huge fan of revenge in general, but we're with you, Samwise. Whatever you decide."

The rest of the evening blurred a little. We sat, we drank tea, we talked about everything except the impending plot to upend the Kristiansen hold on Genetix. We ate half a box of lemon cookies and made jokes about how Joey would someday destroy the world by inheriting his father's penchant for revenge and his mother's ridiculous IQ. Eventually, I left, wrapped in a cloud of borrowed warmth and assurance.

On the walk home, I looked up at the dark autumn sky and tried to picture what my life might look like if I went through with it. If I said yes.

I thought about Andreas, about the look on his face when he'd asked me to be his daughter, about the way he'd seemed frustrated about it. Or maybe that was my imagination. Or perhaps I was the one who was frustrated.

Whatever. You've already decided, my brain whispered. *You're just stalling.*

I stopped under a streetlamp, took out my phone, and stared at the new contact labeled simply *Andreas*. My thumb hovered over the call button.

Maybe tomorrow, I told myself, and slipped the phone back into my coat.

The wind was still biting, but I barely noticed.

[9]

INHERITANCE PATTERNS

Samantha

The next morning, I woke up on the blue corduroy sofa in the apartment's family room and I had zero recollection of how I got there.

But I'd had that dream again, the one where Andreas and I were building a blanket and pillow fort and we'd turned into adult versions of ourselves. But instead of asking me to marry him, this time Andreas had told me he'd already adopted me. And then right after saying the words, he'd died.

Last thing I remembered before falling asleep last night, I'd been on my bed reading an article about ancient microbiome DNA. I'd been wearing a sleep shirt, undies, and nothing else. Now, I was in jeans and a backward, inside-out T-shirt, sitting on the couch, covered in a chunky fleece blanket that smelled like citrus and old bagels, and someone—probably Diya—had set a glass of water and two ibuprofen on the coffee table in front of me.

I reached for the water, my hand trembling a little, and chugged half the glass before the first wave of disorientation passed. My mouth tasted sour. My arms and legs felt like they'd been disconnected and reattached. I squinted at the clock on the wall: 5:32 AM.

Sleepwalking. Again. I didn't want to think about it, but my brain, like a bad roommate, always ignored closed doors and boundaries.

Instead, it replayed last night's series of decisions, starting with the walk home from Kaitlyn's, followed by the usual ritual of brushing my teeth, setting my alarm, etc. This time, there'd been an addition to the ritual. Sitting on the edge of my bed for a solid forty minutes, staring at my phone and hovering over Andreas's number, willing myself to call and agree to his scheme.

I never did call him. I fell asleep on my bed and now I was here.

Standing, and ignoring the twin protests from my spine and my sense of mental stability, I shuffled to the kitchen for more water. I heard the hiss of the shower from the hall bath and figured Nakita was gearing up for an early shift. I didn't know where Kendra or Diya were, however.

My backpack was on the floor by the front door, right where I'd left it last night. I shouldered it, poured another glass of water, and—after a moment's debate —went to my room and grabbed the towel and shower caddy from my closet, placing them in a duffel bag. I had a huge task list today and I couldn't afford to allow myself to freak out about the troubling reemergence of my sleepwalking.

I simply need—

I needed to start taking better care of myself and avoiding anything in my life that caused stress. And maybe . . . maybe my subconscious knew the right answer before the rest of me did.

* * *

MOSTLY JOGGING TO WORK, I made a beeline for the women's locker room. Once there, I showered, scrubbing my skin with more aggression than usual. I tried to lather off all the weirdness and disruption of the last few weeks, tried to wash away the greasy film of sleep deprivation and bad memories.

For once, I used the fancy pomegranate shampoo Diya had given me for my birthday. I shaved my legs, even though it was November and nobody would be seeing them, not even me. I also exfoliated, which I hadn't done since law school.

After drying off, I spent a long moment in front of the mirror, examining my reflection the way a pathologist might examine a suspicious cell line. The usual pale skin, brown hair pulled into a wet bun, blue-gray eyes underscored by dark circles.

I put on the clean underwear set I kept in my locker for emergencies, then my scrubs and lab coat. I even dabbed on a little concealer and mascara since I wouldn't be running any samples in the secure lab today. The makeup made my eyes pop but also hid the dark circles. For the first time in months, I felt a flicker of actual, non-caffeine alertness.

The cotton pants were too short at the ankles, and the shirt was a touch too baggy, but at least I looked and smelled like a functioning human.

I walked the length of the building's main corridor, my sneakers squeaking on the linoleum. My plan was to call Andreas before I got sucked into spreadsheets. I'd decided this in the shower, the same way I sometimes convinced myself to go to spin class. I always seemed to make my most responsible choices while taking a shower, as though good-decision inertia buoyed my motivation and self-control, especially when it came to doing something difficult.

The plan was to call, say, "Thanks, but no thanks," and then block Andreas's number and hope we never ran into each other ever again.

Or at the very least, tell Andreas that, after careful consideration, I'd decided to let the past stay in the past and focus on my future. And then block his number and hope we never ran into each other ever again.

No matter how airtight the legal strategy, no matter how delicious the revenge, no matter how badly I wanted my father's company, I'd spent the last ten years, since I'd turned eighteen, trying to put my past behind me. Turning down the adoption meant I would truly and finally let it all go. If I didn't let it go now, once and for all, then I feared I'd continue to sleepwalk; I'd continue simmering in hurt, disappointment, and anger; I'd allow an obsession in the past to ruin my present and future.

Plus, to a much lesser extent, I couldn't come to terms with the visceral wrongness of Andreas adopting me and me being tied to him forever. There was no denying my attraction to him in the present. And, I finally admitted, there was no denying that a younger version of me had deeply loved and cared for a younger version of him.

That was enough reason to put an end to this. I didn't want to be tied to anyone. Ever.

Silly? Maybe. But also facts. Moreover, my sleepwalking agreed with me. My subconscious thought it was a bad idea and there was no arguing with one's subconscious.

I turned into the hallway that led to my cubicle, intending to find a quiet corner to make the call. Instead, my phone buzzed with a new text. Not from Andreas.

It was from Dr. Hauser, my PI. I stopped in my tracks, thumb hovering over the screen. The message was terse, even for her.

Dr. Hauser: Please see me in my office when you arrive.

My first thought, she wanted to discuss my latest sequencing run. Maybe there was a problem with the dataset?

I squared my shoulders, made a U-turn, and walked to her office. The door was half open, as usual. Inside, Dr. Hauser sat at her desk, typing on her laptop. She wore her hair in a tight French braid and her glasses on a chain around her neck. She looked up as I entered.

"Sam," she said, and gestured to the chair opposite her.

I sat.

She closed her laptop, folded her hands, and looked at me with the steady, intelligent gaze that made her both a brilliant scientist and an intimidating mentor. I'd known her for almost four years now, and in that time I'd never seen her hesitate to do the right thing or take responsibility for a mistake. She was the only person in the department I respected without reservation.

"Is everything okay?" I asked, hoping to get the bad news out of the way first.

She nodded, but her lips pressed into a line. "Sam, I want you to know that I fought for you. I did everything I could."

My heart, already unsettled, performed a backflip. "Fought for me?"

Dr. Hauser sighed. "I'm so sorry to tell you this, but I was informed yesterday afternoon that all my funding, including the Teaching Assistantships, has been suspended, effective immediately."

For a moment, her words didn't parse. They hit my brain like a virus, searching for a receptor dock.

When they finally connected, I said, "But—but—why? What happened?"

She leaned back, glasses dangling from the chain, her fingers steepled. "I have no idea. The dean called and said it was temporary, just for the next six months to a year, but he couldn't give me any other information. The foundation account for my lab is under review."

"That makes no sense," I sputtered. "You're the top grant recipient in the department. You bring in more money than the next three PIs combined."

She shrugged, a sharp, angry motion. "Apparently not for the next six months to a year." She paused, then added, "I'm not the only one. It's department-wide, but for some reason, they targeted my lab and two others first. The other two professors have tenure. I do not."

I stared at her. "So . . . I'm out? I don't understand. I thought the university covered Teaching Assistantship positions once I've been accepted into the program. Isn't that standard?"

"Yes, it should be. I have asked this question and was told that your Teaching Assistantship—specifically—has been placed on hold."

"I've been removed from the program?" My voice pitched high.

"No. That's what doesn't make sense. I don't understand this either and I'll push for more answers. In the meantime"—she picked up a folder from the edge of her desk and slid it toward me—"don't worry. I've spoken with James, and he's agreed to take you on. You might be aware, but his postdoc just left. This won't be a postdoc position, obviously. But he was happy to step in and help."

I picked up the folder, but my fingers barely worked. "James Nieminen?"

"Yes. He's the only one with private funding who can take you on without a gap until we can get answers regarding your Teaching Assistantship and continuation in the program. He'll get you the hours you need, and he's agreed to let you continue your research as a side project, provided you help with his upcoming publication deadlines."

My jaw clenched. I wanted to scream. *Of course.*

Instead, I said, "Will I continue to report to you?"

"Unfortunately, no. Dr. Nieminen will be your PI for the time being. He'll need to have you do some work on his projects to justify the funding through his grants, and—as I said—it won't be a Teaching Assistantship until we can get some answers." She gave her head a quick, frustrated shake. "I apologize. This is a mess. I wish I could give you more information, but I don't understand what's happening either. You might need to get another part-time job elsewhere, and this will likely delay your dissertation."

"Why do you think this happened?"

"I have no idea. Maybe a major donor or alumni called and requested an internal review, or something like that. Honestly, I'm at a loss. I've only seen this happen once before, when a professor angered an important lobbyist and that lobbyist pulled strings in Washington. It's incredibly unusual, but these are unprecedented times."

"I understand," I croaked, confusion giving way to cold certainty, because I did understand. I understood perfectly.

Tobias Kristiansen.

He was responsible.

Hadn't he threatened to do this very thing?

Dr. Hauser watched me for another long moment, then softened, her voice dropping a notch. "Sam, I know this is a setback. But it's not permanent. As soon as everything is sorted, you'll be back working with me, no question."

I nodded. "Thank you."

She smiled, the first time in this meeting. "You're a good scientist. Don't let this stop you."

I stood, folder in hand. "I won't."

Outside her office, I walked the corridor in a straight line, barely seeing the world around me. All I could think was, *This is Tobias. This is Tobias, and this is how he plays dirty. If you won't take the carrot, he'll take the stick to everyone you care about.*

The more I thought about it, the more it made sense. Tobias's threat had been surgical, precise. He didn't even have to pull Kristiansen funding from the department, that would reveal him as the puppet master behind the scenes. He only needed to request a review of funding, not just from my position, but from anyone who he thought might help me. He'd cut off my way forward, and now, if I wanted to finish my PhD within the next decade, he thought I'd have to play by his rules.

The rage was slow and cold, like dry ice. It spread from the base of my skull to the tips of my fingers. I could feel my pulse in my teeth.

If this is how Tobias wants to do things, then I will teach him the definition of playing dirty.

Not only would I allow Andreas to adopt me, and thereby I would inherit the controlling shares in Genetix, I would uncover Tobias's role in framing my father fifteen years ago. I would dig up every single piece of dirt on that asshole and ensure he rotted in prison for the rest of his life.

High on rage, I took out my phone and found Andreas's number.

Samantha: I agree. Let's meet ASAP.

Andreas's response was almost instantaneous.

Andreas: Name the place.

I stared at the screen, my anger settling into a sickly sort of vindication. I would gladly sleepwalk for the rest of my life if it meant exacting revenge on Tobias, Henrik, and Oskar and their accomplices. My subconscious could go take a flying leap.

Tobias didn't want me around Andreas? Fine. Not only would I destroy Tobias, I would strut around with Andreas like a friggin' male peacock, shoving our renewed relationship in that mayonnaise-colored dipshit's face.

Samantha: Text me your address. I'll come over tonight.

A moment later, Andreas's address came through.

I put my phone away and walked to the women's bathroom, locked myself in a stall, and sat on the closed lid. I didn't cry, because I'd stopped crying years ago. Instead, I replayed my conversation with Tobias last week over and over, studying all his threats, analyzing each statement for a potential weakness. When I finished with him, he'd wish he'd never been born.

This was it. This was the moment.

I flushed the empty toilet, left the stall, washed my hands, and went to work.

* * *

IF YOU EVER WANT TO KNOW WHAT it feels like to operate your own body on autopilot while your brain runs a continuous background loop of wrath, try waking up to the knowledge that your entire life has been puppeted by two generations of sociopaths, and that your only way out involves being adopted by your former childhood best friend.

I got through the rest of that day like a woman possessed.

Task list: pulverized.

Experimental run: so flawless, I double-checked the calibration because I suspected a supernatural intervention. I'd removed my makeup so I could enter the lab because I had a feeling today was the day those little bastards bent to my will.

Nieminen's hand on my thigh during our "transition review" meeting: ignored. (I set a personal record for not cringing. If this had been the Olympics, I would've gold medaled in Disassociation in a Professional Setting.)

I even survived Dmitry's worried hovering at lunch, where he watched me eat a granola bar in clinical silence and finally asked, "Are you okay?"

"Yes," I said. "Never been better."

He frowned, then returned to his quinoa salad, occasionally shooting me glances as though he expected me to mutate at any moment.

I should've won a fucking Oscar for my portrayal of World's Most Unbothered Grad Student Whose Funding Has Abruptly Ended and Who Has Been Forced to Work for a Sleezy Professor Who Won't Stop Touching Her.

By 5:01 PM, I'd finished my work, closed out my samples, and actually left the building at closing time, a feat unheard of in my department. As I walked down the steps into the blue evening chill, my phone vibrated with an automated reminder that my monthly health insurance payment was due. I ignored it and focused on the plan.

Step one: cash withdrawal.

I hit the ATM, yanking three crisp hundreds from my grandmother's account. I tried not to think about the promise I'd made her ("Don't use this money for anything stupid or self-destructive, like revenge") as I pocketed the bills. Given the events of this morning and the level of Tobias's evilness, I would gladly break this promise. And part of me hoped Grandma would understand. Even if she didn't, nothing would stop me now.

Step two: outfit.

I walked thirty blocks east to a store whose name I will not mention, because it was a discount luxury boutique that only locals know about. The store catered to online influencers and women who had never paid full price for anything, ever. I fit right in, in my faded black jeans and a hoodie that said "I HAVE BACTERIA ON MY MIND." Nobody looked at me twice.

There, I bought a little black dress so tight it looked vacuum sealed, a set of thigh-high stockings in a shade called raven, and a jewelry set composed of black glass drops and gold. The saleswoman said, "Excellent choices," in the dry tone of a former Soviet judge, but she gift wrapped the lot and even threw in a lipstick sample.

Step three: transformation.

Back at my apartment, I locked myself in the bathroom and stared in the mirror for a long time, memorizing my own face. I'd lost weight this semester, and with the way my cheekbones now jutted, I looked faintly starved. *I need to eat more nutritious foods.*

I wiped the remains of the day off my skin, then spent the next forty-five minutes blow-drying my hair, taming it into a glossy, brown-goldish sweep. I applied two layers of makeup. One to erase, and one to repaint. When I zipped myself into the dress, I felt like a different person.

I dug through my closet for my favorite stilettos, the pair I'd bought for a law firm interview and never worn. They were black leather, with a single, elegant ankle strap. I put them on, wobbled once, and then remembered how to walk in three-inch heels.

I added the new jewelry, the shiny drops cold against my collarbone. For the finishing touch, I draped my long, black wool overcoat across my shoulders—open at the front, I didn't want the dress to go unnoticed—and wrapped my grandmother's red-and-pink silk scarf from Paris around my neck for courage.

Staring at myself in the full-length mirror by the door, I didn't recognize the woman who stared back. It was a former version of me, one I thought I'd—sadly— left behind in undergrad. I loved her then, I loved her now, but I'd thought I didn't have much time for her these days.

That changed now.

I wished I could claim that I did this all for myself. I wished this was—at least in part—a way to pamper and take loving care of Samantha Sylvia Jarlston. But this was not the case. I knew I was being watched, and *that* was both the point and the reason for this costume change.

It was all for Tobias Kristiansen. For Henrik. For Oskar, even if the old man was probably hooked up to life support. I wanted them to see me—the version who would walk into their world and burn it down with her bare hands, or at least in heels—and continue to underestimate me.

With one last look in the mirror, I grabbed my clutch (which I'd emptied of everything but an ID, keys, some cash, and a lipstick), and walked out the door.

It was only a fifteen-minute walk to the address Andreas had texted, but the heels made every step feel like a conscious act of defiance. The city was dark now, the wind biting, but I didn't feel cold. In my mind, I pictured the way Tobias would react when he got the report that I'd arrived at Andreas's apartment at this hour despite him cutting my funding.

That thought kept me warm all the way to Andreas's building.

The doorman was a thin man with perfect posture, and when I approached he looked me over once, then gave a tiny, involuntary-looking bow.

"Good evening, miss. May I help you?"

I set my jaw and said, "I'm here to see Andreas Kristiansen."

The man's eyes flickered—maybe at the fact that I didn't introduce myself—but he didn't lose his composure.

He held the door for me. I entered. Once inside, he picked up a corded phone, dialed an extension, then spoke in a low, respectful voice. "I believe the guest you've been expecting, Ms. Jarlston, is here."

The doorman listened, then nodded, then hung up. "He's expecting you. The elevator will take you to the top floor. Straight ahead, then right."

I thanked him, giving the lobby a cursory, but shallow, inspection. The marble glowed gold, and the crystal chandeliers shone in the mirrored paneling like the inside of a jewelry box. The elevator was also mirrored, and as I rode up, I caught myself rehearsing the conversation in my head, rapid-fire, like a verbal chess game.

What was I supposed to say in greeting when I saw Andreas? Maybe, "Hi. Let's destroy your family," or "Welcome to the revenge zone!"

The elevator doors opened into a private vestibule, dimly lit and silent. I took a breath, then walked down the hallway, my heels sharp on the marble.

At the end of the hall, a pair of double doors. I rang the bell.

It took maybe ten seconds for the lock to click and the right door to open. Andreas stood in the entry, backlit by warm light, wearing a light gray dress shirt and a pair of black slacks that probably cost more than my laptop. His hair was damp, as though he'd just showered, and his feet were covered in black socks on the wood floor. The contrast made him look both absurdly formal and completely unguarded.

He looked at me. For a moment, there was nothing else in the world. His eyes —grayish green in the overhead light—swept over me from my hair to my heavy makeup to the open lapels of my coat hinting at the dress beneath to my shoes, then back again.

His lips parted. His eyebrows pulled together. He said nothing, just stared like he'd never seen me before. Or maybe like he was seeing me for the first time.

"May I come in?" I smiled, stepping over the threshold before he could answer. Tugging the scarf from my neck, I rolled it up and stuffed it inside my coat pocket.

"Of course." He closed the door behind me, then stood awkwardly, perhaps unsure what to do next. From what I could see, the apartment was vast, every visible wall covered in paintings and polished wood and midcentury modern—probably Danish—walnut-and-white furniture and antique dark red, hand-knotted rugs. It was exceedingly stylish, and if an apartment could be described as sexy, it was that too. But I fought a smirk because a baby would totally trash this place with their sticky fingers.

Can you imagine? A white couch and a toddler? Yikes.

There were no visible photos, and nothing I recognized that he might've inherited from his family. But there was a chessboard on a big, black, round wooden table. The entire wall of the living room beyond the entry was floor-to-ceiling glass, and the city sprawled outside, an infinite grid of lights.

He offered to take my coat. I shrugged it off, and when he saw the rest of the dress underneath, he made a short sound. When I turned over my shoulder, I caught a glimpse of his wide eyes before he looked away so quickly I almost laughed.

Andreas hung the coat neatly in a closet and returned slowly, standing a polite distance away with his hands shoved in his pockets, his gaze never settling on me for long.

I stared at him, letting him stew in whatever emotion had him looking so entirely disconcerted. He needed to get used to this version of Samantha, because she wasn't going anywhere anytime soon.

His cheeks had turned an adorable shade of pink and his mouth formed a flat, determined line. But then, jaw tight, his eyes finally met and held mine, and only then did I speak.

"Let's get down to business."

[10]

ORGANISM REPRODUCTION

Samantha

Andreas's round table in the living room looked like it had been custom-made. It was a dense, glossy black wood, about six feet in diameter, and ringed with matching chairs. At the table's center was a chess set with odd-looking pieces carved out of tan and dark brown wood, arranged in a game that had clearly been abandoned mid-slaughter.

Andreas pulled out a chair for me, pushed it in, then sat opposite. There was a legal-paper-sized envelope on the table with the word "ADOPTION" written neatly across the front. In block letters. Not at all subtle.

I crossed my legs, fighting to keep the hem of my vacuum-sealed dress from inching too high even though the table obscured my lap and legs from view.

"Here it is," he said, placing a pen atop the envelope and nudging both forward with one elegant finger. "Drafted by my attorney. Read it before we proceed."

"When did you have it drafted?" I glanced between Andreas and the folder.

"Before I came to your apartment. I wanted to have it ready as soon as you agreed." He relocated the chessboard to his right, leaving the space between us clear except for the envelope.

"You were so sure I'd agree?" I set the pen to one side and withdrew the document, already skimming the cover letter.

"Not sure. Hopeful."

At his answer, I didn't look up. I settled in to read the adoption packet.

Or rather, I tried to read it. Andreas didn't move, yet the air between us felt dense, charged. I endeavored to ignore it, but the dress I'd worn was having none of my logical resistance. It clung everywhere, making me acutely aware of my body and my pulse. After a full minute, I sensed that while I had my eyes glued to the contract, he had his glued to me.

I looked up.

He didn't avert his gaze.

Instead, he sat there, like a patient wolf in a human suit, eyes unblinking.

Before I could blush or notice how incredibly *fine* Andreas looked tonight, I reminded myself that James Nieminem was now my boss because Tobias Kristiansen was a mayonnaise-colored incubus who I'd vowed to destroy until my last dying breath, and noticing Andreas's attractiveness was a pointless distraction and a complication I didn't need or want.

Inhaling a deep breath, I returned my attention to the contract. Sure, it was difficult to focus on the words with him openly staring at me. It had also been difficult to resist the urge to break James Nieminem's hand earlier today when he'd set it on my thigh.

Anger helped me concentrate. The legal language was dense, yet even a cursory glance told me it was all very standard and likely taken directly from the forms provided by the State of New York.

The adoption would be sealed and private, and the paperwork contained all the typical template sections I would expect from an adult adoption legal document: *The parties agree to assume toward each other the legal relation of parent and child. Adopting Parent will henceforth treat adoptee as if she were the natural child of adopting parent. Adoptee will henceforth . . .* and so forth about treating each other as natural relatives, plus the stark warning that all ties with my previous parents and biological family would cease to exist once the adoption was approved. Since both of my parents were now dead, this part seemed superfluous.

An addendum contract spelled out that I would not be entitled to any other Kristiansen property, nor would I be financially responsible for Andreas or any of his blood relatives, current or future. Though it would be difficult to enforce, it was, in short, the kind of agreement that attempted to protect both parties and leave no wiggle room for the sort of fuckery that had defined our families' interactions fifteen years ago. But, again, difficult to enforce due to intestacy laws.

Technically, as his adopted child, his family automatically became my family.

Fighting a shiver of revulsion at the thought, I skimmed page after page, noted all the sections I needed to complete, then, as I flipped to the last piece of paper, I glanced up and caught Andreas still watching me with an intensity that made my skin prickle against my will.

There was nothing cold about him now. His gaze lingered on my clavicles, dropped lower, then cut back to my face. When our eyes met, something flickered behind his. This wasn't analytical intensity. This was something sharper and more personal, a sort of slow, simmering heat.

I guessed I wasn't the only one wrestling with an inconvenient attraction.

"Do you want to take a picture?" I asked, not hiding my impatience and needing to break the tension.

"Sure," he ground out.

I snorted a laugh and shook my head at his immediate, but aggressive-sounding, response. "Are you okay?"

His left eyebrow twitched. "Why wouldn't I be?"

"You seem . . ." I searched for the word. "Distracted."

He studied me. "Do you have dinner plans after this?" The question almost sounded like an accusation.

I blinked. "After what?"

He lifted his chin, gesturing at me, at my dress. "You are dressed for dinner, or perhaps an event. Or perhaps you have another engagement after our meeting?"

I looked down at myself. The black dress was sculpted, cut to show my collarbones and cleavage, definitely more than I'd shown in the last four years.

I let a smile show. "If you want to take me out to dinner, just ask."

For the first time since we sat, his expression shifted to something other than smoldering displeasure. "Would you accept?"

"Sure. Why not?" I leaned in. "But for the record, this dress is not for you."

Something sharp and quick flashed in his eyes. "Then who is it for?"

"Your brother." I didn't say which one, because it should be obvious. "He cut off my PI's funding today and for the next six months. I figured, if he wants me to stay away from you, then I'll do the opposite. And I'll make a big show about it."

At my response, his posture seemed to relax and he leaned back in his chair. "This is defiance against Tobias and his threats? To show you will not be bullied." Andreas no longer sounded irritated or aggressive.

"That's right." I collected all the pages of the adoption packet, tapping them upright against the table to tidy the stack. "Do you mind if I have my lawyer look at this?" I asked, keeping my tone light.

"You have a lawyer?"

I shrugged. "I do. Is that a problem?"

He shook his head. "No, not at all. That is . . . good. You should have someone to look out for your interests. Just tell me where to send your copy."

"I'll hand carry it in." I scanned the cover letter again, then looked up at him. "There is one other thing I'd like to discuss, and it's related to the adoption."

His intense but bored mask—the one he'd worn when we first met and also in my apartment—slammed into place. "Proceed."

I found myself smiling at his formality. "Even if we do this adoption thing in total secrecy, it still looks suspicious that you and I are suddenly in each other's lives after a fifteen-year hiatus. Tobias, at least, is already watching me."

He tilted his head the barest degree, eyes lighting with something I could only describe as admiration. "You want to create a diversion."

Martin had said it didn't have to be me, and it probably would've been better—safer for my mental health—if it weren't me, but how could I ask some random woman to feign a relationship with Andreas as a red herring just so I could exact revenge?

Also, logistically, the fewer people who knew about our plan and deception, the better.

"Exactly." I leaned forward, letting the pendant on my new necklace catch the light. "We need a smoke screen. Something to explain why you and I have been meeting."

He stared at me, considering. "What do you suggest?"

I drew a deep breath, then said, "We fake an engagement."

His reaction was fascinating. For half a second, his mask slipped and something complicated flickered in his eyes, too quick for me to decipher. Then it was gone, replaced by that patented patient stillness of his that he wore like a favorite sweater.

"You want to use my original proposal as our smoke screen," he said, "while in reality, we pursue the adoption. This would satisfy the addendum to the will and draw their attention away from our real strategy."

"Exactly." I let the silence stretch. "Do you have a problem with that?"

His answer was instantaneous. "No, not at all. It is a good idea. We should."

"Good. Then—"

"But I have some conditions."

I wasn't surprised, I figured he might. In fact, I'd been waiting for him to discuss stipulations and conditions relating to the adoption contract as well. Andreas was famous in the chess world, and—to an extent—in the non-chess world as well. His fame had a global reach. A sealed adoption coming to light after his father died wouldn't bring him good press, nor would the eventual reveal of a fake engagement.

"Fine." I folded my hands. "Let's hear them."

"If we are to pretend to be engaged, you will need to move in here."

I almost burst out laughing, but he looked so serious that I tried to stifle it. "I'm sorry, what?"

"If we are engaged, logic dictates that we should live together." He made the statement sound entirely reasonable. "Otherwise, it would appear suspicious. My brothers will not believe we are together if we are not living together, and I doubt you have time for fake dates, to make more shows"—he gestured to my dress again —"for their benefit. Living together will save us both time. Otherwise, without evidence of our engagement, they will question it."

I considered this. He had a point, even if it was delivered with all the warmth of a robot reading a weather report. His tone didn't matter, but the pragmatic evaluation and solution to a potential problem did.

Not to mention the possible value of this opportunity for me—and my inconvenient attraction problem—personally. Hadn't I always said, attraction fades fastest with either no exposure or too much exposure? Moving in here, seeing Andreas daily and witnessing all his gross habits, because everyone had gross habits, would certainly cure my attraction to him.

Yes, moving in together was a good idea for many reasons.

"Where would we live? Here?" I glanced around, spotting a hallway behind me, then looked back at him just in time to catch his eyes widen slightly.

"You . . . agree?" He sounded surprised.

"Sure. Your reasoning makes sense. How many bedrooms do you have here?"

"I have three bedrooms. You may take whichever you want."

I squinted at him. "Even the main bedroom?"

He arched an eyebrow, the first real sign of amusement I'd seen since I'd arrived. "If you wish."

Leaning back in my seat, I studied him and his request. Certainly, exposure to Andreas never putting the toilet seat down or cleaning up after himself would solve my attraction problem quite nicely. Or, conversely, maybe he was an anal-retentive control freak and couldn't handle a pair of socks on the ground for five minutes. Either would suit me just fine. Then my brain and my body could friend-zone him with no issue.

Logistically, however, moving in here would be complicated. What about my roommates? I couldn't simply leave without finding my replacement. And would I still pay rent in the meantime? What happened when people discovered he'd adopted me? This felt messy.

I must've taken too long to reply because Andreas leaned forward and placed his elbows on the table, asking, "What worries you?"

"I think it would be wise for us to define our concerns and conditions now. In fact, what if we both made a list, about the adoption and the fake-fiancé arrangement?"

"That is agreeable, as long as we set a goal to have everything finalized within three days."

"Why three days?"

He tapped his fingers on the table, a movement that looked absentminded. "I have been alerted my father's will might be shared with my brothers next week."

"Might be?"

Andreas dipped his chin. "My contact did not provide any other details. Only that we need to move quickly, if we are going to do this."

"Okay, then. No time like the present." Flipping over the cover letter, I picked up the pen and began writing. "I'll jot down my immediate concerns and conditions now. You should get a piece of paper and do the same."

He made a small sound that could've been a laugh or a sigh, but then stood and left the table, only to return a moment later with his own pen and paper.

My list was already quite long:

1) Giving my roommates notice before breaking my rental agreement with them (I still have 8 months).

2) I have to find my own replacement for Diya/don't want to leave her hanging.

3) How much is rent on this place?? Can't afford rent on two apartments. Need breakdown of rent, utilities, etc. for this apartment.

4) How public to go with fake-fiancé agreement? Public PDA as evidence of smoke screen? How much? Rules around PDA seem like a good idea. Related, see number 5.

5) Won't it be weird for you when people find out you've adopted me but we've been acting like we're dating? How's that going to work for your image? Hire a PR firm?

6) Your brother threatening me: If I eventually lose my funding, I might not be able to pay rent here. Need plan for this.

7) Rules for the apartment? Bringing people over? Cleaning duties? Can I have shelves in the fridge and pantry? What rooms can I use?

8) What are you like to live with? Do I need to be quiet during certain hours? What do I need to know about being your roommate?

Reading back over the list, I frowned, because a very obvious thing was missing. Deciding that we were both adults and it would be better to spell things out and be honest than hope everything just magically worked out, I added:

9) No physical contact unless it's in public and only for the purposes of reinforcing the claim that we're engaged. No avoidable contact in the apartment at all and—

"That many?"

Andreas's question pulled my attention away from the list and I glanced at his paper, which—from where I sat—only appeared to have three items.

Setting my pen down, I slid my paper toward him. "This is as many as I can think of right now. I like to have everything clearly spelled out before making a decision. Setting realistic expectations from the beginning will save frustration and disappointment later."

"Are you expecting me to disappoint you, Samantha?" His eyebrow raised slightly. He also slid his paper toward me while accepting my list.

I picked up his paper, not caring how my cleavage pressed against the neckline of my dress—or how his eyes darted to my chest then quickly away—as I reached forward with my fingertips.

He needed to get used to me being in his space in various states of clothed. Roommates had to deal with that kind of stuff.

"I am not expecting you to disappointment me, Andreas. Not if we set realistic expectations."

His eyes narrowed marginally, then shifted to my list.

I glanced at his. He hadn't numbered it.

Samantha moves in with Andreas.

Samantha will have one or more bodyguards.

Samantha will not speak to the press about Andreas; Andreas will not speak to the press about Samantha.

My mouth dropped open at the second item. "Excuse me? A bodyguard?"

Andreas lifted just his eyes and stared at me with a bleak sort of intensity. "You underestimate my brothers. Tobias is ruthless, but he prefers psychological warfare. Henrik is unpredictable and often resorts to physical violence. If we are to publicly pretend that we are a couple, you will become a target. I do not want your safety to be jeopardized."

I inspected him, endeavoring to parse whether he believed a guard was truly necessary.

Before I could push the issue, he shook his head. "This is nonnegotiable."

Letting his succinct list fall to the table, I sat back and crossed my arms. "Then I have a counteroffer."

He watched me, waiting.

"The guard can follow me home from work, or be nearby if I'm out at night, but they can't come into my office, my lab, or anywhere else on campus. For one thing, it would be incredibly awkward, and for another, they don't have the necessary clearance or training to enter the lab."

He considered, then nodded. "Acceptable."

Frowning, I gave him a single nod. "Fine. Bodyguard is approved. But then"—I reached forward, my palm up—"I need to add more to my list."

He gave me one slow blink. "Just tell me. I will write it for you."

"Who will pay for the bodyguard?"

Andreas seemed to contemplate me for a long moment before setting down my paper. "I propose, for all the expense-related items, we split the cost of everything —lawyers' fees, living expenses, bodyguard, and so forth—fifty-fifty, after you inherit Genetix. For now, I will shoulder all financial burdens."

I turned my head slightly to the side and examined him. "What if our plan fails and I don't inherit?"

"Then I will accept the financial fallout and cover the cost of everything."

"Why would you?" As I asked the question, I wondered again how this arrangement benefited Andreas. Why approach me at all? Was this actually about correcting an injustice? If so, then wouldn't it make more sense for me to cover all the expenses should we succeed rather than split everything fifty-fifty?

"This is my idea, all of it. And I approached you. Of course I should be the one to take the financial responsibility." He said this like it was the most obvious thing in the world.

Still, it didn't sit right.

"Tell me something, Andreas."

A pause while he stared at me in solemn silence, then, "Anything." He sounded entirely sincere, his tender tone completely at odds with the mask of boredom donning his features.

"Why? Why are you doing this? What are you getting out of it? You say you're going to take financial responsibility, but why? As I've spelled out on my list of concerns, won't this whole thing make bad press for you when it comes to light? The woman you've been pretending to date is actually your adopted daughter? That sounds like a scandal."

As I spoke, his gaze grew more distant, reserved. But when I said the word *daughter* he made a face of distaste. "You will not be my 'daughter.'"

"In the eyes of the law, I will be. It says you and I will treat each other like natural—"

"In the eyes of the law, you will be my direct inheritor and the first grandchild of Oskar Kristiansen." He spoke over me.

"Okay, fine. Semantics. But you still haven't answered my question." I pressed my index finger against the first page of the adoption packet. "Why bother doing this at all? Why reach out to me after fifteen years? Why not ask a woman you fancy to make a baby with you, then let your real child inherit?"

"Did I not—" he began, but then clamped his mouth shut and exhaled through his nose, his stare mutating into a glare. After a few more rises and falls of his chest, he spoke. "It should go without saying, what my family did to you and your parents was reprehensible. My father literally stole everything from your family. Genetix should be yours. How could I live with myself if I let this opportunity pass by? Isn't that reason enough?"

Biting the inside of my lower lip, I scrutinized the remoteness of his expression and the coolness of his words, which all seemed to support my previous hypothesis: Andreas was doing this because he cared about justice, and approaching me was merely about righting a past wrong. Granted, it was a big fucking past wrong.

"Huh," I said, feeling oddly disappointed by his answer. But at least I knew for certain the source of his motivations. "Well then, how about this: If we fail, you cover all the expenses. But if we succeed, I cover all the expenses."

"Why not split—"

"That's my final offer." I sat back in my chair again. "I'll move in here and you'll foot the bill for the apartment and living expenses, you pay for the bodyguard, and so forth, because we both know I can't. That answers a lot of my questions and concerns about the logistics. But if we succeed, I pay you back for everything. Take it or leave it."

The calculating quality had reentered Andreas's gaze. "This offer sounds unnecessarily transactional. As though you are paying me for services rendered."

I shook my head. "No, I am *reimbursing* you for services rendered. There's a difference."

As if at all possible, his features grew colder, and I was reminded of that infamous meme of Andreas, staring at an opponent over a chessboard, with the words: "My mouth may not say it, but my face definitely will."

Yeesh. If I didn't have memories of him bawling over the cadaver of a baby bird, he might've been sort of scary right now.

Finally, after a prolonged period of frosty contemplation, he said, "Then I have more conditions."

I picked up my pen, poised to add another item to his list. "What's that? I'll add it for you."

Folding the piece of paper with my list on it in half, he gave his head a slight shake and stood. "No. We will discuss over dinner tomorrow. In the interim, I will write down my additional conditions along with responses to yours. The summary of 'realistic expectations' will be finalized at that time."

Attempting to stand as gracefully as possible given the tightness of my dress, I shrugged. "Fine. But it'll have to be a late dinner. I have a meeting tomorrow evening with my—uh—work colleague." James Nieminen had requested that we meet tomorrow at 6:00 PM. Who schedules a meeting at 6:00 PM on a Friday night? Such a dick move.

"No problem. What time shall I arrange the car?" His tone was solicitous and soft, once more at odds with the frostbite of his stare.

"You'll meet me at my work?"

"Yes." His gaze moved over me again, his expression still calculating. "I will send over something for you to wear and I will make sure the table is by the window."

"Okay. Then seven thirty should be fine." I slid the adoption packet back in the envelope and picked it up. "And I'll take this to my lawyer."

"Let me know if you require any changes to that as well. My attorney is flexible." Andreas adjusted the chessboard he'd pushed aside earlier back to the center of the table.

I nodded, momentarily mesmerized by his long, elegant fingers resetting the pieces, and said without thinking, "That's a pretty chess set."

He met my gaze briefly. "Would you like to play a game before you leave?"

I eyed the board. "Only if you promise not to go easy on me."

His hand holding the black queen paused for a beat before he placed her on a dark square. Lifting his eyes to mine, a faint smile curved his mouth. "I never go easy on anyone."

"Really?" I tilted my head to the side and set a hand on my hip. "You used to be such a softy."

Andreas shoved his hands in his pockets, his gaze never leaving mine, and said quietly, "Only with you."

I made a face of disbelief, but let his comment go. He used to be a softy with nearly everyone. All the staff in his father's house had babied him because he was so sweet. Maybe he liked to think of himself as tough and intimidating now—and no doubt his cold stares absolutely were—but I'd likely never stop seeing flashes of the sensitive, soft boy he used to be.

The one I loved.

Tensing at the thought, I tore my eyes away from his and gave myself a mental shake. "Right. Well. Let me get out of your hair."

Pointing then walking toward the entrance, I wracked my brain trying to remember where he'd put my coat when I arrived, ignoring the tingling sensation running down my spine at the sound of his steps behind me. Once I reached the entrance, I sorta spun in a circle until I found the closet.

Not looking at him, I pulled my coat from the hanger where he'd left it. "I guess I'll see you tomorr—"

Andreas was suddenly next to me, taking my coat and helping me put it on.

Then he reached inside the closet and withdrew another coat, the camel-colored cashmere one from the time he'd cornered me outside of my department building so many days ago.

"What are you doing?" I watched him push his arms through the sleeves.

He glanced at me, then pulled out a pair of slip-on, yet exceedingly fancy-looking, black loafers. "I'm walking you home."

"Why are you—"

Feet now ensconced in shoes, Andreas stepped close, pulled my grandmother's scarf from the pocket where I'd stuffed it earlier, and draped it around my neck. He then turned and grabbed the doorknob. "What kind of fiancé would I be if I allowed my future wife to walk home alone at this hour?"

I stared at him and his aloof expression, contemplating his terse-sounding words while he opened the door.

"You know," I said, "I walk around the city by myself all the time, even late at night."

"And?"

I rocked back on my heels. "So, I know how to keep myself safe. You don't think Henrik is already planning an offensive, do you?"

"No. But this is not just about safety." He gestured for me to go first.

Exiting his apartment, I asked over my shoulder, "Then what's it about?"

He pulled his door closed and it beeped. "Never too early to make our relationship appear real. As your soon-to-be fiancé, I will use this and every opportunity."

Confused, I frowned at his profile, then at his back as he walked around me and pressed the call button for the elevator. "Use for what?"

He glanced at me, a hint of incredulousness pulling his eyebrows together. "Samantha, people who want to marry each other usually also want to spend as much time together as possible."

"*Ohhhh*." I walked forward slowly to stand next to him. "Yeah, of course. I know that."

He sorta smirked, the incredulousness persisting, and faced the elevator doors.

A sensation of unease prickled down my spine. I'd always ended my situationships if or when the guy started doing these types of things. Calling me or texting me frequently, wanting to hang out every day, telling me about his feelings, hopes, or dreams. No matter how upfront and transparent I'd been about my lack of interest in a committed relationship, this sometimes happened. Not every time, but sometimes.

How funny. Now I'd have to do it with Andreas. And it was all fake.

The elevator dinged, announcing its arrival, and again he gestured for me to go first. I did, and then pressed the lobby button. He stepped in next to me and we stood quietly as the elevator descended, the same thick energy from before in his apartment making the surrounding air feel heavy while I actively avoided the sight of our reflection in the paneled mirror.

At least, it felt heavy to me. It felt like hasty decisions and a precursor to regret. But it also felt like a means to an end and the beginning of my revenge against his family, and that's what I focused on. All of this charged atmosphere and these awkward elevator rides would be worth it, in the end.

As the doors slid open revealing the lobby, I moved to exit. Before I could, Andreas smoothly slid his palm against mine and entangled our fingers, making my heart stutter and my feet stumble at the sudden, electric contact. Just like at the café, a jolt of something warm traveled up my arm at his touch and I struggled against the instinct to prolong the contact. This inability to pull away meant I allowed him to grasp my hand and lead me out of the elevator, the lobby, and the building. The doorman I'd spoken to earlier might've greeted us. But I didn't hear what he said.

I continued being led by Andreas down the sidewalk for two blocks before I finally found my voice and whispered, "Why are—must we hold hands?"

"Do you want the smoke screen to look real?" He spared me a side-eye.

I sighed, resolving to add a new condition to my list when we met tomorrow: *Plot out every incidence of PDA before it occurs in order to mitigate prolonged contact. And absolutely no kissing!*

My stomach twisted at the thought of kissing Andreas. I shivered.

He looked at me. "Cold?"

Obviously, I wouldn't explain. I nodded.

Eyes skating over my upturned face, Andreas lifted my hand in his grip and put both of ours in the pocket of his coat, giving my fingers a squeeze. "Better?"

I caught a whiff of rosemary, which I now assumed must've been his shampoo, and nodded again with a small, tight smile as I thought, *No. Worse. Much, much worse.* The man was painfully handsome, and he smelled so good, and his hand felt so good and strong and warm. And this was torture.

But this torture would be worth it, in the end.

[11]

GENETIC VARIATION

Samantha

The biology building felt extra haunted after dark. Tonight, being the Friday night before Thanksgiving week, it was all but abandoned.

A chemical lemon scent trailed behind the janitorial staff, and the green exit signs burned with a weird radioactive intensity. By the time I packed up my notes and shut down the projector in the conference room, it was 6:55 PM and the only light came from the glass-walled corridor outside. Enough to make the space dim, but not bright.

Dr. Nieminen sat across from me, shoes planted just wider than his knees, pecking something into his laptop with two fingers. I'd expected him to try some uninvited shoulder squeeze, or maybe a breathy "Can I get you a drink, Sam?" as soon as he arrived for our 6:00 PM meeting, but he'd been nothing but professionally friendly all meeting, a pleasant surprise.

The most personal statement Dr. Nieminen made thus far was, "I'm told the venue is cold, so bring a sweater." I even caught myself letting my guard down toward the end of my presentation. My notes from the meeting—mostly reminders to email the poster draft to the co-authors, asking for their citation lists and preferred schedule for presentation times—were scrawled with my normal legible handwriting, not the aggravated micro-script I used when forcing myself to concentrate.

Dr. Nieminen's entire agenda this evening had centered on the conference next month in Boston. So, an actual agenda. And one I was prepared for because I'd drafted a presentation last month just in case Dr. Hauser had wanted me to attend and present.

Presently, eyes still on his laptop, he said, "Your presentation is fine, but I want it in abstract format. For the poster, we'll need to unify our graphics, make sure everyone's using the latest template, fonts, and so forth."

I nodded.

"And I'll rely on you to check everyone's citations, make sure they're not taking any shortcuts. Oh! And Dr. Merkle is extremely anal about kerning, especially for titles and diagrams. Sorry."

"Understood." I scribbled another note, *Check letter spacing.*

"I want to thank you, Sam, for how quickly you've adapted to the change in circumstance." Dr. Nieminen finished whatever he was typing, snapped his laptop closed, and smiled at me, that confident, square-jawed American smile he used in all his lab group photos. "I was worried you'd need more time to adjust, but you're approaching your new duties with such, ah—" He paused, as if consulting an internal thesaurus. "Enthusiasm. It is admirable."

I gave him a tight smile, my stomach tense, not because there was anything wrong with the compliment, but because there was *nothing wrong with the compliment*. I genuinely couldn't process the lack of an ulterior motive.

"Thanks," I managed, twisting my pen between my fingers. "It's all pretty similar to what I was doing for Hauser as her research assistant, just with more, you know, product."

He laughed. "You mean more work."

I offered a slightly wider smile. "But more work means more experience, so I'm not complaining."

Dr. Nieminen stacked his laptop, his notebook, and his phone into a tidy, rectangular pile. He then stood, slinging a backpack over his shoulder. "You say that now, but just wait until you see what international peer review is like. It's nothing but stress and disappointment." His tone was dry, but not unkind. "Anything else before we go?"

"No, I think I have everything for now. I'll let you know if the conference organizers need anything else from our end." I almost added, *Thank you for taking me on, for helping me keep some funding at the university,* but caution won out and I decided against vocalizing any gratitude. I didn't trust that his motives were altruistic yet, despite how straightforward and professional he'd been during this meeting.

"Excellent." Dr. Nieminen picked up his stack of items and gripped them to his chest. "What do you think about making our usual meeting time six on Fridays? It seems like the only time the conference rooms are available. Are you free Friday evenings?"

"Usually, yes. That works for me."

"Great. Then I'll see you later." His grin was pleased. "I won't be here next week, visiting my parents for the holiday. Oh yeah. Happy Thanksgiving by the way."

"Thank you. Happy Thanksgiving."

"Any plans?" His head tilted slightly to one side.

"Nothing major," was all I felt comfortable admitting even though I planned to come in every day and take advantage of the empty lab over the holiday. Dr. Nieminen and I weren't friends. Even if we were, I tended to err on the side of caution when sharing details with anyone other than Kaitlyn.

Yeah, yeah. I know. I have trust issues.

With a quick smile and friendly wave, he left.

Meanwhile, I was left frowning at his departing form, feeling slightly adrift. And muddled. But also relieved he hadn't done or said anything that made me uncomfortable. *Maybe I've been unkind. Maybe he's not . . . so bad.*

Eventually, I turned to gather my things, surprised by the direction of my thoughts. This whole situation with Andreas, his brothers, and the addendum to Oskar Kristiansen's will left me twisted in knots.

Last night, Andreas walked me all the way up to the door of my apartment. I told myself it was for appearances, for the benefit of anyone Tobias had sent to follow or photograph us. However, no one was photographing us inside the stairwell of my apartment building, and yet I'd held his hand the whole time. His fingers were warm, and his palm was large and it fit mine so perfectly that letting go had been quite difficult.

Which was why, when I saw him tonight for our late dinner, I was going to insist on a list of acceptable public displays of affection and have them all written down and signed off on. But not notarized. Notarizing that kind of list would be weird. However, I wasn't about to get blindsided again by random hand holding.

Thus, and in retrospect, perhaps I'd overreacted about or misunderstood Dr. Nieminen's hand on my thigh yesterday. *Maybe he's just a touchy-feely guy . . . ?*

I rolled my eyes at myself. He wasn't just a touchy-feely guy. James Nieminen had been interested in me for a while, that was no secret. But perhaps he'd finally taken the hint and decided to back off now that he was my boss and signed off on my paychecks. It seemed possible I was the problem and saw villains where none existed.

Fine. As long as Dr. Nieminen continued to be professional—like today—I would do my work diligently and we would have no problems. But if he crossed the line again, I'd add his name to my People I'm Going to Ruin list, right below Tobias Kristiansen's.

* * *

I'D ALWAYS CONSIDERED myself an exceptionally pragmatic person, even when I was a child and the other kids on my block wanted to play "wedding" or "FBI" or whatever. I preferred more constructive games, like researching all the pharmaceuticals in my parents' medicine cabinet, or creating elaborate natural disaster scenarios for my Barbie dolls to understand concepts like lava flow, structural integrity of buildings during earthquakes, or the impact of hurricane-force winds on an elaborate hairstyle. The only time I ever did anything truly irrational was when I let myself believe, for a six-month period in middle school, that if I were simply attractive enough, if I wore cute enough clothes and did my hair and wore makeup, I'd feel happy and all my problems would be solved.

That delusion had returned with a vengeance tonight.

After I quickly showered, I blow-dried my hair upside down to maximize volume, then flat-ironed it in sections so that it fell, glossy and heavy, over my left shoulder. Then I did my makeup—full, maximalist mode, with shimmery eyeshadow and a perfect, lethal cat eye. I even did the thing with the contour and highlighter, which I'd watched an online tutorial for back in undergrad and practiced until I'd perfected it.

The dress itself was a slinky, bloodred silk that looked like it should be on a Bond girl. It had been a gift from Andreas. Well, not really a "gift," but a mission-critical apparatus. It arrived by courier in a box with a typed note that read: *Wear tonight. I will match. —A*

The color, a deep burgundy, made my skin appear even paler than usual. I couldn't decide whether the paleness looked good or bad. Either way, the contrast of colors was definitely dramatic.

The cut of the dress was both elegant and indecent in the way that only ultraexpensive things can be. The hem stopped mid-thigh, the neckline was low but not slutty—sadly—and when I zipped myself in, I could feel the silky fabric hugging the curve of my hips and thighs like a second skin.

I put on the same black stilettos I'd worn last night, mostly because I was broke and couldn't justify new shoes. Underneath, I wore the nicest underwear set I owned, the bra so delicate and lacy that it should've been classified as "wishful thinking" rather than an actual undergarment.

As I got dressed, I thought about the fact that tomorrow I'd wake up and it would all be the same. I'd still be broke, still fighting to keep my place in the program, still obsessing about how to make the Kristiansens suffer. But tonight, with the clock ticking down to the first of potentially many public dinners with Andreas, my lips painted to match the dark red of my dress, I was going to enjoy myself. I deserved a break, a treat (that wasn't ice cream) to celebrate the fact that I'd fully embraced my revenge era.

*Rather, a treat that didn't involve *just* ice cream.*

By the time I finished, I felt good. Energized. *Ready.*

Slipping on my black coat, I grabbed the envelope with the finalized adoption contract. Martin had been kind enough to send his lawyer over for a breakfast meeting with me this morning and we'd completed all the details over coffee at the fake-foliage café across the street. Checking the screen of my phone, I saw it was 7:25 PM. I had enough time to get to the curb and collect my wits before Andreas's car arrived.

The hallways in the biology building were now totally deserted, echoey in the weird way only abandoned academic buildings get. When I stepped out into the street, the air was sharp and so dry it stung my nose. The sky was clear and the streetlamps bled orange halos onto the concrete. At the far curb, a black Mercedes SUV idled, windows tinted to near-opacity. I squinted at it, wondering if this SUV could be Andreas.

Obviously, I wouldn't approach without confirmation. Only dumb Marty Sues and Mary Sues walk toward mysterious idling, black Mercedes SUVs.

Instead, I checked my phone. No new messages. Sliding it back into my clutch, I scanned the sidewalk and decided I would text Andreas after five more minutes. To my right, in the shadows cast by the building's decorative columns, something flickered in the corner of my vision. Movement.

I tensed, scanning the darkness. But then, when I saw nothing, I relaxed. Except, I looked again. And I could've sworn I saw a flash of blue. The same blue as the jacket Dr. Nieminen had worn earlier.

I frowned. Why would Nieminen be here? The man was a machine, but even he didn't keep office hours this late on a Friday, especially not the Friday before Thanksgiving. Maybe he'd forgotten something and had come back to get it? Or maybe—my skin crawled—a completely unrelated creep was lurking outside the biology building.

I debated for a full five seconds whether to call over and say, "James, if that's you, you're being a weirdo," but I didn't want to risk being wrong if it were a lurking stranger.

Instead, I turned away from the column, preparing to text Andreas that I'd arrived, when I heard my name.

"Samantha."

It was Andreas's voice, unhurried and flat, but pitched lower than usual.

I looked up. He stood at the rear of the Mercedes I'd noticed earlier. Relieved and grateful that he was already here, I walked toward him.

Andreas watched me approach and, as I drew closer, I saw that his black overcoat was open, revealing a suit. I suspected it was the exact color of the dress he'd sent me, a dark burgundy, with a black shirt underneath. Once again, he looked like he'd been peeled off the cover of an Italian fashion magazine. Maybe that was deliberate, but it still made my brain short-circuit for a second.

There was something almost aggressively attractive about how much he didn't smile, or blink, or do anything besides track my every movement with his intelligent eyes.

I stopped just short of him. "Uh, nice suit," I said as neutrally as possible.

His eyes flicked down my body, mostly hidden by my black coat, then back to my face. "Did you get the dress?"

Unbuttoning the front of my jacket, I held open one flap to show him a peek of the sheath dress beneath.

His glanced away, clearing his throat before saying, "A simple yes would have sufficed."

I almost laughed. Not because it was funny, but because his cheeks were now pink and I didn't think it was from the cold.

I think he likes me . . . Hmm.

No. More accurately, *I think he likes the way I look.* No worries. Once we moved in together and he was exposed to all my weird, disgusting habits, I felt certain any and all attraction to me would fade.

Buttoning my coat, I drifted closer. "Are we on time?"

He checked his watch. "We have exactly eighteen minutes. Please." Andreas motioned toward the car with a little wave of his hand, giving the open back door of the Mercedes a wide birth.

I walked forward and let myself in, scooting all the way over to the seat behind the driver. Inside, it was warm, and the faint smell rosemary tickled my nose— *Andreas's shampoo*—along with expensive cologne.

Shoving away this recognition—that I now knew what Andreas's shampoo smelled like—I glanced up and met a pair of pretty eyes in the rearview mirror. The driver was a woman. I blinked.

She had light brown hair and, from what I could see of it, a pleasant, open face. The woman looked to be around my age, maybe a few years younger.

"Hi," I said, uncertain of the protocol for greeting a driver who wasn't operating a taxi or a ride-share.

She turned over her shoulder and looked back at me, her eyes crinkled with a smile. "You must be Samantha. I'm Tara."

I blinked at her again. She . . . sorta looked like me. Actually, she looked a lot like me.

"Tara will be your driver," Andreas said, sliding in behind the passenger seat and shutting the door. He didn't glance at me as he spoke. "She is also one of your new bodyguards."

"Nice to meet you, Tara." I moved to the edge of the seat and offered my hand for a shake.

She took it. "You too." Tara grinned, then faced forward.

Andreas's finger hovered over a panel set in the door. "To the restaurant, please."

Tara nodded, then pulled away from the curb, merging the car into traffic so smoothly I barely felt the movement.

Andreas pressed a button on the panel and a sheet of privacy glass lifted, separating us from Tara. Once it was in place, silence engulfed us for a minute, which was fine by me. I took the time to fish my contract envelope out of my purse, smoothing my hands over the exterior.

After a few blocks, Andreas glanced over briefly, the lines of his profile perfect enough to be an ancient Roman statue. He reached into his coat and produced a single folded sheet of paper.

"Answers to your conditions." He held it out.

I took it, instantly noting the neat, precise block handwriting. I scanned down the list, seeing my own words summarized, followed by his responses, each numbered and concise.

1) & 2) Giving notice to roommates and finding replacement: Do whatever is necessary. But you need to move into my apartment within the next three days.

3) Rent and expenses: Already resolved. I pay unless you successfully inherit. In which case, you reimburse.

4) PDA rules: To be discussed.

5) Concerns regarding my public persona: Since what we are doing is not illegal, it will not impact my career in any substantive or adverse way.

6) Threats: I will cover any loss of employment or related expenses due to my family's behavior, including previous financial commitments, student loan repayments, etc.

7) Apartment boundaries/ rules: Full use of all shared living spaces. Guest policy will be determined together. Cleaning and chores: Not required. I have a service.

8) Living with me: I don't know. I've never lived with anyone before. Quiet hours to be discussed.

9) No physical contact unless necessary for public display: Acceptable.

Beneath this numbered list of my conditions, Andreas had written his three conditions from last night along with one new one: *Our engagement must be public and take place ASAP.*

I looked at him, holding the paper in both hands. "This all looks more or less fine. We can negotiate the guest policy and quiet hours, I have no problem with that. And I can move into your place within three days, maybe even this weekend. That shouldn't be an issue since Thanksgiving is next week and it's a slow time of year. But while 'no touching when we're alone' is here and you've agreed it's acceptable, you wrote 'to be discussed' next to the public displays of affection stipulation. What—specifically—needs to be discussed?"

He turned toward me fully, the movement casual but focused. "I fully agree with the sentiment, but we need to discuss the details of our public displays of affection."

"What—what does that mean? You agree with the 'sentiment'?"

"I agree, a strategy for public affection, discussed and defined prior to planned public excursions, seems most efficient. In order to avoid"—his eyes flicked over me—"surprises. If you agree, I will run my suggestions by you for this evening before we arrive."

I blinked. "You already have a list of suggestions for tonight?"

One corner of his mouth curved upward. "You underestimate how often people photograph me in public. It would be suspicious if we never touched, but it would also be suspicious if we went overboard. We must strike the correct balance."

I stared at him, impressed and maybe a little annoyed that he'd already thought all of this through.

"Okay." I refolded the paper. "What are your suggestions for tonight?"

"First, in general, for all outings, I suggest frequent hand holding. At any public dinner for example, I may put my hand over yours and vice versa. If we walk in or out of a venue, I will offer my arm or place a hand on your back. That is it."

My eyes widened. "Wait. That's it?" Why was my stomach sinking?

"Yes. I will never initiate any additional public displays of affection without your advance agreement, and I ask the same of you. If you wish to initiate without prior agreement, I give you permission to do so at your discretion, but please give me a signal first so I am prepared."

I stared at him, nonplussed. "You've seriously thought about all this." For some reason, in addition to my sinking stomach, my neck felt hot. Like I was embarrassed. But I wasn't embarrassed. In fact, I didn't know what I was.

"I have," he said evenly. "I do not want either of us to be uncomfortable. If we are not at ease, our act will not be convincing."

There was a pause. The car slowed as Tara navigated a turn, then merged back into traffic.

I needed to say something, so I asked half jokingly, "Are you always this thorough?"

He tilted his head. "Always."

"Mmm. That's, uh, good. That's good to know." I glanced out the window, watching the city lights streak by while I wrestled with a wave of emotion I didn't understand.

Why did I feel like I'd just been rejected? Truly, my brain made no sense. I'd been the one who wanted to define acceptable PDA. I should be relieved.

"Does that sound acceptable?" Andreas asked after a time. "Any concerns?"

I shook my head, glancing at him then back out the window. "Nope. That sounds good. Good talk."

My reflection in the glass looked weirdly alien, the makeup and my earlier confidence all floating above my own skin like an overlay. I wondered if that's how he saw me, too. Something constructed, but also functional. A girl-shaped object. I was tempted to ask him, but the words stuck in my throat.

For a while, neither of us spoke.

Then, out of nowhere, he said, "There is one more thing to discuss."

I turned forward, bracing myself to face him again. "What's that?"

"We should decide on the appropriate PDA for tonight, as it is a special circumstance."

"Is it?" I gathered a deep breath, then met his gorgeous, half-lidded eyes.

"Yes." He nodded once. "I am going to propose to you tonight."

[12]

HUMAN GENETICS

Samantha

I choked, actually choked, on the nothing I was breathing and stared at him with shocked, wide eyes. "I'm sorry, what?"

Andreas simply looked at me, unblinking, totally serious. "We are having dinner at Maison Lavande. It is a favorite spot of my family's, and they will expect something significant to occur."

"But—but why so fast? Couldn't we—"

"My brothers will imminently know about the addendum to my father's will. It is possible they already know. If I wait, it will look suspicious. If we hurry, it will seem real."

"Then can't we just say we're engaged?"

"I added a public engagement to the list as my final condition." He gestured to the folded paper on my lap. "The more public the proposal, the more difficult it will be for anyone to question it later."

My brain fought to find fault in his statements. Unfortunately, all his points were good ones.

But discomfort also meant I felt compelled to tell a joke. "Okay, I agree, but only if there's an obscenely ostentatious ring involved."

"Yes, I have it here"—he patted his side pocket, clearly not comprehending my attempt at humor—"but you do not have to wear it unless you wish to. The size of the spectacle tonight will be in accordance with your comfort level."

99

I couldn't seem to form words as I watched Andreas reach into his pocket and produce a small, navy blue velvet box. He set it on the seat between us.

I stared at it, then at him, then back at the box. "Uh, well. I guess . . ." I scratched my neck. "I'm sorry, could you repeat the question?"

His eyes narrowed, but he sounded infinitely patient as he spoke. "What level of PDA, and spectacle, are you comfortable with tonight? I have reserved the entire restaurant. Flowers, a cake, champagne, candles, rose petals, and musicians are planned. The waitstaff will be our witnesses and our table is near a window. If Tobias has sent someone to photograph us, they will have a clear view. But scaling back the spectacle will be easy, everything except the flowers. Those have already been delivered and placed."

"But . . . are you absolutely sure a public proposal is necessary?" I croaked.

"It is necessary." He nodded at this statement. "Tobias will have someone there to observe from outside, certainly, but also likely a member of the waitstaff. It would be suspicious if I did not take the opportunity to move our relationship forward."

I inhaled a shaky breath, then reached for the box. I opened it. Inside was a simple, but beautiful and huge, square solitaire diamond set in a delicate platinum-colored band. It looked antique and expensive. Like, it could pay my rent for five years maybe.

"Is this real?" I croaked, peering up at him.

"Yes. The appraisal is in the safe of my apartment if you would like to see it."

"That won't be necessary." I tried to smile but wasn't sure I pulled it off. Closing the box, I placed it back on the seat between us and rubbed my forehead, speaking in a stream of consciousness. "Regarding the level of ostentatiousness, I think you should go with whatever you—as yourself—would typically do. If you put on a big show but you're not a showy person, it would look fake. Right?"

Andreas's eyes lost focus for a second, ostensibly in deliberation, then he nodded. "A fair point. I will tell the maître d' to scale it back to candlelight and champagne."

Ugh. That sounds so nice.

"And for the, um, PDA . . ." I found I had to exhale past the strange tightness in my chest and reaffix my eyes to the interior of the car—so, not Andreas—in order to approach this question with the appropriate amount of detachment.

You're a scientist, for God's sake. Be analytical!

Without giving it too much thought, I added, "We should hug and kiss for sure. If we don't, after a proposal, that would seem bizarre. And like, an actual kiss. Not a peck." I peeked at him. "Is that okay with you?"

He smiled, just a little. "I concur."

Oh. You concur, do you? Based on his tone of voice and his word usage, I suspected he didn't quite understand what I meant.

Facing him fully, I spoke to both him and myself as I said resolutely, "I'm serious. If there is one time we should go overboard with the PDA, it's tonight. Okay? So, gird your loins. I'll probably kiss your face off."

Andreas's smile seemed to flatten even as his lips twitched. "Noted."

"I'm trying to prepare you." I lifted my index finger and pointed at him. "Expect tongue. Lots of it. And my hands will be grabby. I'm a grabby kisser."

He gave me a single, slow blink.

But I wasn't finished. "I also bite."

All traces of his smile vanished.

"That's right, I'm a biter."

He faced forward and cleared his throat.

"And a licker. And—"

"I understand. No need to continue." He interrupted me, shifting in his seat, his tone flat.

"But—"

"Please stop."

"But—"

He held up a hand. "I consider myself duly prepared. I assure you, no further descriptions are required."

I was just about to push the issue when I noticed the car had slowed. Glancing out the window beyond Andreas, I realized Tara had pulled alongside the restaurant and I bit the inside of my bottom lip. The lights within—mostly candlelight—were golden and warm, and vases and baskets of red roses had been packed into the space. The interior appeared free of customers, but I spotted a few servers.

Andreas cleared his throat again, bringing my attention back to him. "Ready?"

It took me a second, but I nodded. "Yeah. I'm ready."

He opened the door, paused as though thinking, then turned back to me. "You should hold my hand, as you exit. Let me help you out."

I nodded, steeling myself for the feel of his hand in mine again. That decided, Andreas then fully exited the car and stood just outside, hand extended.

I hesitated, then accepted his fingers, ignoring the spike of warmth jolting up my arm, and let him lead me out onto the sidewalk. The air was cold, but I didn't feel it.

Silly me was already flushed, thinking ten steps ahead to the moment when I'd have to kiss him.

* * *

ANDREAS and I were deep into a passionate argument about which era of *Star Trek* movies was superior when the server, clearly not wanting to interrupt, hovered at the edge of the table like a shadow. I ignored him. I was on a roll.

"How can you argue with the whales?" I leaned forward, pressing my palm to the top of the table. "*Star Trek* four has the whales! And it takes place in the eighties. Oh! And! And! Time travel. Huh? Right? I'm right, right?" Crossing my arms, I nodded.

Andreas, who'd maintained the facial expression of an automaton—granted, a sexy, smoldering automaton—during most of our meetings since our renewed acquaintance was now actually showing signs of life tonight. His new repertoire of facial expressions this evening had been a revelation: eyebrow flickering, a faint crease at the corners of his mouth, even a real smirk of amusement when I described *The Original Series* crew as "a fleet of accidental gay icons."

Presently, he also crossed his arms, dangerously close to a smile that would show teeth, and shook his head. "You can't tell me *Star Trek* four is better than the 2009 reboot."

I gasped, even though I already knew this was his position on the subject since he'd said so minutes ago. "It's like I don't even know you. Tell me the truth, were you taken over by the Zetar? Lieutenant Romaine, are you in there? Do you have Zetarian spirits inside you now?"

We'd already finished our main courses—mine, a fillet of perfectly rare steak with truffled brussels sprouts; his, a warm French lentil salad followed by a seitan bourguignon—and we were working our way through a bottle of Côtes du Rhône AOC rosé that I would never be able afford under any circumstances. But Andreas didn't seem to notice the prices.

Dessert was somewhere in our future. For now, our little round table was a battlefield of quips, pop-culture references, and the occasional flicker of what felt like dangerous chemistry.

If I were to provide an objective, scientific analysis of the evening thus far, I'd say it started stiff and mannered, with both of us trying to perform normally in front of an audience that, as far as I could tell, consisted solely of the manager, a friendly sommelier, and a rotating cast of waiters so discreet thus far, they might've been deployed by the CIA.

And then, about halfway through the first glass of wine, I'd asked Andreas whether he still built pillow forts. And just like that, the ice had cracked.

I'd forgotten how intensely he could focus when talking about something that mattered to him. It was honestly intoxicating. For a long time, I let him monologue about the internal politics of the chess tournaments, the way social media had commodified all the top players, and why he'd decided to stop allowing comments on his posts and photos after strange conspiracy theories and shipping wars broke out between his fandom and another grand master's.

That's right. Members of Andreas's legions of fans had started shipping him with another grand master, another nonfiction human. And, apparently, there were fanfics.

Mental note. Look those up later. For reasons.

His face, usually a monument to European stoicism, had become animated as he explained the different flavors of cheating, mostly having to do with vibration devices planted in shoes or—*ahem*—shoved up buttholes. This portion of our conversation had me laughing so hard, I'd almost snorted rosé out of my nose. Good times.

But the best part? He actually laughed. Not once, but twice. And each time it startled him so much he immediately tried to cover it up by taking a sip of wine or running a hand through his already-mussed hair or dipping his chin down. Watching him try to hold it together was maybe the best thing I'd experienced in months.

"Okay," I said, topping off my own glass and leaning across the table, "but if you had to choose: *Next Generation* or *Deep Space Nine*?"

Andreas's eyes narrowed in mock seriousness. "An unfair question. They are fundamentally different."

"Coward." I pretended to be disgusted. "Cop-out. You have to pick one. Gun to your head."

He considered this, his expression serious and unfocused, as though giving it intense deliberation. Abruptly, his eyes sharpened on me. *"Deep Space Nine."*

I put a hand over my heart. "God, that's a power move. They're not even on a ship."

He grinned, the smile quick and real, like my praise pleased him immensely. Andreas opened his mouth, then shut it again, lips pressed together to hold back another smile. "You are," he said after a beat, "just as fun to be around as I remembered."

"Flattery will get you everywhere." I winked and drained the last of my wine.

We fell into a silence, not awkward, just comfortable. I glanced down and realized my hand was resting on the edge of the table, fingers curled in a way that practically begged to be held. It wasn't intentional, but it also wasn't not intentional. Andreas's hand—long fingers, knuckles like marble—lay close enough that if I reached just an inch or two, I could bridge the gap.

For a second, I considered moving my hand away, but then I remembered the rules. Rules which we'd drafted together and which stated quite clearly that hand holding was not only permitted, but expected.

Good thing he doesn't know about my hand kink.

Giving in, I reached over and put my hand on top of his, soft and casual, like it was no big deal. Like I'd done it a million times before.

He immediately turned his palm up, catching my fingers in a loose but inescapable hold. Then he pulled my hand closer, into the narrow space between our wineglasses, and for the next few moments, he absentmindedly traced circles on the back of my hand with his thumb while we debated the finer points of the time loop movies.

If I'd been a spectator, I would've bet money that we were very much in like—and lust—and not, as was actually the case, running a long con against a cabal of corporate sociopaths. I wanted to give myself a high five for my acting prowess. Except none of this felt like acting. It was just easy. Fun. Comfortable and exhilarating.

More than that, I thoroughly enjoyed trying to make Andreas lose his composure. Not just because it was a challenge—it absolutely was—but because every time he let his guard down, even a little, the world got about twenty percent less bleak and I felt, for a few precious seconds, like I wasn't just someone orbiting in his gravity well, but an equal. A true partner. Perhaps even a friend.

The waiter appeared with a miniature lake of vegan crème brûlée and set it between us, necessitating that we stop holding hands. *Alas.*

I picked up my spoon and broke the sugar-crust top. "Tell me something." I scooped out a spoonful, eyes on Andreas. "What's the dumbest thing you've ever done to impress a girl?"

Andreas set down the spoon he'd just picked up and studied me for a moment, the tiniest hint of a smile tugging at his lips. "This. Right now."

I made a noise, half laugh, half snort, and nearly inhaled a mouthful of burnt sugar. "You realize you're supposed to say something like, 'Bought a sports team' or 'Fought a bear.'"

"I have never fought a bear," he said, straight-faced.

"That's too bad," I replied. "Women love a bear fighter."

He laughed. It was a real one, low and gravelly and full-bodied, and I felt it like a jolt down my spine. Almost immediately, he tried to stifle it, shaking his head. "You are ridiculous."

I beamed at him, enjoying the victory. "Why do you do that? Why do you try to stop yourself from laughing?"

He blinked, caught off guard by the question. "I do not stop myself."

I raised an eyebrow. "You literally just did. Three times."

He looked away, as if the wall of Bordeaux bottles behind me could provide an answer. "I suppose I am not used to it."

"That's tragic," I said, shaking my head in mock sympathy. "You used to laugh all the time, back when we were kids."

Andreas picked up his wineglass, swirling the pink liquid before taking a measured sip. He seemed to really consider my statement, perhaps parsing it for subtext. When he finally answered, his voice was softer. "Maybe. I think I laugh now, too, just not . . ." He trailed off, maybe searching for how to best explain. "Just not with everyone."

"Just with people who are funny?"

Andreas nodded, not looking at me.

"Is this your way of saying I'm funny?"

He glanced up then, and for the first time all night, his expression seemed to open. His eyes moved over my face, then my neck, then the neckline of my dress, which—let's be honest—didn't leave a ton to the imagination.

"Very," he said, gaze sliding up from my chest to my neck, my lips, and eventually tangling with my eyes. "Among other things."

The words landed somewhere between my heart and my stomach and lit a little fuse. I had to fight a blush. Blushing was for people who didn't know better. Yet, the look he gave me, the directness of his stare and the obvious meaning behind his words, made my head spin a little.

He's a good actor.

As if on cue, a member of the waitstaff approached, moving with a careful, almost reverent gait.

"Is everything to your liking?" he asked Andreas, but his gaze flicked to me for a split second, as if checking for signs of distress.

Andreas never took his eyes from mine. "Yes," he said, voice low. "I believe we are ready."

The waiter gave a tiny, satisfied bow and retreated.

I placed both elbows on the table, chin in my palm, and regarded Andreas over the rim of my glass. "So," I said in a conspiratorial whisper, "is it happening now? Are you going to propose?"

He stared back at me with those mesmerizing green eyes and gave the tiniest nod.

I grinned even though this was a farce and we both knew it. But there was something thrilling about it, too. Like being on a rollercoaster you knew was perfectly safe. For a moment, I let myself imagine it was real and risky. That someone would actually propose to me, here, in this beautiful restaurant, and that I would say yes, and that we'd live a perfectly normal, boring life together, free of drama and academic warfare and corporate sabotage.

But then I remembered that the only thing I'd ever wanted less than academic warfare was marriage. If anyone ever proposed to me in real life, I'd probably change my phone number and move to a different state. And if I ever saw them walking down the street, I'd walk the other way.

Still. I understood why people did it. I understood the desire to be seen and known, to claim and be claimed, to say, "This is my person. This is the one I want forever."

But I also understood, maybe more than anyone, that nothing actually lasted forever. And I'd rather be alone and unbroken than risk loving someone so much it would eventually destroy me when they died, or left, or lost interest.

Andreas reached across the table and plucked my hand from beneath my chin, holding it between both of his. His grip was warm and firm. I could see his jaw flex with tension, yet his touch was gentle.

He leaned forward, so only I could hear, and whispered, "Ready?"

I swallowed, my throat tight because this man used to be my best friend as a kid, and my first real crush as a preteen. And now he was going to fake propose to me and I was going to fake accept. How absurd was that?

I nodded anyway.

Andreas stood. He took a breath. He didn't look at anyone but me.

Then he got down on one knee.

My eyes widened and I felt a hush fall over the room, probably born of my own imagination. But I hadn't expected him to kneel. Not in a million years. I was supposed to be acting, but my surprise at his gesture was genuine.

Andreas, still kneeling, took the small velvet box he'd shown me in the car earlier from his pocket and opened it. The diamond sparkled and looked like a fantasy.

He gazed at me, features deadly serious, and said, "Samantha, I think I have loved you from the first moment I saw you. It is one of my earliest memories, branded in my mind and on my soul. You wore burgundy, like tonight, and pigtails, and I recall thinking you were the most amazing, brilliant, interesting, fascinating person in the world, and every moment spent with you since has only reinforced this belief. I cannot believe I am lucky enough to ask you this question."

Heat erupted in my chest and stinging liquid emotion rushed to my eyes. I found I had to blink to keep Andreas in focus.

He paused, only for a second, then asked, "Will you marry me?"

The room was silent. I felt eyes on us. And then I did the stupidest thing I'd done in a decade. I started crying real tears.

It wasn't a sob, not at first. My chin wobbled. One single, traitorous drop rolled down my face. I tried to laugh it off, but the laugh cracked and shattered and became a gasp.

Andreas's face, usually so unreadable, changed. He stared at me, visibly uncertain, his lips parted. There was a flash of alarm, and I realized he was afraid he'd upset me, even though this was all a game.

I forced myself to nod, once, then again, harder, so everyone in the room could see.

"Yes," I said, voice barely a whisper.

Exhaling like he'd been worried I might say no, Andreas stood, slipped the ring onto my finger, and before I could think about it, I also stood and threw my arms around his neck. I hugged him with everything I had. He hugged me back, tight and close, like he meant it. And for a second, my cheek pressed against his neck, I let myself believe he did.

The room erupted in applause, presumably from the waitstaff, and I tangentially wondered if they'd been paid to clap.

Pulling back, I'm sure tears streaked my makeup. Andreas caught my face in both hands, cradling my cheeks. There was a moment of silent negotiation. *Should we kiss now?* his eyes seemed to ask.

We had to, obviously. It was expected. It was required.

Andreas leaned in. I closed my eyes. Our lips met. And this first kiss was nothing like I'd imagined it would be when we'd discussed it in the car.

I'd expected his part to be cold, calculated pressure, a kind of mechanical lip touch that was only technically a kiss. Instead, his lips were soft, lingering, warm. He kissed me slowly, like he was savoring me, and for a second the world went fuzzy at the edges. My heart slammed against my ribs so hard I thought it might bruise, and I felt my body melt into him. When he eventually pulled back, I was legitimately dizzy, and I was certain my face was flushed, and I had only one thought in my head.

Jesus fucking Christ, he has amazing lips.

Something greedy and reckless took hold of me. I grabbed the lapels of his suit and pulled him closer, intent not just on playing my role but on giving myself something I'd never forget. I wanted him, to know if the memory of his mouth would match the daydreams of my youth. My lips crashed into his, not gentle or tentative, but decisive, demanding. I pressed into him, feeling the solid, unyielding line of his chest through my dress, and let my tongue trace along the seam of his lips.

For half a beat he tensed, as if surprised by my boldness, then surrendered without hesitation. But then, I'd warned him there'd be tongue. Hadn't I?

His lips parted and I pushed inside, the heat of him igniting something ferocious within me. Andreas made a low, involuntary sound—somewhere between a moan and a gasp—a tiny, startled noise, the kind I'd only ever heard in moments of genuine surprise. The fact that I'd ripped it out of him made adrenaline zing down my spine and I pushed for more.

He responded in kind. His hands, previously gentle and scripted for the crowd of restaurant staff, clamped onto my lower back with purpose. His grip was solid, fingers digging into the silk of my dress and hips, pulling me flush against him until there was nothing between us, no room for anything but the incendiary heat of our bodies. In that moment, I was hyper-aware of the way his forearm flexed along my side, the hard tremor of his ribs against my own, even the delicate scent of the cologne he wore, now mingled with the citrusy tang of wine.

This second kiss was so much wetter, so much noisier, so much more ravenous. My hands climbed to the nape of his neck, threading through the soft hair, and I felt the shiver run all the way through him. I was distantly aware of movement in the background, a clink of glasses and the hum of waitstaff blurred together. But the only thing that really existed was the hot slide of his tongue against mine and the pressure of his body pinning me to the moment.

He broke away just enough to catch his breath, but when he tried to pull back, I chased him, biting at his lower lip. I felt him smile, felt his teeth graze my own, and that was enough to make me laugh out loud, giddy and breathless. He swallowed the laugh, mouth returning for another kiss, and this time he took control, grabbing my hair and angling my head back with a yank so he could kiss me deeper. I let him, because I wanted it—I wanted it so badly my pulse was thrumming in places I'd been neglecting for years. His tongue flicked against my own and my whole body lit up with goose bumps. I heard myself make a soft, desperate noise, and I would have been embarrassed if I'd had the capacity for shame.

His hands moved, one splayed across my back while the other cupped my jaw, thumb stroking down my neck, hot palm sliding to my shoulder, fingers playing with the strap of my dress. I opened my eyes for a second, saw his were still closed, and suddenly I was terrified, because for an instant I wasn't sure if he was still acting or if this was real, if he could possibly be feeling even a fraction of what was detonating inside me.

That thought had me pulling away, my lungs burning, and I blinked at him. He stared back, pupils blown so wide, his eyes looked almost black. His lips were swollen, his face flushed with heat, and for a flicker of a second, I thought he was going to say something, actually say something real, but instead he just yanked me forward, quick and sharp, and kissed me again. I felt the ring on my finger press against his cheek.

I couldn't have said how long we stood there, locked together in the center of that restaurant, kissing each other. For all I knew, we had stopped time itself. I slid my hands down from his hair, traced his jaw with my thumbs, tried to memorize every detail of this moment because I knew it wouldn't happen again.

It is a special circumstance, he'd said.

Which meant, this was it. This was my one and only chance to kiss him. He'd agreed in the car. This was allowed.

And, worse, this was the best kiss of my life *by far*, a fact that was so dismaying I almost laughed just to keep from crying. Because I'd promised myself I'd never let anyone get under my skin like this, never allow myself to get carried away.

But hadn't Andreas Kristiansen always been the exception? He'd been grandfathered in, before my life had gone to hell, and I'd cared about him so deeply before I understood the potential danger, before I—

Abruptly, there was a loud *pop.* We flinched apart, Andreas's hands still locked on my back. I blinked at my surroundings, spotting the waiter and the sommelier from before standing nearby, holding a silver bucket with an open bottle of champagne. The friendly sommelier was smiling, the waiter trying desperately not to.

Mercifully, Andreas let me go, just enough to turn and face the onlookers. He slid his hand down my arm, threading his fingers through mine, and I let him. I also let him kiss my hand, soft and old-fashioned. For a second, I fought the desperate desire to pull him back in for another round.

I had to remind myself why we were here, what this entire spectacle was really about. With this reminder, the world snapped back into focus. I glanced past the sommelier, scanning the room for anyone who seemed out of place, anyone who might be watching for Tobias or Henrik, and spotted a waitress behind the manager slipping her phone back into her pocket, her eyes shifty.

Mission accomplished . . . *I guess.*

Meanwhile, Andreas's thumb slid over my knuckles, slow and deliberate, and the sensation was so intimate I almost forgot my own name. I let myself lean into him one last time, pressing my cheek against his shoulder, breathing him in. He rested his chin lightly on my head, and I said goodbye to the fantasy. Mourned it. Because out-of-control longing wasn't for me.

But it had been lovely to pretend, if only for a little while.

The waitstaff descended upon us with congratulations, the bottle of champagne, and two flutes already filled to the brim. The manager offered her own best wishes, beaming at us as if she'd played a role in our engagement. I tried to smile, to play along, but I felt hollowed out, like a building gutted by fire. I didn't dare look at Andreas for fear of what I'd see there.

Or what I might show him in return.

[13]

DNA TECHNOLOGY

Samantha

Thirty-one minutes after accepting a fake marriage proposal, I sat in the back of the Mercedes SUV staring holes through the seat in front of me. The privacy window was down and Tara drove with both hands on the wheel, posture immaculate. I sat directly behind her and the middle seat between me and Andreas was left vacant. Andreas, whose own back was pressed flat to the leather, kept his gaze fixed out the window as the city blurred past in electric streaks. He hadn't said a word since we'd left the restaurant. He also hadn't touched me, not even an accidental graze.

I kept waiting for some kind of follow-up. A postmortem of the proposal. A joke. Instead, the only reminder of the whole spectacle was the diamond on my finger, a sparkling star that winked whenever I turned my hand. I still wasn't convinced it wasn't a prop, the weight of it felt obscene.

The proposal, the champagne, the public make out so hot it still echoed beneath my skin, all of it played on a loop during brittle quiet of the car ride. For reasons I couldn't name, I felt like crying. It wasn't sadness, more like sheer *overwhelm*, the way one might cry after narrowly avoiding being hit by a bus.

Tara checked on me in the mirror, watching me with open curiosity. I attempted a smile, but it died halfway up my cheeks.

She caught it anyway. Her own smile flashed, then vanished as quickly as it came.

Andreas was the first to speak, his voice smooth and impassive. "Do you want the movers to come tomorrow, or Sunday?"

I flinched slightly at the sudden sound. "Um, tomorrow's fine," I said, and forced myself to unclench my jaw. "I should be finished packing before noon."

"Do you need boxes?" His eyes were still pointed out the window.

I shook my head even though he wasn't looking at me. "No. I have stackable bins for moving. I've done it so many times that I just keep them in my closet. It'll be four bins and a suitcase. The furniture stays."

At this, Andreas faced me wearing a confused-looking frown. He studied me for a long moment, like he had several follow-up questions. But eventually, the tiny crease that had formed above his nose smoothed, and he redirected his gaze out the window again. "I will tell them to come at noon, then."

That was it. No further conversation. Tara, perhaps sensing the silence had crystallized, turned on a playlist that apparently consisted of only cello covers of pop songs. "Wrecking Ball" had never sounded so apt.

The car ate the blocks between Midtown and the far side of the park. I counted every stoplight, every jogger, every office worker fumbling with their phone late on a Friday night. I wondered what they'd think if they looked through the tinted glass and saw me, diamond ring on my left hand, hair still flawless, makeup less so, and dead-eyed with the particular numbness that follows a massive adrenaline spike.

Maybe they'd think I was some trophy wife on the way home from a charity ball. Or maybe they'd see what was really going on, a girl who'd just sold her soul for a shot at poetic justice, and now had to pretend like the consequences weren't already gnawing at her.

When we pulled up to my building, Tara put the car in park and looked over her shoulder. "Do you want me to wait?"

I'd already started to reach for the door, but Andreas caught my wrist before I could open it. The contact startled me, not because it was rough, but because it was so careful.

"I will walk Samantha up to her apartment." His words sounded coldly polite. "Please circle the block until I return."

Tara gave a little salute. "Sure thing, boss."

Andreas exited first, walked around the back of the car, and opened my door for me. He offered his hand. I took it and our fingers fit together. His was a little clammy, and mine was probably freezing. I let him lead me to the door and studied his posture as we walked. He appeared entirely at ease, his movements unhurried.

At the front entrance, I typed in the security code. He didn't let go of my hand as the door buzzed open and we crossed the threshold.

Inside, the stairwell was dim and quiet, the scent of old radiators and paint chips mixing with the faintest whiff of the bakery down the block. I paused, at a loss for what to do next.

Andreas finally released my hand, stuffing both of his into his coat pockets. He looked up the stairs, seeming to contemplate each one individually, like the act of walking me up to my apartment was perhaps the most complicated situation he'd ever encountered.

I shifted my weight, fished through my bag for keys I didn't quite need yet, gave up searching for them, and tried to think of something casual to say. "You know, it's four flights. You really don't have to walk me all the way up."

"I do not mind."

"It's not dangerous," I pressed, feigning exasperation I didn't feel. "I don't need an escort. Honestly, it's fine. I'll just go up from here."

I wanted him to leave. Not because I didn't want him around, but because the moment he left, I could finally collapse and let the tears—tears I didn't understand and didn't want to explain—have their way with me. Diya should be at work unless something in her schedule had changed last minute. Kendra was at her boyfriend's. And Nakita had left this afternoon for her parents' place outside of Boston. I'd have the whole apartment to myself.

But Andreas didn't leave. He looked at the stairs, then at his shoes, then back at me. "I need to wait here for fifteen minutes."

That threw me. "Why?"

"It would be strange"—his gaze locked on a spot above my head—"for me to sleep alone tonight after that proposal."

It took a few seconds for the logic to sink in. Then it hit all at once. He was performing for an audience we knew existed, and was watching, and was likely outside the building. One I'd already forgotten about in my post-kiss haze. If anyone had followed us to my building—likely one of Tobias's underlings—they'd expect Andreas to spend the night.

I felt a laugh rise in my chest, but it came out bitter. "Right. Of course."

And then, because my brain always insisted on poking holes in plans, I asked, "What if they spot you leaving after fifteen minutes? Won't that look suspicious?"

He cleared his throat, but didn't answer. For once, the strategic genius had no ready move. I could almost see the gears grinding behind his stoic mask.

I took a step up, then stopped and turned, arms folded. "Should you just spend the night, then?"

His eyes snapped to mine. If I hadn't been staring, I might have missed the way they widened, just for a second, with what looked like astonishment.

"Do you want me to spend the night?" The question hung between us, utterly flat and uninflected.

I opened my mouth, then closed it. Thoughts tumbled in. The taste of his mouth, the smell of rosemary, the way his hand had fit against the small of my back and made me feel like my bones were electric. I remembered, too, the rules. No physical contact when alone. No room for the real thing.

I shrugged, hoping it looked cool and unbothered. "If there's a chance you'll be spotted leaving and it messes up our plan, then yes. I'll text Diya and see if she's coming home tonight. If not, you can have my bed, I'll take hers. Otherwise, you can sleep on the couch."

Andreas's eyebrows pulled together in not quite a frown. "Is that what you want?"

I should have said, *It doesn't matter what I want. The plan is all that matters.* But the thought of him in my apartment, of waking up and seeing him there, even as an act, sent a pulse of longing through me that was so strong I wanted to kick myself.

"It's fine," I said tiredly, and started up the stairs. "Whatever makes sense." I paused, thumb hovering over my phone, and shot Diya a text.

Sam: Home early. You have an overnight shift, right? Need to know for . . . reasons.

While waiting for her reply, I continued climbing stairs. I'd ascended two flights before I noticed I was climbing them alone. I stopped, turned, and looked down. Andreas was a full flight below me, face angled up, standing motionless on the landing.

He wasn't winded. In fact, he looked like a malfunctioning Roomba, immobilized by indecision, calculating alternate routes. His face was marble, unreadable except for the barest tightness in the line of his jaw.

"You okay?" I asked, pitching my voice as low as I could, wanting to irritate my neighbors as little as possible.

His gaze shifted to mine and he nodded once. Then he started up the stairs, climbing in a steady, silent cadence until he reached my level.

We walked the rest of the way together, no more than a step apart, neither of us speaking. My thoughts scurried in a dozen directions. Why had he stopped? Did I do something wrong? Was he regretting the whole public display at the restaurant? Had I bitten him too hard during the kiss? Did he realize, suddenly, that he would have to sleep on my sad, lumpy mattress and was recalculating the entire trajectory of his life up to this moment?

I checked my phone at the landing. Diya hadn't replied to my earlier text, so I fired off another.

Sam: Hey, if you won't be home tonight, is it cool if Andreas stays over? I'll sleep in your bed, he'll sleep in mine. LMK if you're coming home tonight.

I sent it, then fumbled for my keys. Andreas reached out—quick, efficient—and took my clutch before I could drop it. Then he held it open so I could use both my hands to find my keys. For some reason, this tiny, proactive gesture sent a shock wave of embarrassment down my spine.

He was so . . . thoughtful.

Muttering thanks once I'd found my keys, I moved to the locks. He followed me to the door, standing close enough for me to catch the faint hint of cologne beneath the more assertive scent of his rosemary shampoo.

I unlocked the top dead bolt, then the middle one, then the bottom, aware that each click ricocheted and echoed down the hallway.

Pushing open the door, I stepped inside. "Why don't you—"

Nakita's voice rang out, surprising and interrupting me. "Who's home? I'm in the kitchen. Don't be alarmed by the smoke." Her inflection was cheerful, so I assumed the smoke coming from the kitchen was purposeful.

But I stiffened, because she wasn't supposed to be home, which meant I half hollered, half screeched, "What are you doing here?! Aren't you supposed to be in Boston?"

Shit. I hadn't excepted anyone. And of my roommates, Nakita was the one I wanted to see the least right now considering she was the hardcore chess fangirl.

"Sam?"

I looked at Andreas's face; he wore his usual unemotional mask as I called back in a more modulated tone, "Yes. It's Sam, and—"

"Oh my God, Sam!" Nakita bellowed. "I have a bone to pick with you. I can't believe you actually know Andreas Kristiansen! Why wouldn't you tell me that you know the sexiest man in the world?"

Andreas stood perfectly still, holding my bag in one hand. Meanwhile, I cringed. With my whole body.

That's right. *A WHOLE-BODY CRINGE.*

Nakita continued, "That man can fill out a pair of pants, am I right? So hot. And don't even get me started on his chest and hands. Jesus Christ, I didn't expect him to be so tall! I wanted to climb him. Please tell me you're going to hit that—"

Belatedly finding my voice, I cut her off, loud and frantic. "He's standing right next to me, Nakita!"

Dead silence.

I peeked at Andreas again. His features hadn't changed, but there was a suggestion—just a suggestion—of mortification in the way he kept his eyes glued forward. For Andreas, and what I was coming to understand about his lack of external expressiveness, this felt like a big reaction.

Andreas had been a bit arrogant about his chess abilities the last time he was here, but Nakita's objectification now seemed to distress him greatly.

Is this modesty?

He had to know how handsome he was. How could he not?

Modest about his looks but arrogant about chess.

I unwrapped my scarf from my suddenly hot neck, whispering, "Sorry. I'm sorry. Are you okay? Do you want to leave?"

Andreas shook his head wordlessly, issuing me an exceedingly small, tight smile, and set my bag down on the entry table. I studied him as he shrugged off his coat, folding it over one arm with slow, precise movements.

"Andreas." I stepped closer, my voice just above a whisper while I barely resisted the urge to place a hand on his forearm. "We can go. I didn't know anyone would be here tonight. We can—"

He shook his head again, a calculating gleam entering his eyes. "No. This might be for the best."

I stared at him. "Uh, how so?"

Before he could respond, Nakita's quick footsteps interrupted our whispered conversation. She rounded the corner, her hands ensconced in oven mitts, the perfect portrait of domestic instability. Her cheeks were flushed, her braids pulled back into a haphazard bun, and her eyes were wide with apology.

"Oh. Hey, Andreas. I, uh, didn't know you were here." The words tripped over each other, and she sounded completely mortified. Gaze wide with obvious worry, she blurted, "I am so, so sorry. That was gross and rude and uncalled for and I'm sorry."

Saying nothing, Andreas lifted his chin in acknowledgment. Thankfully, he looked slightly less embarrassed than he had a second ago. Nakita turned to me, her eyes screaming *HELP*, and I mentally sent her a sympathy card. But also, she needed to learn: Don't say anything behind a person's back that you wouldn't say to their face. Ever.

Think that kind of shit to your heart's content, but don't say it.

"Where is the bathroom?" Andreas asked, voice low, attention sliding to me.

"Down the hall, first door before my bedroom. Leave your coat on my bed if you want." I lifted my chin in the direction of my room.

He nodded, then sedately strolled away, eventually vanishing behind the door of the restroom, which closed with an unhurried, soft *snick*.

The instant the door closed, Nakita whirled on me. "Oh my God, I'm so embarrassed. Why didn't you say he was here? I sounded like a total idiot. I literally called him the sexiest man in the world." She smacked her lips with her oven-mitt-clad fingers. "I'm so stupid."

Her embarrassment and worry cracked through my cloak of numbness and suddenly I was fighting a laugh at her discomfort. "You apologized. And he probably gets it a lot from people who don't apologize."

"No," Nakita said, shaking her head, "nobody gets that a lot. People don't just casually say that kind of thing in real life. Or they shouldn't. Oh my God. Please tell him I'm not a gross lecher."

I patted her arm, letting the contact linger. "You're not a gross lecher. You're just . . . aggressively fangirly and inappropriate."

Nakita gave me a wincing smile, then, with the finely honed skill of a lifelong gossip, scanned me from head to toe. "Speaking of sexy, what are you wearing? Holy hot sauce, Sam. You look incredible."

I looked down at myself. The dress still clung to me, the color now more dark-pool-of-blood than burgundy in the dim entryway. My heels felt less "elegant" and more "torture device" with every passing minute, but I tried to stand up straighter.

"It's a nice dress, right?" I said, voice tight, glancing toward the bathroom and wondering what to do if Nakita asked again about what was going on between Andreas and me.

You'll lie, of course, and tell her you're engaged. My stomach tried to sink. I wouldn't let it. Lying to my roommates would likely be the least of my deceptions over the coming months. I needed to get used to feeling icky.

"It's more than nice. Is that what you wore to dinner with him? Please tell me you just got back from a date, because both of you look like you stepped off a catwalk." Nakita took a step back and clasped her oven-mitted hands together. "And his suit matched!"

The weight of the ring on my finger became a black hole, compressing every nerve ending in my hand into a singularity. I thought about hiding it, then decided hiding it would only make things worse later. Better to get this over with.

I took a deep breath. "Actually, there's something I should tell you."

Nakita leaned in, eyes bright, hungry for gossip. And, boy oh boy, did I have a whole damn seven-course meal to feed her. She was about to get heartburn.

Seeing no reason to delay, I held up my left hand, ring finger exposed. "We're engaged."

Her mouth fell open, her eyes bugged out, and for a long moment she stared at me wordlessly.

Again, I actively worked to feel okay about lying. Strangely, I didn't have to try very hard. *Huh.*

"Engaged?" she finally squealed. "You're engaged?!"

I nodded, pasting on a large smile. I didn't feel like nodding or smiling, but I also didn't feel like I had any other available options. That said, the lie didn't even taste like a lie. It tasted oddly sweet, like the first sinister step toward my revenge.

* * *

AFTER MY REVEAL, Nakita worked her way through the five stages of gossip grief. She started with denial ("You're messing with me. No way you're engaged. Is this a prank? I'm not falling for it, Sam."), then anger ("This is so unfair, I tell you everything and you hold out on me like it's a state secret!"), then bargaining ("If you make me a bridesmaid, I'll plan your bachelorette party."), then depression ("Am I going to lose you? Are you going to move to Europe? Will you even visit?"), and finally, acceptance ("Fine, I don't need to be a bridesmaid. But I'd like an invitation.").

What made this progression truly remarkable was that it all took place in the two minutes before Andreas exited the bathroom.

Now the three of us were sitting in the family room, Andreas and me on the couch, Nakita in the armchair. She seemed to be attempting banal chitchat, and I wondered if the only thing keeping her from a full-scale inquisition was her earlier foot-in-mouth moment. That, or the fact that Andreas and I, after sitting next to each other on the couch for a solid five minutes, had yet to make any physical contact. Not a single graze of fingers, not a foot nudged, not even a moment of mutual eye contact.

We probably looked, in a word, estranged.

Nakita must've noticed, of course. She noticed everything. The more we failed to act "engaged," the deeper her frown lines became.

My palms were sweating. This was not how a newly engaged couple was supposed to act. And since Nakita was the gossip in our group, she'd definitely tell everyone about our odd behavior.

Looking between us, she leaned forward, elbows on knees. "So, how did you propose? Sam's never told us anything about your relationship. I want all the details."

I opened my mouth, but Andreas beat me to it. "At Maison Lavande, after dinner." He shrugged, voice even. Understated, but entirely believable. "I am not very original."

Nakita's eyes doubled in size. "Are you kidding? Maison Lavande is legendary! That's so romantic. Sam, did you cry?"

I didn't have to fake the blush. "A little. It was a surprise."

"She cried," Andreas confirmed, tone so dry it could have desiccated a houseplant.

Nakita's frown intensified and her gaze shifted between us, full of suspicion. Apparently recovered from her earlier embarrassment, she asked, "Did you two get in a fight already? Is it about Sam's propensity for sleepwalking?" The question was obviously asked as a joke, but her eyes were sharp.

"Samantha sleepwalks?" Andreas's question sounded so earnest and innocent.

Before I could respond, Nakita's stare sharpened. "You didn't know?"

"It's no big deal." I shrugged, avoiding both Nakita's and Andreas's gazes. "Just once or twice. Probably because of stress at work." I felt Andreas's continued attention on my profile.

Damn it.

Something had to be done. I wasn't certain what, or how to clear it with Andreas before doing it. There'd been a shift since that kiss in the restaurant, a new hyper-awareness—at least on my side. Now, I couldn't bring myself to initiate contact with him again.

So, I did what any rational, fully grown adult plotting revenge would do: I devised a plan.

Step one: Get Nakita out of the living room, even if just for a few minutes.

Step two: Have a whispered strategy session with Andreas so we could agree on a baseline level of "believable PDA" for this situation.

Step three: Behave as a credible couple by the time Nakita returned.

It was a solid plan.

Now, what excuse can I give for our present awkwardness and what will get her to leave the room . . . ?

"Uh, so." I scratched my neck and did a passable job of looking self-deprecatingly embarrassed. "We came here sorta last minute without a plan. I know I didn't clear it with anyone first, sorry about that."

Her gaze moved between us. "Oh, that's fine. Don't worry about that."

I leaned forward, my voice dropping to a conspiratorial whisper. "To be honest, I told Andreas no one would be home."

Nakita blinked and I was pleased to see a light of understanding in her eyes. "Oh, so you two thought you'd have the place to your—"

"Sorry, that was inconsiderate of me. But since we're here"—I put my hand on Andreas's knee without looking at him and felt his thigh muscle flex at the contact—"do you mind if we stay?"

"Not at all!" Her attention flickered to where my hand sat on his leg then back to me. "Sorry if I ruined your plans."

I waved her apology away. "Are you kidding? I'm the one in the wrong here.

But, the thing is, for Andreas to spend the night, I need pajamas for him. Do you think Kendra's boyfriend—"

"Kendra has some of her boyfriend's clothes in her bottom drawer," she said, jumping up. "He's about the same size as Andreas, right? Tall, but, like, not gym tall?"

"Yeah, I think so." I stood too, twisting my fingers. "Do you think she has anything?"

"Sure! I'll grab a pair of sweatpants and a T-shirt. Is that okay?" Nakita was already backing up toward the bedroom she shared with Kendra.

"That should work, if you're sure—"

She disappeared down the hall, her voice calling back, "I'm sure! And I'll be right back. Don't go anywhere!"

I plopped down on the sofa again and inspected Andreas. He didn't look comfortable, but he also didn't look uncomfortable. How did he do that?

Leaning in, I whispered harshly, "We're not acting very engaged right now."

Andreas sliced me a glare so sharp it could've cut a watermelon in half. "What do you want me to do?" he hissed through his teeth. "We have not yet discussed what PDA would be appropriate for this situation, and your conditions state—"

I leaned closer, my nose almost bumping his. "Obviously, we're going to have to improvise!"

His jaw flexed, and he said, low and tight, "I do not know where I am allowed to touch you."

My brain ran through all the possible answers and hurriedly settled on the only one that wouldn't lead to a lengthy negotiation.

"Touch me anywhere you want, okay? Just make it look real. Nakita is already suspicious, and if we want her to—"

The sound of footsteps cut me off, and before I even realized what was happening, Andreas reached over, grabbed my arm, and hauled me across the couch. In one fluid, dizzying motion, he maneuvered me into his lap, spun me to face him, and anchored my hips down with an ironclad grip.

Suddenly, I was straddling Andreas Kristiansen on my own living room sofa, my knees on either side of his thighs, my hands braced against his shoulders, not a single second to spare a thought for how indecently high this position had pushed my dress up.

I froze. We both froze, gazes clashing. Then, his hands—one on my thigh, the other at the nape of my neck—pulled me forward.

He kissed me.

Not a peck. Not a gentle brush of lips. A full-on, open-mouthed, hungry, wet, and breathtaking kiss. His tongue sweeping inside me with a confidence that brooked no hesitation. I didn't even tense for a nanosecond, instead immediately melting against him like a heat-activated polymer.

My arms wound around his neck, and my fingers tunneled into his hair. I could feel him, between my spread legs, growing harder and longer, and my heartbeat jackhammered against my chest, which, incidentally, was now pressed flush to his. I wondered if he could feel me, too. The tightness of my nipples and the wet heat between my legs just as obvious as his erection pressing into me.

Don't do it. Don't grind down. Don't. Don't. Don't—

I did and it felt so fucking good, essential. Andreas groaned, the sound a rumble reverberating from his chest to mine, his hand at my neck gripping harder. The kiss was so hot, so electric, that it must've fried every synapse in my brain. All the rules and boundaries and self-imposed restrictions evaporated. The only thing that existed was the urgency of his mouth on mine and the strong, commanding grip of his hands on my thigh and neck, and how much my body needed—

"Oh! Yikes! Gosh, sorry!"

At the sound of Nakita's reentrance, Andreas pulled away slightly and dipped his chin to break the kiss. He pressed his forehead against mine and we shared a few ragged breaths before he swallowed, leaned to the side, and looked—or rather, glared—at Nakita.

"Pardon. We will move this elsewhere."

[14]
BIOCHEMISTRY AND THE MOLECULES OF LIFE

Samantha

Wrapping an arm around my upper body and standing, Andreas didn't give my brain a chance to catch up with his intentions. Torso supported, my legs gradually slid from his hips to his calves until he bent slightly at the waist, setting my feet gently on the floor. I was about to untangle my arms from his neck when he leaned to my ear and whispered, "Hold on."

The heat of his breath falling against my bare skin made me shiver, but I complied, holding him tighter. Placing one arm under my legs, he scooped me up. Unsure what I was thinking or feeling, I buried my head in the crook of his neck and squeezed my eyes shut, focusing only on regulating my breathing and battling this overwhelming, drug-like daze of arousal.

I heard him murmur, "Thank you."

Andreas then carried me around the couch and down the short hallway to my room. I sensed him pause inside. He shifted. I heard the door close.

I felt his chest rise and fall with a sigh. "Are you alright?"

I nodded, my arms loosening. "Can you put me down, please?" My voice sounded odd, rough, small.

He bent and it didn't occur to me until he set me down that, due to the shortness of my hiked-up dress and the method of his transport—one-armed bridal-style carry—I'd likely just flashed Nakita.

Oh well. She can thank me for the free show later.

Rolling my eyes at myself, I felt my face go red, not because I'd flashed my roommate but because I'd been too turned on to notice. In a scramble to preserve any shred of dignity, I spent a frantic few seconds yanking my skirt down while stumbling away from Andreas, trying to remember what decorum even was.

Decorum. *What is: A word my grandmother used that I never learned, for $500, Alex?*

Still blushing so hard I thought my face might combust, I turned stupidly in a half circle, desperately wanting to fill the tense silence. "So, uh, you'll take—you'll sleep there." I pointed to my bed. "I should change the sheets."

"No need." Andreas walked toward my mattress and, in the dim illumination provided by the city lights coming in through the window, I realized he held a bundle of clothes. He lifted a pair of sweatpants. "These should fit."

Kendra's boyfriend's clothes. Andreas had likely one-arm carried me so he could accept the pajamas from Nakita without letting me go.

I did my level best to pretend the last ten minutes hadn't affected me by clearing my throat and attempting a nonchalant nod. "Good. And if you're cool with the sheets, fine. They were washed recently anyway." The effect was spoiled by the fact that my fingers visibly shook when I darted past him and fumbled with the light switch by the door. "I'll just—I'll go brush my—"

He was next to me in a flash, his larger hand covering mine on the switch. "Wait."

I went statue still, a now familiar jolt of electricity shooting up my arm at his touch.

"Don't. Your roommate is out there, and it would appear strange if you turned on the lights or left now, after . . ."

I made a short sound of agreement, like an ahh, and removed my fingers from the light switch.

A long, awkward moment passed where neither of us moved or spoke. My ears strained to listen for movement beyond the room, but the sound of my own heart beating between my temples made that impossible. And I was too turned on. Rather than allow my breathing to grow shallow or labored again, I held air in my lungs then forced myself to exhale carefully, slowly, silently through my nose.

"Samantha," he whispered roughly, breaking the silence, still standing too close but not touching me anywhere. "Are you . . . upset with me?"

"No," I croaked, then cleared my throat again before adding on a whisper, "Not at all. Are you upset with me?"

Daring to glance over my shoulder, I peeked at him. His back was to the window, his features were mostly in shadow, but I felt his eyes on me.

Finally, after a protracted period, he rasped out, "Not upset, no."

Those words sounded like a riddle. Instinctively, I turned, lifting my chin and searching his face, or what I could see of his features, which wasn't much. But his eyes seemed to glint.

It was on the tip of my tongue to ask what he'd meant when Andreas stumbled a step forward, as though he'd been pushed from behind. His hands reached out and gripped my waist, tugging me forward. His fingers flexed on my sides. The movement felt restless. I heard him exhale a ragged breath as his forehead connected with mine.

"I need—" he began, then shook his head, his arms abruptly embracing me. "May I hold you? I only need—only for a moment."

My arms were already returning his embrace before he'd finished speaking, wrapping tightly around his chest. I felt his erection against my stomach, hard and insistent, but I ignored it, and a long exhale left my lungs. Holding him right now felt necessary, a relief, an outlet for the buzzing electric energy beneath my skin. I closed my eyes, squeezing him tighter.

Ear pressed against his wide chest, I listened as his racing heart gradually slowed and our breathing synced. Eventually, I felt him swallow. He lifted a hand and gently pressed his palm to the crown of my head, as though encouraging me to snuggle closer, to relax into him. My arms loosened but I kept my fingers locked as I melted against his body, sinking into the warm strength of his arms.

We stood there so much longer than a moment, holding each other in the dim light. I didn't know what he was thinking and I made no effort to guess. Abruptly aware of how exposed I felt, both physically and otherwise, I knew I was being ridiculous and I needed to get my head on straight.

The sound of Nakita's bedroom door closing is what finally broke us apart.

I stepped away. He let me go. Then I turned my back to him and stared at my dresser, at the pile of unfolded laundry, at my poster of Rosalind Franklin glaring at me from the shadows with supreme judgment.

"If you're going to stay, you should change clothes." I moved further away from him. "I'll go get you a new toothbrush and lay it out in the bathroom. Let me give you some privacy," I said, a little too fast, a little too loud. I then grabbed my own pajamas from the drawer, bolted out the door, and shut it behind me.

Making a beeline for the bathroom, I ignored the sound of Nakita's laughter echoing from behind her closed bedroom door. Once inside, I turned the lock, found a new toothbrush, set it on the sink, and stared at myself in the mirror.

Somehow, my makeup had mostly survived the double onslaught of tears and tongue. My mascara was only slightly smeared, and my lipstick, while gone, had left behind a faint berry stain.

A laugh bubbled up, but it came out as something brittle and desperate.

I stripped out of the dress and shimmied into my pajamas—baggy, blue, and covered in cartoon mitochondria—then sat down on the edge of the bathtub, buried my face in my hands, and tried to process the events of the evening.

We'd had a *really* nice dinner together. In fact, if tonight's dinner had been a real first date, it would've been the best one I'd ever had. And then everything that came after . . .

This was dangerous. This was uncharted territory. I was the one who'd insisted on boundaries, on rules, on avoiding any scenario where I might get in over my head. And now, I was the one who couldn't get her heart rate below 160.

I needed to talk to Andreas, be honest, and put it all out there. I needed to clarify. To define. To make sure that what happened in the restaurant and on the sofa were simply one-time-only—er, two-time-only—mission-critical incidents, and not gateway grope fests that would lead to . . . something else.

But first, I needed a few more minutes alone.

Pressing my palms to my eyelids, I attempted to memorize the feeling of his hands on my hips, his mouth on mine, the dizzying, impossible heat of his body beneath my open legs. I tried to memorize it so I could lock it away forever, file it under "Miscellaneous," and get on with the task at hand: burning it all down and coming out the other side unscathed and triumphant.

Unfortunately, there was also the small matter of *the hug* in my bedroom just now. Unscripted, unnecessary, and very private. Some part of me had desperately craved that embrace from Andreas, and had been craving it since he first approached me outside my department building. All this strange wistfulness I'd been trying to shove aside and ignore, longing I'd labeled as simple attraction, when my feelings were so much deeper than surface-level desire.

But, so what? What could be done about it? Sure, I'd have to confront it, talk it out, establish new boundaries, especially since we'd be moving in together tomorrow. But I could never allow myself to act on this wistfulness and longing. Too much was at stake.

I had a fake fiancé in my bedroom, a roommate who probably thought I was two weeks from eloping, and an entire empire of lies to maintain until Oskar Kristiansen kicked the bucket, whenever that might be. I couldn't let pesky *feelings* get in the way.

Finally, I stood, splashed cold water on my face, and forced myself to smile. When I failed to achieve what could pass as a genuine expression of nonchalance, I stopped trying.

Inhaling deeply, I decided we'd have to discuss everything tomorrow. Not now. Not when I felt so exposed, not when my desire felt this close to the surface, clamoring for attention and satisfaction and *him*.

Yes. *Tomorrow.* I nodded at my reflection in the mirror. *I'll figure it out tomorrow.*

* * *

PACKING up my entire life took under three hours and only because I had a load of laundry to do. This fact made me either an ascetic or a minimalist. One sounded prudish, the other sounded chic, and neither prudish nor chic sounded like me.

By 9:30 AM, I'd consolidated all my possessions into four stackable plastic bins (with snap-tight lids), a single battered duffel, and my backpack. The task required so little time that by the end I found myself wandering the bare perimeter of my side of the room, mildly unnerved by its echo and emptiness. The blank walls and the empty desktop where my stuff had squatted for four years were bizarre to me. It was the first time in adulthood that I'd had the occasion to move out of a place and leave others behind. Usually, I was the one being left.

Was this a victory? Or a sign of my congenital inability to commit to physical objects and, by extension, people . . . ?

Whoa, whoa, whoa. That's too deep, Sam. Step away from the psychoanalysis paralysis and hop on over to the coping-strategy dance party.

I'd just dropped my last handful of hangers into the giveaway box when Nakita appeared at my door, arms laden with a plastic-wrapped bundle of bagels and a three-pack of full-sugar Red Bull. Her braids were looped into a crown on top of her head and she wore a tank top featuring a cat, also in a crown, captioned "Purr-fect."

"I got you some parting gifts, so—wow!" Nakita blinked into my room like she'd been expecting a mess. "That was fast. Did you burn all your stuff? Or do you only own, like, three shirts?"

I shrugged. "You know my secrets now. I rotate the same three outfits and use a cape for shock and awe. It's a trick I learned from Batman."

She deposited the bagels and drinks onto the edge of my now-empty desk. "You didn't even ask for help," she said, then spotted the empty closet and added, "I feel very weird about this."

"Don't feel weird. Feel wonderful." I waved a hand through the air dismissively. "Now you have one less person vying for the shower."

"Don't lie. You never showered."

"Hey!" I laughed, moving to hit her, and she stepped out of my reach before the back of my hand could connect.

She also laughed, but added, "This is all too sudden. And where did Andreas go? Is he coming back to help load and move stuff? I didn't see him leave."

Turning away from her and clearing my throat before speaking, I said, "He left super early, but he's arranged for movers. They'll be here around noon."

By the time I'd come back to the room last night, Andreas was already lying in my bed under the duvet, his back to the door. I'd thought about reminding him that I'd left a toothbrush out for his use, but decided against it. Minimizing interactions while in a dark room with two beds felt like the smarter option.

When I'd woken up after a fitful night's sleep, Andreas was gone, the clothes from Kendra's boyfriend were neatly folded on the bed, and the toothbrush in the bathroom was untouched, making me suspect he'd left in the middle of the night as soon as I'd fallen asleep. He had texted me this morning.

Andreas: Movers are arranged for today at noon. I will be home when you arrive, and we can scan your fingerprint for the door.

Presently, Nakita flopped backward onto my stripped mattress, arms out like she was about to make a snow angel. "So," she said, "how do you feel? Like, for real. I can't believe you're moving out, just like that." She snapped her fingers. "Have you told Diya?"

"I texted her. She hasn't messaged back." Diya hadn't responded to any of my texts since last night, which meant she was slammed.

The load of laundry I needed to do this morning consisted of Diya's sheets and my sheets. I'd slept in her bed. It only felt right to clean up my messes before I left.

"You texted her." Nakita voice was deadpan. She rolled her eyes at me. "You two have been roommates for four years and you texted her that you're leaving. Did she have any idea? About you and Andreas and how serious things were between you? Or will she be as shocked as I was when you told me this morning that you're moving out?"

"She'll be fine. I'm paying my share until a replacement can be found. If anything, she'll be thrilled to have a room to herself for a while." I tried not to let Nakita's words make me feel guilty.

It was true. Diya and I had been roommates for four years. That meant Diya knew how I was, how I didn't like getting attached. But it wasn't like I was leaving the country and would never see her again. I was moving fifteen blocks away—give or take a block.

Nakita's eyes moved over me. "How long have you two been dating, anyway? I thought for sure you'd never get married. And now you're engaged to a literal chess prodigy who is also, I cannot stress this enough, a billionaire's son. This is high-key the plot of a CW drama."

I snorted a laugh at her description. "Right? I keep expecting a team of lawyers to appear and offer me a check to walk away and never speak of it again." Though the statement was meant to sound like a joke, a team lawyers showing up to threaten me was definitely within the realm of possibility. In fact, I was sorta surprised one hadn't arrived yet.

Nakita grinned. "Or a film crew, or paparazzi. Just so you know, if a film crew offered me five hundred dollars, I would leak your entire internet search history. For science, obviously."

I sat next to her. "It doesn't feel real yet," I admitted, which was the truth. "It's like I'm watching someone else's life, but through my own eyes. Very out-of-body. Maybe it'll hit me when I see Andreas again."

"Hot take, but it's probably for the best," Nakita said, glancing sidelong at me. "If it were me, I'd already have blown up my social accounts, oversharing and bragging." Her face sobered. "You're good at being chill, Sam. Respect."

"I'm not chill," I said, looking at my own hands. "I'm just really, really good at pretending. My whole teenagerhood was, like, training for this moment.'"

Nakita's lips pressed into a line. "What do you mean? What was your adolescence like?"

I shrugged, staring forward. "When my dad died and we lost everything, the people who came after the bankruptcy judgment took everything. They even took the family photos on the wall—not for the pictures, but for the frames. My mother had to fight just to keep the photographs . . ." I blinked, realizing what I'd just said, how much I'd shared, and shifted my gaze to Nakita.

My words obviously surprised her. Nakita's mouth was open and her eyes were wide. I rarely told people about my family's financial apocalypse. Only Kaitlyn, and only after seven years of friendship.

Nakita sat up, cross-legged, and peered at me. "You never told me that."

"It's no big deal," I said dismissively and fiddled with the ring on my finger, twisting it around. My chest suddenly felt too tight and my stomach was sour. *Regret. This is oversharing regret.*

"It's ancient history." Standing once more, I lightened my tone. "I don't even think about it, but I guess . . . moral of the story: I don't get attached to things. If you only own stuff that fits in your suitcase, no one can take it from you."

Nakita's face did something that made my chest hurt even more. Standing also, she grabbed my hand and gave it a squeeze. "You know I was joking about selling your search history, right? Even if the paparazzi do come eventually, or reporters, I won't reveal anything."

I nodded, managing a close-lipped smile, but I didn't believe her. Nakita wasn't a bad person, and she was trustworthy to a point, but the allure of gossip was her Achillies' heel.

She increased the pressure of her fingers around mine. "And you know, you're allowed to keep things, right? You're allowed to have things, Sam."

Withdrawing my hand, I twisted to the side, making a show of stretching out my back. "I know. I'm just used to not wanting to keep things now, and it makes life so much tidier. Anyway! Let me finish cleaning in here, the movers should arrive soon." Walking around Nakita, I picked up my phone from the otherwise empty side table and checked the time.

Even with all my dillydallying while talking to Nakita, I still had over an hour until noon.

No word yet from Diya.

But that was fine. I would clean while the movers loaded my stuff, and would do my best to leave no traces of myself behind.

[15]

BINARY FISSION

Samantha

Nakita left when the movers arrived. They finished grabbing and loading everything in less than ten minutes. I knew they were used to working in the city because they'd double-parked, brazenly blocking the street rather than futilely hunting for a legitimate spot.

I finished cleaning around 12:15 PM. Checking my phone one last time for a message from Diya and finding none, I ultimately decided to head into work rather than go directly to Andreas's, telling myself I needed to get a jump start on cross-checking the citations for the upcoming conference presentation.

My decision to go to work had nothing at all to do with my desire to avoid seeing Andreas, but everything to do with my desire to avoid *talking* to Andreas.

The next time we spoke, I knew I'd have to put all my uncomfortable feelings out there, explain how I was attracted to him for reals, convince and assure him that mine was an unwilling and unwelcome attraction, and request we brainstorm how best to navigate this inconvenient situation moving forward.

For the record, I still hadn't given up hope that once we lived together, and I was exposed to all his unpleasant habits, thoughts, and beliefs, I might be cured of this unwieldy attraction.

If I was lucky, maybe he would cite the manosphere to justify a belief of why all mRNA vaccines were dangerous, or quote Grok as a reliable source of information about literally anything. If so, I would be cured of my attraction at once.

Or, even better, perhaps Andreas was an avid follower of Jordan Peterson or Andrew Tate. My repulsion would likely register on the Richter scale and I'd immediately go from giving him googly eyes to side-eyes. *Bing bang boom, shrivel my womb.*

Or, more effective, it would be great if he pontificated to me—a geneticist—that there exist only two genders, completely ignoring the existence of Turner's syndrome, androgen insensitivity syndrome, genetic steroid disorders, and science. And then it would be great if he called science or human rights a "political issue." That kind of thing would definitely do the trick. *Don't be cautious! Make me nauseous.*

Yeah. *Sigh.* Any and all of that would be so, so great. Convenient. And tidy.

To my surprise, as soon as I left my building, I spotted Tara waiting for me in her black Mercedes. I'd almost forgotten about her acting as my bodyguard and driver.

"If you're going to drive me everywhere from now on, I guess should join a gym." I met her eyes in the rearview mirror after settling in the back seat. She hadn't wanted me to sit in the front passenger seat, claiming the back seat was safer.

"Is walking to work the only exercise you get?" she asked, the corner of her mouth lifting.

"It is," I confirmed with a beleaguered sigh.

"Not a fan of gyms?"

"Not a fan of exercising just for the sake of exercising," I explained. "Makes me feel like a hamster. I played tennis in college, on scholarship. So, I don't mind training for a purpose, but not for, you know, health." I refrained from putting air quotes around the word *health,* but just barely.

I was the type of person who would spend all day cleaning a house without complaint, help an acquaintance move apartments, or walk a dog for hours, but couldn't find the motivation to get up from their desk for a breather, to take a mental break, or to stretch during the workday.

After a silence lasting two blocks, Tara said, "If you want, you could join my gym."

I stared at the back of her headrest and blurted stupidly, "You own a gym?"

Her eyes flickered back to me in the mirror, crinkling at the corners with a smile. "No. But I teach kickboxing at a gym. It's closer to Mr. Kristiansen's apartment than your previous address. Just let me know. You could try out a class. If you like it, join."

I stroked my chin like I had a wizard beard. "Kickboxing, eh? That sounds like a useful skill. When are you teaching next?"

"I'll text you a link to the schedule. Mr. Kristiansen sent me your number."

"Excellent," I murmured and tented my fingers, liking this notion more and more.

Andreas had warned me that his half brother Henrik preferred physical intimidation tactics over Tobias's mind-and-life-fuckery approach. Just the thought of learning how to effectively—should the opportunity present itself—kick Henrik in the face—or balls . . . *or both!*—brightened my mood.

Tara paused the Mercedes at the sidewalk next to my department building and, without cutting the engine, turned on her hazards. She then walked me to the entrance while sending me the promised link to her kickboxing class schedule. Before leaving me, Tara asked that I call or text ten minutes before I was ready to be picked up.

I saved her number in my phone and labeled her "Tara, Kickboxing Teacher." It felt less *Black Mirror* or *Twilight Zone* than "Tara, My Doppelganger Bodyguard."

Depositing my bag and clothes in my locker, I changed, badged into my work area, and quickly lost myself in converting all valid citations to ANSI/NISO standard terminology. I was so absorbed that when my phone buzzed, announcing a call, I sucked in a startled breath and almost choked on my saliva.

Diya's number flashed on my screen. I took a moment to gather my wits before answering, breathing out, then in, mostly to clear my airway. "Hello?"

"You're engaged? And you moved out? Have I entered an alternate timeline? Who was elected president?"

"Yes to the first two questions. I can't be certain regarding the last two questions."

I heard my roommate—er, former roommate—exhale a loud breath. "I know better than to ask too many questions. So, can you answer two more for me?"

"I'll do my best," I hedged and sat back in my office chair, feeling like I needed to mentally prepare myself.

"First, when can I see you? I'd like to say a proper goodbye. I like you, Sam, and I'll be honest"—she huffed a tired-sounding laugh—"I'm going to miss you—"

"Awww—"

"—and all the shirtless guys you used to parade around the apartment."

I snorted.

"CrossFit guy, we barely knew thee." The lingering smile in her voice was unmistakable. "Seriously, though. When can we get together? Let me buy you lunch or something."

My grin also persisted. "Absolutely. I'll send you some dates after the holiday." Spur of the moment, I suggested, "And we can try to make it a monthly thing. Sound good?" I wondered if I would later regret suggesting a standing lunch commitment, but I didn't think so.

I liked Diya, too. And I would miss her. She was good people.

"Sounds great," she said, the words almost obliterated by the sound of a siren from her side of the call.

I waited until the noise faded before asking, "What's the second question?"

"Are you happy?" She'd lowered her voice to ask this and I detected a note of worry. "I mean, with Andreas. Does he make you happy? Do you actually want to marry him?"

For some reason, in that moment, I didn't want to lie to Diya. I didn't want to answer according to the plan just to get her off the phone. But I couldn't explain the complexities of my feelings either.

Thus, I settled on a version of the truth, both to ease her mind and to reduce my guilt. "Honestly, there is no one else in the world I could see myself marrying other than Andreas."

* * *

BY THE TIME I left the biology building, it was after 7:00 PM and my brain felt like a microwaved burrito: hot, overcooked, and liable to burst at the seams with one careless squeeze.

I called Tara from the women's locker room just before changing back into my normal clothes. Her black Mercedes idled at the curb when I exited the building, and I spotted her through the front windshield, brown hair pulled into a neat ponytail, the blue glow of her phone screen illuminating a face that looked enough like mine to make me do a double take.

She saw me and immediately killed the engine, opening the driver's-side door and stepping out into the cold. I waved, but before she could round the car, I opened the back door myself, tossed my backpack in, and then hesitated, half in and half out, caught by the friction of inertia. If I'd had a more poetic soul, I'd have called it "resistance to change." More accurately, it was the genetic legacy of a thousand generations of let's-just-wait-and-see-if-the-bear-leaves caution.

Eventually, I got in.

Tara adjusted the rearview and met my gaze. "Ready?" Her voice was unreasonably chipper. Probably all those kickboxing endorphins.

I wanted to say, *Define "ready."*

Instead, I said, "Sally forth."

She grinned, then pulled out into traffic. The silence between us was comfortable, like she understood that my primary need right now was mental preparation and recalibration.

I watched the city slide past, each streetlight blurring into the next. After three blocks of silence, I realized I'd been gripping my phone in my lap so tightly my hand had gone numb.

I turned the screen on: 7:14 PM. Zero new notifications. I was both relieved and irrationally disappointed that Andreas hadn't texted me since this morning.

Perhaps he hadn't texted because he knew where I was. Tara, as my shadow, had likely filled him in. I considered this, that Tara and any other bodyguard assigned to me would probably be reporting my movements to Andreas.

This thought didn't make me resent Tara. It didn't even make me resent Andreas. It made me resent Oskar, Tobias, and Henrik for being societal sepsis. If only Oskar hadn't been an evil, greedy little virus of a humanoid, perhaps—

Perhaps Andreas and I would be getting engaged for real . . . ?

I rolled my eyes at myself and shook my head. Alternate universe, indeed.

After I'd finished working on the citations, I'd spent an hour helping Dmitry troubleshoot a genetics pipeline issue he'd emailed me about last week but I'd been too deep in my own drama to reply. There was also a backlog of Hauser's undergrad lab reports to grade, which was not technically my job anymore but felt like an anchor to the world I was rapidly losing.

Time collapsed. At some point I ran samples in the secure lab and cleaned up after myself with military precision, mostly because I knew the next person to use the space would be me again, and if I left a mess, it would just be my own future self who suffered. I liked to think of it as a recursive act of kindness.

All day, I'd been stalling. And now, in the darkness of Tara's back seat, I was still stalling. Waiting for me at the end of this ride was an uncomfortable conversation about feelings—*great, yay feelings*—and a new, likely jarring, shift in my reality. I'd never met anyone who embraced sudden shifts in reality without some instinctive resistance and at least a little crankiness.

Tara pulled up to the curb outside Andreas's building. She didn't immediately reach for the locks or say goodbye. Instead, she turned around, elbow draped over the back of her seat, and looked at me with a subtle intensity.

"You okay?" she asked.

"Sure," I said, then, after a beat, "I've been worse."

She laughed, low and genuine. "Want me to walk you up?"

"No," I said, then caught myself. "Yes. Wait—no, I'm fine. I've been here before."

She nodded, studying me. "Okay," she said, but didn't move to start the car again. "Text me if you need anything. I'll be in the garage across the street until ten."

I gave her a thumbs-up, but my hand trembled so badly I had to turn it into a wave. I fumbled the handle, stepped out, and closed the door with a gentleness that sounded like an apology.

At the entrance, the doorman clocked me immediately. He gave a curt nod, then opened the door before I could even raise a hand in greeting.

"Good evening, Ms. Jarlston," he said. The way he pronounced my name was clinical, almost like it was a password. "Welcome home."

I wanted to correct him—explain that I wasn't really "home," I was just "here," and only because of a paperwork anomaly and a series of questionable life choices. Instead, I nodded, mumbled a thank-you, and walked through the vestibule.

The last time I'd been here, Andreas held my hand, and I remembered the exact pressure of his palm and the scent of his coat, and how it made me feel weirdly exposed and helpless. I shook the memory loose and marched to the elevator, punched in the code Andreas had given me, and rode in silence to the penthouse. I made a game of staring at my own reflection in the mirrored walls, trying to will my face into something more serenely composed and less emotionally constipated.

When I stepped out, the hallway was empty. I hovered outside the apartment door for a full minute, rehearsing different greetings in my head, then finally raised my hand to ring the bell.

The door opened before I could touch it.

Standing in the doorway was a tall, broad-shouldered guy with pale blond hair and blue eyes so bright they were legit alarming. He wore mesh basketball shorts and a slightly sweat-dampened long-sleeved T-shirt, and looked like he'd stepped straight out of *Prep-School Quarterly* (not a real newspaper as far as I knew; but if it existed, this guy would be their spokesperson, founder, and president).

I blinked, taking an involuntary step backward. "Uh, hi?"

The man smiled, a tiny curve of his lips. "You must be Samantha?" His accent was subtle, American Southern.

"That's me," I said. "Who's asking?"

He stepped aside, and gestured for me to come in. "Roman. A friend of Andreas's."

From somewhere deep in the apartment, a female voice with a faint British-sounding accent called out, "He's not a friend. They're archrivals."

My eyebrows nearly shot off my forehead. Roman gave me a small, conspiratorial smile, then leaned in to stage-whisper, "We're not actually rivals. But the internet thinks we are."

A woman appeared at the end of the entryway, drying her hands on a towel.

She was petite and sharp-boned, with thick, long black hair pulled into a high ponytail and a beauty mark perfectly placed below her right eye. She wore black yoga pants and a gray exercise shirt. Even in casual wear, she radiated a kind of intimidating composure that made me instantly want to look up and listen to her TED Talk. Assuming she had a TED Talk.

"Hi." She offered her pale hand. "I'm Jackie Cheng."

I shook it. Her grip was precise, not too firm, not too soft.

"Nice to meet you," I said a bit robotically, only because I'd already been overwhelmed prior to entering the apartment. And now, suddenly faced with unexpected *people*, my nerves were fraying.

Jackie held on to my hand a beat longer than necessary, then pulled me into the apartment with a smooth, practiced motion. "Come in, Andreas is in the shower. We just got back from the gym. Roman insisted we had to squeeze in one last session before his curfew."

"Curfew?" I repeated, not sure if I was missing a joke.

Roman nodded. "I have to check in with my host family at ten sharp, or they send out the search party." He said it with a straight face, so it was either true or a level of deadpan I could only aspire to.

Jackie rolled her eyes. "He's in town for a few days, doing a chess camp with the local kids. They treat him like he's a big celebrity or something."

"I'm not a celebrity," Roman grumbled.

Jackie ignored him and steered me into the living area. "Sit down. Want some water? Juice? I think there's kombucha, but it's homemade."

I perched on the edge of the couch. "Water's good, thanks." After I said the words, I marveled at the fact that this woman had just offered me something to drink in the apartment where I was now currently living. *Ahhhh! New realities suck!*

Roman sat at the far end of the sofa, angled toward me but not so close as to invade my space. He watched me with a kind of directness I found both flattering and disorienting.

Jackie disappeared into the kitchen, then called back, "How was your day, Samantha?"

I thought about the hours spent hiding in the biology building, the way my stomach had twisted all day in anticipation of this very moment, only to find Andreas's friends welcoming me instead of my fake fiancé.

"Uneventful," I said. "How about you? Did you, uh, have a nice day?"

Look at me, chitchatting like a chitchatter. Would wonders never cease?

Jackie returned with three glasses of water, handed one to me, one to Roman, and kept the third. "You work in genetics, right? PhD candidate?"

"Yes," I said, surprised she knew so much about me. "Final year. Or it should be."

Roman sipped his water, then asked, "What is your dissertation about?"

I blinked at the question, thrown by how sincerely interested he sounded. "Uhh. Well, originally, it was epigenetic markers of stress inheritance in CRISPR-edited lines of drosophila."

Jackie made a face of pure delight. "Ooh, I love fruit fly people. They're always the most dramatic at conferences. Nothing like a five-millimeter bug to turn a scientist into a gladiator."

I found myself laughing even though her words confused me. "I'm not sure what that means. But, um, I changed my focus after one year. My dissertation is now on bioremediation of ocean plastics via genetically modified microbes."

"Oh. Cool. Isn't the island of trash in the Pacific Ocean larger than Texas? Or is that a made-up fact? Where did I read that?" Jackie pointed her gaze at Roman. "He's the real scientist here. Chess is just his side-hustle."

Roman's mouth tugged up on one side. "I'm not a scientist. But I do like puzzles."

Jackie rolled her eyes, like his statement was a shared joke. I decided I liked Jackie a lot, and Roman maybe even more, but in a way that was less "be friends" and more "he's interesting to observe."

"So"—Jackie sunk into the armchair across from me—"do couples in America typically move in together only after getting engaged?"

My mouth went dry, her question catching me off guard. For some reason, I felt wholly unprepared to discuss the American societal norms surrounding engagements.

Roman bailed me out. "There's no such thing as typical in the USA. Some folks wait until marriage to move in together, some wait 'til engagement. Some move in without ever planning to get married at all."

Jackie nodded, absorbing this information, then glanced at me. Perhaps she misread my wide eyes as confusion because she explained, "I'm from Singapore. We sometimes have marriage requirements surrounding housing. Or rather, before applying for a flat. Sorry. I was just curious."

Roman grinned, a tiny flash of teeth. "Jackie travels a lot, but doesn't get out much."

She wrinkled her nose at him. "This is my first time to the USA and I don't want to take for granted that American television is indicative of reality."

"It's not," both Roman and I said in unison, then the three of us shared a grin, with Roman adding, "Especially—ironically—reality television. Reality television is less reflective of American society than most scripted TV."

"What a relief," Jackie chuckled.

Feeling myself relax a bit, I took another sip of water and floundered for an acceptable subject to discuss with Andreas's friends even as curiosity swelled within me. I surmised that Roman and Andreas competed against each other in tournaments and were colleagues. But how did Jackie fit in?

Before I could figure out how to frame the question casually rather than blurt out, *How do you know Andreas? Are you good friends? How long have you known each other? Did you date?* Jackie glanced at her watch, then abruptly stood up.

"Shoot, we have to run. Roman's curfew is real. And I have an online match at eleven."

Roman also stood and turned to me with a small smile. "It was nice meeting you, Samantha."

"You, too." I set my water glass on a coaster and straightened from the couch, wondering if I should walk them out.

I should, right? Technically, I live here. It would be polite.

While I was still engaging in my internal debate, Jackie crossed to me and pulled me in for a brief hug, saying as she leaned away, "Andreas said if he was still in the shower when you got here, to give you this." She handed me a sealed envelope that she'd seemingly pulled out of thin air. "Instructions, probably. He loves instructions."

I took it, a little surprised at the weight of it. "Oh . . . thanks," I said, but she and Roman had already left the room, walking themselves out.

I waited until I heard the door snick shut before I opened the envelope.

Inside was a printout, double-sided, with a list of building employees, hours for amenities, the procedure for picking up packages, and emergency phone numbers for the night managers and staff. At the bottom, in Andreas's neat, all-caps handwriting, it read:

We need to program your thumbprint into the door pad tonight so you can come and go as you please. I had your things placed in the main bedroom, which is off the living room to the south. —A

He gave me the main bedroom? I frowned at the note, reading it again. The fact that he'd given me the main bedroom—which had likely been his bedroom—was at once confusing and irritating. Was he trying to be chivalrous? Now I'd have to live and sleep in a room that likely smelled like him.

I exhaled. The silence in the apartment felt heavy.

I thought about refusing the main bedroom, potentially sleeping on the couch tonight, but that seemed juvenile. Instead, I walked to the room he wanted me to take and peeked inside.

The movers had delivered my things. They were stacked neatly against the wall, untouched. The bed—a California king—was covered in an off-white-and-pink duvet cover that didn't belong to me. It looked expensive, maybe mulberry silk? The furniture also looked expensive, a minimalist yet sturdy maple. The walls were the color of sandstone and appeared to be paneled with fabric. Or perhaps an extremely high-end wallpaper. The light and airy aura of this room struck me as extremely different from the apartment's entry and living rooms, with their dark red antique carpets, floor-to-ceiling paintings, dramatic leather couches, and dark wood furniture.

In contrast, this space felt undecorated, a blank canvas with tasteful, subtle bones. It didn't feel empty or cold. Rather, it felt warm and ready. *Huh.*

Meandering further inside, I noted that this bedroom was likely bigger than the entirety of my previous apartment, the one I'd shared with three roommates. A view of the city through floor-to-ceiling windows contributed to the sense of expansiveness. My attention fell on white closet doors, currently closed and gleaming with the promise of a storage space I would never fill.

Frowning thoughtfully, I sat on the bed, unsurprised to find the duvet was fluffy and feather, and the mattress was heavenly. Conflicted, I let my mind go blank.

This is my life now. This is where I live. Even if I didn't accept the main bedroom, I would be living here, in this ridiculously huge apartment with my ridiculously attractive fake fiancé, for an undetermined period of time.

I was about to check my phone for the time—somehow, I was convinced it was way later than it actually was—when I heard a door open from somewhere in the apartment followed by approaching footsteps.

I stood, braced myself, and walked back into the living room.

Abruptly halting mid-step, I grimaced at the offensively gorgeous sight before me. Andreas appeared from the opposite hallway, hair damp, a black T-shirt clinging to the muscles of his shoulders, and—you guessed it—a pair of soft gray sweatpants low on his hips.

Well, well, well. *Lucky me.*

Swallowing a mouthful of lusty saliva, I fought a laugh as I cast my eyes heavenward. Was he trying to seduce me? Probably not. Was I seduced? Undoubtedly so.

"When did you arrive?" he asked, voice even but pitched low.

I swallowed, feeling my own pulse thud in my throat, and forced myself to meet his beautiful green eyes. "Just now. Jackie and Roman let me in. And Jackie gave me the envelope."

He nodded, then leaned against the large, black circular table set by the window, still applying a towel to his hair. "Did you have dinner?"

I opened my mouth to respond but then snapped it shut, needing to think for a moment. *Wait. Did I have dinner?*

"Does a bag of Goldfish count?"

He made a face. "Are you hungry?"

Instinct wanted to turn his question into a double entendre and approximately one hundred suggestive retorts floated through my brain. Some were cheesy, a la, *For you? Yes*. And some were sensually ambiguous, such as, *Only if it tastes good*.

I stymied the reflex, saying instead, "Caloric sustenance would not be rejected," which might've been the least sexy reply in the universe. And that was the point.

Lifting an eyebrow at my response, Andreas seemed to fight a smile. "I ordered food. It should be here soon. If you are hungry, there will be more than enough to share."

Was I hungry? I couldn't tell. All I felt was the weird, humming tension that had followed me all day, and the urge to say something—anything—that would make the next moment easier.

But there was no easy. There was only the truth.

Gathering a deep breath, I squared my shoulders and said, "We should talk."

Andreas didn't move, but his eyes sharpened. "Now?"

"Yes," I said, because if I didn't do it now, I never would.

"Okay. Let's talk," he said, blinking once, slowly, giving me the impression he'd expected this.

Or perhaps, he'd been anticipating it.

[16]

CELL REPRODUCTION: MITOSIS

Samantha

I felt . . . uncomfortable.

Presently, we sat at the same black, circular table where I'd reviewed the adoption paperwork and where we'd discussed the initial stages of our plan, the details of the smoke screen, and our conditions for the subterfuge. Thinking back, I marveled at my previous bold aplomb, showing up here in a skintight dress and stilettos, demanding that we get down to business.

Tonight, the dynamic felt incredibly different, and yet also exactly the same, which made no sense.

Peeking at Andreas, I took note of how his gaze moved over me now, dressed as I was in an old baggy T-shirt and equally baggy ripped jeans. His eyes held the same flavor of intensity as before. And this realization gave my usually imperturbable heart spikes of pause, confusion, and panic.

And that's when the doubt crept in. *Perhaps I assumed too much that night.*

Glancing down at my T-shirt, I confirmed it was not at all sexy. I frowned and peered at him again, a new hypothesis forming, leading to a new conclusion. *Perhaps this is not heat and interest in his gaze at all, but rather this is simply his normal expression . . . ?*

Had I misinterpreted his interest two nights ago, and then again during our fake engagement dinner? Was this attraction I felt entirely one-sided? I swallowed around a parched throat, my previously controlled thoughts bouncing around the inside of my head like Ping-Pong balls.

"You wanted to talk." Andreas's flat statement pulled me out of my queasy contemplations.

I nodded. "Yes. Yes, that's right." Folding my hands on the tabletop, I couldn't help but continue to study him.

His gaze felt laser focused on me, and just as hot as it had two nights ago. And yet, after the long day I'd had, I knew I looked like an untidy, dusty, tired mess.

What is going on?

Andreas dipped his chin and raised his eyebrows. "Samantha? Are you well?"

I nodded again, bringing my hands to my lap where I could twist my fingers without him seeing.

Forget it. Who cares if the attraction is one-sided. All you need to do is tell him that you find him irresistibly attractive, you have real feelings for him, and ask him to help you get rid of these feelings.

Inhaling deeply for courage, I mentally prepared myself for the necessary words, but instead what I said was, "So, Andreas. What are your thoughts on Jordan Peterson?"

Andreas's expression changed from what I'd previously—and potentially, incorrectly—labeled as *hot and interested* to *bemused* with a single blink. "Pardon? Who is that?"

I twisted my mouth to the side. "You don't know who Jordan Peterson is?"

"No." His gaze flickered over me. "Should I?"

"What about Andrew Tate? Ring any bells?"

"No." There was no recognition in his eyes. "Are you considering them for roles at Genetix? Are they scientists?"

Frowning dejectedly, I shook my head. "Not even a little."

"Then, who are—"

"Forget it." I waved a hand in the air, batting away any follow-up questions, then let it drop. "Tell me, what are your thoughts on mRNA vaccines?"

He blinked twice, once more looking bemused. "Uh, I do not—I mean, should I not be asking you?"

"What is that supposed to mean?" I searched his words for a possible offensive meaning and frustratingly found none.

"You are the geneticist and know more about this subject than me." When I continued to glare at him, he added, "What I mean is, I play chess for a living, an occupation that has nothing to do with medical science. Why would I think I know more about mRNA vaccines than a PhD candidate in genetics? That would make me a fool."

I nibbled the inside of my bottom lip, growing more and more irritated by his lack of delusions of grandeur and his trust in highly educated experts. "Fine," I bit out. "Then, how about, where do you stand politically on racism, as an example."

He frowned at me, visibly confused, and exhaled a short laugh. "Okay, racism is not a political issue. It is a moral, ethical, human-rights, fear-based, lack-of-education issue, and should not be justified or condoned by political affiliation."

Huffing, I gritted my teeth and turned my head away from his stupid handsome face. He had to possess at least one reprehensible, and therefore unattractive, opinion. Why couldn't he just *cooperate?!?!!*

"Who is your . . . favorite . . . member of The Beatles?"

Now he narrowed his eyes on me, the side of his mouth tugging slightly upward. "George Harrison."

DAMN IT!

"What about BTS?"

"RM or V."

My lungs filled with the fire of exasperation because no one was this perfect. Placing my hands flat on the table, I leaned forward, preparing a rapid-fire question assault.

"Favorite flavor of ice cream."

"Chocolate."

I made a face, surprised. "Really?"

"Yes, vegan cashew chocolate ice cream is the best of the vegan flavors."

I didn't have any experience with vegan ice cream, so I moved on. "Charles Darwin or Karl Marx?"

"Darwin," he answered immediately. "In my opinion, Marx misinterpreted natural selection to justify his philosophical and political ideologies."

"Dog or cat?"

"Both. If you recall, I love animals."

Shoot. That's right. Unable to stop the question, I asked, "Is that why you're vegan? Because you love animals?"

"No. Not really. It is mainly for health reasons." He seemed to hesitate before continuing. "My mother died of colon cancer when I was eleven, she was just thirty-two. And her father died of colon cancer at twenty-nine."

"Oh, Andreas." My hand came to my chest where a sudden ache had made breathing difficult. "I'm so sorry. I didn't know about your mom." I fought the urge to rush over and hug him.

He shook his head, jaw clenching, and dismissed my concern. "It was a long time ago. But peer-reviewed studies have shown that a vegan diet greatly reduces the risk of colon cancer. Also, honestly, I do not enjoy the taste of meat or dairy."

GAH! He'd mentioned *peer-reviewed* studies, not just *research studies*. Get a load of the size of this guy's media literacy, ladies. *Be still my heart.*

But he'd also mentioned not liking dairy, and that was something I could work with. "Not even cheese?" I questioned. "You're telling me you don't like a good Camembert? Nothing alluring about Gouda? Really?"

He gave me a small smile. "No."

I examined Andreas for a long moment, wondering if his opinion about cheese was enough to temper my attraction to him. *Unfortunately, it's not enough.* Andreas was more beautiful, smarter, and cooler than my affinity for cheese, shockingly.

Now, if only he would say something rude about coffee . . . But no. The first time we met weeks ago he'd ordered coffee. He liked coffee.

Sitting back in my chair, I rubbed my forehead. This was getting me nowhere.

Desperate, I tried for a more direct approach. "Tell me something, Andreas."

"What would you like to know?"

"Tell me something unlikable about yourself." I peeked at him, letting my hand drop to my lap again.

His eyes were on me, but they were unfocused, like he was in deep contemplation, attempting to decipher the riddle of my question.

"I do not und—"

"I'll start." I crossed my arms and leveled him with a frank look. "I still like watching old movies even though—when viewed through today's lens—they are often incredibly problematic. I don't care. I still like watching them. In fact, I enjoy the heck out of *Some Like It Hot* and I do not care that some people tell me it's high-key sexist and homophobic. See? I'm a terrible person."

Andreas's eyebrows lifted until his forehead wrinkled. "I do not think that makes you a terrible per—"

"Also, when I'm really busy, I don't shower for days and days." I gave him a flat look. "Sometimes longer than a week, and I kinda like the smell of my own stink."

His eyes widened and he snapped his mouth shut.

"Gross, right?" I wasn't finished. "I would rather be late for a party than arrive on time, but without makeup. I hate going to parties without wearing makeup, but I procrastinate putting it on, which means I'm often late. Yet, I'll likely never change this about myself. Also, I forget to check my mail and have a bad habit of missing important documents and letters, letting them pile up for over a month. I don't enjoy small talk and usually refuse to do it. This means I frequently come across as abrupt or judgy, and I'm really okay with that." I paused, thought about that last one, then added, "Probably because I am both abrupt and judgy, so that's on me. But, again, I'm okay with that."

Andreas had leaned forward as I spoke and placed an elbow on the table. Most of his mouth and chin were obscured by his hand, his thumb and forefinger resting to either side of his nose. His half-lidded gaze seemed to bore into me, giving me the impression that he was listening intently.

"Let's see, what else . . ." I tapped my chin. "Uh, sometimes people don't like my face, or my aura, or my vibes. I get that a lot. I know I sometimes say really stupid and ignorant things. But since that's something everyone does, I'll give myself a pass and try to do better. I also get mad and vindictive when I feel slighted or taken advantage of. Oh! I drink too much coffee and then complain when I have trouble sleeping at night. I also doomscroll on my phone if I have insomnia, and then complain even more about having trouble sleeping at night. It's insufferable."

"You have trouble sleeping at night?" Andreas tilted his head slightly to the side.

"Yes. But here's another one. I suffer from making the fundamental attribution error *all the time*. You know, that thing people do where their own mistakes can be explained away by circumstances outside of their control, but then they unilaterally decide other people's mistakes are obviously due to faulty character traits? I do that. I actually really hate this about myself and I've gotten so much better about recognizing it as I've aged." I looked up at the ceiling, thinking the matter over. "So, let's call that a half-unlikable thing."

Andreas made a short sound, pulling my attention back to him.

His hand fell away from his mouth. "Samantha, why are you telling me all this?"

"Because I want you to tell me something unlikable about yourself, so I figured I would share first."

"Why? Why do you want to know something unlikable about me?"

I stared at Andreas, hoping he'd simply play along without making me explain myself. I stared for so long, I was forced to blink several times. And still he returned my stare, seemingly content to wait me out.

Well, this flex of superhuman patience is certainly unlikable.

Eventually, I glanced away, my eyes moving over the interior of his apartment while my attention shifted inward. No more stalling. I was going to have to tell him about my unwelcome feelings, about this attraction I didn't want and for which I needed his help dispelling. There was no getting around saying it now.

"So, here's the thing." I crossed my arms again, determined to approach this subject as analytically and dispassionately as possible. I could not, however, immediately lift my eyes higher than the tabletop. "As it turns out, and quite against my will, I find myself in a precarious situation."

Hazarding a glance, I noted how his gaze had grown narrowed and powerfully intent. I didn't miss how Andreas leaned forward. Nor did I miss how wooden and useless my tongue felt, and how dry my mouth was, and how courage was beginning to taste like cowardice.

And yet, despite the sudden sweatiness of my palms, I forced myself to continue, because I was an adult. "And I fully admit, I am to blame, obviously. Feelings aren't facts, but they exist, nevertheless"—I swallowed convulsively, telling myself to slow down even as words cascaded out of me like a waterfall—"and despite my attempts to neutralize this—this issue, sometimes emotions exist outside of the Venn diagram of intentions and willful choices. And so, what I want to make you aware of before things take an unintentional turn for—"

The sound of the front door chime cut off my rapid monologue and I flinched, my eyes darting toward the entryway. Despite my best efforts, my heart had taken off at a gallop and I suddenly became aware that my stomach was swimming. *Ugh. I feel like I'm going to throw up.*

"The food." Andreas sounded mildly irritated by the interruption. He pushed away from the table and straightened slowly. "I will be right back. Do not leave."

I nodded automatically. But then, as soon as he disappeared from view, I asked myself via a whisper spoken out loud, "What the hell am I doing?"

Was I really going to confess like this? I'd never confessed having feelings to anyone because I'd never caught feelings before that were worth confessing. Who the hell did I think I was?

Placing my palm over my now thundering heart and staring forward, my brain began to bargain and advocate for an alternate course of action. Because this was freaking *scary.*

It felt like . . .

It feels like . . .

Like what I imagined a wild animal felt when their paw was stuck in the jaws of a steel trap. Was I really going to wait for the hunter to return and explain with reason and logic how I didn't want my paw to be stuck in a steel trap, and would he please release me so that I could go back to being free and wild?

NO!

No, absolutely not. An animal does not try to reason with a hunter. Worst-case scenario, the hunter felt sorry for the animal and shot it on sight. Whereas, best-case scenario . . .

Wait.

Who was I kidding? There was no best case! Was I insane?

I stood abruptly from the table, the chair making a muffled sound on the red carpet as it fell over behind me. Andreas reentered the room, two tied plastic bags dangling from his fingertips, and froze mid-stride when he spotted me and the toppled chair.

A pause, then, "Are you okay?"

I nodded, sucking in oxygen as I turned and forced my fingers and arms to right the chair. "Mm-hmm. I'm fine. I'm good."

Haltingly, he asked, "Do you want to eat now? Or we can wait."

I closed one eye, scrunching my face. "Um, you know—" I stopped myself and cleared my throat because the two words had arrived extremely high-pitched. Remodulating my voice, I tried again. "I'm not hungry. But you should eat."

My mind thrashed around in my own stupidity, struggling to find a viable point to make, one that could take the place of my scary confession.

"Are you sure?" Andreas closed the distance to the table and set the bags on its surface. "I ordered quite a lot."

"I'm sure." I nodded tightly, my brain finally latching on to an alternate argument in place of my inadvisable admission of *feelings*. "I can talk while you eat."

His eyes moved over me, his expression quizzical. But all he said was, "Okay," as he reclaimed his seat.

I did not sit. I had too much adrenaline coursing through my system.

Instead, I folded my arms over my chest like armor and lifted my chin. "All I was saying was that I don't think it's right for me to take the main bedroom. This is your apartment and that room is too big for me and I don't think it makes any sense for me to take the main bedroom when this is your apartment, after all. I'd like to move my stuff into one of the other rooms and sleep there. Tonight. If that's okay. That'll save us from having to change sheets in the morning."

Andreas had begun untying the knot in one of the bags as he sat. But by the time I'd finished speaking, his hands were still and his eyes were affixed forward. Silence engulfed us, making me feel like I'd been swallowed by a sea creature that excreted awkwardness as a pheromone.

I watched his chest rise and fall, listening to the slightly stunted yet audible sound of his exhale. He seemed to be parsing through my words again, evaluating them, maybe searching for hidden meanings. Who knows?

I'd tricked myself two nights ago, believing I knew what he'd been thinking, and now I was paying the price with pride as my currency. Like hell would I assume I knew what he was thinking ever again.

At length, Andreas abandoned the bag and stood, slowly lifting his eyes to mine. "This is what you wanted to talk about?" His voice was oddly gruff.

I nodded.

His jaw seemed to work, giving me the impression he was running the tip of his tongue over his back teeth. His chest rose and fell again, another audible sigh. "Pick any room you like," he said, the words low and rumbly.

"Oh. Thank you." I kept on nodding. "I will."

Refocusing his attention on the food, he frowned. But instead of untying the knot, he picked up the two bags and strolled away toward the kitchen. As soon as he disappeared from view, I slouched, allowing myself a quick moment of relief and reprieve.

A breathy laugh tumbled out of me. *Yikes*. That had been close. Thank goodness I'd stopped myself.

Fascinatingly, the sudden sensation of relief was enough to buoy my spirits anew, because I was nothing if not a problem solver. I didn't need Andreas to help me fix my attraction. I could do it myself. I'd relied on no one but myself for a long, long, *long* time. I loved Kaitlyn, but I didn't actually need her.

Yeah. That's right. I'll do it myself.

I would figure this out and mercilessly cauterize it before I allowed anything as frivolous as attraction to interfere. I didn't need Andreas to expose his unlikable traits, fixing myself wasn't his responsibility. I simply needed to focus on what really mattered.

Revenge.

For my dad, for my mom, for myself. Everything else should be background noise.

Determined, I strolled to the main bedroom with my head high and grabbed my suitcase. It contained all my clothes and toiletries, everything I needed for tonight and tomorrow. The rest I could grab at some point later, or leave in the bins. No use unpacking more than necessary, no reason to settle in.

I would pick a different room and leave Andreas to his palatial suite. It didn't matter where I slept as long as I didn't let myself get too comfortable.

This, him, his apartment, it was all temporary.

Yes, best for both of us if I reminded myself of this fact rather than burden Andreas with my irrelevant feelings.

[17]

FROM FOSSILS TO NEO-DARWINISM

Andreas

Sleep would not come. Not for lack of exhaustion. Nor for lack of opportunity.

The real, unpalatable explanation: Samantha slept here, under my roof, and now every nerve within my body had chosen to organize itself around her proximity, like a citywide blackout except for the single column of light that burned for her, and only her. There existed not enough darkness in the world to convince my body to power down.

Two hours since she'd retired to her room, two hours since I'd heard her methodically moving her shampoo and other items into the hall bathroom, and yet the sum of my progress toward sleep was nil. I lay on my back, eyes fixed on the stippled darkness of the ceiling, and forced myself to replay old chess matches, then count backward from one hundred, then a thousand, then attempt the old trick of imagining myself on a frozen lake, letting the silent cold and emptiness smooth my thoughts into nothing.

Didn't work. In the end, I tried imagining myself as the ice, and she was the body of water below, forever churning, breaking, threatening to warm, melt, and consume me.

Unsurprisingly, this did nothing to propel me toward sleep.

Every five minutes, I checked my phone, hoping for a trivial update from any of the night staff, or, failing that, some sign of familial unrest that might require my attention and thus distract me from the problem at hand. My notifications remained empty.

Earlier, when I wasn't cataloguing the sounds of Sam's movements—shower, teeth, changing, light on, light off—I reviewed the order of the previous night's events as we'd faked our engagement, frame by frame, rewinding over every minute detail. The way she looked at me across the table, the tremor in her hands, her voice when she told me to expect tongue, the impossible heat of her body in my lap at her apartment. Her eyes and smile when she laughed.

She'd always laughed easily. As a child, she'd howled at every low-effort joke, even the ones meant to sting, tossed at her by my brothers. But that laughter had been a type of rebellion.

Making her laugh—truly laugh—used to be the most reliable method of pulling her out of a dark mood. I'd spent hours, sometimes days, strategizing and arranging situations to make her laugh. And when she did, when my well-laid plans came to fruition, it had always made me feel . . . powerful. In a way that wasn't about control, but about being seen. And appreciated. And enjoyed. Useful. Now, I missed it.

I missed her.

Last night, I'd caught only glimpses of it—her laugh, her joy—through a wineglass filled with rosé, darkly, and only when she felt safe enough to lower her guard. The rest of our time together, she'd been tense, wary. I remained convinced she still distrusted me. Or, at the very least, she did not wish to be alone with me.

If she'd asked, I would've left the city, the country, the planet, just to prove she could feel safe here.

She'd chosen the farthest bedroom from mine. The "service suite," a twenty-square-meter room designed for a housekeeper or a guest I'd never invited. She'd taken her suitcase across the threshold and closed the door with a finality that felt less like a boundary and more like a verdict.

I wasn't a fool. My opening strategy had been clumsy, assuming too much after too many years apart. But this second strategy, adopting her as my plan B, had backfired. I shouldn't have cared about the distance between our bedroom doors, but I did.

I wanted her to want this room. It had been stripped and redecorated. I'd arranged for a designer while I attended meetings, interviews, and practice sessions yesterday and today. I'd instructed them to discard anything Samantha might notice or object to, to make the space a blank slate for her. I wanted her to feel comfortable changing anything and everything to her liking, paint the walls, break the windows, gut the closet. I wanted her to possess whatever she wanted, including a sense of control.

Including me, in the unlikely event . . .

Abruptly, I realized I was hard, embarrassingly so, and rolled to my side to hide it from no one. I told myself I should go for a run downstairs in the gym, burn off the excess energy, or take a cold shower. I didn't move. I couldn't. Thoughts of her in that black dress from two nights ago had me reaching under the covers and inside my pants.

A door shut softly, somewhere down the hall. I stilled and listened. A beat passed. The silence like a held breath.

Waiting, rigid and alert, all my attention funneled down the hallway, anticipating her next move. Nothing happened. A full fifteen minutes passed, maybe more. Time became elastic, every second stretching into an eternity.

It must've been after two when I heard the creak of a floorboard beyond my door. Not loud enough for the average person to notice, but I'd spent enough hours in this apartment to form a familiarity with every minor defect. My heart doubled its pace, then tripled. I endeavored to control my breathing, to calm the surging blood in my veins.

The knob on my door turned, ever so slowly. The door opened enough to allow a slip of dim light from the living room, which added to the city lights coming in from the large window. For a second, nothing. Then she was there.

Samantha stood in the doorway, silhouetted in her oversized shirt, hair down around her face and shoulders, eyes half open. Her feet bare and her posture strange, a little slack, as though this room's gravity were heavier than the rest of the world's. She did not speak.

I sat up in bed, all the air gone from my lungs, and managed, "Samantha?"

She did not respond, instead shuffling into the room, not quite looking at me, gaze pointed just above my head. Samantha paused at the end of the bed, hands loose at her sides, then climbed up—one knee on the mattress, then the other—and crawled over the covers until she drew even with me.

Stunned, my body did not know what to do. My brain had already been spun into glass, and now I suspected that, at any movement, the entire scene might shatter into a dream.

Samantha lay beside me, facing me, close enough that I could see the sheen of sweat on her temple. She burrowed into the pillow. Then, with a kind of delicate desperation, curled herself against my body. Her leg wormed between mine, and her hand found its way to my stomach beneath my shirt. Her breath was warm on my throat.

All the muscles in my body tensed at once, locked in a state of absolute incredulity.

She pressed her face against the side of my neck and let out a long, shaky exhale, then, as if it were the most natural thing in the world, she relaxed completely, melting into me.

I did not breathe. I did not move.

This was the opposite of anything I'd ever imagined. In every scenario where she ended up in my bed, it had been a complete fantasy, divorced from reality. What else could it have been? Sleepwalking? Which—wait.

Hold on.

Is Samantha sleepwalking?

A wave of suspicion broke over the shock and arousal. Her roommate had mentioned that Samantha sleepwalked. Certainly, she wasn't awake now. Had she come here on purpose, to tell me something, to ask for something?

If I said her name again, would she hear me?

I swallowed, felt her arm tense at the subtle movement, and risked it. "Samantha?"

No verbal response.

Instead, she tightened her grip around my chest, and slid her hand further under the hem of my shirt such that her palm pressed flat to my stomach, hot and real. I wanted to capture her hand and move it lower. I wanted to entangle our fingers together and slide them into her underwear.

I wanted to roll on top of her, strip her naked, kneel between her thighs, and devour her whole.

But I did nothing. I remained still.

She wore a shirt—baggy, covered in cartoon blobs that were likely science based. I focused on the pattern as a mental distraction. Her thigh, bare and warm, pressed tight to my leg. The pressure of her head on my shoulder, the weight of her body draped over me, felt somehow urgent.

Samantha's breathing evened out. After a minute, I recognized the pattern. Deep inhale, long slow exhale, with a tiny tremor at the end, as if she were recovering from an earlier bout of crying. This perplexed me.

Had she been crying? Had she come to me for comfort?

No. Samantha coming to me for comfort was wishful thinking. She was, in fact, truly sleepwalking.

I considered waking her, but the memory of her earlier admission—about trouble sleeping—kept me in place. I told myself she deserved rest. She deserved peace. If that meant I was her prisoner for a night, then so be it. I would not move until she let me go. It was the very least I could do.

Carefully, gently, I placed my arm around her shoulders and held her there. I wanted to kiss her hair, but did not. I let my lips hover a centimeter away. My cock remained hard, an unyielding iron bar between us. She did not notice.

Time passed. Maybe five minutes. Maybe an hour.

I thought about every moment of our shared history, and every time I'd failed her, and every way I wanted to make it up to her now. I wondered if she would ever know what she did to me, what she meant to me, if I'd ever get a chance to tell her. If she would one day forgive me.

But then, Samantha shifted, just a little, nuzzling her face deeper into my neck. My eyes closed and I gritted my teeth, commanding myself not to move. She made a sound, a quiet mewling noise, then pressed her nose to my skin and inhaled deeply, as if she were drawing something out of me. Then she stilled again.

Samantha smelled like gardenia and something else, something I could only describe as silky and warm and fucking addictive.

Her hand, still under my shirt, flexed against my stomach, and I realized I held her too tightly. I loosened my grip immediately, worried I might hurt her.

She settled again, head heavy on my bicep, hair tickling my jaw. I memorized each sensation, catalogued every detail. Her breathing grew slower. A wet patch of tears, maybe sweat, formed on my shirt where her face pressed against me.

I would not sleep tonight. I would suffer instead.

But, I reminded myself, suffering with her close seemed so much better than suffering in her absence. This kind of pain, I would pay any price for it. To have her here, in my arms, even for a single night, a luxury I did not deserve.

Oh well. *Lucky me.*

When the sun rose, I would make her coffee, and I would make it strong, and I would never tell her how completely she'd undone me.

I would let her believe it was nothing, no big deal.

And, eventually, I would let her go.

But not yet. Not . . . tonight.

[PART 2]

REPRODUCTION

[1]
ENDOCRINOLOGY, BRAIN, AND PITUITARY GLAND

Samantha

Sunlight. Actual, golden, warm-on-my-face sunlight. My first coherent thought of the day was, *So, this is what it's like to sleep soundly through the night and wake up after sunrise.* The next was, *I feel fucking awesome.*

For the first time in two years, I was well rested and not fighting a caffeine-withdrawal headache.

Maybe I'd died and this was the afterlife, a high-thread-count sheet, a cocoon of perfect warmth, and a brain empty of intrusive thoughts but full of serotonin, the type only made possible by an appropriate length and number of REM cycles. I allowed myself the decadence of drifting there, savoring the delicate pressure of a memory-foam pillow against my temple, the gentle weight of a duvet across my hips, and the luxurious sense of not having a single place I needed to be.

I let myself enjoy this blissful state for exactly eight seconds before my limbs, traitorous as ever, craved movement. So, I began to stretch, arching my toes. But before I could fully commence a morning starfish, I froze. Because my left hand was palming the undeniable reality of another human being.

There's a microsecond between "that's a person" and "which person" that, for most people, might be raw panic. For me, however, it was pure professionalism. I had a procedure for this.

Step one: Assess level of nudity. My left hand, still frozen mid-stretch, confirmed bare skin, but not below-the-waist bare. Chest, maybe? Arm, maybe? Stomach, *definitely*. And a muscly one.

Step two: Identify the person. Keeping my eyes closed, I mentally replayed the previous twelve hours. Had I gone out? No. Had I let anyone into the building? Also no. Had I, at any point, consumed more than the recommended daily allowance of alcohol? Negative.

So, no hookups. No midnight social calls. No one should be in my bed.

Yet, this warm body next to mine definitely existed. And this wasn't a dream, I wasn't asleep. Someone warm and solid and occupying a scandalous percentage of my mattress.

Step three: Confirm position. With the meticulousness of a bomb technician, I moved my fingertips. Male, for sure. Hairless chest, ridged with muscle. Not moving, which meant asleep or possibly dead. Breath? Yes, regular, slow, and deep. So, not dead. I could feel his chest rise and fall beneath the new position of my left hand.

Step four: Open eyes, assess the scene, and—*oh my God!*

This wasn't the afterlife. This was a penthouse apartment in the Lower East Side of Manhattan.

And I was spooning Andreas Kristiansen.

Not just spooning, but aggressively spooning. I was *ladling* him, as though sometime in the night I'd turned into an octopus and decided his body was my favorite rock to cling to. My left leg hooked over both of his, my left arm splayed across his chest and under his shirt, and my face nestled in the crook of his neck like a needy baby possum.

My stomach folded itself into an origami crane. *How did this happen?*

Meanwhile, Andreas, for his part, either didn't mind or hadn't yet noticed. He lay mostly on his back, turned slightly toward me, the soft sound of his breathing barely audible. Shifting backward and reversing out of his neck, I tilted my head and readjusted my temple on the pillow. His face was less than six inches from mine, so close I could see the individual eyelashes resting on his cheek, the faintest pink flush along his jaw.

Step five: Detach with minimal jostling.

I tried. I really, really tried to execute an elegant, silent disengagement. What happened instead was I pulled my arm back, but in my haste, whacked him square in the solar plexus. Andreas grunted and flinched, which caused me to overcompensate. I attempted to roll away and simultaneously kick off the duvet, but gravity betrayed me. *Damn gravity, always letting me down!*

I tumbled off the edge of the mattress and landed on the carpet with a muffled thud.

For a moment, I just lay there, listening to the pounding of my heart in my ears, contemplating how in the heck we'd ended up in bed together.

Above me, I heard Andreas take a deep breath. A moment later, he peered over the edge of the bed. He blinked, hair sticking up in sleep-wild directions, and regarded me with what felt like cool, clinical detachment. "Are you injured?" he asked, voice husky from sleep.

I scrambled to an upright sitting position, heat flooding my cheeks. "No, I'm fine," I lied, even as I clutched my tailbone, which would absolutely be bruised by lunch.

Andreas's gaze did a quick vertical scan, pausing at my legs, then darting back to my face. "Good," he said stiffly, an unmistakable yet faint blush blooming over his cheeks.

Is he embarrassed? Good! Who did he think he was? Climbing into bed with me?

I pushed my hair out of my face, indignance flaring in my chest. "I, uh—why are you in my bed?" I demanded.

Sitting up fully, Andreas righted his shirt in a way that felt oddly modest and careful, and then cleared his throat. "You are mistaken. This is my room."

I looked around. Oh my God!

He was right. The massive window, the bare walls, the sheer size of the bed—I was in the main bedroom. His bedroom.

I pressed my palms to my eyes. "Oh fuck. I sleepwalked again."

"Correct. You came in around three. You did not respond to verbal cues."

Dropping my hands, I refused to feel mortified as I assessed the situation. Yes, I'd sleepwalked into his room and climbed into his bed and ladled him aggressively, but he just stated that he'd been aware of my invasion for several hours, and was cognizant when it happened, and had done . . . what? Anything? He just let me *sleep* with him?

"You tried to wake me up?" I squinted at him.

He nodded, still stiff and serious. "Only at first. Then I remembered your roommate said you were a sleepwalker, and you told me yourself you have insomnia. It can be dangerous to wake a sleepwalker, so I let you sleep."

Hmm. There was some logic there. *And yet—*

"So, your solution was to let me"—I gestured, indicating the proximity of our bodies—"occupy your personal space all night?"

The pink on his cheeks burned brighter and he cleared his throat again, saying with a hint of defensiveness, "It seemed to work. You slept well."

I stared at him, noticing, to my utter incredulity, how this expression he currently wore made him look ridiculously adorable. *What is he thinking? What is this expression?*

Not quite embarrassed, but something like it. Not regretful. Definitely not ashamed. More like . . . bashful?

That's it.

Huffing a short laugh, I rolled my eyes at myself, even as my lungs burned with confusion. I didn't understand him. Why would he be shy about it? Wasn't he the one who let me sleep in his bed? WHATEVER!

Since I was still on the floor, I checked to ensure my oversized T-shirt covered me to mid-thigh and did my best to ignore my lack of pants. "Well, then"—I forced a calm confidence into my voice I didn't quite feel—"I apologize for sleepwalking into your bedroom last night. I will barricade my door from the inside to keep it from happening again."

"Is that safe?" Andreas stood, tugging on the front of his button-up, long-sleeve pajama shirt. I noted against my will that Andreas wore a dashing matching blue-and-white pin-striped pajama set. You know, the ones with the mother-of-pearl buttons, piping at the wrists, and a pocket at the left breast. Basically, they were the pajama equivalent of an expensive suit.

In that moment, the stark dichotomy between us struck me. Andreas in his suit of fancy pajamas, likely costing more than my entire wardrobe, and me in my oversized, four-dollar cotton T-shirt. The last fifteen years had taken us on completely contrasting paths. We were not the same.

Andreas reached for his phone while I mused over our surface level differences, but also the invisible ones. Our upbringing, education, and life experiences. Suddenly, I felt immensely curious about him, where in the world he'd been, what he'd been doing, who he'd met, who his friends were. Had he gone to college? I had no idea.

I could look it up online, but I didn't want to read about Andreas. I wanted to know about his past from him.

I was so busy with my own thoughts that I didn't notice he'd extended his hand to me until he said, "Do you need help standing?"

"Um—" I didn't need a hand, but his hand was so nice. Therefore I did what any self-respecting hand aficionado would do. I accepted his fingers.

He hauled me up, steady and effortlessly. But instead of releasing me, he held on. "Are you sure you are not hurt?" he asked, voice suddenly softer.

My brain short-circuiting on the gentleness of his tone, I blinked at him dumbly for several seconds. But then I caught my reflection in the mirror behind him and my hair was in a full-blown Einstein-on-MDMA situation. Yeesh.

Extracting myself from his grip, I crossed my arms and backed up a step. "I'm fine. And I think I'm late for work."

His eyes flicked down to my legs, then back up, and he straightened his spine before speaking. "You have to work today?"

"Yes."

Andreas's eyes narrowed. "Today is Sunday."

Aw crap.

"That—that's right." I spoke and nodded haltingly while fumbling with improvised bravado. "But for a PhD student who has to fight for lab time, there is no such thing as a weekend. So, I better get to it."

I marched around him, but then spun in the doorway, remembering something I'd meant to ask yesterday. "Oh, so. Andreas. Was the adoption paperwork filed? When will it be final?" For good measure, I tacked on some humor. "Just want to know when to start addressing you as *father dearest.*"

I noticed his jaw tighten at my joke. Pushing his hands into his pajama pockets, he leveled me with his trademark bored stare. "Unlike PhD student labs, courts recognize weekends and are closed until Monday." He sounded calm, but I sensed an undercurrent of odd aggression. Or maybe my vibe-checker was on the fritz this morning. Highly possible given my unconscious brain's choices.

He went on. "I have pulled some strings to get it fast-tracked. Everything should be finalized before Thanksgiving."

"That's good. Thank you." This felt like the first real, official step toward revenge. The engagement was all a show, but this adoption was legally binding. Perhaps my subconscious would avoid his bedroom once everything was final.

On that note. "Oh, again, since I'm apparently sleepwalking, I should barricade my door—"

"Do you think that's safe?" He shuffled a step forward.

"—but you should probably lock your door at night. If I somehow get past the barricade and door, I don't want to impose on you again. I am really sorry about last night."

Andreas openly inspected me. The silence stretched for so long, I thought he might not respond, and I was just about to leave when he finally said, "I will keep that in mind."

Hoping that statement was his way of politely agreeing, I nodded, then darted out, speed walking back to my side of the apartment. Once safely in the sanctuary of the bathroom, I braced my hands against the cool countertop, stared into the mirror, and tried to process the previous five minutes.

My hair was a fright. My shirt was askew. I still felt the ghostly imprint of Andreas's hand on my skin.

One night into living with him, and I'd already been betrayed by my subconscious brain. I had to get a handle on myself. I was an adult. A scientist. A woman with a mission and that mission came first.

And yet, the only thing I could think about, as I stared at my reflection, was how good it had felt to be held by him. Even if he hadn't meant it that way. Even if he was, very soon, going to be my legal father.

I groaned into the sink, then splashed water on my face. "Get it together, Sam," I whispered.

But my skin still tingled where his hand had touched mine, and somewhere in my chest, something soft and dangerous took deeper root.

* * *

IF I WERE BEING HONEST, I needed the cold late-autumn air. I needed the sting, because my brain had been running a fever since approximately 8:45 AM, which was when I'd tumbled out of Andreas's bed.

I hadn't even managed to put on my shoes before fleeing the apartment, waving off Andreas's offer of coffee. Instead, I'd clutched them to my chest like a security blanket. Tara, who seemed to have the tact of a Buddhist monk and the judgmental restraint of a golden retriever, merely greeted me when I appeared on the sidewalk.

"I'm teaching a kickboxing class tonight. Want to come?" Tara asked as soon as she pulled into traffic.

"Yes. Please. What time?" Anything to postpone going back to Andreas's apartment.

"Nine."

I thought for a moment. "That works. I'll finish up work around six, grab a bite, then we can head straight there? I'll digest while I check out the gym."

"Sounds good." Tara flipped on her turn signal and the remainder of the drive passed in silence.

I spent it recalling all the boys I'd left before, every strategy for extracting inconvenient feelings or letting them die on the vine. Usually, disentangling myself was as easy as identifying a man's most repugnant opinion and, if necessary, blowing it out of proportion until I couldn't see the good anymore. But Andreas hadn't cooperated last night, sharing none of his repugnant opinions.

My second strategy was typically foolproof and involved asking myself: What was so special about this guy, anyway? What did I actually like about him?

I mean, sure. Andreas was handsome. So were lots of guys. And he was a kisser of rare talent, so that was something special. And he was thoughtful, smart, and strategic. And he seemed to genuinely care about doing the right thing, even if it made his life difficult. And I've known him forever. *And his hands . . .*

DON'T THINK ABOUT HIS HANDS!

Squeezing my eyes shut, I gave my head a quick shake to dispel the image of Andreas's gorgeous hands and decided to talk myself out of liking him later. For the remainder of the car ride, I stayed busy by making a mental task list of all the work waiting for me at the lab.

But the lab was even less successful as a distraction. My hands shook so badly during pipetting that I had to recalibrate the digital reader three times, which is, for anyone keeping score, three more times than I'd ever miscalibrated it during all my years of grad school. By 2:00 PM, I'd gotten so little work done, I abandoned the blessedly empty lab and worked instead on a project Dmitry had emailed to me last week. He'd asked me to read through his methods section. I edited it for him instead, adding new citations and fleshing out a few of his placeholders.

The only thing that kept me grounded was the knowledge that, after work, I'd hopefully get to burn off at least a fraction of my anxious energy doing violence to some heavy bags in Tara's kickboxing class.

That was my new plan: punch things.

When 5:30 PM rolled around I figured enough was enough. I texted Tara, changed in the locker room, and made my way downstairs. Standing just outside the front doors of the biology building, blue scarf wound up to my nose, I searched the curb for the familiar hulk of Tara's Mercedes. The wind had me blinking against the cold.

Movement flickered at the edge of my vision. A man, tall, moving forward purposefully, strode up the far side of the street. His suit was an expensive blue-gray, not the fun blue of a retro car but the cold, almost metallic blue of a winter sky right before it snows. He wore a cashmere overcoat that looked incredibly soft. It reminded me of Andreas's. *Don't think about Andreas!*

Refocusing on the man, I noted his hair was cut close on the sides, styled just enough on top that it seemed to mock lesser men who dared to try the look. *Huh. He sorta looks like Andreas . . .*

Before I could chide myself for thinking about Andreas again, I registered who this man was, and every neuron in my prefrontal cortex fired at once.

Henrik Kristiansen.

Andreas's half brother, the one Andreas had described as "unpredictable and often resorts to physical violence."

Henrik's stare locked on me at exactly that moment. A pulse of adrenaline had me standing straighter.

Run.

[2]

THE FEMALE REPRODUCTIVE SYSTEM

Samantha

Henrik's eyes were glacial and blue enough to make you believe in recessive gene dominance. His gaze met mine with an energy so openly malevolent it was practically scented with testosterone.

I tried not to look rattled. My hand went for my campus badge a full second before my brain gave it the order. Henrik's stride lengthened. He cut across the sidewalk without once glancing for traffic, because obviously the cars would stop for him. They did.

"Samantha!" he called, voice friendly and entirely at odds with the felony violence in his gaze. He lifted a hand, palm up, as if inviting me to a sociable game of Russian roulette.

I took a step back toward the biology building, thumbed the badge, and held it at the ready. "Henrik," I called back, forcing calm into my voice. "Didn't realize you were allowed outside of a cage without a leash."

He grinned, flashing teeth. My fear made them look both whiter and sharper than possible. "Rumors of my incarceration have been greatly overexaggerated."

As he approached, I did my best to hide my movements and intentions. The moment he got within ten strides, I scanned in, pulled the door open, and slipped through, letting it close with hydraulic slowness between us as he ran to grab the handle.

167

Too late. It clicked shut with me on the inside and him on the outside. Thank God.

Henrik's features twisted with anger and he pounded on the glass door. Internally, I gave myself a high five for not flinching. Outwardly, I slowly crossed my arms and pasted on an unperturbed smile. Apparently resigned to the impenetrable partition between us, Henrik huffed a laugh and placed one palm flat against the glass. The look he gave me belonged on a National Geographic special.

"What, not even a handshake?"

"I don't like being touched by violent offenders." I shrugged.

He huffed another laugh and pushed away from the building, his eyes scanning me openly. I took the opportunity to calm my racing heart and inspect him as well.

Up close, Henrik looked older than Tobias. Less pretty boy, more "CEO of Fight Club." His nose had clearly been broken more than once, but rather than diminish his beauty, it only enhanced the suggestion that he was dangerous. His hair was much lighter than Andreas's, but not quite the golden white of his older brother's.

His smile widened as it settled on mine again. "You're a coward, Samantha. Just like your father."

If he wanted to anger me, he succeeded. I'd always suspected Tobias and Henrik had something to do with what happened to my father. I decided to take his current statement as proof.

I smiled back, showing all my teeth. "Oh? Most people just tell me I have his eyes."

Henrik leaned in again, forehead nearly touching the glass, his blue eyes boring into me. "You're not as clever as you think. Or as safe. I'd have caught you, if I wanted to."

I pretended to check my phone, though my hands shook so much I almost dropped it. "Then why didn't you? Worried I'd get blood on your expensive coat?"

Henrik chuckled. It was a deep, rolling sound that might have been pleasant in another context, like, say, a commercial for luxury vodka, or an ad for a private island. "You know, listening to Andreas is a mistake. He makes promises he can't keep, and he doesn't know anything about taking care of a woman." Henrik gave me a quick, lascivious once-over, licking his lips as he added, "Maybe you and I could reach an agreement instead. Unlike my little brother who has no experience, I know what I'm doing."

I cringed at the thought, an honest expression, and shook my head. "No, thank you. I prefer my men to walk upright." I gave him a look, then turned my back on him for two seconds, just to see what he'd do.

What he did was pound once, hard, on the glass with the side of his fist. It made me flinch and triggered a wave of heat down my spine.

I spun, holding my phone like it was a can of mace. "Leave. Or I'm calling the police."

He pressed his hands together, prayerlike, then splayed them wide in a performance of mockery. "You don't even want to know why I'm here?"

"No."

He looked over both shoulders, scanning the sidewalk. "It's good you're cautious. It means you actually understand what's at stake."

That, for some reason, angered me more than anything else he'd said so far. "I know exactly what's at stake." I'd lived through losing everything. It was time for this psychopath to know how it felt.

Henrik grinned again, and there was something feral about it. "I know about the addendum." He sing-songed the statement like a taunt. "To the will, right? You plan to have a baby. Are you two already trying?"

For a moment, I literally could not speak. My ears rang with an icy static, and every drop of blood in my body tried to leave at once.

He knew about the will. And about the grandchild clause. Andreas had been right to be paranoid.

Henrik laughed at my silence. "You're not even denying it?" His eyes dropped to my stomach. "Are you knocked up already?"

I managed to get my tongue unstuck. "Henrik, why are you here? You don't need to stalk me to know what's happening. Just text Tobias and get your briefing."

He leaned back, clearly enjoying himself. "Tobias doesn't know how to get things done." Then he lowered his voice to something deeper. "And because I want you to hear it from me that nothing is guaranteed. Nine months is a long time. Anything can happen."

I did not respond. There was nothing to say to that.

His smile faded, replaced by a darker and flatter expression. "I'm not going to let my Genetix be inherited by a fucking fetus. So, if you have a death wish, keep playing house with my little brother. But don't get too comfortable."

Henrik didn't move, not at first. He just let his words hang in the cold air, hands pressed to the glass, mouth twisting in the approximation of a smile. I stayed where I was, just on the other side of the door, thumb still white-knuckled around my phone, wondering why I hadn't called the police yet.

If he wanted to intimidate me, he was succeeding beyond his wildest expectations.

I watched as he pulled a phone from his coat, thumbed a text or maybe took a photo. Then, like he'd grown bored with the whole "terrorize Sam" event, he took a step away from the door, rocked back on his heels, and surveyed the street. For a heartbeat, I thought he'd leave. But instead, he pivoted on one shoe and scanned the sidewalk, head cocked in a way that was at once predatory and weirdly expectant.

I followed his gaze and saw why.

Not too far away, a black Mercedes pulled up, then idled. A moment later, the driver's-side door popped open and out stepped Tara, all five foot, eight inches of her, hair up in the same efficient ponytail as mine. She wore a navy windbreaker, dark leggings, and sneakers, but the way she moved made the clothes look tactical.

Henrik squinted at her. I watched, fascinated, as the gears turned in his head. For a second, I wondered if he would assume Tara was me. As Tara walked toward us with long, unhurried strides, Henrik started forward, his interest likely piqued.

At fifty feet, his shoulders bunched and he glanced back at me with unmistakable confusion. But then he turned back and met Tara halfway up the steps to the building.

"Hey," Tara called out, voice calm.

Henrik stopped, shoulders rolling back, and for a moment I thought he might just bowl her over. Instead, he put on that same flat, professional smile. "You're not Samantha," he said.

"Nope," Tara agreed, shifting her weight, then continuing to walk up the stairs and around him with a casual authority. "Just a friend."

The words hung there as Henrik turned back toward the building, watching her. Eventually, he released a laugh that didn't touch his eyes. "Well, since Samantha won't come out to play, maybe I could play with you."

"I wouldn't advise that," Tara replied, inspecting me, then mouthing the words, *Are you okay?*

I nodded, but then shifted my focus back to Henrik, not wanting to take my eyes off him for even a second.

She turned her back to me and he looked her over, top to toe, and I saw a flash of something—caution, maybe, or the animal calculation that precedes an attack. "Why? You some sort of ninja or something?"

"Something like that," Tara said, and took one step closer.

There was a stillness then, the kind of hush that comes before an avalanche. Henrik continued openly sizing her up, then darted a glance at me through the glass. I tried not to look like I was cowering, but there was a zero percent chance I was fooling anyone.

"Tell your friend to come out and talk like an adult," Henrik said, voice still soft but edged now.

"Nah."

Henrik's smile dropped. "'Nah?'"

"That's right. Nah."

He laughed again, but this time it was short, almost a bark. "You're serious."

She said something that sounded like "Deadly," but since she faced away from me, I couldn't be sure.

And then, as if they'd been following pre-rehearsed choreography, they both moved.

It was fast. I barely registered the blur of Henrik's hand as he reached for Tara's neck, or the way Tara stepped inside the grab, twisted his wrist, and drove a knee into his gut so hard it lifted him an inch off the cement. He doubled over, more from surprise than pain, but Tara was already behind him, one arm around his throat, the other pinning his wrist. Henrik tried to elbow her but she shifted, swept his feet, and brought him down in a controlled sprawl on the cold concrete.

He thrashed, kicked out, tried to roll. Tara let him, but only enough to humiliate him further, and then—when he growled and went for her ponytail—she caught his arm, bent it backward, and held it at an angle that seemed impossible.

Henrik let out a curse so loud it reverberated through the glass.

"Let. Go," Tara said.

Henrik, to his credit, tried one last time to flip her. She let him get just enough leverage to think he had a shot, then shifted her knee into the small of his back, and he went face-down with a yelp.

"I told you to let go," Tara said, voice steady, not even breathing hard.

Henrik's reply was a string of expletives in what sounded like Swedish, though it might have just been the universal language of defeat. Tara let him go, slow, never giving him her back. To his credit, he didn't even try to stand. She stepped away and kept her eyes on him, posture relaxed but ready.

In that moment, I really, really wanted to go to Tara's kickboxing class.

Tara straightened, brushed her hands together like she'd just finished a particularly annoying round of weeding a garden, and said, "He's not armed. You can come out, Sam."

For a few heartbeats, I just watched Henrik, face-down, still trying to recover his dignity if not his wind. Then I pushed open the door, adrenaline burning through my veins, and hurried down the steps. I gave Henrik as wide a berth as the stairs allowed.

He looked up at me, eyes glassy with rage and, maybe, confusion. "You think you're safe? You're not," he spat.

"Get in the car, Sam," Tara said, never looking away from Henrik still sprawled on the ground.

I did as she instructed, rushing for the door, opening it, and catapulting myself inside. I had never wanted anything more in my life than to be inside a locked Mercedes, surrounded by reinforced steel, and speeding away from this entire encounter.

What felt like seconds later, Tara slid in behind the wheel, yanked her own door shut, and had the car in gear before I'd even managed to get my seat belt buckled. My hands shook so hard I had to use both of them to thread the latch through the buckle.

"Are you really okay? Did he touch you?" she asked, eyes darting between me and the road.

"He didn't touch me, and I am okay," I said, and not believing it. The adrenaline was leaving my system and now I was shaking all over. "Thank you."

Tara gave me a smile, but it looked tight. "May I suggest I take you home now and you skip kickboxing tonight?"

"Uh . . . okay." I nodded, agreeing with her. I would go, just not tonight.

She grinned, the real kind this time. "Come next week, okay?"

I nodded again.

We merged into traffic, leaving Henrik behind. The car was silent except for the muted thump of tires over potholes and the steady thrum of my pulse, which refused to slow down.

I was shaken, and scared, and my hands weren't going to stop trembling for at least a year, but there was something else under the surface—a kind of bright, savage relief. And, deep down, a quiet, vengeful satisfaction. Henrik had fallen for the smoke screen. He thought we were trying for a baby.

The truth would never occur to him, not until it was too late. And by then, Genetix would be mine.

[3]

THE MALE REPRODUCTIVE SYSTEM

Samantha

I sensed Tara's gaze move over me every so often in the rearview mirror as I pressed my palms together, knuckles white, and tried to will my heart to slow. She said nothing, bless her, and seemed to be unbothered by the altercation with Henrik. Meanwhile, I was playing it on loop in my brain. She'd thrown a grown man to the ground and made it look easy. And now, she behaved as though roughing Henrik up was the same as assisting an innocuous, little old lady cross the street. Maybe, to her, she had. Maybe I was an innocuous little old lady.

We drove in silence for a block, then two, the hum of the engine and the rhythmic tick of the turn signal the only sounds besides my own ragged breathing. At the next red light, I spoke without planning to.

"Can you drive around for a bit before heading back to the apartment? I just need a few minutes." My voice sounded too thin, almost childlike. I hated that, but didn't have the energy to make it tougher.

Tara nodded, eyes flickering to me in the mirror. "Sure. But I'll have to let Andreas know. I just told him we were on our way and if we're running late, he'll want to know. Is that okay?"

For a second, I bristled at the idea of being surveilled, but the feeling faded just as quickly as it arrived. I had no problem with Andreas keeping tabs on me. Not after today. He was right about his brothers and he was right about Henrik in particular. It wasn't paranoia if it was warranted.

"Yes, of course. That's fine." I exhaled and tried to melt my spine into the seat.

Tara thumbed her phone at the next stoplight, probably sending a perfectly bland update. It dawned on me that this was my life now. Status reports. Driver/bodyguard. The prospect didn't even feel dystopian; it felt reasonable given the stakes.

The Mercedes glided through city blocks where people in expensive yoga pants jogged with their dogs and didn't have to wonder whether some Scandinavian sociopath was plotting to end their nonexistent pregnancy. I envied them, a little. Or maybe a lot. I'd never admit that out loud, even under torture, which I now suspected Henrik would be happy to provide, gratis.

After two turns, Tara spoke again, voice pitched low. "You handled yourself really well. I know you're probably shaken, but you kept your head." She paused. "Most people don't."

I tried to snort, but it sounded more like a hiccup. "I hid behind glass, Tara."

"And you didn't run. You made him work for it. I've seen plenty of people freeze up or faint, or try to punch back and end up with a concussion. You, though —you got out of the situation, kept your wits and your phone, waited for me, stayed focused. Good job."

I didn't know what to say to that, so I just nodded.

By the third left turn, my hands had stopped shaking. The adrenaline ebbed, which meant a wave of exhaustion washed over me, threatening to knock me out cold right there in the back seat. I watched the city scroll by through the tinted window and let my mind go blank for the first time since I recognized Henrik's face.

The thought emerged, *Why had Henrik called my dad a coward?* I didn't know. Either way, the next steps were clear. I had to be smarter, meaner, and better prepared. There was no room for error, not when people like the Kristiansens existed.

I waited until my pulse slowed, until I could speak without feeling like my tongue would tie itself in a hangman's knot, before instructing Tara, "You can take me back to the apartment now."

Tara caught my gaze in the mirror, checked my face, then nodded. "Got it." She steered us into traffic and in five more minutes we were pulling up outside the apartment building.

By then, I felt almost like myself again. I thanked Tara, even though I knew she didn't need to be thanked, and grabbed my backpack from the floor. I lifted my hand to the door handle when I caught sight of Andreas on the sidewalk.

He stood with his arms folded, eyes on the Mercedes, body angled toward the street like he was preparing to intercept a riot or maybe chase down a rogue food truck. He wore a charcoal sweater that probably cost more than my monthly rent at my old apartment, and for some reason, the sight of him, there, clearly waiting for me in the dwindling daylight and cold, made me want to cry.

Before I could even pull the door handle, Andreas was at the back window, knocking. The knock was polite, but the force behind it suggested he was two seconds from tearing off the whole door.

Tara unlocked the car, and he pulled the back door open, his silhouette momentarily filling the frame. His eyes, usually half-mast and unreadable, were liquid and alive. There was a tightness in his jaw and a wildness in the way he scanned my face, like he was searching for injuries or evidence of trauma that might not be visible to the naked eye.

He did not speak, not right away. The air inside the car seemed to freeze, and then, suddenly, he reached inside, grabbed me by the shoulder, and pulled me out.

I stumbled but he caught me. I was now pressed against him, my chin nearly to his chest, his arm locked around my back, his hand fisting the fabric of my jacket. It was a full-body hug, the kind meant to keep a person from falling apart, or maybe to keep the world from taking them away.

He seemed to be vibrating. Not a lot, just enough for me to notice. His heart was a trip-hammer, beating through his chest so fast it made my own skip a few measures.

He held me, and only after a long moment, did he speak. "He didn't hurt you, did he? Did he touch you?"

I shook my head, unable to find words. My throat was blocked by something big and jagged and stupid. Tears burned behind my eyelids, but I refused to let them fall. I could smell his skin and his cologne and, faintly, the chamomile tea he must have been drinking when he got Tara's text.

He stepped back, but only enough to look me in the eyes. "You're sure?"

I nodded again, trying to manage a reply, but all that came out was, "I'm okay. I'm fine."

His hand tightened on my upper arm and his voice dropped to a whisper. "You have to stay inside the building until your guard arrives from now on. Promise me. God, if something had happened to you, if he had hurt you . . ."

That nearly undid me. He sounded so genuinely upset, so real and so raw, that I had to look away. My vision swam for a second, and I realized my entire body was cold, except for the spots where his hands gripped me. They were warm, unreasonably so.

"It's okay," I managed, but it sounded pathetic, even to me.

He shook his head. "It is not okay. I am sorry. I—" His words jammed together, tangled and sharp. "I will not let it happen again."

My chest hurt with the effort it took to not cry. For a moment, I wondered if this was all for show. But the pulse pounding under his skin, the way he kept glancing at my face and then away, like it was physically painful to see me scared, told me otherwise. He was afraid. For me.

That, more than anything, made me feel oddly safe, safer than I'd felt in a long time. I had someone looking out for me, checking in, waiting for me to come home.

Not allowing myself to think too much about it, I buried my face in his chest and let myself be held. I was so tired, so wrung out, that I didn't care if the whole city watched. The pressure of his embrace was grounding, a force field against the rest of the world.

Tara stepped away, silent and invisible as a shadow, giving us space. For the first time in a long time, I let myself be comforted. I let myself believe that maybe, in this one thing, I wasn't alone.

We stood like that for a long time, not speaking, just breathing each other's air, until my heart slowed and my thoughts grew quiet. When I finally looked up, Andreas's eyes were less wild, but the concern in them hadn't faded.

"You're really okay?" he asked, softer this time.

"Yeah," I said. "I'm okay now."

He nodded, but didn't let go. If anything, his grip tightened for a heartbeat, then loosened just enough for him to tuck a lock of my hair behind my ear, an oddly delicate gesture.

He glanced toward the doorman, who had come out of his booth and now stood a respectful distance away, pretending to be interested in the curb. "Let us go inside," Andreas said, but didn't move.

I stepped away first, feeling steadier, and walked through the lobby. He followed and hovered at my side like a satellite, orbiting, always within arm's reach. I didn't mind. The further we got from the sidewalk, the less I felt the urge to look over my shoulder.

We entered the elevator, and only then did he speak again, voice low and meant for me alone. "Tara texted me that you did everything right. She said you were smart and you kept your head."

I tried to smile, but my lips wouldn't quite obey. "Mostly I just didn't want to be the star of a true crime documentary."

Andreas almost smiled. "I would not let that happen."

The elevator chimed and we walked in silence to the apartment. He opened the door and ushered me inside. For a second, I stood there, taking in the warmth of the space, the faint aroma of coffee and whatever savory dish Andreas was having for dinner.

I dropped my bag in the entryway and turned to look at him. He studied me for a moment, then closed the distance and wrapped me in another hug. This one was less urgent, more careful. It felt like a promise, or maybe an apology.

I let myself relax. I let him hold me up. And there were no cameras here. This wasn't for show.

"Thank you," I whispered, not sure if I was thanking him for the hug, for worrying, or for being exactly who I needed in this moment.

He didn't answer, but he didn't need to. He just held on, and I held back, and for the next minute, that was enough.

* * *

AFTER AN INDETERMINATE PERIOD of time spent hugging in the hallway, I finally talked myself into pulling away. I'd had a shitty night, and accepting comfort, leaning on Andreas was appropriate given Henrik's threatening antics—but only to a point!

Now it was time for me to pull myself together, even if he was warm and smelled good and his body felt amazing. I needed to rely on myself.

Andreas won't always be here to comfort me.

Extracting my body, I gave him a vague smile, then stepped out of his orbit. Kicking off my shoes by the door, I picked them up and placed them in the closet, hung up my jacket, and ditched my backpack. I then drifted to the living room wordlessly, gravitating to the couch not out of conscious thought, but because it was the first surface that promised softness. The cushions were unfamiliar but not unfriendly, and I let myself sink into the plush expanse, arms crossed tightly over my stomach.

I sensed Andreas hover for exactly three seconds, standing behind the couch, before vanishing. I heard him moving in the kitchen. Glass clinking, something ceramic rattling, the faint, deliberate pop of an electric kettle's button.

I focused on the sounds he made while I scanned the interior of his apartment. I hadn't taken the time to really look at this room before. Taking note of the details now felt therapeutic, pulling me out of my head, forcing me into the present. The living room had the kind of curving, expensive lines you see in extremely old houses, and the books on the shelves were battered and dog-eared and grouped in weird little cliques, not for aesthetics but for accessibility.

I also noticed a collection of sheet music, which stood out to me since it was the only sheet music on the shelf. The sheets were lovingly stored between layers of acid-free paper and were within a black linen box. I soon realized why he owned the collection. The composer was his mother, Augustina Loretto, and there were notations and scribbles in the margin of the first page. I assumed these notes were her handwriting. The sheets of music felt precious and private, so I didn't look through them. I put them back safely on the shelf where I'd found them.

On the coffee table, a single remote lay on a glass tray which also contained a pitcher of water, four stacked glasses, four white linen napkins, a blank notepad, and a single fountain pen. The windows swallowed half a city block and spit it back in watercolor versions of itself. It was all so . . . intentional. And elegant. And functional.

I wonder what that remote controls? There was no TV in the room, not that I could see.

Andreas returned with a tray holding two mugs and a small plate, each item selected and positioned with so much care that I wondered if he'd spent the better part of the last fifteen minutes searching the internet for "appropriate beverages and snacks for traumatized guests." He set the tray down on the table, keeping it a safe distance from my knees, then sat on the opposite end of the couch, not quite facing me. Three feet of high-grade leather sofa between us.

"Thank you." It came out unsteady, too loud. I picked up the mug—the light golden liquid inside was, I assumed, tea—grateful for the anchor, and stared at the plate of cookies. After a long pause, I leaned closer and inspected them, the gears in my brain moving sluggishly.

"Are these . . . shortbread with jam?" I finally managed.

Andreas nodded, not looking at me. "Yes. I recall, those were your favorite when we were kids."

I squinted at the cookies, then at him. Then, on autopilot, I picked one up and took a bite. The taste yanked me instantly back to the memory of a kitchen in the Hamptons, my mom humming and rolling the dough into balls, little dots of red jam in the center of the thumbprint I made with my own hands.

The flavor was exactly right—lemony, buttery, with the sharp hit of raspberry jam on the roof of my mouth. The nostalgia gut-punched me so hard my eyes stung, but all I did was chew in silence. They tasted *exactly* the same as my mom's. Even the jam, which she'd make every summer over the Fourth of July from raspberry bushes she'd grown at our home in Connecticut. She'd then bring jars to the Hamptons and make shortbread in the Kristiansens' vacation home kitchen.

How'd he do that?

"How did you do that?" The question tumbled out of me. "These taste just like my mom's."

His face a composed mask, Andreas fidgeted with his mug, then set it down without drinking. He glanced sideways at me, then away, then back. Tension stretched between us and had become its own entity—less a cloud, more a flock of birds with nowhere to land.

He cleared his throat. "Do you regret it?"

I licked a crumb off my thumb, then stared at him. "Regret what? Eating the cookie? I never regret cookies."

He didn't blink. "No. Agreeing to this plan. To inherit Genetix. Now that you know what Henrik is like."

I studied him, trying to figure out if this was a test, or a trap, or simply raw honesty. "No. If anything, meeting Henrik and seeing for myself firsthand how unhinged he is, makes me even more certain that taking over those Genetix shares is the right thing. I can't imagine someone like him being in charge of my father's company. Tobias is bad enough, but Henrik . . ."

I let the thought trail off, not because I didn't have a million adjectives to tack on, but because I'd already reached the upper limit of my emotional output for the day.

Andreas nodded. "He is very dangerous." He spoke without inflection, as if reading from a file. Or a police report. Or a court record.

I sipped the tea, which was hot and herbal and probably blended for maximum relaxation. My hands had stopped shaking, but my insides still felt wobbly.

"He's been arrested many times," Andreas continued, voice low. "My father's connections and money have kept him out of jail, mostly."

"Has he ever killed someone?" I asked, surprising myself with the bluntness of the question. But I felt like it was an important one.

Andreas went very still, his profile sharp in the light from the huge window. Eventually, he met my gaze. "No. Not quite."

The phrase hung in the air, grim and striking me as both vague and precise. Andreas kept saying Henrik was dangerous. I wanted to quantify it so I could prepare myself.

"What do you mean, 'not quite'?" My stomach twisted again.

"He beat someone so badly, they almost died. But not quite." Andreas sounded clinical, not cold, but like he'd spent years reciting these facts to himself.

"And he was never punished?" I pressed.

Andreas shrugged, though it was more a collapse of the shoulders. "Oskar had the case dropped and buried, paid off the family, and placed Henrik under a type of house arrest for almost two years afterward. But when Oskar's illness progressed, no one was paying attention. Henrik has been more or less unchecked since my father fell into a coma. So, a few months now."

I exhaled and rubbed my forehead, a headache pooling behind my eyes. "If anything, I think maybe I should have more bodyguards."

I sensed Andreas move. When I glanced up at him, he seemed to have perked up and now sat straighter.

"I can make the larger team more visible."

I gave him a sidelong look. "You already have a larger team?"

He blinked once, and then his eyes dropped. "Uh . . . I do."

I squinted. "Please explain."

Andreas's chest rose with a deep inhale, giving me the sense that he'd decided something, or was surrendering to something. "The truth is, you have four bodyguards already, but only Tara is obvious to you. Whenever we have been together, we have a team of six. I have requested that they be discreet, so as to not make you uncomfortable."

Setting down my tea, I laughed. But it was a shaky, bewildered sound. "Even when you walked me home on Thursday?"

"Yes," he said. His tone held an edge of belligerence. Or perhaps it was defensiveness. "And even prior, I placed a team of four on you before we had coffee at the café. As soon as I made first contact through my assistant, Elio. By making contact, I knew I had potentially opened you up to my brothers' scrutiny. I wanted to be certain you were safe."

I simply looked at him, mind whirling through every moment of the past few weeks, searching for any sighting of a security detail. I hadn't noticed a thing, and what did that say about my lack of spidey-senses? Was this a compliment to Andreas's security team, or an indictment of my own observational skills? Or both?

Perhaps I was too tired at present to muster outrage at this news, or perhaps my pragmaticism immediately recognized the logic and prudence of his actions. Whatever it was, I didn't feel irritation. I felt resigned.

"I guess I should thank you." I reached for and took a sip of my tea.

Andreas looked up, uncertainty flickering in his eyes. "Are you angry with me?"

Tilting my head, I thought about it, wanting to be certain before responding. "No. Actually. I'm not even a little angry. Thank you for keeping me safe. And if I haven't thanked you for this yet, then allow me to say, thank you for helping me gain controlling interest in my father's company."

His relief was nearly palpable, though he tried to cover it by taking a careful sip of his own tea.

"Are you open to having a larger visible team?" he asked, his tone striking me as carefully conversational.

"Maybe if I'm in a public place for a long time." I debated the matter. "And I think I should probably warn the building security at my department to keep an eye out. What do you think?"

Andreas nodded immediately. "Yes. I agree. I will make arrangements."

He hesitated, then set his mug down again. "Are you sure you do not regret agreeing to this inheritance scheme?"

I set my mug down too, thinking carefully. "No. As I said, I'm really glad—relieved, even—that I finally agreed to it. Again, if Henrik were to inherit Genetix, I can't imagine how he would treat the employees, or how he'd use the wealth and power gained in his sadistic pursuits."

Andreas nodded, but it was a slow gesture. "Yes. I agree. I felt—I feel—similar. Which is why I pushed you so hard. I apologize if, at the time, I—"

"I get it now," I cut in. "You were right to push. You were right to place a security team on me as soon as you made first contact. And I probably wouldn't have listened to you about Henrik or Tobias until I experienced their maliciousness firsthand. I'm sorry I was so resistant. And I really am glad we've teamed up to take them down."

He still looked like he wanted to say something else, but instead he nodded, apparently accepting my words.

A shiver ran through me, originating somewhere deep. I realized I still felt rattled, still floating a few feet above my own body, watching myself from the ceiling.

Perhaps Andreas noticed because he asked, "May I hug you again?"

I lifted an eyebrow at him, then gave in to the impulse to make a joke. "Do I smell that good? It's just soap. I'll give you the name of the brand."

A faint smile ghosted his mouth, but he shook his head. "It must have been frightening for you. But, truthfully, this is for me. I am also shaken, just thinking about what might have happened."

I stared at him, and the urge to make another joke disappeared. Not letting myself think too much about it, I scooted forward on the couch, and opened my arms.

He didn't hesitate. He closed the distance between us in a single, smooth motion, sliding to me, and pulled me into a tight, two-armed embrace. His body felt rigid at first, as though he might be afraid of breaking me, but then I felt the slow, deliberate loosening of tension, the way he let his chin dip down to rest in the curve of my shoulder, the way his fingers flexed and then stilled on my back.

I let myself be held, but after a moment, I squeezed him back, firmer, the way you'd hug a friend after a funeral. I wanted him to feel comforted, too, not just obligated to protect me or keep me from falling apart. I wanted him to know I saw him, and his fears, and for this moment at least, we were both safe.

Neither of us moved. Like before in the hallway, it could have been two minutes or twenty. The city beyond the windows glowed and shifted, but inside, the only movement was our breathing.

[4]

SEXUAL DIFFERENTIATION

Samantha

Sunlight tickled my eyelids, which was strange, because my bedroom didn't face east and—hold on.

I wasn't in my bed.

This pillow felt too solid, too warm, and, if I really paid attention, way too much like human muscle. There was the clean scent of laundry detergent, yes, but also a deeper, spicy note. Rosemary, cologne, and warm skin. My left arm was numb from the angle, and my right leg was slung over something firm and unyielding, with my heel pressed hard against the outside of a knee that was definitely not my own unless I'd suddenly developed superhuman flexibility skilz.

I opened one eye and found an expanse of blue silk immediately in front of my nose. It shimmered in the morning light. I recognized the exact shade, not cornflower, not navy, but the rich, almost iridescent blue reserved for high-end men's pajama suits.

Of course. Because the my subconscious could always be trusted to make things maximally weird. *I sleepwalked. Again.*

Shifting incrementally, I confirmed the following: My face was smashed against Andreas Kristiansen's shoulder. My body was three-fourths on top of him, one-fourth on the couch, like I'd lost a wrestling match with both gravity and personal boundaries. My left arm was threaded beneath our rib cages, and his right arm was wrapped all the way around my back, palm splayed flat and proprietarily across my bottom.

He was asleep. Or—as I lifted my head from his chest—he looked asleep. He could have been dead, but the steady rise and fall of his chest, plus the faint sound of him breathing, suggested otherwise. My thighs, like some kind of traitorous heat-seeking missiles, had made themselves very much at home straddling his. For a moment I marveled at the contrast; his legs, thick and hard, compared to my own, which were encased in the jersey cotton sleep pants I'd thrown on last night.

Tilting my head back and staring at the ceiling, I tried to reverse engineer the sequence of events that had deposited me in this arrangement. Last night, after the Henrik incident, I'd sat on the couch with Andreas. We drank tea, ate cookies, talked in a way that was two degrees too honest, and then, at some point, we'd hugged. I distinctly remembered hugging him.

Then I went to my room, changed into pajamas, brushed my teeth, took the time to do my entire skincare regiment—which was unusual for me, I mostly considered the purchasing of cosmetic items aspirational in nature—and then I went into my room, barricaded the door with furniture and the bins full of my stuff, and I went to sleep.

But then I must have left my room and sleepwalked, right on top of Andreas.

And he must have, for whatever reason, decided it was preferable to let a full-grown woman use him as a pillow rather than disturb her. *He's so weird.*

My psychiatrist was going to have a field day. The time had come. I couldn't put it off. I had to schedule an appointment. I would call her first thing when I got to work, insurance be damned.

Closing my eyes, I weighed my options.

Option A: Extract myself from this sexy European cuddle trap without waking him. This would require flexibility, stealth, and possibly a team of riggers from Cirque du Soleil.

Option B: Accept my fate, go back to sleep, and deal with the fallout later. Pros: no immediate effort. Cons: inevitable awkwardness.

Option C: Use the opportunity to analyze Andreas until I spotted a flaw. Did he snore? Was he a sleep-talker? Would he, if I yelled "Fire!" abandon me for the nearest exit? If I stared at him long enough, would his face reveal a previously unseen defect? Was he, in the immortal words of Cher from *Clueless,* actually a Monet—put together from far away but a total mess up close?

I decided on option A, only because the sun was rising rapidly and I needed to get to work sooner rather than later.

I began the detachment process—disengage left arm, lift head, and pivot right leg off his lap. What I failed to account for was the fact that Andreas's grip on my butt was, even in sleep, tenacious.

As soon as I tried to slide away, his arm cinched tighter, and his other hand came up to grip my upper thigh, pulling me flush against him. I froze. Because, ladies, he had a massive third-leg situation going on. Andreas's unmistakable erection pressed indecently—but so delightfully—against my vagina, and the last tendrils of my sleepiness fled in an instant.

Then, quite suddenly, Andreas awoke. One moment comatose, the next his eyes flying open, expression blank. He blinked several times, then his gaze zeroed in on me, wide and fuzzy, but not surprised.

"Good morning," I said, because what else does one say in this situation? There is no script for waking up on someone's lap, unless you're in an anime, and I lacked the requisite blue hair, DD cup size, and accidental panty flash.

Plus, being totally honest, since last night, when he'd hugged me on the sidewalk, I now felt this low hum of tension, something like electricity, when we were together. A hyperawareness. It made thinking difficult and kept getting in the way of clever word choice.

Andreas blinked at me again, and I watched as his brain caught up with the situation, specifically the time, place, person, limb arrangement, and hand position. His cheeks did that fascinating thing where they turned pink and the color bloomed outward. With a flinching motion, he loosened his grip, his hands flying away, and he took a deep breath.

"Samantha." His voice was so hoarse I wondered if he'd slept at all. "Did you sleep well?"

"I . . . think so?" I scootched backward, away from his mast of morning wood. His hands returned to my body as though to steady me, settling lightly on my waist. "What happened?" I asked, fairly certain I knew, but I wanted to hear his side.

"I was sitting on the couch after you left, reading. Around midnight, you came out of your room, sleepwalking again."

I groaned and covered my face with both hands. "Did I—oh God. Did I say anything? Or do anything weird? I mean, other than sit on your lap."

He considered this, then shook his head. "No. You were walking to my room, I think. I called out your name. You stopped, stood there for a moment. You turned and walked over to me. Then you, uh, you sat on me, as you are now, and went to sleep. Or, I guess, stayed asleep, but in this position." He swallowed, the sound audible and oddly endearing.

"So, you just . . . let me sleep on you. All night." I could feel the flush creeping up my own neck now, both from frustration and a growing sense of something less platonic. And, you know, the aforementioned hyperawareness.

Andreas nodded, turning his head away to yawn. When he finished, he glanced back at me, and for a split second, his eyes flicked down to my mouth. It was subtle—blink and you'd miss it—but I didn't miss it.

Oh no! Does my breath stink?

I covered my mouth as more upsetting possibilities unsexified situation. I must've drooled on him. Or snored. Or, worst of all, ground my teeth. Nothing sexy about teeth grinding.

I needed to say something. Anything. But without letting him smell my morning breath.

"Are your legs okay?" I blurted, still holding my hand in front of my mouth like a female judge on *Iron Chef Japan*. "Can you feel them? Will you ever walk again? Have I paralyzed you?"

He regarded me with a mixture of what looked like amusement and something I couldn't name, glancing at the hand covering my mouth and lifting an eyebrow. "They are a little—uh—stiff," he said, and the way he said it, slow and deliberate, sent a little shiver down my back.

I snorted, then cringed. Nothing sexy about snorting. Or cringing. I mean, name one situation where it's sexy to cringe.

And yet I still sat on his lap, straddling him, and I knew—though I could no longer feel it due to my earlier scootch back—his very hard cock was mere inches from my very open legs.

Yeeeeeah. I needed to get off his lap. Like, right now.

"Anyway!" Turning my face to the side to point my morning breath elsewhere, I set my hands on the couch behind him and pushed, forcing my legs to work even as they protested. My hips spasmed, obviously not liking the position my unconscious brain had preferred for last night's sleep.

I felt Andreas's hands on my waist tighten, probably thinking I might face-plant without assistance, but then he let me go. Ungracefully, I dismounted his lap. My inner thighs ached, reminding me of that one time in elementary school when I'd been forced to ride a horse for six hours. *THE WORST!*

Finally separated from the ridiculously sexy man I shared an apartment and revenge destiny with, I pushed my back against the arm of the couch and brought my knees up, wrapping my arms around my legs.

Once I was off, he immediately reached to the side and placed a throw pillow on his lap, clearing his throat. Andreas was in another fancy pajama set. I suspected the top had been perfectly pressed last night before he'd donned it. Perhaps it had also been buttoned up to his collarbones, but the top two buttons were undone now, hinting at the smooth skin beneath and the elegance of his bone structure. And, boy oh boy, did he give good clavicle.

Tearing my eyes away, I made a mental note to one day count how many pajama sets this man owned, because so far I'd seen two, and each looked like it came with a monogrammed handkerchief and a complimentary monocle.

Thank goodness I'd put on a huge long-sleeve T-shirt and baggy sweatpants last night. In all honesty, I'd chosen these clothes just in case I did sleepwalk. I didn't want to wake up pantsless like yesterday.

But . . . *Hmm.*

Maybe I should do the opposite tonight? Perhaps if I felt uncomfortable going to bed I wouldn't sleepwalk. Maybe I should sleep in a negligee, just to see if my subconscious was less likely to parade around the apartment in lace and silk.

I peeked at him and caught him watching me. Andreas's eyes dropped and he straightened his posture, folding his hands on top of the throw pillow. His cheeks, for the record, had still not faded back to their baseline hue. If anything, they'd gone from pink to red.

That hyperawareness buzzed beneath my skin and twisted in my stomach, making me speak before I'd vetted the words. "Sorry again for, uh, invading your personal space. We should put a bell around my neck so you can hear me coming," I joked, and then internally reprimanded myself for the stupid joke.

I hated this. I was second-guessing everything coming out of my mouth. Horseback riding for six hours wasn't the worst, this was *the worst!*

He shook his head. "There is no need to apologize. The last thing I want is for you to feel like you must restrict yourself here. This is your home, too. Please." Andreas hesitated, as though thinking through his words carefully before saying them, then continued. "I know this situation with my brothers is extremely stressful. If this is how your brain chooses to cope, I am glad to be useful."

My eyebrows bounced upward. "Useful?" Goodness. I could think of a few ways to use him, but none of those seemed at all appropriate.

He looked me in the eye, then away, then back. "I want to be useful," he said quietly.

He had no idea where my dirty brain was going, so I asked, "You're telling me you're okay being my personal mattress?" which was the cleanest way I could think of describing my current thoughts. And I made sure to flavor the words with all the incredulity I felt.

There was a beat during which I honestly had no idea what he was thinking and my heart hammered in my chest. He wasn't looking at me anymore. He stared forward, his face in profile.

My whole body tensed because, *Is he thinking what I'm thinking? Is he going to propose a friends-with-benefits situation?* I held my breath, waiting. Waiting. And hoping.

Eventually, Andreas's usual mask of bored indifference slipped over his features.

So . . . that's a no.

I was suddenly, viscerally aware of how close we still were on the couch. The entire living room, for all its square footage, shrank to a four-foot radius of us. Silence became uncomfortable—for me—so I scrambled to redirect the conversation.

"Uh, so, on a scale of one to ten, how awful was this for you?" Hopefully he would accept my olive branch of self-deprecation. I didn't want to live in an apartment with someone who felt awkward around me. I didn't want to become Andreas's Dr. James Nieminen.

Andreas glanced at me, apparently considering the question with the seriousness of someone reviewing an offer of employment. "Zero," he finally said. And when my mouth parted and my forehead wrinkled with genuine confusion— because how could that be?—he added, "It is only embarrassing if you are uncomfortable. I am not, was not, uncomfortable."

Staring at him and his serene, dispassionate expression, I realized that he was totally unaffected by what had happened last night and this morning. Maybe women fell asleep on his lap all the time. This was old hat for him. An everyday occurrence.

Okay then.

I will say, his honesty was disarming. It made me want to ask a hundred follow-up questions. Likely, those follow-up questions would reveal too much. Being me, I defaulted to banter instead.

"Well, if you're a zero, then I'm a zero. You're a really good mattress. Like, ten out of ten, would recommend."

Holding my gaze, he said, "Glad to be of service," pitching his voice deeper, quieter than it had been up to now.

What's this? What's he doing? What's that mean?

Ugh! This really was the worst. Did liking a person mean I would always be this frazzled and on edge around them? Second-guessing and picking apart their words? I hated this.

Our gazes remained locked for a full five to ten seconds before the tension grew so thick—*again*—it spurred me to stand. Ignoring the renewed protests of my thighs and hips, I made a show of stretching, lifting my arms over my head and faking a theatric and very loud yawn until I felt certain my legs would carry me back to my room. Now I just needed to—

Somewhere down the hallway, the sound of my phone ringing saved me from coming up with a clever post-cuddle exit line.

"Let me get that!" I darted around the couch, nearly kneeing the coffee table in my haste to leave, and jogged toward the bedroom where I should've been sleeping last night. I wouldn't usually rush to answer a call, especially not this early in the morning, but fleeing the scene of my own subconscious crime was a top priority.

When I finally found my phone, it was on the nightstand in the bedroom, still plugged into the charger. I answered with a breathless "Hello?"

"Sam! It's Diya!" Her voice was bright and familiar and a welcome interruption.

"Diya! Hi! HOW ARE YOU?" For the second time that morning, I cringed. This time at the unintentional loudness and breathlessness of my voice.

"Are you—did I interrupt you running a marathon?" She dropped her voice to ask, "Or were you in the middle of something else?" The suggestion in her tone was unmistakable.

"Neither," I said flatly, hating that I felt myself blush. I wasn't a blusher. I never blushed! "Just sprinted across the apartment for the phone. What's up?"

"How are you? How are things? How's engaged life?"

"It's all good. I'm just . . . adjusting." For some reason, Henrik's enraged face from last night picked that moment flash behind my vision. *Psycho.*

"Are you sure you don't want to come back? Pretty sure I heard rats unionizing in the walls yesterday. Sorry you missed it."

I snorted a laugh, which made her laugh. The sound of her laughter grounded me, made the world feel less sharp. In the background, I heard the shouts of hospital workers and the low rumble of what must have been an intercom. She was at the hospital, which meant she'd carved out time for this call in the middle of her insane day. It must've been important.

"Did I leave something behind? Or, why are you calling? Is everything okay?"

"Everything is fine! And, as far as I could tell yesterday, you didn't leave any trace of yourself behind. It's like you were never there. So weird." Her voice trailed off on this last part and I heard her take a deep breath before she continued, "So, the reason I'm calling is because the girls and I want to invite you and Andreas out to dinner Wednesday night. Everyone is still in town. It would just be the four of us. Well, five, including Andreas."

I kicked one of my still-full bins that was parked in the middle of the room. "Dinner Wednesday night with all the ladies? Uh, let me check with Andreas to see if he's free."

From somewhere in the apartment Andreas called out, "I am free Wednesday night for dinner with your friends."

Before I could say anything, Diya said, "Oh! That's great!" Obviously she'd heard him. "We'll eat at Kendra's restaurant. Nakita said that Andreas is vegan?"

I had to clear my throat before I could speak. "Uh, yeah. He is." Kendra worked at a vegan barbecue restaurant not far from Andreas's. "Okay, fine. What time Wednesday?"

After we'd finalized the details (7:00 PM, Smokin Greens BBQ, New York casual) Diya said, "I have to tell you something funny. I was talking to my grandpa and telling him about you and Andreas, and—"

"Wait." I stood up straighter. "You were talking to your grandpa about me?" Did people have those types of relationships with their grandfathers?

I felt a pang of longing for my own grandfather, but then immediately shoved it away.

"Yes. Anyway, just listen. So, I told him that you had gotten engaged to some chess guy, and he asked for his name, and so I told him, and he knew who Andreas was! Isn't that crazy? But then he reminded me that in his hometown, there are a ton of chess grand masters. It's a big deal there, as it should be honestly. But I'd forgotten and I love that. So, my grandpa says congratulations."

"Huh." I felt a sliver of unease at the realization that my friends were unknowingly spreading this lie I'd started. Was I making a liar out of Diya if she didn't know she was lying?

"Are you still there? Sam?"

"Yes! Sorry. Yes. I'm still here. Please, uh, tell him thank you for me." It was all I could think to say. I'd known and accepted that I would have to lie to my friends, but my stomach felt a little queasy at how large this lie had already ballooned.

After promises to see each other soon, we hung up. Lowering my phone, I thumbed through my notifications and saw that I'd missed two texts from Kaitlyn.

Kaitlyn: You're coming over for Thanksgiving, right? I'm counting on you to bring cranberry sauce and mashed potatoes.

Kaitlyn: And I saw a photo of you with your "fiancé" online. I guess that's happening???? Martin and I want you to bring Andreas if he's up for it. Be prepared to spill tea.

The first text made me smile. The second one made me break into a cold sweat. Not only did Diya's sweet grandfather now think we were engaged, my fake engagement was the subject of online speculation too. And possibly a meme. I'd never been memed before. *But Andreas has.*

This reminder did not improve my mood.

Uncertain how to respond to Kaitlyn, I placed my phone back on the nightstand and surveyed the damage in the bedroom. My sleepwalking self had been busy last night. The bin I'd just kicked was one of four that I'd stacked against the door, a barricade I vaguely remembered constructing before going to bed in order to keep myself from leaving the room. All four bins were now strewn around the room, the door wide open. My suitcase, which I'd propped as an additional security measure, now sat upright and open, clothes spilling out.

I was impressed. My subconscious had the strength and determination of a bison. For the record, I would take any opportunity to compare myself to a bison. Theirs is the most delicious of the red meats. Also, they are freaking majestic animals. So much more majestic than a cow or a yak.

While I ranked the majesticness of hooved animals, Andreas appeared in the doorway. He now wore a plush, navy blue bathrobe that looked like he'd stolen it from a five-star hotel, and man-slippers. You know, the tan ones with a wool-lined interior.

He peered around at the chaos in my room, then at me while I worked to quell the fluttering in my stomach. That same stupid electric hyperawareness returned.

"You really did try to barricade yourself last night." His voice held unadulterated awe.

"I said I did." Not knowing what to do with my hands, I set them on my hips. "I honestly don't want to keep bothering you."

Ignoring this, he asked, "Where is dinner on Wednesday? I need to let the security team know."

"A place called Smokin Greens BBQ. My old roommate Kendra works there. It's vegan barbecue. Even the sauces. But you really don't have to—"

"Is it the one with the meditating, neon dinosaur in the window?"

"Yes." I sucked in a deep breath, wishing this awareness of him would disappear just as quickly as it had appeared. "Have you been there?"

"I have not. But Elio swears it is the best vegan barbecue in New York. Possibly the world."

"Good to know. I guess we'll find out on Wednesday."

He nodded but didn't leave. Instead, he lingered, surveying the wreckage of my barricade.

I tried to ignore the butterflies that hatched in my stomach as I watched him. He looked both cute and sexy standing there in my doorway. The bathrobe giving him both a boyish and grandpa-ish aura, which shouldn't have been both adorable and sexy but—God help me—it totally was.

"Do you need something else?" I asked, knowing it was best that he leave so I could quash the butterflies.

"Thursday is Thanksgiving. Do you have plans?"

I hesitated. Did I want Andreas to meet Kaitlyn? She and baby Joey were the two most important people in my life. Did I want Andreas to know them?

When I said nothing, Andreas prompted, "Your grandfather is still alive, is he not? Do you—"

"No. We don't speak." I turned my back on Andreas. The butterflies had evaporated at the mention of my grandfather.

My mom's dad was the only biological family left to me, which had certainly simplified my decision to allow the adoption with Andreas and therefore cut all legal ties with my biological family.

He still reached out to me every so often, but I just couldn't bring myself to return his calls and letters. He'd left my grandmother three years after my mom died, the month she was diagnosed with cancer. I simply couldn't forgive him for that.

"I see," he said from someplace behind me. "So, you have no plans? If so, I thought—"

"Uh, I do have plans. I usually spend holidays with my best—um, my roommate from college." Rubbing my forehead, I spun in a circle, looking for something to do, and nearly tripped over one of the bins I'd strewn about the room while sleepwalking.

"You two are close?"

Picking up the bin I'd almost tripped over, I placed it against the wall and then moved to pick up another bin to place on top of it. "We are close. Really close."

Stop overthinking and just tell him. Invite him. Have him come if he wants. It'll be worth it to watch Andreas beat Martin at chess.

"And you should come!" I straightened, suddenly decided. There was no reason for Andreas not to come. He'd been invited. Plus, watching Martin get absolutely destroyed at chess would pay the mortgage on any regret I might feel later.

Andreas had placed his hands in the pockets of his bathrobe, his usual mask of detachment in place. "I do not wish to—"

"She invited you, actually." I crossed my arms, like the matter was settled.

A crack appeared in his façade of indifference, his eyes widening just a tad. "She did? Your friend did?"

"She did. She saw a photo of us online, from the night of our engagement, and she said you're invited. So"—I lifted my hands in the air and then let them drop against my thighs—"you're invited. And if you don't have any plans, we'll go. But I have to make cranberry sauce and mashed potatoes."

He nodded, still inspecting me. "Then I am very happy to come with you, if you do not mind."

I felt warmth crawl up my neck. "I don't mind at all. And they have a cute baby."

His mouth twitched at the corners, his eyes growing again for a split second. "They have a baby?"

Inwardly, I groaned. Outwardly, I asked, "Don't tell me, you like babies?"

He looked abashed, scratching the back of his neck. "Of course. Who doesn't like babies?"

The butterflies re-alived themselves and performed a synchronized routine, then collapsed in a heap. For reasons I didn't want to examine, the fact that Andreas liked babies made me feel gooey and hot in equal measure.

A slightly hysterical laugh tumbled out of me at the whiplash of my own emotions. Enough. I needed to get ready for work. That wasn't an excuse.

"Okay, I have to clean this up and then get to work. Out." I gathered an armful of clothes from the floor in front of my suitcase and gestured toward the door.

He didn't move. Instead, he reached forward and caught my hand, pulling me up as I tried to shoo him away, his grip surprisingly gentle. I felt immobilized by the shock of warmth traveling up my arm at the contact.

"Do not worry about the bins. I will take care of it. But, what I wanted to tell you, I should let you know, I have to leave Thursday night for a trip."

This news broke through the haze. "What? Why?"

He still held my hand, his thumb tracing a slow arc across my knuckles. "I have a tournament in London. I have to fly out a few days before it starts to acclimate to the time change."

"Oh." I was surprised at how disappointed I sounded. My chest felt empty but tight, airy but hot.

"I will be gone just over two weeks."

The disappointment dug in deeper. "That's . . . obviously fine. Thanks for letting me know."

His gaze moved over my face and he licked his lips before asking, "Do you want to come?"

The question blindsided me. For a moment, I imagined myself in London— watching Andreas play chess, wandering city streets, eating scones and clotted cream, and perhaps wearing a bowler hat for some reason. The fantasy was so vivid I almost said yes.

But then reality swooped in. "I can't. I have too much to do, especially with my switch in PIs." With as much gentleness as he'd reached for me, I pulled my hand away. Going to London and playing house with Andreas wasn't an option.

Andreas leaned against the doorjamb, his features giving away none of his thoughts. "PIs?"

"Principal investigators," I explained. "Remember when Tobias came to my office and threatened to get me expelled from my program? Well, it appears he called in a favor and I had to switch PIs because Dr. Hauser—my original PI—her funding was frozen."

His face darkened and his eyes lost focus, presumably his thoughts turning inward. "I see . . ."

I shrugged and went to my suitcase, rifling through it for pants. "My new PI is —well, he seems okay now."

"This new PI, does he treat you well?" Andreas's voice sounded careful.

"Since I've been reporting to him, he's been fine." I tried to come across as confident, as if the whole thing was an upgrade and not a shakedown.

I felt Andreas's eyes on me as I gathered my stuff, then he said, "You have to tell me if he mistreats you."

I chuckled. "Why? What will you do? Challenge him to a duel?"

"Something like that," he said, his eyes flicking away. And his expression was strange.

Peering at him, I decided this was weird. He was suddenly acting weird. That statement from him, it was weird. He almost sounded like Tobias. And what could he do in reality if my PI was a dickhead? Stare at him with those judgy little eyes?

Crossing to the bed, clothes in hand, I said, "Okay. I'm getting dressed. So, unless you want a free show, close the door."

His eyebrows shot up abruptly—comically, actually—and he grabbed for the doorknob, stuttering, "Of course—sorry. I apolo—sorry, yes. Sorry."

As soon as the door clicked shut, I shook my head at his gentlemanly bashfulness. My opinion of him improved by at least twelve points this morning. Seriously, he needed to start spouting ignoramus opinions about the polio vaccine. And soon.

Just as I'd pulled off my sleep shirt, Andreas's voice drifted back from beyond the door. "Can I make you something for breakfast?"

My spine stiffening with the knowledge that he was on the other side of the door and I was both shirtless and braless, I called back, "I'll have whatever you're having. I'm not picky."

A pause. "I bought you eggs. How do you like your eggs?"

Distracted, I rushed to put on a bra. "I don't care. Whatever is easiest."

A longer pause. "But you must have a preference. Scrambled? I can make an omelet."

Glancing up at the ceiling, I called back, "I honestly have no preference."

It was quiet for a moment, then he said, "Do you like omelets?"

Why was he was so fixated on eggs? "Sure. I like omelets. But that seems like a lot of work. Hard-boiled is fine."

"I'll make you a spinach, tomato, and goat cheese omelet," he said, as though that were a perfectly reasonable way to start the day.

My mouth immediately watered. I had to swallow before responding, "Thank you. That sounds good."

I heard his footsteps pad away and I clutched my forehead in my hands. How did he know Florentine omelets were my favorite omelet? There was no way he could know that. It must've been a lucky guess.

Shaking out my limbs of nerves, I dressed, pulled my hair into a ponytail, and decided not to think about how I'd sleepwalked into Andreas's lap last night, or how I'd slept in his bed the night before, or how his cheeks had turned pink both times, or how I felt when he held my hand just now and his thumb had rubbed over the back of my knuckles so tenderly.

I decided I would save all these fluttery feelings and this hyperawareness for later. Much later. After I inherited Genetix.

And hopefully by then, it would all have stopped for good.

[5]

PUBERTY

Samantha

I will say this about the world's friendliest bodyguard-slash-chauffeur, Tara knew when to give a girl space.

I sat in the back seat of the black Mercedes, hands clutched to my messenger bag, fighting the urge to ask Tara to just circle the block another twenty times. People streamed by on the sidewalk, many in heavy jackets, some in business casual, one or two in actual evening wear because New York is chaos, but all of them seemed to move with a purpose that I envied.

My former roommates were inside, likely with Andreas. Adjusting the engagement ring on my finger, I took a deep, bracing breath.

Unwittingly, I'd begun playing a perverse game of chicken over the last two days, where I tried to see how long I could go without making a total ass of myself in front of a man who had, for some reason, decided to be tremendously sweet to me. I'd constructed a meticulous schedule where our time at the apartment rarely overlapped, save for a critical intersection at breakfast. He was awake before me no matter what time I got up, had made himself some kind of perfectly balanced vegan meal, and was waiting for us to eat together—having made me an insanely delicious non-vegan breakfast—by the time I stumbled out of the hallway.

It was, objectively, the best living arrangement I'd ever had. Even better than rooming with Kaitlyn. She never cooked.

It also didn't hurt that, true to my planned experiment and hypothesis, I'd decided to dress for bed in a scandalous pink negligee on both Monday and Tuesday nights, just to see if my subconscious would be too uncomfortable to sleepwalk if it meant parading around the apartment in see-through lace. And, miracle of miracles, the system worked. Two nights, zero sleepwalking. My subconscious was more modest than me. Not necessarily a high bar, but still. Go figure.

Anyway. Tonight was the first time I'd see Andreas in public since his hug on the sidewalk after the incident with Henrik. It was also the first time I would see him since the Monday morning sleep-lap-straddle-cuddle encounter. There would be friends, food, and—God help me—conversation.

Checking the time, I realized I was now officially two minutes late.

I exhaled, gripping my bag, and pushed out into the cold. "Thank you, Tara," I said.

She gave me a little wave. I shut the door behind me. The Mercedes didn't pull away from the sidewalk. I knew she wouldn't leave until I was inside. I wondered if she'd already texted Andreas that I was here.

The wind had that metallic edge peculiar to late November, the kind that promises snow soon. Smokin Greens BBQ sat on the corner, its windows glowing warm and amber in the dusk, and every wall inside was papered over with concert posters and flyers for local events. In the window, a neon sign in the shape of a brontosaurus advertised plant-based brisket, which I found delightful.

Opening the door, I found the inside air thick with the scent of hickory smoke and something tangy—possibly kimchi?—and the place was so full that the noise of conversation pressed against my ears even before I crossed the threshold. Five tables, all packed. At table two, directly under a painting of a stegosaurus grilling presumably tofu kabobs, sat the entire population of my former apartment: Kendra, Diya, Nakita, and, in the seat with the best view of the door, Andreas.

None of them saw me come in.

Instead, all four were hunched over the table in a configuration that suggested a classified briefing, heads bent, shoulders overlapping. It was Diya who drew my focus first, because her hands were in motion, gesturing wildly with a fork in one and a napkin in the other, and some of her words carried over the hubbub of the room.

". . . skin dryness," she was saying, "you really can't go wrong with a retinol product as long as you're also using glycol and a moisturizer with vitamin C during the day. Oh! Don't forget the SPF."

The others listened like acolytes at the feet of a particularly attractive and knowledgeable prophet. Andreas had his phone out, thumb poised above the screen. Kendra and Nakita nodded with the seriousness usually reserved for our discussions about corruption in the federal government or campaign finance reform.

I stood there, momentarily invisible, and took the opportunity to stare at Andreas for a full, guiltless ten seconds. He wore a charcoal turtleneck and what looked like slate-colored slacks, hair artfully messy, and a watch I would bet my student loan balance was handmade by horological monks in the Alps or something like that. His posture was impeccable even though he leaned forward, and the line of his jaw was relaxed.

He was, infuriatingly, still extremely attractive. I sighed. I kept wishing that the next time I saw him, I would feel less mesmerized by him. It hadn't happened yet. So, I let myself enjoy ogling him for one more beat of my heart, then steeled my nerves and approached.

Halfway there, Nakita said something like, "And I think gardenia, because I have a hand lotion that's gardenia and she said it smelled really good every time I wore it."

Andreas, still typing, eyes on his phone, asked, "Was it a white floral, or more powdery?" There was the tiniest sliver of an accent in his voice tonight, which I only noticed because I was hyper-tuned to every aspect of his existence like an idiot.

Drawing to a stop beside the table, I cleared my throat and said, "Hey. What's going on?"

Four heads whipped around in unison, Nakita's braids swinging so forcefully they nearly knocked over the water carafe. For a half second, no one spoke, then all three girls shouted my name and surged to their feet.

There was a sequence of hugs. Nakita first with a squeal, then Kendra with a tight squeeze, and finally Diya who seemed to pat me down as though searching for injuries. Acutely aware of him, I felt and saw Andreas watch the whole rigamarole, eyes crinkling at the edges, waiting until the others finished before moving forward and drawing me in for a quieter, longer embrace.

"Hi," he said, and, without warning, took my hand and kissed it. Not a joke, not a flourish, just the faintest touch of lips against the back of my hand, then a gentle pull to lead me into the seat next to his.

I could not feel my knees.

Once seated, I tucked my legs under the table and placed both hands in my lap, partly to hide the trembling and partly because they were cold. Andreas reached over and grabbed my hand under the table, holding it between both of his as though to warm it.

My insides were rioting, my chest too tight, my brain in disorder at his closeness and casual touch. He likely had no idea what he did to me. Forcing myself to look around the table at my friends, and not him, I did my best to act normal, whatever that was.

For their part, my former roommates all grinned at me like they were lottery winners.

"Sorry I'm late," I managed. "How long have you been here?"

Nakita flapped a hand. "Please. You're right on time. Kendra and Diya only got here, like, ten minutes before you. Andreas was the early bird."

Diya, eyes sharp as ever, cut in, "How's work? How's the new PI? Do you like him? Do you want us to kill him?"

I laughed. It sounded weak.

"She's had enough excitement," Kendra said, saving me from answering. "Let's not give her a reason not to return our calls." She smiled at me, then leaned over to squeeze my arm. "It's so good to see you, babe. You look incredible."

"Agreed," Nakita said. "Is that a new lipstick? It looks bomb on you. You have to tell me the shade."

I glanced at Andreas. He simply watched us, still holding my hand under the table, a tiny smile on his mouth. I willed my heart to slow down. My neck felt hot.

"Uh, yeah. I guess I'm wearing makeup," I said. "Decided to dress up for the occasion."

"How's engaged life?" Diya asked, a glint in her eye.

I forced another laugh. "Exactly the same as unengaged life, only with more paperwork."

Andreas, without missing a beat, said, "You forgot about the breakfasts."

Nakita leaned farther forward. "Wait. He makes you breakfast? Every morning?"

I opened my mouth to respond but my brain couldn't immediately think of a single thing to say. An awkward pause passed. But before I could decide what to say, Kendra spoke. "I hope you guys are hungry. I already put in an order for the barbecue platter. But if you want something else, the cornbread is life-changing."

"I have never had vegan barbecue before," Andreas said, his tone dry and polite and gentlemanly. "Thank you for inviting me. I am looking forward to it."

"It's legitimately the best," Kendra said. "Every sauce is made from scratch and the owner is a vegan pitmaster legend."

"Andreas, I have a question." Diya took a sip from her glass. "What is your accent? You're from Norway, right? Is that Norwegian?"

Andreas made a short sound of consideration, tilting his head slightly to one side. "It is not. I am not really from anywhere, honestly. My mother was from Italy, and my—uh—father"—Andreas darted a glance at me, then back to Diya—"was from Norway. But I spoke English early, and many of my chess coaches from a very young age were Russian. We communicated in English and Russian. I think I must have picked up some of their pronunciation of certain words, as I most often get asked if I am Russian. Do I sound Russian?"

All three of my roommates shook their heads, with Diya speaking for the group. "No. Well, maybe. But sometimes you don't have an accent at all and sound like you're from the US. And sometimes I can hear the Italian, I think. I was just curious. I hope I didn't offend."

"Not at all," he said graciously. "I am a bit all over the place, yes?"

"What language do you think in?" Nakita placed an elbow on the table and set her chin in her palm.

I listened in as they asked Andreas questions about himself, attempting to slot myself back into the group's rhythm, but finding it hard with Andreas's hands still wrapped around mine. My brain kept snagging on where our skin touched, like a sweater catching on a nail, pulling me out of the flow. The warmth, the steadiness, the way his thumb traced idle, absentminded circles on my skin.

During a lull in conversation, and trying to snap out of my own awkwardness, I said, "So, what were you all talking about before I came in? I caught something about retinol?"

"Nothing really. Skin routines, that kind of thing." Kendra's eyes darted to Andreas's then away as she reached for the pitcher of water. She topped off everyone's cup, then held her glass up. "A toast! To Sam and Andreas. May your wedding be a destination one, preferably someplace warm."

Diya rolled her eyes, but Nakita said, "Here, here! And may we all be invited."

I joined in on the toast and sipped my water to buy time. I needed to recalibrate. This was my first dinner with a fake fiancé—a fake fiancé I had very real feelings for—and I should've come up with a game plan before walking in the door.

As the first round of vegan barbecue and sides arrived, the table conversation shifted to plans for Thanksgiving. Kendra was working a double at the restaurant; Nakita was doing a Turkey Trot in Queens then spending the day with her family; Diya had a rare Thanksgiving off and planned to spend half of it sleeping in and the other half at her brother's place in Connecticut.

Catching me off guard as the conversation turned to strange Thanksgiving side dishes, Andreas leaned close, voice low in my ear, and said, "You look beautiful tonight."

I choked on a bite of black bean brisket, which prompted Nakita to thump me on the back with enough force to realign my vertebrae. "Are you okay?" she asked, eyes wide.

I coughed, nodded, and gave Andreas a side-eye that I hoped would convey confusion. Why would he say that? They couldn't hear him. He could've whispered anything, nonsense, the recipe for hollandaise sauce. Why tell me I look beautiful?

Wait. Were we being recorded? Was there a bug at the table?

Meanwhile, Diya grinned, probably at the way my cheeks had just turned very, very red. "Okay, but you two are too cute. I mean, look at you. Sharing plates. Whispering. Kendra, are you seeing this?"

Kendra made a show of dabbing her eyes with a napkin. "It's true. I was skeptical at first, but the chemistry is undeniable."

Andreas didn't react, but I could feel his posture relax, like he was happy to let the girls run wild with the narrative. *Maybe we are being recorded right now.*

Surreptitiously, I glanced around at the other patrons, looking for someone who could be Tobias's spy.

After finding no one suspicious, it occurred to me belatedly that I was the only one not playing along. I was too busy second-guessing myself, filtering every word before I spoke it, afraid to say anything that might make me look foolish in front of Andreas.

WHO AM I RIGHT NOW?

Before I could answer this question, Andreas released my hand to pull out his phone. He frowned at the screen flashing with a number. "Sorry, I need to get this. It is about my trip tomorrow. I will be right back." Before leaving, he placed his hand on my shoulder and gave it a gentle squeeze, a gesture so sweet and old-fashioned I barely resisted the urge to follow him like a lost puppy.

As soon as he was out of earshot, Nakita leaned in and said, "Girl. I don't know what kind of magic spell you put on him, but I'm obsessed."

Diya chimed in, "Seriously, Sam. I've never seen you like this. So quiet, and calm."

Kendra snorted. "That's not calm. That's what it looks like when you try really hard to be normal for an hour."

"Shut up," I said, but I was laughing because she was right, and it felt good to laugh and be known.

Nakita tapped her glass. "I love the way he looks at you. It's like you're the only person in the room."

I rolled my eyes. "He looks at everyone that way. It's just the Italian intensity from his mom's side."

"No," said Diya, "it's the 'in love with you' intensity. Don't try to science this one, Sam."

I had no response to this, so I just drained my water.

The table fell quiet for a moment, and I felt, for the first time since I walked in, genuinely happy to be here, even if my entire romantic life was an elaborate legal ploy and I was lying to them. I hoped they forgave me, when it all became public.

Kendra nudged me. "You look like you need a drink. You want a drink? I can get you a shot of whiskey if you want."

"Yes," I said, too loudly, "please."

She flagged down the server, who took my order of a double without judgment.

When Andreas returned, he slid back into the seat next to mine and smiled at the group. "What did I miss?"

"We're drinking," said Nakita, winking at me. "Whiskey. Want one?"

He looked at me, eyebrow raised. "You sure?"

I pressed my lips together in a smile. "Positive," I said, then under my breath I added, "I think I need it."

[6]

REPRODUCTIVE AGING

Samantha

Two hours after the first alcoholic beverages went down, the world had softened around the edges, the way it does after not enough sleep. Kendra's boyfriend, whose name I kept forgetting and replacing with "Keith" because I was convinced he looked like a Keith, had arrived about an hour ago with his work friends, and they brought reinforcements in the form of new energy and conversation.

By 9:00 PM, we'd annexed three-quarters of Smokin Greens and the party had metastasized from a catch-up dinner to a legitimate, full-scale celebration of everything that was and ever would be worth celebrating. Friendship, promotions, graduations, vegan brisket, selling a boat, good hair days, weddings, babies, vacations, and tofurkey that actually tasted like turkey.

I was more than tipsy, past the humming, happy phase and floating on that upper stratosphere where time is an accordion and entire conversations disappear into the memory foam of your brain before they even finish. I knew I was beyond tipsy because every time I blinked, the restaurant shifted a few centimeters to the left. I also knew I was past tipsy because I'd allowed myself to slouch sideways and press my temple against Andreas's shoulder. His arm was around me, holding me to him. His other hand had laced with mine and was resting on my lap. I cradled our joined fingers with my free hand and caressed the bones of his like I was sculpting them.

205

Kendra and Nakita had long since abandoned our table in favor of the big round one, and Keith and his army of software developer clones (I think one of them was literally named Clive) filled in the remaining seats. Diya, ever the MVP of social events, was alternating between dispensing rapid-fire medical trivia ("Yes, you can die from eating too many carrots, but only if you're a rabbit") and aggressively setting up rounds of shots. Andreas, to my enduring amazement, took it all in stride. He seemed utterly unbothered by the chaos, never once glancing at the time, or at his phone, or at the door. Instead, he fielded questions, laughed at jokes, and every once in a while, when the noise level dipped, he'd turn to me and whisper some observation that made me want to go home with him and never come back out.

But that would never happen, because we weren't a real couple even though we played one on TV.

Also, he smelled unfairly good tonight. A new cologne, something expensive and alive, cedar and citrus. His hand in mine felt solid and generous and warm. I found myself repeatedly stroking his knuckles with my thumb, fascinated by the structure of them. Part of my brain was narrating a National Geographic episode: "Observe, the majestic male, perfectly evolved for the manipulation of chess pieces and, apparently, the hearts of emotionally unavailable women."

I tried to listen to the conversations at the table, but my attention kept circling back to the reality of my body, of how good it felt to be leaning against his chest and torso, and how I didn't want to escape my own skin. I was so at home in this moment, I would've signed a lease.

The group dynamic was better than I could have hoped. My friends, for all their varied credentials, were softies at heart and clearly delighted to have Andreas among them. Every time Nakita made a joke, he'd tilt his head and smile, the ghost of a dimple appearing at the edge of his mouth. When Diya, emboldened by her third vodka soda, challenged him to a game of speed chess using only soy sauce bottles and ketchup packets as pieces, he demurred with gentle grace. Kendra, ever the ringleader, decided Andreas should be in charge of the music for the table, which led to him requesting (with dry, deadpan conviction) the entirety of *ABBA Gold* as the only acceptable playlist for the rest of the night.

It was, by any metric, a flawless integration. Too bad it wasn't real.

And yet, through the haze of alcohol and noise, I could not stop thinking about the way his hand fit in mine. About how easy it would be to tip my face up and kiss him in front of all these people, and how absolutely zero percent of my pickled brain thought it would be a bad idea.

And, on that note, why was sober me so resistant to the idea of a real relationship? Why did every instinct in my sober body scream at me to run when all I wanted to do right now was stay, and maybe even—God forbid—let myself love someone for more than three consecutive business days? These were the kinds of philosophical queries you should not, under any circumstances, attempt to answer while three whiskeys deep and riding a contact high from your childhood turned adult crush. And yet, my brain would not stop circling the drain.

I kept thinking: If I don't tell him how I feel, if I don't propose right here at this table to make it all real, then what the fuck am I even doing? But then another voice, the one that was allegedly in charge, reminded me that I was drunk, that nothing I said tonight would survive the morning, and that this was precisely the kind of disaster my psychiatrist had warned me about. Emotional decisions under the influence of dopamine and alcohol were not, generally, sound or strategic.

So, I decided to wait. I would wait until tomorrow, or at least until I sobered up, to address the growing suspicion that I wanted, more than anything, to make this the last first date of my life.

At one point, Diya and Andreas got deep into conversation, just the two of them, and their voices rose above the clamor, a duet of quick, bright syllables and the occasional cross talk about chess and gene sequencing and the merits of kimchi. It was only when Diya leaned forward, her eyes lit with what seemed to be wild curiosity, that I tuned in fully.

"Half the chess grand masters in India come from Tamil Nadu. My uncle says it's the water, or the weather, or maybe the local Wi-Fi," Diya said, gesticulating with her dessert spoon.

Andreas nodded with a small, admiring smile. "Tamil Nadu is beautiful. I have visited many times for tournaments in Chennai. They study and make it their life, and they are very good at identifying and fostering talent. Your uncle is incorrect, however. It is not something in the water. But perhaps it is the food?" His tone had turned teasing. "The food is what really made an impression on me."

Diya grinned. "I'll have to take you to my aunt's next time she's in town. She makes a dosa that'll ruin you for life." Then, abruptly, her phone buzzed on the table. She checked it and her face changed; she excused herself with a quick apology, and slipped away to take the call.

With her gone, the table's conversation splintered into smaller groups, and I became aware that I was still, possibly for hours now, petting the back of Andreas's hand in my lap like it was a beloved pet.

I chanced a glance at his face. He watched the room with a serene detachment that made me wonder what was going on behind those eyes. Was he bored? Was he counting down the seconds until he could escape? Or was he as deliriously content as I was, just sitting here, being present, not needing to fill the air with words?

I couldn't tell. I'd never been able to read him well. But I wanted to. So, I squeezed his hand.

He looked down at me, and when our eyes met, he smiled in that slow, unreadable way. Then he leaned over and pressed a kiss to my forehead that made my heart spike with heat. It wasn't hurried, but not lazy, either. It was so out of nowhere, so gentle, that it fried my brain for a moment.

"How are you feeling?" he asked, his voice pitched for me and me alone.

I inhaled a shaky breath, registered the smell of him, and exhaled. "A little drunk."

He made a noise low in his throat, almost a laugh. "You had three whiskeys and a glass of wine."

"Yeah, yeah, yeah." I slouched even further, my cheek pressing into his sweater. "Don't let me drink anymore, please. I will do things I'll regret."

His arm tightened around my shoulders, just enough to let me know he'd heard. Then he kissed the top of my head again, sending my heart to my throat, and said, "Okay."

My eyes fluttered closed. I could've slept there, in the restaurant, if not for the crescendoing volume of the conversations around us and the small, persistent voice inside my head reminding me I needed to go to Kaitlyn's tomorrow, and that the next time I woke up, it would be Thanksgiving.

I felt the weight of his hand shift in mine, and then, slowly, he lifted my fingers to his lips and kissed the back of my hand. A simple, old-fashioned gesture, but when his mouth touched my skin, it sent a supernova up my arm and straight to my heart.

Opening my eyes, our gazes met again. This time he held my eyes, not letting me go even when my face went hot.

"Do you want to leave?" he asked, so quiet I almost missed it. "It is getting late, and we have your friends' Thanksgiving tomorrow."

I thought about it. I weighed the prospect of leaving this perfect, timeless, alcohol-glazed moment against the inevitability of waking up tomorrow. But if life had taught me one lesson, it was that all good things always, always, *always* came to an end.

"I think we should," I said, but didn't move to stand.

He nodded, then let go of my hand just long enough to help me up. He was so gentle, it felt like being picked up by a breeze. He pulled my coat from the back of my chair, helped me slide my hands through the armholes, and took a moment to button it for me while I stared at his mouth. His movements were slow and precise, almost ceremonial.

Andreas offered his arm, and I took it, which made everyone at the table pause and turn in our direction. Diya, who'd returned at some point and was now grinning, caught my eye and gave me a double thumbs-up. Kendra shouted, "Don't be a stranger!" and Nakita blew me a kiss. Or maybe she blew Andreas a kiss. Mostly probably, it was for both of us.

Andreas was the opposite of awkward as he made his excuses. So smooth. He thanked Kendra for inviting us, told Keith and Clive it had been a pleasure, and said something to Diya in what did not sound like English, Norwegian, or Italian. I didn't know what it meant, but Diya laughed so hard she nearly fell out of her chair. *What language was that?*

Diya must've caught my confused look, because she said, "It was Tamil. And I am very impressed."

So perfect, this guy.

Andreas escorted me to the door, pausing every so often to steady me when I started to veer off course. The outside air hit me like a wall, but instead of sobering me up, it made everything feel softer, like the world had been dunked in fabric softener. I clung to his arm and let him guide me down the steps and onto the sidewalk, where Tara waited beside the Mercedes, arms folded and eyes scanning the street.

"Hi, Tara. You're awesome," I slurred, but she just smiled and held the car door open for me.

Andreas ducked inside with me, his hand warm on my lower back as he helped me in. Once we were seated, he leaned across my lap and fastened my seat belt for me, the side of his face just inches from mine, the line of his jaw so crisp I wanted to bite it.

I closed my eyes as the car started to move, but then, because I was at that stage of drunkenness where all consequences are theoretical, I turned my face into his neck and planted a gentle, deliberate kiss just above his collar.

"Thank you," I whispered against the skin of his neck, "for being so great with my friends." It sounded embarrassing the moment it left my mouth, but I didn't care.

Andreas went perfectly still. I felt his pulse under my lips, fast and sharp.

When I pulled back and looked at him, his eyes were dark and focused, fixed on mine. He didn't move, not right away. Maybe he was waiting to see what I would do next. Or maybe I'd upset him?

But my head was heavy and my body was even heavier, so instead of parsing the tension between us, I let my cheek fall to his chest and curled up against him again, sighing in contentment.

After a moment, I frowned because he felt tense instead of yielding. I wiggled and shifted, demanding, "Loosen up! And let me cuddle your big, sexy body."

It sounded like he gave a short, stunned laugh. Or maybe he coughed. Then, after a pause, he wrapped his arm around my shoulders and held me as I fell asleep.

* * *

THANKSGIVING MORNING, I woke up in Andreas Kristiansen's bed.

Correction. I woke up alone, in Andreas's bed. Both better and, paradoxically, worse than waking up sprawled all over him.

Worse, because I remembered, with spectacular—albeit, hungover—clarity, being carried by the man himself last night. The brutally vivid memory of my own idiocy played in my head. He'd physically lifted me from the sidewalk, bridal carried me through the lobby, into the elevator, and into the apartment. We'd paused at the bathroom as he helped me brush my teeth—*ohmygodIamtheWORST!*—and then he'd deposited my limp, drunk body onto my mattress in my room. I remembered all of it.

What I didn't remember was walking in here and taking over his bed. Again.

I groaned, kicked the air under the sheet, and tried to will myself out of existence. Failing that, I rolled over and attempted to die face-down in the pillow. This plan was immediately complicated by the sharp, masculine scent of Andreas that lingered on the pillowcase. Cologne and soap, plus the unmistakable base note of "damn it, why does he get me so hot."

I tried to reconstruct all the events of last night. We'd gotten back from Smokin Greens at, what, ten? Before that, we'd left the restaurant together and in the car I'd kissed him. Not on the cheek, but on the side of his neck.

I shot upright in bed, clutching the duvet to my chest, horrified.

Oh no. Oh no no no!

I'd kissed his neck, right under his jaw, and then—I groaned again, this time louder—called his body "big" and "sexy" in the back seat of the Mercedes. That memory, clear as HD, was followed by a blank patch. I'd probably fallen asleep in the car.

I groaned again, reached for the nearest pillow, and started whacking myself on the forehead with it.

"Stop sleepwalking into his bed. Stop sleepwalking into his bed," I chanted, punctuating every word with a fresh pillow whack. "Never drink around Andreas again. Never drink again, period. Never speak again, actually. Monastic vow, effective immediately."

I took a breath and surveyed the damage. Still in the clothes from last night: jeans, T-shirt, and—oh, I must've gotten cold, because I wore his enormous gray sweater, which was now stretched out from where I'd probably tried to cocoon myself. My hair, which I could only see by its shadow on the white duvet, was a haywire mass. My mouth, at least, tasted like peppermint toothpaste. But also regret.

The only logical solution was to strip the bedding and do his laundry as an act of penance. Hauling myself out of bed, legs shaking, I gathered the sheets into a ball while chastising myself.

I wasn't used to being a hot mess. I was used to being the chick who had her shit together, who others asked for advice, who showed up on moving day to help no matter what, and who visited friends in the hospital. I'd baked seventeen freezer casseroles for Kaitlyn after baby Joey was born, for God's sake! I'd done their laundry for over a month and cleaned their guest bathroom with a toothbrush. I was CAPABLE!

But now, I didn't know this person who drank too much and kissed necks and sexually harassed their revenge partner. *Get yourself together, Sam!*

It was only after I maneuvered the comforter off the duvet cover that my thoughts quieted down enough for the sound of voices in the living room to reach my ears.

Specifically, the low rumble of Andreas's voice, and the soft, polite laughter of someone else over the phone. The odds that Andreas had heard me pillow thumping my own skull were very, very high.

Sigh.

Well, that's just freaking . . . great.

[7]

THE HUMAN SEXUAL RESPONSE

Samantha

Steeling myself and breathing through the bundle of nerves in my chest, I wrapped the sheets, comforter, and pillowcases into my arms, attempted to smooth my hair, and tiptoed out of Andreas's bedroom.

He sat at the big circular table in the living room, dressed in black lounge pants and a black T-shirt, hunched over a chessboard with a mug of coffee steaming beside his left hand. His phone was set next to the chessboard and was lit up with a call.

Andreas's eyes flicked up, pinning me in place for a long moment. His face didn't move, but his brow creased at the sight of me emerging from his room, arms full of bedding.

"I will call you later, Elio." Not waiting for a response, Andreas ended the call and leaned back in the chair, gaze moving down then up, giving me the sense he might be looking for injuries. "Good morning," he said.

"Uh. Good morning." Not recognizing the diffident quality in my own voice, I clutched the laundry tighter. "Sorry. I'm going to wash these."

Andreas continued to stare without giving any of his thoughts away, then returned his gaze to the board. "That is not necessary."

I didn't want to insist out loud. Actually, I didn't really want to talk to him at all since I felt so ashamed of myself. Thus, I swallowed and scuttled past to the laundry room. There, I deposited the sheets, started the load, and retreated to my

213

own bathroom, avoiding my reflection in the mirror. I knew I looked like a meth-addicted raccoon, okay? I didn't need to actually see the evidence.

After a mercifully hot shower, during which I practiced my apology over and over, I emerged from the hallway, dressed in leggings and an oversized hoodie.

Andreas was still in the same position, giving me the impression that he hadn't moved. But the fresh pot of pour-over coffee sitting on a tray in the center of the table along with a second mug dispelled this assumption. In the spot next to Andreas was also a plate enclosed with a metal cover, a glass of water, utensils, and a linen napkin.

Approaching on light feet, I sat across from Andreas and folded my hands on the table's surface, preparing my speech and starting with "I apologize for last night." My voice emerged steady and even. Good.

Andreas took a measured sip from his mug, then glanced at me over the rim. "For which part?"

I exhaled a long breath and couldn't help but duck my head. "You're right. I have a lot to apologize for."

He frowned. "I did not say that—"

"But I'm saying it." I gave him a tight smile. "So, here's a list. I'm sorry for the unexpected hug, the neck kiss, for speaking to you disrespectfully in the back of the Mercedes, for getting so sloppy drunk you had to carry me up here and help me brush my teeth. And I'm sorry—once again—for sleepwalking into your room and invading your personal space."

He huffed and glanced away, his jaw ticking. "Samantha—"

I lifted a hand since I wasn't finished. "I will not drink alcohol again during our cohabitation. And I promise not to cross any boundaries from now on, as much as it is in my power to not cross them. But, the sleepwalking . . ." I held his gaze for a moment, a sense of real helplessness building within me.

Giving into the urge, I pushed my fingers into my hair and then covered my face with my hands. "Since this is apparently a chronic problem," I said, voice still steady despite the volcano of frustration beneath, "maybe we should talk about—uh—changing the doorknob on that bedroom to lock from the outside?"

Andreas blinked at me, then set his mug down. "No. Locking you in your room is not safe."

"I think it's a better option than to keep ending up in your bed," I said, trying to make it sound a bit like a joke even though it was serious. "What if one night I get even more creative? Sleepwalk into the downstairs neighbor's hallway? End up in the lobby?"

He appeared to consider this, steepling his fingers. "I can lock us into the apartment at night with a code."

I shook my head. "We both know I'd find a way around that. My subconscious is a criminal mastermind."

He tilted his head. "What if only I had the code?"

I laughed, because I couldn't believe we were now plotting against my unconscious brain. "You're leaving tonight. Am I going to be locked in the apartment for two weeks?"

"It is programmable and accessible remotely, and could self-lock between certain hours, which will keep you inside the apartment at least. And I can arm or disarm it from my phone no matter where I am."

"Then let's put a similar lock on my bedroom door—"

He shook his head resolutely, obvious frustration making the line of his mouth flat and grim. "No. I do not want you trapped in your room, that is nonsense. What if you have to go to the bathroom?"

I leaned back in my seat and crossed my arms. He had me there.

"Are you sure you cannot come with me to London?"

"There's no way. And besides, what would that solve? Is it better for me to sleepwalk into your bed at a hotel than it is in this apartment?" Scratching at the uncomfortable heat crawling up my neck, I looked away.

We sat in silence, the only sound being the intermittent drip of the pour-over coffee.

At length, Andreas stood and grabbed the covered plate, napkin, and utensils sitting next to him. He carried them over and placed them in front of me, seeming to arrange them carefully. Once everything was neatly set, he lifted the metal cover, revealing eggs Benedict.

My mouth dropped open even as it watered. "You . . . is this for me?"

"It is supposed to be good for hangovers." He set the metal cover to the side, then leaned over the table to grab the water glass he'd left behind.

"How did you know eggs Benedict is one of my favorites?"

He shrugged. "Is it?"

"Thank you." I swallowed and picked up the utensils. "This is very kind of you. You didn't need to, but I really appreciate it."

Andreas's movements stilled briefly, then he placed the water to the left of my plate. "No need to be so formal. I make you breakfast every day." An edge of annoyance had entered his voice.

I pressed my lips together to keep from saying something that might irritate him further. Given my wonky behavior and everything he'd put up with since I'd moved in, the man was basically a saint.

And here I was, a world-class succubus.

Andreas poured me a cup of coffee and set that next to the water glass while I stared at the plate. Then, with no dignity whatsoever, I dove in. The first yolk was perfectly runny, the sauce creamy and lemony, the muffin toasted to a golden brown. I made a small, involuntary moan-whimper of delight. "Ah. It's so good!" I forked and shoved another bite into my mouth.

"What time do we need to be at your friends' place? And should I prepare anything?" Andreas's questions sounded almost chipper.

The sudden change in his tone had me looking at him. He'd just poured himself more coffee and set down the pot. Gazing at me from across the table as he sat, the side of his mouth hitched, eyes warm.

I dabbed at my mouth with the napkin and waited to respond until I'd swallowed my bite, just barely refraining from moaning again. "We need to arrive around eleven and I've already made everything. The mashed potatoes and cranberry sauce are in the fridge. Again, thank you for the use of your kitchen."

"It is your kitchen, too."

"For the time being," I muttered under my breath. It was mostly a reminder to myself, which stung, but was necessary. Nothing about this was permanent.

He drank from his mug, watching me with that serene, analytical stare, eventually saying, "Since you cannot come to London, what if Tara slept here while I am gone? She could lock the exterior door to keep you from wandering, if you sleepwalk again." He made it all sound so reasonable, like we were discussing the logistics of traveling uptown rather than babysitting an adult woman while she slept.

"If Tara is up for it, then sure. I don't want to impose, but that's a good idea." Examining him, sensing that he seemed to be genuinely concerned for me, I decided to share something personal, hoping it would set his mind at ease. "Look, I did call my therapist. I have a virtual appointment with her on Monday. So, I'm working on addressing the root cause."

He nodded, seeming pleased to know this information, and added, "You should sleep in the main bedroom from now on. It is larger, and you—or, at least, the you who sleepwalks—prefer it."

I laughed, shaking my head and cutting into the second poached egg. "Sure, okay. That's very . . . generous of you." I wasn't sure if I would take him up on this offer. For obvious reasons, I preferred to sleep in my own bed.

Andreas mumbled something like, "It is not generosity," his attention on his coffee cup as he arranged it just so on the table.

I finished my breakfast while he fiddled with his chessboard. Once I drained the last of the coffee, I sat back, feeling marginally better about the day, if not the future. Glancing over at Andreas, I let myself watch him for a few moments, marveling at the intensity of his focused gaze, like perhaps he expected the chess pieces to shift squares if he so much as blinked.

Clearing my throat as a precursor to breaking the silence, I slowly stood and gathered my plate. "May I ask, are you playing against yourself?"

His eyes flickered to me then back to the board. "Replaying the Spassky–Fischer match."

I wasn't sure what that meant, so I made a mental note to look up "spasskyfisher," and carried my dishes to the kitchen. When I finished hand-washing them, seeing that Andreas had already cleaned up after making me breakfast, I wandered back into the living room. Still staring at the chessboard, Andreas rolled the black knight over his fingers, flipping it back and forth with his thumb.

I didn't want to interrupt his concentration, so I turned for the hallway, stopping short when he called out, "As I said on Monday, I am not bothered by you sleepwalking. The only thing I care about is that you are safe and comfortable."

There was something about the way he said it—no inflection, no humor, just absolute certainty—that made me want to believe him.

Fiddling with the sleeve of my hoodie, I faced him. "Andreas—"

He cut me off, dipping his chin and deepening his voice. "Do you recall when we were young? I would find any excuse to sleep with you. I slept in your bed most nights. Remember?"

I'm sure I looked confused, because what did that have to do with anything?

"Just consider this a repayment, if that will make you feel better," he said, biting his bottom lip while we locked eyes.

I tried to keep my thoughts from my face, which were mostly flavored by skepticism and bewilderment. The two situations weren't comparable. We'd been kids back then. He'd been seeking comfort from a friend. Everything between us had been innocent and platonic.

But now, we were adults. And my feelings for him? Well, let's just say, I'd be lying if I said my feelings for Andreas were innocent.

* * *

To say that Thanksgiving at Kaitlyn and Martin's was a circus would be an insult to circuses, which at least have OSHA standards they're supposed to adhere to. The only constant was the perpetual motion of baby Joey, who rotated from lap to lap like a hot potato with a self-destruct timer, pausing only to attempt suicide off the edge of the sofa or scream in protest when denied a third dinner roll. By the time we finished dessert, the entire apartment looked like an explosion in a bakery, with dollops of mashed potato welded to the hardwood, and what I prayed was gravy crusted into the tabletop.

Through it all, Andreas managed to monopolize Joey. I don't know how he did it. There were four adults and a baby in a palatial three-bedroom penthouse, but somehow Andreas spent the majority of the afternoon holding, soothing, or otherwise interacting with a seven-month-old as if he'd been training for it. He'd swing Joey with one hand while sipping tea with the other, bounce the baby on his knee as he and Kaitlyn discussed Italian composers (turns out, Andreas's mother was one of Kaitlyn's favorite composers), and when Kaitlyn needed to run to the bathroom, he wrangled Joey's diaper situation with a dexterity that suggested past-life experience as a neonatal nurse. The baby, for his part, gazed up at Andreas with starry-eyed worship, giggled when he made faces—oh my God, Andreas made so many adorable faces!—and fell asleep against his chest in a feat of trust I'd never seen Joey display toward anyone but Kaitlyn herself.

It was obscene. It was unfair. It was, on a molecular level, illegal to be that good with children while also being devastatingly attractive. My latent competency kink reared its ugly head and roared. The only saving grace was that Kaitlyn's husband, Martin, looked even more jealous than I was.

Right now, Joey was asleep in his crib. Andreas and Martin had vanished into the kitchen to wage war against the mountain of dirty dishes, leaving Kaitlyn and me on the couch with nothing but a throw blanket and our secrets.

She tucked her feet under her and used the remote to increase the volume of the stereo. Kaitlyn cast a glance toward the kitchen. Dishes clinked, water ran, the men were out of earshot. She leaned over, blanket slipping down to her lap.

"Okay, let's finish our discussion. You moved in on Saturday and then started sleepwalking into his bedroom? How did he react?" Her voice was a whisper.

I sighed, bracing myself for this part of my story. I'd been giving Kaitlyn the CliffsNotes version of my last week in scattered, five-minute bursts between rounds of vegetable roasting and diaper changing. The goal had been to keep her from dying of curiosity while also minimizing the odds of Martin or Andreas overhearing. It hadn't quite worked. She'd nearly asphyxiated on a carrot when I told her about the show Andreas and I had put on for Nakita at my old apartment. Martin had stormed into the kitchen when he'd heard her choking, sending me a vicious look, like I was trying to murder his beloved spouse.

Then, when I told Kaitlyn about the sleepwalking, she'd gasped so loud, both Martin and Andreas had run into the nursery to ensure nothing was amiss.

Now, with the evening winding down and only the kitchen as our buffer, Kaitlyn wanted the director's cut.

"He seemed a little bashful about it," I said, picking at the edge of the blanket.

"Like, I woke up on his bed, and he just sort of blinked at me, then his cheeks got all red and he went full android. Very formal. Lots of 'It's no big deal' and 'Please, don't be embarrassed'—which, as you know, is the number-one way to make me more embarrassed."

Kaitlyn's eyebrows jumped high on her forehead. "Really? He told you not to be embarrassed?"

"Yeah. I mean, he keeps saying it doesn't bother him, but how can it not? I keep waking up in his room like a poltergeist with boundary issues. Even when I try to keep to myself, it happens anyway. He even tucked me in last night and, this morning, I somehow ended up nested between his sheets again."

She grinned. "He's not upset you keep sleeping with him?"

I shook my head, letting the memory replay. "He never says he's upset. He's just—stiff, sometimes? He'll get all quiet and his jaw goes tight. But then, if I apologize, he tells me it's not a problem, or says something so . . . nice that I want to die."

Kaitlyn nudged me with her foot. "Give me an example."

I exhaled. "Sunday night, I ended up sleepwalking and fell asleep on his lap. Like, literally, across his thighs. I woke up and he had his arms around me. Instead of making it weird, he just said, 'I want to be useful.' Which is simultaneously the most wholesome and the most unhinged thing I've ever heard from a man."

She reached over and gave my arm a gentle squeeze. "Sam, it's not like this is something you can control. You need to stop apologizing for existing. When I was in the kitchen with him earlier, he asked me all kinds of questions about your preferences, what you like, what you don't. And I've been watching him today, how he looks at you. It seems like he's really into you."

I made a face. "He's doing that to keep up appearances. Darn it, I should tell him the truth about you knowing so he won't feel obligated to pretend we're engaged."

Kaitlyn drew back. "'Darn it'? Did you just say 'darn it'?"

I groaned. "It's the strangest thing, but I find myself very much caring what he thinks of me. Like, actually caring. I don't even cuss around him because his manners are so good. I wore makeup to dinner last night. Voluntarily."

Kaitlyn's lips twitched, but she played it straight. "What does that—what do you mean? You care what people think."

I rolled my eyes. "Sure, but not like this. Usually, if someone doesn't like me, I'd think, okay, their loss, and move on. But with him, I keep nitpicking everything I do and say. Whether I smell good, whether I said something dumb, whether my laugh is too loud. I even find myself censoring my dirty jokes. Can you imagine?"

Kaitlyn snorted. "You? No sex jokes?"

"It's a tragedy. My therapist would say I'm repressing my authentic self."

She was quiet for a second, then suddenly made a face of discomfort, her hand going to her chest.

"What's wrong?" I leaned forward, inspecting her face.

Kaitlyn had been dealing with bouts of mastitis since Joey was born and had even been hospitalized for it once. When she first showed me her cracked and sore nipples, I'd almost fainted from friend-empathy.

I knew she'd struggled with breastfeeding but had persevered, hiring a lactation consultant. Things had improved, but were nowhere near perfect. I would be forever in awe of women who breastfed.

Kaitlyn shook her head, giving me a reassuring smile. "It's fine. Just boob issues."

"Are you sure?"

She nodded. "I'm sure. Breastfeeding is not my favorite." She then studied me in that unique way she had when attempting to determine the truth of a matter. Kind but unsparing. "Sam. Do you think you might really like Andreas?"

I stared at the pattern of the blanket and, after a moment, nodded. "Yes," I said, and sounded extremely melancholy about it.

Kaitlyn covered her mouth, and her eyes glinted with suppressed laughter.

"Stop it," I hissed, smacking her shoulder. "It's probably just residual and unresolved crush feelings from when we were kids."

Kaitlyn cocked her head. "I don't know. He's pretty crush-worthy now. How many languages does he speak? That is some sexy shit."

I laughed, but it also sounded melancholy. "Well, he's leaving tonight for two weeks, so that'll give me some time to get my head on straight, at least."

She didn't let the topic drop. "Do you want to sleep here?"

I was touched by the offer, but I shook my head. "No. I told you about Andreas's brother Henrik earlier, right?"

"The scary guy who chased you into the biology building?"

"Yeah. I don't want him bothering you guys. And Andreas's apartment is like a fortress. I have security and everything, so I don't want to mess things up. Plus, Andreas can auto-lock the door so I don't sleepwalk outside the apartment."

Kaitlyn frowned. "I don't know, I feel like someone needs to stay with you."

"One of my bodyguards, a nice gal by the name of Tara, will probably sleep over while Andreas is gone."

She brightened. "That would make me feel better."

"Anyway," I said, eager to steer the conversation away from my trainwreck sleeping habits, "speaking of Henrik, he said something fishy when he was on the other side of the glass, trying to goad me out of the building."

Kaitlyn perked up, eyes wide. "What did he say?"

"He said my dad was a coward. But it was how he said it, you know? Like he had experience with my father, working with him, or some firsthand knowledge."

"Did they ever work together? At Genetix? How old is Henrik?"

I'd already done a little research on this, so I rattled off, "I think Henrik is not quite ten years older than Andreas, so that would make him something like thirty-five now, twenty then. I did a little digging and Henrik interned at Genetix while in college, under Oskar, who was the CFO at the time."

Kaitlyn's eyes narrowed. "That's something worth exploring. Do you think Henrik had something to do with the fraud charges against your father?"

"It's possible, right? But what could Henrik do as an intern? I've tried looking into the fraud charges before—if you remember, it's why I wanted to go to law school, to understand what happened—but since those charges were dismissed after my father died, the only resource for the proceedings are the board minutes at Genetix, when my dad was voted off the board and stripped of his shares."

"Let me tell Martin about this. He has *people* and can look into it without drawing any attention. Maybe he can reach out to Genetix about investment."

I grimaced. "I don't want you guys getting involved. These guys are dangerous. And you have Joey now and everything is so good between you two. I'll handle it."

Kaitlyn was about to say something else, but the click of a cabinet and the sudden clatter of plates announced the return of the menfolk from the kitchen. We exchanged a look that promised: to be continued.

Martin entered first, wiping his hands on a dish towel. He dropped onto the couch beside Kaitlyn and, with the world's least subtle body language, nudged and positioned her until she leaned against him—her back to his front—and his arms came around her torso. She didn't seem to notice, or maybe she was just used to it.

Andreas followed and as soon as he entered the room, my heart took an aching leap toward him. That same buzzing, electric tension ignited beneath my skin whenever we were in a room together and suddenly I was fighting to breathe normally. I was still mulling whether to warn him about Kaitlyn knowing the engagement was fake when he sat next to me, placed his arm around my shoulders, and pulled me closer to place a kiss on my forehead, the motion transferring a staticky jolt through the blanket to my skin.

"Andreas." Kaitlyn lifted her chin toward him. "I was wondering, do you own your mother's compositions now? Or, are they being held in a trust? A musician I work with tried to obtain licensing rights a while back but ran into a dead end of lawyers."

"Oh. Uh, I am not surprised." He gave his head a small shake. "My mother's music is part of my father's estate. When she died, as her husband, he inherited the entire catalogue."

"I see . . ." Kaitlyn's gaze shifted to me and she wisely let the matter drop. She knew my history with the Kristiansens.

"I am sorry to say, I have to be going soon." I looked at Andreas and found his eyes on me as he leaned back, gaze dropping to my mouth. Then, unexpectedly, he bent forward and placed a light kiss on my lips, stunning me momentarily speechless.

"Oh. That's too bad," Kaitlyn said, but her voice held a smile.

I turned my head to glare at my best friend. Her pretty gray eyes twinkled as they moved between us.

"My flight out leaves in three hours."

Finding my voice, I asked, "Do you need to go home first and grab your bag?"

He shook his head. "No. Elio has already collected it. He will call me when he is downstairs."

As if on cue, his phone buzzed. He pulled it out with his right hand, still keeping his left arm draped around me.

"That is him now," Andreas said, with a slightly apologetic tone. "I should go."

Martin pushed himself up, and Kaitlyn followed. I started to stand, but Andreas caught my hand and gave it a gentle squeeze, then rose to his feet with a grace I envied.

Andreas exchanged goodbyes, with Martin giving Andreas an actual hug instead of a bro-hug, which surprised me, and Kaitlyn embracing him with genuine warmth. When it was my turn, Andreas hugged me tightly and, into my hair, murmured, "Will you walk me down?"

I nodded, and he released me. To Kaitlyn, I said, "I'll be right back."

We walked out of the apartment, and when we entered the elevator, he faced forward. The ride down was spent in silence, my head all over the place. In the lobby, he grabbed my hand again as we crossed to the vestibule. A black Mercedes idled at the curb, headlights cutting twin blades of white through the early darkness.

Once we were outside the building, he stopped suddenly and turned to me. "Sam." His voice was quiet and almost swallowed by the sound of New York traffic, his eyes seeming to search mine. "We should kiss goodbye, just in case someone is watching."

Surprised by the suggestion, I opened my mouth to reply. But before I could, he kissed me. Not the kind of peck you'd give a fake fiancée, but the kind of kiss that made my toes curl in my boots and threatened to melt my knees into the sidewalk.

At first, his lips were warm and sweet, but the press of his hands on my back felt hot. Once the immediate surprise wore off, my brain told me to make the most of this moment, and so I did. I slid my fingers up into the back of his hair and kissed him deeply, wondering if he could taste my selfishness or the urgency in how my tongue sought his and explored his delicious mouth. He groaned, yanking me closer, and the kiss turned hungry as he angled his head to one side, chasing my mouth even though I wasn't going anywhere. Fireworks exploded in my stomach. I loved how tightly he held me, how every pass of his lips felt like a demand rather than a request, and how his hands shifted lower with each passing second until they completely palmed my backside.

When he pulled away, he didn't step back immediately. He rested his forehead against mine, breathing in, breathing out.

"I will really miss you," he whispered, so low I wondered if I'd imagined it.

And then he was gone, striding to the car, slipping inside, and leaving me on the sidewalk feeling like a pin had been yanked from some critical axis in my chest.

I blinked around the sidewalk, trying to get my bearings and not knowing what to expect, but nobody had been watching us. Or, if they had, they were pretending not to now. I spotted a couple guys in suits, loitering by a hot dog stand across the street. I recognized one of them as the security detail, which made me feel a little safer.

As the Mercedes pulled away, I watched the taillights for a long time, then turned back to the lobby, planning to squeeze a few more hours of friendship out of Kaitlyn before returning to my own fortress. And, maybe, to my own self, if I could figure out who that was anymore.

The elevator doors opened and I paused, thinking about what Kaitlyn had said. About the way I was acting. About how, even after everything, the person I wanted to talk to was the one who'd just left.

I pressed the button for the penthouse, and as the elevator climbed, I found myself grinning, stupid and secret, at the thought of seeing him again, already counting down the days until he returned.

It wasn't until I was right outside of Kaitlyn and Martin's door that the bubble burst on the fantasy.

This is fake. That was fake. *Everything about us is fake.*

Fighting to draw in enough air past the tightness in my chest, I couldn't help the traitorous thought: *Then why does it feel so real?*

[8]

PROCREATION

Samantha

Sunlight filtered in through the heavy blackout curtains. It took me a minute to realize where I was.

This is not my room.

No, this was Andreas's room—the main bedroom—because of course. After only one day with Tara as my night watchman, I'd already failed at Operation Sleep in My Own Bed.

Though I had sorta agreed to sleep in the main bedroom when Andreas and I had discussed it yesterday morning, I'd started the night in my own room last night, hoping against hope that I would stay put.

Stifling a groan, I reached for my phone, which was perched on the marble-topped nightstand, and thumbed it to life. The notification bar was a record of my weakness. Six unread messages: three from Kaitlyn with photos of a happy baby Joey; two from Dmitry asking me when I planned to be at work on Monday; one from Andreas.

I stiffened, bracing myself before clicking to open his message.

Andreas: How did you sleep

No punctuation. No emoji. No appurtenance that might give me any insight or clue as to his intended inflection or thoughts. Typical.

I lay there, staring at the message, debating how best to respond and how much to admit. This indecision lasted maybe a full minute, then restlessness took over and my fingers began to type.

Before I answered, though, my brain—ever the helpful parasite—replayed the events of the previous twelve hours. After Thanksgiving at Kaitlyn and Martin's, Tara picked me up at exactly 8:01 PM, walked me to the car with the discretion of an off-duty Secret Service agent, and drove me to Andreas's apartment. No questions, no conversation. I'd been thankful for her silence since I'd still been trying to process Andreas's sneak-attack kisses.

At the apartment, Tara made sure the perimeter was secure, then explained that Andreas had arranged for her to sleep over every night for the next two weeks. "This way, if you sleepwalk again, I can help redirect you," she said, her voice a warm blend of casual and commando. She even offered to walk me through some basic jiujitsu moves before bed, should I wish to "relax" before hitting the hay.

I laughed at the time. But now, as I rolled over and found the empty, perfectly made side of Andreas's bed, I realized that somewhere in the night, despite my best efforts, I'd migrated like a very determined barnacle from my own mattress to his.

The only possible explanation was that my subconscious preferred this bed. *Yep. That's the only explanation.*

I disputed the pros and cons of a lie. I could just say, *Slept great, thanks!* and leave it at that. Or I could admit the truth, which was that I had once again invaded his personal space.

I decided to keep it vague.

Sam: I slept very well

There. A statement that was not a lie.

My phone buzzed, his reply instant, like he'd been waiting for me.

Andreas: Where did you sleep

I frowned at the screen. Was this a trick question? Had Tara reported back to him with a full incident report? Did Andreas know already and he was just baiting me into an admission? Was there a security camera I hadn't noticed? *Nah. He wouldn't place cameras around without telling me. That would make him a super creeper, and nothing about him broadcasts creeper.*

Technically, I fell asleep in my own bed. Also technically, I woke up in his. Not that I had any memory of the transition.

My fingers hovered. I tried to assemble my response and make it sound as non-sus as possible. Once again, I settled on not a lie.

Sam: I fell asleep in my own bed

Which was, for the record, true.

I watched my phone, waiting for his response. Five seconds passed, then ten. Then, finally, it appeared.

Andreas: Where did you wake up

I made a noise—a sort of compressed laugh-scream—and flopped back against the pillow, phone resting on my chest. The embarrassment was total. Apparently, technical truths had no effect on Andreas.

Reluctantly, but with *feeling* and while gritting my teeth, I replied.

Sam: In your bed

I punctuated the confession with a self-owning emoji that looked like the monkey covering its eyes. And then, just for good measure, a pile of poop.

The three dots appeared as he typed. Then they disappeared. Then appeared again. Eventually, I gave up waiting for a reply and rolled out of bed.

The apartment was as silent as a cryogenic freezer. The only sign of life was the faint click of the smart thermostat adjusting the ambient temperature to "optimal living conditions." I padded down the hallway, careful not to disturb Tara, who was supposedly sleeping in the guest room. I had no idea what time it was—my phone said 6:04, but the light outside the windows was the kind that only happened on winter Fridays, when the sun doesn't so much rise as it does negotiate with the clouds.

I peeked into the guest room, just to be sure. The door was open a crack and Tara was sprawled on top of the covers, one arm above her head, mouth slightly open. She looked peaceful, which was weird considering she could probably kill a man with her pinky. Deciding not to risk waking her, I crept down the hall to the bathroom and turned on the shower.

The water pressure was water-pressuring, which is how I liked it. As I soaped myself, I replayed every glance, every micro-interaction with Andreas since this whole thing began. The more I tried to categorize what we were, the less I understood it. We'd gone from mostly strangers to co-conspirators, to maybe friends, to . . . whatever this was. I didn't have the right vocabulary for it. I wondered if he did, since he seemed to know every single language.

After I finished showering, I dried off and headed back to my room, determined to at least get dressed before I had to interact with humans. I pulled on a soft T-shirt and jeans and my phone buzzed as I was twisting my hair into a bun.

Andreas: We should schedule date nights. We'll look more like an engaged couple if we go on dates.

I sat down hard on the edge of my bed and spent several minutes staring at the message. My thumbs hovered over the keyboard, not knowing what to type. The air felt electric, and for a minute, I just sat there, feeling my heartbeat echo in my chest.

After a long pause, I responded.

Sam: Okay

I stared at the word, then hit send before I could overthink it.

* * *

IF YOU PUMPED ALL the world's agitation into a single floor of a university building, you'd get my department on the Monday after Thanksgiving. The halls smelled like burnt coffee and sadness, and every colleague I passed looked like they'd only barely survived their own family dinner. Some had the thousand-yard stare of people who'd spent the break explaining, for the fourteenth consecutive year, that no, they weren't going to be a "real doctor" but were in fact a "PhD," which was "different" but "still a doctor, Uncle Bob." Others had the hollow eyes of those who'd failed to meet a single writing deadline, or, worse, had met the writing deadline and now awaited the bloody aftermath of reviewer comments.

I, on the other hand, sat at my desk grinning like an idiot at my phone because I was, in fact, engaged. Not in the classic sense, but in the "I am currently engaged reading the plethora of texts my fake fiancé keeps sending me" sense.

Andreas had left for London Thursday night, but he texted me every day. Multiple times a day, in fact. He sent good-morning messages every morning. He sent me photos of London. He sent me photos of him around London. He asked me how I was, what I was doing, he asked my opinion about scarves, ties, gloves, jackets. He'd gone shopping on Saturday and I'd participated via text message. At one point, someone took his photo while he modeled a suit and he'd asked me what I thought.

I couldn't text him back what I really thought—which was that, though he looked mighty sexy, I suspected he'd look even better out of it—so I responded with two thumbs up. Today, before I was awake, he texted me a photo of a pigeon eating a croissant off a chessboard in some park. The accompanying text had been "She's my main competitor here."

I'd snort-laughed.

It was exactly the right kind of dry humor and passive-aggressive adorableness that I'd always wanted in a pen pal, only this pen pal was in fact my fake fiancé. Who I missed, which was deeply concerning, but here we were.

I glanced around the office, making sure nobody was peering over my shoulder, and scrolled through our thread. It was almost exclusively photos and text plus a few emojis from me when I was at a loss for words. He'd only sent one emoji. It had been in response to a picture I'd sent of me after Tara's kickboxing class on Saturday at her gym, grinning while wearing a sports bra and black leggings, beet red and sweating like a pig.

The emoji he'd sent in response was of a queen chess piece. I'd spent well past midnight trying to decipher its meaning. Did this imply that I was a queen? Or powerful? Or . . . what was he saying?

Tara was, as it turned out, the perfect roommate. She got up early, made magical protein shakes, and coaxed me into self-defense practice every night before bed. When I'd attended her Saturday night kickboxing class, she gave me a "Hell yeah!" and within ten minutes had taught me how to break someone's nose using the heel of my palm. "Just in case Henrik shows up again," she said, not at all joking. I knew she wasn't joking because, after I got the movement right, she'd added, "I can't wait. The crunch of a nose breaking is incredibly satisfying."

Then, she'd winked.

I'd gotten used to having her in the apartment. More than that, I liked it. There was a particular comfort in knowing someone slept nearby whose main professional skills were violence and discretion. I also liked that, despite being a total badass, Tara had no shame in binge-watching British reality shows and giving running commentary on everyone's wardrobe choices.

Also, I'd given up sleeping in my own room after waking up in Andreas's on Friday morning. Truly, I'd surrendered to sleeping in his bed every night. And let me tell you, I'd been sleeping like a wee little baby. Never better. Snug as a bug in a rug. Legit.

Thus, it was with a weird mix of well-rested contentment and adrenaline that I started my Monday, sipping the last of my sad office coffee, reading Andreas's latest message ("My tournament started today. I am free to talk after noon your time if you want a call"), and prepping for the day ahead.

I was mid-response to Andreas when Dmitry's pale, stubbled face appeared over the cubicle divider, a can of some indie-brewed coffee in his hand, complete with a sad little red bow on top.

"My dear future Dr. Jarlston," he intoned, voice like a melancholy cello, "I know you already have a JD, but I'm talking about your future PhD, my friend. How can I thank you enough for all your amazing help last week? You rewrote my methods section and now it isn't shamefully inadequate."

He held the can aloft like a tiny Olympic torch. "Please accept this can of gourmet coffee as a humble token of my gratitude. It is all I can afford."

I accepted the coffee. "Thank you, Dmitry. 'Twas nothing."

"In that case, may I have it back?" he deadpanned, hand over his heart. "I was late this morning and haven't had coffee yet."

I hugged the can to my chest. "Buzz off, ingrate. It's mine now."

Dmitry shrugged, unoffended, then peered at my hand, which still donned the diamond ring. "Wait. What's this? Are you engaged?"

"Oh, uh . . ." I glanced at my hand. "Well. Yes." Setting the coffee can to the side, I slipped the ring off and put it on the chain around my neck, tucking it under my shirt as I spoke. "I forgot to take it off this morning in the locker room."

He narrowed his eyes. "That's it? You're not going to give me any more details? Who is the guy? Or girl? Or non-binary human?"

Caught, I stared at Dmitry, wondering how much to say. It was one thing dragging my friends into this farce. I didn't like it, not at all, but I understood why it was necessary in order to enact revenge and sell this smoke screen Andreas and I had created. I hoped that they would understand my motivations once everything was settled.

But this was work. Dmitry was my colleague. I would never expect a work colleague—or ask a work colleague—to give me the benefit of doubt.

Dmitry seemed about to press for more details when Dr. Nieminen materialized in the doorway of my cubicle, his ever-flawless hair and jawline radiating influencer energy.

"Sam! You're back." His voice boomed across the whole aisle. "How was the holiday? Do anything fun?"

Instead of pointing out that I wasn't *back* because I'd been in the office and lab every day last week except Thanksgiving, I said, "Nothing of note." Lord help me, but I still didn't want to have a sharing kind of relationship with Dr. Nieminen. Something deep inside me still didn't trust the guy. "Did you receive my email with all the cross-checked citations? I sent it to the group."

"Yes! Thank you for doing that so quickly." Dr. Nieminen pulled out his phone to show me the calendar. "We're on track with the poster. Are we still on for our Friday evening meeting? I have it on my schedule. Does that time work for you still? No plans?"

I nodded. "That time works."

Dr. Nieminen grinned wider. "Awesome. Awesome. I have to run to a meeting, but let me know if you need anything, okay?"

He left as abruptly as he'd appeared, leaving behind a cloud of expensive cologne. Dmitry, perhaps sensing that I truly had no plans to return his can of coffee, tossed a thumb over his shoulder. "I need caffeine. Can I get you anything?"

I shook my head. "Thank you, no."

He waggled his eyebrows and left.

For a brief moment, I allowed myself to bask in the normalcy of it all. Office banter. Group projects. The comfort of old routines. I could almost forget that I was now a pawn in a multigenerational revenge plot.

You're not a pawn. You're a bishop, at least.

And then my desk phone rang.

"Sam here," I answered.

The voice on the other end was monotone but polite. "Ms. Jarlston, this is building security. We have a VIP visitor for you at the main entrance."

My heart stuttered. "Did they give a name?"

"Let me check." The line went quiet for a moment, then the security guy returned and said, "Tobias Kristiansen."

[9]

GAMETE TRANSPORT AND FERTILIZATION

Samantha

I didn't even finish hanging up the phone before I texted Tara.

Sam: Come to the lobby. Kristiansen the Elder wants to see me. Can you be here in five? I'll let you in.

My compulsion to use humor wherever possible demanded that I include an emoji. Tara responded with a thumbs-up less than thirty seconds later. I pocked my phone, squared my shoulders, and tried to remember every breathing exercise I'd ever learned in thirteen years of therapy.

This was it, a showdown. The sequel nobody asked for but the universe, in its infinite sense of humor, had green-lit anyway.

On my way out of the office, I made a point of passing the coffee lounge and swiping the free mini-donuts on the counter, because if I was going to face Tobias again, I wanted to be heavily fortified by fried dough and sugar. I also considered taking the elevator, but decided to walk the stairs for the sake of dispelling my nervousness. Four flights down, my heart was pounding out a bossa nova in my chest and I had to stop, lean against the stairwell wall, and check my phone to see if Tara had replied with anything new.

She hadn't, but as I rounded the last flight to the lobby, my phone buzzed. It was her.

Tara: Andreas doesn't want you to meet with Tobias.

233

I stopped short, reread the line three times. Then, because I couldn't help myself, I immediately typed a reply.

Sam: I'm meeting him. Please come to the building and I'll let you in. I want you with me.

My finger hovered over the send button for half a second, but then I hit it. The message was direct and honest. A second later my phone buzzed.

Tara: Okay. On my way.

I slipped the phone into my pocket, trying to ignore the simmer of annoyance in my gut. Maybe Andreas had good reasons for wanting me to avoid Tobias. But he hadn't communicated them to me clearly. I saw no reason why meeting Tobias would be risky, especially with Tara present.

And if I was ever going to get closure on what happened to my dad—or even just a scrap of information that I could chew on—this was an opportunity I couldn't let pass.

I reached the glass doors that separated the lobby from the second badge-access area and stepped to the side, hiding myself from the main area. Through the doors, I spied Tobias waiting near some midcentury modern couches with the exact same bored expression as last time, except now he was scrolling through his phone and occasionally looking up to glare at the security guard on duty behind the desk. He wore a suit that was only slightly less well-tailored than Andreas's but made up for the sloppiness by being a loud shade of periwinkle.

I watched him for a second, and used the time to remind myself that Tobias Kristiansen was not the real threat. His mind games wouldn't work on me. He could threaten and cajole and I would remain unshakable. Unlike Henrik—who was unpredictable and unhinged—Tobias's penchant for manipulation seemed to stick to the established playbook of following up threats with behind-the-scenes machinations. Which meant that if I could just get him talking, he might let slip something useful about my father's fraud case.

Tobias walked over to the security guard and said something. The guard stood and gestured for Tobias to follow. I assumed they were heading to the same private area where we'd met the last time he'd paid me a visit.

Movement outside the building caught my eye. Tara pulled up at the curb and parked in a space that definitely wasn't legal. Seemingly unperturbed, she strode across the sidewalk. Making eye contact with me through the glass, she nodded once and waited for me to open the door.

I pushed open the second access door and jogged across the lobby to open the main entrance for Tara. She stepped in, pulled off her gloves, and eyed the scene like a SWAT team leader prepping to breach.

"You want me in the room?" she asked, voice low and calm.

"Definitely," I said, matching her volume. "You can punch him if he tries anything."

She grinned, and the energy in the lobby shifted in my favor.

I led her down the corridor to the side office where I'd met with Tobias previously, and we passed the security guard on the way. He didn't give us so much as a double take. It was like stepping into a time capsule of discomfort.

Tobias turned as we entered, and his eyes flicked over Tara, then back to me. "Bringing body doubles everywhere you go now?" he asked, his voice sliding off the vowels like they'd personally offended him.

"Actually, yes," I said, seeing no reason to sit down. "What do you want?"

He shrugged, then set his phone on the table in the middle of the room and crossed his arms. "It seems you didn't take my advice last time. Have you forgotten? I can make the rest of your academic career very, very uncomfortable."

I almost laughed, it was such a weak opening gambit. "How very innovative. This is the same threat you made last time, and see how well that went?"

He leaned back on his heels, lips twisting. "You don't think I'll do it?"

"I don't think it'll be any more effective this time," I said, deadpan, channeling the ghost of every grad school office hour I'd ever attended.

His face didn't change, but his eyes narrowed a little. "I haven't done anything yet. Don't test me. One phone call is all it takes."

This tripped me up. I was under the impression that Tobias had already made the phone call, already twisted the arms and greased the wheels that got Dr. Hauser's funding frozen. So why the veiled threat again? Why not just say, "I did it. Here's what you get if you don't play nice"?

Unless there was more leverage he could apply . . . ? Or maybe Tobias was just fishing for a reaction. I was about to confront him when he withdrew an envelope from his inside pocket and placed it on the table next to his phone.

I rolled my eyes so hard I worried I might detach a retina. "Are these more pictures of me with Andreas? Are you making us a photo album for our wedding?"

Tobias's mouth twitched. "This envelope contains a contract you might find interesting, but I do have some new pictures, from last week. I believe my younger brother paid you a visit, yes?"

I froze. *Henrik.*

The name landed like a barbell on my chest. Suddenly the world was too bright and every sound felt amplified, like my ears were trying to track every molecule in the room. Tara must have noticed because she shifted her weight next to me, shoulders tensing as if to intercept a thrown punch.

I managed to speak, but it came out hoarse. "Did you put Henrik up to that?"

Tobias shook his head, lips curling with what I assumed was mock disgust. "No one puts Henrik up to things. He has his little hobbies, and fucks things up all on his own."

The envelope sat between us like a land mine. I forced myself to look at it, to focus on the reality in front of me rather than the panic mounting in my throat at the reminder of Henrik's visit.

"What's the contract for?" I asked, keeping my voice steady only through raw will.

Tobias didn't touch the envelope, but he tapped the table next to it. "I can get Henrik under control, but I want control of my father's shares. I know about the addendum." His eyes crawled over me, evaluating. "Are you already pregnant? Henrik said he didn't think so, not yet anyway."

The blood in my body stopped moving. "What is the contract for?" I repeated.

He drummed his fingers on the table. "Walk away from Andreas, from our family, and I will make it worth your while. You could start your own company with the amount I'm offering you."

"That's what's in the envelope?" I said, letting the disbelief saturate my tone. "You're trying to pay me off so I'll leave Andreas?"

"That's an ugly way to put it, but yes," he said, not the least bit abashed.

I looked at Tara. She watched Tobias with a mixture of obvious professional disdain and plain personal contempt.

I turned back to Tobias. "I'm not interested."

He shrugged, like he didn't expect me to say yes anyway. "Don't blame me if Henrik's clumsiness makes you lose something precious." His voice had gone soft and creepy.

I took a step back, my body demanding that I escape. "This conversation is over."

I didn't wait for a response. I turned, grabbed Tara's sleeve, and practically ran for the door. Behind us, Tobias called, "My offer has no expiration date, come to me anytime."

Once we were around the corner and out of sight, I leaned against a wall and bent my head, trying to regulate my breathing. *Damn it!* I'd gotten nothing valuable from Tobias. Not a single thing.

Tara placed a gentle hand on my shoulder and asked quietly, "Are you okay?"

I wanted to say yes. I wanted to say I was fine, that none of this fazed me. But the truth was, the second Henrik's name came up, my brain stopped working and adrenaline had flooded my body. I'd meant to pump Tobias for information about the fraud, about the addendum, about what steps he was taking to stake his claim on the shares, but instead I'd let fear short-circuit my entire personality.

Forcing a smile, I pushed away from the wall and shook out my hands. "I'm fine. I should get back to work."

Tara eyed me for a long moment, then let her hand drop. "I'll be here when you're ready to leave. We can go at any time."

I nodded. And I couldn't stop the disloyal thought from creeping into my mind. *I wish Andreas were here.*

* * *

I DECIDED to head home early and take the virtual call with my therapist from the apartment. There's a feeling I experienced sometimes, especially after a taxing day, where my thoughts were both tangled and muted, where silence sounded like background static and I wanted to escape it by doing something unproductive but engrossing, like an internet search for my fake fiancé to see if he was trending on the chess subreddit. Not that I was about to actually do that.

The call with my therapist had ended a while ago and now I was lounging in Andreas's bed, horizontal across the mattress with my laptop glowing at quarter-brightness, the room dark except for a pencil stripe of late-afternoon sunlight crawling in through the drapes.

I hadn't called Andreas today. I hadn't texted, either. For the entire afternoon, I'd done a spectacular job of not thinking about whether I should reach out, or if he was mad at me for meeting with Tobias, or if our goodbye on the curb last Thursday meant something to him. It had to, right? No one kisses like that without it meaning something . . . right?

Except, we'd kissed like that on the night of our fake engagement, and it had meant nothing then.

Instead of checking the subreddit, I spent forty-five minutes reading back through our text string and not spiraling over what it meant that he'd hearted the text message I'd sent yesterday wishing him good night, a fact I'd missed until this afternoon. For the record, it was a really good text. Funny, but not try-hard. Then, I'd spent another hour on a resale site for yachts, judging rich people for not having three full bathrooms on their ten-million-dollar floating McMansion.

Setting the laptop to the side, I rolled onto my stomach, resting my cheek against the pillow. There was no trace of Andreas's cologne or shampoo in the sheets. I'd made the mistake of washing everything the day he left, since I'd slept in his bed with my clothes on. Now I regretted it. If I could wish for one additional coping mechanism tonight, it would be the ability to smell a man who was several time zones away and pretend, for a minute, that everything was fine.

My therapist had been less than impressed with this wish.

Our virtual session earlier today started exactly on time, as always, and lasted precisely fifty minutes. When I'd told her a lot had happened since our last visit, Dr. Glass had blinked once behind her large, aggressively round glasses and said, "So you're not sleeping. Tell me about that. Let's start there."

I explained the sleepwalking. The relocation from my bed to Andreas's. The sense of being a passenger in my own body.

She wrote things down on her tablet, and then, when I was done, asked, "When did this first start?"

"The very first time was years ago, after my dad died," I said, and realized I hadn't rehearsed that answer at all. "I was thirteen. I'd get up, move things around the house. Sometimes I'd wake up in the backyard."

"Did your mother address it with a doctor?"

"She was, uh, a little busy being nonfunctional." My laugh was brittle. "But after a while, she put a lock on my door. She didn't want me wandering outside."

Dr. Glass digested that for a minute, then nodded. "There's nothing abnormal about stress manifesting in these kinds of dissociative episodes. Especially if you experienced a sudden trauma at a formative age."

It was so clinical I almost wanted to hug her. God, I loved her analytical approach. She always made me feel less broken in a critical sense and more fixable in a pragmatic one.

"Have you ever tried medication for it?" she asked.

"I'm already on sleeping aids," I said. "But I don't like to take them too much."

She nodded again, scribbling. "I agree. Sleepwalking while on sleep aids can be dangerous. Have you tried meditation? Or grounding exercises?"

I told her I'd tried everything: deep breathing, progressive muscle relaxation, counting sheep, counting backward from ten thousand, listening to classical music, binaural beats, actual brown noise, guided meditation apps, and once, in a moment of true desperation, those ASMR videos where women whisper compliments at you like you're a child in need of a sticker.

None of it worked. Or at least, not well enough to keep me from getting up in the middle of the night and sleepwalking into the bed of the world's sexiest chess master.

She said, "I think your current situation is unique in that you're dealing with multiple stressors. The inheritance. The security threat. The pressure to perform at work and academically. And on top of all that, you're living with a man you may or may not be in love with. And for the first time in your life, you're open to the idea—albeit, just a slight opening up—of a committed relationship with that person. This is a lot, Sam."

"Thank you. That's a relief to hear someone else say. I was worried it was all in my head."

Dr. Glass smirked kindly at my poor attempt at a joke and prescribed more self-care, less caffeine, and a list of meditation apps that I'd already tried but would try again. She also said, "May I suggest—since you said he's okay with it—you continue to start the night sleeping in his bed? Let's see if this reduces your sleepwalking. Keeping you safe is the top priority here. And give yourself time to adjust to the new normal. You are not responsible for fixing everything at once."

Now, as I lay in Andreas's bed, I opened my phone and flicked through the meditation apps, then gave up and typed "London chess tournament standings" into the search engine. The coverage was, as you'd expect, less than riveting. *The Chess Master* blog recapped each round like it was a boxing match for the criminally nerdy. Andreas was, of course, undefeated, but the write-ups focused mostly on his rivals' self-destruction. There were only a few candids of him, and in them all he was staring at the chessboard with that same intensity I'd witnessed Thanksgiving morning, like the pieces might move if he blinked.

I watched a video clip of his most recent game, not because I understood chess, but because I liked to watch his hands when he played. I discovered he had this habit of twirling the pieces between his fingers, never slamming them down but always moving with an economy that was so . . . Andreas. The video was annotated by some bespectacled British guy who talked a mile a minute.

"And you see Kristiansen here, arriving with less than a minute on the clock, which, frankly, you never see at this level—most players, you give them a thirty-minute clock, they'll use all of it—but Kristiansen, look at him, he sits, shakes hands with his opponent, stares at the board, and bang, bang, bang, executes the first ten moves in less than five seconds. It's like the man was playing from memory."

I paused the video, rewound it, and watched again. He did sit down late. He did shake the hand of his opponent. And then he just, almost absentmindedly, destroyed the guy.

I tried to imagine what it must feel like, to be so certain in your next move that you don't even bother to look up. To know, before anyone else, exactly how the game will end.

The phone was heavy in my hand. I wanted to text him, but what would I even say? How's the bird with the croissant? Try on any other suits? Please come home soon . . .

Instead, I set the phone aside and pulled the duvet up to my chin. It wasn't cold in the apartment, but I wanted the extra weight. I counted backward from one hundred, as Dr. Glass suggested, and I was halfway to fifty-six when a sharp rap at the door pulled me upright.

"Come in," I said, voice embarrassingly hoarse.

Tara entered with the confidence of a woman who'd once subdued a drunk hedge fund manager using only a plastic spoon and her own elbow. (True story. She'd told me about it on Saturday after our kickboxing class.)

The woman wore actual pajamas, a cartoon-print T-shirt and plaid pants, and held a box in one hand. She set it at the foot of the bed and said, "Something came for you."

I sat up completely, pulling my legs under me. "What is it?"

She shrugged. "It's not a bomb. I already checked. It's from Andreas. He texted me yesterday and said it was coming."

The box was heavier than it looked, and taped shut with precision. I picked at the tape, then gave up and used my keys by the bed to slice it open.

Inside was a blue-and-silver tin of Scottish shortbread, a box of herbal tea called Nighty Night Relaxation Blend, and, on top, a card. My name, written in Andreas's neat, almost typewritten print. No heart, no flourish, not even a "to" or "from." I opened it.

The note inside read,

Thinking of you. I hope you have sweet dreams.

—A

I stared at the card for a second, my face doing that thing where it tries to express seventeen feelings at once and lands on none. I wanted to laugh because it was such a short message for him to rush across the sea. I wanted to cry a little because he remembered that I liked shortbread cookies. Mostly, I wanted sniff the card just in case it held traces of his rosemary shampoo.

Tara watched me, arms crossed. "Cookies and tea?"

I held up the tin. "Want one?"

She narrowed her eyes. "No, Sam. These are for you, not us."

I frowned, confused.

She shook her head. "You're weird, Sam. Why would Andreas rush a package of tea and cookies? These are meant just for you. You're the one he's in love with."

Before I could formulate a response to that, she yawned and padded back out the door, leaving me alone with the parcel and the echo of her words.

I opened the tin. The cookies were arranged with geometric precision, three rows of four, each one stamped with a pattern. I picked one, then another, and arranged them into a triangle on top of the tin. I stared at them for a long time, thinking about what Tara said.

Andreas obviously hadn't told Tara or any of the other bodyguards about the nature of our arrangement. If one wants to keep a secret, the fewer people who know, the better.

And I knew that if I didn't come clean soon regarding how I'd consulted Kaitlyn and Martin about Andreas's proposal before I'd accepted it, I would start sleepwalking again. I felt certain I would. Thus, I resolved, right then, to call Andreas tomorrow and tell him.

I picked up my phone, debated for a second, then sent him a photo of the cookies, arranged in the shape of a smiley face. Underneath, I typed out a message.

Sam: Thank you for the cookies and tea.

I hovered over the send button, then pressed it, and immediately buried my face in the pillow. I should've called him earlier today instead of avoiding it after Tobias's visit. I shouldn't let Tobias—or Henrik—factor into my relationship with Andreas.

When I surfaced, there was a reply already.

Andreas: Let me know if you want bedtime company. For tea.

My heart did the thing, the swoop and fly thing. Was he flirting with me?

I think so, yes. This is, what the kids these days call, the flirting.

Before I could formulate a response, he texted me again.

Andreas: I need to go to sleep. Don't want to be late tomorrow. Call me when you're free.

I smirked at his reference to being late, then I exhaled a long breath. I liked this. I liked his check-ins and I liked knowing about him and what he was up to. Setting the phone on the nightstand, I lay down and stared up at the ceiling, imagining a chessboard there, all the pieces in their perfect rows, waiting for someone to move.

I would call him tomorrow. I would tell him the truth. But for this evening, at least, I could let myself rest, and dream of the one man who, for better or worse, always seemed to be five moves ahead of me.

[10]

REPRODUCTIVE HEALTH

Samantha

The next morning I woke up with my alarm, before the sun had managed to brighten or color the sky, and rolled out of bed. The thick wool carpet beneath my feet felt plush and warm, making me wish I didn't have to traverse the wood floor between Andreas's room and my bathroom across the living room and down the hall. But I did.

Tara was probably already gone. Regardless, I decided to tiptoe to the bathroom. Then I ran through a shower, brushed my teeth, and stood for a solid three minutes trying to decide what to do with my hair. There was no reason to do anything with my hair. And yet, my hair existed. Thus, the question remained. Bun? Ponytail? Down? I split the difference and left it a damp mess around my shoulders. There, decision fatigue solved.

I used Andreas's fancy espresso machine. It felt more approachable than his pour-over contraption, and I sipped it standing at the kitchen counter, staring at the digital clock on the oven. It was 5:18 AM East Coast time. In London, it would be just after ten in the morning. He'd probably been up for hours, already destroying some unfortunate international grand master, or whatever it was they did during the early rounds of chess tournaments. He hadn't texted me yet, but that was normal; he always waited until after 7:00 AM my time.

The knowledge that every time I'd texted him so far, he'd sent a near-instant reply, felt oddly . . . comforting. Like a safety net. Maybe that was why I felt nervous about calling him today. Because I was about to cut that line, or at least threaten it, by telling him what I'd put off saying since Thursday.

I paced the apartment for twenty minutes, then padded back to the kitchen for a second shot of espresso. I opened the fridge, looking for the oat milk, and was greeted by a single row of vegan yogurts, each container organized with military precision. How did he even do that when he wasn't here? Had he called Tara and asked her to alphabetize the fridge? Had he bribed the cleaning service? Did the food arrange itself when he left the room, like *Toy Story* but with probiotics?

Stop stalling and just call him!

I shut the fridge and drank the coffee black. The bitterness helped focus my thoughts. Grabbing my phone, I went to his bedroom, which I still couldn't enter without a fluttery, dumb feeling in my chest. Shutting the door, I sat cross-legged on the edge of his bed, and opened our message thread. I stared at the last text he'd sent.

Andreas: I need to go to sleep. Don't want to be late tomorrow. Call me when you're free.

I smiled despite myself, then forced my face back to neutral. I needed to focus. I needed to be honest. I texted,

Sam: Hey, can we talk later today? Not urgent, but I'd like to call you.

Less than sixty seconds later he responded,

Andreas: I can be free whenever you need me to be free.

That was so him. An immediate, all-in commitment to my whims.

Sam: How about now?

There was a brief lag—maybe a minute—then my phone rang, and there he was: ANDREAS KRISTIANSEN calling.

I let it ring twice, just to take a deep breath, then answered.

"Hello?" My voice sounded rough. I cleared it and tried again. "Hello."

He was somewhere busy; the background was a low thrum of voices and the tinny sound of plates clattering. But his voice was calm and immediate. "Hi. Are you okay?"

I hated that this was the first thing he asked, but also, I loved it. No hello, no small talk, just a direct line to my internal status.

"Yeah, I'm fine," I said, swallowing. "I . . . I wanted to tell you something. Before I lose my nerve."

He made a small hum, not impatient but maybe a little wary. "What happened?"

"Nothing bad," I rushed to clarify. "It's not bad. I—well, it's something you should know. About Kaitlyn and Martin."

The line was silent for a beat. "Yes?" he prompted, when I didn't immediately continue.

"I told them," I said, all in a rush. "About us. Before I agreed to anything with you, I needed to talk it over with someone, so I talked it over with them. Or, well, Kaitlyn, but Martin was in the next room and he eavesdropped, so he found out, too."

There was another silence, but it was longer this time. It didn't feel like an I'm-about-to-yell-at-you silence, but more like an I'm-recalibrating-my-assumptions silence.

I hurried on, "They haven't told anyone, I promise. But I feel bad for not telling you sooner. It was bothering me. I wanted you to know. I trust them completely. But I should have told you before."

I heard a sound like a door close, and then all the background noise suddenly stopped. His side was so quiet I wondered if the call had dropped.

I gripped my forehead. "Are you still there?"

"Let me see if I have this correct." His tone was calm but struck me as precise. "They knew about our arrangement, even when I came for Thanksgiving?"

"Yes, they did." I gave into my urge to wince. "Are you mad?" I asked before I could chicken out.

His response was quick. "No. No, I am not at all mad." He let out an audible breath, then added, "But why did you not tell me when we were there on Thursday?"

This, I had rehearsed. "Because it completely slipped my mind, honestly. And then you were there, and you started pretending—kissing my forehead, holding my hand—and that's when I remembered—that I hadn't told you—but I didn't want to make you self-conscious about it, not when we were already there. It's been really bothering me since, that you still didn't know. I want us to be honest. That's why I'm telling you now. I didn't want to wait any longer. I'm sorry."

He was quiet again, but—thankfully—this time the silence felt less loaded. "It is fine," he said. "Thank you for telling me."

I let out a breath. "You're really not upset?"

"No. I am glad you have friends you trust. To be honest, I am somewhat glad I did not know on Thursday. Meeting your good friends, I was already very nervous. But being your fiancé gave me a good reason to be there. Otherwise, why would I deserve a place next to you?"

His tone sounded matter-of-fact, but something about the way he said it made my insides tighten. "What are you talking about? Kaitlyn is the best. She wanted you to come. You were invited. You don't need to be my fake fiancé to have a place at the table. You're my friend. That's enough."

He was very, very quiet. Then, softly, he said, "It is good to know you consider me a friend now."

I blinked. "Of course we're friends! Do you not want to be my friend?"

There was another pause and it struck me that Andreas had paused and considered his response for a significant period of time nine out of ten times so far on this call. Whereas, I hadn't paused and considered my responses at all. Usually, I wasn't this reckless. Only with Kaitlyn, who I trusted completely.

Eventually, he said, "Knowing one's position on the board is imperative before making the next move."

I snorted, and the tension that had been coiling in my gut all morning started to unwind. "Everything is chess with you."

"It is what I know," he said.

"I'm so glad you're not mad. It's important that we trust each other completely, right? We're in a very precarious situation. If I couldn't trust you, I wouldn't know what to do." My confession, and therefore vulnerability, settled around me with a hush. I'd stopped short of admitting to Andreas that the level of trust I'd decided to place in him was monumental for me. It felt scary, but also strangely good. I found myself smiling at my phone screen like an idiot.

Again, he said nothing for a while, and the silence didn't feel awkward at all. It felt like the inside of a snow globe, muted by something gentle and invisible.

"Are you sure you're not mad at me?" I asked again, because I needed to hear his assurance again. I'd really done a number on myself this morning, twisting my worries into a noose.

"No," he said, his tone intoxicatingly gentle. "I am not mad at you, Samantha. Not even a little."

But there was an odd edge in his voice this time, something almost sad.

Instinct demanded that I try to cheer him up. "Is everything okay there? Any challenging matches? You sent me cookies and tea from London, and all I can do is sit here in your apartment and eat them without you. I wish I could send you something in return."

"All is well here, but . . ."

I gripped my phone tighter, waiting with anticipation. "What? What can I do?"

"You could send me more photos."

I laughed. He must be joking. "Of what? You live here. You already know what New York looks like in winter."

He cleared his throat. "You could send me photos of what you are doing. You do not have to, of course, but . . . I spend a lot of time at the tournament waiting. It can be boring."

His voice was weirdly gruff, like he was embarrassed by the request. My stomach did a weird summersault at the reemergence of his bashfulness. "Then I'll send you photos meant to entertain."

"As long as you are in them."

I tried to ignore the way his words made my chest tighten, and endeavored to dispel my body's reactions with a joke. "I'll dress up in a clown costume and have someone record me juggling petri dishes."

He laughed, the sound low and lovely. "By the way, I meant to say, thank you for helping me pick out the suit. You know, I can also help with that kind of thing, if you want."

"Helping me pick out clothes?" I asked, amused.

"Sure," he said, like it was the most natural thing in the world.

"Is this your way of saying my wardrobe needs an upgrade?"

"I am saying, your style is very American."

I cackled. "I'll have you know, half the girls in my department consider my ten-year-old skinny jeans awesome cosplay."

"You deserve better than a costume." His voice held a smile. "We should revisit this. It would not be strange for a fiancé to buy his beloved clothes, do you not think?"

"Do not buy me clothes, Andreas."

"Why not?"

"Because I'll have to reimburse you, and you have expensive taste. It's a slippery slope from one nice sweater to a closet full of cashmere."

With supreme confidence, he said, "You will be able to afford my taste and more once you inherit. And I am not going to listen to you on this. Expect clothes."

"Andreas!" I said, half laughing, half warning.

I heard a new voice on the other end, someone saying his name. Andreas's line fell quiet for a minute.

Then he returned and said, "I have to go. I am fifteen minutes late for a match."

"What?!" I stood from the bed. "Then why did you call me?"

"I only need five minutes with this guy," he said, dry as the Atacama Desert. "We will talk again soon, okay?"

"Okay," I said, smiling like a doofus as he hung up.

Sitting back down on the edge of his bed, I hugged my knees and let my feelings simmer without trying to name them. I didn't have the right vocabulary anyway.

Eventually, I got up. I made breakfast for both Tara and me. She drove me to work. I spent several hours in the lab, catching myself staring into space and grinning. And when I returned to my desk, every time I glanced at my phone, I again smiled like a dope, replaying the words, the tone, the laughter of our call.

I hadn't ruined anything. We were more in sync than before.

* * *

THE FIRST FRIDAY—AND first snow day—in December, and I was still at work at 6:45 PM, listening to Dr. Nieminen enumerate my own accomplishments like he'd been the catalyst for all my success. Not even the anticipation of knowing that, at this precise moment, Andreas Kristiansen was likely past security in Heathrow and would soon be on a flight home from London, could save my mood.

The tick of the conference room's analog clock sounded disproportionately loud for some reason. Perhaps because it was the countdown to my freedom. I'd been sitting in this chair for forty-three minutes, and the two most meaningful things I'd managed to accomplish—really, the only two things—were not falling asleep and not losing my temper.

"Your time logs are thorough," Nieminen said, flipping a page. He wore a navy quarter-zip and, as always, looked like he'd just come from a corporate retreat where the team-building activity was silently judge your subordinates. He had a stack of papers at his elbow, the top one marked in his fine blue pen: "Jarlston, S. – November."

Nieminen flipped through two more pages and gave a tight nod. "You're quite productive for someone who's lost their funding and was saved by a new PI in the middle of the semester."

"Thanks," I said, though it didn't feel like a compliment. The way he'd said the words, he'd put the emphasis on "lost their funding" and "saved" as though to remind me that my place here had more to do with his generosity than my ability.

Or maybe you're just reading menace into his words where none exists because you simply do not like the man.

It was a possibility. Nothing he'd said was false, even if I didn't like the words.

Stop assuming the worst of Dr. Nieminen!

I'd tried. I'd really, really tried. Honestly, he'd done nothing tangible I could object to since taking over my funding.

Yes, over the last two weeks since Thanksgiving break, he would frequently and randomly check in on me during the day, something Dr. Hauser never did. And he would lean over my shoulder to peer at my computer screen while I showed him evidence of my progress. In our smaller department meeting last week, he'd said "we" instead of naming me specifically when giving credit for the fast turnaround of the poster presentation, a la, *We were able to confirm all the citations before the break.*

I was a junior member on *his* team. Thus, he could technically say "we" and take public credit for all my work if he wanted. That was how academia worked. Dr. Hauser never did that, she'd always given the specific person credit for their contributions, naming them in public. Sadly, Dr. Hauser seemed to be the exception.

Presently, biting my tongue, I tuned him out as he continued reciting out loud all the tasks I'd completed in November, and let my mind drift to more pleasant thoughts. Namely, my reunion with Andreas and the ever-expanding collection of gifts he'd mailed to the apartment since leaving New York.

The collection was, in a word, absurd.

Every night for the last ten days, I'd come home to one or more surprise parcels. After the tea and cookies, the next package contained a pair of Italian-made pajamas, a lady version of his gentlemanly suit of sleepwear. The next day brought a tiny, perfectly wrapped box of perfume that smelled absolutely divine— like fresh gardenias at first, but then with a dark, velvety scent after, one I couldn't quite place, like sweet cedar but better. I'd considered bringing it into the lab and running an analysis on its chemical composition.

After that, a stationery set so beautiful I couldn't imagine ever using it, along with an actual fountain pen that wrote smoother than any pen had the right to and felt magnificent in my hand. Next, a beautiful new scarf in the exact shade of my eyes, with a note that read, "To keep you warm while I'm away." And I'd gasped upon opening an antique copy of Darwin's *On the Origin of Species*. He also sent an entire suite of skincare items that even Diya would've approved of.

To my surprise, some of the gifts originated from close by. A kombucha brewed locally that I quickly became addicted to. (I didn't even know I liked kombucha.) Pickled vegetables from the Bronx that I started putting on everything because they were so spicy and tasty. A crusty sourdough loaf from Queens that Tara and I polished off in two days. He'd even sent a yummy charcuterie spread last Saturday night with olives, almonds, fancy cheeses, cured meats, and a bottle of Italian red.

I felt so spoiled. The only people who had ever given me gifts like this were my parents and grandparents.

And then came the clothes, always with a note requesting I send a photo of me wearing the item. "To ensure they fit," he'd explained in his note. "If they don't, I can send a new size."

More than once, usually after unwrapping that evening's box and marveling at how much I loved whatever was inside, I would wonder why Andreas was sending me gifts at all. He'd explained them away on the phone as expected since the world thought we were engaged, but that excuse didn't fully explain his constant and effusive lavishing. Every item was thoughtful, personal, and indulgent, clearly chosen specifically for me. If he'd simply wished to put on a show, then he could've sent the same item every day. Or jewelry. Or flowers. Why go to such trouble?

Not quite understanding the impulse, I began leaving work on time and stopping by shops on my way home. Visiting four different vintage resellers and two antique shops, I found myself searching for something Andreas might like, trying to find the right thing, only to walk away empty-handed, except for a tiepin shaped like a rook that I worried he'd think was tacky.

It wasn't until the night before last, standing in the back of a dusty used bookstore on East 12th, that I found it: a complete, signed set of Bobby Fischer's chess writings, the spines brittle but the dust jackets intact. I'd nearly fainted when I opened the first volume and saw the signature, because I suspected what it would mean to Andreas. Based on his library, he obviously loved books, and I'd snooped around his collection enough to know he didn't have signed versions of these.

Using grandma's account to pay for the—ahem—extremely expensive set didn't even faze me. It seemed like something she would want me to do, like an expense she'd heartily approve of. I'd wrapped it in tissue, hidden it under my bed, and planned to present it as casually as possible so as not to seem too eager.

Apparently, I was more concerned with the appearance of chill than reality. But what could I do? I'd never given a man I was interested in a gift before. This was new territory for me.

". . . and the rest looks good," Nieminen said, yanking me from my thoughts as he loudly set down his pen. I blinked the room back into focus and found him giving me a faint smile. "There are only a few weeks left in the term. Your project proposal is strong. Let's just make sure you keep hitting your time benchmarks, okay?"

"Will do," I said. I began packing my laptop away, a move he either didn't notice or chose to ignore. I had half a mind to ask if he needed anything else, but I was worried he'd find something.

Instead, as I slowly stood and zipped my bag, I waited for him to say, "Thanks for coming in," or "Enjoy your weekend," or, God willing, "You can leave now." He didn't move, simply kept watching me. Since I'd finished packing my things and he still hadn't spoken, I decided to take that as implicit permission to skedaddle.

I'd just placed my backpack on my shoulder and reached for the door when he said, "Oh, yeah—"

"Yeah?" I turned to face whatever Dr. Nieminen's "one more thing" was.

Dr. Nieminen, standing now on the other side of the table, reached into his bag and pulled out a thin blue folder. He slid it across the table to me. "I got us two tickets for the show tonight," he said. "If we hurry, we can get a quick bite to eat before curtain."

[11]

FERTILITY AND ITS CONTROL

Samantha

I stared at Nieminen, then at the folder. His words didn't compute.

"A show?"

He smiled again, a flash of white teeth and cleft chin. "I overheard you mention to that guy in the cubicle next to you that you haven't been to any Broadway in months, and I had an extra connection with the box office. It's Company, at the Bernard Jacobs. The reviews are excellent."

I picked up the folder. Inside were two tickets, row J. I was so confused. "This is for tonight?"

"Of course," James Nieminen said, like it was the most normal thing in the world to randomly spring a Broadway show on an colleague less than an hour before curtain, let alone a *boss* springing it on an *employee.*

I blinked, then tried to recover. "Uh, Dr. Nieminen, I can't. I have other plans tonight."

He cocked his head to the side, lips pursed. "You have other plans? But I thought—when we scheduled these meetings, you said you didn't have other plans on Friday nights."

I stifled a strangled bark of laughter. "I agreed to meet you in the conference room, not to go to a Broadway show."

He frowned. "You said you were free. You didn't mention anything else."

"I'm not—I mean—" I glanced at the wall behind him. "I am free Fridays, but only for this meeting. I have plans after work." My face was getting hot. With anger.

James exhaled loudly through his nose, shoulders going rigid. "Sam, I wouldn't have bought these tickets if I'd known you weren't available. Are you telling me you can't change your plans?"

The phrasing, the sudden shift from genial to weirdly controlling, made the inside of my skull itch. "No. I can't."

James's face went flat, the smile gone. "Fine. With whom do you have plans that can't be canceled, if you don't mind me asking?"

This was too much. Even my least chill hookups had never interrogated me like this. I summoned every ounce of petty I had, which, to be fair, was enough to run a midsized petty kingdom where petty trees were logged and made into petty paper at a petty mill.

"I'm having dinner with my fiancé."

James stared at me, unblinking. "You have a fiancé?" The way he said *fiancé* told me he thought I was lying.

Which I was technically, but still. Whether I had a fiancé was none of his business.

"Yes." The lie came so naturally, it shocked even me. "And he can be very jealous, controlling, so I don't like to provoke him." Internally, I wondered why I'd never made up a jealous, controlling fiancé before now. Fictional controlling men were so hugely handy in a pinch.

James's eyes dropped to my hands, which, to be fair, were empty of rings of any kind. "Where's your ring?"

"In my locker," I said, without missing a beat, because that was the truth. I took it off on days I knew I'd be in the lab.

For a second, I thought he might laugh or otherwise let it drop. Instead, he just stood there, staring with a sort of clinical dissatisfaction, like I was an unexpectedly recalcitrant cell culture.

James eventually shook his head. "I didn't know you were seeing anyone. You never mentioned it before now."

I shrugged, wanting to leave and never think about this again. "I keep my personal and professional life very separate," I said, which was not just true, it was extremely true.

James was silent for a moment, then asked, "Are you sure you can manage the increased responsibilities of your position, Sam? I'm not convinced you can keep your commitments. Or that you're being completely truthful with me."

I didn't know whether to laugh or smash his face into the table. Instead, I could only look at him blankly and try to keep my voice pitched as detached as possible.

"I'm happy to continue meeting the obligations you set for me, as long as we keep things professional."

"I'll think about it." His voice was tight and cold.

Not bothering to smile or offer a parting salutation, I placed the tickets back on the table, turned, and walked out of the room, hearing him huff loudly just before the conference room door closed behind me.

I left the corridor as quickly as I could, taking the side stairs to the women's locker room. The building felt empty now, each echoing step in the cinder-block stairwell rebounding back at me in a hollow, rattling syncopation. Once I made it inside, I sat down on a bench and put my face in my hands. My cheeks were burning, and my heart was pounding so hard I could feel it in my throat.

I wondered how many other times James had tried this move on other grad students. I wondered how many of them had given in, terrified that they'd be blacklisted or kicked out of the program if they said no. I thought about the way James had looked at me, the sudden withdrawal of praise, the veiled threat about funding. I thought about his postdoc who everyone whispered about and dismissed as *dramatic* because he'd said so. I thought about how little control I would have over the narrative, how easily a man's expectations could be treated as fact. I thought about the last fifteen years of my life, about watching my father be destroyed by liars, about my mother's body wasting away, her giving up because no one would listen to the truth.

When she'd denounced the Kristiansens publicly, would people have taken her more seriously if she'd been a man? My father had died before he'd been allowed to plead his case, before he'd even made a public statement or given an interview.

But if he'd lived, would he have been believed? Would his word carry more weight because of his chromosomal arrangement and phenotypic sex? *Yeah. Probably.*

Standing from the bench, I walked to the sink and splashed cold water in my face, certainty taking hold in my bones. Discovering the truth about my father and the charge of fraud against him now felt more important than securing Oskar Kristiansen's shares upon his death. Proving that my dad had been framed wouldn't only absolve my father, it would also vindicate my mother, show the world she hadn't been hysterical or lying about the Kristiansens before her death.

Thank God for Andreas. Thank. God.

Thank God he'd pushed me to take revenge. Thank God he'd found a way to make it happen that didn't involve bringing an innocent child into the situation. Even if I discovered all of their secrets on my own, I would never be able to confront Oskar and Tobias and Henrik openly with the truth or go to the press, not even with rock-solid proof. Without Andreas to back me up, I'd have to use some other surreptitious means. Because women weren't believed. Somehow, I'd have to trick them into confessing, or otherwise trick them into destroying each other.

But with Andreas, he'd arranged the pieces masterfully, our subterfuge with the engagement making me appear like a pawn instead of the queen.

They will find out soon enough, I promised myself as I glared in the mirror. They would all find out soon enough. Including Dr. James Nieminen.

* * *

I ZIPPED my parka all the way up after waving goodbye to the dude at the security desk in the lobby. As I approached the glass doors of the main entrance, I scanned the street for Tara's Mercedes beyond. I never left the building until Tara arrived. Per protocol, she generally showed up ten minutes after I texted her, which I'd done in the locker room right after placing the engagement ring on my third left finger.

Pulling my hand out of my pocket, I studied the twinkle of the large stone in the dim light. I honestly didn't know precisely why I'd put it on my hand. Usually, I wore it on a chain around my neck if I wore it at all. But for some reason, after telling James that I had a fiancé, wearing it on my ring finger just felt right.

Faint sound and movement beyond the glass doors had me lifting my head. I spotted Tara's Mercedes pull up to the curb, hazard lights blinking. That was my sign that it was safe to leave.

I had barely reached the first step down when a voice said, "Where are you going?"

James Nieminen materialized from behind one of the columns. Apparently in full stalker mode, dressed in a dark wool coat and leather gloves, he looked me up and down.

"Just heading out," I said, faking cheer. Then, because I'm a petty queen, I couldn't resist adding, "You should get going if you want to make that show."

Ah. Sam. You are your own worst enemy.

I shifted my weight and looked past James toward the waiting black car, which had just been joined by a second SUV. From the passenger side of the Mercedes, Tara climbed out, eyes locking on mine. I gave my head a faint shake, hoping she'd stay put. The last thing I needed was James claiming that he'd been harassed by my security team, then I'd have to explain why I had a security team. He was a dipshit, but I didn't consider him a physical threat. I didn't need Tara this time.

Meanwhile, James smiled, and I didn't like how much teeth it showed. "I realized we didn't finish discussing the distribution of tasks for the conference poster. There's a lot to do, and I decided I want you to draft my section."

"You want me to draft *your* section?" Quickly, I scanned the sidewalk and I spotted two other security detail people who I recognized. Both glanced at me, then at Tara. Obviously, they were following her lead, hands in pockets but stance alert. They fanned out, silent as bats, and started inching toward us as though they were simple strangers passing by.

"That's right," James said, leaning closer, "you draft it, I'll edit it. That'll save me time." He stepped fully into my personal space, the gap between us narrowing to "intimate conversation" range. I could smell his cologne, citrus and chemical, and the tang of it made me want to sneeze.

I backed up a half step. "Sure," I ground out. "I can send a draft tonight."

He smiled even wider. "Good. I know you have a lot on your plate, but this is something you should've proposed to me, not the other way around. I need you to be more proactive if this is going to work."

I stared at him, my anger suddenly sharper than the cold. "In that case, if this is going to work, you'll need to give me more of a heads-up before assigning major tasks like this. I would've thought, as the lead for the poster, you would've already created a first draft of your section. Especially since mine is done and it's due for everyone else on Monday."

He shrugged, all faux casual. "Things change. You can work on it tonight, or wake up early and do it. I don't care. But it has to be done by tomorrow."

I opened my mouth to tell him where he could put his poster, but in that exact moment, approaching movement caught my eye at the curb.

Andreas walked toward us, long strides, hands in the pockets of his camel-colored cashmere coat. Underneath, he wore a blue sweater and dark gray pants. His hair was perfectly styled, his jaw shaven, and his skin much more hydrated than I would expect for someone who'd just flown in from England.

Currently, Andreas wasn't looking at me. The entire weight and force of his glare was on James. He wore the same flat, predatory stare that he'd employed during the chess matches I'd been stalk—er, watching online from the London tournament.

He'd won, by the way.

He'd won the tournament. He'd barely smiled when he'd been presented with the £750K check, and his short interview afterward had made me laugh.

Because when the interviewer had asked, "Are you relieved that you won?"

He'd said, matter-of-factly, "No. It was expected."

Drawing even with us, Andreas stopped beside me and his gaze shifted to mine, suffusing with warmth. "Are you ready, Samantha?"

Dear. Lort. His voice was deep and smooth and gentle and just magic.

Not waiting for a response, Andreas reached out, took my backpack off my shoulder, and slung it easily over his arm, the side of his mouth tugging adorably to one side. "Where are the mittens I got you? Your hands must be cold."

I felt my eyes narrow with confusion because—as far as I knew—Andreas had never bought me mittens.

Regardless, using his teeth, he tugged off his left glove and fitted it over my fingers, his thumb giving the ring on my third finger a little twist as he did so, his smile growing more obvious the moment he spotted it.

I couldn't speak for a second. Despite being irrationally angry mere seconds prior, my brain was now busy rerouting all available blood to the part of me that was in charge of appreciating how utterly, dangerously hot Andreas looked and how overwhelmingly happy I was to see him.

I finally managed a weak, "I am ready to go."

Giving me one last warm almost smile, Andreas turned his attention back to James, who was now blinking rapidly and trying to recover his composure.

Andreas extended his gloved right hand. "Andreas Kristiansen," he said, in a tone so incredibly flat and unfriendly. After a beat, he added, "Samantha's fiancé."

James stared at him, face slack. "Kristiansen?" he repeated, the word a croak.

Andreas's handshake was brief but obviously punishing; I saw James's knuckles blanch, and when Andreas let go, James cradled his hand for a second before hiding it in his pocket.

I cleared my throat. "This is James Nieminen. My new PI."

James was still looking at Andreas, and his skin had lost all its color despite the cold. "Are you—uh—by any chance, are you related to the Genetix Kristiansens?"

"I am."

There was a moment of silence so thick it felt like the world had been soundproofed. I didn't want to laugh and ruin it, so I rolled my lips between my teeth and bit down lightly, wishing I could snap a photo of James's face.

Nieminen licked his lips, eyes wide. "Nice to meet you. I—" He broke off and cleared his throat, likely needing another minute to collect himself. At length, he repeated, "Nice to meet you."

Andreas's lips curled at the edge, but not in a way that suggested humor. "I could not help but overhear that you want Samantha to finish a task by tomorrow morning? Assigning work on a Friday night, after hours? Seems like poor planning." Every word was cut with ice.

James's face went red, then white. "I was just—" he said, then caught himself. "I was joking. Obviously, she can do it on Monday."

Andreas stared at him for a moment longer, then nodded, as if dismissing him from the conversation.

James stood there for another heartbeat, looked at me, then at Andreas, and then said, "Have a good evening, Samantha. Nice to meet you, Mr. Kristiansen."

He turned and left, shoulders hunched and pace just shy of a jog.

The moment he was out of earshot, I said, "That was . . . I'm not sure what that was."

Andreas didn't look at me, just watched James's retreating figure. "He is your new PI?"

"That's right."

"Does that man bother you at work?"

I hesitated, then shrugged, not really wanting to talk about James Nieminen, not when Andreas was finally home. "I should be able to handle it."

Andreas said nothing, but I saw his jaw clench. Then, finally, he looked at me, eyes scanning my face. "If you want, I can get rid of him."

The way he said it, so calm and practical, made me laugh out loud. "That's not necessary. Besides, I think you just inadvertently solved my problem for me. He's terrified of you."

He seemed to consider my words, then nodded. "Good."

I felt like laughing again, but this time with frustration. No matter how competent I was, no matter how good of a job I did, all my efforts were nothing compared to the power of the Kristiansen last name. *Sigh.*

"Shall we?" Using his left hand, Andreas reached for my right one and entwined our bare fingers together, bringing them both into the pocket of his coat, the movement smooth and natural.

I couldn't believe he was here, and so the question slipped out of me. "When did you get back?"

Andreas didn't break stride. "I took an earlier flight. I came here from the airport. Are you hungry?"

"A little." I caught myself staring at his profile and grinning, thus I rapidly tore my gaze away.

"We will go on a date."

"A date?"

"Yes. You agreed last week. We should go on dates, as an engaged couple. I saw you are wearing the ring."

"Aren't you tired? The time zone shift must be brutal."

"I want to go and I already made a reservation." Andreas stopped short and turned to me, his forehead wrinkling. "Wait. Are you tired? We can go home if you are tired."

Shaking my head, I gave his hand a little reassuring squeeze. "I'm not too tired. We can go on a date."

He seemed to study me, as though to ascertain whether I told the truth. His forehead clearing, he turned back to the car and we walked the last few feet. Tara stood at the hood and sent me a small smile, but I noticed when her gaze shifted to Andreas the smile evaporated.

He opened the back door for me, and I slid inside. Instead of following me in immediately, he leaned down in the open door. "Give me a moment please, I need to speak with Tara."

Wondering what he wanted to discuss that either couldn't wait or had to be discussed without me, I nodded and settled back against the bench seat. *I'll ask him during our date.*

With a quick smile and a promise to be fast, Andreas shut the door, leaving me in the quiet car with my own thoughts, which consisted mostly of replaying the incident with James over and over in my head. Most especially, I enjoyed the look on James's face when Andreas had introduced himself, and the particular shade of white—ghostly white—when James confirmed Andreas was one of the Genetix Kristiansens.

But then my mind snagged on a particular detail of the interaction and I frowned.

Andreas had given me his left glove, leaving my right hand and his left hand without any protection from the weather. And then Andreas had used his right hand —which was still gloved—to shake James's hand.

Hmm.

The glove musical chairs hadn't all been a calculated maneuver so Andreas could hold my bare hand, but avoid touching James, had it?

. . . Nah.

Who thinks so many steps ahead? Just to ensure we held hands but also to avoid touching James?

That would be truly diabolical.

[12]

BRAIN SEX

Samantha

Fifteen minutes after Tara pulled away from the biology building, Andreas and I were in a booth at Del Vino, one of those Lower Manhattan wine bars where the walls looked like they'd been imported from Tuscany and the food menu consisted of "lite bites." Even though this place was only a block from Andreas's apartment, I'd never entered it or any other wine bar in New York before. Wine bars weren't in my budget.

The host had shown us to the most public booth after confirming Andreas's reservation. Located right up against the window, it was practically a diorama for the passing parade of New Yorkers. Andreas seemed immune to the idea of passersby watching us, and he had his jacket, scarf, and glove off, already rolling up the sleeves of his cable knit sweater as soon as he slid in across from me.

Forearms. I tried not to stare as I took off his other glove and passed it to him.

A server materialized to take our order for "something to nibble," and gave us our wine-dispenser cards. I barely registered what Andreas ordered—some kind of cheese and nuts, roasted olives, charcuterie? Sure, all of it sounded like food. The reason my brain was on vacation was because, less than three feet away across the table, Andreas Kristiansen's eyes settled on me with a focus and intensity I hadn't mentally prepared for. Because he wasn't supposed to be back until tomorrow.

Presently, he was trying to deduce my taste in wine, a subject about which I was both ignorant and, apparently, also abysmally unprepared for.

"Italian?" he asked, hands folded on the table. "Or Argentinian? Or New Zealand, perhaps?"

I shrugged. "The last time I drank was with you, house red at Smokin Greens." After a brief period of internal debate, I decided to stop censoring myself and just tell the truth. "Usually, it's in a box and cost six dollars. I'm not sure I have a region."

Ugh. I just admitted that. But I had to stop pretending to be someone I wasn't whenever we were together, like I'd done before he left for London. So what if I embarrassed myself? I was embarrassing. Plus, it's not like this was an actual date.

Andreas considered my words with a faint smile tugging at his lips, his eyes feeling warm as they moved over me. "You paint quite a picture."

"I don't know how to paint unless it's with my fingers," I said primly, picking up my water for a sip. There. Another honest answer. *I'm a plebeian. So sue me.*

Andreas's grin instantly claimed his mouth, and his laugh surprised me. Entranced, I watched him and slowly set my water down. I found myself smiling in response to his smile, basking in his twinkling green eyes, his features soft and unguarded.

"Come now, you must have a preference," he pressed, voice low and ridiculously sexy.

"Honestly? No." I lifted my hands, helpless. "If it's red and doesn't taste like battery acid, I'll drink it. If it's white, I'll also drink it, but less happily. If it's rosé, I'm just as clueless as with the other two." I shrugged. "I've had good wine before, just not often. And I did like the rosé we had for our engagement dinner, which I actually recognized because Martin once ordered it when I went out to dinner with him and Kaitlyn."

Andreas stared at me, his smile lingering, then stood and held out his hand. "Come with me."

Before I could respond, he reached for my hand with his, pulling me from the booth. Predictably, I fought a jolt of hot awareness as Andreas took my hand, not in a let's-go-couples-bowling way, but in a very deliberate, fingers-laced, this-is-mine way. Aware that we were being observed (by both the host and the three women at the next table who were definitely ogling Andreas, but who could blame them?), I tried to walk like a person who belonged in expensive restaurants and not like an imposter lost in a Neiman Marcus while searching for the bathroom.

He led me through the open corridor that separated the main dining area from the wall of wines. There were racks and racks of bottles, arranged by country and varietal. Opposite the racks, a row of glass-doored dispensers with little digital readouts and shiny metal taps, like a self-serve soda fountain but with—you know

—alcohol. The aroma of cold, damp stone and wood mingled with the acidic perfume of three dozen open reds.

Andreas guided me to the middle bank of dispensers. Bringing me with him, he slowly paced the row, perhaps cataloguing the options. The light was dim and golden. The way it caught in his hair reminded me of candles and firesides and all the other things I associated with fictional romantic rendezvous.

"Do you like robust flavors?" he asked, not breaking his relaxed stride. "Or softer, lighter?"

I considered the question. "I like my coffee black. Does that help?"

He almost smiled, head tilting as he read another label. "What about fruit? Berries or citrus?"

"Uh. Berries."

"Cherry, blackberry, raspberry, blueberry, or strawberry?"

"Cherry . . . ?"

"Dark chocolate, right?"

I nodded. "Yeah."

"And on pancakes, maple syrup rather than honey or powdered sugar."

I leaned back, giving him a suspicious side-eye. "How do you know that?"

Andreas grinned at me, his gaze sweeping over my face before he leaned close and whispered, "Let us try something bold, then."

Yes. Let's.

His words paired with the intonation of his voice had me imagining all sorts of dirty and delightful things. Making out behind a row of wine dispensers; his hand down the front of my jeans at the end cap; sex against the imported Tuscan wall.

Sadly, Andreas was clearly talking about the wine. But he did lift my hand and press his lips to the back of it, holding my eyes as he did so.

Then, he turned a bottle for me to read. I was instantly, irrationally aware of how much I'd missed this over the past two weeks, our pretend PDA, the way he invaded my personal space. My body felt lit from within and my hand, which should have been limp and dignified, instead twitched and then gripped his.

He seemed not to notice my hand spasm. Or if he did, he was very gracious about it. "This is a Brunello. Sangiovese grape. It is high in tannin."

I nodded, as if those words meant something. "Great. Let's try it."

He dispensed a tiny pour into a stemless glass and handed it to me. "Tell me what you taste."

I sipped. It tasted like wine. Like, a little more sophisticated than the six-dollar box, but still—wine. "It's fine."

He arched one brow. "Fine? No leather and tobacco?"

I tried another sip. Now that he'd said "leather and tobacco," it was all I could taste. "Huh. You're right. That's exactly it."

He turned to me. "Do you want me to pick a few different kinds of wine that are representative of different flavor profiles? Then you can eliminate the ones you do not care for, and we can narrow down which might be your favorite?"

It was adorable that he wanted to optimize the process for my enjoyment, but I wasn't really here for that. "We could do that," I said. "Or, we could just pour two glasses of random wine and compare notes."

His eyebrows lowered a smidge. "What if you select a wine you do not like?"

"I'll just drink it. No big deal."

Andreas seemed to stand straighter, as though taken aback by my words. "You should never have to accept something that you do not like or want, Samantha."

His tone was so earnest that I nearly snorted a laugh. I mean, come on. It was just wine.

And yet, I held back the laugh. His face was all gravity, as though I'd confessed to a grave personal failing.

Instead of saying exactly what was on my mind the second it occurred to me, I took a page out of his book and I let the moment breathe, gathering my thoughts before responding. "Andreas, it's not feasible to only go through life having exactly what I want. That's impractical and impossible."

He frowned, like I'd said something in need of urgent correction. "So, you drink the bitter wine? That is not acceptable, you deserve so much better than that."

His oddly touching statement was also vaguely annoying. "It's not that I want to drink bitter wine." I lowered my voice. "But if that's the drink life serves me, shouldn't I make the best of it? What would you have me do, throw the wine out and not drink at all? Isn't that like cutting off your nose to spite your face?"

He took the stemless wine glass from me and set it down on a nearby tray. He then gathered my hands in his and, frowning, his gaze somewhere between determined and concerned, he said, "Let me bring you all the wine."

Now I did snort laugh. "*All* the wine? You're going to bring me every bottle of wine that ever existed?"

"Yes." He nodded once firmly. "You do not deserve to make the best out of a situation, you only deserve the best situation. And then you choose which you like, and accept only those. You only drink the best wines, and the ones you actually want, from now on."

I wanted to argue that always getting exactly what one wanted eventually led to never being happy with anything. Humans needed struggle, we needed discontent, we needed something to strive for and rally against. Otherwise, where did character come from? And humor? Especially dark humor.

Andreas stepped closer. I felt the heat from his chest and the subtle pressure of his thumbs on the backs of my hands. The scent of his cologne and his rosemary shampoo invaded my senses, making my heart ping and my head light.

"Please," he said, not a demand but an entreaty. "Please let me do this for you. I want to do this for you."

I didn't have the vocabulary for the feeling that swept through me, but I nodded. "Sure," I said, voice steadier than my pulse. "Sure. I'll try your wines. But don't let me drink too much unless you want a repeat of what happened before Thanksgiving."

Andreas flashed a half smile. "These will be very short pours, so you can taste them. You do not need to drink them. There is a container on the table for those you do not wish to swallow."

I immediately censored a dirty joke about spitting and swallowing. Yes, I wanted to be more my true self without editing my words before I spoke them. But that didn't mean I needed Andreas to enjoy every single irritating thing about me.

A little bit of self-censoring goes a long way, and if more men understood this concept, the "male loneliness epidemic" in this country wouldn't exist.

But I digress.

"Return to the table." He released my hands after one last quick squeeze. "And I will select the first flight of wine for you."

Resigned to my fate of sampling expensive wine hand-selected by my incredibly hot, smart, and thoughtful fake fiancé—*woe is me*—I made my way back through the labyrinth of tables to our booth. Awareness prickled at my skin, and I scanned the other patrons as I passed, finding at least two parties watching me with a sort of fascinated detachment. Maybe they'd recognized Andreas? Or maybe wine people were like birders, always scanning for an odd species.

As I slid into the booth, my mind wandered, and I ended up replaying the tense car ride from the biology building to the wine bar.

When Tara and Andreas had returned to the car after their little talk on the curb, both had been stone-faced. At the time, I'd decided whatever business they'd discussed was best not brought up in the frosty air of the Mercedes. I figured I'd ask about it later, maybe after a glass of wine, when Andreas's tongue was looser and his inhibitions adequately marinated.

I liked Tara. A lot. I'd been attending her kickboxing class three days a week and loving every session. I'd also decided, once Andreas and I were no longer living together, I'd ask Tara if she wanted or needed a roommate. Obviously, if I inherited Oskar Kristiansen's shares of Genetix, I would be able to afford a place of my own. But I liked having roommates. I didn't like living alone.

Andreas appeared at the table with the same ease he did everything, this time trailed by a server holding a long tray with twelve stemless glasses of wine, each filled to the level of a swallow or two. The server set the tray on the table with a flourish, handed us a small notepad for tracking our favorites, then melted away.

Instead of sitting across from me, Andreas slid into my side of the booth, his body angled so his thigh pressed against mine, which made my heart twist. Before I'd recovered, he picked up my hand, thumb stroking my knuckles, and then, as if it were the most natural thing in the world, kissed the back of my hand. Again.

The effect of this touch paired with his closeness was chemical and immediate. I fought the urge to squirm, instead forcing myself to focus on the wine tray.

Once more I found myself asking what this was. Was he pretending still? Or was this real? I was so confused. And every time I convinced myself that Andreas was flirting, or truly interested in me, I'd gain a little distance and perspective and talk myself out of that belief.

Was this what other people did when they really liked someone? And if so, how did one exit this spin cycle of surging hopes and soul-eating self-doubt?

Cutting into my disordered thoughts, Andreas started with the first glass, describing it in a way that made me wonder if he'd studied as a sommelier. "Pinot noir from Oregon. Silky, with notes of black cherry and spice." He handed it to me, then watched with rapt attention as I sipped.

The flavor of the red wine burst over my tongue, though I lacked words to describe it. Peeking at Andreas's expectant expression, I sighed, setting it down. "It's good, I like it. But if you're waiting for me to tell you what it tastes like, I'm going to say 'good wine.'"

He smiled. "That is great, that is what I am hoping for. You tell me, good or bad. And that is enough."

I narrowed my eyes. "Are you sure? Because I can pretend."

His grin widened and he bit his bottom lip, eyes dancing over me. "What would you say? If you were going to pretend?"

Effecting a snooty and very bad pseudo-British accent, I cleared my throat and sat taller in the booth. "Notes of ripe candied melons sifted with pickled pepper residue and bee's anus dusted with honeysuckle pollen."

Andreas's eyes widened as I spoke and so did his grin, his features betraying his expectant anticipation. When I finished, he tossed his head back and laughed *heartily.* I mean, the man chortled. I set my elbow on the table and covered my mouth with my hand while I watched him, barely holding in my own laughter while also enjoying his.

When he gave his eyes back to me, they were shining, and he wiped away tears of hilarity while sniffing. "Oh my goodness. You are—I love how funny you are, Samantha. I love it so much. Please, never change."

Inhaling deeply to stave off the wave of nervous happiness, I shrugged, but discovered I had nothing to say to his praise because my brain was stuck on the word *love.*

He loves me!

No, doofus. He loves how funny you are.

. . . or, was this also part of the act? Was this still part of a performance?

I deflated, my confusion circling the drain of my confidence. I really hated this, not knowing what was real and what was fake between us. I needed to talk to Kaitlyn. I needed a sounding board who wasn't my therapist.

My therapist would tell me to be brave. SQUARE!

But Kaitlyn could be counted upon to advocate for caution. She'd been in a similar situation with Martin before they'd married. They hadn't fake dated, but she'd felt confused about his feelings for her, whether they were real or imagined. I now had newfound sympathy for my friend and her plight.

While I stewed in my whiplashing mood, Andreas moved on to the next wine, and the next, and over the course of an hour, we'd sampled all twelve wines. Sometimes I could catch a hint of whatever note he described—"graphite," "earth," "stone fruit"—but other times it was simply "good," "bad," "sour," or "sweet."

At some point during the second flight, my inhibitions dropped just enough for me to stop overthinking whether Andreas's behavior was fiction or nonfiction. I allowed myself to observe the apparent ease with which Andreas had settled next to me. His hand, still entwined with mine, remained on my thigh throughout, except when he needed it to refill my water or jot down a quick check mark next to a favorite on the notepad. I realized, with a slight start, that I hadn't felt this warm or this cozy in a long, long time.

Even if it was all ultimately for show, it was nice.

At the end of the second flight, Andreas ordered a glass of my favorite—some big, juicy blend from Paso Robles, which I promptly forgot the name of but remembered for its immediate, heady effect—and sat back to let me savor it. I nursed the glass, cheeks warm, pleasantly buzzed but not even close to drunk.

"I'll drink this glass slowly," I said. "In fact, I should probably have more water."

He reached over, topped off my water glass from the bottle, then handed it back. "It is good to hydrate."

I smiled easily, then watched as his face shifted from what looked like playful to intent.

Andreas angled his body more toward mine and, with a gentle seriousness, asked, "So, this James Nieminen who is now your PI. Why is he your PI?"

I froze, not out of fear but because I wasn't expecting the pivot to Real Talk. But it was clear Andreas had been turning the question over in his mind for a while.

I took a steadying sip of water. "I've already told you this."

He frowned. "You did?"

"Yeah."

His frown increased. "I apologize, but could you tell me again, please?"

Sighing, I fiddled with my wineglass. "Do you want the short version, or long?"

"Start with the short," he said, voice soft.

I reminded him of Tobias threatening me at the university; how he'd then pulled strings to freeze Dr. Hauser's funding; how, with Hauser's accounts on hold, I'd been transferred to Nieminen's lab because James had the only opening and was willing to cover part of my funding.

Andreas listened, features composed and unreadable, though his eyes seemed to darken when I mentioned Tobias and James. Or maybe his eyelids just seemed heavier.

When I finished, he took a sip of his own wine, then set the glass down with a quiet finality. "I am sorry."

I was thrown by the apology. "Why are you sorry? You didn't freeze Dr. Hauser's funding."

He shook his head, the smallest smile at the edge of his lips, but not a happy one. "I am sorry you have to deal with Tobias and Henrik and this Nieminen, and that my actions and wishes instigated all this trouble for you." He glanced around the bar, then back at me. "Samantha, let me know if you want me to get rid of him. I will leave it to you."

Now I frowned, blinking once. The way he'd said "get rid of him," I didn't know what he meant.

"Are you—" I shook my head, trying to clear it of wine and the cobwebs induced by my proximity to Sexy Andreas. "Are you saying you'll get rid of Dr. Nieminen if I ask you to? Like, remove him from his position in the department? Is that what you're saying?"

He nodded, his mouth opening, giving me the sense he wanted to say more. But then he pressed his lips together in a flat line. I watched his chest rise and fall with a deep breath before he finally settled on, "You let me know. I will do whatever you want."

[13]

ADULT FEMALE AND MALE
REPRODUCTIVE SYSTEMS

Samantha

We left the wine bar and walked through the lightly falling snow, neither of us in a hurry. The air felt more like powdered sugar than ice; it didn't bite so much as dust and then vanish. The only sound was the click of my boots on the concrete and Andreas's steady, careful pace beside me. I wore his left glove, which swallowed my hand, and he gripped my right hand in his bare left, tucking it deep into the pocket of his coat. It was possibly the most effective means of preventing frostbite ever invented, and it was also unfairly cute.

Most of the world had clocked out for the evening. Rows of apartments stretched above us, with windows like little yellow beehives, people moving and living inside each frame. For blocks, it was just us and the odd taxi, the hum of the city distant and muted by the snow.

We didn't talk. I kept waiting for Andreas to say something, but his eyes were on the street, like he was trying to memorize the shapes of the shadows or the traffic cones, or maybe he was playing some internal game of urban chess, seeing moves no one else could. He only broke the silence when we turned onto his block, pausing to scan the avenue up and down.

"Is it too early to put up Christmas decorations?" he asked with a seriousness that made me look twice.

I followed his line of sight to the lampposts, which were now draped in silver garlands and had huge, cartoonish snowflakes affixed at the tops. Every other building had pine wreaths or string lights over the awnings. Now that I took a moment to notice, it struck me as magical.

"It's the first Friday in December," I pointed out. "Christmas is less than twenty days away."

He nodded, absorbing this information with an almost anthropological interest. "What do you want to do for Christmas?"

It wasn't the kind of question I'd expected. "Do you not have any family you want to spend it with?"

He shook his head. "No."

I studied his profile. *No lie detected.* "Not even on your mom's side?"

Andreas considered this for a moment, then shook his head again. "No."

We crossed the street in tandem. I tried to remember if I'd ever actually spent Christmas with anyone in my adult life, or if it was always a hodgepodge of roommate dinner parties and Skype calls with Kaitlyn. "I go to mass on my own," I said. "And then, not much. If any of my roommates are around, we'll have dinner together. Kaitlyn is usually in California with her parents."

"What do you think about getting a tree for the apartment?" He made the words sound like he was proposing a research collaboration.

The last time I'd had a Christmas tree was when Kaitlyn and I lived together in our first off-campus apartment. I'd made gingerbread cookies and burned half of them, and Kaitlyn had decorated the tree entirely in purple tinsel, mostly because she'd gotten it for free. We'd even tried to make eggnog from scratch.

I'd forgotten how much I missed that, the precious little rituals.

I squeezed Andreas's hand inside his pocket. "Sure. Yeah. Let's get a tree."

His smile was small but instantaneous. But then he tore his eyes from mine and wiped all expression from his features while clearing his throat, eventually saying, "Then we will."

We arrived at the glass-and-steel awning of his building. Mr. Costa, the doorman on duty, held the door and smiled as we passed.

"Samantha. Hello," he greeted me warmly.

I returned his smile. "Mr. Costa. I hope you're staying warm."

Shifting his attention to Andreas, he offered a more formal sounding, "It is good to have you back, Mr. Kristiansen."

Andreas gave the man a small nod and responded with a simple, "Thank you."

We walked through the marble lobby and waited for the elevator, Andreas still holding my hand in his pocket as he glanced over his shoulder toward the front of the building. "Do you know the doorman?" he asked me.

My cheeks were warm, and it wasn't just the change in temperature. "Yes. Well, sort of. I introduced myself to all of them over the last two weeks and brought whoever was on duty hot tea and cookies in the morning when I left." Lifting my chin toward the building's entrance, I explained, "That's Mr. Costa. His wife works at the United Nations and he's a sixth-generation New Yorker. He gave me some good tips on the best Puerto Rican bakeries near our—I mean, your apartment."

Andreas nodded lightly, as though absorbing this information and deconstructing it into pieces. His gaze grew unfocused as he did so and he repositioned our hands in his pocket, fitting our fingers together more tightly.

When the elevator arrived, we stepped inside. Still, he kept my hand, holding it in his, our threaded fingers tucked in the pocket of his coat like we were smuggling contraband affection.

"Will you help me decorate the tree?" Andreas pressed the button for our floor.

"Yes." I smiled despite myself, and my reflection in the elevator's mirrored wall looked almost deranged with how wide the smile was. I couldn't remember the last time I'd felt so thoroughly flustered by someone simply standing close to me.

"Do you get any time off around Christmas?" he asked, tone conversational.

"Yes. The week between Christmas and New Year's."

"I have a tournament right after Christmas." Voice neutral, he glanced at me, then away. "In Rome."

There was a catch in my chest. I tried to ignore it, but it was there. A twinge of discomfort. "Oh?"

He didn't say anything more. But he did remove our joined hands from his pocket and look at them, as if calculating the odds of something he didn't want to say aloud.

The elevator deposited us at his floor, and as we exited. My palm had suddenly gone sweaty at the continued discomfort in my chest. I gently withdrew my hand, telling myself I'd done it so he could unlock the apartment. He did with his thumbprint, then gestured me in first, ever the gentleman.

Inside, the air was warm and smelled faintly of the cookies I'd made earlier in the day for the morning doorman, Mr. O'Brein. Andreas wordlessly helped me with my coat. Then I unzipped my boots, also without speaking. The mood between us suddenly felt introspective instead of comfortable.

"Thank you for letting me borrow your glove," I said, trying to mimic his good manners. Pulling off the borrowed glove, I handed it over to him.

Eyes on the offering in my hand, he took it, holding both gloves in one hand. "You should come with me. To Rome."

Looking up at him, I inspected his features. That mask he wore when we were alone together was now firmly back in place. Stoic and bored.

"For the tournament," he went on as though to clarify. "Since you have time off work, would it not look strange for you to stay here alone? We need to be careful and convince my brothers this is real between us. I do not think you want to open the door to suspicion. If you were my fiancée, you would travel with me." He set his jaw, the line of his mouth slanted downward.

The change in his demeanor from friendly to standoffish knocked the wind out of me. Not only that, but his reason for suggesting that I go to Rome with him—not because he wanted me there, but because we needed to keep up the charade—made my stomach turn cold. I'd been feeling so light, so comfortable in my little holiday fantasy, and now the idea of being together with Andreas in Rome simply to perpetuate our fake engagement sent all those swirling hopes straight down the drain.

This is all fake. And everything tonight, all the touching and joking and closeness, has also been fake.

My throat felt tight and I didn't trust myself to speak quite yet, so I made a short humming noise and stalled by lining my boots up neatly in the closet. Needing space, I then walked to the kitchen, filled a glass of water, and sipped it slowly. I wasn't drunk, but the leftover buzz from the wine made everything feel dreamlike, a little less real.

To put it bluntly, I didn't trust myself not to say something I'd regret.

A moment later, I sensed Andreas enter the kitchen behind me. A quick glance over my shoulder revealed him hovering at the entrance and leaning against the doorjamb.

He waited until I finished the glass, then said, "I am sorry."

I twisted at the waist, inspecting him again. He still wore the same expression, eyes half-lidded, gaze unreadable.

I faced the sink again. "What are you sorry for?"

"I overstepped, asking you to come with me to Rome. Of course, you should spend your free time as you see fit."

I laughed, a short, confused sound. I was too tired to keep up with him, his offers and apologies. So, I made another humming noise, hoping he would interpret my "Mmm" as he saw fit, and I rinsed out the water glass.

I didn't know how to exist in this gray area between what was pretend and what was real. No matter how much of a crush I had on Andreas, the constant confusion wore on me. What was performance and what was genuine?

Some of it has to be genuine . . . right?

Muddled and too much in my own head, I walked past him into the living room, plopping down onto the couch. He followed but didn't sit, instead standing at the edge of the rug, hands shoved in his pockets. I sensed his eyes on me, but this time I didn't glance at him to confirm.

It was strange, this behavior from him. Andreas was the picture of confidence and charisma in public, a master of social and literal chess, every move and every word calculated yet perfect. But in the privacy of his own apartment, when he had no audience, he withdrew into himself. He was quiet, almost sullen. The difference gave me whiplash.

Eventually, he spoke. "What are you thinking?"

Not wishing to share my actual thoughts, I searched for a subject change. My gaze snagged on the errant remote on the coffee table and I picked it up. "What does this remote go to? Both Tara and I tried using it and nothing happened."

He crossed to me and extended his hand. "May I?"

I gave him the remote, careful not to touch him. Andreas pressed a series of buttons and the large glass window that overlooked the city instantly went from clear to solid black, a privacy setting I didn't know existed. He pressed another button and a TV lifted from the floor, rising smoothly until it faced us.

I stared. "Whoa. So that's where the TV is." *What else is hidden in this apartment that I cannot see?*

In my peripheral vision, I saw him nod, then set the remote back on the table. He finally sat down on the sofa, albeit several feet from me. The distance felt like a gulf.

Again, I sensed him watching me before he spoke. "I would like to get a tree with you, for the apartment."

I looked at him then, confused by the repeated request. "Didn't we agree we would? Downstairs?"

Andreas set his elbows on his knees, leaning forward, and studying his hands. "It is hard to know what is true when we are in public. I did not know for certain if you meant what you said, or if it was for show."

A tingling heat disrupted my blanket of numbness and I turned, drawing my legs up. I felt a flicker of hope. He'd just broached the topic I hadn't been brave enough to bring up, and now I felt like he'd given me the perfect opening to clarify things without sacrificing too much of my pride.

"I'm actually really glad you said that." Staring at the pattern on the pillow, I attempted to choose my words wisely. "I—uh—feel the same. It's hard to know, when we're in public, what's real and what's not. I'm not sure if—for example—when you held and kissed my hand at the wine bar, was that something you felt like you had to do? Or was it something you, uh, wanted to do . . . ?"

A blush rose over his cheeks, giving off that same bashful aura from weeks ago, and he peeked at me. "If I do anything you do not like while we are in public, I hope you would tell me. And if I have made you uncomfortable, I am sincerely sorry. It is never my intention. I know we are being watched, and it is important for us to be convincing. But if it bothers you, or feels too real, I can—hmm—dial it back."

I examined him as he spoke, and the coldness returned in my stomach, extinguishing the earlier tingle of hope. My heart fell through my ribs. *Ah. I see.* I'd misunderstood. This was a warning, right? To remind me that all the flirting and touching was just for show, that I shouldn't read into it.

I breathed a short sigh that probably sounded like a laugh, but it was actually a sort of melancholy relief. At least now I knew. "Don't worry, Andreas. I know you're a gentleman. And furthermore, I know it's fake and you see me only as a friend. I won't get carried away with the fantasy or whatever."

He visibly stiffened, his eyes snapping to mine. "I—pardon? I only see you as a friend?"

I busied myself by standing and refolding a throw blanket unnecessarily. "What? Are you saying you don't even see me as a friend?" I tried to sound teasing, but the ache in my chest made it come out brittle.

He stared at me, wide-eyed and lips slightly parted, like my statement or my reaction was something he couldn't compute. I immediately regretted speaking.

Scrambling to break the tension, I wracked my brain for a joke. Eventually, I shrugged and said, "I guess you believe fathers and daughters can't be friends, hmm? The moment that adoption paperwork was filed, you turned into an authoritarian parent. Figures. *Yeesh.*"

Andreas stood abruptly, as if propelled by a sudden jolt of electricity. He was suddenly all nervous energy. Staring at me, he tore his gaze from mine, turned away, then back.

Finally, he blurted out, "It would not be a good idea for us—for you—to get involved for real. Not now. You shouldn't be—you should not think of getting involved with me that way."

The words hit me hard, and the rejection clothed as a warning stung like a motherfucking hornet. "I understand. No worries." My throat was full of rocks and I couldn't speak any further without risking stupid tears. Thus, I grabbed my phone and headed for my bedroom.

I heard him follow, his footsteps soft but determined. He stopped at the threshold of my room. Meanwhile, I found someone—Tara probably—had brought my backpack into my bedroom. She'd likely dropped it off after taking Andreas and me to the wine bar earlier. I assumed she'd then collected her things and gone home to her own apartment now that Andreas had returned. No need for her to babysit me anymore.

I picked up the backpack and dug inside it for no reason other than to focus my attention somewhere.

A pack of tissues.

That pen I thought I'd lost.

A ruler. Why do I have ruler? How long has this been in here?

"You do not want to be with me," he said, voice low and rough from behind me. "Please, trust me on this."

I nodded, not looking at him. "Got it. Message received."

He made a strangled sound, something between a sigh and a groan, and stepped into my room and into my side vision. He seemed to struggle with the words before settling on, "You should not be my friend. I am not worthy of even that. Samantha, you deserve—you deserve everything. I am not good enough for you."

He reached for my fingers. Reflexively, I yanked them away. "Okay. Like I said, message received. You can leave now."

He covered his face with his hands, then let them fall, the movement drawing my attention. His eyes were red-rimmed, his jaw set in a way I'd never seen. When he looked at me, I saw a storm of emotion. Maybe longing? Definitely pain and regret. And something else I couldn't name. Or maybe none of it.

Where correctly deciphering Andreas and his motivations were concerned, I didn't trust myself.

He seemed to wrestle with himself for a long moment, then said, "I want to be your friend, of course, and I have wanted you—to be your friend again—for so long. But if I am allowed to be honest and selfish, I want to be so much more than that to you, for you. You are—you are my—I know you will never—my father and my brothers—and I would never ask you to—I would never ask that you make any commitment to me when you do not—when I am—"

I tried to parse his broken thoughts and sentences, the words a stop-start rush of what appeared to be completely unplanned statements. What I could gather: He did like me; he wanted to be with me, but he didn't think he was good enough for me? Because of his family, because of what his family had done to mine.

I took a step forward, swallowing around my own surging hope, and lowered my voice, a counterweight of calm to his chaotic speech. "Andreas, I know you are not like your family. I know you aren't one of them. You're trying to help me."

He grabbed my hands, holding them tightly, and closed his eyes. Andreas shook his head, his jaw tight, but didn't let me go.

I kept talking, hoping my words would make a difference. "I would never put you in the same category as your family."

He looked at me then, his face etched with misery. "I do not deserve you."

I sighed. "Well, I'm not giving myself to you. It's not like we're really engaged. And, to be clear, I'm not asking for a commitment from you, nor am I offering one. In fact, I'm not sure I'll ever want a committed relationship with anyone. I never have before. But, allow me to be just as honest here, I am *extremely* attracted to you."

Andreas grew very still, his eyes searching mine, wide and frantic. They seemed to be filled with hope and reluctance in equal measure.

So, I added, "I like you. *A lot.* I think about you all the time. I missed you when you were gone and checked my phone obsessively for your messages. I've never felt this way about anyone. And, so, the idea of a romantic commitment is frightening to me. So, if you're not ready for one, that's a relief."

He seemed to stop breathing, and the raw desire in his gaze made my heart soar.

"We don't have to commit to each other," I said soothingly, lifting my hand to cup his face. He leaned into my touch, his cheek hot. "But we are here in this apartment together for the foreseeable future, and I don't see why we have to torture ourselves by holding back what it seems like we both want."

His breath came shallow, his gaze fixed on my mouth. "What are you proposing?" he asked, voice barely above a whisper.

I took a deep breath, sent a quick prayer upward for emotional bravery, and told him the truth.

"We both agree, we'd like to be friends, right? And we both agree, we want more than that. So how about we try something low pressure? How about being friends with, you know . . . benefits?"

[14]

SEXUAL DIFFERENTIATION AND DEVELOPMENT

Samantha

Andreas stared at me as though he waited for me to continue, as though *friends with benefits* couldn't be the entirety of my proposal. The way his eyes roved over my face, my neck, my chest—where my heart was hammering—left no ambiguity as to what he was thinking. Or, rather, what he wanted.

Say yes.

The air between us felt thick with tension, the silence heavy. It elongated, pulling the moment taut, stretching it until my nerves began to singe with anticipation. And, honestly, lots of lust. LOTS OF LUST!

Andreas was so sexy, so epically attractive in every possible way. I wanted him, all of him, so badly. I recognized my suggestion had been a tad reckless. Feelings—clearly, on both sides—were already involved. But he didn't think he deserved me and I was afraid of commitment. Thus, other than a no-strings, friends-with-benefits situationship, what was left? Walk away from each other? Call the whole thing off?

I was about to say something—anything, a joke, a question, a dumb comment about snow—when Andreas swallowed hard and rasped out, "I have never done that before."

He said it like a confession, every word precise and heavy.

"You mean friends with benefits?" I kept my voice gentle, like I was talking to a nervous undergrad on their first day of lab.

277

He nodded, very slowly.

"What about a one-night stand? Or hookups?"

He shook his head. I felt a jolt of affection for him. He looked both vulnerable and a little resentful. The admission about his lack of experience with noncommitted relationships had obviously cost him something.

Since he'd been vulnerable, I figured the least I could do was meet him halfway. Tilting my head, I studied him and asked, "Are you interested? With me?"

His answer came so fast, so automatically, that it had to be true. "Yes. Of course."

I smiled, I couldn't help it, the tension breaking for just a second. I genuinely hadn't expected that level of urgency or conviction, not from him. Perhaps he'd been restraining himself even more than I had.

Andreas watched me, and I thought I detected—no, I was sure I detected—a note of disbelief as he asked, "Are you interested? In me?"

Instinct, or maybe bad habits, wanted me to tease him. To drag it out, say something about how he was obviously the sexiest thing in a thousand-mile radius and he knew it. But if he currently felt even a tenth as brittle as I had moments ago in the living room, I didn't want to contribute to prolonging his suffering.

So instead, I stepped close and dropped my voice to just above a whisper. "Absolutely. So, why don't we give it a try? Hmm?" Unable to help myself, I pressed a light, teasing kiss to his lips, aware that this was our very first kiss without an audience. My stomach filled with rainbows and unicorns when Andreas swayed forward upon my retreat, as though his mouth were magnetized to mine.

"We're both adults," I continued, whispering, wanting this to be the real secret between us. "I want you. You want me. We already live together."

He remained silent. But in his defense, he looked entirely overwhelmed. I got the sense he half expected me to take back the offer, or say, "Kidding, this is a joke." Or maybe he thought this moment might be a dream and he was doing his best to stay asleep a little longer.

I reached up and cupped his face, pulling him gently into another kiss—just a brush, a soft invitation, nothing more. But when my lips caught his, he gasped, and then he took my hand in his, squeezing and pressing it to his jaw as though to anchor himself.

When I broke the kiss, his eyes were wide and raw with emotion and such visceral longing, my heart stuttered. He wanted this. Clearly, he did. So why was he still hesitating?

"Do you want me?" I asked. Perhaps he needed to say it out loud.

"Yes." It was a whisper, but it might as well have been a roar. "Very much," he added, as though he couldn't help himself.

The thrill that shot through me was electric. I wanted to laugh, to leap into his arms, to do every stupid thing I'd always made fun of in romantic movies and TV shows. Instead, I withdrew my hand from his face and brought it to the first button of my shirt. I unbuttoned the first button, then the second, then the third.

He watched my hands with a predator's focus. Abruptly, with a shake of his head—like he was physically shaking off restraint—he caught my wrists and stilled them. "May we—do you mind if we go slow?" he said, voice rough and uncertain.

My fingers went still on the fourth button. I looked up at him, searching his face. "Not at all."

His eyes dropped to my mouth again. "May I kiss you?"

"Please do," I replied, and this time it was me who leaned in, arms going around his neck. He responded instantly, his hands slipping to my hips, then my lower back, and then he pulled me to him, tight enough that I could feel the heat of his body everywhere we touched.

The kiss was different than the ones we'd performed in public. Softer, but also somehow more desperate. Desperate in the way one is desperate for air after being underwater for too long. He cradled my face in both hands, thumbs brushing my cheekbones as though trying to memorize the shape of me. And I realized there was nothing, absolutely nothing, fake about the way his mouth moved over mine, or how he shivered when I pressed up against his chest. Nor, I further realized, had there been anything fake in our previous kisses. He'd wanted me just as much then, and my heart cracked a little at how he must've suffered, waiting for me, pretending it was all pretend.

I felt his cock grow and lengthen, hard and insistent against my stomach, and couldn't help but smile into the kiss. When he pulled away for air, his breathing was ragged, his eyes glassy.

"I'm—I'm sorry," he stammered, as though his body's response was something to apologize for.

"Don't be," I said, and with one smooth movement, I reached down and slid my palm against the front of his pants.

Andreas's mouth felt open in obvious and silent shock and his entire body shook. His eyes fluttered closed, and for a second, I thought he might actually pass out.

"Do you want me to take care of this for you?" I murmured, grinning at the honesty and intensity of his response, fingers pressing lightly against the ridge beneath his zipper.

His eyebrows pulled together in something close to pain, and he nodded once, dazed.

He was so hot, so wound up, I wondered if it would take nothing at all for him to reach climax. I felt a rush of heady power at the thought, at the evidence of his desire for me. But I didn't want to overwhelm him; if anything, I wanted to see just how slowly I could make him unravel.

Dropping to my knees was not a move I'd ever considered especially romantic, but for some reason, doing it for him, in this context, felt like doing it for *us*. A particular kind of intimacy, one I'd never experienced, where giving meant receiving. Slowly, I unbuckled his belt, looking up at him as I did, and when I popped the button of his slacks, he flinched, like the sound was a gunshot.

"Wait," he said, voice strangled, eyes the size of quarters. "What—what are you doing?"

I grinned. "Taking care of this," I said, echoing my earlier words.

"You don't need to—you shouldn't—" he started, but I cut him off with a gentle tug at the waistband of his boxer briefs.

"Give you a blow job? What if I want to?" I teased, stroking my hands up and down his thighs. The fabric was expensive and soft, but the muscle beneath was hard as stone.

He said something then—something I didn't understand, a series of rapid syllables that sounded distinctly not English. Italian, maybe. I liked the way it sounded, dark and desperate.

Andreas bent down and forced me to stand, pulling me gently by the elbows until I was back on my feet. His face was red, his jaw clenched tight, and he covered his face with both hands again.

This was not the reaction I'd been expecting. This was beyond shy, beyond bashful. This looked like shame.

Holding my hands close to my chest, I asked haltingly, "Are you okay?"

He nodded, but didn't move his hands. "I have never done that before, either," he admitted, voice muffled.

I stared at him, stunned. "What? You've never received a blow job?" It came out louder than intended, but I couldn't help it. I was genuinely shocked.

Andreas shook his head, still not looking at me.

Who were these women who weren't giving Andreas blow jobs? I mean, maybe one or two of his previous relationships would've deferred, sure. No shade, no judgment. But *all* of them? Every single one? How was that possible?

I frowned, unable to let the question go, and was about to ask how many girlfriends he'd had, when another thought occurred to me.

I stiffened, suspicion smacking me across the face like a brick to the brain. "Andreas," I said, feeling unaccountably breathless. "Andreas, are you a virgin?"

His fingers speared violently through his hair, then laced together behind his neck. He dipped his chin, hiding his face. Silence.

I didn't know what to say. But now I understood what he'd meant by going slow. He didn't mean no intercourse. He meant kissing. Making out. Over the clothes. Eventually rounding bases, taking our time like we were new to this.

Because he was.

"I get it now," I said, softly, stepping closer. "I am sorry. I will go slow. *Actually* slow this time. Not, Mustang slow, but Cadillac-Fleetwood-75-driven-by-my-grandma-in-the-left-hand-lane slow."

He didn't answer but he did huff a laugh. It held humor, but it also held a fair amount of bitterness. He was so tense, so plainly mortified, that I felt a pang of protectiveness.

I reached out and pulled his hands away from his neck, encouraging him to lift his head. His cheeks were flushed, and his eyes were bright with what looked like frustration. I pressed a kiss to his cheek, unable to help myself, and then another featherlight one to his lips.

He immediately chased my mouth and kissed me back with a hunger I'd never felt from anyone before. He grabbed me, held me tight, and for a moment, the world spun. It was dizzying, the way he kissed me. No hesitation, just pure, unfiltered need. Like he wanted to hide himself in the kiss, escape his feelings.

But I did break away first, gasping for much-needed air. But I also broke the kiss because my knees felt wobbly and I didn't trust them to hold my weight if he kept kissing me like that. I backed him up until his legs met the bed. He followed where I led, hands grasping on my body. And when I encouraged him to sit down, he did, eyes never leaving mine.

Straddling his lap felt normal and natural, perhaps because we'd already found ourselves in this position twice. "We're going to go slow, okay?" I said. "I'll go real slow. We're just going to make out."

He nodded, eyes wide, so full of trust it made my heart ache.

"If at any time you feel uncomfortable, or I'm going too fast, just say—uh—checkmate. Okay?"

Some of the haze of panic cleared from his eyes, replaced by a tiny flare of amused confidence. "Should be easy for you," I added, "since you say it so often."

He gave a miniscule smile, finally meeting my gaze fully. There was so much in his face—relief, gratitude, hesitation, concern, and something that looked suspiciously like awe.

Settling more firmly onto his lap, I kept my hands light on his shoulders and kissed him softly, then trailed a line of kisses down his neck, lingering at the pulse that pounded just below his jaw.

He groaned, the sound vibrating through his chest. His fingers dug into my lower back, strong but tentative, as if he were afraid I might break. Or disappear. Or change my mind.

He slid one hand up, slow and hesitant, to the back of my head, threading his fingers through my hair and pulling me back to his mouth. The kiss was again urgent, teeth and tongue, but always gentle. Always careful.

I could feel his hands drifting toward my chest, then diverting at the last moment to my hips, my back. I got the sense that he was strategizing every touch, trying to calculate the optimal sequence.

Pulling back, breathless, I said, "Just do what feels good. You don't have to plan every move. I want you, okay? And I'll tell you if I want you to stop. Trust me."

He stared at me for a moment, and in those seconds I saw every flicker of worry, every strategy, every last-ditch plan run through his mind and get torched by the pure, incandescent need that was currently holding him hostage. Then he surrendered to it, to me, with a short, helpless sound, and kissed me again. Deeper this time, but no longer frantic.

I let him take the lead for a while, marveling at the way he seemed almost shocked by his own desire, the way his hands gripped my waist tighter than before, as if anchoring himself to a reality that was quickly coming apart at the seams. But curiosity—and maybe a little cruelty, and horniness—compelled me to see what would happen if I just . . . nudged things along.

I took his hand, which was clinging to my hip like a lifeline, and guided it upward, sliding it over the curve of my rib cage and settling it directly onto my breast, over the fabric of my shirt and bra. He froze, eyes wide, mouth parted in a stunned little O. For a long, silent moment he simply stared at where our hands met, as if he'd never quite believed this was something I would allow him to do outside of his daydreams.

But then, with a cautiousness so at odds with the ferocity of his earlier kisses, he began to move. His palm flexed against me, fingers curling, thumb gently tracing slow, painstaking circles that set every one of my nerve endings on high alert. The sensation was at once infuriatingly gentle and almost unbearably intense. I couldn't help it. I shivered, and my own hands clamped down hard on his shoulders for balance.

He watched that reaction, catalogued it, and then started to experiment. Testing out a firmer squeeze, a change in pressure, the migration of his thumb along the edge of my bra. I realized, with a stab of something strangely tender, that he was learning me, in the same way you'd learn the layout of a new city or the steps of a complicated dance. He was methodical, deliberate, but never cold. It was the chess genius at work, except instead of pawns and bishops he was strategizing flesh and bone.

It shouldn't have been so hot. But it was. *Fuck.* It was.

He tilted his head, eyes still on my chest, and then looked up at me as if seeking permission before adding his other hand to the equation. I gave an encouraging nod, just to see what he'd do next. The answer was a lot. He slipped both hands under my shirt and ran them up my back, fiddling with the clasp of my bra.

I was about to offer to undo it myself when I felt it unhook. And then, after a moment's hesitation, he glided his hand back around front, under my shirt and bra, skin meeting skin for the first time. He sucked in a sharp breath, almost a gasp, and swore in what I assumed was Italian—another one of those dark, beautiful series of liquid words that made me want to bite his mouth just to taste the sound of it.

Perhaps he was cursing at how good it felt, how badly he wanted it, despite all his previous restraint. I was suddenly, weirdly proud of myself, for being so tempting that this tightly controlled mountain of restraint had crumbled. I wanted to push him farther, just to see how far he'd go, but I held back. *Go slow.*

He kissed me again, softer now but less careful, like he'd decided to stop analyzing and just experience. His hips rolled, the movement plainly involuntarily, pressing his hardness against me. There was nothing tentative about it, nothing shy. The move was pure instinct, and the sound he made—low and ragged, vibrating up from deep in his chest—was the hottest thing I'd ever heard. Period.

My own body responded on autopilot, pressing down, grinding into him, and I could feel the wetness gathering between my thighs, slick and hot and insistent. The tension in the room spiked, and I could tell from the way his hands shook that he was fighting a losing battle with himself.

I bent my head, mouth tracing a line from his jaw down the column of his neck, pausing at the hollow of his clavicle just to see if he'd shiver the way I had. He did, and then some, his hands tightening at my sides, dragging my shirt up high enough that the cool air hit my bare skin and made everything sharper, more urgent.

He muttered something in Italian, and I laughed, feeling drunk on the entire situation. I licked the pulse at his throat, tasting salt and adrenaline, and he groaned again.

His hands roamed, greedy now, cupping my breasts, kneading and stroking until I was practically vibrating. And when he slid his hands under my bra again and roughly pinched my nipples, I gasped so hard, my cheeks flooded with heat.

He paused, panic flickering briefly across his face, but I shook my head and kissed him hard, reassuring. "Don't stop," I whispered, and the relief in his eyes was almost comical.

The next few minutes (hours? years? time was a flow state) were a blur of hands and mouths, skin and heat, the two of us tumbling and rearranging ourselves until I straddled him, shirtless and flushed.

He was still in his slacks and sweater, but barely—his belt was off, button undone, zipper halfway down. I hooked my fingers in the waistband, tugged, and he lifted his hips automatically to help me slide them down, never letting me go. He wore black boxer briefs, and the sight of him, tented and straining against the fabric, made me lick my lips.

One day, I promised myself, *one day you will be my popsicle and I will lick you like there's a heatwave.*

"Is this okay?" I asked, pausing, giving him one last out. Because with so few layers between us, an orgasm was coming for one of us. Actually, probably for both.

He nodded, breathless, eyes gone pitch-black with want.

I leaned down and kissed him, slow and deep, while my hands slid lower, exploring the cut of his hips, the sinew of his thighs. He trembled under my touch, every muscle in his body taut as a violin string.

I pressed my palm against him, over the cotton, and he arched up into my hand, gasping. I stroked him through the briefs, gentle at first, then harder, and he clung to me, one hand wrapped in my hair, the other digging into the flesh of my back, his mouth on my breast, wet and sucking.

He whispered my name, not once but over and over, each time softer, more desperate. "Samantha, are you—are you sure? Samantha . . ." It was like he was terrified this moment would vanish if he let go, and the sound of it did something to me that I couldn't quite articulate.

I slid my hand under the waistband, a new skin meeting skin, and wrapped my fingers around him. He was hot and hard and already leaking, and the way he shuddered when I stroked him was the purest thing I'd ever felt.

He tried to reciprocate—tried to unzip my jeans, to touch me, to explore—but I batted his hands away with a grin. "Let me take care of you," I whispered.

I worked him with slow, deliberate strokes, watching his face the whole time. Every hitch of his lungs, every flutter of his eyelids and eyebrows, every muttered curse or prayer in a language I didn't speak—it all added up to more *real* intimacy than I'd never experienced before. There was no performance here, no script. Just raw, unfiltered feeling.

Within what seemed like seconds, he was panting uncontrollably, hips bucking up to meet my hand, jaw clenched as if he could somehow will himself to last longer. But he was too new, too overwhelmed, and I knew the end was close.

"Samantha," he gasped, his voice breaking. "I think we should—have to—"

But before he could finish the sentence, his entire body went rigid. He grabbed my waist, holding on with an almost bruising intensity, and buried his face in my breasts as he came, hot and sudden, spilling across my hand and his stomach and my jeans.

The sound he made—half groan, half growl—ripped right through me, and the sight of him undone like that, so completely lost in sensation, made my own climax snap tight and sharp. I ground down on his hard thigh, seeking friction, and finished with a reckless, greedy desperation that was nothing like anything I'd done or felt before.

It was wild. It was messy. And it was—*he was*—completely perfect.

[15]

SEX DETERMINATION

Samantha

I didn't know how long I clung to him, maybe a minute, maybe an hour, maybe the half-life of a radioactive isotope. Time seemed irrelevant. There was only Andreas's heartbeat under my palm, the slick press of his arm at my back, and the warmth of our foreheads knocking gently together.

He was still breathing hard. As was I. My lungs were desperate for air. Every breath felt like it might be the one that reminded me of who I actually was, as opposed to who I became when he touched me. Or maybe this was who I actually was, a person with needs and feelings and a desire for this man that was so strong, it terrified me.

He lifted his chin and we kissed, slower and softer now, the rhythm of it tender and sustained. Then, some part of my rational mind—buried under the volcanic crust of post-orgasmic bliss—remembered the basic facts of anatomy and causality, namely that Andreas had come, spectacularly, and it was all over his gorgeous sweater, my hand, and my jeans.

Romantic, I know.

I shifted my weight to the side and managed, with an awkward crab-scoot, to avoid smearing even more of the evidence across my chest. It was only as the dopamine started to ebb, as my heartbeat began to slow, that a particular sensation rushed in. Not shame, not exactly, but a sort of dread, like a cold front arriving out of nowhere. The voice in my head piped up. *What have you done? You just made*

287

out with your fake fiancé like a desperate, horny teenager and it was the most fun you've had since . . . FOREVER.

My previous hookups—such as they were—had all been transactional and efficient. Maybe a few minutes of foreplay, then straight to the business, because why drag it out?

With Andreas tonight, going slow had definitely been hot, but it had also been . . . deeper, somehow. It felt less like eating fast food in a parking lot and more like feasting at a table with endless gourmet courses, each one better than the last, and finishing with the knowledge that I hadn't yet sampled the full menu yet.

Oh crap. Did this—did we just—did this mean something?!

It did. It had meant something. I hated that it meant something. I hated even more that I was terrified of what it meant.

I felt his arms squeeze me a little tighter, and I could tell he wanted to say something. The words seemed to vibrate in his chest, just waiting to be expelled. But I was not ready for words. I was not ready for analysis or debrief or, God forbid, a check-in about feelings.

"Here," I said, my own voice embarrassingly raw. "Let me go so I can clean up."

He flinched as though he'd just remembered I was naked from the waist up and covered in bodily fluids. "Oh. Yes. Of course."

I peeled myself away from him—careful to keep the mess corralled—and scuttled toward the edge of the bed, my hand held away from my body. "I'll just go take care of things," I mumbled, grabbing my discarded shirt with my clean hand and trying to cover myself.

I did not look at him. I could feel something like panic spreading from my chest to the tips of my ears and the backs of my knees. I did not want him to see it. In the hallway, I clutched the shirt to me, wrapping my clean arm around my torso in a vain attempt to feel less exposed. Hurrying into the bathroom, I locked the door and went straight for the sink.

For the first twenty seconds I did nothing but stare at my hand under the running water and try to catch my breath. Then I washed my hands thoroughly, and the memory of his voice in my ear, his hands on my breasts, the way he'd come apart under me—like I'd done something powerful and beautiful—came rushing back. It returned so bright and urgent it made me dizzy. I gripped the edges of the sink for balance.

When my pulse returned to something resembling a resting state, I splashed cold water on my face. Only then did I glance in the mirror. My hair was a disaster, a horizontal comet tail. My cheeks were blotched with red, and my chest and neck bore the unmistakable evidence of our lovemaking, a constellation of love bites and handprints covered my skin, and—

AHHHH!

Lovemaking?!

I scolded myself for calling it lovemaking, even in my own brain. It was not love. It was friends with benefits.

Yeah, yeah. That's the ticket.

I stripped off my jeans and climbed into the shower, setting the temperature to hot but not scalding. The water felt amazing and I washed everywhere, twice, even though there was nothing left to wash away except the memory of his skin against mine. While I stood under the spray, I realized that the thought of facing him again made me more nervous now than I'd been before we'd taken things to sexy town.

Why? Why would seeing him be so much scarier now? I tried to puzzle it out, tried to analyze my feelings the way I would a bizarre result on a gel electrophoresis, but the answer eluded me. All I could do was focus on the fact that, in a few minutes, I'd have to see him again.

After the shower, I dried off and wrapped the towel tight around my chest, tucking the corner in so it would stay put. Peeking out of the bathroom, I saw no sign of Andreas in the hallway; he must've retreated to his own room. I sprinted the short distance to my bedroom and shut the door. Rifling through my drawers for the baggiest, most amorphous sweatpants I could find, I tugged them on plus my old undergrad hoodie with the paint stains on the sleeves.

Dressed in full emotional armor, I sat on the edge of the mattress—which Andreas must've stripped of covers—and tried to steady my breathing. *You are fine,* I told myself. *This is the ideal scenario. Friends with benefits is exactly what you said you wanted. No strings, no feelings, no expectations. It's a system that has been mathematically proven to work for you. I have an adequately powered sample size!*

So why did it feel like my heart had just been scooped out and left to air-dry on the radiator?

I stared at the ceiling, debating the merits of remaking my bed, crawling under my covers, and—

That was when I heard it. The soft thump of footsteps in the hall.

Andreas's voice, quiet but clear, called out, "Samantha, may I talk to you?"

The sound of my name in his voice was like a defibrillator to my insides. Instantly, every nerve ending buzzed. I pressed my hand to my chest, wishing I could forcibly slow the arrhythmia, and tried to compose myself. I had a job to do. I had to be cool, calm, and at least plausibly collected.

"Yes," I called out, voice only shaking a little. "Be right there."

I took a few deep, centering breaths, then patted my cheeks to see if the flush had faded. It had not. That was fine. I could be pink. There was nothing wrong with pink.

Walking out of my bedroom and down the hall, I found Andreas in the living room, seated at the black table with a notebook open in front of him. When he looked up at me, his features weren't masklike and detached, nor were his eyes weren't cold or unreadable. They were full of warmth and interest and anticipation.

I melted. I straight-up, puddle-on-the-floor melted.

I stopped a few feet away and managed a small, shy, "Hi." The word sounded alien coming from me. I was not a person who said hi in a small or shy way.

Andreas stood up and crossed the distance between us. "Hi," he said, his voice not at all shy. It was deep and loaded with meaning.

He took my hand and kissed the back of it, eyes holding mine, the faint smile on his lips never quite leaving his mouth. I felt like I was living inside a classic romance, the kind where the guy is tall and dangerous and very European, and the girl is . . . not me.

He didn't let go of my hand as he asked, "Where are you sleeping tonight?"

I blinked at him, caught off guard. "I mean, should I sleep in my room? Now that you're back? Right? Or—"

He interrupted, "You should sleep in my bed. Since you do not sleepwalk when you start the night in my room."

"Oh," I said, voice a little high. "Then where will you sleep?" I bit my lip to keep from adding, *I hope it's with me.*

He seemed a little uncertain, like he hadn't anticipated the question. That made two of us.

I blurted, "Sleep with me." The words hung in the air for a beat before I realized how they must have sounded. "I mean, just sleep. Obviously. Because we're going slow. And I've already showered."

I cringed so hard my soul left my body and hovered near the smoke detector.

But Andreas grinned, his shyness from the before-sexy-times replaced by something both confident and sweet. "If you do not mind, then I think we should sleep in the same bed."

I squeezed his fingers, smiling so widely I was sure my face would be sore tomorrow. I had never, in my entire life, felt anything quite like this.

As we stood there, close enough for the heat from his chest to reach me, I realized the truth. I was in so much trouble. I was definitely falling for Andreas Kristiansen.

Or maybe, I already had.

* * *

THE NEXT TIME I opened my eyes, it was because something hot and heavy was pressed against my bottom, and there was the soft sound of breathing in my ear. For a luxurious, floaty moment, I lay still and allowed the sensation to register. The weight behind me was not, as I'd half dreamt, a particularly dense body pillow. It was a person—a six-foot-plus, brilliant and sweet, abnormally considerate Norwegian-Italian specimen—and that specimen was spooning me with the kind of thoroughness normally reserved for vacuum sealing.

Andreas's entire body was a study in contrasts. His arms were wound around me, one under my neck and the other slung lazily across my chest, hand splayed against the fabric of my hoodie, which I'd slept in and which now, thanks to entropy, was rucked up almost to my rib cage. His body radiated heat, and his leg hooked over mine, pinning me in place. The rest of him pressed to my backside, and—yep—there was something unmistakably hard nudging into the soft curve of my ass.

It was the textbook definition of being trapped in a good way. I didn't even try to move. If I so much as twitched, I risked shattering the illusion that this was a perfectly ordinary thing to wake up to. But the only thing I felt, aside from the urge to never ever move again, was the smallest, tiniest spike of pure, uncut bliss. And possibly something else, but I refused to identify it without a second opinion.

Andreas was still asleep. His breath was warm on my neck, the slow, deep kind that suggested total relaxation. But then he shifted and his hand slid up, finding its way under my hoodie. He cupped my breast, skin to skin. My nipple, traitor that it was, gradually went stiff as an ice pick in his palm. I was half tempted to reposition him, or at least see if I could nudge his hand back to a more neutral territory, but instead I lay still, eyes shut, and tried to see how long I could go without doing anything to disturb the moment.

Not long, as it turned out.

Andreas moved behind me, stretching just enough to arch his back and press his erection more firmly against me. I sucked in a breath. Quiet, but not imperceptible. He must have felt it because the hand on my breast flexed, then relaxed, then resumed its gentle, absentminded hold. I could not, for the life of me, remember ever being this turned on before. Even the memory of what we'd done last night paled in comparison to the feeling of being pinned beneath him, helpless and wanted by his subconscious.

That's when his breathing changed, the rhythm of it, and I knew the precise moment he awoke. Furthermore, I knew the precise moment he knew I was awake. His body went rigid, and the air around us went from languid to charged.

"Are you awake?" His voice was a whisper, still thick with sleep and just a little rough.

I meant to say, "Yes," or maybe, "Barely." Instead, what came out was an incoherent, "Mmm-hmm," that sounded an awful lot like a moan.

There was a beat of silence. I could feel the indecision, the hesitation, in every muscle of his body. I decided to shortcut the deliberation by shifting my hips back, just enough that the hard line of him slipped between my thighs, pressed up against the warm spot where I was already embarrassingly wet.

I expected him to freeze again, to say something polite, to maybe roll away in a fit of virginal moral fortitude. What happened instead was that his fingers tightened on my breast, and then he pulled both hands away from me at once, as if burned, and rolled onto his back with a groan of what sounded like genuine torment.

"Sorry," he said, voice muffled as he scrubbed both hands over his face. "I did not mean to—"

I rolled onto my back, stretched languidly, and reached for his hand. "You can touch me," I said, trying to sound casual and maybe missing by a few octaves. "I like it. You don't have to—"

He caught my wrist before I could finish and, in one smooth move, rolled on top of me, pinning my hands to the mattress above my head. His face hovered inches from mine, eyes searching, alarmingly hungry, but still so full of restraint I could've screamed.

"You like it," he repeated, voice soft and curious. "How much do you like it when I touch you?"

Feeling heat rush to my cheeks, I admitted on a squeak, "A lot."

His smile was immediate and he bent his head, brushing his lips over my throat, my jaw, my earlobe. The smallest, most calculated touches. It was like being edge-of-orgasm tickled with a feather dipped in liquid nitrogen.

"I do not want to hurt you," he whispered against my ear, his breath sending a shiver straight down my spine.

"You won't," I promised, and I arched up to kiss him, hard, messy, desperate. I wanted him to lose control again. I wanted both of us to lose it, at least for a little while.

For, you know, science.

He groaned into my mouth, and I felt his hips grind down, his cock pressing into me through the layer of my sweatpants and underwear. I moaned again, louder this time, and wriggled my hips, teasing him, urging him on. In a move that was both infuriating and deeply sexy, he shifted his weight to the side and brought his hand to my waistband, watching my face as he slowly, torturously, slid it down and inside.

"Okay?" he said, his eyes locking on mine.

I nodded several times.

He took his time, fingers gliding over my clit, then lower, then back, barely touching, making me feel crazy. For a minute or an hour I just lay there, panting, not even pretending to have chill.

Andreas watched my reactions, studying every shiver, every shift of my hips, and seemed to adjust his approach accordingly, switching from delicate to rough, slow to fast, until I writhed on the bed. He slipped a finger inside me, then two, pumping slowly, curling at just the right angle, and I nearly blacked out from the sensation.

He moved faster, mouth coming down to my neck, nipping and licking, and the combination of pleasure and tenderness was too much.

"I'm gonna—" I started, and then the orgasm hit. My back arched off the bed, and I clung to his arm, not trusting my body to stay anchored to earth. It was a full-body, brain-melting climax and the man had barely touched me. As I came back to myself, I realized I'd grabbed his hair at some point and currently held his face tightly against my neck.

"Oh my God," I managed, voice shaky as I released him. "I am so sorry—can you breathe?"

As he lifted his head, Andreas grinned at me, wide and delighted, his hair wild from my clutching. "I can breathe," he said, and he looked so genuinely proud of himself I started laughing, shaky and a little hysterical.

"You are so sexy, I l—" I stopped myself just in time, but I felt my face go nuclear. I hadn't finished the sentence. Even so, I wondered if he'd caught the implication. For me, it hovered in the air like a hazardous chemical cloud.

Andreas's smile softened, and he leaned down to kiss me, slow and sweet, then trailed his lips down my neck, lifting my hoodie as he went, and encouraging me to sit up just enough for him to take it off. I complied and was immediately rewarded with his mouth on my breast.

Not only that, his fingers returned to my underwear, gentle now, stroking, teasing. "Do you think you can go again?" he whispered, voice low and reverent. "I want to taste you."

"Mmm-hmm," I said in my now-signature moan of acquiescence. If he'd asked for a kidney, I would have handed it over, no anesthesia required.

He coaxed my sweatpants and underwear off, leaving me naked to his gaze, and propped himself up on one elbow to look at me. The way he did it—no smirk, no arrogance, just awe—made me shiver.

Andreas kissed his way down my stomach, hands tracing over my ribs, my hips, and then he spread my thighs, holding them open and wide.

The anticipation was unbearable, an ache, a static, a humming in every nerve. Andreas met my gaze from between my spread thighs, and for a split second, the world froze. Soft orange-pink light streamed in through the curtains, the sharp scent of his soap and sweat, his eyes on mine full of emotion I didn't dare name. Then he broke eye contact, his lashes lowering as he ran a single finger up the inside of my thigh, slow and gentle. My breath caught. He pressed a kiss to the side of my knee, then another, traveling closer, each one hotter, rougher, more deliberate.

The first pass of his tongue was tentative, exploratory, as if he were mapping the landscape of my desire in case he needed to draw it later from memory. I twitched, unable to stifle the gasp, and in response his hands tightened on my inner thighs, anchoring me, making it clear—without a syllable—that there was nowhere else I was allowed to be.

The second pass was nothing like the first. He licked me with greedy, unapologetic hunger, his tongue slick and soft and then, suddenly, hard and pointed, tracing circles around my clit with precision. The sensation was overwhelming, a scramble of pleasure flooded my thoughts and left me clawing at the sheets, at his hair, at my own skin. I became aware, in the most abstract sense, that I was making noises—unladylike, undignified, almost animal—and that Andreas was moaning in concert, the vibration of his voice making me lose my mind.

My body rebelled against the rules of muscle control; my thighs clamped tight around his head; my heels dug into the mattress; and my hands, acting independently of my brain, twisted into his hair and pulled, hard.

He sucked my clit between his lips, and the sound I made was so loud I was momentarily embarrassed, but then his hand pressed flat against my stomach and he groaned, "God, you're perfect," and I didn't care about anything except coming apart in his mouth. He repeated the word—"Perfect, perfect"—between licks, like he was programming it into my DNA.

The orgasm hit me sideways, unexpected and sharp, a heat-lightning strike that started at the base of my spine and radiated outward until I was nothing but aftershocks and stardust. The world went out of focus. I felt myself dissolving, my body a field of fireworks and trembling muscle, and I didn't even realize I'd sobbed out his name until his grip on my hips loosened and he nuzzled his face against my thigh, humming proudly.

I was still floating, unmoored, when he started again, this time with more patience and less urgency, as if he was savoring the slow, inexorable buildup for its own sake. He drew out the sensation—long, teasing strokes, punctuated by gentle bites that made me shudder. My third orgasm of the morning was nothing like the other two. It was slower, but more intense, like a wave lifting me higher and higher until I lost all definition, until my vision fuzzed at the edges and the only thing I could see was the flash of his eyes every time he looked up to see what he was doing to me.

I lost track of my limbs, lost my grip on everything but the sheets. My entire being reduced itself to one point of contact, one axis of pleasure, one spiral of sensation that kept climbing, kept fracturing, until I was babbling his name and clutching at his shoulders just to be sure I hadn't floated away altogether.

He slowed, finally, and rested his cheek against the inside of my knee, hands rubbing gentle circles up and down my thighs, as if he was coaxing me back into my body, reassuring me it was safe to return. I felt emptied out, like a glass flask rinsed clean and left to dry.

Damn. What a frickin' overachiever.

When I finally came down, Andreas slid up the bed and gathered me against his chest, kissing my hair and murmuring soft nonsense in my ear in a language I didn't understand. I'd never been held like this before, post-orgasm. It was weird, but in the best way.

I pressed my face to his collarbone and tried to slow my heart rate, aware that I was one careless word away from confessing something dangerous and irreversible.

I did not, under any circumstances, want to be in love with him.

But God, did it feel like that's exactly what was happening.

[16]

PHENOTYPIC SEX

Samantha

Two hours after I'd sworn off ever moving again, I was moving—down Fifth Avenue, hand in Andreas's. Manhattan in December was its own kind of Grimms' fairy-tale setting. Wool coats in every Pantone-neutral shade, the low and ceaseless whine of traffic, and the hint of holidays floating through the exhaust haze like cinnamon sprinkled on a garbage fire. My lungs burned and my thighs prickled from the cold, but I walked on. I wanted to make a joke about Brownian motion and city particles, but honestly, I was still processing the fact that, not an hour ago, I'd straddled the most brilliant mind in chess and tried (and failed) to convince him to let me reciprocate his boundless oral enthusiasm with at least one —ONE—act of service.

Nope. Andreas wanted to spend the entire morning making it about me, which sounded hot in theory but was, in practice, deeply aggravating. Every time my hand wandered below the waistband of his fancy pajamas, he'd detour me with kisses, or nuzzle my stomach, or grip my wrists and pin them above my head. He was too strong for my cleverest work-arounds.

I'd even tried logic. "You do realize this is supposed to be a two-way street, right?"

He'd just smiled, then gone back to methodically mapping my erogenous zones with the kind of attention to detail you only see in astrophysics or, well, chess.

By ten, I'd called it. "We need to leave this apartment or I'm going to combust."

He'd nodded, still panting slightly, and stiffly stated that he needed to shower. Then he'd rushed off to his bathroom. I did not peek to see if he went cold or hot, but I had my suspicions.

Presently, Andreas and I were headed north, our destination Central Park. I didn't bother to ask if there was an end goal. I was just happy to have this, whatever it was.

At the corner of 74th and Madison, we waited for the light, the pedestrian swarm eddying around us like we were a couple of decorative bollards. I took the opportunity to check his profile, the sharp nose, the gold-shadowed cheekbones, the hair that looked tousled and deliberate. He stared at me, too. Actually, he stared at me so intently that I felt myself grow self-conscious under the scrutiny.

"Is there something on my face?" I asked, which was a fair question. I'd skipped makeup and gone for a hat that could generously be called elf adjacent.

Instead of answering, he stepped forward, hand warm at my elbow, and bent to kiss me on the mouth. Not a peck. A real, intent, you-will-think-about-this-at-inappropriate-times kind of kiss. It lasted through the red light, past the walk sign chirping, and into the next cycle of traffic. Pedestrians flowed around us in an indifferent stream.

He only broke the kiss when a wet, heavy snowflake splatted on his cheekbone and began to melt down his neck. Andreas blinked, then produced a sleek black umbrella from the depths of his coat like a magician. He snapped it open and tucked me under his arm, both of us shielded in the bubble of warm breath and umbrella fabric.

"You realize this is the world's worst snow," I said, glancing out at the wet-ice downpour. "It's not even snow. It's acid slushy."

"I do not think it is so bad," he replied, leading me off the curb and onto the crosswalk. "It gives me a reason to keep you close."

I let that pass without comment, but I did slide my arm around his waist, snaking my hand under his coat and looping my thumb through the nearest belt loop.

We walked for several blocks, the city becoming progressively whiter and slipperier. The avenue ahead looked like it had been glazed with cornstarch. After a while, Andreas leaned his head toward mine, so close that his breath made the fuzz on my hat stand at attention.

"I apologize," he said quietly.

I cocked an eyebrow up at him. "Why are you apologizing?"

He answered, stone-serious, "We agreed we would discuss public displays of affection before engaging in them." For a second, I thought he was genuinely worried he'd broken our agreement, but then I caught the twitch at the corner of his mouth. Andreas, the king of the deadpan.

I slid my hand down beneath his coat and pinched his butt, hard. His eyes went cartoonishly round. Looking down at me, mock-offended but actually clearly delighted.

"That was before we agreed to a friends-with-benefits situation," I said, not even trying to hide my grin.

He considered this, head tilting, then asked, "Does that mean I do not need to ask before kissing you?"

"If you're uncertain, feel free to ask. And I'll do the same. Otherwise, just kiss me."

He nodded solemnly. "What about when we are alone," he asked, "can I touch you without asking?"

I waggled my eyebrows. "Again, if you're uncertain, just ask. Otherwise, just touch me."

He mulled this over as we crossed into the park, where the grass was still that eerie, too-green-for-winter color but the trees and railings had already been decked out in blue and silver Christmas lights. A massive menorah and a giant blow-up dreidel stood next to a line of wire-frame reindeer. *Only in New York*, I thought.

Or maybe just in the USA? I had no idea. I'd never traveled outside the country.

The path narrowed, and the snow got deeper. Andreas shifted the umbrella so that it covered more of me, which meant he had to lean down, almost folding himself in half to fit under the dome. We walked like this for a bit, not talking, and I realized I liked the silence. It was soft and companionable, not the awkward kind.

After a few more yards, he said, "What is the difference between what we are doing and actual dating?"

The question startled me so much that I nearly tripped on an icy patch. "What?"

"I mean," he clarified, "if we are friends, but we also have benefits, but we are not dating—what is the difference?"

I was about to say something glib, like "It's marketing," but instead, a more interesting question slipped out of my mouth: "Have you ever dated anyone?"

He nodded. "Yes. I have dated a few people."

This was not the answer I expected. "But you never went all the way with them?"

He shook his head, matter-of-fact. "No. But they were long-term, committed relationships. However, my traveling got in the way, and so . . ." He let the words trail off, as if the rest was both obvious and irrelevant.

I couldn't help myself. "How far did you go with them? I mean, in the sex department."

He answered easily, without embarrassment, "Just a few kisses."

I frowned, trying to line up my understanding of him with the data I'd just been given. "Your decision or theirs?"

He thought for a long time, lips pursed, eyes squinted. Then he said, "Mostly mine, I suppose. I am not . . . I am not a very affectionate person, I think."

I had to bite my tongue to keep from bursting into laughter. I was currently being held, umbrellaed, and generally coddled within an inch of my life. He'd spent the entire morning worshipping my body like it was the lost ark. But he considered himself "not very affectionate"?

"Yeah," I said, "you're a real cold fish." I didn't bother hiding the sarcasm.

He glanced down at me, as if to see if I was joking. I grinned back up at him. His eyelids lowered, his expression looking half annoyed and half smiling, and then he bent his head to my ear and whispered, "That is not what you said earlier."

I nearly tripped again, but this time it was because my knees gave out a little. The way he said it was so low and intimate I could feel it in my teeth.

"I surrender," I said, laughing but also gasping a little when he nipped the edge of my ear. "We are in public. You have to behave."

He looked at me, eyes bright and hot. "We should have just stayed in bed all day."

I tried not to smile, but it was impossible. "We should change the subject," I said, more to myself than to him.

He sighed, as though the effort of talking about something that wasn't us in bed was genuinely painful. "Fine. Then tell me, what is the difference between dating and what we are doing?"

I glanced up at the skeleton trees and the gray sky, trying to organize my thoughts. "When you date, it's my understanding that you're in a monogamous—unless discussed and agreed to be otherwise—emotionally committed relationship. But friends with benefits means you're not in a relationship other than a friendship and there is no expectation of genuine feelings developing between the two people. It's just for fun."

He listened closely, brow furrowed. "So we should not develop feelings for each other, right?"

I nodded, because my throat felt suddenly tight.

Andreas mumbled something I didn't quite catch.

Neither of us spoke for a while. We walked deeper into the park, the snow collecting on the umbrella, weighing it down so that Andreas had to occasionally shake it off with a flick of his wrist. I was grateful for the break from talking, but I also wanted desperately to say something that would lighten the mood.

So, after wracking my brain, I settled on a subject I'd let drop last night. "Hey, I've been meaning to ask, when I got in the car last night, you spoke to Tara on the sidewalk before we left for the wine bar. What was that about?"

He kept his gaze forward. "I wanted to make a slight change in your security coverage and wished to discuss it with her before I forgot. That is all."

I nodded, not sure if I believed him but not wanting to press.

He looked over at me. "Do you have any other questions?"

I thought about this. Did I? There were so many, it would take a lifetime to answer them. But one rose to the surface, a little buoy of curiosity in the murk of my self-doubt.

"Yes. Actually, I do."

He smiled, just a small one, and said, "I will tell you anything."

I took a deep breath, not sure how to start. "Tell me about you."

He blinked, surprised. "Me?"

"Yeah. After my father's funeral, I never saw you again, not until you showed up outside my department building. Tell me, what was your life like? Did you go to college? Or what was high school—or secondary school—like for you? Where did you live?"

He looked at me for a long time before responding, "This information about me is available on my Wikipedia page, I believe. Are you saying you never looked me up?"

I dodged the question, because of course I'd looked him up. But just once. "I want to hear about it from you. Will you tell me?"

He met my eyes, inspecting me. Eventually, he nodded, serious and open.

"As I said, I will tell you anything," he said. "You only need ask."

* * *

On Monday morning, I'd showered at home, washed my hair, shaved, exfoliated, and then—on a lark—put on a swipe of eyeliner and a hint of mascara. I even did the thing where you blow-dry while holding your head upside down, so my hair actually had some volume. By the time I'd eaten breakfast with Andreas, laced up my shoes, and stepped outside into the cold December rain, I decided that Mondays were underrated.

This feeling persisted, even as I badged into the biology building and took the stairs instead of the elevator up to my floor. Exiting the locker room still feeling fantastic, I did not walk; I sashayed, twirling the chain of my necklace as I walked, the engagement ring strung on it clinking against my sternum with a very faint, satisfying thwack. I hummed as I made my way down the gray cinder-block hallway to my cubicle, and the tune wasn't even from the radio or my phone, just a musical outburst from unknown origins.

A postdoc in the hallway looked up, startled, as I chirped, "Good morning!"

She blinked twice, then replied with, "Good morning. And congratulations!"

I did a double take but kept walking, only faltering for a half step. "Thank you?" I called over my shoulder, because I had no idea what she was talking about. Maybe it was a general congratulation, like, "Good job, you showered!"

As I approached the grad student bullpen, I passed two more people in the corridor, both of whom gave me the exact same look. A bright smile, eyes up and down my body, then a nod and a "Congratulations!" One of them even tacked on, "That's so exciting!" before turning into a copy room.

Now, I was really confused. Had I won some kind of grant lottery? Was there a rumor that I'd been awarded a Nobel? (Haha, as if.) Was there a secret plot among my colleagues to haze me with relentless praise? Or had someone uncovered my supersecret weekend activities, and this was the department's passive-aggressive way of expressing their jealousy?

Thinking about the weekend made me blush. Not just a little, but all over. In point of fact, the weekend was the single greatest forty-eight hours of my adult life. Saturday and Sunday mornings had started with mind-blowing and multiple orgasms. On Sunday, we'd transitioned into a few hours of nearly naked cuddling and eating breakfast foods in bed while we watched cartoons or random old chess matches on YouTube. Andreas did disappear for an hour or two to do, presumably, chess grand master things, and then came back to the apartment.

On Sunday night, he'd convinced me to try strip chess, which turned out to be less a contest and more a rapid-fire exercise in undressing me with maximum efficiency. I was naked after less than five minutes, but I didn't mind. In fact, I'm not sure I'd ever been so thoroughly, blissfully owned in my life.

He did *not* go easy on me. Not on the board, and definitely not off it. But for reasons beyond my comprehension, he was obsessed with making me come as many times as possible. The only thing that bothered me was that he barely let me reciprocate; any time I tried to make it about him, he'd just flip us over and start again. The man had stamina. I, meanwhile, walked around the apartment Sunday night on legs that felt like very tired Twizzlers.

But I'd lost count of how many cold showers he'd taken. I didn't want to push him to do more than he felt ready for. And yet—perhaps for the first time ever—I couldn't wait to make a man orgasm. I thought about it, making him come apart like he'd done to me over and over, all the time. Andreas, his body, and especially the parts of himself he withheld, felt like they were starting to become an obsession.

Maybe I need a hobby. I should learn to knit.

I was still a little sore when I reached the open office. Three people glanced up from their monitors as I entered. One raised a coffee cup in salute. Another said "Good morning!" and the third nodded and muttered, "Morning, Samantha." These were people who usually only offered a faint nod.

Confused, I made my way to my desk. Except—someone was already sitting there. Dmitry.

He slowly spun in my chair to face me, elbows on the armrests, fingers steepled, giving him an air of Bond villain meets mafia consigliere. "Good morning, Samantha. I have been waiting for you."

"Good morning, Goldfinger," I replied, lifting an eyebrow at his theatrics, and dropped my backpack at the foot of my desk. "Do you know why everyone is offering me congratulations this morning?"

Dmitry stood, tilting his head slightly to the left then right as though considering my question. "Hmm. Well, it could be one of two things as far as I'm aware, unless you also won the lottery. It could be—" Before he could finish, a shadow loomed over the cubicle divider. James Nieminen. He looked as though someone had rung him out like a wet sock.

"Congratulations, Sam," he said, voice so clipped it could have doubled as a surgical instrument.

I stared at him for a beat, eventually saying, "Thank you," and doing my best to sound pleasant and unbothered, which seemed to infuriate him.

He made a sound like he was going to spit, but held it in. "Since I'm no longer your PI, I'll need you to hand over all the projects you've been working on by the end of the day. You can just leave anything that's hard copy with my secretary and everything else can be emailed directly to me." He waited a second, for what purpose I had no idea.

I nodded, saying nothing, because I didn't know what he was talking about. Since when had he ceased to be my PI? My nonresponse seemed to disappoint him. He turned on his heel and stalked off, the back of his white coat flapping behind him.

I watched him depart for a full three seconds before looking at Dmitry, who was blinking at me with a mixture of compassion and high-quality-gossip hunger.

"What is he talking about?" I asked.

Dmitry shrugged, not quite meeting my eyes. "So, that's the first thing. It's all over the department. Dr. Hauser's funding was restored and her accounts were unfrozen over the weekend. You're now her number one researcher and teaching assistant extraordinaire again. She's not in town today, so she asked Carter with the administrative pool to tell you when you arrived. But Carter's such a gossip, he told everyone he saw on his way here and asked me to fill you in when you got to work."

It took a second for this to sink in. When it did, I lost all semblance of chill. "What? You're kidding. That can't be—that's—oh my god, that's—"

I hugged Dmitry. I literally leaped into his arms. He didn't reciprocate, but stood stiff as a post and offered a tepid "Yay."

I didn't care. I did a little dance in place, hugged myself, then threw my arms around Dmitry again. "Yay!" I squealed, unable to contain my exuberance.

He let me hug him but offered no further reaction, just looked vaguely to the side, as if waiting for me to finish.

I did, eventually. "Sorry, sorry. I got carried away." Folding my hands under my chin, I grinned at him. "Thank you for letting me celebrate. Now, what's on your mind? You seem preoccupied."

He squinted at me, as if weighing whether to ask what he wanted. After a second, he grabbed my upper arm and pulled me a half step closer, lowering his voice to a conspiratorial hush. "I thought you would never ask. Is it true that you are engaged to Andreas Kristiansen?"

I flinched back, nearly upsetting a mug of pens and pencils. "Who told you that?"

"James Nieminen," he said, shaking his head in disgust. "He's been circling around your desk for the last hour like a pickpocket. And when Carter came by to tell me about the funding restoration with Dr. Hauser, Dr. Nieminen snidely told us that the reason Dr. Hauser's funding was restored was probably because you, Sam, are engaged to the youngest son of the Kristiansen family, billionaire endowment supporters and controlling shareholders of Genetix. Is this true? Please tell me it's true. Even if it's not true, tell me it's true. But prepare yourself. Because Carter is definitely going to tell everyone that too."

I groaned and rubbed my forehead. "It's very complicated. Let's just say I understand why James believes that. But I have no idea why Dr. Hauser's funding was restored, and I certainly didn't have anything to do with it."

He nodded sagely. "But what about the other part? About you being engaged to Andreas Kristiansen. Is that true?"

I opened my mouth to respond, but before I could, Dmitry grabbed my hand with both of his and locked eyes with me, wild and intense. "I am a huge fan. I have followed Andreas's chess career since I was in middle school. Do not judge me for my parasocial relationship desires, but I have always wanted to be his best friend. If you are engaged to marry him, then you have to set us up so we can become best friends and I can live out my childhood fantasy of playing chess with Andreas while we sip martinis and him telling me I'm not a terrible player just before he beats me resoundingly. Can you do this for me? Will you make my dreams come true?"

I held back the urge to laugh admirably. Truly, I deserved a metal. With my free hand, I patted his. "I do know Andreas, and I will introduce the two of you. He is picking me up today after work, so you can meet him as early as today if you want. But whether or not you become best friends is entirely up to your sparkling personality."

Dmitry made a face I couldn't interpret, but I was a little worried it was his O face. Then he said, tone as flat as a pancake, "This is the happiest moment of my life."

I covered my mouth, again trying not to laugh, and he must have noticed because his grip on me tightened for a second before he let go and composed himself. "Thank you. I am so glad I never talked bad about you behind your back."

This time, I did laugh.

[17]

HUMAN REPRODUCTIVE BIOLOGY

Samantha

The rest of the day passed in a blur of grant paperwork. By four o'clock, my email inbox had been ambushed by no less than nine congratulatory GIFs, including a dancing gnome and a Mariah Carey that looped in perpetual vibrato.

I changed out of my scrubs in the nearly empty locker room and checked my reflection at least three times. Then, upon opening the door, I nearly walked right into Dmitry, who had apparently been waiting outside like a bouncer at a very selective night club.

He stepped back, gave me a very obvious up-and-down, then let out a low, unfeigned whistle. "When did you become so fashionable?"

I looked down at myself and, before I could stop the words, the truth fell out of my mouth: "Oh. Thank you. Andreas bought these for me."

Dmitry's eyes went wide, then almost crossed as he processed the statement. "You're using the best chess player in the world as your personal shopper?"

"He is not my personal shopper," I said, but the way it came out sounded false.

Dmitry fell into step next to me as we started down the hall toward the elevators, shaking his head in a way that made his glasses slip down his nose. "The kombucha drink you were raving about earlier today, didn't you say that Andreas bought that for you first?"

"Yes, but that doesn't make him my personal shopper." I tried to sound resolute, but my voice did a little trampoline bounce at the end.

Dmitry pressed the elevator button and fixed me with a side-eye. "He seems to know your tastes better than you know yourself. Didn't you say last week that your fiancé picked out the perfume you've been wearing recently? I assume you only have one fiancé."

Once we stepped inside the elevator car, I pressed the lobby button and made a low noise of defeat. "Yes. Fine. He did pick out the perfume, too."

"How long have you two been together?" The elevator doors closed, sealing us in with the hush of a confessional.

I deflected. "I've known him for a really long time, since we were kids."

Dmitry nodded. "Apparently so. For him to know exactly what cut and shape of clothes look best on you, and what color those clothes should be to flatter your complexion and bring out your eyes, and what food you'll like even before you try it yourself, and what perfume scent not only smells like heaven mixed with your unique pheromones but also uses your favorite flower, you two must've known each other since birth and he's been taking notes the entire time."

The elevator doors parted on the ground floor, and I said, "Cut it out. He should be waiting for me outside. Stop teasing me if you want to meet him."

Dmitry raised his hands, surrendering, but couldn't resist a last volley as we crossed the marble floor toward the security desk. "I'm just trying to point out, you are getting married to someone who loves you very much. A man does not pay this close attention to a woman unless he plans—or hopes—to spend the rest of his life making her happy."

My heart did a little twist and flutter, and I felt an unexpected blush prickle up my neck. Once upon a time, the thought of someone falling in love with me would have triggered a biological panic response. I would have ended the situationship. But Dmitry's words about Andreas didn't scare me. In fact, they made me . . . happy. Giddy, almost.

We passed the security desk, said goodbye to the guard, and walked straight for the main glass doors. Andreas stood waiting for me just outside, eyes on something in the distance. He wore a dark wool coat and a navy scarf, his hair swept back with the kind of effortless style that cost actual effort. I felt a tiny, irrational spark of joy at the sight of him.

"Are you ready? Your boyfriend is outside," I said, nudging Dmitry.

He stumbled for a second then hissed, "Only say nice things about me. Do not embarrass me in front of him. Or else."

I cackled. The sound actually startled a nearby student.

As we stepped outside, Andreas's gaze swung toward us and instantly focused on me. For a split second, his eyes did that thing where they got very bright. Then his gaze slid to Dmitry, and the corners of his mouth dipped slightly.

"Dmitry, this is Andreas Kristiansen. Andreas, this is Dmitry Bortnik, one of my fellow PhD candidates and my work husband." I grinned.

Andreas's frown deepened, but before he could say anything, I added, "That just means he's like my best friend at work, and I trust him, and he's very good to me."

Andreas's forehead cleared, and the side of his mouth pulled upward in a not-unfriendly way.

Dmitry shot me a look. "You should have called me your work brother, not your work husband."

Andreas took off his glove and extended his hand to Dmitry. "No, work husband is better. I do not get along with my brothers. It is nice to meet you. I am Samantha's soon-to-be real-life husband."

I tucked my chin into my scarf to hide my smile.

Dmitry gripped his hand. It was a very firm handshake but without aggression, the kind that telegraphed mutual respect. "I have followed your chess career for many years. You obviously already know this, but it is truly an honor to meet the best chess player in the world. I wouldn't let Sam marry anyone less impressive."

I did a double take at the chill in Dmitry's voice, like he was meeting an old friend for a beer and not the person he'd been fanboying over since—as per his own admission—he was a kid.

Dmitry continued, "I have to get going, but if you ever want to beat an amateur chess enthusiast, I am at your service."

Andreas grinned, a real, dazzling grin. "If you are free after the break, perhaps we could have you over for dinner."

Dmitry nodded, king of being unconcerned. "I will look at my calendar and get back to you."

As Dmitry started to walk away, I made a face at his retreating back, equal parts disbelief and admiration at how unshakable he was acting in the presence of his literal idol.

I waited until he was out of earshot before shaking my head.

"Was I nice to your friend?" Andreas asked.

"He is so weird. He's like your biggest fan and yet is all chill, acting like he has plans and needs to check his calendar before playing chess with you. What a weirdo."

Andreas's eyes sparkled. "Not all Russians are the same, obviously. But I had many chess coaches who were Russian, and my experience is if they said, 'Good job,' it was like getting a round of applause from anyone else. He seems similar. Understated."

I slotted my arm through his. "Enough about Dmitry. Why did you insist on picking me up this evening? Are we going on another date night?"

He tilted his head, feigning offense. "Did you forget? We're going to go pick out a Christmas tree."

I gaped. "We're doing it tonight?"

He nodded, entirely serious. "It is already past the first week of December. I made a list of tree vendors within walking distance."

I grinned, letting myself be led down the sidewalk. "Have you ever picked out a Christmas tree before?"

"No," he said. "I will have to defer to your superior experience."

"Indeed," I said, fairly certain my cheeks were going to be stuck in a smile for the rest of the night.

* * *

FOUR HOURS after Andreas had reduced my body to a grinning machine, we were locked in a silent domestic standoff in his apartment. The Christmas tree—our pride and sorrow—stood at one end of the living room, still oozing pine sap onto the plastic tarp we'd finally remembered to put down after the fourth try. At the other end, Andreas was slumped on the couch, arms crossed over his chest, a scowl engineered to repel all attempts at cheer.

"See? Doesn't it look great?" I said as brightly as I could without setting off his sulk sensors.

He glared at me, a thundercloud of discontent, and made a noise that might have been "Mmm."

I admired our work. The tree was lopsided. A quarter of it faced the wall because that's where the branches were the most anemic. Several strings of lights ran in drunken ellipses, not the crisp Fibonacci spiral I'd intended, and the stand oozed sticky sap onto a fortress of doubled garbage bags. I stood back, hands on my hips, channeling every suburban dad.

"Look at it this way," I said. "We couldn't enjoy the wonderfulness of this moment if we hadn't lived through the pain and suffering of setting it up."

The scowl deepened. Andreas might have been plotting to torch the tree and salt the earth with the charred remains.

Truthfully, the evening's pain and suffering had not been minor. We'd left my department together, hand in hand, and found a Christmas tree lot on the east side of Central Park, just as the sun dipped behind the buildings and threw the world into blue shadows. We had agreed on a tree in less than four minutes—a record that should have been immortalized on a plaque—but then our differing philosophies of logistics clashed like tectonic plates.

Andreas wanted to hire professionals. "I will call the building. They can send staff to pick it up and install it for us. There is no need for us to carry it," he'd said, already dialing the number.

But the whole point, I'd tried to explain, was to carry the tree ourselves. "Have you ever seen *When Harry Met Sally*?" I'd asked. "There's this part where they carry the Christmas tree back to Sally's apartment and it's iconic."

I'd pressed my case, citing romantic comedies and the importance of seasonal tradition. In the end, Andreas caved. He always caved when I made irrefutable arguments. Or, in this case, when I kissed him on the mouth until he lost the will to argue.

What followed was an hour of abject humiliation as we tried to drag a seven-foot balsam fir through the city without killing any pedestrians or ourselves. The net result was a trail of needles through the lobby, an irritated doorman who might've threatened to fine us for sap stains if I hadn't brought him so many cookies over the last few weeks, and several hundred calories burned in passive-aggressive bickering.

Then came the tree stand. Andreas had bought the most expensive one on the internet, which claimed to "self-center" and "lock in seconds." It didn't. It took us forty-five minutes to get the tree vertical, and it listed like a ship half flooded. Andreas's mood, which had started at "mildly testy," decayed in half-lives to "active volcanic rage." He began shouting in Italian. Eventually, we figured out how to fill the reservoir for water without unleashing a tidal wave onto the parquet.

We high-fived when it finally stood upright and didn't immediately topple. The moment lasted exactly three minutes, until we realized we hadn't put anything down to protect the floor. Which meant: remove tree, empty stand, mop, line with plastic, then repeat all prior steps. I'd laughed through most of it, which Andreas did not appreciate, but even he couldn't deny that the result—one haggard, needle-dropping, fully upright tree—was impressive.

But now, with the post-holiday-trauma haze settling, he looked at me like I'd personally invented Christmas for the express purpose of making him suffer.

I walked over and straddled his lap, resting my hands on his shoulders. He was all angles and tension, a physical object lesson in stubbornness. As soon as my butt hit his thighs, his hands automatically migrated to cup it, holding me in place like he'd been born with that evolutionary adaptation.

"Thank you for setting up the tree with me," I said, and kissed the tip of his nose.

He maintained eye contact, refusing to smile, a gesture of resistance that made my insides fizz. I lowered my mouth to his neck and whispered, "I'd like to show my gratitude, if you'll let me."

The hands at my backside slipped up under my shirt, fingers tracing bare skin at my lower back. His voice was wary but hopeful. "What do you have in mind?"

I licked his earlobe, slow and deliberate, then breathed, "Anything you want."

A full-body shiver passed through him, like a seismic wave. His hands roved upward, pausing at my ribs, then higher, fingers skimming the band of my bra. He found the clasp, flicked it open with deft precision, and said, "I would like very much to taste you."

I frowned, just a little. Not because I disliked the offer—far from it—but because I'd been trying to get him to let me reciprocate for days, and every single time I attempted to put my hands or mouth on him, he'd redirected the focus to me. His generosity was infuriating. I wanted to worship his body, to have him at my mercy, and he just kept giving and giving until my bones felt like they might dissolve.

I kissed down the side of his neck, letting my hair fall across his jaw. "Can we focus on you tonight?" I whispered. "I miss your body."

He exhaled, a hot rush of air against my temple, but didn't reply.

"Can I unbutton your shirt and touch you?" I murmured, letting my hands drift up the planes of his chest.

He hesitated—just for a beat—and then, voice rough, said, "Yes."

I slid my fingers down the row of buttons, popping them open one by one. As his shirt parted, I saw the flushed line of muscle down his sternum, the ridge and shadow of each ab. I could feel him getting hard, urgent and insistent against my inner thigh. The sight sent a thrill through me, and I had to lean back to really take him in. He was so beautiful, so perfectly put together, and yet right now, under my hands, he trembled.

I finished the last button and ran my hands over his skin, savoring the heat and the way he flexed beneath my touch. "Where else am I allowed to touch you?" I asked, half teasing, half daring him to answer.

He swallowed, throat working. "Anywhere you want."

Emboldened, I spread his shirt wide and let my palms roam, fingers mapping his chest, down his stomach, stopping at the waistband of his pants. "May I unbutton this?" I asked.

He gritted his teeth, seeming to wrestle with himself, and then nodded. "If you want."

I wanted. God, did I want. I slid my hands lower, unfastened the button, and began to unzip his pants. He watched, transfixed, cheeks blotched with heat and something else. Hesitation?

I reached inside, found the soft fabric of his boxers, the outline of his erection straining beneath. I stroked him, gentle at first, then more firmly, but before I could do anything meaningful, he caught my wrists.

"You do not have to," he said, the words squeezed out like he was in actual pain.

I tried to keep a frown from my forehead. "I want to. But if you're not ready, we can do something else."

His grip on me loosened slightly. "Like what?"

I considered, genuinely. What could we do that wouldn't be all about me, but also wouldn't push him past where he wanted to go? I bit my lip, then said, "You could watch me touch myself."

His eyes opened fully, dark and sharp, and his eyelashes fluttered as if the concept had winded him. For a long second, neither of us moved. Then I gave him a slow, sweet kiss. When I broke away, I easily twisted my wrists out of his lax hold and began to unbutton my own shirt.

"Would you like that?" I asked, just above a whisper.

He nodded, the motion small, his gaze molten.

I smiled, then moved to stand, but he caught my waist, grounding me to his lap. I kissed his jaw, then leaned in and whispered, "Let's move to the bed."

This time, he let me go.

I stood and slowly unbuttoned my shirt, letting it fall to the floor. Then I unzipped my jeans, shimmied out of them, and left them puddled by the couch. My bra was loose, barely holding on, so I let it slip off my shoulders and tossed it onto a chair. I was now in nothing but underwear and a cocky smile.

I walked to his bedroom, well aware he was following, and once inside, I flicked on the light and glanced over my shoulder to see if he was still watching. He was. Every step, every movement, his eyes tracked me with a hunger that bordered on devotional.

I sat on his bed and patted the spot next to me. "Sit wherever you want."

Instead, he stood in the doorway, arms at his sides, chest rising and falling. I lay back on the bed, parallel to the headboard, legs dangling off the edge. For a minute, I just let him look.

Then, with deliberate slowness, I cupped my breasts, rubbing and pinching my nipples, rolling them between my fingers. I could feel his eyes on me, like a current of heat, and I let myself imagine what he saw. My flushed skin, my hips pressed into the mattress, my hands working myself into a shudder.

I sucked my middle finger into my mouth, getting it wet, then slid it under the elastic of my underwear. The touch was electric, I barely needed to move before I began panting. I kept my eyes closed, wanting to memorize the feeling of his gaze, and started to work slow circles around my clit.

I heard him step further into the room, the sound of his feet soft on the floor. I cracked opened my eyes and saw him looming over me, shirt open, pants hanging half undone. His face was flushed and his mouth was open, as if he couldn't quite believe what he was seeing.

I got close, so close, the ache building and building. Kicking off my underwear, I brought my heels to the edge of the bed, and opened my legs wide. I slid a finger inside and let myself moan.

Andreas dropped to his knees next to the bed, face level with my body, his eyes burning with something primal. "May I?" he asked, voice hoarse and thick.

"Tonight isn't about me," I said, fighting to keep my hand in place. "I wanted to do something for you."

He licked his lips and said, "This is for me." Then, without waiting, he gently pulled my hand away and replaced it with his own, touching me with the perfect pressure, the perfect rhythm. "You are so wet," he murmured, almost reverent.

I almost came right then, the sight of his hand moving and his eyes fixed on my body was enough to push me to the edge. Before I could protest or even process, he bent forward and licked me, slow at first, then with intent.

My whole body jerked, a shock of pleasure racing up my spine. I tried to brace myself, but Andreas was relentless. He slid his thick finger inside me, curling it just so, while his mouth worked in wet, greedy laps. He groaned into me, the vibration like a tuning fork, and the sensation sent me spiraling.

I tried to hold back, to draw it out, but I couldn't. I came hard, knees locking around his head, fingers tangling in his hair as I bucked against his mouth. My voice echoed in the room, wordless and raw, and the orgasm just kept going, wave after wave, until I was certain I'd left my body behind and was now just a field of pure, radiant energy.

He didn't stop until I physically had to push him away, my skin so sensitive it hurt. He kissed his way up my stomach, lingered at my breasts, then settled over me and kissed me deep, tongue tasting me, hands cupping my face like I was something precious.

Andreas's hand drifted back down between my legs, and he stroked me, gentle and patient, coaxing. He looked down at me, his eyes hopeful and greedy all at once, whispering, "Do you think we can do that again?"

I laughed. Not a full-bodied laugh, but the soft, incredulous kind, and spoke my mind. "Don't you want me to go down on you?"

His whole body stilled. The question hung in the air, visible and vibrating. For a second, he looked shy, speechless. Utterly bashful.

I sat up, propping my arms behind me, and arched my back just a little, because if he was going to stare at me, I might as well give him a show.

He slid backward, away from the bed, and then knelt on the carpet at the edge of the mattress. He looked up at me, licking his lips. The movement was small, but it felt almost dangerous, like a warning that things were about to get very, very interesting.

"Andreas," I said, drawing his name out, "don't you want me to make you come?"

He closed his eyes and shook his head once. Not a no, but an attempt to clear it, to get back to the topic at hand. When he opened them again, the look on his face made my insides twist. It was desperation.

I let the silence bloom. I wanted him to say it, or at least admit it to himself.

Then, softer, I added, "I don't have to use my mouth. I can use my hand, like before."

He inhaled through his nose, then exhaled slow, nostrils flaring just a bit. I waited, studying the tension in his jaw, the lines of muscle along his neck.

Finally, while still kneeling, still refusing to move, he nodded. Once. Just enough to confirm that he'd heard, and he wanted. A thrill ran up my spine.

I watched him a second longer, then cocked my head and said, "Do you want me to use my hands or my mouth?"

He looked up at me, eyes wide and vulnerable. He took a deep, shuddering breath, then he said, "Your mouth," and it sounded like the words were forced out of him, a confession.

I suppressed a smile and stood up, still naked, and reached for his wrists, gently encouraging him to stand. He did, but looked uncertain, so I took charge and gave him a slow come-hither gesture toward the bed, pushing his pants all the way down his legs and turning him.

I pushed his shoulders gently and Andreas sat on the bed. Kneeling between his knees, I lowered my gaze. He still wore his black boxer briefs, but the fabric was already tented. For a second, I just looked at him, loving the way his entire body was wound up, his muscles tense, his fists gripping the mattress.

I met his eyes and didn't break contact as I reached under the waistband and tugged the boxer briefs down his hips. He lifted himself off the bed automatically, like he'd been trained in this. The second the fabric slipped over the head of his cock, it sprang up, full and flushed and utterly, beautifully exposed.

He was big. Not comically or cartoonishly, but enough that my first thought was, *That is not all going to fit in my mouth*. The shaft was perfectly straight, but with a slight curve at the end, the head thick, a slick bead of precum already gathered at the tip. The skin was smooth, and I realized with another jolt of pride that I was probably the first person to ever see it like this, up close and in the wild.

My mouth watered. I mean, literally. I swallowed, then smiled up at him, and wrapped my hand around the base. He sucked in a breath, lips parting, and his eyes rolled back for just a second before he brought them back to mine, still desperate looking.

I stroked him a few times, slow, just to get the feel of him. He was heavy, hot, the pulse of blood in the veins like a tiny earthquake under my palm.

He tried to speak, voice wrecked, and choked out, "I am not a good person."

I almost laughed, the words so out of left field I thought maybe I'd misheard. But he looked dead serious, like he genuinely believed his body was a weapon of mass destruction. Instead of arguing, I just leaned forward and, without breaking eye contact, pressed my lips to the tip of his cock.

He groaned. But then in the next moment, he shook his head and reached for me.

"No. I can't. We—we can't," he said.

Before I could say anything, Andreas grabbed me by the waist, hauled me up onto the bed, and crushed me against his chest. He kissed my neck, my jaw, my shoulder, everywhere he could reach, speaking in that frantic, beautiful language, and this time I was sure it was Norwegian and not Italian.

He kissed my breasts, my collarbone, my lips. He held my hands down so I couldn't touch him. And when I tried to speak again, ask him why he'd stopped me, he kissed me deeply and wouldn't answer.

[18]

THE NEONATE AND THE NEW PARENTS

Samantha

The Friday before Christmas, Kaitlyn's apartment was a zone of clutter and chaos. Packing cubes and zipped pouches covered every square inch of the sectional and ottoman. Every open surface bore witness to at least one pile. Baby onesies in a pastel avalanche, an unsettling number of travel-size Clorox wipes, industrial-strength diaper paste, and a dizzying array of chargers, cables, and adaptors.

I'd spent the day running interference on a fifteen-pound screaming potato so Kaitlyn could do recon at the shops and come home armed for her flight to California.

Now, in the late afternoon, the apartment was a battle between two competing energies. Kaitlyn, coolly methodical, folding and zipping and stashing with the efficiency of a veteran general; and Joey, who'd managed, against all odds, to wedge his entire body under the living room coffee table and was making a series of wet, determined noises that suggested the imminent birth of a tooth. But then he cried. It was his tired cry, not his wet-diaper cry. So I made him a bottle of stashed breast milk and rocked him to sleep.

When I came out of the nursery a half hour later, I felt *tired*, but determined. My job, as I saw it, was to be a sounding board and also to keep Joey from swallowing anything not on the pediatrician's approved foods list. I was failing at

317

the second one (at last count, he'd gnawed the corners off two foam packing blocks), but I was crushing it at the first.

Because all during Kaitlyn's packing session, there had to be an emotional component. It was required by law, like how TSA makes you take off your shoes even if you're wearing Crocs and have a TSA PreCheck tattooed on your forehead. Kaitlyn's emotional component was, "Tell me everything about your sex life, and don't leave anything out."

Earlier, I'd tried deflecting. ("Don't you want to talk about Martin?") But Kaitlyn had batted that aside. ("You already know everything.")

Now she was on her fourth packing cube, expertly shuffling pajama sets and toddler socks, when she said, "So, as you were saying before you put down Joey, you're going to Rome on Monday. What's the plan—just watch him play chess and drink espresso?"

I shrugged. "There's a spa at the hotel. He's got matches, interviews, and press the whole time. I'll mostly be making sure he eats and sleeps and maybe helping him avoid the international chess paparazzi." I paired the word *paparazzi* with jazz hands. "It's going to be a lot of room service and weirdly elaborate breakfast buffets."

Kaitlyn eyed me over the rim of a Ziploc full of charging cords. "What's on your mind? Something is bothering you."

I hesitated. I hadn't planned to say any of this out loud, not yet, but it was Kaitlyn. So, why not.

"It's weird," I said, picking at a stray Cheerio glued to my thigh. "We sleep together every night, and always end up cuddling. And then, in the morning, he's—like—extremely ready to do something as soon as I wake up."

Kaitlyn snorted. "Martin is the same way. It's like, as soon as I crack an eyelid, his hands are all over me."

I shook my head, not sure how I wanted to put this next part. "But with Andreas, it's strange. He only ever wants to give me orgasms."

She stopped stuffing pajamas and looked at me, full attention now. "What do you mean?"

"He's obsessed with my body," I said, feeling both ridiculous and, if I was being honest, smug. "He stares at me all the time. Like, it's not even subtle. It's like he's memorizing every square inch for a quiz. But he never lets me return the favor. It's like he's . . ." I trailed off, realizing I didn't know how to finish.

"He's shy?" Kaitlyn guessed, still folding but now mostly on autopilot.

"I don't know if that's it. He's a little shy, I think." I stared at the ceiling, running through all the data points. "But it's more than that. Like, I know he really enjoyed it when I gave him a hand job, but I get the sense he's denying himself for some reason. He's put up this internal boundary that he doesn't let himself cross."

Kaitlyn finished a cube and zipped it with a flourish, then set it on top of the suitcase with a thunk. "That's understandable. If you remember, I was very shy when I first started becoming intimate with Martin. I hated being naked in front of him, and not because I disliked my body. It's just, it felt weird, and not good-weird. It made me feel vulnerable, like it was a risk. Do you think that's what's going on with Andreas?"

I considered this. I'd shared everything with Kaitlyn, because all people needed someone they could talk to about absolutely anything, and Kaitlyn had always been that person for me. Likewise, I had always been that person for her. So, I knew she'd listen with full seriousness.

"Maybe," I said.

Kaitlyn abandoned the pajamas and perched on the edge of the coffee table. She watched me for a second.

"Have you asked him about it?" This was the most obvious solution.

I made a noise like a deflating tire. "I don't want to push. I figure he'll tell me when he's ready, right?"

Kaitlyn smirked. "I guess you just have to accept him giving you multiple orgasms every morning and every night until he's ready to tell you why he's holding himself back from reciprocation."

"He's taken so many cold showers, he actually got a cold last week," I said, and we both laughed, but I felt a little bad for him, too.

Kaitlyn pressed her lips together and said, "Poor baby. He's got it bad for you. Why won't he just let himself feel good?"

I shrugged. "I don't know. The only thing I can do is be patient."

She seemed to study me for a moment, eyes narrowed as if looking through a microscope. Then she said, "Have his brothers harassed you again?"

I shook my head. "No, thankfully. I haven't seen either of them for weeks. Are you suggesting that the threat from his brothers could be giving him psychological cock-block?"

"Hmm. I don't know. And what about his father. Any news?"

"No. In fact, Andreas hasn't heard anything for days, which is strange, so he sent someone to investigate. He should hear back today or tomorrow."

"Then, do you think maybe Andreas is being cautious because of the 'friends-with-benefits' and 'no-strings' thing you two have going on?"

I blinked at her. "What do you mean?"

"Maybe he's falling in love with you and he doesn't want to be devastated when you leave. So, he's holding himself back, reserving parts of himself."

My heart picked up pace, and I felt my cheeks flush. "Do you think so?"

Kaitlyn nodded. "If it were me, I would do the same thing."

I fumbled for a counter-argument. "What? Hold yourself back?"

"Yes," she said. "Because why would I give myself—my body—fully to someone who doesn't also want all of me? That's how I think, but maybe that's not how Andreas thinks."

She went back to her packing cubes, folding and stacking, but I could tell she was watching my reaction out of the corner of her eye. I stared forward, feeling a weird combination of guilt and longing.

After a minute, I blurted, "I think I'm in love with him."

Kaitlyn froze. The pajamas in her hands sagged to the table, forgotten. She turned to look at me, her expression raw and shocked. "Are you serious?"

I nodded, because anything else would have been a lie.

She said, "Oh my God," and sat down hard next to me.

"I know!" I picked up a throw pillow and pressed my face to it, muffling a scream.

Kaitlyn set her hand on my knee, squeezing until I looked at her. "Are you going to tell him?"

I nodded, still half buried in the pillow. "Yes. I feel like I'll burst if I don't tell him. And it's not fair, right? It's not fair of me to keep calling this no-strings when I want strings. We're heading to Rome for his chess tournament on Monday. I think I'll tell him in Rome."

Kaitlyn smiled, real and big, then pulled me into a hug. "You're not feeling squeamish anymore about him legally adopting you?"

I shook my head. "No. Not at all, actually. I haven't thought about that in weeks. Besides, it's all for revenge. It doesn't mean anything, it's just paperwork, and I certainly don't consider Andreas a father figure *at all*."

"Have you talked to your therapist about this? This is huge for you."

"Yes. And she agrees. I should be honest with him. And, she didn't say as much, but I get the sense she approves of him."

Kaitlyn laughed, and the sound was warm and safe, like a heated blanket right out of the dryer. "For the record, I approve too. I think he's great, and I love how he pampers you. You deserve pampering."

I smiled and felt a little overwhelmed by my happy feelings, which were rare and precious.

Waving my hands in the air, I said, "Let's change the subject. I'm already too obsessed with him as it is. Let's talk about something else."

"Okay . . . How's work? You haven't talked about work in ages."

I gave her the quick version of the drama that happened with Dr. Hauser and

James before and after Thanksgiving, hitting the highlights—the funding reinstatement, the departmental gossip, Dmitry's campaign to befriend Andreas.

When I finished, Kaitlyn shook her head. "I can't believe all of this was happening and you didn't tell me!" She smacked me with one of Joey's onesies. "You really are obsessed with Andreas. You didn't even tell me about something so important. Oh! Speaking of important. Wait right here."

She jumped up and disappeared down the hallway, then came back less than a minute later, carrying a pile of folders and papers. On top of the stack was a thumb drive.

"I know you told me not to, but I had Martin's people do some investigating about your dad and this is everything they found, in hard copy and digital."

I stared, stunned. I'd been so swept up in my romance with Andreas that I'd forgotten to do more digging into my dad's fraud case, a fact that now made me feel like a traitor.

"Oh my gosh," I said, clutching the folders. "Thank you. Thank you so much."

Kaitlyn shrugged, modest but pleased. "I figured you've been busy and I know how important this is to you. It's everything from the initial fraud complaint to the bankruptcy filing—I think you had that already, right?—to his death certificate. I also had them pull Genetix's initial corporate filing paperwork, just in case. I hope you find something helpful."

"Seriously. Thank you. This is amazing." I set the pile to one side and gave Kaitlyn another hug, tighter this time.

She said, "I just want you to be happy."

After the hug, I picked up the pile again and said, "Let me go put this next to my phone. I'll be right back."

I carried the folders and thumb drive to the kitchen counter where my cell was sitting. I realized, with a pang, that the phone was dead. I plugged it in and called back to Kaitlyn, "My phone is dead, I'm using your cable to charge it."

She called out, "Sounds good. Take your time."

I hovered, waiting for it to reboot. When the power finally came on, I had several missed texts, including a few from Diya, one from Tara, and one from Andreas.

I checked the one from Andreas first.

Andreas: Please message me when you get this. Oskar died four days ago and I've just been notified today. I'm on my way to the airport and will fly out immediately for the funeral, which takes place tomorrow in Oslo. Tara will pick you up this evening. She has your travel and hotel information. You need to be in Paris for the will reading Sunday morning.

I sat down at the kitchen table and reread the message several times before it truly sank in.

Oskar was dead. I couldn't believe it. I didn't know what to think. I'd thought we had more time. And now . . .

Shaking myself, I texted him back.

Sam: I am so sorry I didn't get your message until just now. My phone was dead. I will do as you've said and see you at the will reading on Sunday in Paris. Please take good care of yourself. I miss you.

I considered texting, *I love you*, but decided against it. Not yet. Not on the day he found out his father died.

I set the phone down, and for a long, long time, I just stared at the kitchen wall, trying to process the fact that everything had changed. My world had been turned upside down by a missed text message while my phone was dead.

Silently. And with no warning.

* * *

I'D TEXTED Tara from Kaitlyn's apartment and she'd appeared outside within twelve minutes. Now, thirty minutes after I read Andreas's message, I was in the back seat of Tara's Mercedes, staring out the window at the city, feeling oddly wired. I kept checking my phone, freshly revived and plugged into the charging port in the center console. No new messages from Andreas.

As the Mercedes sliced through the damp cold, the reality of what I was about to do caught up with me like a slap. I should have been thinking about the logistics of packing and getting to the airport, asking about travel arrangements once we landed in Paris. But all I could think about was Andreas, how he must have found out, what he was feeling right now, whether he'd had anyone to talk to on the way to the airport.

I wanted to be the one holding his hand, or at the very least the one texting him back within a reasonable timeframe, not after my phone spent six hours dead on the kitchen counter. I felt, for the millionth time, the bone-deep guilt of missing his messages, of not being there to offer a single goddamn word of comfort.

For the tenth time since Tara had picked me up, I opened the messages app and scrolled to the top, hoping for a late-breaking missive from Andreas. Nothing. But just below his thread, I noticed the messages from Diya that I hadn't yet checked.

Diya: Your grandfather came looking for you at the apartment today. I hope you don't mind, I told him your new address. He said he would call you and arrange a time to meet. It didn't occur to me until after he left that maybe you didn't want him to know where you live? If so, I am so sorry!

Diya: Please message me back.

I reread Diya's words three times, trying to parse them. The last time I'd seen my mom's father, he was packing everything that had been legally determined to be his into a moving van after my grandparents' divorce. He'd tried to hug me. I'd pushed him away.

He'd raised me from age fourteen to sixteen, and then filed for divorce the month my grandma was diagnosed with cancer. I'd never forgiven him for it. I wasn't sure I ever would.

"Hey." Tara's voice floated back from the front seat. "You want a protein bar or anything? Have you eaten? This traffic is dogshit."

I looked up at the rearview mirror. I could see the outline of her head, the edge of her ponytail, her eyes flickering to meet mine for a split second. "No, thanks. I'm good," I said, which was a lie, but she didn't press.

The car lapsed back into its private storm of engine noise and bad thoughts.

I pulled out the thermos of tea Kaitlyn had given me before leaving her apartment and tried to take a sip, but my hands were trembling too much to unscrew the lid. I jammed it back between my knees and turned my attention to the world outside. Bridges, overpasses, the blur of holiday lights in shop windows. All I could think about was Andreas's face, and how I would find him at the Paris hotel, and whether I could say anything that would make any of this less terrible. I knew he had complicated thoughts about his father, but the man was still his father.

When I next looked up, we were gliding to a stop outside Andreas's building, the familiar stone-and-glass box on the Lower East Side. I blinked, surprised at how quickly we'd arrived, then realized that my sense of time had been completely scrambled by the chemical cocktail of stress and shock. Tara double-parked and turned around in the front seat to face me.

"Can you wait here for a minute before going in?" she said. "There's someone at the door talking to Costa. Not one of our people."

I craned my neck and looked out the tinted window. Standing on the front steps, next to the doorman, was an old man in a navy peacoat and gray slacks, a heavy wool scarf knotted at his throat. He was hunched against the cold, hands shoved deep in his pockets, his head inclined toward the doorman as if listening to a secret. The angle was bad, but even at a distance I recognized the shape of his jaw, the stubborn set of his shoulders. My grandfather.

"That man is my grandfather," I said, my voice flat.

Tara raised her eyebrows, then looked out the window again. "Want me to take you around the back? Or wait until he leaves?"

I shook my head, surprising myself with the intensity of my own answer. "No, it's fine. I should see him." The words tasted bitter and unfamiliar, but I knew they were right.

Tara paused, studying me for a moment. "You sure? We can circle the block until he's gone."

"No," I said again, this time more certain. "I want to talk to him."

"Okay," Tara said, and put the car in park. "But Peter will meet you in the lobby to take you up to the apartment while I park. I'll be right behind you. If you want privacy, I'll keep the team away, but they'll be watching."

I nodded, grateful. "Makes sense. Um, can you bring up these files when you come up?" I gestured to the folders that Kaitlyn had given me, which now sat on the seat next to me. I'd placed the thumb drive in my bag.

"Sure thing," she said.

I opened the door and stepped out into the air, which felt like it had become colder over the last half hour. My legs were still wobbly from adrenaline, but I forced them into motion and walked up the steps to where my grandfather stood. He was arguing with Costa in the amiable, practiced way of old men who have spent years perfecting the art of polite combat.

He saw me first. His whole body snapped to attention, and for a second he looked exactly as I remembered him—sturdy, confident, more granite than flesh. But then I saw the age in his face, the slack at his jaw, the thinned patch at his hairline. His mouth worked for a moment, unsure what shape to make, and then a small, hopeful smile tugged at one corner.

"Hi," I said, stuffing my hands into my own coat pockets, suddenly fourteen years old again.

He nodded at Costa, who tactfully stepped inside to give us privacy. "Hey, kid," my grandfather said. His voice was softer than I remembered, a little worn at the edges. "How you doing?"

I shrugged. "I'm okay. How are you?" The words felt rehearsed, but it was the only thing I could think to say.

"I was in town and thought I'd look you up," he said, eyes skittering away from mine and then back again.

I felt my throat tighten, but I pushed past it. "I'm sorry I haven't been in touch. It's been—" I gestured to the city, the sky, my entire existence.

His eyes glistened, but he didn't look away. "Oh, it's okay. I know you've been busy."

I nodded, then blurted, "I have a plane to catch tonight, so I only have a few minutes."

His face fell just a hair, but he rallied. "That's okay. I just wanted to see you, make sure you're alright."

There was a silence, the kind that's both too short and too long, and I realized I wasn't angry at him anymore. Or maybe I was, but it was drowned out by the greater urge not to waste another second.

"I'm coming back in a week," I said. "Will you still be in town? Would you want to meet up then? Or, I don't know, maybe talk on the phone before that?"

He smiled, and this time it stuck. "Yes. Anytime. I can fly out here, too, if you want. Whenever you want."

He fumbled in his pocket for a phone. "Can I get your number? I, uh, only seem to have the old one."

I recited it, watching as he typed, then listened as he called the number. My phone, which was still in my hand, buzzed with the new contact.

I held it up and flashed the screen. "That's me."

He laughed, a little sheepishly, and then said, "I'll let you get going. But I'd like to see you. When you get back."

"Yeah," I said, and this time I meant it. "I'll call you."

He nodded, his smile going shaky at the corners. "Thank you, Sammy. I really miss you."

The words hit harder than I expected. I felt my eyes sting, and before I could second-guess it, I closed the distance and hugged him, hard. His arms came up around me, strong and warm, the same way they used to when I was a kid. He smelled like his usual aftershave and cold air, and for a second I wanted to take him with me upstairs and tell him everything.

But instead, I just said, "I missed you, too," and let go.

As I walked toward the lobby, I felt lighter, not because I'd let go of anything, but because I'd decided to carry it differently. I didn't know what would happen with my grandfather, or whether we'd ever be close again, but for the first time in years, I was done pushing people away. I wanted to believe that we all could change, including me. I wanted to believe that they wouldn't let me down, that they wouldn't leave. That it was safe to love someone.

As I greeted my guard and followed him to the elevator, I said a silent thank-you to Andreas. Without him, I wasn't sure I would've ever opened myself up again.

I felt . . . optimistic.

[19]

DYSFUNCTION

Samantha

Approximately thirty hours after I hugged my grandfather, I was sitting in a Paris hotel room, regretting every time I'd ever fantasized about waking up on another continent.

It was just past 9:00 AM on Sunday, which, if you did the math, made it about 3:00 AM New York time, or the eternal Now of jet lag. The hotel suite looked like the inside of a Fabergé egg, all gold moldings and white marble and so much velvet you could have upholstered an army of Marie Antoinettes.

I'd taken a midnight direct from JFK and my traveling companion had been Tara. We'd landed at Charles de Gaulle just after 2:00 PM on Saturday afternoon, and from that moment I had given up any hope of understanding what the fuck was happening, electing instead to simply follow Tara's lead. She produced a car from thin air, and then spirited us to a hotel so swanky I was half convinced they were going to kick me out if I ventured into the lobby.

The suite itself was another world. Two bedrooms, each with a king bed and a bathroom bigger than my undergrad dorm room. A private sitting room with a view of the Eiffel Tower so close it looked fake, like one of those Instagram filters that superimposes the Taj Mahal behind your backyard barbecue.

In any other circumstances, I would've been thrilled.

I spent the first five minutes after arrival in a sort of fugue state, staring at the pair of black dresses that had been left on the bed in my room. Both in my size, both with designer tags. One was a Givenchy, the other a Chanel. And I was supposed to pick one for the will reading, which made me feel like a paper doll dressed by a particularly chic god.

The next ten hours were a blur of attempts to sleep (fail), attempts to eat (triple fail), and increasingly desperate attempts to locate Andreas, who had not so much as texted since leaving for his father's funeral.

Earlier this morning, around 6:00 AM, Tara had claimed that his flight should have landed, and that he was probably "handling things," but as the minutes wore on and the silence grew, I became concerned something terrible had happened. What if Henrik had done something? Or Tobias had arranged for an unfortunate accident?

By 8:00 AM, I'd given up on checking my phone and moved to the sitting room, where I sat cross-legged on a cream brocade settee, clad in the less threatening of the two dresses, my hair styled and makeup applied.

My gaze strayed to the bundle wrapped in paper under the oval coffee table. For some reason, I'd brought Andreas's Christmas gift with me to Paris, the set of signed Bobby Fischer books. Now I felt strange about it. But Christmas was just days away. Even if we didn't celebrate while in Paris, I'd thought maybe I could give them to him, something to cheer him up.

Rolling my eyes at myself and how inadequate of a girlfriend I might theoretically make some day, I refocused my attention on my computer. I should have been reading over my father's files, aka Kaitlyn's gift to me. Instead, I'd been sitting with my laptop open, scrolling through the PDFs in a cycle of diminishing comprehension, never reading more than half a page before scrolling to the next.

Then, there was a knock on the door.

It was not a soft, French-hotel knock, but the kind you'd use if you were serving a warrant or delivering news of a tornado. I startled upright, staring at the door.

From inside the other bedroom, Tara called, "I'll get it. Stay put." She appeared in the corridor two seconds later, already in a black suit and boots, her light brown hair slicked back.

She opened the door.

I leaned to the side, peering around her, and saw Andreas standing in the hallway. My heart did an actual, audible restart. I set the laptop aside and bolted to the door, nearly tripping on the corner of an antique rug.

Tara started to say something, but I didn't let her finish. I shouldered her out of the way, which was sort of like shoving an iceberg, then threw my arms around Andreas's neck.

For a split second, his body went rigid. Eventually, he wrapped his arms around my waist and pulled me tight, so tight I thought maybe I'd never breathe again, and honestly, I was fine with it.

I kissed his neck because it was the only part of him I could reach without letting him go. "I am so sorry," I said, and the words came out in a rush, unplanned. "Let me know what I can do. I am sorry." I rubbed his back, which was taut and hard as a carved statue, and he shook his head, as if to say, *There is nothing.*

I heard Tara say, "I'll be in the next room," just before a door closed quietly behind us.

She was gone before I even registered the words, a true professional.

I pulled away and took Andreas's hand. He let me. I led him toward the sitting area, then shut the door behind us for privacy. I looked at his face for the first time and saw that the skin under his eyes was gray and bruised, like he'd spent the last thirty hours awake. There were faint white lines at the corners of his mouth, the kind that only appear when you've been frowning for days.

"When did you get in?" I asked, my voice soft so it wouldn't break.

He didn't answer at first, just stared at our hands like he was counting the bones. Then, all at once, he dropped my fingers and took two steps back, shoving his own hands in his coat pockets. "We need to go," he said, voice scraped raw. "Are you ready?"

Something about the way he said it—so flat, so unlike him—made me go stiff. But then I reminded myself that his father had just died. I told myself to be patient. Be normal. *Don't make this about you.*

"Yes. Let me put on my shoes and get my coat," I said, and went to fetch them. I could see him, reflected in the antique mirror above the fireplace, standing there like a dark pillar, unmoving.

I pulled on the shoes, leaving the straps at the ankles dangling, and I found the matching wool coat, shrugged it on, and turned to face him.

"Is there anything I should know?" I said, trying to keep my voice steady. "About the will reading? Anything I should be prepared for? Or is there anything I can do to support you and make this easier?"

He stared at the carpet, then at the chandelier, and then, finally, at the wall behind my head.

He spoke without emotion. "Tobias has a child. A daughter, by a woman he was involved with a few years ago. He tracked them down. He believes this daughter is the oldest and first grandchild."

I blinked, processing. "Wow."

Andreas continued, "He will be very surprised and unhappy when I show him your adoption papers. Henrik, likewise, will be unhappy, since Tobias has always taken care of Henrik, in a way. I will encourage the woman and the child to leave the room before Tobias or Henrik lose their temper, but I need you to not intervene."

I nodded, feeling sick for the woman and the girl who would have to be present for what was about to happen. "Understood," I said. "I won't intervene. But if you need me to do something, you just have to look at me."

He didn't reply, but his jaw unclenched, and I took it as a win.

Then, for the first time since he'd entered the room, Andreas looked directly at me. His eyes were cold and bright, but his expression was grave. "It is imperative that you stay close to Tara and the team. No matter what is said, or what my brothers do, or what I say, stay with Tara and the team."

I nodded, matching his seriousness, and bent to fasten the ankle straps of my shoes. "I will."

Some of the tension drained from his face, but not all. There was still something else, a thick, invisible layer of ice between us, and I didn't know how to melt it. *Be patient.*

I finished with the last strap of my shoe and straightened. Only then did I realize that every single item I was wearing—dress, coat, shoes, even the tights—had been bought for me by Andreas. And every piece fit perfectly. He'd chosen everything so that I would look the part, and now, walking toward him, I felt a bit like an accessory, one he'd designed for today's purpose.

"Tara. We are leaving," Andreas called, turning away from me.

Tara exited her room seconds later, but she hung back, her face a mask of professionalism.

Andreas opened the suite door for me, not meeting my eyes. I walked past him into the hallway, feeling the heavy thud of each heartbeat, and heard him let the door close behind us after Tara exited.

He walked in front, not beside me, setting the pace. I thought about reaching for his hand, then decided against it. Tara and four other guards who'd been waiting outside fell into step around me, a human wall.

We walked, the seven of us, through the silent, perfect corridors of the hotel. I wondered, not for the first time since reading his text message on Friday, what it would be like if I just ran away with Andreas to a place where none of this could reach us. But that wasn't reality.

Reality was a will, and a company, and two sinister brothers who would likely be blindsided, and therefore unpredictable.

Tara nudged me, a tiny, invisible reassurance, and I squared my shoulders. It was time to play my part.

As we reached the elevator, I looked once at Andreas, hoping to catch his gaze. But he was focused forward, jaw set, eyes fixed on the future.

* * *

IN THE BACK of another Mercedes, this time a limo, I tried not to sweat through my dress. Not because it was hot—it wasn't, it was very cold—but because I was so nervous. Tara sat next to me along with the four security guards from the hotel. The Parisian sky was the exact shade of the mother-of-pearl buttons on my coat.

I'd assumed I'd be in the same car as Andreas, that we'd go to the will reading together, but apparently not. Logistics had been handled with the same precision as a hostage exchange. Two identical cars, two sets of bodyguards, two separate routes through city traffic to the lawyer's office in the 16th arrondissement.

Through the window, the city unspooled in wet, gray ribbons—cyclists hunching past, children in wool coats dragging parents toward boulangeries, impossibly thin women chain-smoking under the eaves of apartment buildings. I didn't know if it was the jet lag or the situation, but the city looked haunted. Every block was like a different timeline, each building a monument to some secret history. It made New York look like a freshman attempt at culture.

The lawyer's building was an old limestone hulk that looked like it should have been repurposed as a museum or the headquarters of the Illuminati. The Mercedes rolled to a halt in a semicircle cobbled drive, and immediately the doors opened, Tara barking orders and the guards forming a phalanx around me as I stepped out. There was something deeply embarrassing about being flanked by five security professionals when you yourself were the farthest thing from an international asset, but Tara seemed to relish the moment.

Inside, the lobby was cold and sterile, the kind of place where the receptionist's lipstick was the only color in sight. I caught a glimpse of myself in the glass. Pale, overdressed, a little hollowed out around the eyes. Tara was a step behind me, and in her black suit and earpiece, she looked like a bulletproof shadow.

Then I saw him. Andreas. He was ahead of us, near the elevators, standing ramrod straight in his dark suit. He had no security detail now, just himself, hands folded in front of him, jaw set.

He looked back, saw us, and did not smile. Instead, he pressed the elevator call button, then turned away, as if to telegraph that we'd be taking different elevators. And we did. Andreas got into the first elevator alone, doors closing on him. Tara guided me toward the next set of elevators, then leaned in and whispered, "We're taking a more secure route. Mr. Kristiansen doesn't want to take any chances with your safety."

The way she said it—"your safety"—made it sound like I was the target of assassins. I suppressed the urge to laugh because Henrik Kristiansen was no assassin.

We rode in silence. At the twelfth floor, the elevator doors opened to a long, echoing corridor lined with gold-leaf mirrors and the sort of furniture that looks like it's only meant for looking at, never for sitting. As a group of six, we walked the last fifty feet to the double doors at the end.

Tara stopped in front of the doors and checked her watch. I could hear voices inside, faint and heated. Then, the doors swung open and someone who I assumed was a lawyer beckoned us in.

The conference room was so opulent it was offensive. The table was a single, carved slab of something dark and old, long enough to seat thirty. The chandeliers above dripped with crystal, refracting the winter light into a haloed glare that made my head throb. The windows were so tall and thick that you could barely hear the city outside. For a second, I wondered if that was the point, to make the whole will reading feel like it happened outside of time or worldly worries.

Henrik was already in the room, seated at the far end of the table. He wore a suit, but the tie was off and the top button undone. He looked like he'd spent the night drinking bleach. His eyes were red-rimmed, and as soon as he saw me, he started to grin—an ugly, hungry grin that made me want to throw up.

Tobias stood at the head of the table, hands braced on the wood, talking in low tones to a man I assumed was the lead lawyer. He was short and trim, with silver hair and a face like an old coin. He wore the most beautiful suit I'd ever seen, and spoke French in the rapid, clipped way I used to think was beautiful. Tobias gestured wildly, then shot a glance at Henrik, and then at me. His eyes didn't register me as a threat, and I felt a perverse sense of satisfaction at being so thoroughly underestimated.

Andreas entered the room last, as though he'd timed his arrival to coincide with ours. For the first time since I'd known him, he looked small—not physically, but in the way he moved, like he was trying to take up as little physical space as possible. He glanced at me once, then at Tara, then nodded to the lawyer.

The lawyer stepped forward and greeted Andreas in French. Andreas, likewise, responded in flawless French. The exchange was smooth and struck me as friendly. *Did these two know each other well?*

Meanwhile, I hadn't even known Andreas could speak French.

Tara led me to a spot at the long table as far from Tobias and Henrik as possible. She pulled out a chair for me, and as I sat, I could feel Henrik's eyes boring into me.

The lawyer conferred with a second attorney. There was a flurry of document shuffling and whispered strategy, then the one I'd assumed was the lead lawyer seemed to call the room to order.

Henrik leaned over to Andreas and said something in Norwegian, low and rapid-fire.

Andreas barely turned his head, then replied in English, crisp and flat, "No. Sam is not pregnant."

Tobias rolled his eyes. "Then why all the security?"

The lawyer said something in French, then switched, mid-sentence, to English so flawless it barely carried an accent. "I apologize, Ms. Jarlston. I will use English from this point forward." He bowed his head toward me.

I gave him a small smile of gratitude.

Tobias sneered, "Why pander to the childless American? The heir is Norwegian." He gestured with a dismissive wave toward the far end of the table, where a woman sat with a small child on her lap. The woman looked shell-shocked, her face locked in a stone mask of compliance. The child—maybe two—wore a miniature sailor suit and clutched a sippy cup in both hands.

I stared. The woman wouldn't look at me, and for a moment I wondered if she was here of her own free will, or if she'd been coerced.

Tobias spoke to Andreas, his tone smug. "And now father's shares belong to my child. Likewise, father's personal holdings and estate, which include all your mother's compositions, belong to me."

I stiffened. The last part was news to me. I settled my attention on Andreas, who was looking at the table, fingers laced together like he didn't have a care in the world.

The lawyer glanced from Andreas to Tobias to Henrik, clearing his throat as he did so. "Let us sit and discuss the matter thoroughly, yes?"

Tobias took his seat with an exaggerated sigh. "I guess what they say about sleeping around not paying off is all a lie, hmm? I can't wait to license your mother's songs for car commercials." He barked a laugh, then turned to the lawyer and said, "Isn't that right? Since I fathered the oldest grandchild, according to father's addendum, the personal estate passes to me, and that includes every piece of physical property that belonged to my dearest youngest brother's mother and every piece of intellectual property as well."

I shifted my attention back to Andreas again, and this time, he was smiling—but not in a way that suggested happiness. It was more like he was enjoying a private joke at everyone else's expense.

I tried to mask my confusion as my brain tried to make sense of what was happening. Meanwhile, Henrik—who must've noticed Andreas's smirk—shifted in his seat and glared at me. "Wait. What's going on?"

Andreas sat down slowly, folded his hands on the tabletop, and turned to the lawyer. "Shall we proceed?"

Henrik pointed at the lawyer and yelled, "What the fuck is going on?"

The little girl at the far end of the table started to cry, loud and abrupt. The mother whispered something in her ear, rocking her, but the noise only increased.

Andreas, calm as ever, said, "You might want to ask your child and her mother to leave."

Tobias stood up, hands braced on the table, and leaned in toward Andreas. "You've lost," he said, but he didn't sound so certain or smug anymore. For a second, I thought he was going to vault across the table and strangle Andreas.

Andreas sat there, eyes on Tobias, expression serene. "Allow me to introduce you to your niece, who I adopted last month." He lifted a hand to me. "She is now the controlling shareholder of Genetix, and is of legal age. Thus, she will be inheriting and have control of those shares as of today."

It was like time stopped. Henrik and Tobias just stared, mouths open, eyes bouncing from me to Andreas and back again. Even the lawyers seemed to freeze, reminding me of rabbits when they suspect a nearby predator.

Andreas continued, "And since I am the legal father of the oldest grandchild, all of Oskar's personal belongings—including my mother's compositions and property in Italy—pass to me."

A beat of silence. Pure, soundless suspension, a vacuum of air and atoms and time.

And then all hell broke loose.

Tobias lunged, overturning his chair, and screamed something in Norwegian that even I could tell was a collection of the most inventive curse words in the language. Henrik, instead of going for Andreas, actually went for the lawyer, grabbing him by the lapels and shaking him. The woman at the table shrieked, clutching her daughter to her chest. She stood and stumbled away from the kerfuffle.

Someone was calling for security. My guards didn't move. They simply stood in formation around me amid all the chaos outside the bubble of their protection. And inside the bubble, where I sat miring in my own chaos while stupidly staring at Andreas, I watched this man I thought I loved grinning triumphantly in the face of his eldest brother.

I realized, with no small amount of despair, that I had also been played by Andreas Kristiansen.

When I'd asked him all those weeks ago why he wanted to help me take over Genetix, he'd told the truth. He didn't want Genetix, he never had. He didn't care about the company.

But he'd also lied.

Andreas wanted his mother's legacy, her property, the rights to her music. *That's* why he'd sought me out. That's why he'd adopted me.

Perhaps that was also why he'd bought me gifts and meticulously won me over with nostalgia and sweetness and thoughtfulness and shy smiles. He'd seduced my mind, my body, and my heart. And I'd let him.

What had I been to him? A pawn? This whole time, had I been nothing but a disposable piece in his game? He'd lied to me. And he'd gotten exactly what he wanted from me. I thought I was so smart, but I was nothing.

No. I was less than nothing.

I was a complete fool.

[20]

UNSTABLE ENVIRONMENTS

Andreas

I'd been standing some distance outside Samantha's suite for five minutes. To my left, a tall blue vase loomed above the white marble pedestal like a flowerless cenotaph. To my right, a row of four security guards spaced at measured intervals along the hallway, each pretending not to see me, each one shifting in place with the periodicity of metronomes. I loitered exactly fifteen feet from her door. I'd measured it in paces when I first traversed the distance this morning.

These men worked for me. I'd hired them. Or, at least, I'd given the order for them to be here. The gracelessness of my idling in their presence didn't faze me. What I had not counted on was the pain in my stomach. The actual, physical sensation of needing to vomit and being unable to do so. The last time I'd felt this kind of visceral discomfort had been at my mother's funeral.

The hour was just past ten, Paris time. Lights in the hotel corridor were dimmed except for the spots immediately above each door. The walls were lined in blue silk the color of sea glass, and it made my black suit and shoes look funereal. I supposed, for this occasion, it was appropriate.

That moment at the will reading, when I'd revealed the truth to the room, played on repeat inside my head. Specifically, I recalled the way Samantha looked at me. Not with anger or betrayal. Not even with hurt. Her gaze exuded emptiness. As though I were a stranger, someone she didn't know and didn't wish to.

It had always been possible that Samantha might not forgive me. I'd approached her months ago with this knowledge, but it hadn't seemed to matter . . . *then*.

We'd been strangers, more or less. That we would—that I could, and almost from the very first moment I laid eyes on her, grow to care for her again so deeply after fifteen years apart seemed ludicrous. Standing outside her department building on that early fall morning, she'd unknowingly wrapped me around her finger; and she'd twisted me into knots in that café with effortless ease. But, it wasn't until the night she'd showed up at my apartment—bitter and sweet, dressed in black and stilettos—that I suspected I might be dealing with a queen instead of a pawn.

Closing my eyes, I exhaled, fighting the urge to crawl on my knees in front of her and beg for forgiveness, for absolution. Samantha would not want that from me tonight. She would despise it, and me, for being weak and inconsistent and continuing to lie, and she'd be right. She'd see through the performance.

Forgiveness wasn't what I wanted from Samantha.

However . . . *Later, perhaps*. In the fullness of time, Samantha Jarlston might someday permit me to kneel at her feet, and in that event, I would be more than happy to oblige. And if she wanted me to be sincerely sorry, if it would make any difference, I would—sincerely—be sorry. Yet, only if repentance won me her heart in the end.

But first, consequences. Pain and suffering. Which I assumed would culminate in either objects thrown at my head or a slap across the face by her own hand. Perhaps screaming. Possibly tears.

I hope it's not tears. I had no countermove for tears. No plan, other than to surrender. And I didn't want to surrender. I wanted *her*.

Squaring my shoulders, I checked my watch again (10:07 PM), and approached the door, ignoring the attention of her guards. I lifted my hand to knock and hesitated. What if she was already asleep? She slept fitfully under the best circumstances. I didn't wish to wake her. But I was also not a coward. Cowardice was a learned behavior, a vestige of too many years in the company of men who mistook ruthlessness for virtue.

Whereas, I was ruthless. But did not consider myself virtuous. Obviously.

I knocked, three precise raps, then braced myself.

The door opened after four seconds and Tara appeared, her face unreadable. She wore the same suit as earlier, but had lost the tie, and her arms were folded across her chest.

She looked at me and said, "She's in her room." No pleasantries.

"Is she awake?" My voice came out gravelly. I was not surprised. I'd been forced to shout over Henrik when the Police Nationale had arrived to take him into custody for aggravated assault against our father's favorite lawyer.

Tara shrugged. "She is not asleep. I'm going to take a walk. Text me when you're done."

She stepped aside to allow me entry and, as I passed her, I caught the faintest trace of—what? Pity? Disgust? I had the suspicion Tara wished to maim me, and also that she would have been entirely justified in doing so.

Tara closed the door to the hallway, leaving me in the darkness and silence of the suite's entryway. I took two deep breaths and walked into the suite proper.

The suite had two bedrooms, and the main bedroom was at the end of a short corridor lined with mirrors and low, blue-lit sconces. I walked slowly, careful to keep my steps light. Sam's door was ajar, and from the crack of it, I could see the square of bright light from her laptop screen, and her form hunched in bed, shoulders up, head down.

I stood there for a moment, staring at her, the way her long hair curled at the edges, the angle of her jaw above the collar of an old sweatshirt. She scrolled with one hand and picked at her thumbnail with the other, something she did when she felt overwhelmed. A tell, I speculated, she wasn't aware of.

Abruptly, she glanced up and spotted me in the doorway, our gazes clashing. Yet, her expression didn't alter at all.

I knocked softly, pushing the door open wider, and said, "May I come in?"

She closed the laptop with a snap. "I'll come out." Her voice rang neutral and monotone.

I retreated to the sitting room and waited for her to appear. This was not a sensation I was familiar with. In chess, you lost, and then you immediately began analyzing the defeat for lessons, weaknesses, patterns. I had never been checkmated in love before, the irony being that I'd checkmated myself. The rules were unfamiliar.

Samantha entered the sitting room and stood ten feet removed from me, hands pushed into the front pouch pocket of her sweatshirt, hair falling around her shoulders. She regarded me with what I wanted to believe was blankness, but in reality was probably contempt.

"I know it's late," I said.

She didn't move, didn't nod. Just waited.

"Before we discuss anything else," I said, "I have something important to tell you."

She blinked, her features softening just a little, eyes seeming to spark to life. "Go on."

I exhaled, surprised at my own nervousness, but forged ahead. This confession would, hopefully, be the worst part. "I am the one who froze the funding for your PI, Dr. Hauser, back in November. That was not Tobias, that was me."

She stared at me for a beat. Her face went slack. I recognized that she required a moment to process this news and I braced myself for her reaction to my manipulation. *Please, no tears. Anything but tears.*

But Samantha didn't cry. She smiled. It was a bitter, twisted thing, and it made me wish she'd cried instead.

Then, she laughed, short and sharp, and turned, walking to the window and wrapping her arms around herself. She stood with her back to me, looking out at the city.

"After what happened today," she said, her tone steady, almost academic, "I wondered if it had been you. Tobias told me, when he came to see me that second time after Thanksgiving with a bribe, that he hadn't done anything to me yet. And then, when you and I went to that wine bar, you asked me if I wanted you to get rid of Dr. Nieminen. It struck me as strange at the time, but I never would've suspected you until today."

The urge to apologize, or at least to explain myself, bombarded my better judgment. But I knew both of those pathetic displays would only make her hate me more. I stood there in silence, hands at my sides, breathing through the sting of it.

After a long pause, she said, "You did tell me once that you were not a good person. I should have believed you."

I gritted my teeth. The memory of saying those words, of believing myself to be the villain, was suddenly, acutely real. I was a villain. I'd almost let her put her mouth on me because I'd wanted it more than I'd wanted my next breath in that moment. I'd wanted her so badly, I'd almost let it happen. I didn't regret stopping her. If I hadn't stopped her, I would truly be a weak-willed coward. And I'd hate myself just as much as she hated me now.

Telling her, as she lowered to her knees, that I wasn't a good person didn't absolve me of any sins. But absolution wasn't my goal. What good would that do me? I didn't want her to move on, I wanted her stuck, just as I was stuck. Truthfully, pathetically, I wanted her even if she hated me. Even if she never forgave me. And I would settle for any part of Samantha, at any time.

That was now my goal. A sliver of her attention. A bone thrown in my direction at her discretion. Given my sins, just that would be a miraculous victory.

Her back still to the room, she cleared her throat and said, "I think I know why, but tell me anyway. Why did you have Dr. Hauser's funding frozen?"

I'd rehearsed an answer to this question. "I knew, if your position were threatened and you thought Tobias was responsible, you would accept my proposal to let me adopt you. I knew Tobias interfering in your life would anger you and lead you to seek revenge against him." My statements were one-hundred-percent honest and also provided just enough detail and type of information to paint a clear picture of the situation without me self-indulgently explaining additional context for my decisions. Context would only sound like excuses.

What I'd done was ruthless and without virtue, even if the end result meant Samantha inherited the shares of Genetix that should've been hers by birthright.

She was silent again. I could see the tension in her shoulders, the way her hands curled into fists at her sides. I waited for her to say something, anything.

She didn't.

I swallowed, and found I had to focus in order to keep my voice steady. "Do you have any additional questions for me? I will answer anything."

She shook her head, slow and methodical. "No. I think you covered everything else this afternoon at the will reading."

There was a sharp, literal pain in my chest. Her dismissiveness and lack of curiosity hurt me. I wanted to say her name but knew it would sound like an entreaty, which she would likely view as deceitful.

Anything I said beyond the relaying of factual, verifiable information would be discounted, derided, filed under manipulation. Thus, appealing to her now on any personal level, or with any emotion, was not a viable strategy. I knew this.

I forced myself to swallow the hurt silently and reached into my coat pocket. I pulled out a bank card and flicked it between my fingers. "This account contains approximately the same amount of money that was in your parents' bank accounts before the fraud allegations, before the bankruptcy. The pin is your birth year and month."

She turned slightly. I could decipher the reflection of her profile in the window's glass, but she didn't look at me. "You can leave it on the table. And it goes without saying, I think, that I will not be paying you back for any expenses incurred while we lived together."

I nodded, blinking against a sudden stinging in my eyes, and masked my tone in equanimity. "I would not accept it, even if you did try to . . . reimburse me." I placed the card on the table and added, "The security team is with you for another six months, fully paid. And I have arranged for an apartment for you in New York, the lease is paid through the end of next year."

She nodded, arms still around her middle. "Looks like you covered everything. I assume my things are already out of your apartment?"

"Not yet."

Samantha seemed to pause, like this information surprised her. Then she turned and looked at me, eyes finally meeting mine, and asked, "Why not?"

"I did not wish to touch or move your things without your consent."

She barked a laugh, then shook her head. "That's funny. That's a good one."

I felt my jaw clench and grind with the effort it took to remain silent, to not explain myself or my reasoning. I'd led us here. No one but me. And if she wished to laugh in my face, she deserved the distinction of being the only person I would ever allow to do so.

When her laughter tapered, we stood in silence for a long time, simply staring at each other. I wondered what she saw, or if she suspected how carefully I'd planned this interaction.

If I weren't a villain, this would likely be where we said goodbye. I would apologize for using her and lying to her. I would let her go. This brief interaction would be the finite end of our acquaintance.

That had been the original plan because she was never supposed to care about me, or want me, or even like me. Obviously, the original plan had changed that first night she'd sleepwalked into my bedroom. I began bargaining with myself and formulating new schemes, ones where she eventually forgave me and we remained in each other's lives in some capacity. I'd studied her preferences, asked her friends for information about her, studied her partialities and dislikes, selected items as gifts I felt certain she would adore, hoping to make myself indispensable.

But that night I'd returned from London, Samantha had annihilated all my assumptions about us, about what might be possible in the future. I'd never considered the possibility that she might want *me*. And so, I'd stopped focusing on how to earn her forgiveness and friendship and began plotting how to keep *her*.

This meeting—this conversation—was part of my new plan. A necessary, albeit painful, step for us to move forward. Each move orchestrated, each statement prepared. I hadn't expected it to hurt this much, but letting Samantha go was impossible now.

If my father had just lived for another three months, I might've strategized a solution, mapped out how to tell her the truth without losing her in the short term. I might've convinced her to love me, to keep me. But the timing was off.

"I leave for the tournament in Rome soon," I said, and covered my urge to grimace at the banality of my words by glancing down at my shoes.

"I'm sure you'll win. You always do." Her emotionless statements were like ice water down my spine.

I had one more thing to say, and then I would leave. I simply needed to speak.

Yet, I couldn't force my mouth to move. I didn't wish to leave her, not even for a few days or hours. And the urge to beg, to plead, again pressed forward against my better judgment, sending my heart to my throat. My vision blurred. My breathing grew labored. I felt myself waver.

Please. Please love me back. Please forgive me.

Suddenly, Samantha tore her gaze from mine and turned away. "If there's nothing else . . ." Giving me no chance to respond, Samantha walked to her bedroom and closed the door behind her with a gentleness that cut more than the violence of a slam ever could.

I stood there in the blue-lit silence, staring through blurred vision at the closed door beyond the corridor, the blood rushing between my ears a dizzying commotion, drowning out all other sounds. Then, without warning, I crumpled to the floor.

I covered my face with my hands and struggled to breathe. I thought I might cry. I didn't. Just waves of numbness, followed by excruciating pain, over and over.

Eventually, I stood. Feeling lightheaded, I sat on the sofa and clutched my forehead, breathing in deeply through my nose and out through my mouth. Tomorrow, I would begin again. I would stay the course I'd set, employ an improved strategy.

I would win her over in some capacity. Eventually. Because the alternative felt unfathomable.

[PART 3]

EVOLUTION

[1]

THE HISTORY OF EVOLUTIONARY BIOLOGY

Samantha

Sitting in my old apartment's tiny kitchen, I tried my best to listen as Nakita performed a play-by-play of last week's online chess drama. She stood at the counter, grinding gingerroot and peppermint leaves using a pestle and mortar. Every now and then, she punctuated her monologue with a clatter of marble against marble, or the tap of her phone, like a one-woman percussion section with strong opinions about a global fandom.

Kendra was out, as usual—still spending most nights at her boyfriend's place—and Diya, my favorite person in the world who currently hated me, was still sleeping off a night float rotation and was due to wake up any moment. Thus, presently, it was just Nakita and me, plus a kitchen table that was approximately the size of a cafeteria tray, and a new, monstrous Edible Arrangement I'd brought as another peace offering.

The arrangement squatted on the stovetop like an alien queen head, bristling with pineapple stars and chocolate-covered strawberries, shedding flecks of coconut onto every available surface. It was, in a word, ridiculous. But it was also one of Diya's favorite things to receive as a gift.

"—so then they said, if you read all the An-Romic fic, you'd know that it's not even about the chess, it's about the unresolved sexual tension," Nakita was saying as she scooped the peppermint and ginger mixture into a tea infuser. "But then obviously the An-Romval stans had to weigh in, and you know they're feral about

347

historical accuracy, so it's just all-out war at this point with the An-Romvals on your side."

I tried to focus, but the bouquet kept drawing my eye, its bamboo-skewer spine slouching to the left. It looked like it was leaning in, listening with interest to Nakita's summary of how the online chess fandom was reacting to the latest news this week of Henrik and Tobias's lawsuit against me. Also, as far as I could follow based on Nakita's descriptions, someone had snapped a photo of Andreas and Roman Buckley walking together in Central Park recently and it had caused a fervor of speculation.

Were they official? Were they finally dating now that Andreas's fake engagement had been made public? Were they scoping out apartments together? Were they planning to get married and adopt children? Rumors were swirling like mad and Nakita was all over it.

"Sam," Nakita said, waving a hand in front of my face. "You spaced. I just told you, the An-Romics are not very happy with you at all."

I blinked and tried to rejoin the conversation at the last noun I remembered. "An-Romics?" I echoed, which bought me a solid three seconds as Nakita pulled off the little foil freshness seal on the bear-shaped plastic honey dispenser with her teeth.

"You know, the Andreas and Roman shippers. The An-Romics? Have you been listening at all? For someone who's basically the main character in this whole debacle, you're really bad at keeping up with your own discourse."

Nakita finally plopped down at the table, slopping a mug of tea for me dangerously close to my left hand, and shoved a napkin toward me.

I made a face. "Sorry, I can't keep up with all the names. And I still don't understand why the Andreas–Roman shippers are called An-Romics when you told me the couple name for Andreas and me is Sam-Dreas, which makes a lot more sense, right?"

Nakita rolled her eyes, the way only someone who had, in her own words, "devoured three hundred thousand words of chess RPF in two days" could (where RPF stands for Real Person Fiction).

"Because there's two sets of Andreas–Roman shippers. Those that want them to be romantic—the An-Romics. And those that love them as archrivals—the An-Romvals." She counted them off on her fingers, then reached over to the stove without even needing to stand, plucked a chocolate strawberry from the food bouquet, and crammed half into her mouth. "It's a taxonomy, Sam."

I smiled at her joke as I processed this. Forcing myself to feign interest, I asked, "But I thought you said the An-Romvals want them together as well?"

Truly, the last thing in the world I wanted to talk about was Andreas Kristiansen. But I couldn't blame Nakita for constantly bringing him up to me.

The last two months had been a constant, headlong trip through the minefield of self-loathing. After the new year, I'd invited myself over to the apartment and come clean to my former roommates about my lies, but none of the truly private details were disclosed. Nothing about Andreas's deceiving me about his reasons for approaching me initially; I didn't tell them about Henrik and Tobias's antics either, only that they opposed my inheriting the shares; and no mention of Andreas manipulating my funding with Dr. Hauser.

This was also the same amount of information I'd shared with my grandfather and—more or less—anyone at work who asked. I shared just enough factual information about the will and inheritance law to explain why I'd lied about the engagement as a cover for the adoption.

In my grandpa's case, we were just starting to get to know each other again. He'd been upset that I'd allowed myself to be adopted by anyone—especially someone with the last name of Kristiansen—and I didn't want him worrying about me because of Henrik and Tobias. But also, I didn't particularly trust him yet. One step at a time.

Thus, Nakita thought Andreas and I were still on good terms and had no idea how uncomfortable these conversations were for me. But so what? I'd been the bad friend who lied. If Nakita wanted to talk about Andreas and the chess global online fandom, I would listen. I considered it penance.

Nodding as she chewed on the strawberry, she said, "Yeah, but the An-Romvals want Andreas and Roman together as enemies. They want them to be together, but —like—have them hate being together. You see?"

"I see," I lied, sipping my tea. The peppermint hit my tongue like a fluoride treatment at a dentist's office. "Thank you for the explanation and your patience with me."

Nakita raised an eyebrow, then did a head-tilt squint as her gaze moved over my face. "Have you been sleeping? No shade, but you're looking really tired these days."

I considered deflecting, then decided it was less work to just say, "Not really. The new apartment has been an adjustment. I guess I'm not used to living alone." This was true, but not the entire truth.

I wasn't used to living alone and over the last two months since the will reading in Paris, I'd discovered that I did not like living alone. Also, I was sleepwalking again. Not every night, or even every other night, just enough to stress me out and make me dread my own bed.

But I didn't want to tell Nakita about the sleepwalking for fear it would end up in a chess fandom RPF.

She sent me a sympathetic look. "Yeah, I totally get that. I would hate living by myself. Where is the apartment? Close by?"

I nodded, though I didn't elaborate on exactly where. I hadn't moved into the apartment Andreas arranged for me. I couldn't bring myself to do it even though it appealed to my thrifty sensibilities. Instead, upon arriving back in the United States, I'd checked into a Marriot near JFK and stayed there for two weeks during the holidays since all the other moderately priced hotels in New York City were booked.

I knew I wouldn't be welcomed back here with my old roommates, not after all my lies, so I didn't even ask. After the holiday break, Kaitlyn insisted I move in with them until I could find a permanent place.

In the end, after a month of searching, Martin and Kaitlyn—but mostly Martin—pulled some strings and helped me get an apartment in their building.

Only Kaitlyn and my security team knew where I lived. I hadn't told anyone else. As mentioned, Nakita was not known for her discretion, especially with strangers, or acquaintances, or taxi drivers, or people online. After all the media attention since the will reading, the fewer people who knew where I lived the better.

Nakita gave me a squintier look, then changed track. "So, have you been able to make any headway with Diya? Is that why you're here today?"

"Not yet, but I'm not just here to see Diya. I wanted to see you, too." I tried for a little smile, but the best I could do was a brief uptilt at the corners of my mouth.

After I broke the news to my former roommates that my engagement to Andreas was fake, Diya had gone full ice queen. She'd stopped replying to my texts, didn't acknowledge me in the group chat, and never referred to me directly when we were in a room together. Nakita and Kendra were both pretty mad, but nothing like Diya.

Nakita had started talking to me again within a month, and Kendra shortly after, but trying to get through to Diya was an ongoing struggle. Her sense of betrayal had the force of a neutron star.

But I got it. I did. I completely understood her perspective. If I didn't understand, I would've been a huge hypocrite instead of just a moderate-sized hypocrite. I'd lied to them about Andreas being my fiancé. We'd gone out to dinner with them before Thanksgiving as an engaged couple and put on a lovey-dovey show. No one likes being lied to.

Ask me how I know.

I wasn't going to let my friendship with Diya go without a fight. Nakita, Kendra, and Diya were important to me. I was in the wrong and I needed to make it up to them.

Nakita sipped her tea, saying, "Just give her time. I'm sure when she sees this big fruit basket you brought over, it'll soften her a little. It's all her favorite things. She's always talking about how she wants more pineapple and less cantaloupe. Thank you for the tea, by the way!" She gestured to the tin on the countertop near the sink.

I'd brought Nakita a fancy tin of loose-leaf Assam, and for Kendra I'd brought a cozy wool throw blanket because she was always complaining that the apartment was too cold.

"You don't need to thank me," I said, meaning the words.

I'd been compulsively sending gifts to all three of my former roommates for weeks, unable to resist the urge to buy their goodwill one macaron tower or cold brew subscription at a time. Retail therapy, except the therapy was for my own guilt and the recipient was always someone else.

Nakita swirled her mug, then returned to her favorite topic. "Anyway, the Sam-Dreas shippers don't even care that he legally adopted you. Once I explained how you two used to know each other and that he was just trying to do the right thing by making sure you inherited your family's shares, they totally came around. Like, overnight. There's even a new board called the Inheritance Trope Safe Zone, and you are their queen." She grinned, like this should be good news.

I did my best to school my expression, but I could feel my cheeks heating up anyway.

The biggest mistake I'd made while explaining myself to my former roommates was not explicitly telling Nakita to keep it all a secret. Within days, she'd shared the details online, which led to a cascade of posts and, eventually, emails from real-life journalists asking for comment. Not that I'd ever had much of an online presence, but I'd gone completely underground after that, deleting all the accounts I did have and avoiding social media and online news. I also had to block reporters and screen all my phone calls.

Tara still worked with me, which had been a huge blessing. We'd started dressing in identical outfits. Both her competence and the fact that we looked so much alike had saved me more than once. She was great at running interference with anyone who tried to approach me, mostly outside my work, by pretending to be me and leading reporters away so I could safely walk from the car to the biology building or vice versa.

Last week an influencer with a chess-adjacent online following had staked out the biology building, waiting for me to emerge so she could get "a reaction video" to the news that Andreas had been spotted in Central Park with Roman Buckley. Tara darted away and the influencer had followed.

Basically, I was grateful for Tara every single day.

"Hey," Nakita said, plucking another strawberry from the fruit bouquet and popping it into her mouth. "So, have you heard from Andreas?"

I forced a noncommittal smile as a cold lump formed in my stomach. "No."

This was not a lie. I hadn't spoken to him once since Paris. But every time I saw Nakita, she always asked me about Andreas. My answer was always some variation of the same response.

No. I'm sure he's very busy.

No. We don't really know each other.

No. We're not actually friends and don't keep in contact.

No. He helped me, and that's basically it.

Nakita squinted at me, and for a second I wondered if she could read minds. "When's the last time you heard from him?"

"I'm sure he's busy," I said, picking up my tea for a sip.

"I know he's busy, but when is the last time you two spoke?"

I shrugged. "Uh, just after the will reading, right before Christmas." Which was true, if you didn't count the emails from his personal assistant, Elio. Which I didn't.

Elio had emailed me several times since the new year, usually with some random piece of information or paperwork related to finalizing the transition of my father's Genetix shares. He had also been the one to send me the *real* version of Oskar Kristiansen's will.

Most recently, Elio had emailed about logistics for the lawsuit brought by Henrik and Tobias contesting my inheritance of the Genetix shares, and whether I wanted to retain their preferred law firm.

"Of course," he'd typed, "Mr. Kristiansen is anxious to help you fight this frivolous claim in any way possible. All you need to do is reach out."

Of course.

Every message from Elio was formal and signed off with, "Mr. Kristiansen wishes you the very best." At first the messages made me so damn mad, especially when I'd read the real will. But more recently, they made me cry. The last one in particular had sent me straight into a bubble bath of feelings. I hadn't allowed myself to think about why. It felt too big, too dangerous, and too unwieldy to contemplate.

"Andreas hasn't called you at all?" Nakita continued to press.

Maintaining my unconcerned smile, like this was very normal and fine, I modulated my voice to indifferent. "Like I've mentioned before, we're not close. At all. He helped me with this one thing, that's it. I honestly don't even know him very well." This, obviously, was also true.

What did I know about Andreas Kristiansen truly? Nothing.

When I looked back at the almost two months we spent together, I realized that he'd never communicated anything meaningful about himself. I knew about his childhood because we'd grown up together during our shared summers. But any time I'd asked him about himself during those weeks we'd spent in his apartment, he either gave me basic answers or redirected the conversation back to me.

Even so, I missed him. I missed him so much it made my stomach hurt whenever I let myself think about him.

Nakita finished her tea and sat back in the chair, openly studying me. "Well, have you called him? Because he's been basically off the radar since losing the Italy tournament to Roman. I think this is the longest he hasn't posted anything on social media."

I blinked. "He didn't lose the tournament in Italy, he came in second," I said, before I could catch the words.

Nakita raised both eyebrows. "For him, that's losing. First time he hasn't won a major tournament in years. Are you sure you don't want to call him?"

I shook my head, then realized Nakita was waiting for more explanation. "No. I've been busy, too. I haven't really had any time." I set my mug down, wishing I could crawl under the kitchen table and never come out.

Nakita made a noise that was half annoyed, half disbelieving. "You're so stubborn. He literally got you your father's shares back, and you can't even check to see if he's alive?"

I wanted to laugh, but knew it would sound bitter. So, instead, I spoke the truth. "Nakita, as I've said several times, we aren't that close. I'm not someone he wants to hear from. I'm honestly nobody to him."

Nakita watched me for a minute, then sighed. "He hasn't been doing any online matches or appearances either. Instead of showing up, he's been donating money to multiple animal rescue charities for every missed match, including his own charity."

I frowned. "His own? He has a charity?" Again, asking the question before I could catch myself.

Nakita looked at me like I'd grown a second head. "You know, his charity? The one he started for animal rescue and rehabilitation?" When I shook my head, she looked genuinely shocked. "Huh. Maybe you guys aren't that close. He never talked about his animal rescue work? He's, like, infamous for donating to shelters and personally funds an exotic animal rescue in upstate New York. They had a spread about it in *American Chess Quarterly*."

This was news to me. I tried to think back. Had he ever mentioned animal rescue work? He was vegan, but had said it was for health reasons.

I remembered when we were kids, how much he'd loved animals, how he'd cried when that bird died and how we'd held a funeral for it. I'd meant what I said when we went on that wine bar date after he returned from London. I didn't want to look up information about him online. I wanted *him* to tell me about himself. Now, it seems, since he never told me and I'd never internet stalked him, I still knew basically nothing about Andreas Kristiansen.

Whatever. Just another thing about himself he'd never wanted to share with me.

"Let me have your phone," Nakita said, placing her hand on the table, palm up.

I hesitated, then reached in my leggings pocket and handed it over. She unlocked the browser and started typing, narrating as she went. "You have to see this. It's literally adorable."

I heard a bedroom door open up somewhere and my heart leapt to my throat. *Diya is up*. Turning around in the chair, I waited and listened to the sounds of Diya moving around. Another door opened then closed. A few moments passed before she appeared, likely stopping by the bathroom first before shuffling into the kitchen.

When she caught sight of me, she stopped dead in her tracks, her hazy, sleepy gaze turning hard.

I waved, not allowing myself too much hope. "Hi. It's good to see you. I brought you fruit."

Her attention flickered to the alien-queen-head Edible Arrangement on the stove. She sighed. Loudly.

Silently, Diya walked past me to the refrigerator.

Meanwhile, Nakita tapped through a few links, and without looking up said, "Did you sleep okay? Were we too loud?"

"I didn't hear you at all. Thanks for keeping it down." Diya directed her sleep-roughened voice toward the interior of the fridge. "Where are my leftovers?"

"Behind the OJ," Nakita responded, then turned my phone so I could see the screen.

An exotic animal rescue website home page was revealed, a study in professional branding, with a blue and white color scheme, and understated serif fonts. In the header, a photo of Andreas crouching next to a small, besuited capuchin monkey. The monkey perched on his shoulder, tugging at his hair, and

Andreas was smiling. An actual, unguarded smile, the kind I'd only seen on him a handful of times.

Below the banner was a product carousel featuring, among other things, a resin Andreas Kristiansen Chess Set. The pawns were meerkats, the bishops were owls, the rooks were turtles, the knights were panthers, and the kings and queens were modeled after wolves in miniature.

Nakita scrolled down to the donation stats. "He's raised over three hundred grand in the last month. Every time there's chess world drama, the animal rescue gets a ton of money. It's so weird but also kind of brilliant."

I stared at the photo, at the way the monkey was yanking Andreas's hair and he didn't even seem to mind, and my heart did a sad little deflating thing in my chest, like it had been punctured by sharp regret, a longing for something I didn't wish to name because it was so entirely out of my reach.

"What's wrong with you?"

I glanced up and found Diya looking at me. And . . . talking to me? *Whoa.* Diya acknowledging my existence was a huge improvement.

Straightening in my seat, I allowed my hope to balloon. "Nothing. I'm fine. How are you?"

Her expression flattened and she shut the fridge, muttering under her breath, "You're clearly not fine, but whatever. Forget I asked."

I glanced at Nakita, hoping for some help, but discovered she was still holding my phone and—from my vantage point—appeared to be poking around my contacts.

"What are you doing?" I asked.

Nakita stood up and moved away from the table. "You need to call Andreas."

Panic detonated in my chest and I shot up from my chair. "Don't—no. He doesn't want to hear from me."

Nakita, who was much faster than I'd ever be even when I had a full night's sleep, held the phone high over her head and danced out of reach as I tried to snatch it back. "I don't believe that. You two were obviously much closer than you're letting on. He could be waiting for you to call and say thank you for helping get your father's company back!"

I darted around the table, but Nakita had a good four inches and ten pounds on me, and she used both to her advantage. She pressed Call before I could even form a coherent protest. This was happening too fast, it felt like she'd knocked the wind from my lungs.

"I don't—please—don't—" I wheezed, but then the ringing started, and my brain went to static.

Nakita grinned. "Talk to him. He just lost his dad, he lost the Rome tournament. I'm sure he wants to hear from you. Trust me."

The phone rang once, twice. My palms went slick and my heart banged against my rib cage. By the third ring, I felt certain he wouldn't answer and I started to relax. If it went to voicemail, Nakita might drop this issue once and for all.

But on the fourth ring, there was a click, and then a voice on the other end of the line, clear and unmistakable.

"Hello?" Andreas said. "Samantha?"

[2]

EVOLUTION AND GENETICS

Samantha

I froze, the kitchen, the fruit bouquet, even Diya and Nakita blurring out of focus. I had not heard his voice in weeks, but it was exactly the same as I remembered—precise, careful, but with an edge underneath.

I could not breathe.

Nakita mouthed, *Say something!* but my throat had sealed itself shut. I waited, hoping maybe he'd think it was a spam call or a butt dial. Maybe he'd simply hang up and I could have plausible deniability.

"Samantha?" he said again, and this time there was something about how he'd said my name that made my heart crack open, just a little.

I drew in a breath and opened my mouth to speak. My face went hot enough to fry eggs. Why had he answered?

Nakita leaned back and shouted at my phone like she was far away from it. Or maybe in a canyon trapped under a heavy object. "Hi, Andreas! It's Nakita. I'm using Sam's phone but she's right here. We were just calling to check on you, make sure you're okay, after the tournament and your dad and every—"

I lunged forward and snatched the phone out of Nakita's hand, a surge of strange protectiveness for Andreas and his privacy catching me off guard. I gave Nakita the kind of dirty look that would sterilize a petri dish, then took the call off speaker.

There was a second of breathless silence on the line. I pressed the phone to my ear and forced myself to croak out, "Sorry to disturb you. Nakita took my phone from me and called you without my knowing. It won't happen again. Bye."

I started to hang up, but Andreas said, "Wait, wait. Don't hang up."

I didn't hang up. Of course I didn't. The rational part of my brain screamed at me to end the call, but my thumb hovered over the screen like a chicken at the edge of a crosswalk. So dumb. And chickeny.

More silence, then, "How have you been?" The words were gentle, full of an earnestness that made my vision blur. I had not expected gentleness. I had not expected anything. I honestly hadn't even expected him to answer. *Why did he answer?!*

I didn't know how to respond to his question. There was nothing I could say that wouldn't betray the fact that he'd messed me up more than anyone had in over a decade. I stared into the middle distance of the old kitchen, trying to breathe through the knot in my throat and the tightness in my lungs.

I felt both Nakita and Diya watch me. They were waiting for me to say something, to give some sign of life. Instead, I just stood there, letting the seconds tick by.

Andreas shifted on his side of the call, the faintest scrape of plastic against a cheek, then said, "Elio reached out to you, about my brothers' lawsuit. Have you received the messages?"

I managed a "Mmm-hmm." I did not trust my voice beyond that.

"I can help you," he said, his voice deepening. "Remember the woman and child Tobias brought to the will reading? I have information that proves—"

"Before I let you go," I interrupted, my heart aching like a motherfucker at his words.

This was the first time we'd spoken in months and all he wanted to talk about were his brothers? I asked the first thing that came to mind, the question tumbling out, "What was the name of the kombucha drink? The one you bought that was brewed nearby?"

A pause. Then, a tentative, "You want the name of the kombucha from Brooklyn?"

"Yes."

He cleared his throat. "Uh, it's called Andromeda. But, listen, that child—"

"Thank you," I said, cutting him off, my voice shakier than I would've liked. But given how agitated I felt, it was a miracle I could form words at all. "I appreciate the information. Sorry for the interruption. Mmm-hmm. Okay. I won't call again. Sorry again. Bye." Saying this last part for Nakita's benefit, I hung up before he could speak another word.

I stared at my phone, my hands trembling, and navigated immediately to my contacts. "See, Nakita? He doesn't want to talk to me. He asked me not to call again," I lied as I blocked his number, then deleted his contact card.

Just like that, he was gone. It felt less like cutting a cord and more like tearing out an organ, but I did it anyway. He was never going to apologize. He didn't care about me. It was always going to be about his brothers and his sick, twisted family. I never wanted to see him again. Ever.

Logically, I knew this was impossible. I would have to see Andreas—and Tobias, and Henrik—at the major shareholders' meeting in a few weeks. But maybe I could get away with never actually speaking to him again. Maybe I could—

"Sam . . . are you okay? Are you—did he really ask you not to call?" Nakita said, her voice genuinely worried now, which almost made me want to forgive her for everything she'd just done.

Before I could answer, I felt Diya grab my wrist and yank me toward the hallway with force. I let myself be dragged, stumbling after her. Diya pulled me into the bedroom we used to share, then shut the door behind us. Once we were next to my old bed, she pushed me down until I sat.

Diya also sat, perched next to me, crossing her arms. "Okay. Let's start from the beginning. And don't give me any of this bullshit about Andreas Kristiansen being a saint and helping you get your family's shares back by adopting you and you insisting on pretending to be engaged. I don't believe that's the whole story."

I buried my face in my hands, squeezing my eyes shut, but the tears started anyway. "I am so sorry, Diya."

"I'm not comforting you or forgiving you until you tell me the truth," she said, her voice gentle but implacable. "The whole truth, Sam. I know there's more to the story and, I have to be honest here, I'm so damn tired of guessing with you. I spent four years trying to climb over these walls you've built and I'm freaking tired of it. Either you trust me and we're friends, or you don't trust me and we're not friends. You can't have it both ways."

I sniffled. "I do trust you."

"Listen, I understand why you're not being forthright with Nakita." Diya's tone softened, just a little. "But, honestly, you can trust her, too. You just have to tell her what's public and what's private. She's great, but she doesn't always know unless you spell it out. She's an oversharer even about her own stuff, that's just how she's made. Think of her like—like a journalist. Everything is on the record unless you invoke the cone of silence ahead of time."

I nodded, wiped my nose on my sleeve, and gave myself a second to pull it together. "You're right. I didn't tell you the whole story."

"I know." Despite her statement that she wouldn't comfort me, her hand came up and rested on my shoulder. "And I also know that whatever you're about to tell me is super top secret. I won't tell anyone, not even my grandpa."

The tears were flowing fast now, saturating my face and wracking my body with sobs. I wasn't necessarily surprised. I hadn't let myself cry yet. I'd raged when I told Kaitlyn. I'd tried to be logical when I spoke to my therapist. But I hadn't really allowed myself to be sad.

"I'm not mad you lied to me—to us—about the engagement." Diya started rubbing circles on my back. "I was mad, but when I read the news about how your father died, how your family lost the shares of the company *he* founded due to a civil suit after his death, how your mom died, then your grandma, I completely understand you doing whatever was necessary to get those shares back. I do. It wasn't the lie about the engagement; it was the realization that I didn't actually know anything about you. I can't be a good friend to you if you're so stingy about sharing parts of yourself. Does that make sense?"

I nodded. "Yes. Yes. I'll tell you."

Diya's arm came around my shoulders and she squeezed. And I took a long, ragged breath, then let it all go.

* * *

About an hour later, Diya and I were still in the old bedroom, sitting cross-legged on the mattress, both of us staring at a point on the opposite wall. I'd just finished telling her everything. Not the sanitized, Wikipedia version I'd given Nakita and Kendra, but the raw dataset. All of it.

When I'd started, Diya's arm around me had been comforting but her body had been removed and stiff. As I got deeper into the mess, she'd softened. By the end, she was sitting so close our knees touched and she allowed me to rest my head on her shoulder. She listened without interrupting, except to occasionally ask for clarification or blurt out, "Are you serious?" like a shocked TV judge.

When I got to the part about Paris, and the will reading, and Andreas explaining everything that night in the hotel, and especially the part about Dr. Hauser's funding, she didn't even try to hide her rage on my behalf. In the end, she pulled me into a full hug and muttered, "If I ever see Andreas Kristiansen again, I'm going to punch him in the scrotum. And his evil brothers, too."

After the hug, we sat there for a long time, just breathing.

Finally, she said, "I hope you have a good lawyer. I hope you prove your father was innocent."

"I do have a good lawyer. In fact"—I breathed a laugh at the absurdity of what I was about to admit—"I have a whole legal team now. They're going through the documents Kaitlyn obtained about the fraud charges against my father, the civil suit Oskar Kristiansen used to take the shares away from my mom after my father died, the original incorporation documents, and the publicly available IPO paperwork, and they think they've discovered some serious inconsistencies. They think Oskar framed my dad."

"That's great!" Diya jumped a little, but then gave her head a quick shake. "Sorry, I mean, it's not great that Oskar framed your dad. But it's great that it looks like you'll be able to clear things up and prove your dad is innocent."

"Just not yet. The civil suit was based on the indictment, and it looks like the evidence used for the indictment was either falsified or misleading." I felt my throat constrict with tangled emotion. "I need access to Genetix's internal files first, though. I should be able to get everything I need after the shareholder meeting at the end of the month."

"What a relief. So . . ." Diya openly studied me. "What are your thoughts, then? What are you thinking about Andreas? Are you going to forgive him?"

I let out a dry, bitter laugh. "He hasn't asked for my forgiveness. Like I said, after the will reading, he showed up at my room, explained that he was the one responsible for freezing Dr. Hauser's funding. He'd let me think it was his brother when it happened. Then he told me he'd arranged an apartment and security for me, gave me money, and that was that."

Diya squinted at me, as if examining a particularly mysterious rash. "How did he seem? Was he calm or—?"

"I don't honestly know," I cut her off. "I'd calmed down by the time he came to the hotel room that night. Yes, during the will reading, I was shocked that he'd lied to me about why he'd approached me in the first place. But I honestly got over that part pretty fast."

"You did?" Diya raised an eyebrow, skeptical.

"Of course he'd want his mother's intellectual property, her music, and would do almost anything to get it. That's how I felt about getting the shares of Genetix. If I didn't understand his perspective, I would be a huge hypocrite. Look at how I lied to you all, and you're my friends. I was basically a stranger to Andreas when he first made contact."

"But he could've told you the truth," she said, voice still soft. "He had weeks to tell you the truth while you two lived together."

"I know, I know. But I also know myself, so I understand why he didn't. I'm not a trusting person."

Diya's lips quirked up. "Oh really? You don't say."

We shared a look, and for the first time since the beginning of the conversation, I huffed a laugh.

"If I were him," I said, "maybe I wouldn't have told me the truth either. How could he trust me not to lose my shit when I was so untrusting of him to begin with. It took over a month for me to agree to speak with him at first. Not to mention, by the time we were living together, he'd already maneuvered things with Dr. Hauser."

"I get the sense that's the main thing you're really angry about," Diya said. "Andreas not being forthright in the beginning makes sense, sure. But him manipulating you by freezing Dr. Hauser's funding, and then letting you think it was his brother Tobias is, like, next-level villain stuff."

I nodded. "I was—I was so mad. That moment after he told me, I couldn't think straight. I couldn't even see him, not really. So, I guess I can't tell you whether he was calm or upset or what he was feeling that night. My recollection tells me he was cold and distant, but maybe also anxious? Probably to get the conversation over with."

Diya shook her head. "I can't believe he entered into a physical relationship with you while lying to you the whole time."

That one hurt. I felt my eyes burn again, but I kept my voice steady. "It was no strings from the beginning. I told him I didn't want a commitment. I said there would be no feelings."

"That doesn't really make it any better, Sam. He used you."

I sighed. "This is where my brain keeps stumbling. I was the one who said no feelings, but I already had feelings. I was just too much of a coward to admit how I felt out loud. I encouraged him to think of things between us as no commitment even though I'd already fallen for him. Every time after the first time we were together, he made it all about me. And whenever I tried to reciprocate, he turned me down."

We fell silent, each of us lost in our own thoughts. What I didn't tell Diya was that Andreas's hands-on experience with sex and physical intimacy had been basically nonexistent. I'd told Kaitlyn, only because I'd needed someone to talk to about it at the time. But there was no reason to reveal Andreas's prowess status to Diya now.

Back then, I'd suspected that the sexual side of our relationship was a lot for him. He'd said he wanted to go slow, and I told myself at the time that I was respecting his boundaries. But had I really? How many situationships had I ended because the guy caught feelings?

If Andreas had used me physically, then I'd definitely used him too. At the very least, I'd been extremely dishonest about what I really wanted from him.

After a while, Diya said, "I know you've probably talked to your friend Kaitlyn about this. What does she think?"

"I did talk to Kaitlyn, when it all first happened and I was just really angry. We spent a long time cursing him out together. But she's been sick off and on this last month, so I didn't want to bother her with my stupid ongoing drama as my feelings have evolved."

Diya made a short, impatient sounding noise. "What about your therapist then? I know you've been in therapy for a while."

"Yes. I've been covering this with my therapist weekly."

She nodded approvingly, as if my therapy attendance record counted for something. "Good. What about your grandfather?"

I lifted an eyebrow, surprised by her question. How did she know I'd been speaking to my grandpa?

Diya gave me a tight smile. "When you were here last week, I overheard you on the phone with him. I know he was in New York before Christmas and wanted to meet with you. How does he feel about you being adopted?"

I heaved a huge sigh. "I mean, he's not happy. He and my grandmother didn't agree on much, but they did agree that the Kristiansens framed my father for fraud at the company. They also blame the Kristiansens for the death of their daughter, since she became so despondent after my dad died. In retrospect, I think my mom died of a broken heart partially because of my father's sudden passing, but also because no one believed her. No one would listen to her about the Kristiansens. She sorta just gave up."

"What did he say when you explained about getting your father's shares back?"

"It didn't make much of a difference. He doesn't care about the company. But when I explained that, with the shares, I would have access to Genetix's internal files and might be able to clear my father's name—and therefore prove that my mom was right all along—that seemed to make him come around. He liked the idea of his daughter being vindicated."

"And you two are still talking?"

I nodded. "Weekly. He got the day and time mixed up last week, that's why we were on the phone here."

Diya squinted at me, her gaze assessing. "How's the sleepwalking? Is that still happening?"

"It is, but only when I sleep in my new apartment. Mostly, I'm still sleeping on Kaitlyn's couch at night." I hadn't bought any furniture except a mattress for the new apartment, and even that wasn't being used except as a place to sit. I didn't sleep great on Kaitlyn's couch, but I also didn't sleepwalk if I slept in her apartment. I did, however, always sleepwalk when I tried to sleep in my new, big, empty apartment.

"Hmm." Diya inspected me. "You look really tired. What if—and let me know *honestly* what you think—what if I moved in until the sleepwalking situation improves? You shouldn't be alone."

I felt tears prick at my eyes again. "That would be—that would be so great. Thank you."

Diya reached over and gave my hand a squeeze. "My schedule is crazy, but if I'm not working at night, I can sleep at the apartment with you."

Exhaling a fair bit of relief, I nodded.

Gaze growing scrutinizing again, Diya asked, "I hate to repeat the question, but what are you thinking about Andreas now? I only ask because your sleepwalking seemed to start when he reentered your life. Maybe if you can resolve your feelings for him, it might go away. Just a thought."

I shrugged. "I try not to think about him at all. Obviously, my feelings were all one-sided. Obviously, he never cared about me at all. I was nothing but a pawn in his game against his family."

"Why 'obviously'?"

I rolled my eyes. "Come on, Diya."

Diya held up a hand. "Yes, based on the fact that he hasn't reached out, I agree with you. But I was there that night before Thanksgiving. I saw how he looked at you. He was a man completely, pathetically besotted. I don't think he's that good of an actor. No one is."

I was already shaking my head before she'd finished speaking. "If he felt anything for me, wouldn't he have contacted me before now—and not through his PA, but called me personally? Wouldn't he have apologized? At least once? Wouldn't he be buying me fruit bouquets and Assam tea and cozy wool blankets? Wouldn't he be trying everything in his power to make it up to me?"

Diya stared at me for a beat, then conceded, "You make good points."

"No. When I told him no strings, he took me at face value. That's on me. I'm hurt, but a lot of this was my own doing. He lied, he manipulated things so he could secure his mother's intellectual property, but he never told me he loved me. He never said he wanted to be with me, or made any commitments. In that at least, he was honest from the beginning. It was me who lied about feelings." I lifted a hand toward the kitchen where my fateful call with Andreas had occurred less than an hour ago. "The first time we speak in weeks, he wants to talk about his scheming brothers, not about us? He doesn't give a shit about me. As far as he's concerned, there never was an *us*."

We sat quietly for a stretch, just the hum of the heater and the distant, muffled sounds of Nakita in the other room.

Eventually, I said, "I'm so sorry I didn't tell you the entire truth after the new year. I'm so sorry I lied to you at all. I am so sorry I'm a terrible friend, but I want to make it up to you. I will do anything to make it up to you, I promise. I don't want to lose you."

"You're not going to lose me." It was Diya's turn to sigh and she squeezed my hand again before tugging me forward for another hug.

This time the embrace lasted a lot longer and it felt so good to hold someone, and be held by someone I trusted.

When we broke apart, Diya smiled. "You're not going to lose me, but you're going to have to keep wooing me."

I laughed and then sniffled. "Sounds great."

Diya patted my shoulder. "I want our relationship to be a two-way street this time. It can't be me sharing everything and you sharing nothing. I want a real friendship."

"Me too."

We let the silence settle again. It wasn't heavy or awkward anymore, and I felt so grateful for her willingness to hear me out, to forgive me.

After a minute, Diya stood and stretched. "After hearing the whole story, I guess I agree with your conclusion to keep Nakita in the dark with the details about this. If the guy were literally anyone else, I would say invoking the cone of silence would be enough. But she's got this . . . well, she has strange ideas about her chess celebrities, and I don't quite understand the parasocial relationship thing she has going on with them."

I also stood, reaching around her for the tissue box sitting on my old desk, and grabbed a tissue. "Do you think she would post about it if I told her? Even if I explicitly asked her to keep it a secret?"

"My guess is she wouldn't post, but she'd probably write a fanfic about it."

We both laughed at that, which felt so much better than crying.

When the laughter faded, Diya picked up the entire tissue box and passed it to me. "So, what's going on with the lawsuit, then? Do you think Andreas's brothers will eventually be able to take your father's shares back?"

"No. I don't think they will." I dabbed at my eyes. "But they'll drag it out for a while. Don't worry. There's nothing they can do about the shares in the long run. But in the short term, them contesting the will means I have to nominate a proxy to vote the shares until the case is settled."

"Ugh. That sucks. I'm sorry."

I shrugged. "Doesn't matter. After the shareholder meeting, I'll be able to access Genetix's internal files. Like I said, once I have evidence that my father was wrongly indicted, I'll be able to clear his name. Plus, there's something else weird, not related to the company files."

Diya's eyes widened. "Really? What did you find?"

I hesitated, not because I didn't trust her, but because I needed her help and we'd just made up.

"Or is it something you can't tell me?" she asked.

If I was going to trust Diya, I might as well go all in. "I actually have a favor to ask. Is that okay?"

"Yes! Ask!" She laughed lightly. "People who like you want to help you. Ask for more favors."

"Would you mind looking at my father's death certificate?"

"His death certificate?"

"Yes. There's . . . well, there's something odd about it, and I'd like your professional opinion."

[3]

THE ORIGIN OF MOLECULAR BIOLOGY

Samantha

Three days after my conversation with Diya, I sat across from Dr. Hauser in her office. One of the admin assistants had made us hot tea and had been overly solicitous regarding every aspect of the brewing process. Was tap water okay? Organic peppermint or English peppermint? Leaves or bag? Teacup or mug? Cream or milk? Vegan or dairy? Sugar or zero-calorie sweetener?

I hadn't been asked so many questions since my graduate school interview.

Dr. Hauser sat at her desk. She wore her favorite black turtleneck, which I took as a good sign. Usually, she was in a good mood if she wore the black turtleneck and I had a favor to ask, a big one.

She looked up at me from the folder she'd been reading when I walked in, eyes tired but sharp. "Thanks for taking the time to meet with me today."

"Of course. Is this about the samples I ran over the weekend?"

"No. This is actually about a decision that was made by the department." Folding her hands on top of the folder, she leaned forward. "At the last small faculty meeting, the dean asked me if it would be possible to fast-track your dissertation, Sam."

She said it like she was dropping a granite block onto my head, but with a professional kindness that told me she knew exactly how heavy it was.

I blinked. "I see . . ." It was not what I expected, and my face must have gone slack because she half smiled.

The last few weeks at work had been progressively weirder since I came back from winter break. The Monday after New Year's, when I'd first shown up in the fourth-floor biology suite, I'd thought I could slip in and out of the cold room with my trays of samples like any normal anonymous grad student. I could not. Every office and common area was wired with a low-grade current of gossip, and the second my coat brushed a doorknob, the energy shifted. Hushed voices would drop a register, eyes would find sudden interest in the ceiling tiles, and there would be a measurable dip in the ambient oxygen content until I passed.

At first, I'd attributed this to the fact that everyone had read about Oskar Kristiansen's will in the news. The fact that I'd inherited fully fifty percent of Genetix—a publicly traded company—was big financial news all on its own. However, by week two, it was clear the story most people cared about was whether my engagement to Andreas Kristiansen had been fake, and specifically why we'd faked it, and when I'd been adopted by someone two years younger than me.

But no one ever asked me directly. Not even Dmitry, who, if anything, was even more chill than before. He didn't seem at all surprised when I'd told him, and had taken it in stride. But he did voice mild disappointment that he wouldn't get a chance to play chess with Andreas.

The secret truth was that most people in science can only handle gossip in microdoses, like a vitamin supplement. When exposed to the full blast of a tabloid-style scandal, they responded the way bacteria do when you set the temperature to four degrees kelvin. They grouped together, barely moved, and slowed their metabolic rate.

So, when Dr. Hauser delivered this news about my dissertation, I shouldn't have been shocked, but I was. The idea of being "fast-tracked" out of grad school sounded less like a gift and more like being loaded onto a rocket and aimed at the sun.

I tried to smile. "Is this . . . something the department wants, or—"

Hauser cut me off, her voice businesslike but not unkind. "The news of your—uh—change in circumstances and all the media attention surrounding it has made it clear that giving you more time to work on your dissertation is what would be best for the department."

I let that land, then asked, "Best for the department, or best for the donors?" I regretted it instantly, but the words were out, and I saw a ghost of approval in her eyes.

She shrugged. "Genetix is a major partner of the university, Sam. You are now —or are very soon to be—its main shareholder. Please don't make me spell it out."

We exchanged a smile, brittle but real.

Dr. Hauser leaned back in her chair. "Not that you asked, but I also think it's for the best. The sooner you graduate, the sooner things can get back to normal around here."

I nodded, trying not to dwell on the word *normal*. It had lost all meaning for me.

Hauser moved her cup of tea aside to read from a sticky note she'd placed on top of a folder. "From now on until you finish, you'll have dedicated lab space and the dean has requisitioned an office for you to use. Likewise, you won't have any more TA duties."

I felt my stomach drop. The TA gig wasn't glamorous, but it meant contact with other humans and access to the always-warm lecture halls, which I'd come to love. Plus, grading undergrads' attempts at explaining the cell cycle was free comedy.

"But what about the support work for publications?" I asked, voice almost desperate. "Will I still be allowed to help with those?"

Hauser tilted her head, considering. "Of course, if you want. We just don't want to overwhelm you with obligations."

"I do want." I know I sounded eager. "I honestly love research and I'd be very disappointed if I was cut out of publication and grants support."

She smiled again, this time wider, almost proud. "Then I'll keep sending you tasks for our ongoing projects. But mainly, you need to be focused on finishing your dissertation with an eye toward graduating at the end of the summer, at the latest."

My head spun, but I nodded. In the context of my new life, this actually felt like a reasonable request.

Hauser set her hands flat on the desk. "Okay, I have a call coming up this afternoon I need to prepare for. Is there anything else?"

I hesitated, but then recalled what Diya had said to me three days ago. *People who like you want to help you. Ask for more favors.*

"Actually, yes." I gathered a deep breath for courage. "I have a favor to ask. I know this is a big ask. I've wanted to broach a topic with you for a while—for the last week or so—but I wasn't sure how to bring it up."

She did not break eye contact. "What is it?"

I exhaled. "The two eldest Kristiansen brothers are challenging the will and my inheritance of the shares that have been held in trust since my father died."

She blinked, absorbing. "Are you saying the shares you inherited actually belonged to your late father? You told me that your father and the late Mr. Kristiansen were business partners, but I didn't realize the shares you inherited were your father's."

"Yeah." I tried to figure out how to explain without using a ton of legal speak.

"It's a very long story. But, the short version is that my father and Oskar Kristiansen founded Genetix together, and part of the initial incorporation documents stipulated that if either of the founding members were to undergo a felony criminal investigation related to the company, the shares held by that member would be placed in a trust until after the member was found not guilty or the member was convicted. If convicted, the shares would stay in the trust and could only be inherited after the death of the other member. So, not sold or traded, used for collateral, or voted."

Hauser nodded, her brain already several moves ahead. "I think I follow. So, basically, when your father was indicted for fraud relating to Genetix over fifteen years ago, his shares went into a trust? But your father was indicted, never convicted. How did the shares end up with Oskar Kristiansen?"

"After my father died, the government obviously couldn't move forward with a conviction. So, Oskar Kristiansen filed a civil lawsuit and gained control of the trust—the shares—that way, on the grounds of the indictment and charges filed."

"Ah. I see . . ." Dr. Hauser nodded, and I saw her brain work through the implications of this. "Forgive me, but didn't your mother also pass soon after?"

"Correct." I found myself sitting up straighter.

Her eyes narrowed. "But Oskar Kristiansen couldn't sell the shares, or trade them, or otherwise touch them. He could only designate who inherited them upon his death. Do I have that right?"

"Also correct," I said. "This is not an unusual practice in corporate partnerships. It's meant to discourage one founding member from falsely accusing another member, because what would be gained if the shares can't be touched or used? But it also keeps company shares with the founders and their families."

Hauser's lips pursed, a sign that she was intrigued. "That's interesting. So, what's your big ask?"

"As I said, Oskar Kristiansen's two eldest children are contesting the will, which means, for at least the short term, I need to nominate a proxy to vote the shares on my behalf. They can't be sold, transferred, or traded until the will issue is resolved. But they can be voted." Glancing down at my hands, I swallowed. "I'm hoping you will agree to be my voting proxy for the shares. Or at least allow me to nominate you as my proxy to the board. They're meeting at the end of the month."

I peeked at her. Hauser sat back, hands flat on her desk, blinking twice. She didn't speak for a full ten seconds, which felt like an eternity.

"This is—what you're asking, this is a big responsibility," she said at last, her voice even. "Not that I'm ungrateful, but . . . are you sure I'm the right person?"

I nodded, maybe too fast. "I trust you. You have my respect and I consider you one of the most honorable individuals I've ever met. And it shouldn't take too much of your time. There are no major issues coming up in front of the board for at least six months. You would just need to attend the meetings."

She squinted at me. "But didn't you inherit fifty percent of the Genetix shares? Who is the next highest shareholder?"

"Each of the Kristiansen children inherited approximately one third of their father's shares, or what was left of those shares after the public offering thirteen years ago." I found myself weirdly energized by the conversation and the thought that Dr. Hauser might agree.

She raised a hand, as if signaling a time-out. "Hold on. I thought—please correct me if I'm in error—that the youngest, Andreas, was the one who inherited the estate of his father? That's what I read in the news."

"Yes, the personal estate did pass to, uh, the youngest. But the shares were not part of the personal estate. They were part of Oskar's business holdings, which were always going to be split among the three children equally."

Hauser picked up a pen and tapped the desktop with it, the motion rhythmic. "But the shares in trust, those are the ones that passed to you? Sorry for all the questions."

"I don't mind explaining. It's all very twisted." I tried to parse through only the necessary details, eventually explaining, "Oskar Kristiansen wrote an addendum to his will before he died. Apparently, it stipulated that the shares held in trust would pass to the oldest and first grandchild of Oskar Kristiansen."

I said "apparently" because I'd received the full text of the real will and its real addendum the week after Paris, and that's when I realized Andreas had never shown me the actual addendum. The version he'd let me see in that café so many months ago was a carefully drafted printout that left out several important details: that the personal estate—meaning all his mother's music, her home in Italy, Oskar's personal accounts and property—would go to the parent of the first grandchild. Which, through legal Tetris, meant Andreas alone.

But what became of the business holdings owned by Oskar outright—his remaining shares after using twenty-three percent of his original half for the IPO filing thirteen years ago—was all spelled out in the main will.

Hauser asked, "Can I have some time to think about this?"

"Of course." I exhaled my relief that she hadn't flat out turned me down. My only other option was Kaitlyn's husband. "In the meantime, may I send you some materials my lawyer drafted on what you can expect as the proxy?"

She nodded. "Please do. The more information the better. I promise I will give the matter serious thought. In any case, thank you for thinking of me, Sam."

We exchanged a friendly goodbye, but just as I stood to leave, Hauser called to me. "Oh, and the department manager will show you where your new solo office is. Please see her on your way out."

I nodded and headed for the door, grateful to have that conversation done and over with.

In the corridor, the air felt lighter, like the pressure had dropped twenty millibars. I walked past the small faculty efficiency kitchen and almost made it to the elevator before I heard the quick, staccato footfalls of someone in a hurry.

Turning, I spotted James Nieminen. His hair was especially shiny, as if he'd used a liter of conditioner and windshield water repellant. He did a double take when he saw me, then switched directions mid-stride to intercept me.

I braced myself. More or less, he'd kept his distance since the run-in with Andreas way back at the beginning of December. I had no earthly idea why he'd go out of his way to talk to me now.

He greeted me with effusive warmth, the type usually applied to billionaires and infants. "Ah, Sam! A pleasure to see you. I was just on my way to check in with Dr. Hauser. I hope your meeting went well?"

I pasted on a smile. "It did, thanks." I had no idea why he would know I'd just met with Dr. Hauser.

James exhaled, as though sagging with relief. "Well, that's great. So exciting that your dissertation will be fast-tracked. Congratulations!"

Before I could respond, he redirected his game-show-host energy to someplace beyond me and waved. "Pardon me, I'm late for a meeting. See you later." As he jogged past, he added, "Let's grab coffee and catch up!"

Perplexed, I walked down the hall, half laughing at the memory of how James had popped out from behind a column and snidely called me "Miss Jarlston" on the front steps of the biology building back in December, as though he were some sort of villain in a Jane Austen novel. Now, after months of avoidance, his familiarity and friendliness were as strange as they were off-putting.

All things considered, I wished he'd go back to avoiding me.

* * *

I DECIDED to leave work early. Kaitlyn's text from after lunch still flickered in my mental status bar.

Kaitlyn: Another random fever last night. Please, if you can come over tonight and babysit for a bit, I'd appreciate it.

The word *please* in Kaitlynese was basically code for "please for the love of God, help."

I texted her back right away.

Sam: Have you been to the doctor? Is it mastitis again?

Kaitlyn: I think it's a UTI this time. My back and sides hurt. But maybe it's just a cold?

I noticed she hadn't responded to my question regarding whether or not she'd gone to the doctor. Thus, I texted Tara shortly after, alerting her that I planned to be outside and ready for pickup by 4:30 PM.

Quickly changing into gym clothes in the locker room—because babysitting my godson was like going to the gym—I entered the stairwell at 4:27 PM. For sure, I'd end up dirty, wet, and red-faced tonight. But I loved Joey, the little stinker.

As I clattered down the linoleum stairs, a list of what to grab from the corner bodega began forming in my mind. I wanted to make her dinner, something hearty and warm, give Kaitlyn a break. But I also wanted to get to her place as soon as possible, just in case she was waiting to go to the doctor until I arrived. Martin was off on a business trip to the West Coast and I knew Kaitlyn didn't want to take Joey with her to the doctor. I mean, who—while feeling awful—would want to take a baby with them to a doctor's appointment? That sounded hellish.

Withdrawing my phone, I thumb typed the shopping list into Notes even as my eyes tracked the landings ahead. Movement caught my attention, and I spotted Dmitry three flights below, descending the last flight of stairs in his signature trench coat and fingerless gloves.

He had an uncanny ability to spot me or sense my presence, so I was surprised when he didn't look up, didn't so much as pause on his way to the door. Maybe he was sleep-deprived? He'd texted me last night around 3:00 AM about some disaster in the new yeast stock and his desperate plan to fake results "so the postdoc wouldn't cry." I knew he would never fake results, he just needed to vent.

But he didn't respond to my answering text asking if he'd finished reviewing my methods outline yet. And he'd clearly been avoiding me all day. If I wanted his feedback before tomorrow, I would need to corner him now.

Speed walking down the last few flights, I attempted to catch him, my shoes slapping the steps. At the bottom, I pushed out the stairwell door, rounded the corner, and was surprised by how many people crowded in the lobby. There must have been a lecture letting out; students clustered by the coffee cart, everyone talking loud enough to bounce their voices off the tile and into my skull. In the crowd, I could just see Dmitry's dark hair in the sea of winter hats, heading for the glass double doors.

I thought about calling out, but didn't. I'd learned early on that yelling "Dmitry!" at him in public always drew a full 180-degree pivot from the man himself, followed by an annoyed squint, as if he was deeply disappointed that you'd forced him to acknowledge his own name. And if I yelled now, half the lobby would look, too. These days, I would rather eat glass than have that many eyes on me at once.

So, I angled for the door, hoping to catch up to him before he left completely. When I reached the heavy glass double doors, Dmitry was already twenty feet ahead, melting into the sunset haze of the stairs and concrete beyond. The heat lamps from the building's overhang haloed the sidewalk in sodium light, and the rest was February gloom and approaching darkness.

Torn, I checked the curb for Tara's car. The Mercedes idled just where it always did, hazard lights strobing, but Tara wasn't outside yet. That meant it wasn't technically safe to leave the building, which was one of the many personal safety rules I now followed. *You do not leave the building until you see Tara standing outside the car, at the curb. If the car isn't there at all yet, you call. If she doesn't pick up, you call the backup number.*

I pressed my palm to the cold door, peering through to scan for the other security guys, spotting them walking along the sidewalk. They always wore subtle suits and stood just close enough to be inconspicuous but not so close as to look like bodyguards. I watched as they made a slow walk past the benches, then nodded to each other.

I hesitated.

Two times since Christmas, both on Tuesdays, Henrik had shown up outside the biology building. The first was six weeks ago—the first week back from winter break—when I'd been reckless enough to walk to the curb alone. Henrik had been leaning against the lamppost, arms crossed, a thin white envelope in hand. He'd tried to talk to me, but I'd gone straight for the car, and security had intercepted.

The second time was two weeks ago. Same spot, different weather. He'd been waiting behind the newspaper box, and again, the security guys had gotten there first. I didn't know if he was doing it to intimidate me, or if he actually wanted to talk, or if it was just another way to remind me that I was always being watched.

My eyes sought out Dmitry. He'd stopped walking and was standing near the bike rack, turning left, then right. I still had time to corner him if I hurried. The security guards were both in sight and seemed to be at ease. Thus, I made the executive decision to break protocol and leave the building before Tara emerged from the Mercedes. My guards were in sight, and I felt much more capable these days of defending myself since I'd started going to Tara's kickboxing class three times a week. Not only that, but Tara had also taken me to a gun range a few times, telling me that I should at least know how to use a gun—and where the safety was located, and how to aim and handle it—if I ever needed to disarm someone.

Leaving the building, the cold hit my face like a slap while I scanned the stairs, sidewalk, and street for anything out of place. Finding nothing, I kept my head down, fingers curled around my phone in my coat pocket.

Dmitry still loitered by the bike rack and I jogged toward him. I was maybe fifteen feet away, his name on the tip of my tongue, when someone else called out, "Dmitry!"

My steps faltered and my entire nervous system seized up at the voice, extremely familiar and not at all expected. I watched, frozen, as Dmitry pivoted. Instinctively, I followed his line of sight. There, not twenty feet away, looking just as brutally handsome and aloof as ever.

Andreas.

[4]

EVIDENCE FOR EVOLUTION

Samantha

The moment my eyes found his face, the rest of the world stopped rendering. The sounds on the sidewalk, the traffic, even the pain from where my backpack strap dug into my shoulder, it all became muted and blurry. Like being underwater with my eyes open. I had the fleeting, irrational sense that maybe my heart had stopped, too. My body took up the slack by flooding every cell and sense with a chemical soup that brought to mind the aftermath of a car accident.

For several long seconds, Andreas didn't see me. He spoke to Dmitry, standing in profile in the sodium glare of the lights, looking exactly as I remembered.

Actually, no.

The funereal pallor that had been glued to his face in Paris continued to shadow his features. His eyes seemed tired, darkened with circles beneath. Andreas's color was off and, judging by the sharpness of his cheekbones, he'd lost a little weight. But his camel-colored cashmere coat was the same precise cut and shade I remembered, and it was open at the front, revealing a dashing navy cable-knit turtleneck sweater beneath. Even with the new outward indicators of weariness, Andreas still looked elegant.

"Are you ready? Have you been waiting long?" He gestured as he spoke to Dmitry, gloved hands loose in the air, all the sharp edges and corners smoothed out by the effortlessness of their movement. Despite the signs of fatigue, he appeared pleased, relaxed at present.

377

Andreas was so close, I could see the seam on his left glove and the way his eyelashes cast little shadows on his cheekbone. My stomach pitched and rolled like a ship in high seas and I felt my internal organs rearrange themselves into a new configuration.

It seemed certain Dmitry would look over and see me. He didn't. I wasn't even a blip on the periphery of their conversation.

Dmitry shrugged, his posture loose and easy, and replied, "No, not at all. I just got here. Let's go."

I blinked my eyes hard once, just in case I was hallucinating. Perhaps I was over-caffeinated or under-slept? Maybe I'd had too many nights dreaming of Andreas—usually the kind of dream that left me wide-awake and staring at my phone, vibrating with a need to call him and then immediately being crushed by the memory of why I absolutely should not—that my brain had just started inserting him into my field of vision randomly during the day.

But then I saw the two of them smile at each other, in the kind of open, genuine way that implied they'd spent enough time together to be actual friends, and the wave of confusion and hurt that rolled through me was so overwhelming, I took a step back to maintain my balance.

I didn't have a right to be hurt. I'd apologized to Dmitry weeks ago for my lie and he'd acted like it was no big deal. I'd told him the same story I told Nakita, Kendra, and Diya, and he'd said he understood.

Dmitry hasn't betrayed me. He has no idea what Andreas did, because I didn't tell him the whole truth.

I commanded myself to look away, avert my gaze and walk calmly toward the car. If I left now, they would never know I'd witnessed their obviously scheduled meet-up. Except, I couldn't get my feet to listen to my brain. I probably looked like I'd just been beaned in the head with a brick. I couldn't move or even blink.

But then, abruptly, it was too late.

Andreas's gaze lifted nonchalantly as though to absentmindedly scan the sidewalk, passed over me, then returned sharply. The impact of it felt like a head-on collision. His smile faltered, then fell completely, all the color draining from his face. His eyes widened, his moment of recognition hitting me like a tidal wave, the force of it sending a hot, sudden spike of adrenaline straight down my spine and limbs.

I faintly registered that Andreas appeared just as surprised to see me as I was to see him, and the words I'd spoken to Diya over the weekend floated back to me. *He doesn't give a shit about me.*

It was too much. I tried to turn again, this time with the singular goal of getting away before embarrassing myself further. Unfortunately, Dmitry was now facing me as well, his sharp eyes squinting, holding obvious but benign confusion.

"Sam?" Dmitry called, his accent coloring the syllable.

Both gritting my teeth and hammering on a small smile, I ripped my eyes from Andreas. "Hi. Sorry. You're busy. I'll catch up with you later."

I spun on my heel, hiked the strap of my bag higher, and started walking as fast as my legs would go without breaking into an outright sprint.

"Samantha, wait—" I heard Andreas call from behind me, surprising me anew, and my entire body rebelled at the sound of his voice.

Stumbling on nothing, I quickly recovered, reminding myself to slow down. It was cold and the sidewalk was slick with patches of ice and rock salt. If I didn't want to end up in the hospital with a concussion, I needed to measure my steps.

On the other hand, if I wiped out, at least I'd be unconscious for whatever came next.

Within seconds, the sound of shoes hitting the pavement at a jog signaled that Andreas followed me. I knew it was him. I didn't have to look.

Why would he follow? What could he possibly want?

He cut in front of me, blocking my path, and I had to stop so suddenly that my backpack fell from my shoulder.

Andreas, his hands held out as though to catch me if I fell, stared at me, eyes wide and serious. "Wait. Where are you—do you want to—" He cut himself off and I watched him swallow thickly, his chest rising and falling before breathing out a whispered, "How are you?"

I ducked to the side and stepped around him, refusing to let him see the tears already stinging my eyes. I hadn't prepared for this. I'd prepared for seeing him at the shareholder meeting, maybe, in a suit and tie, with an entire legal team, a boardroom, his brothers, and a security buffer between us. I had not prepared for this, for his voice, for his face, for the way just being near him could turn my brain into pudding.

He fell into step next to me, and this time, he sounded steadier. "Did you get Elio's messages about Tobias? I tried to call you back on Saturday but—"

I interrupted, "I blocked and deleted your number on Saturday. Don't call me. I don't care about whatever new plot you're hatching against your brothers." My voice arrived shaky, which only served to piss me off.

I sensed him wince subtly and he was quiet for a second. I could feel the weight of his stare on the side of my face as we walked.

Then, gentle as a feather, "I am surprised it took you so long to block me. I assumed you already did, until you called me on Saturday."

I kept my eyes on the Mercedes parked at the curb, a glimmering black escape pod with hazard lights strobing a silent SOS into the quickly darkening February evening. "I didn't call you. Nakita did."

He made a sound almost like a laugh, and I hated how warm it made my ears feel, even in the cold. "Yes, you said so. On Saturday."

We walked in silence for a few paces, the crunch of salt and the slap of our shoes a percussion against the symphony of traffic. I willed myself not to cry, not to look at him, not to do anything that would betray just how completely out of control I felt in this moment.

Tara exited the car finally and walked around to the passenger side, arms folded across her chest, eyes on the front of the biology building at first, but then scanning the sidewalk after a moment. She spotted me and her eyes widened with obvious surprise. Almost at once, they narrowed when she saw who was at my side.

Andreas must've spotted her too, because he tugged at my jacket sleeve as though to bring me to a stop. "We should talk before the shareholder meeting."

"No, thank you." I yanked my sleeve out of his fingertips and continued toward the car, aiming for breezy but landing somewhere closer to openly hostile.

He didn't seem discouraged by my brush-off. If anything—and perhaps I was imagining it—he sounded more desperate. "Have you found a proxy for your shares? If you need help, I have someone—"

Stopping so suddenly that Andreas nearly collided with me, I turned to face him and glared, hating that I noticed how his eyes darted over my face in a way that felt frantic, as though I might disappear. But this had to be wishful thinking.

"I don't need your help." The words came out slightly garbled by emotion, so I cleared my throat.

He inched closer, his body swaying toward mine. "I ask only for a half hour of your time. That is it. Please, let me help." His words were low and urgent, pleading, making my chest expand and contract with heat and tightness.

I didn't understand this. I didn't understand him. No contact for months and now he was chasing me? Looking at me like I mattered to him? Saying please? What the hell was this?

Maybe he needs your help with his new scheme. Maybe you were such an effective pawn, he wants to use you again.

My chin wobbled, and I could see, from the way his own eyes flicked down to my mouth and then back up, that he noticed. His brows pinched together and he stared at me with a look of such concern that my heart shoved itself in his direction, painfully smashing against my rib cage.

I wanted to slap him. I hated him. I hated him so much for making me feel this way. *Why is he doing this? What new game is he playing?*

I needed to get myself under control. Why would I allow this person who didn't care about me at all to dissolve my composure so completely?

Lifting my chin, I squared my shoulders and reminded myself that he'd never —not once—apologized. Not. Once.

He. Doesn't. Give. A. Shit. About. Me.

"Don't you have plans with Dmitry right now?" I gestured behind him, toward the spot where Dmitry still stood, pretending to check his phone. "And why are you now friends with my co-worker?" I asked, allowing my annoyance to pour out into the words.

Andreas stared at me for several seconds, his mouth opening, then closing, then opening again just to say, "I am using him to get close to you."

I blinked, startled, certain I'd misheard him.

"You—you what? What did you say?"

"I am using him to get close to you. But Dmitry knows this and does not mind. He would like to help." Andreas sounded calm, almost resigned, and for the first time in recent memory, I had no idea what to say.

I had . . . nothing.

It felt like the floor dropped out from under me. New tears stung my eyes. I didn't know what to do with the words, or the way he said them, or the way he was looking at me. So, I did the only thing that made sense in the moment.

I exhaled a bitter, ugly laugh, then turned away and walked faster toward the car.

He followed, matching my pace. "Please, Samantha." His voice sounded strained, choked with emotion. "Will you please—"

Tara finally moved to intercept, stepping between us with the efficiency of someone trained to stop professional linebackers and also dangerously tempting men in navy cable-knit turtlenecks. "Hey. She doesn't want to talk to you," she said, her voice measured and reasonable, but edged with a razor.

No steps followed. The relief that washed over me was so profound, I felt dizzy.

I heard Andreas exhale, a sound of pure frustration, before he said, "Tara. It has been a while." The sudden change in his voice quality sent a shiver down my spine. He suddenly sounded so calm, calculated, lethal.

"Not long enough," she replied, her tone echoing his.

Opening the back passenger door, I scrambled inside, shut myself in, and hit the lock button before I even had my backpack fully off. The interior was blissfully quiet, and as the world outside faded into a blur, I pressed my palms to my face and sucked in several shaky breaths.

I could feel the tears pricking again, building, a pressure behind my eyes that wanted so badly to break. But I was so tired of fretting over Andreas Kristiansen. I was done. I was not going to waste another second, another molecule of moisture or neuron signal of thought, on *him*.

[5]
THE ORIGIN OF LIFE

Samantha

The next morning, I arrived at my new office with a fresh head of broccoli from the corner produce stand. The broccoli had been on sale and I hadn't eaten a real, raw vegetable in ages. Before you ask, I do like broccoli. But only when steamed or sauteed and covered in cheese sauce. Taken with the idea of making nauseatingly healthy decisions, I'd bought it, and planned to devour the whole thing for lunch.

Presently, the head of broccoli spent the morning peeking out of my tote like an anxious green meerkat.

Yes, this was another classic Sam overreaction to an emotional crisis. I'd thought Tobias had threatened my PI's funding, so I let Andreas adopt me. I saw Andreas last night meeting with Dmitry, so I planned to eat a head of broccoli. See? It all makes sense.

Last night, I'd gone straight from the car into Kaitlyn's apartment building, refusing even to stop for groceries at the bodega, wanting to get to work being as busy as possible as soon as possible. I'd thrown myself into domestic triage: making soup out of whatever was left in Kaitlyn's fridge, feeding Joey, washing baby bottles, setting up the new humidifier, even refolding all of Joey's clothes in the drawers.

Kaitlyn had returned from the doctor around seven, confirmed that she had a fever and a UTI, wolfed down a bowl of soup, pumped Joey's midnight snack, and then put herself to bed. Once they were both fully asleep and the apartment was spotless, I went downstairs and completed a brutal treadmill run in the apartment gym, hoping to make myself exhausted.

Then, I showered, returned to Kaitlyn's, and crashed on the couch, telling myself it was so I could be available if she needed me. But really, it was because the thought of being alone in my new place made my skin crawl. Somehow I felt certain I wouldn't sleepwalk with a newborn in the apartment.

This morning, I'd changed Joey's diaper, fed him, and made a halfhearted attempt at small talk with Kaitlyn, who was in her own haze. I left only after confirming she was okay with me heading off to work and making her promise to call if she needed me to come back.

Tara drove me to campus under a gray, low-contrast sky. It was technically just a few weeks into the new semester, but the halls were still half empty and weirdly quiet. My new office was on the fifth floor, in an area I'd always associated with visiting professors. I'd only just finished arranging my notebooks when Dmitry's face appeared in the small window of my door.

He rapped lightly, then opened it just enough to poke his head and one arm through. In his hand he held a potted plant with neon green leaves and white spots. A plastic tag poked out like a little flag.

"May I enter?" Dmitry said, looking not at me, but at the ceiling as if he needed third-party approval.

"Yes. Of course," I said, standing and pushing aside a box filled with office supplies. I cleared off the second chair in my office, sending a mouse pad tumbling to the floor.

Dmitry entered while I picked up the mouse pad. He closed the door behind him with a gentle click, and approached. Without further ceremony, he held out the plant at arm's length. I got the sense it was a peace offering.

"It's fake," he said. "Because I know you can't keep a plant alive."

"Aww. Thank you," I said, genuinely touched because he knew me so well.

Accepting the plant, I admired how bright and cheerful and fake it was. I felt suddenly inspired. Truly, I aspired to be as low-maintenance as this plant. It had no needs. Sunlight and attention would only make it fade and fray.

He sat, crossing one ankle over his knee. "Are you okay?"

I set the plant next to my computer monitor. "Yes. I'm fine. Why?"

He leaned back and examined my face with the kind of intensity usually reserved for examining Western blots. "You appear very tired. The circles under your eyes are starting to look like those black smudges athletes wear to avoid sun glare."

I rolled my eyes and flopped into my chair, which squeaked in protest. "I've been sleeping at my friend's house. You know, Kaitlyn? The one with the cute baby? She's sick. I made her dinner and watched Joey—that's the baby—so she could go to the doctor. Then I stayed over and fed him in the middle of the night so she could sleep. That's all."

He squinted, unconvinced, and plucked a pen from my cup, clicking it with a slow, deliberate rhythm.

The silence stretched out a bit too long, so I kept talking, trying to sound casual. "Also, I might have overdone it at the gym last night. I tried out one of those exercise programs on the treadmill where you walk through an ancient city— which means climbing up steep terrain—and the auto-adjust feature moved the deck to a thirty-degree incline unexpectedly. I almost fell off. It was trippy. Have you ever tried it?"

Dmitry shook his head, solemn. "No. I value my knees and dignity too much."

"Dignity is overrated," I tried to joke, but the silence returned. Thicker now.

He broke it with a tilt of his head. "You are not upset with me?"

I tried to remember if there was a plausible reason I might be upset with him and recalled my motivation for chasing him yesterday. "I am upset with you. You never sent your review of my methods outline and it's due tomorrow."

His lips tugged faintly to the side. "I have it done. I will send it today."

I nodded, not actually caring about the status of my methods outline. I knew he wouldn't let me down. Dmitry was reliable like that.

He watched me for another several seconds, and I could tell he was working up to something. As his eyes began to narrow, I braced for it.

"You are pretending to be ignorant. Thus, I have no choice but to ask you directly."

Here it comes.

"Yes?"

He let the pen rest between two fingers and tapped it against his knee. "Do I need to know anything more than what you've already told me? I am speaking, of course, about what occurred between you and Andreas Kristiansen."

I paused, the question landing like bad shrimp in my stomach. I hadn't discussed Andreas's sudden appearance and behavior with Kaitlyn last night. She'd been sick and, honestly, I didn't want to. My drama was so pathetically small compared to her actual physical suffering and the ongoing battles of newborn sleep cycles.

I hadn't told anyone. Not Kaitlyn. Not Diya. Not even myself, really. After it happened, I'd shoved it away, wanting to label the whole encounter as irrelevant. He didn't care about me, and I didn't care to be used by him again. The end.

Dmitry allowed the silence to extend, then broke it with a dry, "I'll take that as a yes."

I sighed. "This is personal stuff, the kind of stuff you and I don't usually discuss. Our domain is work, work gossip and related memes and jokes, and food. I don't want to make you uncomfortable by pulling you into my personal drama."

He nodded, not looking away. "First, thank you for that. Usually, your instincts would be correct. Second, I'm on your side, no matter what, no matter who. Third, given your reluctance to pull me into your personal drama, but also seeing that you have clearly been suffering in silence like an anemic martyr for weeks and it's been a vibe killer to be around, I have to tell you something."

I blinked, worried. "What?"

He crossed his arms, the pen now clutched in his hand. "Do with this information what you will, but Andreas Kristiansen is madly in love with you."

I stared at him, not blinking. My mind went through at least twelve different types of emotional revival and collapse, all of which—I am certain—made it to my face. Then, I laughed. I laughed and laughed.

Through the laughter, I wagged a finger at my old friend. "You are hilarious. And that is impossible."

Dmitry waited for my laughter to mostly subside before saying, "He contacted me over the weekend and asked if we could meet. So, of course, I said—"

"When? When did he contact you?" I interrupted, sniffing and wiping at my eyes. It felt good to laugh. I couldn't remember the last time I'd laughed so hard.

Dmitry raised an eyebrow. "Saturday late afternoon."

My brain immediately spooled back to Nakita's unauthorized call to Andreas Saturday around noon. I felt my smile fade. Andreas had waited a few hours before reaching out to Dmitry.

"Okay. Go on," I said, voice tempered now.

Dmitry leaned in, resting his elbows on his knees. "He was very forthright, and told me that he wished to meet with me because he hoped I could help him with you."

I felt a weird mixture of dread and something else, a flavor on my tongue I'd not experienced since I was a child and my grandmother tried to make me eat sauerkraut and vanilla pudding in the same meal.

"Help Andreas? With me?"

"That's right. He said he did something that ruined your friendship—"

"Friendship?" Now I leaned forward. "He said 'friendship'?"

Dmitry raised a hand. "Let me finish. He said he did something to ruin your friendship, and he needed to talk to someone who knows you well. He said he needed—and this is a direct quote—he needed help figuring out how to repair what he broke."

I pressed my palm flat against the desktop, as if the solid surface might steady me, and spoke stream of consciousness. "I can't believe he called you. I can't believe he asked for your help."

Dmitry's lips quirked. "I can. You and I, we've known each other for years. You introduced me to him as your work husband. And I'm a guy."

I squinted at him. "What does you being a guy have to do with it?"

He smiled, the real thing this time, like he found my question amusing, or cute, or both. "For better or worse, guys are more sympathetic to other guys' plights. Just like you ladies are more sympathetic to other ladies' plights. It's a plight-sympathy ratio based on phenotypic sex that's at work here. Makes sense to me."

I shook my head at both him and myself. "Okay, I guess I see your point. So, what makes you think An—uh, what makes you think he's 'madly in love with me'?"

It wasn't even 10:00 AM yet and I already felt exhausted.

Dmitry ticked off points on his fingers. "Data point one: You two had an argument and ceased communication after the will reading, yes? Right before the Rome tournament. He lost that tournament."

"He came in second! Coming in second is not losing."

His smile returned. "For Andreas Kristiansen, anything other than a decisive first place showing is losing."

I wanted to roll my eyes but I didn't. "Fine. What else?"

He counted off another finger. "He looks worse off than you do. He's clearly not sleeping or eating well."

I shrugged because this was easily explained. "His father just died. And he—uh—like you said, he lost that tournament in Rome and he never loses."

Dmitry shook his head slowly. "I do not believe he is grieving the loss of his father, but whatever. Third point: He is notoriously calculating, cold, and aloof in every interaction he's ever had with anyone, public or private."

"How could you know about his private interactions?"

"Because even his closest friends, when asked if his tournament persona is a façade, for intimidation purposes, they all say no. They all say he is the same in public as he is in private. And I've followed him for years. So, imagine my surprise when you introduce me to him in December and he is not as expected. Around you, he is someone else."

"It was all fake. An act. He is cold, calculating, and aloof. And if that's your third data point, it's a lousy one."

"That was not my third data point, that was merely the introduction and background to my third data point, providing necessary context, which is: When we went to dinner last night, dare I say it, but I believe he overshared. With me. A stranger."

I squinted at this odd news. "What do you mean he 'overshared'? What did he say?"

Dmitry's eyes glinted. "He told me—and this is another direct quote—that he is madly in love with you and would do anything to be part of your life again."

I stopped breathing for a second. The words made something in my chest hitch and trip and then do a little loop the loop before landing on unstable ground.

Why would Andreas do that? Why would he—

I stopped myself from wondering, because Andreas never did anything without an ulterior motive and a long-game strategy. Thus, the answer was simple. Andreas needed me to help him with something—what it was, didn't matter—and his dinner with Dmitry was part of his carefully plotted scheme to dupe and use me all over again.

A wave of exhaustion rolled through my body. It felt like being drunk and sleep-deprived at the same time.

Dmitry waited for me to respond. When I didn't, he filled the silence. "He also said he doesn't need you to forgive him. In fact, he believes it is impossible for you to forgive him, but that he simply wants to know you, see you, and speak to you. And he said all this while sober."

I looked at the fake plant, jealous of its undemanding nature, and I found myself smiling, just a little, because what else could I do?

"Sam?" Dmitry prompted. In my peripheral vision I saw him tilt his head to the side. "Did I do the right thing by telling you?"

"It's fine. Nothing he said matters. It's all nonsense." I waved a hand through the air and gave Dmitry a small smile. "By the way, are you okay after being the emotional repository for your favorite chess grand master?" I asked, desperate to lighten the mood.

He stared at me, solemn, then said, "Thank you for asking. Honestly, I am not okay."

I snorted. "I'm sorry he sought you out just to—"

He stood up, abruptly, which startled me. "Don't be. It was the best night of my life. But it's all downhill from here, isn't it? How can I be okay when I've peaked at such a young age?"

I felt a laugh bubble up and covered my mouth with my hand to keep it inside this time, which made my shoulders shake. This type of laughter felt dangerously close to tears, and I didn't want to cry. Not here. Not in front of Dmitry and the fake plant with no needs or desires, and the stupid broccoli. But there it was. Sadness. Waiting just below the surface. Circling.

Dmitry let me have my moment, then, softer, said, "I don't know what he did, nor do I have an opinion to offer regarding whether or not you should accept him back into your life. I merely came to provide a few data points for your consideration."

I waited until I felt fully in control before dropping my hand and saying, "Thank you, Dmitry."

He nodded, went to the door, and paused, hand on the knob. "There is this saying about friendship in Russian. Roughly translated, it's something like, 'Walking with a friend in the dark is better than walking alone in the light.'"

We looked at each other for a beat before he added, "This is only true in certain neighborhoods in and around Moscow and New York City, obviously. It's better to be alive on your own during daylight than stabbed to death with a friend while walking in the dark together. But what I want to say is, you're a good friend to me, Sam. I like our friendship. And I understand why Andreas—even if he weren't in love with you—would want you in his life."

The laugh that emerged this time was shaky, but also genuine. "You're a good friend to me, too, Dmitry."

He gave me a little two-finger salute, then slipped out the door, closing it gently behind him.

I sat for a long time staring at the fake plant, not knowing quite what to think. It was possible to be finished with someone, and still miss them so much it made your bones ache. It was possible to be furious and heartsick at the same time, and wish things could be different.

Ultimately, despite my wishing and heartsickness, the truth was actually quite simple. I couldn't trust anything Andreas did or said. There existed no possibility of allowing him into my life.

Not now. Not ever.

[6]

THE LAST UNIVERSAL COMMON ANCESTOR

Samantha

By the following Thursday, my new office was no longer empty, but it was nowhere close to organized. I didn't understand how I'd been able to fit so much in my small cubicle. My filing system consisted of teetering piles that I arranged based on how much dismay their contents inspired. I'd also taken to stockpiling small snacks and caffeine sources in random drawers. I told myself that the hoarding was in case of a sudden lockdown.

The real reason was I enjoyed finding yummy surprises whenever I opened a drawer, even if I'd been the one to leave them there.

It was just after 3:00 PM and I'd decided to leave early. Yes. Again. Kaitlyn needed me, and even if I hadn't been caught up with all my work—actually, I was ahead—I would've left early to help her.

The dedicated lab space had been a dream. I'd made more progress on my dissertation in one week than I had during the entirety of the fall semester. And the quiet of my own office had increased my word count and productivity tenfold. Dmitry had promised to cover any of my physical presence requirements at meetings for the rest of the day, provided I brought him a black-and-white cookie tomorrow.

I was just closing up my laptop when my phone buzzed with a message from Nakita. The preview read, "Diya told me to message you about this before I do anything. I just got a call from Andreas—"

391

My stomach clenched and I unlocked the phone and read the rest.

Nakita: Diya told me to message you about this before I do anything. I just got a call from Andreas and he wants to meet for coffee. Diya said I should ask you first if it's okay for me to go or if I should turn him down. Let me know what you want me to do!

The full text was so textbook Nakita that I could picture her pacing her bedroom, aggressively talking to herself while typing with both thumbs.

I texted back almost immediately in a flare of vindictiveness. Not against Nakita, but against Andreas.

Sam: Thank you for asking. Go ahead. Have fun.

I pressed send, then stood at the window for a moment, watching the traffic below, somewhat surprised at my lack of immediate, vengeful satisfaction. If I were a better person, I might've tried to stop Nakita from meeting with Andreas. But, alas, I was not.

Petty queen, wear that crown.

My phone buzzed again, but this time it was a call, not a text. Diya's name flashed on the screen.

I picked up, cradling the phone between my shoulder and cheek as I zipped my backpack. "Hello?"

"Did Nakita text you?" Diya sounded energized. Or maybe rushed?

"Yes. Just now, actually. She also told me that you were the one who asked her to text me. Thank you for that." I paused to stuff a protein bar into the side pocket of my bag.

"May I ask, what did you tell her to do?" Diya's tone became measured.

"I told her she could do whatever she wished."

I heard Diya gasp before she asked, "Did you really?"

I toyed with my zipper. "Listen, Andreas is the one who will suffer here if he meets with Nakita or tries to draw her into his schemes. His request will end up plastered all over online fandom sites and documented—with dramatic flourish— in her latest fanfic."

Diya huffed a laugh. "You're diabolical."

I felt my hackles rise at the label. "If he wants to keep playing games and trying to manipulate the people around me, then this is what he gets."

"Sam, this is a guy who seems to protect his privacy like it's Fort Knox and you're sending him out to a coffee meet-up with Nakita? His biggest fan? While he's emotionally unstable?"

My temper spiked.

Last weekend, I'd texted Diya in a moment of weakness and asked her to come over. It was one of the few nights I hadn't needed to sleep at Kaitlyn's. Diya and I sat together on the floor of my apartment—I still didn't have any furniture except a mattress—and picked apart the entire Andreas situation, start to finish.

We'd also dissected what Dmitry had told me about Andreas confessing his supposed feelings for me. How he'd said he was madly in love with me but didn't think I'd ever forgive him. Diya had been pragmatic and diplomatic, but she'd ultimately agreed with my conclusions. If Andreas wanted my forgiveness, he should ask for it directly. Not use my friend Dmitry as a means to reenter my life.

However, she'd also suggested that Andreas's reasons for meeting with Dmitry might've been sincere. I did not agree.

"He's not, nor has he ever been, emotionally unstable. This—pretending to have real feelings for me—is an act. It's all a ruse! And if he actually wanted me to be in his life again—which he doesn't, not really—I'm not the one who can't apologize. I apologized to you and Kendra and Nakita the very first time we met after the holiday break. Same with Dmitry, I apologized and I explained and I asked for forgiveness. That's what you do when someone is important to you." Realizing I was now angrily fidgeting with my zipper, I released it and crossed an arm over my middle.

Diya went quiet for a moment, but then said, "Playing devil's advocate here, but you've blocked his number. He can't call you. And didn't Tara keep him from talking to you last week? How is he supposed to apologize if he can't contact you?"

"He's a freaking genius who figured out all my favorite things when we were living together, things I didn't even know I wanted. He sent me magical perfume, discovered I loved kombucha before I did, and bought me a closet full of clothes that were exactly my preference, in shades and styles that flattered my body and coloring perfectly. And you're telling me this genius baby-man can't figure out how to freaking apologize? Is that what you're saying?"

Diya's voice softened. "What would you say if he—"

I cut her off. "Listen, I'll see him next week at the shareholder meeting. He could try to apologize then. It's been on the calendar for months. But you know what, if he's supposedly 'madly in love with me,' then he should've thought about all this before he used Dr. Hauser's funding to manipulate me. Or, at the very least —at the very, very, very least—he should've apologized in Paris! He should've made more of an effort before now!" I finished with a whisper-shout.

Diya made a sound that was half sigh, half laugh. "You're right, you're right. Sorry. Remind me never to make you mad."

I barely heard her, my blood pressure had skyrocketed and I was now seeing red. "And technically, I'm not doing anything to him. I didn't give Nakita his number, I didn't tell Nakita anything but the basic information she could already read in the news. I protected him and his precious privacy even after he screwed me over! And what does he do? He knows she's a superfan, and he seeks her out anyway. If he suffers, he did it to himself."

"Okay, subject change only because I'm short on time right now—I have another fifteen minutes before my break is over—but we should pick up this conversation topic later for sure. First, where are you sleeping tonight? Should I come to your place?"

Sighing as I mentally downshifted from rage rant to mild-mannered conversation, I picked up my backpack from my chair and set it on my desk. "Thank you so much for the offer, but I'll be at Kaitlyn's again tonight."

"You've been sleeping there on and off for over a week. What's going on? Is Kaitlyn still experiencing the same weird fever?"

I hesitated, not sure how to describe what was happening since I wasn't a doctor. "Yes, I think so. Martin doesn't believe the antibiotics are working. She's going back to urgent care today to get new ones. Martin is back in town and going with her, thank goodness. He's really worried. So, I'm on baby duty tonight."

"Poor you."

I felt the corners of my mouth tug upward. "Yeah, I know. My godson is so damn cute, I'm constantly snacking on his cheeks."

"Well, tell Kaitlyn if she needs anything to give me a call." Diya's smile was audible.

I stepped around a stack of folders on the floor, hunting for my work keys. "Will do. And thank you again for the sleepover offer."

Diya hummed, then said, "Wait! I'm actually calling for another reason."

Abandoning my search for the keys, I paced over to the fake plant Dmitry had gifted me last week. I'd put it on a shelf. It didn't need sunlight, so it didn't care. "What's that?"

"Do you know how you asked me to look into your father's death certificate? And I had you sign the necessary release forms for his medical records?"

I'd asked Diya to look into my father's death certificate because something about it didn't add up. I'd been told my father died after falling down a flight of stairs, but the death certificate had listed the cause of death as a heart attack. This seemed strange to me. Late last week, I'd signed every highlighted page Diya had emailed over. She'd explained that to get my dad's medical records from fifteen years ago, she needed me to sign as his surviving family member.

Technically, since the adoption by Andreas, I was no longer considered my father's legal daughter. I was an "unrelated party" in the eyes of the law, but I signed the release forms anyway. I really wanted to see those records, and I doubted anyone at the hospital would check whether I'd been adopted by a sexy strategic mastermind two years my junior.

Of course, this was a gamble. Since my name had been all over the news after Christmas, there existed a chance that someone would know I'd been adopted and no longer had the right to request the records.

"Yes." Turning away from the plant, I walked to the other side of the small office, then back again. "Did they send you the records? Did you find something?"

"I received his records—"

I sighed my relief that the ploy had worked.

"—and there is no mention of a cardiac incident at all. However, the certificate indicates cardiac arrest was the cause of death."

I stopped mid-stride. "That can't be right, correct? I was always told he'd fallen down a flight of stairs and that's how he'd died."

She hedged, "Maybe. If the medical examiner conducted an autopsy—which I can't find that he did—maybe he discovered evidence of cardiac arrest. The medical records from the hospital actually indicate that your father's neck was broken when he arrived at the hospital. I guess it's possible that he had a heart attack, fell down the stairs, broke his neck, and so the medical team at the hospital didn't . . . but no."

I slumped down in my chair, staring at the coffee stain on the corner of my desk. "His neck was broken?" I didn't know that.

But then, I'd only been thirteen at the time. No one discussed the particulars of my father's death with me. Only that he'd fallen.

Diya's voice grew more clinical. "When I called over, I couldn't get ahold of anybody who remembered your father's case at the hospital. Which—if you think about it—is not unusual because it was fifteen years ago. So, I tried to reach out to the medical examiner's office."

"What did they say?"

"Your instinct about there being something wrong with the death certificate was right. They've never heard of this medical examiner, the one who signed off on your father's death certificate. So, I tried to track him down but all I could find was a news story from New Haven about a guy with his name losing his medical license. The story was printed a couple years after your father died."

My hands had gone cold and my throat felt weirdly constricted. "Why did he lose his license?"

"Illegally prescribing medication. Turns out he had gambling debts and—yada yada yada—he lost his license. My suggestion is to try and track the medical examiner down and see if he remembers why he was the one to sign off on your father's death certificate, since he lived and practiced in a completely different county. It doesn't make sense to me. But maybe I'm missing something?"

"Thank you so much, Diya. This is incredibly helpful." My hand was shaking as I scribbled the notes on a pad, underlining "broken neck" and "not the county ME" three times.

She seemed to hesitate, then asked, "Not to keep poking at a sore subject, but other than the Nakita situation today, have you heard from Andreas? Or is there anything else new on that front? Even though I'm not coming over, we can talk about it later if you want."

Rubbing my forehead, I said, "Since he met with Dmitry, Andreas hasn't tried to make contact with me as far as I know. But, as you mentioned, I did block his number, so . . ."

Diya made a thoughtful noise. "I wonder if Andreas doesn't know how to stop playing chess, even in relationships."

"What do you mean?"

"I mean, what if he doesn't understand how to ask for what he wants. It doesn't occur to him to try the direct path because everything is strategy with this guy. Everything is trying to stay five steps ahead of his opponent."

Diya and I sat in mutual silence while I listened to the faint office noises that filtered through the door. I mulled her words over and immediately saw the truth in them.

From what I understood firsthand about his childhood, every day had been a contest, survival of the fittest, and he was the youngest. He couldn't rely on brute strength. His brothers were monsters, his father was a black hole of emotional energy, and if you didn't learn to strategize, you'd get crushed.

At least my parents had loved me even if I didn't get to keep them for long. If I had grown up needing to be strategic in order to survive, would I be the same?

My heart twisted with a new kind of melancholy, and I realized suddenly that I actually felt *extremely* sorry for Andreas. Which was annoying.

I shook my head. It didn't matter. Andreas clearly saw me as either a pawn or an opponent, someone to manipulate or to conquer. Diya's point and my compassion changed nothing. Andreas did not care about me as a person, and he definitely wasn't in love with me.

But one day, if he ever did fall in love with someone, he would likely have a hard time knowing how to approach the person with sincerity and vulnerability instead of strategy. And that made me feel sorry for him all over again.

Diya cut into my thoughts, asking, "Didn't you say his assistant keeps reaching out to you about the lawsuit contesting the will? Something about having information that will help?"

I let my hand drop from my forehead. "Yes. I just received another message yesterday, practically begging me to meet with Andreas about it before the shareholder meeting."

"See, that seems more Andreas's style, right? He has information that would help you and he wants to use it as a bargaining chip to stay relevant in your life."

Picking up a pen, I spun it between my fingers. "That does seem like something he would do given everything I know about him. But not to stay relevant in my life. I still maintain he wants to use me for some new plot against his brothers."

She made a noncommittal sound, then said, "Okay. My break's almost at its end. But please let me know what you find about the medical examiner. And text when you need me to sleep over again."

"I will. And thank you."

Diya said bye, then hung up.

I put down my phone, then closed my eyes for a full thirty seconds, feeling the pressure at the back of my throat build and dissipate. Andreas was undoubtedly a strategic genius. But if there was one thing I was a genius at, it was avoiding prickly emotional issues until I could file things away neatly in the correct emotional folders.

After all, I'd had fifteen years of practice.

* * *

AFTER ROCKING my sweet cherub godson to sleep, I busied myself by cleaning Martin and Kaitlyn's kitchen, including the grout behind the faucet. With a toothbrush. I also sterilized two loads of bottles, reorganized the under-sink cabinet, and Windexed the mirror in the guest bathroom.

Kaitlyn and Martin hadn't returned from the doctor's yet, but it was just past 8:00 PM. Last time, Kaitlyn hadn't come home until closer to 10:00 PM. Joey had now been out for over an hour, so there was no point to my continued movement except to stave off my resting thoughts.

I poured dish soap into a bowl and filled it with water, soaking Joey's tiny spoons and watched the bubbles form their little kinetic city. I told myself I was definitely not going to check my phone for notifications from Nakita. Rather, while the suds did their job, I simply picked up my cell to pass the time.

Lies.

In truth, my brain had not moved on from the idea of Nakita meeting with Andreas since her text this afternoon.

The image kept popping into my head: Nakita, vibrating with extrovert energy, sitting across a vegan sausage platter from Andreas, who, despite having an honorary degree in Aloof Studies from every university on the planet, would answer every question in an effort to win her over to his side.

That's what kept tripping the worry breaker in my head. The idea of Andreas sharing anything with Nakita. It would definitely backfire. She always meant well, but she didn't have an off switch. If he so much as hinted at what happened between us or said something about being madly in love with me, she'd run with it. She'd amplify it. There'd be memes and GIFs and maybe even a T-shirt. Within twenty-four hours, everyone in the chess world orbit would know.

I was supposed to be done thinking about him, finished, but apparently my amygdala hadn't received the memo.

He deserves it. If he tries to use her, he deserves what he gets.

And yet, I also knew how much Andreas valued his privacy. He guarded his thoughts and feelings like they were state secrets. He would *hate* having his statements made public like that. And if there existed even a miniscule chance that Diya was right, that Andreas had actual feelings for me, then this public exposure would impact him deeply.

The more I thought about it, the more uneasy I became. Setting the phone down before I could unlock it, I paced the length of the kitchen, pausing as I passed to stare at the baby monitor and then at the cell on the counter. Every time I glanced at the phone, my heart rate jumped.

I considered calling Nakita and telling her I'd changed my mind, I didn't want her to meet with him. But then what if she posted about that? Would that kind of post embarrass Andreas? What if she embellished our conversation? I would ask her to keep it off socials, of course, but what if she—in a fit of impulsive exuberance while misguidedly trying to defend her stance as a Sam-Dreas shipper —posted about it anyway?

No, I can't ask Nakita not to meet with him. The less I talk to Nakita about Andreas the better.

After forty minutes of arguments with myself, I finally caved. I grabbed the phone, walked to the living room, plopped down on the couch, unlocked the screen, and stared at the blocked numbers list for a full minute.

I scrolled to his. My thumb hovered over the Unblock button for a solid thirty seconds.

This was so dumb. Why was I even debating it? If I wanted to warn a person about the human spoiler machine that was Nakita in order to give myself some peace, that was my business.

Decided, I tapped Unblock. A brief spike of shame shot up my neck and into my cheeks. I couldn't help but feel like a sucker. After the way he'd treated me, I couldn't believe I was this worried about him. I set the phone on the couch cushion, then ran both hands through my hair and laughed at myself.

After a few breaths, I picked up the phone again, went into the text field, and began to type a message to his number. And erased. And typed again.

What was the right tone for a message like this? "Heads up, you're about to have your privacy vaporized by a very sweet perpetual secret spiller"? "Meet with Nakita at your own risk"? "Don't say I didn't warn you when your conversation with Nakita is trending"?

In the end, I typed, "Meet with my friend Nakita if you wish, but please be careful about how much you share with her. Anything you tell her will likely end up being posted online."

I hit Send.

Biting my thumbnail, I considered the possibility that Andreas had blocked me in return and he would never get the message. This might've been a silly thought, but OH WELL! So sue me. *I'm silly.*

Still fretful, I navigated to my inbox, found the latest email from Elio, and began typing a message that was similar to the text, only addressed to Andreas's assistant.

Then my phone rang.

I jumped so forcefully at the vibration, the phone went flying into the air and landed behind the sofa with a clatter. Clutching my chest, I sucked down a gulp of air, then folded myself over the couch to retrieve my cell. The screen lit up with a number I knew by heart, despite everything.

For three rings, I stared at it, paralyzed.

Was this a test? What if it was a butt dial? If I answered, would he finally apologize? And if he did, what would I do? On the fourth ring, I decided I wasn't going to answer. I let it go to voicemail. Safer that way. Then he could leave a message and I could spend the next hour debating my options.

The ringing stopped, but no voicemail appeared. I waited. Five minutes passed. Still no voicemail.

Gritting my teeth, I rolled my eyes. *Of course not.* If I mattered to him, if he were actually "madly in love with me" and he realized I'd unblocked him, why not take the opportunity to ask for a chance? Why not say sorry?

Releasing a frustrated laugh, I shook my head at myself. I should've known better. *I'm a silly sucker.*

I was just about to go into my contacts and block him again—so I wouldn't be tempted to do something moronic of this nature ever again—when a text popped up.

Andreas: Can you talk?

I stared at the screen. It felt like the words were sitting on my chest and pressing down, making it feel heavy and hot. I blinked, waiting for something else. Eventually, the three little dots appeared, the universal sign of emotional purgatory, and then another message.

Andreas: Please.

Wiping my palm on my jeans, I considered the "please" for less than ten seconds, then tapped Call. I'd spent all afternoon with my circular thoughts. I didn't want to overthink this. Instinct screamed at me to call, so I did.

He answered before the first ring even finished.

"Hello? Samantha?"

I had to clear my throat before I managed a steady, "Yes?"

I listened as Andreas inhaled an audible breath, then said, "I promise, I have no plans to say anything or reveal anything that might embarrass you. I planned to give her the information regarding Tobias's case against you and his—"

"You're a real shithead, you know that?" The words were out of me before I could catch them, but with my emotions so close to the surface after hours of fretting about his stupid asshole self, I didn't care.

HOW FUCKING DARE HE.

This was pointless. I was not his ally. He did not value me. I was always going to be someone to plot against, to win over by any means necessary, to barter with.

Standing up, I set a hand on my hip and prepared to chew him out. "Listen, I didn't warn you because of *me* and *my* desire for privacy. I warned you because I—like a fucking moron—don't want to see *you* get hurt or blindsided when Nakita documents every word out of your mouth for her online friends. She's a great person. I love her. But she's terrible with boundaries and secrets. And I know you're extremely careful about your priv—wait. You know what? Forget it. I don't know why I even bother!"

I ended the call and immediately blocked his number again. Then, just for good measure, I threw the phone to the other side of the couch.

Storming off to the kitchen, I spun in a circle, looking for something else to wash and mentally cursing myself for my utter foolishness.

As I scrubbed at a baked-on stain on the lid of Kaitlyn's favorite Dutch oven, I tried to pretend that the ache in my chest was merely a side effect of strenuous cleaning, and not the gory aftermath of accidentally getting my hopes up. For nothing.

[7]

THE TREE OF LIFE

Samantha

At 8:00 AM, the lobby of Genetix's glass-and-steel tower was full of the chemical tang of floor wax and the hum of busy people arriving and departing. But mostly arriving. This morning marked my very first time walking to the building that Oskar Kristiansen had built with my father's ideas.

Every conversation seemed to cut off the second I passed, as though photos of me had been passed around ahead of time with instructions to remain silent in my presence. My security team—their haircuts as tight as their neckties—flanked me. One gentleman two steps ahead, the other two steps behind. Meanwhile, Tara hovered at my left and Dr. Hauser, my PI, matched my stride exactly on the right.

My legal team was already upstairs, making last-minute preparations in a conference room that the Genetix board had graciously offered for my use. I'd spent most of the past week fielding my team's calls, reading dense PDFs in the middle of the night, and pretending I wasn't nervous about today's vote.

Since Dr. Hauser had agreed to be my proxy last week, I'd spent the days since avoiding any thought that wasn't strictly about work, the shareholder meeting, or Kaitlyn. That is to say, I spent the week avoiding any thoughts about Andreas. Some unavoidable, uncontrollable thoughts did break through. Mostly, I'd succeeded.

Kaitlyn's deteriorating state was probably the reason.

401

Last night, Kaitlyn's fever had come back after we thought it was finally gone. She'd spent most of the evening sweating and pale. Meanwhile, I'd convinced myself she was dying. I did not share these suspicions with her. She had enough to deal with. But I did encourage both her and Martin to call Kaitlyn's father, who was the dean of the college of medicine at a large California university.

"Are you okay?" Dr. Hauser's voice cut through my thoughts.

I flinched only subtly and forced my face into something resembling composure. "Yes. Sorry. I'm fine. I just—my friend is sick, and I'm worried about her."

Hauser nodded once, her eyes warm but her mouth in a straight line. "Don't worry if you need to go, I'll cover for you."

I managed a grateful smile. "Thank you. I appreciate it."

She returned the smile, then turned her attention back to the closed elevator doors as we waited. I glanced around at the Genetix lobby. Clean, cold, all shiny surfaces and plants that I was ninety-nine percent sure were plastic. Not that I was one to judge. As already established, I adored fake plants.

The elevator arrived with a ding. The doors opened. We boarded. Tara pressed the call button for the top floor. All the while, I did a quick mental check of the seating chart for the meeting: Dr. Hauser as my share proxy would sit next to me, then the two partners from my law firm. Also present would be the CEO of Genetix, the CEO of the Vince Group—a three and a half percent shareholder, the largest non-Kristiansen stake in the company—as well as several other smaller voting groups. On the other side of the table, the three Kristiansen brothers would perch like vultures, along with their own wall of lawyers and fixers.

There was a chance the meeting would end in a quiet procedural vote and a minimum of drama. However, given Henrik Kristiansen's penchant for violence, there existed a much larger chance it would descend into gladiatorial farce.

I must've been lost to my thoughts again because the sound of my name in Andreas's voice startled me.

I looked up and found him standing just outside the elevator, surrounded on all sides by women and men in well-tailored suits, his hand holding the sliding doors open. His green eyes were already on me. They looked wide and hopeful and absorbed by the sight of me. Had I not been expecting to see him, I might've been entranced by how warm his gaze felt, how interested and inviting.

Not this time. *Nah, bruh.*

I knew he'd be here, though I'd hoped to arrive early enough that we wouldn't run into each other. But no problem. I was prepared.

Eyes locked on mine, Andreas took two measured steps into the elevator, clearly testing the water, whether I'd allow him to enter and ride to the top floor along with us. When I made no protest, he gestured for his entourage to wait for the next car. The doors closed behind him, sealing us together in the small capsule of icy silence.

Tara shifted, ever so slightly, her body language a silent "Want me to deck him?" but I shook my head minutely. Let him stand next to me. I didn't care. He didn't matter.

"Good to see you," he said, his voice low and unhurried, as though he were testing the words.

I ignored the way my stomach flip-flopped at the sound of my name from his lips. I had catalogued and accepted over the past month that there were certain stimuli that bypassed my cerebral cortex entirely and shot straight to the lizard brain: the smell of brewing coffee, the sound of Kaitlyn's baby's giggle, and, unfortunately, the way Andreas said my name.

For a second, I almost forgot what I was supposed to do. Then, remembering I had manners, I turned to Dr. Hauser and said, "Dr. Hauser, this is Mr. Kristiansen. He's the youngest of Oskar Kristiansen's sons and, technically, my adoptive parent."

I didn't miss the way Andreas's eyes narrowed and his expression darkened at my use of the word *parent*.

He extended a hand to Dr. Hauser. "It's a pleasure to meet you," he said, voice perfectly civil.

She shook his hand, her own grip certain and strong. "Likewise. This is quite the meeting."

"Yes. Quite," said Andreas. He released her hand and, with a tight nod to Tara, turned to face me fully, his expression again absorbed and what looked like hopeful.

There was a moment's silence as the elevator whisked us up, and I took the opportunity to stare him down while trying to recall all the things I'd rehearsed saying to him if ever given the chance. But the only thought in my head was, *I hate you.*

Something in my expression made his eyebrows pull together and he broke the silence first. "If possible, would you mind giving me a few moments before the shareholder meeting?"

I blinked my glare away from him, redirecting it to the seam of the elevator doors. "I don't have time to—"

"Please," he interrupted, and the word landed with more force than I expected. "Otherwise, you might be blindsided by some changes in shareholder ownership during the meeting."

That got my attention. Involuntarily, I glanced at him and noted unmistakable fatigue etched into the lines of his face, and something else. A haunted quality, worse than the funereal pallor in Paris. The suit was flawless, and the hair, of course, was stupidly perfect, but he looked thinner.

My heart jolted and asked, *What's the harm? What difference does five minutes make? Maybe if you meet with him, he'll finally leave you alone.*

"Okay," I said, voice flat. "Fine."

He inclined his head. "Thank you."

The elevator arrived at the boardroom floor, and the doors slid open. Tara and the other bodyguards fanned out. I followed Andreas through a maze of high-ceilinged corridors, each one lined with what must have been millions of dollars in abstract art. Apparently, the Genetix interior design theme was "aggressive minimalism," which suited the Kristiansen brand of self-mythologizing to a T.

As we walked, I found myself studying his posture, the angle of his jaw as he turned his head as though to ensure I still followed, the way his hands seemed to fidget, something I didn't recall them ever doing before.

The more I watched, the more the notion took hold: Something is actually wrong with him; he is not well; this is not the Andreas I knew.

But he was not my problem. I'd made my decision. *Stay strong.*

Despite the other stressor on my mind, when the unavoidable, uncontrollable thoughts of Andreas did break through this last week, many of the important people in my life had helped me mentally prepare and workshop strategies for dealing with him.

Diya was Team Gentle But Firm. My therapist was Team Healthy Boundaries. Kaitlyn, perhaps due to her fever, thought I should torch his entire life by writing a tabloid-style tell-all and sending it to Nakita to proofread.

Only Martin, who knew less than everyone else, was Team Maybe Have One Honest Conversation With The Guy. He argued that, for some people, strategy and defensiveness were a survival mechanism, a life raft. And that maybe I owed it to myself to hear Andreas out, judge his sincerity for myself, and communicate my needs before closing the book forever.

Bah! Just like Dmitry, I suspected Martin's plight-sympathy ratio based on his phenotypic sex was all out of whack because Martin and Andreas were both dudes. At the time, I'd rolled my eyes so hard they made a sound.

But now, as we approached a frosted glass door at the end of a hallway, I wondered if he'd been on to something.

Andreas stopped in front of the door, glanced over his shoulder, and said, "Please. After you."

Tara brushed past him first, scanning the interior with professional efficiency, then leaned back and whispered, "I'll just make sure it's secure."

Dr. Hauser seized the opportunity to ask Andreas, "Can you direct me to the ladies' room?"

He gave her crisp, unhurried directions, and she peeled off down the corridor. At a gesture from me, one of my bodyguards trailed her at a respectful distance, leaving just me, Tara, Andreas, my other guard, and the unmarked conference room.

Tara emerged and gave me a nod. She stepped back inside, followed by Andreas and me, and my second bodyguard stationed himself directly outside the door.

The room was small and elegant. Pale wood, a gleaming oval table, and maybe six ergonomically perfect chairs. A single water carafe and a stack of glasses sat at one end, and the only color in the room came from a miniature succulent in the center of the table.

I hovered just inside the door, trying to decide where to stand.

Tara waited a beat, then looked to me for instruction.

Glancing at Andreas's fidgeting fingers, I said, "Please wait outside." My voice was steady, but my stomach did handsprings.

She nodded, her expression never changing, and ghosted out of the room, closing the door behind her.

I turned to face Andreas, and was startled to see him looking as off-balance as I felt. His eyes were staring, his mouth slightly open, and his mask was nowhere to be found.

Unsettled, I decided to get straight to the point. "What did you want to tell me about the change in shareholders?"

He took a moment, physically steadying himself by bracing both hands on the back of one of the chairs. "I have bought out Tobias's shares."

I blinked, momentarily thrown. "You now control eighteen percent?" I moved further into the room.

He nodded. "I also bought six percent of Henrik's shares."

I could feel my blood pressure ratcheting with confusion. This was more than unexpected. This didn't make any sense.

I forced myself to sound calm. "Why only six percent? Why not all?"

He exhaled, a little laugh with no humor. "He would only sell me six percent."

I cocked my head, surprised by his appearance of candor. "How could you afford that? That must've been—I mean the stock is worth—"

"I leveraged loans based on my nine percent as collateral. Both Tobias and Henrik were desperate to sell, and I negotiated a price less than a third of the market. They are cash-strapped at the moment."

I did the math. "Why did they not simply sell to the market?"

"Neither of them wanted to devalue the stock since they are absolutely convinced they will be able to successfully contest the will and take your father's shares from you."

I stared at him, incredulous. "Who convinced them of that?"

He hesitated, then admitted softly, "Me. In a way."

I couldn't help myself. "Naturally. So, you lied to them."

"No," he said, his voice still quiet. "I ensured certain incorrect information made its way into their possession."

I huffed a laugh, sharp and brittle, because this wasn't surprising. "I see."

He pressed his lips together, eyes on me, plainly assessing my reaction, then said, "I wanted you to know I control twenty-four percent of the current votable shares and that the Vince Group will vote however I instruct them to vote. After today's meeting, your fifty percent will be votable, but not until a proxy is approved."

I froze, the realization hitting me all at once. With twenty-four percent plus the Vince Group's three and a half percent, Andreas would decide the vote. He would determine whether Dr. Hauser was approved as my proxy.

I folded my arms, frustrated with myself for considering Martin's perspective, that Andreas might be sincere, that I simply needed to give him a chance, to listen and judge his sincerity for myself.

Sincerity wasn't a word in Andreas Kristiansen's vocabulary. Everything was a ploy.

"I'm guessing you're telling me this because you want something, correct? You want to use your control over whether Dr. Hauser is approved as my proxy in order to negotiate with me."

Andreas visibly winced, swallowed thickly, then shook his head. "No." The word was rough, gravelly, as though it cost him to say it. He cleared his throat and added, "But I thought you should know before the meeting starts. I will, obviously, approve whomever you put forth as your proxy."

Nonplused, I walked to one of the chairs and sat down, frantically working to puzzle through this current game of his, what trap he was setting for me. It was no use. He was so much more adept at maneuvering and having patience than I would ever be.

"Okay, I give up." I shrugged, barely keeping my voice level. "Tell me why you did this."

He hesitated once more, then said, "I wanted your proxy to be approved."

I felt the urge to scream. "So you can force me to do what exactly?"

Andreas's eyebrows pulled together again, making his features look pained. He gave his head a little shake. "I do not wish to force you to do anything."

I knew that wasn't true.

My eyes stung. My head throbbed. For months, this man had twisted me into knots, manipulated the world around me, and never once asked for forgiveness or said he was sorry. Now, he stared at me like a kicked dog and expected me to believe him just because he said so?

"You did this so I'd feel indebted to you." I gripped the chair's armrests as my voice trembled with a cocktail of rage and hurt.

He shook his head but said nothing, his gaze tangling with mine.

I leaned back in the chair, closed my eyes, and counted backward from fifty, struggling to keep my composure from shattering. I was so, so tired of not knowing what the hell he wanted, of being his pawn, of playing into his hands.

When I opened my eyes, Andreas stood in the same spot, watching me openly, and his eyes once again seemed to be wide with hope.

Before I could speak, he blurted out, "I miss you."

The words hit me in the chest, a perfect shot to the heart, and I flinched at the impact. An alarm bell rang between my ears almost immediately because these were words I wanted to hear, had desperately hoped to hear months ago, but instead all he'd given me was silence.

I'm not falling for it. I won't fall for it.

Finding the edges of my self-respect, I mentally pulled it around me like a numbing cloak and stood from my chair. "Anything else?" I said, voice flat.

But in my head, I begged him to just apologize. Just once. Maybe I wouldn't forgive him, maybe it was too late for that, but part of me really needed to hear the words.

Straightening from the chair he held, Andreas seemed to gather himself, the mask I was accustomed to seeing on his face finally slid over his features. "I hope —" He stopped, took a deep breath, and spoke with more force. "I hope you know that I will always be here for you, if you ever need anything. I will always want to be of help to you. I will always be on your side. And I will always want to know you."

I couldn't think of a single response that wouldn't lead to an epic argument. Luckily, my phone buzzed at that exact moment, vibrating loudly in the tense silence.

Grateful for the interruption, I glanced down at the screen, and saw a text from Kaitlyn's husband.

Martin: Can you meet us at the er Kaitlyn fell in the bathroom and is still unconscious I couldn't wake her up and since I have Joey I can't ride in the ambulance will send you the hospital information

The world contracted to a pinpoint. Tangentially, I registered the lack of punctuation, which made the entire message just feel more frantic and urgent.

I looked up at Andreas, who was still standing there, waiting for something from me. I couldn't remember what.

"I have to—I have to go," I choked out, and then I bolted.

[8]

DIVERSIFICATION OF BACTERIA AND ARCHAEA

Samantha

ndreas's voice called out from somewhere behind me. I couldn't comprehend the words. I couldn't speak. I couldn't stop. I ran.

The door had barely opened. I already moved through it, not sure which way I needed to go but running anyway. For several disorienting seconds, the only thing I could process was the pounding of my heart and the amplified sound of my own shoes on the corridor carpet.

I don't know if I was crying or just leaking adrenaline, but my eyes started to blur and sting and I wiped them on the back of my hand as I took the first corner too tight and hit my shoulder on the wall.

Someone's hand gripped my arm and pulled me to a stop. "Sam! Sam—wait. Ms. Jarlston! What is it?" It was Tara.

I gulped air, hands shaking so badly I almost dropped my phone. "Please drive me to the hospital. My friend is unconscious and was taken by an ambulance to the ER."

The words came out as a slurred tumble, the edge of panic made me sound hysterical. Tara's face went instantly flat and professional.

"Of course. We'll walk to the car together." Her hand still gripping my upper arm, she steered me and I let her.

My other security guard fell into step next to us as my phone buzzed again. I frantically checked it. A second text from Martin, this time the name of the hospital and instructions on where to meet. I tried to read the whole thing out loud but my throat closed halfway through and I had to try again.

"'Emergency entrance. I'll meet you in the waiting area,' he says. Just drop me off." My voice sounded shrill and unfamiliar, like a bad recording of myself played too fast.

Tara pulled out her phone and, without looking at the screen, started typing as we walked.

We reached the elevators, and the three of us stood there in a triangle, all eyes on the small LED floor indicator as the numbers changed. None of us spoke. I pressed my hand to my chest, hoping the pressure would slow my heartbeat or at least keep my ribs from vibrating apart. The elevator arrived. The doors opened.

I didn't even realize Andreas had followed until—as my security team and I stepped onto the elevator—I heard his voice say, "I will explain the circumstances to the shareholders and Dr. Hauser. We will move forward with the proxy vote. Do not worry about that."

Turning and facing the doors, my gaze connected with his as an automatic "Thank you" slipped past my lips, but I didn't care about the shares or the vote right now.

Andreas nodded, hovering outside the elevator, his face twisting into an expression I couldn't interpret. Tara jabbed at the Lobby button.

Doors still open, he leaned forward, voice rough. "Is it Kaitlyn?"

I nodded. My eyes filled immediately, and my chin started trembling before I could even try to stop it.

Andreas cursed under his breath, a rolling string of syllables. He turned to Tara and barked, "Give her a hug, for fuck's sake."

Then the doors shut and he was gone.

For a long moment, no one moved. I stood frozen in place, jaw set, trying to blink away the hot, suffocating pressure of tears.

Tara hesitated only a second. Then, as gently as she could manage, she wrapped her arms around my shoulders and pulled me in, my face mashed into her blazer and the starched cotton of her shirt. I leaned into her, let my weight rest there, and pressed my forehead to her collarbone.

A tremor ran through my whole body and my chest hitched with the first, traitorous sob. I bit my lip, shook my head, and fought to control it, but the more I fought, the worse it got.

Tara squeezed me tighter, murmured, "It's okay, it's okay, I've got you," and let me sob into her like I was a little kid and not a nearly-thirty-year-old adult whose whole life and priorities had turned inside out in a matter of sixty seconds. I squeezed my eyes shut and begged God, the universe, whoever was listening, to let Kaitlyn be okay.

* * *

I DIDN'T KEEP track of how long it took to get from the Genetix building to the hospital, but it felt like hours compressed into a single, taut pulse. I spent the drive texting Diya, requesting that she pull whatever strings she could to give us frequent updates, and generally failing to keep my hands from shaking. Tara ignored every speed limit and stop sign, cutting corners with incredible precision. The other guard sat in the front, leaving me on my own in the back.

We pulled up to the ER entrance and I nearly fell out of the car in my scramble. My other guard must've switched into the driver's seat and taken the car because Tara was next to me again before I entered the building.

The lobby was an assault of florescent light and clashing noises—monitors beeping, babies crying, the high, tinny drone of an endless TV infomercial. I wove through the crowd, following the arrows for "Emergency Waiting Area" until I spotted Martin in the far corner of a rectangular room with rows and rows of chairs.

He looked worse than I'd imagined, and I'd imagined a lot. His hair was a mess, shirt untucked, eyes red and dazed. He had Joey in his lap, but the baby was writhing, arms flailing and face beet red from constant wailing.

Martin looked up as I approached, and I could see the wild panic in his eyes, the kind of fear that defies language, that lives in the bone marrow.

"How is she?" I asked, my own voice barely above a whisper.

"I don't know," he said, voice cracking. "They haven't told me anything. She hasn't woken up yet."

He tried to bounce Joey on his knee, but I could see the movement was absentminded. The baby only screamed louder. In a fluid motion, I took Joey from him, cradling his little body against my chest and rocking gently. Joey's cries didn't immediately stop, but the rhythm helped me breathe.

"He's just tired," I mumbled to no one, though I knew it was more than that. The baby could sense the terror, the instability, and was amplifying it with every decibel.

I scanned the room for a distraction, something to entertain Joey, but the only thing I spotted was a pile of torn coloring books and a sticky cardboard container of apple juice. I dropped into a crouch, shifting Joey to one arm, and looked under and around Martin's chair for the diaper bag.

"Where's the diaper bag? He probably needs to be changed." My hand at Joey's tush told me the diaper was full.

Martin stared at his own hands, then at the empty spot next to him, and a wave of guilt washed over his face. "I . . . I forgot the diaper bag," he said, and his face crumpled. He put his face in his hands and let out a sound that was half sob, half laugh. "I forgot the fucking diaper bag."

For a second, he seemed to have collapsed in on himself, like he'd lost all muscle tone and was nothing but sorrow and cartilage. Taking the seat neat to Martin's, I set Joey on my knee, holding him steady as I reached out and touched Martin's arm.

"It's okay," I said, and then, because I didn't know what else to do, I hugged him with one arm. Really hugged him, the way I'd hugged Kaitlyn after she'd told me she was pregnant, or the way I'd hugged my mom the night my dad died. Martin clung back, his arms going rigid and desperate, as if I was the only thing keeping him from being swept out to sea.

"Everything will be okay," I said, even though I had no idea if it was true.

Martin sniffed, wiping his eyes with his shirtsleeve. "I should have made her go back to the doctor first thing this morning. I shouldn't have let her go to the bathroom by herself."

I shook my head, rocking Joey, who had ratcheted down to a whimper. "We all thought the fever was finally gone," I said. "It's not your fault."

He pulled back from the hug, and his eyes were still rimmed red, but steadier. "I don't know what to do, Sam. I can't lose Kaitlyn. If I lose her . . . I don't think I can live without her."

For a long moment, there was nothing I could say. No science, no logic could fix this kind of raw animal fear. I held Joey while Martin absentmindedly held on to my arm. And the three of us waited, because it was the only thing we could do.

[9]

PHYLOGENY AND BIOLOGY

Samantha

The next three hours were a blur of semiconscious parenting. I found the nurses' station and begged for diapers. By late afternoon, the hospital waiting room had cycled through several generations of stricken families. There was the toddler with a golf-ball-sized head wound; a woman who sounded seconds away from coughing up both lungs; a set of college-aged kids, who looked related in color-matched sweats, trading turns between the vending machine and the bathroom; and a businessman with a loosened tie pacing back and forth in front of the swinging double doors, visibly negotiating the stages of grief over the course of four hours.

All the while, Martin and I hunkered in the corner, taking turns with Joey and using the three rations of hospital diapers only when absolutely necessary.

I spoke to my grandfather, since Friday afternoons were our designated weekly phone call times, but just briefly. He'd offered to fly out and help. I told him that wasn't necessary, but I did thank him profusely. I also might've teared up. It had meant a lot to know he was willing, and that I still had family out there wanting to be involved in my life, even when it felt like things were falling apart.

Like Martin, I couldn't imagine my life without Kaitlyn.

Tara slowly circled the room, scanning the inhabitants, drifting in and out of my periphery. Every so often, she'd catch my gaze and lift her chin, the

413

international sign for "You good?" To which my answer, every single time, was a single dazed nod, even if the real answer was, "Not even a little."

If I'd been in my right mind, I would've called and had diapers brought via delivery app. Or asked Nakita to drop off some baby essentials. Or called Kaitlyn's close friend, musical collaborator, and maybe the hottest guy on the planet, Abram Fletcher. So what if he was a famous rock star? Smokin' hot musicians are capable of running errands. He could've stopped by Kaitlyn's place to pick up supplies, and then delivered baby food, diapers, butt paste, and burp cloths. And a pacifier. And . . . other things I couldn't remember right now.

But I wasn't in my right mind, so none of this occurred to me, and I didn't call anyone except Kaitlyn's parents to give them the news.

However, sometime around noon, just as we were down to our last diaper provided by the hospital and Joey was trying to eat my shirt, Tara materialized at my side carrying a new diaper bag still with tags. She set it down on the chair, unzipped it, and produced a full array of baby gear: diapers (correct size, brand, and count), wipes, butt cream, three bottles of pumped breast milk (cold, in a mini cooler; whose, I had no idea at present, but never look a gift titty in the mouth), two baby spoons, six jars of age-appropriate baby food, three bananas, two clean onesies, a muslin swaddle, a baby sling, a teething giraffe, a plush octopus, several rattles and toys, disinfecting hand and surface wipes, and—this was the kicker—an exact replica of Joey's favorite pacifier, the one he'd chewed to death two days earlier.

Once she finished revealing the inventory, she zipped it half closed, likely so the bounty wouldn't spill out on to the dirty floor, turned, and began her circuit of the room again, as though she hadn't just summoned a complete baby-care kit out of the ether.

I blinked at the bag, then at Martin, who stared at it like its appearance was a religious miracle.

"How did she . . . ?" he whispered.

"No idea," I said. "Let's not ask questions."

Not fifteen minutes later, just as Martin finished feeding Joey his second jar of sweet potatoes, the doctor finally came out.

The man introduced himself as "Dr. Tomasetti, neurology," but his accent was pure Long Island, and he looked about twenty-seven. He asked if we'd like to do the consult in private.

I said, "No, here is fine," because I felt certain that neither Martin nor I could handle waiting another minute. "Go ahead, Dr. Tomasetti," I said, a little too brightly as I pulled out my cell phone to call Kaitlyn's dad. "We're all ears."

He frowned at the phone with plain confusion, then addressed Martin. "Your wife is stable. She suffered a moderate concussion. The scans look completely clean—no swelling, no intracranial bleeding."

We both exhaled mutual relief then Martin asked, "So, is she up? Did she wake up?"

Kaitlyn's father answered his phone and I put him on speaker, whispering, "The doctor is here. Listen please."

Dr. Tomasetti went on as though he hadn't been interrupted. "She'll be monitored overnight for the concussion, but that's not the main concern right now." He peered at us, waiting for the words to sink in.

I glanced at Martin. He stared at the doctor expectantly and I could see his patience was wearing thin. "Then what's the main concern?" he ground out, and I got the sense he was three seconds from committing assault and battery.

Martin Sandeke had never been known for his cool temper.

"Yes, what is the main concern?" I asked more tranquilly.

Dr. Tomasetti's lips pressed into a line. "She hasn't woken up yet, and she has an infection. We're still trying to pinpoint the source, but it appears to be antibiotic resistant. That's probably why she lost consciousness—high fever, low blood pressure, systemic stress."

Martin's hands tensed around the empty jar of baby food he still held like he wanted to throttle it. "She's been sick for months," he said, voice fierce and frayed. "First mastitis, over and over. Then another infection, then this UTI. She just finished a round of antibiotics."

The doctor nodded. "It's likely this is a secondary infection—maybe related, maybe not. We need to do more tests. But I have to warn you, if the usual antibiotics aren't working, our next options are . . . less ideal." He checked our faces. "Some of the stronger drugs have risks. In particular, it would mean she can't keep breastfeeding your son."

Martin blinked once. Very hard. Like he couldn't believe his ears, or he doubted what he'd just heard. I recognized the look. He was about to lose his shit.

I opened my mouth to intercede.

Before I could, Martin shouted, "I don't give a fuck about that. Fuck your 'ideal options.' Save my wife! Now. Whatever it fucking takes!"

The doctor recoiled slightly. However, I saw the faintest hint of relief flicker across his face, as though he might've been glad this was Martin's reaction and decision.

"Understood, sir. I just have to make sure you're aware of all the factors." His gaze darted between us, then to the phone, as if to ask if anyone else wanted to shout at him.

Kaitlyn's dad, via speaker, said, "Fully agree with my son-in-law. Do what you have to do. Kaitlyn's health comes first."

Perhaps detecting the air of authority from Kaitlyn's dad, the doctor nodded at the phone, and then excused himself.

"I'll call you back when there's more to report." I spoke to the phone.

"We might be on the plane by then," Kaitlyn's dad responded. "But keep us updated via text. Love you both." Then, he hung up.

Martin let out a noise somewhere between a strangled scream and a laugh, then collapsed into the plastic chair, face buried in both hands. Joey, who must have been taking notes from his father, shouted discontentedly. As though he, too, wished to give the medical establishment a piece of his mind.

I got the baby calmed in under two minutes, which was my new personal best. Joey had always liked me, but I think today he recognized me as a fellow traveler on the emotional shitstorm express. And we clung to each other like two survivors waiting for the next aftershock.

Eventually, Martin lifted his head and glanced around the waiting room. His eyes settled on me and Joey. Then, unexpectedly, he reached for my hand and squeezed it. "I'm sorry I lost my temper. Thank you for all your help. Thank you for being here."

I squeezed back, not trusting myself to speak, not sure what to say. Martin's whole body radiated guilt and exhaustion.

He shook his head and added, "But what the fuck do I care whether Kaitlyn can keep breastfeeding? She's unconscious because she has an antibiotic-resistant infection. She's been sick for six fucking months. Joey is perfectly fine. These fucking people are crazy if they think I'm going to risk sacrificing my wife—*my wife*—and choose a more 'ideal option' for fucking breast milk. There are breast milk banks, for Christ's sake. What the fuck is wrong with people."

I patted his hand, finding the right words somewhere below my sternum. "I know the doctor was just doing his job. But if it makes you feel better, I think you made Kaitlyn's father very proud."

* * *

WE MADE it through the next phase of waiting with considerably less difficulty now that Joey's needs were being met and we'd met with the doctor once. Still, we were both on edge, and I imagined we would be until Kaitlyn was out of the woods.

At some point, I realized I hadn't eaten since my oatmeal and coffee at 6:30 AM, and my blood sugar was on a one-way drop. I stood and stretched, planning to rustle up some food, when Tara approached again, this time with two bags of takeout and a twelve-pack of LaCroix. The food was from the barbeque place where Kendra worked—Smokin Greens—and the order seemed so specifically tailored to my preferences (buffalo cauliflower, arugula salad, and lentil chili) that for a moment I wondered if Tara had access to my former roommates' group chat.

Martin barely touched his food, but I ate like I was prepping for the end times. I tried to push some calories on him, but he just shook his head and stared at the wall, the way you do when you're expecting inescapable bad news.

About an hour later, after a second update from the doctor ("Still stable, monitoring closely, more tests coming back"), I handed Joey to Martin, slotted him into the baby sling, and did a slow lap of the hallway to clear my head. Now that I had food in my system, I could think a little better. Unfortunately, with the ability to think came questions.

On my second pass, I found Tara walking slowly in my direction, completing another of her endless circuits.

I hesitated, then sidled up to her. "May I ask you something?"

She didn't look at me, just kept scanning the waiting room, checking the exits, the hallways, the corners. "I called it in, and I have a night-shift security detail ready to go for the next week, if needed. After that, we'll have to get creative. Don't worry about coverage for now."

Smiling at her reflexive train of thought, I shook my head. "It's not that. But thank you."

"Oh. Sure, ask me anything."

I gestured vaguely in the direction of the diaper bag next to Martin and Joey. "Andre—I mean, Mr. Kristiansen the younger. He brought the diaper bag and all the stuff, didn't he?"

Tara spared me a sideways glance. "Yes."

Neither my brain nor my body had any immediate reaction to this news, good or bad.

Keeping pace with her, I asked, "And the food? That was him as well?"

"Yep."

I chewed my lip, struggling to ponder this confirmation of my suspicions and what it might mean. But my mind was slippery with worry for Kaitlyn. Thus, I filed it away for later analysis.

"Thanks," I said, turning to go. But then another question occurred to me. "Wait. Did he request that I be told? That you let me know it was him?"

Tara shook her head. "No. He made me promise not to tell you."

My feet stopped moving. I required several seconds to process this. By the time

I did, Tara had already moved twenty feet away. I quickly caught up with her, asking, "He did what?"

"He didn't want you to know. Made me promise. Got the food from your friend's place, hoping you would assume it was from her." She met my stare with unblinking calm before giving her attention back to the room.

"But you're telling me even though you promised?"

"I work for you, not for him. And I like you better. And since I didn't do it, I didn't want you thinking it was me." She paired this with a shrug. "I don't like taking credit for work or ideas that aren't mine."

I accepted her explanation with a nod. Then, still walking alongside her, I spoke mostly to myself. "Why—I don't understand. Why didn't he want me to know?"

"Didn't say," Tara replied. "But my theory is that he doesn't want you to think he's helping with any ulterior motive. He seemed genuinely concerned when he stopped by and saw the baby crying." She scratched her cheek, adding, "Well, you know. As much as he shows any expression at all. Like, his eyebrows moved a little."

My gaze narrowed. "He was here? He came here?"

"Yep."

I scoffed. "Okay. Fine. He was concerned about Joey. I can accept that, I guess. I . . . I should thank him."

Neither Martin nor I had the capacity to think about things like baby diapers, toys, and food at present. Living moment to moment, unable to proactively plan for whatever came next, I felt certain we both continued to miss the obvious, even now. Having someone who wasn't so emotionally invested in Kaitlyn, someone capable with a clear mind doing the logistical thinking for us was hugely helpful. And if Andreas Kristiansen was one thing, he was capable.

The corners of Tara's mouth turned up, and her eyes softened as they connected with mine. "Sam, you're dealing with a lot right now. Don't make someone else's feelings for you a burden or a distraction. Focus on your friends."

It was so gentle, so unexpected, that I didn't know what to say. I felt the urge to argue, to point out Andreas didn't have feelings for me, he wanted something from me. But the gears in my brain refused to mesh.

After a beat, Tara added, "Andreas will still be in love with you and making an ass of himself after your friend recovers. If you want my opinion, you should exploit his feelings for your own benefit, right? Watch him suffer up close. It might make you feel better."

Studying her, I eventually gave up my attempt to parse through her meaning. "What, specifically, do you suggest?"

"Call him up, drag him down here, and make him help. You could use some extra hands and, like you said, he was concerned about the baby."

A weird laugh escaped me. Suddenly, my vision was blurry. I wiped at my eyes with the back of my sleeve. "I'll think about it. Thanks, Tara."

She nodded, gave my shoulder a squeeze, then continued on her way.

I wandered back to our corner of the waiting room, where Joey dozed in the sling while sucking on a pacifier and Martin stared at nothing. Scrolling on my phone, I noticed that Diya hadn't texted me back yet, which wasn't unusual. Some days she didn't get a chance to check her phone until the end of her shift.

Tara came by once more before my security team's shift change, this time with two soft blankets, a basket full of snacks, and two Americanos from Central Grounds, my favorite coffee place.

She deposited everything in the seat next to mine except for the coffees, which she placed in our hands.

Pointing at Martin, she said, "Don't drink it while holding the baby."

He nodded, placing the cup on the floor just under the chair. Poor guy. Usually, Martin Sandeke was the most methodical and clever person in any given room. But he was basically helpless right now, reckless and thoughtless and completely overwhelmed. It was . . . hard to witness.

To me, she said, "Jerome and his team are taking over."

I nodded.

She seemed to hesitate, then—to both of us—she said, "Did you know they have VIP suites here?"

This snagged Martin's attention and his gaze cut to hers. "What?"

"VIP suites for rich patients and their families. Someone told me that if you speak with hospital administration, they'll set you up. It's wicked expensive, but the rooms have couches and rollaway beds. They can even bring in a crib. If you pay for it, they'll bring you meals and all the suites have private bathrooms with showers. Then you don't have to wait out here, worry about food, or go home. And you can get some sleep tonight."

My expression flattened. "*Someone* told you that?"

The side of her mouth tugged in a rueful-looking curve. "Yeah. Someone."

[10]

GENETICS AND GENOMICS

Samantha

It was the warmth that woke me—radiating through my neck, cheek, and one shoulder, gentle and immovable. I clung to the last remnants of sleep, unsure where I was or who the solid mass belonged to, but certain my face was buried in some combination of expensive wool and aftershave. The wool felt pillowy and scratchy, and the scent was familiar: rosemary, cedar, and that barely there note of ozone I used to associate with thunderstorms and now associated exclusively with *him*.

For a single confused, half-lucid moment, I told myself it had to be Martin. He was the only man I'd feel comfortable enough to collapse on in public, let alone in a hospital. But then my mind clicked through the last few hours and reminded me, slowly and with increasing certainty, that Martin had left me with Joey to go investigate the possibility of securing a VIP suite.

Fighting a series of yawns, I'd changed Joey's diaper, gave him a quick sponge bath in the public restroom sink, and fed him a bottle, the source of which was written on a label affixed to the exterior of the breast milk. It had come from the hospital's breast milk bank. Come on, people. I wouldn't have fed my godson mysterious breast milk. You can relax now.

While feeding him and watching his eyes grow heavy in the sling, I'd felt mine start to drift as well. Tucking him fully and safely inside the sling, I'd rested my head against the wall. My security team watched us closely. We would be safe. And I was so tired. I told myself I would rest my eyes. Just for a moment.

Famous last words.

Presently, I continued resting my eyes while I debated what to do about this persnickety situation, reasoning it was safer to lay there, pretending to be asleep, allowing the weight of my world to be redistributed across Andreas's shoulder. Just for a moment.

Famous last words. Again.

"Are you awake?" The achingly familiar voice vibrated more than spoke, low and just a little gravelly, the pitch of it sneaking in through the spaces of my rib cage.

I swallowed, adjusted my head, and said, "Yes."

A pause followed, not awkward. Suspended.

His arm—which I realized suddenly was around me—tightened, almost imperceptibly. I also suddenly realized one of my arms lay across his stomach.

"Kaitlyn was moved to the ICU and finally woke up about an hour ago. She is still in the ICU. Her parents have arrived and are in there with Martin and the doctors now. The new treatment seems to be working really well, but they want to keep her under close watch for sepsis. She is going to be okay."

Relief washed through me, hot and weightless, and I shot a prayer of thanks upward. My entire body slackened, so boneless with gratitude that I nearly lost my grip on the moment.

After another indefinite pause, I came back to myself and the moment and the reality that Andreas was here with me and I was still curled against him, giving him my weight. I didn't dare move my head; I wasn't ready to look at him directly.

Instead, I inhaled deeply and asked, "What time is it?"

"Two-thirty," he said. "In the morning."

"Where's Joey?"

He shifted slightly, and I felt the movement ripple through his torso. "Right here," he said, and I thought I heard a trace of amusement.

Forcing my eyes open, I blinked the harsh fluorescent light into focus. We were still in the ER waiting area, in the same corner Martin, Joey, and I had spent all day haunting. But we—both of us—were now tucked beneath one of the soft blankets Tara had dropped off earlier.

I glanced down. Joey was curled on Andreas's other shoulder, his bottom half in a baby sling I didn't recognize, a tiny, chubby face peeking out from a cocoon of blue fleece. His impossibly small hand rested against the knit fabric of Andreas's sweater.

Andreas stared straight ahead, gaze fixed. He looked as exhausted as I felt, his eyes rimmed red with what looked like worry, and there was a rawness about his jawline, like he'd shaved in a hurry and missed a few critical spots.

I realized, in that moment, that he'd been awake longer than I had. I'd taken a nap, albeit a brief one. He'd been up since yesterday morning. This information didn't stir anything good or bad within me. Like learning about the origins of the fully stocked diaper bag and take-out order from Smokin Greens, it just was.

"I suppose Tara called and told you to come?" My voice sounded steadier than I felt and I felt grateful for small mercies.

He didn't look at me as he spoke. "She explained how you interrogated her about the diaper bag and food, threatening to fire her if she did not reveal who sent the items."

I felt my mouth betray me with a tiny, traitorous smile. "Is that so?" What a liar.

He nodded. "She also said that you demanded I come and help take care of Joey."

"And you came?" The question was rhetorical. But, perversely, I wanted to hear his answer out loud.

"Yes," he said, finally turning his head to face me.

Our gazes met and clashed with the force of a head-on collision, like they always seemed to do these days, and I could barely stand it. The intensity of his eyes, the way they searched my face, all his concentration pointed at me. My skin prickled; the fine hairs on the back of my neck raised; nerve endings tuned themselves to a frequency filled with tension and anticipation.

After the past eighteen hours, I gave myself permission to be a coward and looked away first, before something in me cracked or—worse—gave in.

Dropping my head to his shoulder again, I set my gaze forward. Somewhere in the back of my mind I knew I was still really, *really* fucking mad at him. Yet, I couldn't deny the relief of having him here. Not just because Martin and I were both running on fumes and needed an extra set of hands, but because he made the chaos feel less chaotic. His presence was reassuring. Andreas exuded steadiness, calm, and when I allowed myself to admit it, I liked his stoicism.

"I didn't threaten Tara." I took in the battered linoleum floor, the splatters of ancient gum, the scuffed edge of his Italian shoe. It was easier to look at the ground, to pretend we were just two exhausted people stuck in a hospital together, not whatever we actually were. "She gave you up as soon as I asked."

He was quiet for a long moment, then said, voice thick, "I suppose she works for you now, and has no allegiance to me."

"I also never instructed her to call you and demand you come help."

I felt him stiffen. Before he could speak, I added, "I don't trust you to have no ulterior motive. So, I'm not going to feel gratitude or indebted, if that's what you're hoping for. If you're here, it's because you want to be. I won't make you leave right now. But if you do leave, that's also fine."

"That is fair." His shoulders rose and fell with a deep breath.

Joey made a small, unhappy sound—a sigh more than a cry—and I lifted my head to look at him. Joey's eyelids fluttered, then closed again. Andreas patted his tiny back, slow and rhythmic.

"I will stay until you ask me to leave," Andreas whispered. To my ears, it sounded like a secret.

The three of us sat there for a long time, not talking, not moving, just breathing together under the unnaturally bright lights. If I'd had a phone or the presence of mind to check the time, I might have noticed that an hour slipped past without anyone noticing. But I didn't care about time or the minutes ticking by. All that mattered was that Kaitlyn was going to be okay.

After a while, the rhythm of the baby's breathing changed, and I realized Joey had fallen deeply asleep again, his lips slightly parted and his tiny back rising and falling in sync with Andreas's chest. I let my own head drop once more. This time not to hide my face, but just to rest. I let myself feel the weight of the blanket, the press of his arm around my body, the heat of his hand on my hip, the faint pulse of his heart against my temple.

I wasn't ready to forgive him. And it hadn't escaped my notice that he still hadn't asked.

* * *

TWO DAYS LATER, I was on my knees, on the floor, kneeling in front of my favorite boy on the planet.

That's right. I was peeling a blowout diaper from Joey's bottom while he stared at me with his round gray eyes, wrinkling his nose as though he objected to the smell. The smell *he'd* created.

"I don't understand. Why didn't Senator Parker just accept the VIP suite?" Tara, who'd returned for her shift this morning bright-eyed and showered, whispered this question to me from where she stood close by. "Why make her son-in-law pay for it if they were offering it for free?"

I glanced up at her, hands wrist-deep in wipes and carnage, and found her standing with a plastic container of cut melon in one hand and a fork in the other, her face equal parts genuine curiosity and "explain this weird human behavior to me, please." She looked at me, but I could tell she was also glancing sideways at Andreas, who was leaning against the wall a few feet away.

He wore black pants and a charcoal-colored button-down today, looking effortlessly chic and oddly better rested than he had when I saw him at the Genetix offices a few days ago. I didn't understand why since I suspected he'd been getting less sleep than me, and that was not a lot.

Andreas had offered to change Joey's diaper, but he'd already changed the last three diapers, and my typically dormant sense of righteousness wouldn't allow me to take him up on the offer this time.

Returning my attention to Joey, I shrugged. How to explain the dynamics of Kaitlyn's family? "It's complicated," I finally said.

The personalities involved were simply too big and set in their ways. Thus, logic didn't always apply.

Martin had inquired about a VIP suite the very same day we arrived and had been told there were none available. Diya, who'd returned my messages Saturday morning, tried to pull some strings to no avail, but she did stop in to check on all of us and translate doctor speak when Kaitlyn's father wasn't around.

Both Andreas and I had also tried to persuade hospital administration to find space in the VIP area. The answer had been the same: We have no rooms.

Until . . .

Kaitlyn's mom was a sitting United States senator and her father was the dean of the college of medicine at a major California University. Once these facts were discovered Sunday morning, the hospital not only had magical availability in the VIP area, they'd offered the suite's use for free.

Kaitlyn's mom did not want to accept the offer. The woman had always been extremely rigid about right and wrong and perception of professional ethics.

Rather than engage in an argument about it, Martin had simply accepted the offered suite, but insisted on paying for it himself, out of pocket, reserving it for an entire month for our use, even though Kaitlyn hadn't yet been transferred from the ICU.

I supposed, in New York, there were plenty of rich people. But in the entire USA, there were only a hundred United States senators, and even less than a hundred who advocated for universal healthcare.

As an aside, the irony was not lost on me that I had a security team of three because of Andreas's brothers, but Senator Parker—who received constant death threats—had no security detail.

"I think at a fundamental level, Senator Parker and Kaitlyn's husband have two extremely different ways of looking at and approaching the world," I finally said in response to Tara's question.

Ignoring Andreas's steady—albeit, slightly frosty—gaze, I grabbed the diaper rash cream and squeezed a significant amount onto my fingers. Joey had a bath last night, but the delay in changing his diaper from two days ago meant he still had little red pinpricks of irritation on his backside.

Tara stepped closer and asked quietly, "I don't get it. Mr. Sandeke paid for the suite and Senator Parker still requested a regular room for Kaitlyn. They even argued about it in the hall." As though appealing to Andreas, she added, "You heard them too, right?"

I didn't see if Andreas nodded or what, but he didn't respond with words.

Smearing the cream on Joey, I shrugged again. "It doesn't matter. Martin is her husband. He gets to make the decision. Kaitlyn will be transferred here, to this palatial VIP suite, when she's out of the ICU."

Martin Sandeke would never be above or below receiving special treatment, and in my opinion, his attitude about always wanting and accepting the best for his wife, himself, and his kid was actually really good for Kaitlyn. He balanced her out.

"But wouldn't a mom want the best for her daughter?" Tara sounded truly perplexed. "Kaitlyn has been through hell recently. What's wrong with accepting the suite?"

Pulling Joey's foot from his mouth so I could fasten the new diaper, I quickly handed the baby a toy meant to distract him and I spoke without thinking too much about my words. "Like I said, it's complicated. Wanting the best for your kids is sometimes ensuring they don't receive special treatment. That's essentially the difference between parents and partners, right?"

"How do you mean?" This question came from Andreas.

My attention flickered to him then back to Joey.

Part of me was surprised at my verbosity in front of Andreas. Though I appreciated all his help with Joey, and how he'd met Diya at my apartment and packed me a bag so I could stay at the hospital, and the calming quality of his steady presence, and how he'd been a great distraction for Kaitlyn's parents and a surprisingly effective sounding board for Martin, we weren't on friendly terms. At all. And that went both ways.

The longer we'd spent in each other's company, the chillier and more reserved he'd grown with me. Perhaps he was finally getting tired of my glares and short answers and cold shoulders.

Good.

But, right this moment, with my hands full of wiggly baby and operating on less than six hours of sleep in two days, I was too tired to care about talking so much in front of him. I didn't have the energy.

"Well, parents—or rather, in my opinion, *good* parents—want what's best for their children, and that sometimes means withholding special treatment when they don't believe it's earned or justified, or if they think it's a corrupting influence. Or, in Kaitlyn's mom's case, an injustice in general. Senator Parker actively advocates for universal healthcare on the senate floor. Of course she's not going to want her daughter to stay in a free VIP suite just because Kaitlyn is her child. I think I've heard Senator Parker say to Kaitlyn a few times, 'Having the best isn't always what's best.'"

Tara snorted softly. "That sounds like my dad. He says that kind of shit, too."

I sent her a quick smile then finished buttoning Joey's onesie. "But partners—and good friends for that matter—are always going to want *the best* for the people they love. They're not wondering if the existence of VIP suites are an injustice, or a corrupting influence. They're simply thinking about how to improve the life of the person they care about the most."

"So, you agree with Mr. Sandeke? I mean, you agree with Kaitlyn's husband?" Tara bent, picked up the toy Joey had just thrown, and set it on the coffee table.

"In this case? Yes. Mostly because we're talking about Kaitlyn, who never takes or asks for the best for herself. She's always putting herself last, because that's how she was raised. She was taught that to those who much is given—"

"Much is expected?" Andreas guessed, drawing my attention again. His gaze had become somehow . . . heavy. And his tone had been ice-cold.

Giving him a quick glare, I redirected my attention to Joey and picked him up with one arm while searching for a new toy from the diaper bag with my free hand, preferring one that hadn't fallen on the floor. "Yes. But also, to those who much is given, they must never put themselves first. They must use their gifts, talents, and money to help those who are in need *first* rather than spending all of it on themselves."

Andreas stepped forward, knelt next to me, and held the diaper bag open wider, asking, "Were you raised that way?"

I reasoned there was no harm in responding. "I guess I was, when my parents were alive. But by the time my grandma became my guardian, I . . ." I sighed.

When I found the toy I wanted, Andreas moved himself from the floor to the couch, reaching for and taking Joey into his arms without asking. "Go wash your hands," he said. "I'll hold him."

Slicing Andreas another dirty look, because under no circumstance was I going to go wash my hands now that he'd told me to do so, I reached into the diaper bag and pulled out the disinfecting hand wipes. I cleaned my hands with them while glaring daggers at Andreas.

Get a load of this a-hole. Ordering me around. Who the hell did he think he was? HE STILL HADN'T APOLOGIZED!

Meeting my dirty look with an absolutely epic one of his own—I mean, the man deserved every meme made about him—Andreas allowed Joey to tug and gnaw on his jaw while he asked, "Do you think your reluctance to have or keep nice things is because you don't believe you deserve them?"

My teeth slid to the side, I blinked once slowly, and I felt my mouth curve in a mean smile. What. An. Asshole.

Meanwhile, Andreas maintained eye contact unflinchingly. Patiently, even. His smile also looking a little mean.

Tara cleared her throat, as though to remind us both that we were not alone. I ignored her.

Apparently, so did Andreas, because he felt the need to add, "You have no furniture in your new apartment."

"I have a mattress."

"And no frame. Why can you not let yourself have nice things? Why do you not let people care for you?"

Zipping the diaper bag closed with more force than necessary, I wadded up the used disinfecting wipes and placed them on the corner of the coffee table. He would hate that I didn't immediately throw them away. Then I sat on the couch next to him and Joey, facing them, and telling myself to ignore his questions because the answers were none of his damn business.

Except, I wanted to answer. Perhaps the impulse was so strong because I was so tired. Or maybe it was due to the emotional roller coaster of the last seventy-two hours.

Whatever the reason, I responded honestly, "I don't think I don't deserve nice things. I think it's because nothing really lasts, does it?"

"Why does that matter? Why deprive yourself of something you want, of something you might love, and all the experiences that come with it, and all the enjoyment, just because one day it might not be there? Then you are left with neither the memory nor the thing."

Joey made a sound of frustration and smacked Andreas on the shoulders.

Impatiently, I reached forward and turned Joey in Andreas's arms. "He likes to face outward, like this."

Andreas allowed me to reposition the baby, but caught me by the wrist before I could withdraw, his eyes narrowing, growing fierce. "Answer my question. Why does it matter?"

"Because the memory of having something good that didn't last is really fucking painful. Why get used to having nice things when they can so easily be taken away? Or turn out to be nothing but a lie?"

Andreas's hand tightened on my wrist and we glared at each other for another exceedingly long and hostility-filled moment.

Peripherally, I was aware of Tara excusing herself, and her departing footsteps. When the door closed behind her, Andreas, Joey, and I were the only ones left in the room. I was about to twist my arm out of his grip, but Joey bent his head, cupped my hand, and began biting and drooling on my fingers.

And then, because he must've wanted my wrath, Andreas said, "I am not the only one who lied."

What. The. Fuck.

Resigned to holding this position until Joey lost interest in my hand, I ground out, "I know. I lied to my friends. And, guess what? I *apologized.* Unlike some people."

"You also lied to me."

I blinked, flinching, feeling my spine go ramrod straight as though I'd been struck. "I—I lied to *you?* What the hell are you talking about? When did I lie to you?"

Joey laughed and clapped around my wet hand, his legs kicking as though he was delighted by the screechy quality of my voice.

"You said no strings. You said no feelings. Friends with benefits." His voice was low and lethal and held more than an edge of anger, possibly even resentment. Tilting his head subtly, his gaze skated over my face, as though hungry for my reaction. "Did you lie?"

[11]

THE ORIGIN AND DIVERSIFICATION OF EUKARYOTES

Samantha

Heat slithered up my chest to my neck and over my cheeks as our eyes locked. He was right. I'd had feelings for him before I proposed a friends-with-benefits relationship. I'd promised "no feelings involved," but I'd lied.

His eyes dropped first, lowering to my mouth as he pushed the issue. "Were we *just friends* before Paris? Was there ever anything else between us? Anything you kept to yourself and refused to tell me?"

I had to both swallow and clear my throat before asking, "Why does it matter now?"

"Because I fell in love with you while lying to you, deceiving you and manipulating you, and I wonder if I am the only one."

I fell in love with you . . .

My heart liked the sound of that, but the rest of me rallied against the words. The truth was, I didn't know what to think anymore. He hadn't apologized. But he'd gone into massive debt buying the Genetix shares from his brothers, and he'd looked after me and Martin and Joey without wanting us to know, and then he'd been showing up every day since even though I knew he had better things to do.

Did he love me? I had no idea.

But I supposed the real question was, did it matter?

His fist around my wrist began to feel like a brand, so I twisted my arm. He let me go immediately, grabbing a pacifier to replace my fingers and distracting Joey with it before the baby could protest.

Picking up a burp cloth, I wiped the baby slobber from my hand and tried to find my place in the conversation while also struggling to bring my heart rate back to normal.

Eventually, I asked, "Are you suggesting I lied to you, and thus manipulated you into falling in love with me?"

"Did you not? When did you begin to have feelings for me? Was it before or after Thanksgiving? Before or after you said there would be nothing real between us?"

My heart jumped to my throat and I stood, placing my hands on my hips, feeling defensive because his points were valid.

And man, do I hate arguing with someone who made valid points.

"Then when did you start falling for me, huh? Before or after Thanksg—"

"In retrospect? The moment I saw you outside your work back in early November." Andreas also stood, twisting slowly at the waist and bouncing lightly with his legs, presumably to keep Joey happy while we argued. "But I am not the one who said—"

"Ha!" I lifted an accusatory finger. "Then you lied about 'no feelings,' too."

"The difference is, I never set out to deceive you about falling for you. When you said, 'no strings,' I believed you. I have never been in love with someone before you—"

"Well, neither have I before you!" I admitted. Thoughtlessly. Like a moron. Realizing too late what I'd said and that, by shouting, I'd startled the baby.

Joey stilled, looking at me silently for a protracted moment, eyes wide with surprise and betrayal. And then he promptly cried.

I huffed, the shrill sound taking all the fight out of my bones. I didn't know what I was doing, what I was saying. This entire situation and conversation felt ridiculous. Was I really going to argue with Andreas about this? Try to defend what I did? The choices I made? My cowardice?

Reaching for Joey, I sighed. "I'm sorry, baby. I scared you. I'm so sorry. I shouldn't have done that."

"I accept your apology," Andreas said, keeping hold of my godson and turning him around to face his chest. Soothing and cuddling Joey, he gave him several cherishing kisses on his pillowy cheek. Joey calmed down almost at once.

Wanting to seethe, but too tired to do so, I shook my head and exhaled a laugh devoid of humor. "I wasn't apologizing to *you*."

"Too late. I have already accepted it." Andreas paced away, bouncing Joey and patting his back. "You are forgiven for seducing me and making me fall irrevocably in love with you. But now, you will have to accept the consequences."

This time when I laughed, it was full of humor. The exhausted kind.

I threw my hands up. "Well then . . . I really do apologize. I'm sorry."

Rhythmic movements halting, Andreas's gaze turned searching. "Pardon?"

"I'm sorry. Especially if I pushed you into something you weren't ready for because I . . . wanted you."

He frowned, looking extremely perplexed, like he didn't understand my words or why I'd said them. It was an expression so entirely foreign on his features, I wondered if he'd ever made it before.

I went on. "Yes, I was already starting to have feelings for you before Thanksgiving. As the person with more sexual experience, I should have been more careful and forthright before pushing you for a physical relationship. I shouldn't have told you it was no strings, no feelings. I can see that I took advantage because I was too much of a chicken to ask for what I really wanted, and I'm so sorry. I'm willing to take responsibility for my recklessness and cowardice."

Andreas's confusion warred with his typical mask of calculation, his brain obviously more alert than mine and likely running through moves and countermoves, strategy I had no energy for.

That's when I felt my lips curve into a small, bitter smile.

Perhaps he did love me, in his own way. I wasn't quite certain when, over the last few days, I'd accepted Andreas loved me, but I now believed him. He did. It wouldn't be enough, however. His kind of love was devoid of trust and faith, and so I guess I had my answer to the earlier question.

Would it matter if Andreas was truly, sincerely in love with me? No. It wouldn't matter.

Looking at him now, I suspected it would never occur to him to apologize like I had just done. To apologize was to take the exposed position, one of vulnerability. He would never, could never, do that.

Joey babbled, breaking through the silence, and we both looked at the baby. The pacifier was long gone, likely somewhere on the floor. He was biting on his fingers, his features pulled in a grimace.

Andreas kept his eyes on Joey, but I got the sense his focus had turned inward because he frowned, his eyebrows pulling together and his gaze slowly dropping without purpose.

Joey made another noise, this time one of frustration and impatience, and Andreas seemed to shake himself, blinking rapidly several times, as though surprised to find the baby in his arms.

"Do you want me to take him?" I asked softly.

Andreas's stare swung to me, his mouth slightly open as though he would speak. He said nothing. His apparent confusion persisted, giving me the sense that my apology had truly thrown him a curveball he hadn't anticipated.

The room filled with the soft sounds of Joey's babbling. I waited, hoping so damn hard that he would take this opportunity to finally apologize, to meet me halfway.

Andreas simply stood there, looking increasingly perplexed—perhaps even angry—with each passing second. His eyes searched mine, but whatever he looked for, he didn't seem to find it, and this only served to aggravate him more.

I wanted to tell him to stop trying to turn everything between us into a game, to stop looking for weaknesses or an area to exploit for leverage. I wanted to tell him that, if he genuinely wanted us to have a chance, all he had to do was simply tell me the truth, apologize for hurting me and those around me, and accept the consequences of his actions. Honesty and contrition without pretext or strategy was the only way we both could win.

He was so damn smart. But faith and trust were clearly concepts he'd never been taught or learned, and definitely never valued.

The door to the suite opened suddenly, shattering the moment. In walked Martin, followed by Kaitlyn's parents. They were deep in conversation, but Martin stopped mid-sentence when he saw Andreas and me standing on opposite ends of the room staring at each other.

"Is everything okay?" Martin split his attention between us.

Andreas walked over to Martin and handed Joey to him. "Samantha just changed him."

Kaitlyn's mom intercepted the baby, snatching him right out of Martin's hands. "I'll take him."

Andreas nodded, then turned to Martin. "I have to . . . I have to go."

With that, he brushed past them and left the room, the door closing softly. I stood motionless, feeling a mix of frustration and sadness. But mostly sadness.

I'd opened myself up. I'd hoped for something more, something real from him. A move with no strategy behind it except honesty. But all I got was silence and a quick exit.

* * *

KAITLYN'S TRANSFER from the ICU to the VIP suite occurred an hour or so after Andreas's departure. The anxiety crushing my chest for the last three days finally lightened enough for me to take a real, unforced breath. I watched two nurses roll Kaitlyn down the hall, her body cocooned in blankets and her hair in a ratty topknot, and marveled at how, even after all her health troubles, she managed to look like a tired, pale woodland sprite.

Martin trailed behind and I could see he was trying his best not to fuss. His gait, which for three days had been something like a caged-animal shuffle, seemed looser now.

I managed to steal a few minutes with her once she'd settled. Kaitlyn was groggy and not entirely herself, but she was lucid enough to recognize me, grip my hand, and say, "Sam? You look like shit."

This made me both laugh and cry.

That was when I knew for certain she'd be okay. Seeing her color come back, even in small increments, did something good to my brain. It allowed me to finally entertain the thought of leaving the hospital and returning to the world.

The plan was for me to go home and sleep in my own bed for the first time in days. Kaitlyn's parents would take Joey home to Kaitlyn and Martin's apartment for the evening. Martin would sleep on the pullout in the VIP suite. Since Martin and Kaitlyn had each other, and Joey had his grandparents, I had no excuse to keep haunting the hospital.

I hadn't heard from Andreas since our argument earlier, which was probably for the best. It seemed to me that we'd reached the end of our game and it had resulted in a stalemate. The only move available to him was one he wasn't willing or didn't know how to make.

So be it.

Packing my tote bag, I made a last round of the suite to say goodbye. Kaitlyn was asleep, her face slack and peaceful, so I just squeezed her arm and whispered, "See you tomorrow."

I gave Joey one last kiss and hug, accepted quick embraces from Kaitlyn's parents, and then met Martin at the door.

He surprised me by pulling me into a full, back-breaking hug. "Thank you so much. I don't know what I would've done without you." The words came out strangled, which also surprised me.

My first instinct was to deflect with a joke. Martin and I had never truly clicked. I didn't like how he'd treated Kaitlyn at the beginning of their relationship, and I also didn't like how quickly she'd forgiven his bad behavior when they did get back together.

But after watching him suffer for the last several days, after leaning on him and encouraging him to lean on me, I knew it was time for me to get over the past. Which, given my track record with grudges and reactionary feelings, felt like a huge leap forward in personal growth.

"Thank you, too," I finally said, pulling back and giving him a commiserating smile. "Don't hesitate to let me know if I can do anything. I'll see you both tomorrow."

With one last nod, I left, closing the door on Kaitlyn and her family. It was time to reenter my own life. Or at least figure out where to start.

Tara waited just outside the door, flanked by the other two guards. They fell into step behind me as I navigated the long hallway out of the VIP area, making me feel, if not important, then at least difficult to assassinate.

As we turned the corner toward the bank of elevators, I caught sight of a figure in the small VIP lounge. Andreas, alone, slouched on a leather chair, staring down at his phone. He looked so different and out of place, I had to check twice to make sure it was really him.

His hair was damp, like he'd just come from the gym or a quick, punishing run. He wore—of all things—sweatpants. Gray ones. He also wore a navy blue hoodie and sneakers, more evidence that he'd come here after a run. The attire made him look much younger, and that's when my brain reminded me that Andreas Kristiansen was only twenty-six.

For once, he actually looked his age.

I slowed my pace, debating my options. I could walk by and pretend I didn't see him. Or, I could walk over and thank him for all his help, and then say goodbye. Other than Genetix meetings, we wouldn't have any reason to see each other moving forward. But as the first and second largest shareholders in Genetix, I reasoned it would do us no good to be enemies. We could be passing acquaintances. It would be rude to ignore an acquaintance. *And he did help these last few days. Quite a lot . . .*

Decided, I turned to Tara. "Can you give us a minute?"

She nodded. "Of course." Without hesitation, she gestured for the other two guards to follow her down the corridor, past the lounge, and to the bank of elevators where she'd be able to see us but not hear us.

Unless, of course, we ended up shouting at each other. But I didn't think that would happen. Not this time.

[12]

MULTICELLULARITY AND DEVELOPMENT

Samantha

I squared my shoulders and crossed the distance to the waiting area and planned what to say. As I approached, I noticed that Andreas was watching a video on his phone. For a second I thought it was of puppies. But as I drew closer I realized the video was of baby wolf pups.

He didn't see or notice me at first, which was more indicative of how absorbed he was in the video than the stealth of my approach. Thus, I cleared my throat, and he jerked his head up, blinking and meeting my gaze. There was mild but genuine surprise in his eyes, which was quickly masked by his usual cool, aloof expression.

"Hey." I meant to tell him thank you for everything and then walk away, but instead my mouth blurted, "What are you watching?"

He pocketed the phone, a trace of something passing behind his expression. "Nothing important."

I felt a flicker of disappointment. Nakita told me a few weeks ago about Andreas's work with an exotic animal shelter. I assumed the video was related to this work. I also assumed he still saw no reason to share this information with me, even when I asked. His current lack of sharing shouldn't have bothered me. But it did. It stung.

I would get over it.

Standing up straighter, I hardened my voice and attempted to mimic an approximation of his stoicism. "Fine. Thank you for your help over the last few days. It was appreciated."

"You are welcome. Before I forget again, and since you have not asked, I want to ensure you are aware: Dr. Hauser was approved as the proxy for your shares on Friday. She is, and you are, all set."

"Oh. I see." I felt suddenly winded at the realization I'd completely forgotten about Dr. Hauser and the shareholder meeting.

When I'd emailed her yesterday that I might not be back to work this week, she'd responded with a simple, "Okay. Keep me in the loop."

It hadn't occurred to me to ask her about the shareholder meeting. Interesting how a life-or-death situation involving my best friend completely wiped my brain of all other priorities.

However, Kaitlyn was on the mend. And now it was time to get back to the real world.

Thus, I continued with the second half of my planned statement. "Uh, thank you for that as well. But, as I said early Saturday morning, I do not feel indebted to you. And you don't need to come back to the hospital. In fact, please don't. Have a nice night."

I turned to go, but before I could take a step, he reached out and caught my hand. He pulled me down onto his lap and enclosed me in his arms.

Then he lifted the phone, set his chin on my shoulder, and unpaused the video. The screen filled with tiny, mewling wolf pups rolling around a patch of straw.

"There is an animal sanctuary I, uh, help. Or work with, raise money for, whatever. And their wolves just had babies. They set up a livestream, so people can see them."

"I see . . ." I managed, still more than a little startled by the abrupt lap sitting.

We watched the pups in silence while my brain struggled to comprehend what had just happened. If there was a way to measure the complexity of a moment—to gauge the number of unresolved needs and unspoken regrets swirling in a single human body—then I was, at that instant, setting some kind of record.

My first impulse was, oddly, to settle in and watch, to let myself be held. The wolf pups were objectively adorable. Tiny, squirming, impossibly soft looking. Their mother, a gray-and-white blur, kept nuzzling them, pushing them into a pile, then circling the perimeter, ostensibly to search for threats. The camera shook a little as it zoomed in, and someone off-screen laughed—a thin, tinny sound that made the whole thing feel more real, less like a nature documentary and more like true surveillance footage.

Andreas kept his arms loosely wrapped around me, his chin balanced on my shoulder, his breath shallow. Maybe on purpose? So as not to disturb my viewing of the wolves.

If I'd wanted to, I could have said something cutting and ended the moment immediately. Instead, I stayed. Maybe it was curiosity, or maybe it was simply weakness. A desire to let the pretense hold for another minute, to accept this thin slice of affection even though I knew it wouldn't last.

Yeah. It's probably weakness.

I tried to ignore the way his body felt under mine. The hospital waiting area, with its bolted-down chairs and infinite echoes, faded into the background. There was just the video, and the warmth of him all around me, and the absurdity of the entire situation.

So we sat like that, the two of us, pretending we didn't notice the way our bodies had mapped themselves onto each other's, and I found myself wondering why neither of us could figure out how to be brave at the same time.

That was when I remembered who I was, and who he was, and who we had failed to be together. My body suddenly and reflexively recoiled, reminding me that, no, we were not in that place anymore, that his right to pull me onto his lap had expired months ago. No strings, no feelings weren't going to cut it. It didn't matter if he loved me or if I still loved him. I needed more than a small slice of Andreas, more than the bare fractions of himself he was willing to share.

I pushed him away and moved to stand.

He released me immediately, his arms falling away from my sides as if they'd never meant to hold me there in the first place. I stood quickly, maybe too quickly, brushing imaginary dust off my jeans and straightening my shirt with mechanical focus. He rose as well, but more slowly, as if his body couldn't quite keep up with the recalibration of the moment.

We ended up facing one another, the only people in a radius of at least ten yards, silence made impossible by the distant burble of an intercom and the occasional squeak of rubber soles on linoleum.

I couldn't make myself look away, and he seemed equally rooted, his green eyes flicking across my face in rapid, uncertain micromovements. My heart beat so loudly I was sure he could hear it. Every detail of the last seventy-two hours—every word, every mistake, every sideways glance—hung between us like holiday ornaments on a dead, undecorated tree.

He shifted his weight from one foot to the other. I realized my own hands were trembling, so I jammed them into my pockets. I wanted to say something—anything—but the words got stuck somewhere between my chest and my tongue. I could tell he was waiting for me to go first, as though he'd decided that after sharing a sliver of his interests with me, it was now my move.

If we'd been in a movie, this would be the scene where the characters kissed and all the tension evaporated, replaced by swelling music and a fade-out. But we weren't in a movie; we were in a hospital, and I was exhausted, and the only thing swelling was the sense of loss expanding in my chest cavity.

He looked down at his sneakers, then back up to me. His features had rearranged themselves into something softer, something that made my insides warm and an alarm bell sound between my ears.

Stop being weak!

In a desperate attempt at strength, I blurted, "Well, goodbye," and moved to leave.

I didn't manage a step before he caught my wrist again, asking, "Have you really never looked me up online?"

I paused, turned back. Seeing no reason to keep the information from him, I said, "I looked you up once, when I was sixteen or so."

"Truly?" He seemed genuinely surprised.

I nodded.

He slipped the phone into his pocket and let go of my wrist. "I have never been to university, never applied for one."

I waited, not sure if this was meant as a confession? A humblebrag? Or . . . what was this?

Andreas shoved his hands into his hoodie's pockets. "All I know how to do, all I was brought up to do, is play chess. Since we last saw each other when I was eleven, all I live and breathe is chess. It is the only thing at which I excel. I am incredibly boring."

"You can cook, though," I said, uncertain why I felt the impulse to defend Andreas to himself.

One side of his mouth lifted. "I like to cook. Otherwise, I would not know how."

I arched an eyebrow. "Are you saying you only do things you like to do?"

He shrugged. "I call it avoidance of time-wasting activities, but laziness is a better word for it. I do not engage in activities I consider a waste of my time, or tasks I do not wish to do. This also means I do not save as much money as I should since I outsource any task I dislike. Cleaning, as an example."

A laugh snuck out of me. "Is that why you pitched such a surly hissy fit when I insisted we carry the Christmas tree and set it up ourselves?"

He was silent for a beat, blinking once, the curve of his mouth looking suddenly wry. "I did not throw a 'hissy fit.' But I concede to being surly, as you say."

"As long as you admit that you were surly," I said under my breath, smirking to myself.

His eyes narrowed. "I hate being laughed at and have difficulty being the butt of a joke. My mind immediately goes to revenge. I am also a sore loser and am bad at losing. Anything. But especially games."

"You mean . . . board games?"

"And card games. Any games. I take them too seriously, and literally. I am a terrible joke teller, I think because I am too serious. My timing is always off and my delivery is terrible."

That pulled a genuine smile from me.

"You are great at telling jokes," he said like he meant the words, but it also sounded like an accusation.

Regardless, I tipped my head in acknowledgement of the compliment. "Thank you."

He inhaled deeply, his gaze moving to some spot over my shoulder. "Let's see, what else? Uh, like you, I prefer old movies. But I do not enjoy any modern TV shows or films. For me, they seem to lack a compelling story, always impatient, going too fast, never deep enough. Never taking the time to make characters real people with real problems. In general, I prefer books. Also, I do not know anything about cars—how to fix them, not even how to change a tire—and I cannot fix anything mechanical. Not a faucet, nothing electrical. I am useless, in this way. In an apocalypse, I would be one of the first to die, whereas I think you are the opposite. I have no life skills, but I do have an intense survival instinct, which gets in my way just as often as it serves me well."

As I listened, it dawned on me that he was doing what I'd done when we first lived together. Andreas was listing his most unattractive traits, offering up his worst qualities for my inspection.

"I have never gone on a hike or gone camping and do not wish to do so. I do not like the outdoors or 'nature.'"

"That's interesting, because you seem to like animals so much."

He shrugged. "In this way, I do not make sense. I love animals. I do not enjoy their natural habitat, though I do believe it should be protected. And Central Park is fine for walks, but I have never exercised for the sake of a workout outside of a gym. I am particular about what I wear, what material touches my skin, what products I use. I am . . . fussy about my appearance."

I stroked my chin. "I have suspected for a while that you are a metrosexual."

He frowned. "What does that word mean? I have never heard that word."

"It's a type of human taxonomy," I deflected, anxious for him to continue. "So, what else?"

His gaze moved over my shoulder again as he continued his recitation of faults. "I know I can be impatient, dismissive, and lack compassion for people who do not catch on to complex ideas and issues quickly. I am too intellectual, too much in my head, and do not enjoy the messy complications of the world. I have always viewed them as burdensome. They make me weary."

"Does anyone enjoy the messy complications of the world?" I asked, trying to keep things light.

He seemed to give the question real thought before responding earnestly, "I think some people do, who thrive on instigating drama and chaos. Take my brother Henrik, for example. I believe he enjoys the messiness of life, but does not enjoy the intellectualism of philosophy, self-reflection, or self-improvement."

I tried not to smile. "My question was rhetorical."

"Ah. See? I took it literally." Andreas's tightlipped smile struck me as self-deprecating, and he glanced down at his shoes. "Related, I know I can be cold and unfeeling toward people who wish to take up my time, which is why—I believe—all my previous attempts at a romantic relationship have failed before they even started. I never engaged in one-night stands or friends with benefits or hookups because I do not trust people. I have been some level of famous since before I was of age. Being careful seemed more important than my physical . . . desires."

I nodded, absorbing this, a puzzle piece clicking into place that I hadn't realized I was looking for. I hadn't questioned Andreas's lack of experience, but I think part of me always found it unbelievable. He was an incredibly attractive guy who could cook. Not to mention, Andreas possessed impeccable manners, was obviously intelligent, wealthy, and famous-ish. He would have no problem finding a quality hook-up, if he so chose.

But as he'd said, the messiness of real life made him weary.

"Related, I prefer the company of animals to people. Generally, again, I do not know how to trust people, not really, and my instinct is always to keep my thoughts to myself rather than share them."

This last confession hooked me so deeply, I took a step closer to him and lowered my voice. "Why? Why is that your instinct, do you think?"

His gaze lifted to mine again, held. "Because I am boring. And I do not wish to bore people."

"I do not find you boring." I didn't think about the words before saying them. They were simply the truth.

He smiled at me. "And I do not find you abrupt or judgy."

I couldn't help my answering grin. He'd remembered my self-proclaimed list of unattractive qualities. Of course he did.

Andreas shook his head. "I am uncertain how to have a relationship with someone that is not transactional, and that includes colleagues and friends. I do not feel comfortable with a person, even as a friend, if I do not feel certain that I am in the stronger position, the more generous one in the relationship. I do not want to be in someone's debt. And I realize this is a wall I put between myself and others. I am uncertain how to . . . change this about myself."

Andreas twisted his lips to the side, a rueful expression, one of resignation and perhaps a little melancholy.

It was, honestly, sexy as hell. The twist of his generous lips made me want to bite them. But I couldn't do that.

Clearing my throat, I gathered a deep breath to unclutter my thoughts. "Okay. Anything else?"

I tore my gaze from his handsome face. But then—unable to help myself—my eyes sought him out again immediately.

Andreas seemed to consider the matter for a beat, then said, "That is all. For now. But if I think of other points, may I text them to you?"

I couldn't not smile at that. "Yes."

His mouth twitched, the tiniest possible curve, and his eyes seemed to twinkle mischievously. "So, that means you can receive my text messages? Am I unblocked?"

I tongued my back molar, fighting a new grin. He was sneaky, I'd give him that. Offering to text me more of his flaws was the perfect way to guarantee I wouldn't block his number again.

"I just thought of another one," I said.

"What is it?"

"You're sneaky. And calculating."

He pondered this, then asked, "Is that unattractive, though?"

I laughed, and it felt unburdened. "Look at you, telling jokes."

He laughed, too, and the sound was so much softer and lighter than my heart had been prepared for. For a moment, we simply stood together, looking at each other, our surroundings becoming a shapeless backdrop. I wanted to say so many things I knew I shouldn't. He'd handed over more parts of himself. Bigger pieces. But what happened next between us, I couldn't guess.

Andreas's eyebrows pulled together and he broke the silence abruptly. "I miss you."

The words hit me with a force that was almost physical, which is probably why I said, "I miss you, too," before I could stop the impulse.

He moved closer, as if he couldn't help it, as though we were magnetized, and his gaze dropped to my mouth. His hands came out of his pockets, lifted slowly. My chest tightened.

"Samantha—"

"I have to go." I gained a step back, not yet ready for this—whatever it was—and so I held up my hands to stop his advance.

He nodded, swallowing thickly and also stepping back, accepting the boundary. "Okay. I understand. Have a nice evening, Samantha."

"You too, Andreas."

Slowly, I turned and walked away, away from the VIP waiting area and to the elevator bank. Tara pressed the call button and I listened as my security detail fell in step with me as we boarded the lift.

As soon as the doors closed, I pulled out my phone, scrolled to my blocked numbers list, and unblocked Andreas's number. Then, on impulse, I added him as a contact.

[13]

DIVERSIFICATION OF PLANTS AND ANIMALS

Samantha

If you had told me last year that come next March I would be driven everywhere in a black luxury car by an entourage of personal bodyguards while getting remarkably close to finishing my PhD while also juggling meetings with my team of lawyers and having weekly bonding calls with my maternal grandfather, then I would've been impressed with the wildness of your imagination.

But there I was, sitting in the back seat of the Mercedes, two guards up front, one in the back with me, phone pressed between shoulder and cheek, having just left work early after making significant progress in the lab today, talking to my grandpa about my father's decision to declare bankruptcy over fifteen years ago, and debating whether to take notes so I could share them with my legal team later.

Tara parked as I searched for a pen and piece of paper, finding neither in the spotless back seat.

"Oskar Kristiansen was the one who convinced him to file for bankruptcy? Are you sure?" I asked, not bothering to hide my skepticism.

He exhaled, and I imagined him rubbing the bridge of his nose. "Yes, I remember this very clearly. Your mother called and told me that Lawrence was going to file for bankruptcy to avoid lawsuits. Genetix customers were suing your parents personally for the data release, for the—the—it was the customers whose information was sold by Genetix. Your father obviously had nothing to do with the data being sold, but since his signature was on the purchase agreement, he was being targeted with the individual civil lawsuits. That's why he filed for bankruptcy. That Kristiansen guy convinced him to do it as a preemptive measure to protect you and your mother from all the scrutiny."

"I had no idea." I kept my voice low as I exited on the same side as my guard.

Briefly, I wondered if Andreas knew this. We hadn't actually spoken since Monday, but he'd added to his list of personal faults via text message. He'd pointed out that he was a picky eater and that he was hard to buy gifts for. This last bit made me remember the stack of signed Bobby Fischer books sitting in the bedroom closet of my new apartment. The ones I hadn't given him, but couldn't bring myself to sell or donate.

For the record, I hadn't texted him back. I'd left him on *read*.

Pretty queen being petty. Admittedly, a big part of me was sore that he STILL hadn't apologized.

Stepping out, Tara and the other guards fell in around me, forming a four-person wedge as we crossed to the elevators.

Grandpa's tone grew more gentle. "Your mother was really upset about it and I think that's about when she began to suspect that man wasn't on their side." His use of "that man" arrived with an undercurrent of loathing.

We waited for the elevator, and I could feel Tara's sidelong glance.

What my grandfather might not have known was that the actual fraud charge against my father had almost nothing to do with the sale of the datasets. Yes, the datasets being sold did cause an avalanche of civil lawsuits against my father. But what got him indicted was the "misrepresentation of value" in documents sent to the SEC and the IRS as part of the Genetix IPO filing. Essentially, *someone* (*cough* Oskar Kristiansen *cough*) had built a paper trail leading to my dad as the scapegoat for inflating the data's worth after it had already been sold, knowing this would trigger an investigation. Overestimating, i.e., misrepresenting, the value of a company's assets is part of what brought down Enron.

Elevator doors dinged. Tara's finger hovered a millimeter from the button that would take us to Kaitlyn's floor until we all piled in.

"We're getting on the elevator, if I lose you that's why." I leaned against the stainless steel wall. "Thank you so much for this information. This is really helpful."

"Anytime. Let me know if you have more questions."

"I will. And, just to let you know, this last week, I spent three days at Genetix, getting copies of emails and internal messages between Henrik, Tobias, and their father." Since the shareholder meeting, I'd been given carte blanche access to the internal Genetix files. I hadn't known Henrik was an intern under my father's department—for a period of six months before my father was accused of fraud—until three days ago. "I've sent everything to my legal team. They're going to scour it for leads."

"Good. That's good." I could hear the smile in my grandpa's voice. "You know both your parents were against the IPO filing, right? Your father wanted to keep the company private. So, why would your father inflate numbers for the SEC in the initial paperwork? That's madness."

"Right. Good point." And I knew for a fact my dad would never sell customer data. That also made no sense.

My grandfather was not finished. "Have you found any information about that doctor fella who claims your father died of a heart attack?"

I closed my eyes for a second. I'd let slip last week that Diya had helped me pinpoint issues with my father's death certificate. "You mean the medical examiner who lost his license? We've been looking for him, but I think I have to hire a PI firm. I can't find him through any of the simple online searches and I haven't brought it up to my legal team. I want them focused on the fraud charges."

Tara's eyes met mine in the reflection of the elevator doors. She didn't say anything, but her eyebrows lifted.

Grandfather gave a tired-sounding sigh. "Keep me updated. I'm . . . interested."

I smiled into the phone. "Honestly, it's like the more I find out, the less sense it all makes."

"When 'the facts' don't make any sense, it means they're not the truth." I could tell he was proud of me for chasing the answers.

Lifting my eyes to the floor readout, I knew my time was up. "I have to go. Thank you for the information. We'll talk next week?"

"Don't be a stranger, Sammy. You know I love you."

"Love you too, Grandpa. I'll keep you in the loop."

Tara let the rest of the elevator ride play out in silence, but as soon as the doors slid open and we exited the elevator, she leaned in close and murmured, "Do you need help finding someone?"

I stopped mid-step, thrown. "Yes. Why? Is this something you can help me with?"

"Not me personally," Tara said, glancing down the length of the hall as we resumed walking. "But I have a friend who can help. If you text me the information, I'll put them on it."

"Thank you so much. That would be great." What a relief.

Tara touched my arm as though to slow me down and leaned closer. "Just a reminder, the temporary night-shift arrangements I made for you ended yesterday. I know you didn't use the guys past Sunday night, but I don't have the option of calling them back in. Just wanted to make sure you were aware. So, if you spend the night here tonight, I don't have anyone scheduled to stay past nine."

"Yes. Absolutely. Totally fine. I have no plans to spend the night here. Thank you for keeping me safe last weekend when I was here twenty-four hours a day. It really helped ease my mind."

Tara released my arm and gave me a short nod of acknowledgement. Our four-person wedge advanced down the pristine, windowless hallway toward the VIP wing. I let myself drift a step behind, texting Diya for the full name and last-known address of the rogue medical examiner. I had the information on my laptop, but figured the sooner I sent it to Tara, the better. Diya responded in under ten seconds, as if she'd been waiting for me to ask this very question. Then she sent a second message.

Diya: I can't come over tonight. Unexpected family in town. Will you be okay? Nakita can come in my place.

My steps faltered for a millisecond as I fought a flicker of worry. I'd sleepwalked twice this last week, but Diya had been spending every night with me. She'd ensured I didn't do anything dangerous, like leave the apartment, which unconscious me tried to do during the second incident.

But what could I say? *No. I won't be okay. Please ditch your family and babysit me while I sleep.*

I typed out a quick response.

Sam: I will be fine! I bought handcuffs (kidding). Have fun with your family!

Almost at once, she responded.

Diya: No. You need someone to stay with you. Accept Nakita's help! Just tell her the cone of secrecy applies.

I knew Diya was correct. Resigned, I texted Diya and let her know I would ask Nakita, then I messaged Nakita, asked her to observe the cone of secrecy, and asked her if she could come over and spend the night just in case I tried to sleepwalk. She didn't respond right away, so I tucked my phone in my bag.

Kaitlyn and Martin were still at the hospital full-time. Kaitlyn's parents were in their apartment with Joey and I didn't feel comfortable asking if I could sleep on the couch as a deterrent for my unconscious brain's mischievousness.

I'll . . . figure something out. I missed December, back when I'd stopped sleepwalking, was getting eight plus hours of sleep, and receiving orgasms every night and morning. Good times.

Rounding the last corner leading to Kaitlyn's suite, I nearly smacked into the unexpected wall of dark-suited bodyguards posted outside her door. Backing up a step, I counted at least four—three men with the builds of disgruntled linebackers, and a woman who looked unassuming yet incredibly intimidating at the same time. They stood ostentatiously at parade rest, not even pretending to blend in.

One of them—bald, but not in a way that suggested hair loss so much as preemptive scalping—held up a hand. "Can't go in, sorry."

Tara went still, her entire body going tight. Saying nothing, my guards stepped forward and went into "us vs. them" formation, shoulders squaring, arms tensing at their sides.

The intimidating woman said, "No one in unless you're on the list."

Tara shot back, "She is the list," jerking a thumb at me.

Bald guy gave me a once-over, his eyes skating over my face, then the hospital badge I'd clipped on in the car, then my shoes. I braced for a second round of denials, but he blinked, recalibrated, and said, "You're Jarlston?"

"That's me," I said, raising my hand like a twelve-year-old at roll call.

"Go ahead," the woman said. "Solo only."

I sensed my guards bristle, but only Tara objected out loud. "Absolutely not. She doesn't go anywhere alone."

"It's fine." I held up a hand. "Really."

Tara gave me a look. She didn't like me leaving her sight when I wasn't at work or at home, but she also didn't like arguing in public. Ultimately, she nodded and fell back.

Stepping past the sentinels—the woman holding the door for me—the noise hit me before I'd even entered. Joey was upset about something and I detected two distinct adult voices. Also, the unmistakable thrum of an acoustic guitar, mid-song.

I walked all the way in and found Kaitlyn perched on the hospital bed, hair in a messy side braid, bouncing Joey on her knee. Her face was still thin, but her eyes were bright and her color was better than it had been all week. She was being serenaded by a guy sitting in a nearby chair, a battered acoustic guitar on his lap, one leg crossed at the ankle, looking for all the world like he lived there.

I felt a little jolt of awareness shoot down my spine because the guy was Abram Fletcher. You know, the Grammy-winning rock and roll lead singer and likely future *People*'s Sexiest Man Alive (after he turned forty-five, it was just a matter of time; but he was nowhere near forty-five yet). Kaitlyn and Abram had met in a for-hire cover band years ago and he'd tried to date her. Unfortunately for him, Martin had been in the process of wooing Kaitlyn back at the time.

However, fortunately for Abram, he began dating his future wife a few years later. By all reports, they seemed epically happy, though I'd always thought they were a bit mismatched. As mentioned, Abram was a rock star. Whereas his wife, Dr. Davinci, was a genius astrophysicist, this generation's Isaac Newton, who would over the course of her lifetime likely develop time-travel technology or figure out how to fuel the power grid with energy from black holes.

But what did I know? I'd only met her once, because she was—arguably—even more famous and busy than Abram. And she'd seemed lovely. Weird. Awkward. But absolutely delightful.

Abram looked up as I entered and offered a lopsided grin. "Hey. Hi. Come to join the party?"

Setting my bag by the couch, I gave Kaitlyn a look, eyebrows up because Joey's complaining increased suddenly in noise level and severity.

She shrugged. "It's been a day. He thought maybe music would help."

Walking forward, I scooped up Joey, who immediately stopped crying and started gumming my index finger before I could object that my hands weren't clean.

"Maybe he's hungry?" I suggested, even though I had no evidence for this. "Or tired. Or angry about the state of the world."

"You and me both, Joey," said Kaitlyn, rolling her eyes at the ceiling. "I literally just fed him. He had two jars—peas and carrots—and a half bottle. I thought he was about to go to sleep, then suddenly he started fussing."

Abram stood and stretched, and I got my first good look at him since the last time our paths had crossed months ago. He was still tall and muscly, with the kind of effortless swagger that made sense for a rock star. Black jeans, black boots, and an ancient Led Zeppelin T-shirt that hitched up as he lifted his arms over his head. I averted my eyes before they could ogle the sliver of six-pack revealed by the action.

Thou shalt not covet the genius astrophysicist's husband, or her cow.

I decided to reintroduce myself with a little wave, just to be polite. "Hi, I'm Sam. Longtime friend of Kaitlyn's."

"I remember you, Sam." He grinned, and I felt a tiny flicker of understanding for why millions of people screamed at his concerts.

Readjusting Joey, I held the baby slightly away so I could turn him to face the room. But then, before I could, Joey, perhaps sensing a lull in attention, hiccupped, which was then immediately followed by a stream of baby vomit that felt akin to being sprayed with a garden hose.

It splattered everywhere. In my hair. My face. Down the front of my shirt. Onto my pants. And when it was over, my first thought was, *There is NO WAY that was just two jars of baby food and a half bottle.*

"Oh my God, are you okay?" Abram ran forward and grabbed Joey, holding the baby away for a moment before remarking, "Huh. He didn't get anything on himself."

Kaitlyn, however, was laughing. Hysterically. The sharp, clear sound echoing off the high ceiling. I was so shocked I just stood there, hands out, dripping, feeling the warmth and stickiness of half-digested pea and carrot puree seeping into the fabric of my clothes.

"Oh, Sam. I'm so sorry. Sorry I'm laughing. But I—couldn't help it. Sorry. I'll stop laughing. But it feels so good to laugh." Kaitlyn wiped tears from her eyes, then reached for a package of wipes from the nightstand. She looked at them, shook her head, then set them back down again. "I was going to offer you some wipes, but you need a shower. I have three changes of clothes in the bathroom closet. Please. Go shower."

Joey, now calm and practically beaming, gave me a gummy smile that suggested he also thought my impression of a swamp monster was hilarious.

I gave in, peeling myself from the floor and heading for the en suite, where I found not only Kaitlyn's clothes, but also a brand-new toothbrush, a razor, and some fancy mini bottles of shampoo and conditioner.

I stripped off the ruined shirt and caught my reflection in the mirror. Kaitlyn had been right to laugh. I looked both gross and utterly ridiculous. Plus, as I turned on the water and stepped in, letting the heat and white noise wash away the residue, I realized that was the first time I'd heard her laugh like that in ages.

* * *

ALMOST THE VERY moment after I turned off the shower, I shivered. Not just because the air in Kaitlyn's hospital suite was frigid enough to hang beef, but because I had exactly three seconds of blissful, steamed-up privacy before the atmosphere was punctured by a knock.

At first, I thought it was a hallucination, auditory pareidolia. But then it happened again, three sharp raps echoing through the tile and out into the main living area of the suite.

I froze, clutching the towel around my chest like I hoped it would morph into an invisibility cloak. But then my brain figured out that the knock did not originate on the bathroom door. It had come from front door to the suite, the sound filtered and dull.

A moment later, I recognized Andreas's voice say, "Hi. Sorry to disturb you. I am looking for Samantha." The low volume and garbled quality meant that he hadn't opened the suite door and had spoken these words from the hall.

I dropped my forehead to the tile wall, internally groaning.

Kaitlyn's response sounded clear, bright, and unfazed. "Come on in."

There was the click of the suite door opening, a quick exchange of pleasantries I missed, then Andreas again: "Is Sam here?"

Kaitlyn, voice flat: "Do you see her?"

There was a pause, as if Andreas might be sweeping the suite for signs of life. I pressed my eye to the tiny gap in the door, but I couldn't see either of them; the angle only gave me a generous view of hospital-grade carpet beyond the bathroom threshold.

Kaitlyn: "Sit down, please. I want to interrogate you."

A rush of self-consciousness skittered up my spine. Why would he come to the hospital to look for me? My phone was out in the main suite area so I had no idea if he'd messaged. I hadn't spotted a message earlier . . .

There was the low groan of a chair being shifted which was interrupted by Kaitlyn: "Are you in love with Sam?"

My hand shot up to cover my mouth.

A long pause. I imagined Andreas blinking at her, maybe weighing the pros and cons of honesty versus deflection.

Then, "Yes."

His answer didn't surprise me nearly as much as the suddenness and directness of her question. Hadn't Andreas already told me? Hadn't he already told Dmitry? Why would he lie to Kaitlyn, my closest friend? He wouldn't.

Kaitlyn, wasting no time: "Then why haven't you apologized for being a lying liar who lies?"

I stifled a laugh-snort, turning and pressing my back against the cool tile. The phrasing was pure Kaitlyn.

Andreas: "First, may I borrow your pen and paper? Just there on the nightstand."

A shuffling, a click of something.

Kaitlyn: "Uh, sure. Here."

There was silence for a stretch.

Then Kaitlyn, sounding curious, said, "What are you writing?"

Andreas: "A note for Sam. Please give it to her when you see her."

Kaitlyn: "Sure thing."

Andreas, his tone going soft: "To your question, why do I not ask for forgiveness? It does not seem fair to ask for something I do not deserve."

Kaitlyn: "What are you talking about? What are you saying you don't deserve?"

Andreas: "I do not deserve her forgiveness."

There was a loud, beleaguered-sounding exhale from Kaitlyn, the prelude to an epic eye roll if I knew her at all.

"Come on. I know you're so much smarter than this. How is you never apologizing fair to Sam?"

Another silence.

Kaitlyn again: "I have two thoughts about this I'm going to share with you. First, maybe you don't deserve forgiveness. But that doesn't mean you can't become deserving of forgiveness. Work for it. Earn it. And second, the apology isn't about you and what you do or don't deserve. It's about what Sam deserves, right? Don't you think Sam deserves an apology? Have you considered the fact that *she* might need to hear it?"

I felt a strange, electric flush in my chest. It was not an unfamiliar sensation, being scrutinized from afar, a fly on the wall of my own life.

Andreas: "You are saying I should apologize—because she deserves my contrition, and to know that I am sorry for hurting her—even though I know it is unforgivable."

My lip curled into a sneer. This was so like Andreas, to treat an apology as an exercise in logic and game theory.

Never venturing too far from the door—so I wouldn't miss their conversation—I moved quickly and quietly through the post-shower steps: toweling off, and wriggling into Kaitlyn's jeans and T-shirt which were two sizes too big, but I didn't care. I kept my movements as silent as possible, not wanting to disturb the delicate tableau outside.

Kaitlyn, her voice rising: "There you go again. Whether she forgives you or not isn't your decision. It's up to Sam. And by withholding the apology, you are still making decisions for Sam, about Sam, just like you did when you froze her PI's funding. Stop making decisions for her and just do the right thing. Why is it so hard to let Sam decide what she wants?"

Andreas: "Does it not make more sense to earn her forgiveness first, become deserving of it first, before I ask for it?"

A pause, then a snort of laughter from Kaitlyn. "You are ridiculous, Andreas. That's not how loving someone works. She's not a doll you can play with, or—or a chess piece on a board. There's no machinating shrewdly or well enough in order to trap her into forgiving you. Either she does, or she doesn't. But the longer you wait, the more you reinforce her perception that you're a scheming, manipulative a-hole."

A sound from Andreas, something like a huff of surprised-sounding laughter. "Admittedly, 'scheming, manipulative a-hole' is a fair description of me. But I see your point."

Kaitlyn: "Which point? I've made so many."

Another chair movement, like someone stood up or shifted position. Then

Andreas: "Specifically, Sam deserves an apology. It matters not if she forgives me, that is up to her to decide."

Kaitlyn: "And?"

Andreas, with a note of humor: "And I need to stop scheming how to stay in her life and allow her to make the decision . . . ?"

Kaitlyn: "Bingo."

Andreas: "Thank you for your time, and the conversation."

Kaitlyn: "You're welcome."

Andreas: "I am glad you are feeling better. As soon as you see Samantha, please give her this note."

Kaitlyn: "Sure thing."

Footsteps, then the soft hush of the suite door opening and closing. Silence. A moment later, Kaitlyn called, "Come out. He's gone."

I emerged from the bathroom, hair wet, cheeks flushed, and crossed to Kaitlyn's bed.

She was propped up in a nest of pillows, hospital tray table in front of her, a blue plastic cup with a straw and folded piece of paper resting next to it.

Kaitlyn picked up the paper and held it out to me. "The note he wrote when he first walked in. I didn't read it."

"Thanks." I accepted the it. "Where are Abram and Joey?"

"Martin showed up right after you went into the bathroom and took Abram and Joey with him to go grab me something that tastes better than hospital food. Which, according to Martin, is literally anything."

I nodded, then gave her a small, grateful smile. "Thank you for . . . talking to Andreas."

She shrugged, her expression wry. "For what it's worth, Martin was just as dumb when we first got together. And I believe you gave me lots of good advice at the time, if memory serves."

I chuffed out a laugh, then returned my attention to the note.

It was a single sheet of hospital stationery, folded three times and bearing my name in his handwriting—a mixture of precise block letters and elegant script.

I opened it, bracing myself.

Samantha,

I know you're in the room somewhere. Your guards are right outside the door and Tara would not allow you to leave without following. As such, I am assuming you will hear my conversation with Kaitlyn, or at least parts of it depending on where you are hiding. I do not blame you for hiding from me, but I wanted you to know I am aware you are listening. I do not wish to lie to you or keep anything from you. I want us to only be honest with each other.

—A

Huffing in disbelief, I dropped my hand holding the note and glanced at the ceiling. "He's unbelievable." I wasn't embarrassed about my eavesdropping. Or rather, I was going to try really hard not to be embarrassed about it.

"What? What does it say?"

I handed the note over and watched her read it. When she finished, she chuckled. "He's a stinker. And I had no idea he knew. But of course, your guards are just outside the door. I don't know why I didn't realize."

Giving Kaitlyn a smile, I accepted the note back from her. "I believe you've had other things on your mind. And Andreas is, like, an apex predator at concealing his thoughts."

Kaitlyn pushed back her covers and stretched her arms over her head. "What are you going to do about him?"

"I'm not sure." Glancing down at Kaitlyn's clothes and my bare feet, I backed up toward the suite door. "First, though, I'm going to ask Tara if she can send someone to the gift shop to pick me up some different clothes. Be right back."

Turning, I closed the distance to the suite door and reached for the handle, saying as I swung it open, "Hey, Tara. Could one of you—oh!"

Tara hovered next to the door along with my other two guards, as expected.

Whereas, not at all expected, Andreas stood on the opposite wall, facing the door, arms crossed, gaze slightly narrowed, a ghost of a smile curving his lips, obviously lying in wait.

GENERATION OF VARIATION BY MUTATION AND RECOMBINATION

Samantha

Ten minutes later, the world had not ended. I was still alive, if slightly less confident in my own skin than usual.

I sat in a leather club chair in the VIP waiting area, hands folded, eyes focused somewhere on the abstract nothingness of the framed art that decorated the lounge, and tried to take inventory of how many small deaths my ego had just suffered.

The scene from the suite replayed, celluloid crisp, through my mind: me opening the door, expecting to make a quick dash to Tara, and instead finding Andreas stationed in the hall like a stone-faced Roman sentry. Arms folded, cable-knit pullover stretched tight, the kind of sweater only the expensively gloomy could ever pull off. He hadn't said a word at first. Just stared. I, having resolved in advance to project the aura of a woman who absolutely did not give a shit about eavesdropping . . . was startled.

I don't remember what exactly I said (probably something acerbic), but I know I did a double take on the sweater. Mostly because the T-shirt and jeans borrowed from Kaitlyn made me feel like I was twelve and about to attend my first slumber party. The only thing keeping me from freezing was residual post-shower steam and indignation.

Without any ceremony, Andreas unwrapped himself from the pullover, handed it to me, and said, "Wear this. You look"—his gaze dropped to my chest, then back to my eyes—"cold."

I'd gawked at him for a second, another acerbic remark on the tip of my tongue, then caved and put it on. The sweater had been warm from his body and, once I'd pulled it over my head, the collar sagged perfectly around my collarbones in a way that was both flattering and cozy.

After a beat, he'd asked if we could talk. I'd said yes.

Thus, we'd walked to the VIP lounge, him three paces behind me like he didn't want to startle a flighty horse. We didn't talk when we reached the empty cluster of club chairs arranged in a half circle near the window, which was where I sat now, ensconced in his sweater that smelled like him, hands gripping my knees.

Andreas returned from the small kitchenette at the back of the lounge, carrying two mugs. He set one on the side table next to my seat, leaving it there like a peace offering.

He took the club chair opposite mine. He didn't sit back or relax; he perched on the edge, his eyes ensnaring mine.

"Thank you," I said, eyeing the mug.

"It's only tea," he replied.

"Still, thank you."

He nodded and ran a hand through his hair. The movement seemed agitated. Then, before I could say anything else, he fixed his gaze on me and said, "I am so sorry."

The words hit me like a pillow when I'd been expecting a bus.

I'd waited months to hear him say anything close to these words; I'd planned out a dozen ways I would respond; I'd even rehearsed them out loud with Diya and, once, Kaitlyn. But now, here, in this blindingly sterile lounge, I felt utterly underwhelmed.

I took a second, waiting for more emotion from myself. When nothing happened, I asked, "What are you sorry for?"

He inhaled, letting it out slow. "I am so sorry I hurt you, and I lied to you, and I manipulated you and hurt the people you care about."

It was so exactly the apology I'd wanted. He'd nailed every point. His answer was the correct one. And yet . . .

I tore my gaze from his, picked up the tea, and studied the surface of the liquid. "You know, when I imagined this moment, I thought it would feel better. Like, emotionally satisfying? But actually, honestly, I feel nothing except tired." I peeked at him.

He nodded, looking acutely restless, watching me, not speaking. But his eyes were fixed on me with a kind of rawness I'd never seen before.

"You can't just say sorry and expect things to go back to how they . . . were," I finished, my voice thin. "It doesn't work that way. You don't just say 'sorry' and expect me to forget about all of it."

He nodded, his focus flickering from my face to the mug, then back again. "I do not expect you to forget it. I know I can never take back what I did."

I set the tea back down again and crossed my arms over the bulge of cable-knit fabric. The sweater was so soft I could've buried my face in it. "You can't. But you can take responsibility. And accept the consequences."

Andreas inhaled and nodded several times. "I will."

We let that hang. Reaching forward again, I took a careful sip of tea. It tasted faintly of ginger.

I set the mug down once more, using the action to gather my composure. "So. What now? I mean, what do you want from me?"

Andreas seemed to hesitate, as though carefully debating his next words, then asked, "May I know, what are the consequences?"

For a second, I had no answer. Not because I hadn't daydreamed about this scenario, but because I never thought I'd get to write the rules.

"I don't know yet," I said. "I'll message you when I know."

He nodded, accepting this with all the gravitas of a convicted, but repentant, criminal. "What can I do in the meantime?"

It was a reasonable question. I tried to think of something equally reasonable, but all I could do was remember how it felt, for all those months, to want an apology and not get one. To crave an ounce of self-awareness from him, just once.

"For the next ten times you see me," I said, "you have to apologize. It needs to be the first thing out of your mouth after hello. Every single time."

He cocked his head, his eyes narrowing with plain confusion.

I leaned forward, giving him the full weight of my frustration. "You should've apologized in Paris, first thing! This is to make up for all the times you didn't say you were sorry and you could have over the last few months."

Andreas processed this, then gave a tiny, single nod. "Okay," he said. "That is fair. Anything else?"

"Yes," I said, even though I hadn't yet thought of anything else.

He waited. I glared at him. He opened his mouth. Then he closed it and waited some more.

A faint muscle ticked in his jaw several times before he said, "Well? What else?"

"I get to keep this sweater." It was an impulsive ask, but I knew right away it was a good one. This thing was so freaking soft and snuggly. I wanted it.

Andreas gave me a single somber nod, but his eyes were twinkling. "It is yours. Is there anything else?"

"I'll make a list. It will be very long. It might be a book."

I watched him fight a smile, then lost to it, the edges of his mouth twitching. I wondered if he found me funny, or if this was his way of signaling submission, showing me he'd let me have the last word.

Before I could test it by actually saying another word, Tara materialized in the doorway to the lounge, hands planted on her hips, face set in lines of seriousness.

"Sorry to interrupt," she said. Then to me, "My friend found that guy you were looking for."

I stood up at once. "Where is he?"

Andreas also stood, tilting his head. "What guy?"

I ignored him. "Where is he?" I repeated.

Tara's gaze flicked from me to Andreas, then back again. "He's right here in Manhattan. The NCI-designated cancer research hospital."

I blinked, doing the math. "He got his medical license back?"

Tara shook her head. "No. He's a patient. In something called the phase one research unit."

I felt a whoosh of air leave me and slumped back into the chair, heat draining from my face. "Oh. Geez." My grandmother had been a terminal patient who'd volunteered for phase one studies before she died. The memory of those days made something inside me recoil.

Tara frowned. "What? What does that mean?"

I rubbed the heel of my palm into my forehead, marshalling my thoughts. "The phase one clinical research unit is where—not always, but often—many terminal patients go to participate in end-of-life medical research studies. So, after an agent passes bench research, it moves to phase one human subjects research, which is where the entire point is to determine whether the agent—er, sorry, the drug—is safe for humans."

Tara's lips pressed together in a line as she absorbed this. "You mean these terminal cancer patients donate their last months while they're alive? Allowing themselves to be research test subjects to see if drugs are safe for humans? Like being a human guinea pig?"

I grimaced at the wording. "That's a very crude way of putting it. Anyone who goes through end-of-life care is brave, whether that be in a phase one unit, in hospice, whatever is right for them and their family. They are remarkable in a way you and I will never fully understand, God willing. What these particular patients do as part of a phase one unit is a huge gift to science and the world and it's disrespectful to them and their sacrifice to call them guinea pigs."

Tara looked appropriately chastised. I also felt Andreas's gaze on my profile, sensed his brain working, calculating.

I didn't have the energy to guess what his calculations yielded, so I went on. "They're testing the next generation of therapies so that maybe future cancer patients might go into remission."

"Okay. I'm sorry. You're right," Tara said remorsefully, adding, "My point is, your guy is a patient. And, get this, he's part of a gene therapy trial conducted by Genetix."

This gave me pause and I felt my eyes seeking out Andreas. He and I shared a look as I said, "Huh. That's . . . very interesting."

She shrugged. "So, you can catch him there if you want to talk to him."

Crossing my arms again, I nodded. "Please, thank your friend for me."

Tara said, "I will. But you should hurry and schedule a meeting. If this guy is a terminal patient, your time might be running out."

* * *

Holding one of my pharmaceutical-grade Americanos in one hand and Tara's wrist in the other, we dodged a biker, a pair of hospital workers, and the scent of boiled street meat on the sidewalk outside the cancer center. It was one of those Manhattan mornings when the sky could not decide whether to rain or bestow sunshine, and the mood matched the meteorology: volatile and uncertain.

Andreas stood waiting in front of the glass entrance, his back to a wall of "No Smoking" signs, glancing at his phone. He wore a lightweight charcoal coat over what was probably, if I had to guess, an obscenely expensive cashmere sweater— *maybe I'll usurp that one too!*—and his hair had a windswept, just-got-out-of-bed look that almost nobody outside of hairstylists could achieve. The man truly was fussy about his looks.

For reasons I couldn't untangle, my first, second, and third reaction to seeing Andreas was relief. Which likely had more to do with the night I'd had than anything else.

Releasing Tara, I rushed up to him. "Sorry we're a little late. Were you waiting long?"

Andreas's gaze lifted, green eyes locking on mine with such sharpness that, for a second, I forgot how to breathe. Then he flicked his gaze to Tara, nodded, and said, "Not at all. I did not wait long. It is completely fine. And I am sorry."

It took me a second to remember why he was apologizing, but then it clicked. He'd promised, yesterday, to apologize every time he saw me. At least for the next ten times. I couldn't help feeling a pulse of satisfaction that he'd not only remembered, he'd complied. I wasn't sure if it made anything better, but it was something.

I gave him a small smile. "I appreciate that."

But Andreas didn't appear to hear me. His eyebrows pulled together as he studied me and I felt his assessment as a corporeal thing as he traced the disaster that was my unwashed hair, my caffeine-glazed irises, and my lack of makeup to hide the bleary circles beneath my eyes.

"You look . . . very tired," he said. "Are you okay? You are not getting sick, are you?"

This is where I should have lied, or at least come up with a plausible explanation for why I looked like the "before" photo in a cosmetics commercial. But instead I sighed, because that was easier than forming an entire sentence, and then I glanced at Tara in mute desperation.

She picked up the cue and said, "She sleepwalked out of her building last night."

I tried to wave it off, but Tara's answer hung in the air, pulsing with implication.

Andreas jerked to attention, his posture going rigid. "Are you serious? What happened?"

"My friend Diya couldn't stay over last night," I fumbled to explain, shoving my hand in my jacket pocket and ducking my head. "She's been sleeping with me all last week, and she always wakes up when I sleepwalk. But last night, she had a thing, so my other friend, Nakita, stayed with me instead. She's a heavier sleeper. I guess she . . . didn't notice when I got up."

Tara chimed in, "Basically, Nakita slept through Sam waking up, walking out of the apartment—"

"It's not her fault," I interrupted, because it wasn't her fault.

Tara kept going, undeterred. "—taking the elevator downstairs, walking out of the lobby and on to the sidewalk. Luckily, her doorman figured out something was wrong because Sam was in her pajamas and not responding."

Andreas's concern sharpened, and he looked at Tara like her recitation of the details personally offended him. "The doorman woke her up? Where were you? Where was her team? And why is it just the two of you now?"

Tara bristled, shoulders climbing an inch. "She doesn't have a shift assigned when she's at home. That would be ridiculous. She's smart. Not going to let anyone inside the apartment she doesn't know. She's been training in self-defense with me at the gym. She's supposed to be safe at home. And it's just me today because I had to pull Chan and Tomar out of bed in the middle of the night to stand guard outside her door, just in case she did it again. Plus, you're here. Your psycho brother won't do anything with you here. We'll be fine."

Listening to the two of them talk over me, about me, in detail, triggered a weird wistfulness. My parents used to have these conversations in front of me when I was a kid, as if the most effective way to solve a problem was to pretend the problem didn't have ears or feelings. I didn't miss that dynamic necessarily, but it still felt nostalgic.

And I did not blame Tara for her bad mood. I'd gotten so little sleep last night, the entire sequence felt more like a fever dream than something that actually happened.

I rubbed my eye with the heel of my hand, fighting the urge to yawn in Andreas's face. "Okay, that's enough. It happened. We need to get going or we'll be late for our appointment."

He caught my arm as I reached past him for the door handle. "What are you going to do tonight?"

I hesitated. I'd given exactly zero thought to tonight, but I was terrified. I didn't want to sleep, or even try, knowing how easy it was for my brain to betray me. But I also didn't want to impose on Diya or Nakita or anyone else who needed rest. There was always the possibility that I could ask Tara to spend the night, but she couldn't watch me day and night forever. The woman had her own life.

"I'll figure it out later," I said, and it sounded as hollow as it felt.

It was time to concentrate. This meeting was important. And my sleepwalking worries could wait until tonight. For now, getting through this interview was all that mattered.

[15]

VARIATION IN DNA AND PROTEINS

Samantha

The waiting area for the phase one unit was full of warm-toned floors, a wall of inspirational photo murals, and two enormous tanks of what appeared to be the world's most chill goldfish. The receptionist buzzed us in without any attempt at skepticism and greeted us with warmth.

Tara gave my name, explained that we were visiting a patient, and were expected. How today's meeting came to be was a bit convoluted and not at all due to the persuasive powers of Tara or myself, but because I'd told Kaitlyn about the situation yesterday afternoon.

Kaitlyn had then called her father and he'd made a few phone calls on my behalf as he was apparently old medical school classmates with the head of hematological oncology at the NCI center. He then texted me that the phase one coordinator had cleared everything with the patient and a meeting had been scheduled for today.

As a result, here we were, not worrying about the rest.

A friendly nurse appeared and led us down a labyrinth of gently humming halls. I counted three separate lounges, all with the same warm decor. Every thirty feet, a hand-drawn sign cautioned against food or drink in patient areas and I felt relief that I'd already finished my coffee on the way up and tossed the cup.

We were shown into a small conference room off a quieter corridor, its glass wall rimmed with faux-wood paneling and the requisite "Privacy Please" sign flipped to the correct orientation. On the table sat three unopened water bottles and a box of facial tissues—a choice I couldn't help but interpret as foreshadowing.

While we waited, Andreas paced. He had a measured walk, as though he needed to map out every cubic inch of space before trusting it. I ran my hands over my jeans and tried to calm the high-voltage buzz in my rib cage. This place brought back memories of my grandmother's last days in a way that felt impossible to compartmentalize. Paired with my lack of sleep last night, my thoughts were slow and muddled and I already felt strangely emotional.

Meanwhile, Tara scrolled through her phone with the patience of a panda, occasionally glancing up at me to make sure I hadn't suffocated on my own anticipation.

The door opened, and the nurse reappeared, this time pushing a wheelchair. I caught myself halfway out of my seat—out of respect, or awkwardness, or something in between—but the man in the chair waved it off.

"I can walk," he said, voice steady and rough-edged. "But they keep us in the chairs for a while after treatment. Hi, I'm David Gounter. I'm so happy to meet you."

He looked like the sort of guy who'd played defense in high school football and then gone straight to med school—he had the build, even with his frame gone a little soft and shrunken from cancer treatment—and he wore a green tartan flannel. Covering his head was a Yankees baseball hat that shaded clear blue eyes. I'd never met the man before, but I recognized him immediately from my internet image searches.

I introduced myself, trying to make my voice sound steadier than it felt. Tara did the same, but I noticed she left out her last name, perhaps a reflex from too many years of military and private security. Andreas was last.

"Andreas Kristiansen," he said, holding out a hand. His accent went more Eastern European when he was on edge, and I could hear it now.

Dr. Gounter accepted the handshake, and I saw something flicker in his face at Andreas's name. Surprise? Or maybe recognition, echoing through time.

I filed it away for later.

The nurse left, pulling the door closed, and the room went very quiet for a beat. Dr. Gounter wheeled himself up to the edge of the table, folded his hands, and scanned our faces.

"I really appreciate you meeting with me," I said, because someone had to go first.

He nodded, once. "When they told me who you were, I jumped at the chance. Thank you for giving me the opportunity to make this right."

I felt the fine hairs on my arms stand on end and all sound seemed to slow, then stop. There are moments in life that you know, even as you live them, will divide your personal history into Before and After. I had a strong suspicion this was about to become one of those moments.

Dr. Gounter rested his elbows on the table, interlaced his fingers, and looked directly at Andreas, then at me. "First, if you don't mind, how are you two here together? I know your father"—he lifted his chin toward Andreas—"did not much care for her father."

I blinked, surprised at the question and his knowledge of our families. Glancing at Andreas, I responded, "The answer to that is quite complicated, but we were friends growing up and have, uh, rekindled that friendship."

He huffed a sound that might have been a laugh, or maybe just relief. "I hope what I'm about to say doesn't ruin your rekindled friendship."

I caught Andreas's gaze again. Level, unreadable, but with something like curiosity underneath.

"I am not close with my family," Andreas said. "I have always been on Samantha's side, on her family's side. Do not be circumspect on my account."

Gounter let out a long exhale, his shoulders slumping. "I am relieved to hear that, because your father had me change her father's death certificate."

For a few seconds, the only sound was the thrum of the building's HVAC and a distant page on the intercom. In the corner of my eye, I saw Tara's hand twitch, and my own pulse slowed to a crawl.

Gounter didn't rush. He took a sip from a water bottle, his hands shaking only a little. When he spoke again, his voice was thick but steady. "I think you probably know by now if you've tracked me down, I made some very bad choices when I was a younger man. I had a mountain of debt and owed money to some very bad types. Mr. Kristiansen—your old man"—he gestured at Andreas again with a bob of his chin—"found me through a friend of a friend and paid off all my debts at the time. All he wanted was for me to change the cause of your father's death to cardiac arrest on his death certificate. This was no easy task, but I got it done."

He turned to me, and in a voice so small and raw my heart ached with empathy, he said, "I am so sorry. I wish I could take it back. I wish I could take back so many things. But this is a big one."

As I returned this man's gaze, I felt a sense of dull gratitude. Someone was telling the truth, finally, after so many years of pretending the truth wasn't out there somewhere, hidden in a file or a memory. I had an answer.

I tried to swallow, but found my mouth dry as wool. "Do you have any idea why Oskar did that? I have my father's medical records from the hospital, the one that received him from the ambulance, and they mention a broken neck, but no other injuries. I was told he fell down a flight of stairs? Do you have any idea why there are so many different versions of events about the cause of his death?"

Gounter looked at me for a long moment, and the way he studied my face made me think he was searching for a reason not to answer. But then he did. "If a person has a broken neck and no other bruises or injuries, they didn't fall down a flight of stairs. And he didn't die of a heart attack."

It landed like a sucker punch, even though it was more or less what I'd come here to hear. The story I'd told myself for years—about my father's accidental death—evaporated.

The room stayed silent for several beats.

It was Andreas who finally broke it. "Are you saying my father killed Lawrence Jarlston?"

Gounter's face was a slow-motion car crash of pain and regret. He shook his head, looking suddenly, horribly exhausted. "I'm sorry, I don't know. But he was killed by someone. And your father paid me to cover it up. I can't tell you how sorry I am. I'm just so grateful that you found me, so I can tell you now and try to make things right."

I didn't understand myself. I should've felt something grand or shattering—a release, or maybe just relief—but what I actually felt was like my entire body had been replaced with an old, unabridged dictionary: a hundred thousand words, and none of them quite right for this feeling.

Looking across the table, at this man who'd carried a secret for more than half my life, there was nowhere for the unnamed emotion to go except up and out. So I let it rise until it hovered in the air above us, a cloud made of all the things I didn't understand, and didn't have the right words for.

* * *

TAPAS, when you think about it, are an elegant justification for indecision. Unable to choose a single dish, you simply order en masse. You can hide behind the pretty little plates and the illusion of Mediterranean moderation.

For lunch, I'd ordered ten plates, meant to be shared between the two of us.

Andreas seemed content to let me do whatever I wanted. His restlessness permeated the table, though he did an admirable job of holding it inside himself. Even now, as he dissected his third pimiento de padrón like a neuroscientist mapping the human mind, I could feel his gaze ping-pong between the table and my halfhearted, if not wholly symbolic, attempts at eating.

The restaurant, Tío Pancho, occupied a shoebox-sized chunk of West 114th. Inside, it was tiled in terra-cotta and glossy stone, the air thick with vibrant smells of things being marinated, baked, broiled, and fried. The tables were crowded elbow to elbow, separated only by mismatched chairs.

Tara was nowhere in sight, having dropped us off and excused herself to call my private security detail and strong-arm someone into reworking my night-shift coverage, which Tara and Andreas agreed among themselves needed urgent rearranging after yesterday's sleepwalking debacle. Since I was so tired, I appreciated the gesture.

This left me with my own thoughts.

I replayed the meeting with Dr. Gounter on a loop, dissecting the way he'd looked at me when he said, "I'm so sorry."

What was one even supposed to do with that? Was it an act of cowardice or bravery, to make a confession fifteen years too late? If I was being honest, it felt like both. Or maybe it was neither, and I was just programmed to forgive strangers their trespasses as long as they seemed sincere. In that moment I realized something about myself: Sincerity went a long way with me.

I still didn't know how I felt about the news that my father had been murdered. There was an entire semantic landfill of unprocessed emotion surrounding the concept, and I couldn't seem to get past the basic act of labeling it. Murder. My father had been murdered, and, at best, the only justice we'd ever get was the cold, unsatisfying fact of knowing it happened. I tried to imagine my mother hearing this news, or my grandfather. I had no idea whether it would comfort or further hollow them.

Or, did they already know and kept it from me? I shook my head. I had no way of asking them now.

Abruptly, Andreas set down his fork, straightened his back, and said, "You should request he be interviewed by the police, get a sworn statement."

I nodded my agreement. That seemed like a logical first step if I wanted to prove my father had been murdered.

Then, he said, "He apologized to you."

It took me a second to realize he was still talking about Dr. Gounter. I glanced up. "Pardon me?"

His eyes caught mine and Andreas spoke without any hint of sarcasm or softness. "That man took a lot from you by helping my father cover up your father's death. We now can extrapolate your father was murdered, either by my father or by someone my father wished to help. And by assisting Oskar in covering up this crime, that man did irreparable damage. To you, to your mother, your entire family. And he . . . apologized to you."

I studied him, fighting an urge to yawn—not because I was bored, but because I was so damn tired—or lose the thread of the conversation. His jaw looked tense, as though he were literally chewing on the idea of Gounter's apology and finding it made of gristle. There was a rage, a righteous indignation in his body language that felt wildly out of step with the blank fatigue I experienced upon attempting to process the situation.

"Why are you so mad?" I asked, mostly because I didn't want to answer the question he'd asked me.

Andreas's face twitched, and he said, "Who the hell does he think he is? One cannot simply apologize for a lifetime of hurt. Are you not angry? Why are you not livid?"

I bit down on a smile, not because it was funny, but because it felt ironic that Andreas was this mad and I . . . wasn't.

I considered this, genuinely. It was true, my first impulse should have been rage, not relief. But my body—my brain—just didn't have it in the tank.

"Maybe I was, for a long time. But today I feel . . . empty. I already spent fifteen years mourning the loss of my father and my family. I think I don't have the energy to be livid about something I was already livid about for over a decade." I set my coffee down but kept my hands wrapped around the cup. I needed to wake up. "Truthfully, I'm not mad at him. Maybe I should be, but I'm not. He told us what we wanted to know without us even asking. This incident has clearly tortured him for fifteen years." I shrugged. "He lost his medical license, his career. He's dying of cancer and probably only took our meeting because he thought it was the right thing to do. Why kick a guy when he's already kicked himself every day for over a decade?"

Andreas stared at me, and for a moment, I wondered if he thought I was lying. But then he said, quietly, "I do not understand you."

I yawned. Couldn't help it. It came out big, stretching my face until I probably looked like I was in the final seconds of a silent scream, but I was too tired to cover it. When I finished, I said, "I don't know what to tell you, Andreas. I don't understand me either sometimes. But I do have compassion for someone who has a desire to make things right, even if it's fifteen years late." I paused, then added, "Honestly, if I were dying and could clear my conscience before I went, I'd want to do it, too. I can't begrudge him for that."

Andreas made a noise—half exhale, half incredulous huff—and leaned back in his chair. He laced his hands behind his neck, a pose that exposed the full length of his arms and made him seem twice as large as usual.

"I would not forgive myself so easily," he said, sounding like someone who'd spent considerable time imagining what he'd do if the roles were reversed.

I picked up an olive and rolled it between my fingers before popping it into my mouth. "That's because deep down you're a masochist."

He glowered at me briefly, but the emotion didn't stick.

We lapsed into silence. The type that's uncomfortable if you let it be, but today, for me, was more of a buffer zone. I let the noise of the restaurant push back against the encroaching tide of what-the-fuck-happens-next.

I yawned again, then felt self-conscious. I reached for the coffee, only to find the cup empty. "I should have more coffee," I muttered.

Andreas watched my hand, then said, "May I make a proposition?"

Lifting my eyes to his again, I fought to keep them open. "The last time you said something to me like that, I ended up adopted."

He huffed a laugh, but said in all seriousness, "Sleep at my place tonight."

The words short-circuited my brain. I blinked, waiting for the punchline or the awkward clarifying statement, but none came. He just looked at me, steady and sincere.

I squinted at him. "Are you worried about me sleepwalking into traffic, or are you just really lonely?"

He considered it. "Both."

Now I huffed a laugh, because I didn't doubt he told the truth. He was worried about me. He was also lonely, otherwise he wouldn't have admitted it. I wondered if I'd ever get used to his new unfiltered candor about absolutely everything.

"You are not safe sleeping on your own right now. You need a roommate. Please, allow me to help in this way."

There was an edge of desperation in his voice, and I recognized it because I heard the same edge in my own voice, sometimes, when talking to Kaitlyn if I felt like she wasn't advocating for herself, or wasn't taking good enough care of herself, or wasn't putting herself first when she absolutely should.

I narrowed my eyes, searching for a catch, a twist, some hidden strategy. "Is this—what's your angle? What would you get out of it?"

His face did not move, not even to blink. "I promise, I will not try anything. We will sleep, that is all."

I stared at him, weighing my options, trying to figure out whether it was pride or self-preservation telling me to say no. If it was pride, then pride was stupid, because the last few days had proven I could not be trusted not to sleepwalk into a manhole or an oncoming SUV. If it was self-preservation, then self-preservation was already at a loss.

Andreas continued looking at me, eyes steady and sincere in a way that made this intimidating man appear anxious and vulnerable. "Please. Stay with me."

[16]

VARIATION IN GENETICALLY COMPLEX TRAITS

Samantha

We didn't speak the whole way to his building, unless you counted my muttered *thanks* when he opened the car door for me. It was after 9:00 PM and dark, but the streets in this part of Manhattan glowed with the iridescent energy of people who'd never missed a meal, and who always assumed tomorrow would show up with champagne. There existed no reason for me to feel anxious about returning to Andreas's apartment again. I knew all the doormen, but none of the neighbors had ever met me, and my name had never been added to the mail slot next to his in the lobby. Yet, the click of my own shoes on the floor of his entryway made me feel unsteady, as if it were made of thin ice and not solid wood.

Andreas set my suitcase down inside the door and said nothing. At least at first glance, the interior appeared unchanged. I shrugged out of my jacket. He took it from me without asking. It was so automatic, the remembered steps to a dance we'd done at least thirty times before. I almost laughed, like my body and his had a sequence of default rituals regardless of what our actual brains thought about them.

He hung our coats up and stepped back, hands at his sides. For a second, despite the stress of the day, I thought we'd crash together in one of those cliché, forbidden-urge embraces. Instead, we simply existed together. Me looking at him while he studied his shoes; then him looking at me while I reacquainted myself with the walls.

473

Part of me wanted to say something clever, or silly. Ideally, both. Cut the tension with my usual scalpel. The rest of me was so exhausted from the last twenty-four hours, all I could muster was, "I should get some sleep."

Andreas cleared his throat. "Do you want any tea first?"

"No, thanks. I think I'll go right to—uh—bed."

He nodded, his gaze flickering up to mine, then away. He cleared his throat again. "Sleep anywhere you like."

I opened my mouth to question him about the strange statement, but Andreas grabbed the handle of my suitcase and carried it through the entryway toward the living room beyond. The quiet echo of his footsteps paired with the gentle comingling smells of rosemary, wood polish, and the spices he used liberally to season his vegan dishes—all of it so familiar and precious in my memory—made me realize that, for all the weeks I'd lived here, I'd never once heard Andreas slam a door, stomp his feet, set a glass down too hard on a table, scrape a chair against the floor, or make any other thoughtless loud noise.

He disappeared around the corner, and I stood alone in the entry, letting the silence settle. Something about the stillness here felt different from my own apartment, or anywhere else I'd lived. It wasn't simply the absence of noise, or even the absence of clutter.

It was Andreas.

He was a quiet, thoughtful, and careful person. His place felt quiet, thoughtful, and careful. Which made me wonder, why would he invite me back into his gentle and peaceful living space? He claimed to love me, but why? What did he even see in me? I wasn't quiet. I was reactionary instead of thoughtful, and not at all as careful as I should be. Logic told me I should frustrate him, not attract him.

Eventually, I followed the sound of his footsteps, catching sight of the huge black circular table that anchored the large living room. It was here that the memory of my last morning in this apartment—stuffing my comforter and sheets into trash bags, angrily sorting out everything he'd purchased for me, folding and refolding my clothes—rose up like a poltergeist.

Similar to the entryway, everything appeared the same. The living room still had the same couch, where I'd woken up straddling his lap, where we'd made out more than once. Even the throw pillows were neatly arranged, just the same.

But as I walked further into the room, I realized something had changed. The Christmas tree still sat in the corner, wedged between the window and the wall, but it was long dead. The needles, once dense and shockingly green, now drooped in sad, brittle clusters, brown as hay. It looked like it would disintegrate if you sneezed on it. The lights and ornaments still wound around the branches, but the bulbs were dark.

I caught myself gaping at it and tore my eyes away, refocusing my attention. Sneaking a peek at Andreas, I realized he'd noticed my staring. His cheeks had turned faintly pink, and his mouth twisted as if he were about to mention the presence of the tree before I did. His mouth opened, then closed, then he gave his head a little shake.

I felt myself wanting to apologize for noticing, but instead I said, "It's still up."

He nodded but offered no explanation.

A joke, a bad one, tumbled out of me. "Waiting until after Christmas in July?"

Andreas cleared his throat a third time and gathered a deep breath. "I could not bring myself to have it removed. Thinking about it not being here . . . hurt. A lot."

Ah, yes. Andreas is in his brutal, blunt honesty era.

As we silently traded stares, I told myself not to ask Andreas any more questions unless I wanted to hear the truth. Complete honesty seemed to be all he would offer me from now on.

Breaking the suddenly tense moment, he pointed at my suitcase. "I put it there for you."

"Thank you." Rushing forward, I picked up the bag. "Well, uh, good night."

"Good night." His voice sounded gruff, strained, but not unkind.

I carried the suitcase toward the back bedrooms, feeling Andreas's attention on me until I walked a distance down the hall past where he could see. The door was cracked to the bedroom that had technically been mine from mid-November to late December. Upon first glance, I—once again—found everything exactly the same. The mattress was still bare. No sheets, no pillows, just a beige slab in the middle of the room.

I frowned at it, then scanned the rest of the space. All the items Andreas had bought me—the stationery, the candles, the stylish clothes—were where I'd left them, stacked neatly on the dresser. Even the little box of tea was exactly where I'd left it. Nothing had been moved or touched.

Setting my overnight bag on the bed, I unzipped it and fished out my phone. A text from Tara, the timestamp from fifteen minutes ago, flashed on the screen.

Tara: I can figure out the night-shift roster if we start in two or three weeks. A month from now would be better. We were already stretched thin when we covered you at the hospital during the overnights last weekend, and I only got the backup then because I said it was a temporary situation. I'll need to negotiate with the boss upstairs in order to get more guys assigned. Get your door lock switched out ASAP so you can sleep at home without worrying about sleepwalking out of the apartment. Sorry I can't be of more help this time.

Tara had been equal parts frustrated and relieved when I'd informed her after lunch that I had decided to stay with Andreas tonight. Andreas's offer was the best, simplest, and most logistically reasonable solution to my immediate dilemma, which was why I'd ultimately agreed.

First of all, he'd volunteered. Secondly, I couldn't keep imposing on my friends and hoping they were light sleepers. Or imposing on Kaitlyn, Martin, and Joey. I needed a sustainable solution that didn't require me to burden anyone else.

Plus, Andreas and I already had a system to keep me inside the apartment should my subconscious wish to flee. Like before Christmas, Andreas would lock the exterior door with a code tonight. I wouldn't be able to leave until he typed in the code.

And this was what Tara referred to in her text when she'd mentioned having my apartment's door lock switched ASAP. If I had the same lock installed that Andreas owned, then I could do something similar at my own apartment. But obviously, not tonight. *Maybe not tomorrow either . . .*

I texted Tara back.

Sam: Please don't worry about it. We'll figure out the night-shift situation if needed. Thank you for all your help. I'll get the lock installed ASAP.

There were no other texts, no missed calls, nothing else in the digital universe that demanded my attention. I set my phone on the nightstand and rifled in the bag for my pajamas—a pair of old joggers and a T-shirt with a faded university logo—and was about to hunt for a towel when I realized, since I'd always used my own sheets the last time I lived here, I didn't know where Andreas kept the sheets, or even if there were any clean ones. Leaving my suitcase on the bed, I padded back out into the hall.

Andreas sat at the circular table, a book in one hand and a glass of something the color of honey in the other. There was a level of tiredness in his posture tonight that made me hesitate asking him for anything. But I needed sheets, a pillow, and a blanket.

Hovering on the threshold, I eventually cleared my throat.

Andreas lifted his eyes immediately and—*is it my imagination, or does he look . . . hopeful?*—tilted his head to the side as if inviting me to speak.

"Where are the sheets?"

His face seemed to fall subtly before he cloaked his expression, arranging his features into their usual calm mask. Setting down the glass and book, he stood. "Oh. Sorry. Yes. I forgot."

He gestured for me to follow and walked to the entryway closet. There, he opened the door, and pulled out a drawer, bending then straightening. He turned, holding a bundle of sheets.

I held my hands out, but he tucked the sheets under his arm. "Since you are my guest, I should be the one to make the bed. You brush your teeth and do whatever else is required while I see to it."

I felt my hands go slack and let them drop to my sides. "Okay. Thanks."

We walked single file back down the hall to the bedroom. I relocated my bag so he could make the bed, then I grabbed my things and left for the bathroom. It was spotless, as always. The towels were perfectly folded on the rack, and all of the old bath and body products that Andreas had gifted me were still lined up along the shelf above the sink and around the shower, including the little bottle of perfume I'd loved. I stared at the bottle, then at my own reflection in the mirror.

It was uncanny, this feeling. Like I'd stepped through a portal into a universe where nothing bad had ever happened between us, where the last three months were just a blip in a dream. Obviously, I knew better. But, as I brushed my teeth, washed my face, and changed into the pajamas, I couldn't help but wonder at the difference between one month ago and now.

Last month, I'd believed him indifferent to me. And now, I knew for certain he wasn't.

Last month, I couldn't imagine ever speaking to him again. And now, I wondered if we might repair what had broken, at least enough to become friends.

I stood in the middle of the bathroom, not wanting to leave, not wanting to return to the bedroom where Andreas was probably still in the process of making the bed. When I finally worked up the nerve to go back, I found him unfurling a cozy-looking comforter on top of the sheets, two pillows already ensconced in pillowcases at the headboard.

My mind chose that moment to recall the first time we'd touched and kissed in private, not for the benefit of putting on a show, but because we wanted to, and had admitted as much to each other. How unsettled and lost he'd looked, how hypnotized he seemed to be by everything I did.

I shoved the memory aside.

Andreas straightened and turned. Catching sight of me, he shoved his hands in his pockets. "All done."

"Thank you." I stepped inside and moved to my suitcase, knowing I needed to place distance between us. The day had been full of upheaval. I felt more than vulnerable. Distracting myself by seeking out physical comfort would solve nothing. And taking physical comfort from Andreas in any circumstance, without clear boundaries and *honest* expectations between us, wouldn't be right.

He nodded stiffly and walked toward the door but paused as he reached it. "Like before, the front door is locked on a code. You will not be able to leave the apartment if you sleepwalk tonight. I have texted you the code, just in case you do need to leave. I mean, when you are awake."

I nodded, feeling my cheeks heat. "Thank you."

He gave me a long look—so long I couldn't catalogue all the emotions within it —and then quietly closed the door behind him.

I let the silence fill the room. I was determined to not cry about the revelations of the day, not even quietly into my pillow. I was also determined to not sleepwalk. Doing anything that interrupted or interfered with Andreas's calm, peaceful, thoughtful existence was off-limits tonight.

Tucking myself into bed, I turned off the light and whispered to the universe, "Please let me not sleepwalk into his room tonight. Let me get through this without being a burden or blurring lines between us."

The universe declined to comment. As usual.

* * *

I woke up groggy but well rested, with the distinct feeling that I was wrapped in something—someone—warm and solid, pressed tightly against my back.

My first thought was: *I do not own a weighted blanket.*

My second thought was: *Fuck.*

Andreas's arm rested heavy over my waist, his chest spooned into my shoulder blades, and one of his legs had managed, at some point in the night, to wedge itself between mine. A classic big-spoon maneuver I hadn't experienced since December. Low, rhythmic sounds, almost a purr, vibrated from his chest. He was still asleep.

Universe, you son of a bitch! You had one job. ONE. JOB.

Of course. Of course this happened.

I lay there, staring at Andreas's open bedroom door, unable to move, because there are some scenarios in life where the only rational response is to stop, collaborate (with your conscious mind), and listen. Obviously, I'd sleepwalked in here last night. I was the invasive species. There was no way to blame this catastrophe on anyone but myself. Or, if I was feeling generous, my treacherous subconscious.

Last night, I'd promised myself to not disrupt Andreas's peaceful life, but apparently my sleep-brain had other plans. Squinting, I attempted to recall climbing into Andreas's bed. I came up empty, as per usual.

Gritting my teeth, I refused to enjoy this feeling of being wrapped in his strong arms, in his big bed, surrounded by his lovely warmth and smell, and instead considered my options. I could try to extricate myself and leave, hoping he wouldn't bring it up later. Conversely, I could simply lie here until he woke up, then apologize and embrace the awkward. Third option, I could live here forever and become the world's least interesting bedbug.

I decided to split the difference between options one and two. Leave now, embrace the awkward later. It was time for me to take responsibility for my actions—subconscious or otherwise—instead of always avoiding uncomfortable truths.

Slowly, carefully, I attempted a forward inch. Andreas's breathing didn't alter, but his arm tightened for a moment. I paused, held my breath, and then tried a more aggressive exit maneuver by rolling slowly toward the edge of the mattress.

He made a small sound and adjusted himself, giving me an opening. I escaped.

Once I stood, I saw his bed was a crime scene of harmony and geometry, sheets perfectly crisp and tidy except for the tiny Sam-shaped trench. The sight made me irrationally angry. Who the heck maintained this level of orderliness in their sleep? Was he a cyborg? Was there a nightly visit from a bed-making Roomba with opposable thumbs?

Tiptoeing out the door, careful not to disturb him or his supernatural sleep hygiene, I maintained my soundless footsteps until I reached my assigned bathroom. There, I started my day as if nothing abnormal had occurred, refusing to look in the mirror longer than it took to brush my teeth. The idea of confronting my own expression right now was too much.

Subconscious Sam is such a disappointment.

But I did take a shower, clearing my mind and focusing on the sensations. The bath products were the same ones I'd left behind months ago, all luxury brands in minimalist packaging Andreas had bought me while in London. Letting the familiarity sink in, I inhaled the steam and scents deep into my lungs, certain this would be the last time I got to enjoy this extravagance. Unless, of course, I took the time to find and buy the products.

Knowing myself, I would never do that.

I toweled off and shuffled back to my old bedroom. Ignoring the piles of beautiful clothes Andreas had purchased for me, I opened my suitcase and pulled out a pair of jeans and a T-shirt. I needed to draw the line somewhere. If I couldn't stop myself from sleepwalking into his bedroom and sleeping in his embrace—just like old times—and using the delightful bath products—just like old times—I could at least eschew his superior taste in women's apparel.

Boundaries. Weak boundaries. But boundaries nevertheless.

I checked my phone—no messages—and then, with resigned determination, headed out to face the music. The smell of brewing coffee was lovely and I followed it, steeling myself for the inevitable embarrassment of what was to come.

Andreas, already at the stove with his back to me, wore a fitted plain white T-shirt and gray sweatpants, both of which left little to the imagination regarding the glorious shape of his body beneath. He looked less like the metrosexual, dashingly handsome strategic genius of my memory and more like an extremely sexy, fit, overgrown college student whose hair was still damp from a recent shower. I also noticed his feet were bare. *Where are his fussy pajamas or Euro-chic casual wear? Who has Americanized him?*

He glanced over his shoulder. "Hi. Coffee is made, if you would like some."

His voice was easy, casual. But I was distracted by the sight of him looking so informal that it took me a second to process his words. *And . . . is he wearing underwear beneath those sweatpants? Because it certainly doesn't look like it.*

"Sam?" Andreas's voice cut through my inappropriate contemplations and I realized I'd been openly ogling him.

"Hmm?" I pressed my lips together, fighting the blush threatening my neck and cheeks. "Pardon?"

The side of his mouth angled up. "Coffee?"

"Uh. Yes, please. I can get it for myself. Obviously." I moved to the carafe and poured myself a cup, relishing the heat on my palms. I didn't add anything—he always bought the good stuff—and anyway, my heart rate was already on a hair trigger. If I wanted cream, I'd have to move within his orbit.

As I took my first sip, he said, "I am so sorry."

I blinked, then remembered the rules I'd set regarding the ten required apologies. This was number two. I felt a tiny, odd thrill of satisfaction, then tamped it down and focused on the fact that I also needed to say sorry for sleepwalking into his room last night.

He remained at the stove, attention fixed on whatever he whisked in a metal bowl, while I struggled with how to bring up my mistake and apologize for it. I had hoped he would bring it up first. Then I could express my sincerest and most profound apologies. I would then point out the obvious, which was that I should find somewhere else to sleep tonight since my unconscious couldn't be trusted with him nearby.

Uncomfortable in the stretching silence, but not yet ready to broach the topic, I asked, "What are you making?"

"Eggs Benedict for you. Rice, black beans, and salad for me."

"Why do you make me things you can't eat?" I asked, genuinely curious. "I appreciate you making me breakfast, but why not just make one breakfast? I can eat rice, black beans, and salad."

He kept his gaze on the stove, but his jaw tensed. "Just because I cannot eat something does not mean I do not enjoy watching you eat it."

I scrunched my face, doing the mental subtraction on his triple negative: not, not, not. "That's . . . Wait, does that mean—"

He set down the whisk. "What I mean is, you enjoy eggs Benedict. I enjoy watching you enjoy things, even if it is not something I am able to experience for myself. I derive enjoyment from your enjoyment." He glanced at me quickly, then picked up his coffee.

Pondering his statement, I asked stream of consciousness, "Is that why you were always going down on me when I lived here?"

He choked. Full-on, spectacularly choked, nearly spitting out his coffee. And as Andreas coughed and sputtered, his shocked stare swung to me, wide-eyed and pink cheeked.

Realizing belatedly what I'd said, I averted my gaze and hid my grimace behind my own coffee. Then I set my mug down and crossed to the sink penitently, filling a glass with water. I walked over and handed it to him. He accepted, his glassy eyes still wide but this time with plain suspicion.

After a moment, when he'd composed himself, he rasped, "Was that a real question? Or were you trying to make me choke on my coffee?"

"Why can't it be both?" I hedged, trying for a joke.

His teeth slid to the side, and he actually smiled, just a little. Andreas turned off the burner, set the pan aside, and leaned his hip against the counter, glaring at me. "Fine. Yes. I enjoy watching you enjoy yourself. *A lot.* And when I am the direct cause of your enjoyment, even better."

His voice dropped on the last word, and the sound of it made my stomach flip. A ridiculous, unwelcome warmth filled my chest. "Good to know."

Again I sipped my coffee, trying to pretend my skin wasn't prickling.

Still glaring at me, he added, "But, when I 'went down on you,' I also enjoyed myself, unrelated to your enjoyment. Immensely. Just like I enjoy myself when you sleepwalk into my bedroom at night. . ." He allowed the end of the sentence to hang between us, not really an ending at all.

Ah. There it was. My opening. *Time to showcase my personal growth.*

Sighing silently, I set the coffee cup down on the counter and faced him. "About last night—"

"It is no big deal." Turning from me, he plated the English muffin, Canadian bacon, and eggs, added a swirl of hollandaise, and handed the dish to me.

I set it on the counter next to my coffee. "But it is a big deal to me. I have very big, unresolved feelings for you. I—I think I'm still in love with you"—*gah! I said it. I admitted it. And I survived*—"and it's not fair to either of us for me to walk into your bedroom at night and complicate everything. I'm sorry. I shouldn't have—"

"You were asleep." Not looking at me, Andreas scooped rice seasoned with saffron onto his plate and covered it with a generous helping of savory-looking black beans, his movements aggressive. "So what if you are in love with me? What is the problem? I am in love with you, too."

My stomach flipped again. "You know it's not that simple. Sleeping with you blurs a line I have no intention of crossing, not right now, maybe never, I don't know yet."

He shot me another glare. It felt full of longing, but also frustrated beyond belief.

Yet, I would not be deterred from my big speech. "And—given how honest you've been, at times painfully honest—I don't want to send mixed signals or—"

Andreas set his plate down and faced me again. "Do not use last night as an excuse to leave. We both knew it might happen, therefore no lines were blurred. I know I am not forgiven."

My heart twisted. "Andreas, it's not that I don't forgive you. It's that I'm not sure if—I'm not sure if I can—"

"You were asleep," he repeated, firmer this time. "And if it happens again tonight, so be it."

"It won't happen again tonight because I can't stay here. It hurts us both, and I don't want to hurt you. Listen, I know how you feel. I believe you when you say that you love me, but I'm not sure—"

His feet carried him a step closer. "Samantha. What are you going to do? Where will you stay? Was Tara able to find evening security for you? Will she sleep over?"

I sighed again, much louder this time. "I'll figure something out. I'll—"

Closing the distance between us, he gathered my hands and held them pressed between his palms, his gaze intensely sincere and imploring. "Please. Please stay. I will have no expectations of you. But knowing you are safe, here—it will keep me from worrying. If you do not stay, then I will not be able to sleep either. Please."

I felt myself waver.

Perhaps sensing my indecision, he shuffled closer, his hands curling around my fingers. "And I promise, I will not take advantage of the situation . . . for at least ten days."

That made me laugh.

He smiled. "Worry-free sleep. This buys you the time needed to sleepwalk-proof your apartment. I will rest easier knowing you are safe. Seriously, no expectations. What do you say?"

Trying and failing to flatten my expression, I glanced down and to the side, searching the kitchen for a reason to say no. Instead, I found my eggs Benedict. If anything, Andreas's yummy breakfasts alone were a reason to stay. *Traitor eggs. Aptly named.*

Sucking in a deep breath, I surrendered. "Fine. Yes. Fine. Okay. Thank you. No expectations. I will sleep here until I figure out a solution and can stay at my place."

Andreas flashed a huge grin, as though he'd won much more than I'd yielded. Almost at once, he said, "Good. You will stay. It is settled," and released my fingers, cheerfully picking up his plate and leaving the kitchen.

Meanwhile, I wondered if I would regret yielding to Andreas Kristiansen.

[17]

RANDOM GENETIC DRIFT

Samantha

Monday afternoon, in the sanctum of my biology building office, after ten nights of exceptional sleep, I was the goddess of bioremediation at the height of my dissertation writing powers.

What stunned me most these days was how much easier everything had become once I was free of shared resources, broken power strips, and unsolicited opinions about post-structuralism from the PhD psychology students who would wander into the communal office area. All it took to triple my productivity was a single-occupancy office and my own dedicated lab space.

Plus, you know, sleep.

My computer screen was a horizon of tracked changes and citation manager pop-ups, the kind of thing you only appreciate after four years of learning how to format figure legends. My desk was arranged for maximum efficiency: laptop dead center, phone to the right of my mouse, mug of emergency pretzels to the left, coffee within reach. Every so often I'd pause, lean back, and bask in the idea that, for the first time in my academic career, nobody could judge me if I wanted to nap on the floor under the desk because they'd never see me do it. *This is heaven.*

Which is why, when a knock hit my door, it felt like a trespass.

I blinked, checked the time, and found it was almost 4:00 PM. Today wasn't a lab meeting day, I wasn't late for anything, and the only person I expected was Dmitry at 5:00 PM. *It might be an undergrad, looking for help.*

"Who is it?" I called, hoping the edge in my voice would serve as an adequate warning that I was not in the mood for "quick questions" about the semester's next animal protocol submission.

"Quinby from HR. Just here for a quick chat, if you have the time, Ms. Jarlston."

The voice was male, with that overly calm, blandly courteous cadence I associated with insurance salespeople. I frowned, saved my document, and wondered what HR could possibly want with me.

"Please come in," I said, and turned my chair to face the door.

It swung open to reveal a man in his mid-thirties, dressed in a mid-gray, mid-priced suit. But the tie looked like it was Italian and expensive. He smiled tightly, then crossed the room and extended a business card to me.

I accepted it—*KENNETH QUINBY, HR Director, Faculty & Academic Divisions*—and gestured to the only other chair in the room. He sat, a tablet balanced on his knee.

"Thank you for seeing me, Ms. Jarlston," he said. "I promise I'll be out of your hair in a few minutes. I'm here for a quick check-in, to ensure you're feeling good about everything, see if there's anything we can do. You know, basic stuff."

"I have never in my life been visited by anyone from human resources, so forgive me if I'm a little confused."

"Well, that's a good thing, isn't it?" He offered the smile of a man who'd been to a lot of webinars about active listening.

I returned his smile with one of my own. "Everything is great. Ten out of ten. Would recommend. No notes."

He nodded, made a scribble on his tablet, and said, "Good. That's good. Well, there is one more thing."

I waited. I'd learned this trick from watching Dr. Hauser. Don't help. Wait and let people fill the silence.

He did. "For a period of time back in November and early December, you were reporting to an assistant professor—just a very short period of time—and I wanted to check in with you about that experience."

I blinked twice, my brain switching gears. "Do you mean Dr. Nieminen?"

Quinby tapped something on his screen. "That's right. This is an informal conversation, off the record if you want, no pressure here. We were just wondering if you had any feedback on James Nieminen, as his direct report. Or perhaps any comments on him as a—uh—maybe a mentor?"

I leaned back and let my gaze drift to the bookshelf behind Mr. Quinby, wondering what this might be about. Had someone said something? *Wait. Did Andreas call someone, like he'd offered to do months ago?*

Almost at once, I dismissed the notion. Andreas and I had been cohabitating for ten nights. I'd sleepwalked into his room almost every one of those nights. And we'd discussed work, his days, my days, food, movies, all manner of things. But not once had James Nieminen come up.

My professional interactions with Dr. Nieminen were brief. I hadn't wasted time or energy on the man since Dr. Hauser took back over as my PI.

"Why do you want to know?" I finally asked. Academia was a very small world. If someone had suggested HR speak with me, I wanted to know who.

Quinby's mouth twitched. "I'm afraid I can't tell you that."

So, this was an investigation. Or at least a prelude to one.

"I suppose if you're asking about his mentorship, I can say I don't have enough information to draw any conclusions."

"Can you expand on that?"

"Well, he didn't give me much in the way of direction or mentorship, and he required extensive daily logs of my activities, which we reviewed every Friday evening even though he had access to my daily logs via the shared drive. But it was a temporary thing. I have nothing to offer about his long-term mentorship skills."

He made another note. "He never asked you to meet him outside of work?"

That gave me pause.

"I'm sorry," I said. "Could you repeat the question?"

"Certainly," Quinby said brightly, then read from his screen again. "Did Dr. Nieminen ever ask you to meet him outside of work? Related, were you ever uncomfortable in your interactions with Dr. Nieminen?"

I thought and blurted my question at the same instant: "Did James Nieminen sexually harass his new postdoc?"

Quinby's eyes went wide, but he held fast. "Why don't you tell me about your experience working with Dr. Nieminen."

Putting my elbow on the desk and propping my chin in my hand, I shrugged. "Fine. He bought tickets to a Broadway show and assumed I would attend with him. He also suggested that we grab dinner before curtain. I said no and told him I wasn't comfortable meeting with him outside of work. In response, he was less than friendly. That night after work, he waited for me outside the building and demanded I complete what I considered a ridiculous amount of work before the next morning, suggesting I quit if I couldn't accomplish the task and that my funding might not continue if I couldn't keep up." I said it all in a tone that, even to my own ears, sounded more bored than aggrieved. But I wasn't going to dress it up for him.

Quinby nodded again, lips pressed together. "Did you tell anyone about this?"

Technically, Andreas had witnessed the conversation outside the building, but something kept me from mentioning him. Why did I need a witness? Why wasn't my word enough?

I decided not to mention Andreas.

"Not really," I said, deciding it was technically true.

Quinby looked disappointed. I guess I'd failed to provide the proper paperwork for my own trauma.

"Why not?" he pressed.

"Well, it's embarrassing, isn't it? And also, at the time, I was a poor grad student who had trouble making ends meet. I didn't want to make any waves and potentially lose my place in the program. Nor did I wish to be labeled difficult or dramatic. The situation wasn't cut-and-dry, right? Maybe I'd misunderstood him, maybe I'd overreacted. I suppose I second-guessed myself and talked myself out of it."

He narrowed his eyes. "But you're not in the same circumstances now. Why not tell someone after your circumstances changed?"

I could have told him that not everything was about leverage or "safe reporting," but instead I said, "Not that it's any of your business, but I've been very busy and haven't given that man any thought since coming back from winter break."

He tried one more time. "But how come—"

I cut him off. "Look. I'm telling you now. Believe me, or don't believe me. But you came here and you asked. And so I told you what happened."

Quinby sighed, typed something. I watched his thumb move on the screen, probably toggling the "difficult" or "hostile" button.

Feeling my temper spike, I added before I could think better of it, "And I'd just like to point out that maybe the reason more women don't 'say something' in these situations is because they're grilled with twenty questions after it happens, and then they're not believed anyway. So, isn't that just a waste of our time? Not only that, but you're asking me to relive something that was truly awful to experience—when all I want to do is forget it—and then you're treating me like I need to convince you it happened."

He shook his head, eyes softening. "Ms. Jarlston, I am absolutely not doing that."

I stood up, my patience at an end. "I don't have time for this. I answered your questions. Please leave."

He also stood, smoothing the lapels of his suit. "Ms. Jarlston, I just have one more question—"

"Fair warning, if you ask me what I was wearing, I might get violent. So, please leave. Seriously, leave."

Quinby drew himself up, like he wanted to say something else, but I had already picked up my mug full of pretzels and turned my back to him, saying, "If you want to talk to me about this, you'll have to speak to my lawyer first. Goodbye."

That did the trick. Saying nothing, he left, and the door closed quietly. I didn't breathe until I heard his shoes recede down the hallway.

Returning to my chair, I set the pretzels down and picked up my coffee. Staring out the window, I savored the peace of my private office.

Other than the dedicated lab space and the solo office, maybe the best thing about inheriting sudden wealth was being able to tell people to speak to my lawyer if I didn't feel like answering their questions.

Lawyers. Buffers for the rich. No wonder most ridiculously wealthy people were Libertarians. No taxes, no regulations, no oversight, no consumer or public safety. They could afford to litigate their way through life, railroading everyone in their path, and simply call it "the free market."

* * *

WHILE STIR-FRYING tofu in a sauce of ginger, garlic, and honey, I decided that I could get used to the domestic life.

Not the long-term, marriage-and-mortgage domestic life. But this. Right now. Making dinner in a Manhattan kitchen with the din of New York traffic humming through the windows, an overpriced bottle of Malbec breathing on the counter, and a very tall, very sexy chess grand master perched nearby, pretending to scroll on his phone while actually watching me cook, and checking out my ass every time I bent over.

Andreas's kitchen was perfect. It was spacious and minimalist. Quartz counters, white cabinets, a "statement" faucet that probably cost more than my old couch. When Andreas wanted food, he made it from scratch, using ingredients that had faces, even if they were only plant faces. When I wanted eggs Benedict, he made it for me, then watched me eat it with a smile that said, *You like it when I spoil you.*

Tonight, however, was my night to cook. We'd been alternating ever since I moved in (temporarily), a ritual as new as it was functional. Mondays were mine. I'd settled on ginger-garlic tofu with bok choy and brown rice, because it was easy, and because I secretly liked the way Andreas's entire body reacted when he tasted something spicy.

He sat with his elbows on the counter, hands folded, looking up from his phone every few minutes to observe my progress. Once again, he wore his relaxed attire.

A fitted black T-shirt, gray sweatpants, and bare feet, a look that should've been illegal for a man with that jawline and . . . other things.

I knew I was being watched, but in a way that made me want to show off. Just a little. I even poured my wine with a flick of the wrist.

Fishing a piece of tofu from the pan, I blew on it, and popped it in my mouth. As the heat hit, I exhaled and said, "So, I had a visit from HR today."

Andreas glanced up, the blue light from his phone tinting the underside of his jaw. "HR?"

"Human resources." I jabbed the wooden spoon at the tofu. "He shows up unannounced and starts grilling me about Nieminen. I guess someone put in a formal inquiry."

Andreas's eyebrows drew together. "How do you mean?"

"The whole thing was so . . . off." I dropped the spoon into the pan, switched hands, and sipped my wine while summarizing the early part of the conversation, eventually detailing what I'd shared with Mr. Quinby.

Andreas's frown grew intense. "You never told me he invited you to a show and dinner."

"It doesn't matter now." I waved the hand holding my wine through the air. "What matters is that Mr. Quinby kept asking me questions, asking if I'd ever told anyone about it, asking why I didn't go to HR when my circumstances changed, etcetera. I got so mad, it's like—this is why women stay silent, you know? Don't give me BS about owing it to *all* women. That's putting the onus on the victim. I don't owe all women anything. If I don't want to bring it up, leave me alone with this malarky. I have my reasons. James Nieminen's shitty behavior is not my responsibility. Stop making men's shitty behavior the responsibility of women!"

Andreas had drifted closer during my rant.

I wasn't finished. "And Quinby came in there and asked me questions—which I answered— and then wanted me to justify my answers? GTFO!"

I liked how "GTFO" sounded in the echoing space of Andreas's kitchen.

"That's unbelievable," Andreas said, voice sharp. "Why ask you if he wasn't going to believe you?"

"Exactly!" I set down the wineglass a little too hard, wiped my hand on my leggings, and held up my palm for a high five.

Without hesitation, Andreas slapped it, palm to palm, with just enough force to be satisfying. The contact lingered for a fraction of a second longer than strictly necessary. Then he let his hand fall, but he didn't stop watching me.

"Eventually," I continued, retrieving my wine and taking another sip, "I told him he'd need to talk to my lawyer if he wanted to discuss the issue with me. For as long as I'm wealthy, I'm so done being forced to have conversations I don't want to have."

When I was poor again, I knew I'd have to do it. But not yet. *Not yet.*

Andreas grinned at me like he thought I was weird but cute. "What do you mean, 'for as long as I'm wealthy'? Are you planning to donate your shares?"

I bit my bottom lip and shrugged, picking up the spoon and spinning it between my fingers. "What if I did? Would you be mad?"

I could admit it, Andreas's opinion mattered to me. However, I would still do what I needed to do to prove my parents' innocence.

He gave me a side-eye that was all affection, a one-corner smile lifting his lips. "Anything else happen today?"

I found those little smiles stupidly sexy and thus tore my eyes away and busied myself with the pan, tossing the tofu cubes so they wouldn't burn.

"Other than making more progress on my dissertation, not much. How was your day? Any more news about the wolf pups? Did they finally name them?"

For all of his purported introversion, Andreas had spent the last week volunteering more personal trivia than I ever thought possible. His favorite animal, his preferred old movies, tons of details about the exotic animal shelter upstate.

He leaned forward on his forearms, arms corded with muscle, phone forgotten. "If you want to buy naming rights, the bidding is still open."

I set the spoon on a trivet, wiped my hands, and cocked my hip. "I've always been partial to the name Bartholomew. It can have so many shortened nicknames. Bart, of course. Then there is: Theo, Mew, Lomeo, Tholo, Barmew."

Andreas frowned with his eyes but smiled with his mouth. "Thomeo?"

"Exactly!"

The rice cooker beeped, and I spun as I portioned everything onto two plates.

Handing Andreas his, I said, "How about Roman? Did you two get a chance to do a livestream?"

He accepted the plate with a thank-you nod, then followed me out to the now-iconic large black circular table.

"We did," he said, setting down his dish. "It was good."

"Who won?" I asked, settling next to him.

He looked at me, eyes hooded, the tiniest arch to his left brow. The look said, *Who do you think won?*

I laughed, scooping rice into my mouth and swallowing before speaking again. "Well, this is your first livestream match in months. How was the attendance? Did many people watch?"

Andreas shrugged. "I did not check. I can ask Roman, if you want."

"You didn't check?" I shook my head at his nonchalance. "Just give me his number. As my love rival, I should have his phone number."

Andreas went very still. Too still. I could feel the abrupt change in pressure next to me, like I'd dropped an ice cube down the front of his shirt.

I opened my mouth to explain it was a joke, but he cleared his throat and said, "How is Kaitlyn? Is she home from the hospital finally? It's been weeks at this point. Over ten days since I saw her last."

The redirect was so smooth I almost laughed, but I let it go. "Martin paid for the suite for a month, but yes. She returned home yesterday. I think her parents will stay for a few more days, just to help out."

Andreas nodded. "And how is Diya? It's been over ten days since you saw her."

I shot him a confused look, wondering why ten days had now become his metric for the passage of time. "She's doing well. I texted with her over the weekend. Her family is still in town, so I think that's been a lot."

"They're still in town? It's been over ten days."

There he goes again.

I set my fork down and smirked at him. "Yeah. But they keep extending their trip. I think they really like the city."

He nodded, then, almost as an afterthought, said, "Before I forget, the sanctuary asked me to come up sometime soon for some publicity photos with the wolves. Do you want to come?"

I sat up straighter. "What? Of course! I'd love it. Will we get to pet the wolves? Or, is that safe?"

He tilted his head, maybe weighing the risk. "Yes and no. We will not be able to pet the adults or the puppies, but the teenage wolves can be touched. Do not wear your hair in a bun, though. They like to bite them. I think they believe buns are little hairy animals."

I nodded, grave and solemn. "Okay. I won't. Is a braid okay?"

He looked like he fought a smile. "Braids should be fine."

We finished the meal in companionable conversation, the clink of silverware and the random creaks of the old building filling the space between us. When I was done, I set my fork down, wiped my mouth, and said, "I'll do the dishes."

Andreas stood, collected the plates, and said, "I will do the dishes. You made dinner."

He carried the plates to the sink, and I rotated in my chair so I could watch the way his T-shirt stretched across his back and his backside filled out the gray sweatpants as he walked away. Then, I sighed happily.

As I listened to the sounds of Andreas cleaning, I reflected on how, in less than two weeks, my sense of "normal" had completely reset. I'd gone from crashing on friends' couches and sleepwalking through my own apartment, to feeling oddly at home in the lair of my onetime enemy, now—what? Friend? Ally? Something more? I didn't know how to label it. And I didn't want to. Not without discussing things with Andreas and defining what we were together.

But I did know one thing. I'd miss this when I left. As soon as the new lock was installed on my apartment door—this Wednesday, if the handyman's text was to be believed—I'd move back, and our fragile little domestic bubble would pop. It was funny how quickly I'd acclimated to the luxury of safety and good company. *And gray sweatpants.*

The fact that Andreas had kept his word, never once making a move or even hinting at wanting more than my friendship, made me like him even more. He'd proven—over and over—that he could be trusted, at least on matters of personal boundaries. He did not exploit my vulnerability or the proximity of our situation. He made room for me, literally and otherwise.

The buzz of my phone broke the reverie. I fished it out of my leggings pocket and saw a call from the head of my legal team. I glanced over at the kitchen, then answered, "Hello?"

"Ms. Jarlston. I have some excellent news." The voice was clipped, but giddy.

My heart thudded. "What is it?"

"We made two major breakthroughs today thanks in big part to the files you sent us from Genetix." Without even taking a breath, she continued, "First, we discovered that Henrik Kristiansen—not your father—was the one who sold the Genetix customer data and forged your father's signature."

I stood up, energy zapping through my limbs. "Are you serious?"

"Yes. We have definitive proof. Not only do we have a confession from the acquisitions firm that handled the sale, we also have video with audio of the meeting where the sale took place."

"How is that possible?" I said, genuinely bewildered by this stroke of luck.

"The manager in charge of the acquisition filmed the meeting secretly. He didn't trust Mr. Kristiansen—Mr. Henrik Kristiansen, to be precise—to keep his word and so he recorded the meeting in order to blackmail Mr. Kristiansen later, if needed. He called it his insurance."

I nearly collapsed back into the chair. My head spun, every cell buzzing with disbelief and a wild, manic joy. "What's the second breakthrough?" I managed, voice barely above a whisper.

"You might want to sit down for this."

I sunk into the chair as instructed. "I'm already sitting down."

"On the recording," the lawyer said, "when the manager asked Mr. Kristiansen what would happen if Lawrence Jarlston—that is, if your father—ever traced the sale back to Henrik, Henrik said that the manager didn't need to worry about that because, and I quote, 'My father wants him dead.'"

The words hit me like a freight train. My heart pounded so hard I could barely hear what the lawyer said next.

I stared at nothing, at the black table, the surface reflecting the city lights through the window, and I was speechless. I was everything and nothing at once, my insides stripped to the quick by the possibility—no, the certainty—that everything I'd suspected, everything that had finally fueled me to accept Andreas's offer last year, was true.

I pressed the phone closer to my ear, holding on for dear life as the lawyer's voice rattled off the next steps, the possible outcomes, the legal terminology and strategic advantages. But it all blurred together.

I kept hearing the same sentence, over and over, repeated in my head.

My father wants him dead.

[18]

POPULATION STRUCTURE

Samantha

When I woke in the night, I was not startled to find myself in Andreas's bed. This was the predictable outcome of falling asleep these days. The only surprise was how effortlessly I'd slipped out of my own bed, traversed the hall, and tunneled into the warm hollow of his sheets like a feral raccoon searching for a heat source.

Andreas's arm was already around my waist, his hand splayed on my stomach, trapping me between the mattress and his body. He spooned me, of course, because apparently he only had two sleep modes: perfect monastic solitude or maximum-contact human burrito. I'd shifted from fully asleep to waking so fast I didn't even try to untangle myself. It wasn't fully dark. I lay there, in the dim light, listening to the distant city noise filtering up from the avenue.

For several seconds, I convinced myself I could fall back asleep in this position and deal with the psychological aftermath in the morning, along with the world's worst case of bed head.

As soon as I started to drift, a soft voice rumbled behind my ear. "Are you awake?"

I considered pretending to be asleep, but that ship had sailed. "Mmm-hmm. Yeah. Sorry."

He pulled me a fraction closer, so my ass fit snug against his hips. "Why are you sorry?"

I could have said any number of things, but in the end, I went with, "My unconscious is a menace."

Andreas made a small, sleepy noise that was almost a laugh, then pressed his face into my hair. The sensation was unexpected but good, like being nuzzled by a big cat who'd decided not to eat you just yet. "I like you here."

This, I realized, was permission to keep making mistakes, which felt both seductive and deeply irresponsible. I briefly entertained the option of extracting myself, slipping from his embrace, tiptoeing back to my bed. Instead, I gave up, gave in, and settled in, the weight of his arm a comfort.

We lay there for a while, neither of us talking, but also not sleeping. At least, I wasn't sleeping. Based on the steady increase in his respiration rate, I doubted Andreas was either. His hand on my stomach was warm, his thumb absently stroking slow circles through my shirt.

Eventually, I let my breath out, slow. "Should I go?"

He didn't answer right away, but then, with measured deliberation, he shifted closer and hooked his leg over mine, caging me more completely.

"No." His mouth was right at my ear, and his voice was a raw-sounding whisper. "Stay."

My whole body prickled, a line of heat tracing from my ear down to my chest and belly. I didn't move. I didn't want to move. And the mood seemed to shift, growing tense with anticipation.

After several more seconds, I cleared my throat and said, "You're still awake, aren't you?"

"Very," he replied, the word a breath.

Now, it was my turn to freeze, because I could feel exactly how awake he was. His erection pressed to my lower back, large and not at all understated about its existence. My pulse spiked, and my pragmatic brain suggested several ways I could ignore this development, all of which were instantly vetoed by the rest of me.

Andreas's hand, which had been content to linger at the equator of my waist, moved up. He shifted back an inch. With careful, almost excruciating patience, he slipped his fingers beneath the hem of my shirt and traced the bare skin there. He didn't say anything, but his fingers broadcasted their intent with all the subtlety of a PowerPoint presentation. Andreas was going to touch me, and unless I explicitly asked him to stop, he would not stop.

And so, I made no protest. I let him.

His palm slid upward, knuckles feathering along my ribs, the pads of his fingers searching for the soft edge of my breast. He cupped it—gently, as if testing the physics of its weight—and I felt my nipples harden so suddenly and sharply, the sensation was almost painful. Still, I did not move. If anything, I breathed slower, deeper, making it more inviting for him to explore.

Andreas squeezed softly, his thumb brushing over my nipple in lazy, deliberate strokes. After a minute of this, he moved his body so his mouth was at my ear again, and whispered, "Do you want me to stop?"

I shook my head. "No. Don't stop."

Andreas kissed the spot behind my ear, a soft, hot press of lips that sent an immediate pulse of electricity to my core. He let his hand wander, alternating between fondling my breast and tracing the curve of my waist, as if he couldn't decide where he wanted to touch me most.

At some point, my breathing got loud enough that I felt self-conscious, so I brought my hand up to cover his, pressing his palm harder into my skin. This provoked an appreciative-sounding exhale from him, which made my thighs clench together in an automatic, instinctive movement.

"I know something that will help you relax and help you sleep," he said, the words so sincere that I nearly laughed. But instead of laughing, I let him slide his hand down, past my stomach, over the curve of my hip, and into the waistband of my pajama pants.

There was a moment of suspense, a question hovering in the air between us, before he moved forward. His fingers crept inside my underwear, skimming over the skin, lower, lower, and then—without ceremony—he touched me, his fingers seeking out the wet, sensitive place between my legs.

I inhaled, a gasp, and pressed my face into the pillow to muffle the sound. He parted me with his middle and ring fingers, not entering but circling my clit with small, firm strokes that made my hips arch, made me want to grind back against him. I didn't. But the need was there, building, tidal.

Andreas's voice was low, hoarse. "Is this okay?"

I nodded, then managed to say, "Yes. God, yes."

He rewarded my approval by slipping a finger inside me, slow and maddingly gentle at first, then building in rhythm as he anticipated my reactions. It was both familiar and new, the memory of him touching me like this months ago colliding with the now. He was gentler than I remembered. Or maybe I was just more desperate.

"I thought you said you wouldn't try anything," I said, wanting to give him an escape if my presence tonight had somehow pushed him into this, made him feel pressured. But it was hard to concentrate on words when my whole body was focused on sensation.

He hummed against my ear. "I said I would not try anything for ten days. It has been ten days."

Well then.

That statement fully addressed any and all concerns I'd had about Andreas feeling pressured. He wanted this. And—as he slid his fingers out, circled my clit with slow, deliberate strokes, and then pressed his palm flat against me, grinding in tiny increments that made my legs tremble—I felt certain he'd planned this.

"Do you want me to stop?" he repeated, his voice darker, the words sounding like a dare.

My response was immediate. "Please, don't stop."

Andreas's breath caught, and I realized how much he needed this, too.

He nuzzled my neck again, his lips soft and damp on my skin. "Weeks ago, when you apologized for seducing me, you said you would accept responsibility. This is the consequence. This is the responsibility you have to accept for making me fall irrevocably in love with you. Do you accept?"

I whimpered, something between a laugh and gasp. "Yes, please."

He pushed his fingers deeper, curling them just so, and with his other hand, he pulled my top leg over his, opening me wider, giving him better access. The audacity of it—his hand buried between my legs, his body spooned up behind me, the casual dominance of the movement—made me dizzy.

He found a rhythm that was all precision, alternating slow circles with insistent pressure, then back again, reading every micromovement of my hips, every gasp, every desperate clutch of my hand at the sheets. His cock, rigid along my lower back, pressed harder against me every time I moaned.

At some point, he whispered, "When I am finished making you come, you will suck my cock." Not a request.

I said nothing, because I was already too far gone. Instead, I pushed back, grinding my ass against his erection, letting him know I wanted everything he was offering.

He groaned—an honest, raw sound—and fingered me deeper, keeping his thumb on my clit, until I came with a stifled cry, my whole body locking up, shuddering, then releasing in waves. The aftershocks made my vision go white, my hands fisting in the pillow.

He didn't let up. He kept touching me, softer, gentler now, kissing my neck, my hair, my shoulder. "You are so beautiful," he murmured. "I love you, Samantha. I love you." The words, at first, didn't register, but then, as the afterglow receded and my mind returned to my body, I heard them, and they landed in a way that made me want to cry.

I turned and rolled over to face him, his hand slipping out from between my legs but staying on my thigh, like he didn't want to break the connection. He looked at me, eyes shining in the pale light spilling in through the open door, and for a moment, neither of us said a word.

Then I grinned. "You know what's next, right?"

He nodded, solemn, eyes huge. "Yes. I do."

I kissed him, hard and messy, and then rolled him onto his back. He lay beneath me and I straddled his hips, pinning his wrists above his head, if only for a second. He let me, watching me with a wonderful kind of awe and reverence.

I kissed down his jaw, his neck, the warm, fragrant column of his throat. I loved how his skin tasted. Clean and faintly salty, like someone who spent a lot of time at the gym and then a lot of time in the shower. Lifting his shirt, I worked my way down his chest, pausing to scrape my teeth over his pecs, then further, following the line of hair down to where his sweatpants tented high and insistent.

I tugged at the waistband, and he lifted his hips to help me, the movement so coordinated it felt rehearsed. The sweatpants came off, followed by the boxers, and suddenly his cock was there, hot and hard, throbbing against his stomach.

I took it in my hand, stroked it once, and watched his eyes flutter closed, his breath hitch. He looked so goddamn beautiful like this. Vulnerable, waiting for me.

I wanted to say something funny, or smart, or biting, but all I could do was stare, then wet my lips, then bend down and taste him. I licked from the base to the tip, slow, savoring the texture, the heat, the softness of the skin. He made a sound, half growl, half groan, and fisted the sheets on either side of his body.

I loved that. I wanted more.

So, I licked again, this time swirling my tongue around the head, savoring the salty-sweet taste of him, then sucked him into my mouth, taking as much as I could, letting my hand stroke what my mouth couldn't reach. I kept my eyes on his face, wanting to see every flicker of pleasure, every tightening of his jaw, every clench of his abdomen.

He lasted longer than I expected, probably because he was trying so hard not to come too fast, but eventually his hips bucked, and he said, "Wait—wait, I'm going to come. If you do not want—Samantha—"

But I did want. I wanted all of it. I sucked him harder, faster, feeling him swell in my mouth, and then he came, hot and thick and sudden. I swallowed all of it, loving the way his body lost control, the way his voice broke when he gasped my name.

I drew it out, sucking gently until he was empty, then licked him clean, planting a kiss at the base for good measure as he flinched away, now too sensitive, a soft laugh slipping past his lips.

When I looked up, he was staring at me, dazed and worshipful, his chest heaving. I climbed up his body and kissed him along the way, and he wrapped his arms around me, pulling me so close I thought we might fuse into a single entity.

Burying his face in my neck, Andreas held me tight, repeating over and over, "I love you, Samantha. I love you so much."

I smiled into his hair, feeling a rush of something fierce and unnameable. "I know," I whispered. "I know."

I didn't need or want to qualify it. I didn't wish to hedge or joke or run away. I let myself be loved. And it was the best, worst, and most terrifying thing I'd ever done.

[19]

THE INTERACTION BETWEEN
SELECTION AND OTHER FORCES

Samantha

The first thing I noticed when I woke up—before the angle of light cutting through the curtain or the ache in my thighs or the fact that the sheets were twisted around my naked torso—was the absence of his body next to mine. The space he'd occupied only hours before had cooled, leaving behind the faintest indentation that still smelled like him.

Everything else was generic morning. The city noise beyond the window, the dust motes floating in a sunbeam, my sudden and urgent need to pee. Surrendering, I rushed into his bathroom, did my business, and then washed my hands. Eyeballing the mouthwash by the sink, I gave my mouth a quick rinse just to escape the taste of my own morning breath.

Then I returned to the bed and stared up at the ceiling for a long time, searching for cracks in the paint, the slow revolutions of the aforementioned dust motes, the trajectory of my own thoughts as they immediately turned on themselves like a pack of rabid dogs.

Regret was the first to strike. Followed quickly by guilt, then worry, then—just as I was about to slip into a full shame spiral—desire, curling itself around the rest like a python and squeezing until everything else was quiet.

Last night had been perfect, which was the problem. Not perfect in the Hollywood sense, with slo-mo kisses and roses and orchestral music, but perfect in the sense that it was exactly what I'd wanted, and had been afraid to want for months. I'd let him in, literally and metaphorically. I hadn't tried to self-sabotage. I'd just let go. And in retrospect, it was scary.

In the clean light of morning, I could already feel the cognitive dissonance setting in. My body was still humming, every nerve ending thrumming with the memory of his hands, his kisses, the way he said, *I love you.* But my brain— treacherous evolutionary relic that it was—wanted to know what came next. Would he act like nothing happened? Would he freak out? Would I?

I pulled the covers up to my chin and stared at the wall, half hoping the answers would be written there in the negative space between the bookshelf and the window. No such luck.

One thing was for certain, we needed to have a serious conversation. In fact, we needed to have a Serious Conversation—proper name—before things between us escalated in any direction.

The sound of approaching footsteps made me freeze. I was, to put it mildly, not dressed for company. Shirtless, in my underwear, hair sticking to my cheek in a way that suggested a minor wrestling match with the pillow, I debated whether I had enough time to find my T-shirt before he arrived. But the footsteps drew closer, and then the door swung open with a small but definite click.

Andreas stood in the doorway holding a tray.

He looked neither sheepish nor awkward. In fact, he looked devastatingly put together. Black pants, olive-green shirt, hair styled to perfection, skin clear and a little glowy. Euro-chic was back with a vengeance.

Andreas balanced utensils, a bowl of fruit, and a toasted bagel with cream cheese on the tray. Incredibly, there was a bright green takeaway cup from Central Grounds, my favorite. The detail made my chest ache.

Smiling slyly, he crossed the room, moving with his usual predatory grace, and set the tray on the nightstand next to me. "I hope you are not awake only because I was too loud in the kitchen."

My voice came out groggy. "I didn't hear anything. I mean, except now." I pushed myself up on one elbow and immediately regretted it, needing to yank the sheets up to cover myself. "Did you, uh, make this yourself?" *What? What was I even saying? Did he make a toasted bagel with cream cheese himself?* GET IT TOGETHER.

"I know how to toast a bagel," he said, deadpan. "But I admit, the coffee is not my creation."

He stood next to the bed, looking down at me, the corners of his mouth clearly suppressing a smile. His eyes roved over my face, my shoulders, the line of my collarbones, and I could feel the blush start at my neck and race upward.

I gave him my very best nonchalant nod, trying to play it cool. "Is this you trying to be the more generous one in this relationship?" This was in reference to Andreas's list of unattractive qualities about himself, and I hoped he considered it a flirty joke rather than an airing of grievances.

His entire face lit up, giving me the sense he appreciated my callback to our conversation in the hospital's VIP lounge. "Even if I wanted to be the more generous one, even if that was a thought in my head about you, I think I would have to spend a lifetime trying to rebalance the equation after what you did to me last night."

Oh. Well. Ahem.

Smiling softly, eyes dancing, Andreas sat on the edge of the bed, leaned in, and pressed a kiss to the side of my neck. The contact was brief but devastating, a spark that lit up every nerve ending beneath every inch of my skin.

He lingered, lips just barely grazing my skin, sending another series of sparks through my body, then whispered in my ear, "I think I am addicted to you."

The way he said it—dead serious, like he'd spent the entire morning contemplating it—made me freeze.

The silence stretched for a second, and then he leaned back and studied me. Andreas's smile grew the longer he looked, teeth bright and sharp, and before I understood his intentions, he lifted the covers to peek underneath.

"What are you doing?" I said, reflexively grabbing for the comforter and yanking it back.

He cocked an eyebrow. "I want to see where else you're blushing."

I snorted, but the blush got worse, which he obviously noticed.

He slid his hand under the covers, dragging them down to my waist, and ran his palm over my bare stomach, fingers tracing the line of my ribs. I shivered. Andreas leaned over me, bracing himself on one arm. The other hand continued to stroke my skin, mapping out the landscape of me like he was committing it to memory.

I tried to summon the resolve I'd felt just minutes earlier, the part of me that had sworn up and down to myself that we would have a Serious Conversation before any further escalation. But that part was nowhere to be found. It had been vaporized by the touch of his hand and the scent of coffee and the relentless, idiotic pounding of my own heart.

He slipped his fingers under the waistband of my underwear and tugged gently.

"What are you doing?" I said, voice barely above a whisper.

He looked me dead in the eye. "I want to taste you."

I gaped at him, caught between arousal and surprise. "That's not a very vegan breakfast," I said. Apparently, the only words available to me were snarky.

He smiled, slow and dangerous, and cupped me firmly over my underwear. "I will always make an exception for this."

Once more, he hooked his fingers around the elastic and pulled. Not hard, but with enough conviction that my hips lifted off the mattress, surrendering. He dragged the underwear down and off, tossing it aside. Then he pushed my knees apart, climbing on to the bed and settling between them.

Immediately, Andreas ducked his head and ran his tongue over me, slow and deliberate. I grabbed a fistful of the comforter he'd removed, white-knuckled, and arched my back slightly. He took his time, alternating between gentle licks and firm pressure, teasing and retreating until I was panting.

And I watched him between my legs. Andreas in his button-down designer suit shirt, perfect hair, glowing skin, and heavily lidded green eyes. The dichotomy of his perfectly put-together veneer licking me beyond the expanse of my naked breasts and stomach, paired with the wet, sloppy, hungry sounds he made, felt overwhelming. It was too much. He was too much.

Abruptly, he pushed two fingers inside, curling them just so, and my stomach tensed even as my legs fell open wider, as though he'd found the hidden override switch in my brain, a button he could press which made me a brainless sex toy for his use and pleasure.

Gradually, I became aware of my own noises—high-pitched, breathless, desperate—but I had zero control over them. Andreas played my body like a damn instrument, and I happily moaned along to his tune.

He looked up, eyes dark and hot, and he lifted his lips just enough to say, "I missed this." His gaze lowered to my open legs and he watched his fingers disappear inside my body. Then he bent and sucked my clit into his mouth.

If last night had been a revelation, this was a religious experience. I lost all sense of time, space, self. I was a single point of sensation, suspended in the air, every muscle locked and trembling. And when I came, it was all at once. Sharp and loud and messy.

He licked and loved and held me through it, mouth never leaving me, fingers still working inside. When it was finally too much, I grabbed his hair and tried to push him away, but he only laughed and licked me again, slow and soft, until I gasped.

Only then did he crawl back up the bed, kissing my stomach, my ribs, my collarbone, and then lay beside me, burying his face in the crook of my neck and inhaling deeply.

We lay like that for a long time, neither of us saying anything. I stared at the ceiling, waiting for my breathing to return to normal, and wondered how it was possible that this person, who, at one time, had been the most infuriating force in my life, was now the only thing I wanted.

Yet, I knew things were still left unsaid between us. The Serious Conversation had been neglected. In the back of my mind, I knew I should be worried. *He could hurt me again.*

Just as this thought entered my consciousness, Andreas lifted his head from my neck, eyes fixed on me, and said, "You are so beautiful, it hurts sometimes to look at you."

His tone was almost clinical, like he'd just discovered a new mathematical constant and wanted to make sure I understood its significance.

I stared at him, feeling too many things, and therefore unable to name any one of them individually.

* * *

THIS PARTICULAR MEXICAN RESTAURANT, where Kaitlyn and I often met for drinks and amazing food, went hard for California cantina meets Brooklyn chic. Exposed brick, succulents in recycled mason jars, tables made out of repurposed gymnasium floors.

And the drinks didn't pretend. The tequila to mixer ratio was legit. Our server had already delivered two margaritas the size of human skulls, sugar crusting the rim in lieu of salt.

Kaitlyn watched me over her glass, eyes sharp with cross-examining energy. "Let me get this straight. You didn't have the serious conversation?"

We'd arrived just ten minutes ago, but I'd already filled her in on all the need-to-know details. And since she was my BFF, she needed to know *all* details.

I sipped my drink. The margarita tasted like lime and I didn't at all mind. "No, I didn't."

She set her glass down so decisively it thudded. "You just let him go down on you and then you ate breakfast, flirted, gave him a hand job in the shower, and then went to work?"

I didn't even have the decency to blush. "Why am I so weak for this man?" It was a serious question.

"It sounds like he's good at giving head." Kaitlyn, ever the queen of deadpan, took another swig through her straw.

Our chips and salsa arrived, set down with a flourish by our waiter, who glanced between us. "Your mains will be out soon. Can I get you two ladies anything else?"

We both shook our heads, mumbled thanks, and he was off.

I picked up a chip, snapped it in two, and said, "He's just . . . so fucking good at it. It's like, it feels like he enjoys it more than I do. He said he's addicted to me, but I think it's the opposite." Thinking about it now, I nearly shorted out my own brain. The memory was so vivid—Andreas's mouth, his hands, the way he operated like a very patient, very determined scientist, mapping out my pleasure centers. Except, he clearly was already in possession of the blueprints and was simply showing off.

Kaitlyn gave me a sly side-eye. "Maybe you're addicted to each other."

I tossed my hands up without dropping the chip, then let them thump on the table. "What am I going to do?" I wanted to laugh at myself, but it came out as a groan.

"That's easy," Kaitlyn said. "Take him to a place where you can't get naked and then have the serious talk."

I blinked at her. "That's genius. Why didn't I think of that?"

"You're in it, you know? It's hard to see solutions when you're deep in the love pit."

"Love pit? More like the sex dungeon." I lifted my eyes to the ceiling, as if divine intervention might drift down through the ductwork. "I can't talk about this anymore. I am so disappointed in myself. No matter how deep I am, I should be more responsible than this."

Kaitlyn reached across the table and nudged my hand. "Sex complicates everything. Don't be so hard on yourself. Just, have the talk sooner rather than later."

I nodded. "I can't believe this is all I can think about given what happened with my legal team yesterday."

I'd already told Kaitlyn about the phone call—the one where my lawyer laid out, in their signature giddy-dour affect, how they now had not just circumstantial, but smoking-gun evidence of Henrik's guilt framing my father. The news had been like a shot of dopamine and bleach at the same time. I was elated, but also hollowed out. There's only so many events you can metabolize before you become numb.

Kaitlyn wiped salsa from her lip. "What are you going to do? I mean, now that you have proof it was Andreas's brother."

I didn't answer right away. I loaded a chip with salsa, too much, so it collapsed in my hand. "Well, with the affidavit and sworn statement of Dr. Gounter—you know, the doctor who faked my father's cause of death on the certificate? With his testimony and this proof, my legal team thinks it's more than enough to open a murder investigation. It's also plenty to contest the civil suit Oskar Kristiansen won against my father's estate after my dad died."

Kaitlyn furrowed her brow. "But, if you contest the civil suit, doesn't that mean your father's estate will have ownership of his shares again?"

"Yes."

She gave me a look as though to say, *And you don't see the problem?*

Narrowing her eyes, she spelled it out. "But you're no longer your father's daughter. You signed away those rights when you let Andreas adopt you. Since Andreas adopted you, you no longer have a right to those shares."

[20]

CONFLICT AND COOPERATION

Samantha

"That's right." I nodded, confirming Kaitlyn's statement. If there existed a Guinness world record for most times a single person could regret a complicated adoption, I was surely in the running.

I sipped my margarita and let the tequila sting.

Kaitlyn crunched a chip. "So, who inherits your father's shares once you hand over all this evidence to the police and overturn the civil suit? And what about Oskar's shares, since it looks like Oskar is the one who committed the felony associated with the business, which triggers the whole removal or freezing of shares clause, or whatever. You know, can't you do to Oskar's shares what Oskar did to your dad's?"

I shook my head, dizzy with the logic loop. "I don't know. This is a strange situation and there's no precedent for this. It'll be up to the judge, what to do, if Oskar is ultimately implicated in framing my dad. It will also depend on what Henrik does after he's—God willing—finally arrested." I drained a quarter of my margarita, then licked sugar off my thumb.

Kaitlyn arched her brows. "You think Henrik will be arrested?"

"Definitely. If not for murder right now, then for fraud, and for framing my father."

"Then back to your father's shares. Who will inherit them?"

I slumped back in my seat. "According to my legal team, they will follow the

509

line of succession that they should've followed had they been part of his estate. They would've gone to my mother. Since I'm no longer in the picture—"

"Due to the adoption."

"Yes, due to the adoption, then they would've gone to my mother's closest relative, which is now my grandpa."

Kaitlyn gave a low whistle. "What do you think he'll do with them?"

I shrugged, the motion feeling heavy. "I don't honestly know."

She leaned in. "So, you could either keep quiet about Henrik framing your dad, and keep billions of dollars in Genetix shares. Or, you can turn in the evidence and the shares will go to your grandfather."

"That's right."

"And you've decided to turn in the evidence?"

"Yes."

Kaitlyn shook her head, setting down her chip. "That's . . . something else."

We sat quietly. It was the rarest of silences, where neither person feels pressured to fill it. The margaritas melted. The table salsa congealed at the edges. I picked at a spot in the lacquer of the tabletop and wondered whether it would have made a difference if my father had lived. Would I have felt less like an imposter? Or more?

"It just sucks"—Kaitlyn broke into my thoughts—"that if you'd been able to figure all this out before Andreas adopted you, then the shares would be yours, fair and square."

"But I never would have figured this out if I hadn't inherited the shares and gained access to the internal files at Genetix. Once I had access, discovering that Henrik worked in my father's department as an intern and had been granted access by Oskar to the customer dataset was easy. It was also easy to retrieve old emails and text messages between Genetix work accounts. Once I passed all that over, my legal team did the rest." I scooped salsa onto a chip and watched it drip, feeling the words pool in the bottom of my stomach.

"It's a lose-lose situation," Kaitlyn said, chewing with zero self-consciousness. "No matter what you do. Either you clear your father's name and prove your mom was right and then lose the shares, or you keep quiet, don't prove your parents' innocence, and keep the shares. I don't know what I would do."

"Yes, you do. You would clear your parents' names." I crunched the chip and, through a mouthful, said, "In fact, when I made this decision, I asked myself, 'What would Kaitlyn do?'"

She lifted her glass in salute, then drank. "I'm just impressed you made the decision so fast."

"I didn't though." I swallowed before continuing. "I made it months ago."

Kaitlyn frowned. "What? When?"

"When I agreed to the adoption. I knew, by agreeing, I'd no longer be in line to inherit the shares if I was able to prove my parents were innocent."

She laughed. "That's right, I forgot you were a lawyer."

I groaned. "I was never a lawyer. I went to law school."

"And you passed the New York state bar."

I let my head thud gently against the exposed brick behind me. "Kaitlyn."

She grinned and chased it with a slurp of the margarita. "What if you asked your grandpa to give you the shares after he inherits them?"

"He can't just give them to me, a nonrelative. Gifts that large are taxed, and I would have no way to pay the taxes."

"Too bad he can't adopt you, then he could put them in a trust and you could inherit them."

I squinted at her, margarita glass halfway to my lips. "No. I . . . if he asks me what to do with the shares, I'm going to tell him I'd like for him to give them to the employees."

Kaitlyn's mouth dropped open. "Are you serious?"

"I think it's what my dad would've wanted, you know?"

She raised a brow. "You think?"

"Yes." I let the word hang, then rolled it around, thinking of my dad, his total disinterest in money, his inability to understand why people needed more than one kind of car or any television larger than twenty-two inches. "He wasn't big on generational wealth, didn't believe it was appropriate for kids to inherit millions or billions of dollars. He was very much a . . . proletariat, if I'm being honest."

"That explains a lot about you."

I smiled, a little flattered.

"I still think you should ask your grandpa to adopt you, though."

Picking up another chip, I asked, "Why?"

"For lots of obvious reasons. You two are family, and are finally starting to act like it. Plus, then if you do finally forgive Andreas, you won't be sleeping with your adoptive father."

I choked on the chip, coughed, and wiped a napkin over my lips. "When you put it that way . . ." I lobbed a corn chip at her, which bounced off her shoulder and landed in her cleavage. She plucked it out, dipped it in salsa, and ate it.

"Not to bring the conversation full circle again," she said, "but what would it take for you to forgive Andreas?"

I propped my chin in my hand and tried to answer honestly. "I think I have forgiven him, I just don't . . ."

"What?"

"I don't trust him yet." I wrinkled my nose. "He's too sneaky, and good at being sneaky. He's calculating and always ten steps ahead of me."

"You need Andreas to stop plotting against you."

"Stop plotting against me, but also stop plotting for me." I lifted my margarita for a sip.

She crinkled her brow. "What does that mean?"

"He bought his brothers out of their shares—well, most of the shares—without telling me, just so he could get my proxy approved without issue at the shareholder meeting."

Kaitlyn's face lit up. "That's a grand gesture if I ever heard of one."

"Yes, but I want to be informed. I want to be consulted. And I want to decide for myself about myself."

"And you don't trust him to let you decide?"

I debated how to answer before settling on, "I trust him to want, and do, what he thinks is best for me at the expense of my free will."

Kaitlyn nodded, wide-eyed, features stark. "He's really taking this adoptive father business too far." Her deadpan was a force of nature.

I whipped another chip at her. "Okay, okay. No more dad jokes."

* * *

TARA DROPPED me at the curb in front of Andreas's apartment, just as the streetlights flickered on and the afterglow of sunset turned the façades a shade of oxidized gold. I greeted the doorman and then stepped inside the building. The lobby was cavernous and quiet, except for the scrape of my sneakers on polished marble. I pressed the elevator call button, feeling the weight of my take-out bag, my backpack, and every unresolved conversation yet to happen tonight.

The elevator arrived with a polite ding. I stepped inside and, as the doors closed, took stock of my reflection in the mirrored panel. I looked fine, but I didn't feel fine. Shrugging at myself, I pressed the button for Andreas's floor.

Halfway up, my phone buzzed. The display read: "GRANDPA CARL." I considered letting it go to voicemail—putting off another (potentially) emotionally fraught conversation until tomorrow—but I eventually swiped answer.

"Hello?" I said, voice soft so it wouldn't echo in the metal box.

"Sammy? It's Grandpa."

The sound of his voice, all New England vowels and world-weariness, made my chest compress.

"Yes. Hi! What's up?"

"I received a call from your legal team today."

I cringed, wishing I could have crawled through the phone lines and prepared him with a hot chocolate and a blanket. "That's right. I knew they'd be calling you. I texted you last night and gave you a heads-up."

The elevator doors slid open to Andreas's floor. I stepped out, phone pressed to my ear, and used my thumb to open the door. I balanced the call, the food, and my nerves as I made my way inside.

"Sammy, they're saying that I'm going to inherit your shares. That can't be right."

"That is right, Grandpa. Those shares are yours." I dropped my bag and coat onto the table just inside the entryway, then toed off my shoes.

I heard a chair scrape in the next room, the faint clink of glass, and then saw Andreas moving at the periphery. He was at the circular table in the living room, laptop open, hair damp like he'd just showered. He looked up at me, eyebrow raised in question, but didn't interrupt.

I mouthed, *It's my grandpa*, and he instantly re-sorted his face into neutral.

My grandfather said, "They're yours. They belong to you. You are Sylvia and Lawrence's daughter. Who am I?"

I moved into the living room, set the takeout on the table, and paced in slow, deliberate circles while I marshaled my words. "Not in the eyes of the law, I'm not their daughter anymore."

Andreas was heading toward me, a gravity I could feel across the room. He closed the distance and kissed me lightly on the cheek.

Grandfather's voice got sharp. "Is it because that Kristiansen boy adopted you?"

I could feel Andreas's entire body tense with the words "Kristiansen boy," but I ignored it. "Yes. But if Andreas hadn't adopted me, I never would've been given access to the documents that proved Dad's innocence, and that Mom was right all along. I couldn't have done any of this if I hadn't agreed to the adoption."

"I hate that you're giving up those shares. Why can't you keep them?" I heard him sigh on the other side of the line, the sound familiar enough to conjure a childhood memory of being walked to the park and fed fist-sized slices of bakery bread.

"Because we have to hand everything over to the police. Once it all comes out, you will petition to have the civil suit overturned and the shares will be yours. Mom and Dad deserve to be vindicated. Once, uh—" I stopped. Andreas stood right in front of me, his arms at his sides, his frown intense.

He'd listened to every syllable, and I realized that this was the first time Andreas had heard any of this information from me. His eyes told me he had opinions.

"Grandpa, let me call you back. Give me an hour. Okay?"

"Okay, sweetie. I'll talk to you in an hour." He hung up.

I dropped my hand to my side and straightened.

"What the hell are you talking about?" he said. "You are giving up the shares? After everything, you're giving them to your grandfather?"

I exhaled, all the air leaving me in a single whoosh. "Listen, I have proof—as of last night, remember the call I received after dinner? I have proof your brother Henrik forged my father's signature on the data sale documents, and that Henrik—and potentially Oskar—were involved in framing him. Once I hand over this proof, Henrik will be arrested for fraud, and then the dominoes will start to fall."

He blinked twice, frown deepening, jaw tight. "Why would you hand this information over to the police?"

I stared at him. "Are you kidding? How else can Henrik be punished? I think he killed my dad."

Andreas responded instantly: "Yes. Obviously!"

That made me stop. I stood very still. "What do you mean 'obviously'? Do you know something you're not sharing with me?"

He paced, hands flexing at his sides. "I have no hard evidence, if that is what you are asking. But who else could it be? Henrik has always been the one to get his hands dirty. It makes sense that it was him."

A cold ripple moved down my back. I didn't think it made me paranoid to worry that Andreas had already set some multistep, 4D scheme in motion, and that by the time the police got involved, Henrik would be in a pine box or the bottom of the Hudson.

Taking a deep breath to calm myself, I said, "Andreas, what did you do? Please tell me you haven't done anything to Henrik."

He stopped and looked at me, face unreadable. "Nothing directly to him. Yet."

"What does that mean?" My voice sounded unsteady.

"The pieces are all in place," he said. "He took your dad's life. Of course he should suffer."

. . . WHAT?

My frustration suddenly detonated. "This is the problem! This is why we will never work!"

His eyes widened and I could see my words genuinely startled him. Andreas reached for me, but I twisted away, heading for the hallway that led to my old bedroom.

He followed, two steps behind. "What? What did I do? Are you saying you do not want Henrik to pay for his crimes?"

I yanked open the closet, grabbed my suitcase, tossed it onto the bed. Andreas stood in the doorway, face pinched with confusion and anger. Then he rushed forward, moving to block me from the closet and grabbing the handle of my bag. "Wait. Talk to me. Yell at me, but please, talk to me."

I growled. "You can't keep making decisions for me."

Setting my bag down on the ground, he said, "I—I do not think of it that way. I am merely keeping your hands clean."

"But I want your hands clean, too!" My voice was harsh, the words ricocheting off the bare walls, and I told myself to calm down. Gripping my forehead, I tried again. "Of course I want Henrik to pay for what he did, and I have concrete evidence that will ensure he does pay. He will be arrested and he will be tried and he will go to jail. But we are handing all the evidence over to the police so that we can do this above board. I *need* to prove my parents' innocence. If you go all vigilante on me, and Henrik is punished outside the bounds of the law, how am I supposed to prove that my dad didn't commit fraud and that my mom wasn't a hysterical, paranoid fool? I can't. Not unless we do this through the legal system."

He listened, breathing hard, and then said, "But if you do that, you will lose all those shares. They belong to you."

I met his gaze, steady as I could. "But they don't belong to me. I did nothing to earn them. I had nothing to do with the creation or the success of Genetix."

He was nearly vibrating with incredulity. "But your father did. Every success that Genetix has is based on your father's work."

I nodded. "I agree. But his work is not my work. I have my own research, my own projects. If I become a millionaire or a billionaire, let it be because I've earned it."

Andreas began pacing the room, from the foot of the bed to the window and back. "I don't understand you, Samantha. After everything we have done, everything we have been through. How can you throw it all away? You say those shares do not belong to you, then who do they belong to? Why do they belong to your grandfather more than they belong to you?"

I braced myself for his reaction, drew in a breath, and said, "I don't think they belong to my grandfather more than they belong to me, which is why I'm going to encourage him to sign them over to the employees of Genetix."

He stopped. He stared at me, stunned. "You are going to give the company away?"

I shrugged, though my heart hammered. "It's what my dad would have done. He believed in science for the public good. It's not about the money. It's about vindicating him. Clearing my mother's name. Restoring what was stolen."

He started to laugh, but it was the kind of laugh you heard at funerals—hollow, shocked, a bit dangerous. He ran a hand through his hair, then sat down heavily on the bed, hands folded in his lap.

I gave him space to process. I didn't try to fix his feelings or make him okay with my decision. I waited until his breathing slowed, until his face softened, and then I joined him on the bed, sitting a careful distance away.

Hesitating, I reached out and placed a hand on his back, feeling the tension there. "I hope you can support me in this," I said, voice soft but unwavering. "As you said, I made this decision a long time ago. And I hope you can agree this is my decision to make, not yours, not anyone else's. I know my own mind, and I feel very strongly that this is the right thing to do."

He nodded, almost imperceptibly, then looked at me out of the corner of his eye. "You have already decided. Nothing I say will make a difference."

"Yes. It has always been more important to me to prove my father's innocence and my mother's stability than it has been for me to inherit those shares. At first, sure, I wanted to believe that they belonged to me. But it didn't take long for me to realize, they didn't. My priority has always been for the truth to come out."

He studied his hands for a while, then finally exhaled, a long, slow release. "I will support you," he said. "But I do not understand it. Not fully."

"That's all I can ask." I tucked my clasped hands beneath my chin, afraid to get my hopes up quite yet.

He gave a wry smile. To me, it seemed half sad, half proud. Andreas reached out to touch my hands. "Okay."

His touch gave me the confidence to add, "Whatever plan or plot you have in motion against Henrik, I want you to put a stop to it."

He stiffened, then nodded. "If that is what you truly wish, then that is what I will do."

"Do you promise?" I squeezed his hand with both of mine.

"Yes. I promise." He squeezed me back, but sounded defeated.

I narrowed my eyes. "No loopholes? Nothing you're not telling me? Do I need to get you to sign a piece of paper or a contract? Is there anything I'm missing or words you're using to make me misunderstand?"

He met my gaze, full on. "No," he said, voice stark. "I promised I would stop my plan and I will. I will do what you want because you are right, this should be your decision and only your decision. I will . . . support you."

Relief swept through me, so physical I nearly collapsed. But before I could savor the moment, he added, "And I know that if I make any attempt to trick you or manipulate you or try to force you to see things my way, it would only jeopardize our relationship and our newfound trust. I would never do anything to jeopardize your trust ever again."

Something in the center of my chest melted. Acting on instinct, I leaned over. I kissed him on the cheek. "Thank you."

He tightened his hold before I could draw away. "You should know, Henrik might be stupid and violent, but he does have eyes and ears inside of Genetix and elsewhere. If you found evidence against him, no doubt he already knows about it. And since he is stupid and violent, this knowledge will make him desperate. You need to be careful. Until he is in jail and stripped of monetary resources, you should increase the number of bodyguards following you. And you might want to keep a guard with you inside work from now on. Tara would be a good choice."

I absorbed his statements, the grim weight of them. "Is there anything else I should know?"

He placed his palm on my cheek, gentle. "I do not know if this will help, but he cannot see out of his right eye. Cosmetically, it looks fine, but he lost his vision after a fight in college. I know you take self-defense classes with Tara. If, despite being careful, he manages to grab you, target his right side. He is slow to react when attacks come from the right."

That, at least, I could file away. "Thank you, Andreas."

He pulled me into an embrace, careful not to squeeze too tightly, as if I was fragile and he didn't want to risk damaging the new trust between us.

I pressed my forehead to his and said, "I know you're not happy about this. But knowing that I can trust you makes me very happy."

He smiled, but it looked melancholy. And intensely grumpy. "Well, as long as you are happy."

He sounded grumpy, too. I was not about to fix it.

Instead, I patted his chest and said, "You need to get used to not plotting for me. Or against me for that matter."

He rolled his eyes. "I would never plot against you."

I gave him my best skeptical glare.

He tilted his head side to side, as if considering, then said, "I might plot to get you naked, to do things to your body, but never to manipulate you or hurt you in a way that means you would have difficulty trusting me again."

I laughed, a real laugh. It felt good. "And you can't plot on my behalf either. Not unless you consult me first and receive my consent."

"Fine." He sighed, long-suffering, resigned, and stood up. Giving me his back, he paced a few steps away. "I guess now would be a good time to tell you that Roman instructed me to wear gray sweatpants whenever you are around."

I blinked, confused. "Wait. Why would Roman tell you to wear gray sweatpants whenever I'm around?"

Andreas turned, looked down at himself, then back up. "Roman claimed gray sweatpants and tight T-shirts would make me irresistible to you. In the interest of full disclosure, I thought you should know."

I looked at his fitted black T-shirt, and then at the gray sweatpants that did, in fact, leave absolutely nothing to the imagination. And I realized that Roman had absolutely nailed it.

Throwing my head back, I laughed. Chess grand masters and their schemes.

Even so, I would definitely be sending Roman Buckley a thank-you note. *For science.* And for everything else.

$$[\ 21 \ ]$$

PHENOTYPIC EVOLUTION

Samantha

Breakfast at Andreas's was always an event, but this morning it felt like the prelude to something cataclysmic.

I sat cross-legged at the kitchen island on a stool, watching Andreas as he juggled two pans, a French press, and a phone call conducted entirely in French. Even after so much time living here, I still couldn't figure out which language he spoke at any given time. Sometimes, I wondered if he switched languages mid-sentence just to mess with me.

Last night, I'd called my grandfather back, as promised. I'd sat in the spare bedroom with the lights off, phone pressed to my ear, and explained, in exquisite detail, how and why the Genetix shares would soon be his. I told him about the affidavits and the recording, the probable cause for the police to start digging, the likely outcome for Henrik (and hopefully Oskar), and how, with any luck, within a few months, my parents' names would be cleared.

I also told him that I wanted the Genetix employees to inherit the shares eventually, because they were the ones who made the company what it was. It took nearly an hour for him to process the idea. There was a lot of silence on the other end, broken only by the sound of him pouring bourbon over ice and muttering "Goddamn" every few minutes.

Eventually, he said that it made him proud but also sad, because he didn't want me to give up anything.

I reminded him I'd never earned any of it. That was the point.

After a long pause, he said, "Well, the shares will go where the law tells them to go. Unless you want me to adopt you again." He was only half joking. I could hear it in his voice.

Before we hung up, he told me he would make me the proxy for his shares, so I could vote at the meetings until all the dust settled.

Honestly, he and Andreas would probably get along great. They shared a belief in the power of arbitrary declarations while ignoring inconvenient realities.

"Eggs on toast," Andreas announced, setting a plate in front of me with a flourish. "And coffee, just how you like it."

"Black as hell, hot as possible, and not a single molecule of actual nutrition." I grinned, picking up the cup and smelling it. "Thank you. This all looks delicious," I said, because it really did. He had a knack for arranging food in a way that made it look like it was plated by a culinary school graduate, even when it consisted of whatever he'd found in the fridge. I picked up my fork and immediately started eating.

Andreas sat down across from me, seasoning his own bowl of quinoa, tofu, and avocado with sriracha. He didn't look at me while he did it, but I felt his attention anyway.

We ate in companionable silence for a while, interrupted only by the occasional clink of fork on plate or the hum of city traffic beyond the window. I tried to focus on the food, but my mind kept drifting to last night, to the feel of his body curled around mine as we fell asleep in his bed.

I wondered if now would be a good time for us to have the Serious Conversation. He seemed to have accepted my decision about prosecuting Henrik and the shares. We'd slept together last night and cuddled, but did nothing else. I didn't have the post-sexy-times fog muddling my mind.

Yes. *The time is now!*

But just as I opened my mouth to begin, Andreas set down his fork, wiped his mouth with a napkin, and said in the most casual, morning-conversation voice, "Are you on birth control?"

I choked on air. Not figuratively—literally. I had to take a huge gulp of coffee.

"Yes," I said, once my airway was clear. "I am on birth control."

He nodded. "I do not have any STDs. Do you?"

"No." I reared back even as I answered honestly.

He reached for his coffee, sipped, then asked, "Do I need to buy condoms?"

It finally clicked that he was running through a sex-prep checklist. Gaping at him, I wanted to laugh. But I also wanted to crawl under the table. Who discussed these things over breakfast?

Eventually, I managed to say, "That's up to you."

He gave me a flat stare. "Do you want me to use a condom when we have sex?"

"You're assuming a lot," I said, trying for indignation but landing somewhere closer to mortification.

"Am I?" he asked, raising an eyebrow.

I wilted. "Actually, no. You're not." And that was the truth.

He laughed, the sound so unexpected and bright it startled me. I threw my napkin at him, but he caught it without looking.

My entire body was flushed. I fidgeted with my fork, restless. Setting it down, I decided that if Andreas could bring up condoms and birth control and us eventually having intercourse over breakfast, then there existed no reason for me to keep dillydallying about the Serious Conversation.

I straightened my spine. "Because I am trying to learn from previous mistakes, I just want to say for the record that you and I are together, boyfriend/girlfriend, strings attached. Agree?"

He didn't hesitate. "One hundred percent."

I nodded, feeling a weird, giddy flutter in my chest, but also strangely deflated since I'd hyped the conversation up so much in my head and it had been incredibly anticlimactic.

But since we were bringing up unusual breakfast topics, I added, "And once all of this is over and the dust settles, I'm going to ask my grandfather to adopt me."

He considered this, then said, "You should start moving forward with the adoption as soon as possible. And you should put some security on your grandfather. As soon as Tobias and Henrik realize your grandfather will be the one taking over those shares, he will become a target. And if it is really important to you that the employees are the ones to inherit the shares, you should move forward with the adoption as soon as possible to establish the line of inheritance."

I gawked at him and how he'd taken everything in stride. "Uh. Thank you. It's really helpful when you share your thoughts with me instead of keeping them to yourself. I just want to let you know, I appreciate you."

He smiled, a little wicked. "Even if I'm sneaky?"

"You say that like it's a bad thing," I shot back, shrugging.

The corner of his mouth tugged upward.

I glanced at my phone and realized I was running later than I wanted. Shoveling food into my mouth, I stood up. "I have to go."

"Are you running late for work? It is not yet seven," he said.

"No, I just want to get there early so I can talk to security about getting clearance for Tara," I said, grabbing my bag and heading for the door.

Before I could escape, Andreas caught my hand and pulled me down into his lap. The force of it made me laugh, but also set off a cascade of nerves from my scalp to my toes.

He moved his hand under my skirt, up my thigh, and cupped me over my underwear, fingers pressing gently but insistently. He leaned in, his lips at my ear, and whispered, "I love you."

It sent a lightning bolt straight through my brain stem. "I love you," I said, and the words felt truer than anything I'd ever spoken.

He grinned against my jaw, slow and smug, and I realized—impressed—that he'd just gotten me to admit it out loud by turning me on. He'd engineered the whole thing.

I tried to scowl at him, but my resolve melted when he started rubbing small, lazy circles with his finger.

"I thought you said you wouldn't plot against me," I said.

"But sometimes you like it," he murmured, not even a little bit sorry. He hooked a finger in my underwear and tugged. "Take these off."

I hesitated for a second, but then slid them down my legs, kicking them off.

He traced a line up my inner thigh, then said, "Unbutton your shirt and unhook your bra."

I did as he asked, working the buttons open with trembling fingers. I unclasped the bra—front closure, thank you very much—and let it fall away, baring myself to him. He ran his hands over my ribs, my stomach, then cupped my breasts, squeezing gently.

"I like that this opens in the front," he said, voice thick with approval.

He bent forward and kissed the swell of one breast, then the other, licking and biting lightly at my nipples until they ached. He kept one hand on the center of my back and the other between my legs, teasing my clit with soft, deliberate strokes.

"Open your legs wider for me." Andreas breathed the words against my nipple between sucking kisses.

I obeyed, heat flushing through me. He slid two fingers inside, curling them perfectly, and rubbed my clit with his thumb, all while nipping and tonguing my nipples like he was starving.

Andreas's hips rocked beneath me, and I could feel the hard line of his cock pressing into my bare bottom through his thin sweatpants.

"This is what you do to me. Can you feel how hard I am?" His voice was scraped raw, like he'd sanded the words against his own teeth just to get them out.

My only answer was an embarrassing, involuntary whimper. The second it escaped my throat I felt my face go hot, but it didn't matter. The look in his eyes said he'd already filed the noise away in some secret compartment of his brain and planned to weaponize it at the earliest opportunity.

"When will you let me make love to you?" he asked, and the way he said it— low, reverent, so unlike his usual clinical detachment—nearly fried my higher reasoning. He punctuated the question with a twist of his wrist, clever fingers curling in a way that made every muscle in my body seize and then liquefy. For a moment, I couldn't remember the English language, let alone the rationale I had ten seconds ago for not just climbing him like a tree right here, right now.

"Not yet," I choked out.

He made a guttural sound, forehead collapsing onto my sternum. His hand never broke rhythm, but his mouth was insatiable—kissing, biting, licking, and suckling my skin like he'd die if he didn't consume every square inch.

"Soon," I amended, and it came out as a kind of sob.

"You have no idea what you do to me," he said, and there was so much longing —and desperation—in his voice. "I want inside you. It is all I can think about. I cannot concentrate. You are all I think about."

My mind became a blank page with only his name scrawled on it in block letters. I was barely even aware of the apartment, the city, the fact that I was half naked, sitting on his lap, legs spread for his fingers, my tits pressed against Andreas's mouth.

He kept stroking me, relentless. His thigh was hard under my knees, his erection pressing insistently against my bottom. His grip on me was unyielding, anchoring me while my body pitched and rolled with every calculated move of his hand.

Abruptly, I seized the collar of his shirt, yanking him up to meet my mouth, kissing him with a kind of feral need that surprised even me. He kissed me back, teeth and tongue, one hand fisted in my hair while the other still worked its magic between my legs. I could taste the coffee on his lips, the faint ghost of toothpaste, and something else—something dark and hungry that hinted at the part of him he never showed anyone else.

He broke the kiss long enough to say, "Do you trust me?"

The question startled me, mostly because I realized I did. I trusted him more than I'd ever trusted anyone, and I was terrified by it. But I nodded, unable to do anything else with the way my body craved his touch. I tried wiggling my hips, rocking them, needing more friction.

"Sit still," he ordered, voice muffled against my neck.

Somewhere in the distance I heard the click of a fork hitting the floor, the crash of a plate sliding against tile, but it didn't matter. The only thing in the universe was the pulse of his tongue against my breasts, the clever, playful pressure of his mouth, the way his hands held me to keep me from bucking off the chair. I felt every breath he took, every shift of his jaw, and my vision went white at the edges as the sensations built and built, a slow, inexorable tide.

I was so close I could taste it. So close I actually clawed at his back, desperate. He must have sensed it, because he doubled down, sucking hard at just the right spot, fingers matching the rhythm, and I came so hard I nearly blacked out. My body arched off his lap, toes pointing, fingers tangling in his hair, and shirt, and whatever else I could grab on to.

When the world came back into focus, I was sprawled in his lap, legs shaking, chest heaving. My face was hot, my lips numb, and my whole body felt like it had been scooped out and filled with fire.

Andreas held me there, arms banded around my waist, face pressed against my chest like he'd run a marathon and needed to catch his breath. He was hard as a rock under me, and I could feel him through his sweatpants. But he didn't move to do anything about it. He simply held me, like he wanted to keep me safe, and with him.

Eventually, Andreas kissed my collarbone, then my jaw, then finally my lips— soft, almost shy. I kissed him back, just as soft, just as shy.

When we separated, he grumbled, "I want to keep you here forever."

I laughed lightly and wiggled off his lap, legs wobbly, and started collecting my scattered clothing. He helped, surprisingly gentle, buttoning my shirt for me and smoothing down my hair like I was a doll he had to return to its shelf after playing with me however he liked.

When I was mostly put together, he tipped my chin up and kissed me once more, lingering this time. "I love you," he said, and it didn't sound like a trap or a power move. It sounded like a promise.

"I love you."

"Can't you call in sick?"

Grinning at his tempting offer and the longing in his gaze, I kissed him quickly on the cheek, and said, "No." Then, darting away, I suggested over my shoulder, "Why don't you go take a cold shower?"

He groaned.

I called back, "Accept your punishment!"

"For what?"

"You know what you did!"

I heard him curse in Italian behind me, loud and frustrated.

                                [22]

                SPECIES AND SPECIATION

                         Samantha

It was a Wednesday and I sat in my office at the desk, deep in the groove where
productivity meets intense focus and critical concentration.

And then someone knocked on my door.

I jumped up so fast I nearly upset my coffee. Tara, who had been sitting in the
spare chair reading a battered paperback and not even pretending to be anything
but bored, raised an eyebrow at me.

"It must be Dmitry," I said, pressing a hand against my chest to calm my racing
heart. "He messaged earlier. He has some news that can't be sent via text message,
so I told him to come over before lunch."

Tara's expression remained unchanged. She set down her book and crossed to
the door.

A few months ago, I would have been self-conscious about being chaperoned
by my own private security detail at work. Not anymore. After the police reviewed
security footage from the building—showing Henrik making multiple attempts to
approach, shout at, and otherwise terrify me—they'd made it a point to recommend
increased protection. In an uncharacteristically generous move, my department
gave Tara security clearance. She could badge in and out, and tail me anywhere on
campus.

The footage from the incident last year was especially damning. Not that I
needed confirmation. I'd lived it. But knowing the authorities were taking it

                              525

seriously, that they had finally started the process of seeking a warrant for his arrest, should have brought me comfort. Instead, it left me jittery, the hairs on my arms permanently set to "goose bump."

Just as Andreas had predicted a few days ago, Henrik was growing desperate.

Tara yanked the door open to reveal Dmitry, exactly as expected. Lab coat, scarf, and the faint smell of clove cigarettes that followed him everywhere.

"I have news," Dmitry announced, repeating his earlier message.

"Come in," Tara said, stepping aside to allow him entry.

He sauntered in, nodding once to Tara. "Hello, Sam's doppelganger."

Tara gave a two-fingered salute. She closed the door and leaned against it.

Dmitry settled himself on the edge of my desk and leveled me with his typical look of frankness. Except this time, there was a hint of sympathy about it. "I am here to tell you that James Nieminen has been suspended for suspected sexual misconduct."

It should have been a relief, maybe even a vindication, but what I felt instead was a strange, hollow disappointment. In myself. *Damn it.*

I should've gone to HR. I should've told Dr. Hauser. If I'd stepped forward earlier, maybe none of this would've happened.

Yes. I know. This was a one-eighty from me. I talked a good game about victim blaming and holding men responsible for their shitty behavior. But at the end of the day, I hated that he'd harassed someone else after harassing me. *Maybe, if I'd been braver, or smarter, or more strategic, I could have stopped him . . .*

"Are you okay?" Dmitry asked, his eyebrows lifting slightly.

Eventually, all I could think to say was, "That makes sense."

"I didn't think you would be surprised." Dmitry gave me a once-over. "But I did want to be the one to tell you."

I sensed that his interest in the topic and wanting to be the one to break the news had zero to do with gossip. Rather, he knew James had given me a hard time and this was Dmitry's way of being a supportive work husband.

Tara, finally interested, uncrossed her arms and leaned forward. "Is that the creepy professor guy who jumped out from behind the column that one time and harassed you? Last December, right?"

"That's the one," I confirmed.

She nodded, as if this tied up a narrative thread that had been bothering her.

Dmitry continued, "Turns out, his new postdoc is the daughter of someone on the board of governors, but she didn't disclose it when she applied for the position. She wanted to get the job based on her merit instead of who her family was, go figure. Lo and behold, Dr. Nieminen thought he could treat her like any of his other postdocs, and that's when he found out who her mother was."

"Serves him right," I said, but my heart wasn't really in it. Sure, it was nice to see karma work in real time, but it was also a reminder that only some women get to be believed. For every postdoc with a board of governors parent, there were a hundred who just wanted to keep their jobs, who had to weigh the risk of speaking up against the certainty of retaliation.

And yet, I still hated myself a little for not speaking up. *Tell me why this makes sense. Tell me why we do this to ourselves.* I hadn't been the one harassing women, so why did I feel such a deep sense of failure about it?

My phone buzzed on the desk. I ignored it, turning back to my bodyguard and confidant. "Should we go grab some lunch?" I felt like I needed cheering up. "It's actually a nice day outside. We could walk somewhere."

Another buzz. I studiously ignored it.

Tara frowned. "I'll have to call your entourage. Now that you have five guards, it might be better to have something delivered rather than try to navigate the sidewalk."

"Fine," I said, reaching for my phone, "I'll order something."

I glanced down at the screen. Two missed calls, both from Martin. There was also a voicemail. My pulse kicked up a notch. Kaitlyn had been out of the hospital for weeks. She'd seemed fine the last time we spoke. But Martin only ever called me when there was something wrong with Kaitlyn.

I tapped the voicemail, my brain already compiling worst-case scenarios. I pressed it to my ear.

"Sam, call me back as soon as you get this," Martin's voice said, ragged with panic. "This is an emergency, I've already called the police. I have a phone call from Henrik Kristiansen and he says that he has Kaitlyn and Joey, and he wants to trade them for you. I can't get through to Kaitlyn and her phone is turned off, so I can't track her location. I'm on my way to your work now and I'm going to try calling you again. If I don't hear from you or can't get in to see you, the police will be stopping by. Call me back ASAP."

The message ended with a click, but the afterimage burned in my mind.

I must have gone very still, because Tara was watching me with the coiled readiness of a pit bull waiting for a command. Dmitry cocked his head, his smile fading.

"Sam?" Tara said. "Everything okay?"

I looked up at them both, my voice barely a strangled scrape. "He has Kaitlyn. And the baby. Henrik has them. And he wants to trade them for me."

* * *

I'D ALWAYS IMAGINED that when someone says, "We have your loved ones, come alone or they die," you'd go into this action-hero trance and become single-minded, invincible, incapable of panic. Instead, my body was so overloaded with cortisol that my gums were numb.

Stuck to the leather seat of Tara's black Mercedes, I compulsively refreshed the GPS dot on my phone as if it could will my friend and her son safe.

It was nearly 12:30 PM by the time we left the campus parking structure. The city outside the car was cartoonish and cruel, too-bright sunlight refracting through dirty windshield glass, people blurring by on their missions of grocery runs and gym check-ins, a dog in a bandana barking at nothing, completely unbothered that my best friend and her baby were being held hostage by a psycho with a grudge.

Tara gripped the wheel with a single hand, thumb drumming rapid fire on the steering column, her focus split evenly between the address I'd punched into the GPS and the black SUV trailing us at a discreet but definitely not subtle distance. That would be the rest of the security team. My security team. At this moment, they felt like a liability more than a comfort.

I tapped out a text to Andreas with both hands, only marginally aware of Tara side-eyeing my frantic thumbs:

Sam: Henrik has Kaitlyn and Joey. Martin will send you Henrik's voicemail. I'm on my way to the address Martin sent. Talk to Martin before calling me. I love you.

There was nothing else I could say. I wouldn't be able to say it out loud anyway. No read receipt. Good. The last thing I needed was a reply that might make me cry when I needed to be brave and strong.

My head was in a blender, every thought fighting for top billing. What if Henrik already killed them? What if I was wasting time with every second I spent not at the address? Was there a way to stall him? Could I trust the police to actually help?

Tara broke the silence. "We're almost there. Two stoplights." She shot a look at me over the top of her aviators, and her face, usually so open and expressive, was locked down and set to grim. "Are you sure you want to leave everyone else behind?"

I didn't answer right away. Instead, I relived the last hour on a loop, as if by narrating it to myself I could make it turn out different the second time.

Martin had called me—no, not called, summoned—with an urgency that had sent every neuron in my skull into red alert. When I arrived downstairs outside the biology building with Tara, he'd greeted me with zero preamble, instead shoving his phone at me and saying, "You need to hear this."

His voice was the scariest thing I'd ever heard. Not shaking, not frantic, just completely emptied out.

He hit play on his phone, and Henrik's voice came through the tiny speaker, thick and menacing and, worse, giddy:

"I have your lovely wife and son with me. If you want to see them again, send Sam Jarlston on her own to the address I'll be texting you shortly. If she comes with anyone else or if you send the police, you'll never see your wife and child again. And that would be a shame, because your wife is very, very beautiful. And if Ms. Jarlston isn't here in . . . let's say two hours, tell her not to bother coming at all."

The click at the end of the message had echoed around us for three full seconds before Martin, looking somehow twenty years older, said, "I have a tracking device for you. It's a prototype I invented, but it's the best I can do on such short notice." He popped a tiny plastic button from a velvet jewelry box. "It's also a camera and an audio recorder. It syncs to my phone and to the security office at my building. I'm sharing the feed with the PD. As long as you're wearing it, we'll know where you are, what you're hearing, and what you're seeing."

I'd looked at the device, then at him. "Okay."

I was almost proud of myself for not laughing or screaming or projectile vomiting. Instead, I let him press the button in place, let him explain how the adhesive backing would fuse to the actual button and how the battery would last at least ten hours.

The device stuck fast, perfectly disguised.

Then Martin said, "I'll be tracking you the whole time. So will the police."

I nodded, choked out, "Thank you," and turned away before I could fall apart.

Now, as we approached the first of the two stoplights, Tara slowed and glanced in the rearview again.

"I want the rest of the team to back off," I said, and my voice cracked hard on the last word. "He said to come alone. I don't want to put Kaitlyn or Joey in any more danger."

Tara nodded, set her jaw. "Next left, then you're on your own. Are you really sure about this?"

I looked at her. "Yes."

She didn't argue. Instead, she pulled into the parking lot of an abandoned laundromat and turned to face me squarely. "I think this is a very bad idea," she said, her voice flat and sincere. "But I know I can't talk you out of it."

I didn't know what to say, so I exited the car, walked to the driver's side, and accepted her unexpected hug. She patted me once on the back, then held me tighter than I expected, her biceps crushing enough to make me think she was trying to transfer some of her own strength through osmosis.

When I finally let go, she gave me a small smile and said, "If you get a chance, stab him in the balls."

"Absolutely." I nodded, feeling braver than I had any right to.

Accepting the keys, I adjusted my collar so the button tracker sat perfectly in line with the others. Tara stepped back, hands in her jacket pockets, and watched as I got into the Mercedes and drove away.

The address Henrik had texted was at the far edge of the city, in a part of the port district so old and irrelevant it wasn't even gentrified yet. The streets were a patchwork of new concrete and ancient cobblestones, lined with razor wire and rusted fences and more "No Trespassing" signs than your conservative uncle's cabin in the woods.

It took two minutes to get there, and my heart rate climbed another ten BPM. By the time I saw the number painted in giant block font on the corrugated side of a warehouse, I was pretty sure I was in the red zone for a stroke.

My phone buzzed with an incoming call, startling me. Cutting the engine, I picked up my cell and read the name on the screen.

Andreas.

I stared at his name, thumb hovering over the green button, but the time mocked me from the upper right corner. If I took the call, I'd have to explain, or hear him beg me to turn around, or admit that I was seconds away from walking into a situation with zero leverage and zero plan. I sent the call to voicemail, muttering, "Sorry, sorry, sorry," under my breath like a prayer.

I left the car running and jogged up the cracked pavement toward the main entrance of the building. It was a massive structure, all dirty windows and steel siding and the faint chemical smell of something burning in the distance. There was a battered sign over the door, but the name had been scraped off, leaving only the faded outline of what I guessed used to be some sort of shipping office.

I was almost to the door when someone called my name.

"Jarlston."

I turned, and a man walked toward me from behind a large truck. He was dressed in all black—black jeans, black hoodie, black gloves—and his face was hidden behind an N95 respirator mask, the kind you'd see on the subway in flu season.

He looked left, then right, scanning the area with the jumpy energy of someone expecting an ambush.

Stopping about six feet from me, he crossed his arms and said, "Are you Samantha Jarlston?"

I nodded, trying to keep my voice from shaking. "Yes. Where are Kaitlyn and Joey?"

He didn't answer. Instead, he stepped forward, grabbed my arm with a gloved hand, and spun me around so fast I almost lost my balance. He pushed me toward the wall, then frisked me, hard and efficient, like he expected to find a gun or a knife or a wire.

When he got to my phone, he yanked it from my pocket, powered it off, and chucked it into the weeds. Then, without warning, he grabbed me by the back of the neck and marched me around the side of the building.

I didn't fight. My only thought was that this was good. He believes I'm alone, with nothing on me, and I'm still alive. *That's something.*

At the far side, there was a battered sedan parked up on the curb, trunk open and waiting. Before I could process what was happening, he shoved me into the trunk—hard, so my shoulder bounced off the carpeted wheel well—and slammed it shut.

The world went dark, except for the single pinpoint of light leaking through the seam of the back seat. For a second, all I could hear was the sound of my own breathing, ragged and echoing in the metal cage.

The car started moving immediately. No hesitation, no time for second thoughts. The ride was rough, every pothole magnifying the cramped, coffin-like space. The smell was industrial and greasy, and with every minute, the air got stuffier and thinner.

I counted my breaths and tried to think. I remembered Tara teaching me how to kick out the rear taillight, how to wave a hand for help, how to scream loud enough that passing drivers might hear. But if I escaped now, Kaitlyn and Joey would suffer.

I also reminded myself of the tracker button and hoped to God that Martin and the police were following every turn.

So, I waited.

It felt like hours, but was probably only twenty minutes, before the car slowed and took a series of hard turns, then came to a stop. I heard voices—muffled, arguing, one of them a woman—and then the trunk popped open, flooding the space with blinding white light.

For a second, all I could see was the sun. But I heard a voice. *Henrik's voice.*

"Well look who it is. Apparently, you can follow directions."

[23]

EVOLUTION OF NOVELTY

Samantha

The next moments played out in jump cuts, as if someone flipped through my life frame by frame. The world tilted sideways when Henrik's fist clamped around my upper arm and yanked me out of the trunk. I must've hit the gravel when I landed because the entire right side of my body was instantly on fire.

I didn't have time to catalogue injuries. Henrik was already dragging me toward a different warehouse with both hands and the subtlety of a sack-throwing butcher. His knuckles dug through my shirt, cutting off circulation. Two men in black followed, both with the posture of guys who were too morally bankrupt for even ICE to accept.

I got one last glance at the sun before the warehouse doors slammed behind us.

The interior reeked of wet concrete and old paint. I got the sense that it had never, not once, been the site of anything wholesome. We moved fast through the front office, past a toppled desk, then down a corridor lined with steel doors, some open, some welded shut. I heard something that sounded like a baby crying, echoing down the hallway. Oddly, the sound firmed my resolve and loaned me bravery.

I demanded, "Where are Kaitlyn and Joey?"

Henrik let out a bark of laughter. "You'll see them soon enough."

He kept walking, but to the guy on my left he said, "Did you frisk her? Does she have her phone?"

533

The guy, whose face was still covered in a mask, like a coward, said, "I frisked her. She's clean, no weapons, and I left her phone at the dock."

Thank you, I thought, *for not knowing the difference between a button and a bug.* I sent a silent prayer of thanks for Martin's tracker and to whatever patron saint presided over law enforcement response times. If I was lucky, there was a tactical SWAT team right now putting their boots on, ten blocks away.

We rounded a corner and the baby's wailing grew louder, then softer again as someone shushed it, a woman's voice, urgent and cracked. I recognized it instantly, and rage detonated in my chest like a Roman candle.

I turned on Henrik as hard as I could, spinning out of his grip. "If Kaitlyn and Joey are hurt, I'm going to kill you."

He laughed again, more genuine this time, and then, with zero warning, backhanded me across the cheek so hard my ears rang. I tasted blood before I could catch my balance.

"And I'm going to enjoy messing up this pretty face," he said, voice flat.

The sting burned through my whole jaw, but all I could think about was what Andreas had told me weeks ago about Henrik's right eye.

I stumbled, half on purpose, and moved to his right side.

"Why are you doing this?" I said, even though I could guess. But I wanted Henrik to talk. I wanted him to say it louder for the police in the back, for the tape, for the world.

He didn't disappoint. "Because you stole what was rightfully mine, everything I worked for."

I scowled. "Are you talking about my father's shares? How did you work for them? How are they yours?"

He stopped walking and, for a moment, I thought he was going to hit me again. Instead, he screamed in my face, "Those shares belong to me. I'm the one who did the dirty work, who made sure they belonged to my family. They don't belong to you, they belong to me!"

He was actually frothing, just a little, at the corner of his mouth.

"Because your father made you frame my father for fraud?" I said, keeping my tone calm, almost bored. The muscle next to Henrik's eye twitched.

"My father didn't make me do anything, I wanted to do it. I was glad to do it. Your father was a spineless, rigid weakling with no ambition. He didn't deserve those shares. He should have been an employee, not my father's business partner. He wanted to stop us from taking the company public!"

The men with us looked uncomfortable, but I couldn't tell if it was the screaming or the content.

Henrik yanked me forward, then through another door, this one opening into a small, dark office. The air was hot and muggy, and in the middle, tied to an overturned file cabinet, sat Kaitlyn. Her face was streaked with sweat and her arms were wrapped around Joey, who was shrieking at the top of his lungs, red-faced and terrified. Kaitlyn looked up and saw me, and the relief in her expression cut through my own fear like a scalpel.

She looked pristine. Untouched. And when she saw me, she smiled, even with tears in her eyes. I saw her faith in me and I felt absolutely humbled.

For her, I would get through this. For her, I would stab Henrik in the balls. *And for Tara.*

I turned back to Henrik. "I'm the one you want. Let Kaitlyn and Joey go."

He grinned, like he'd won a round already. "I will let them go. But first, you're going to transfer ownership of the shares into my name. I have an account—"

I barked a laugh, then interrupted him with as much incredulity as I could summon. "You can't be serious. I have no way to do that."

He grabbed both my arms and shook me hard, the kind of shake that makes your teeth rattle. "You will do it, and you will do it now. I have an account ready to receive them."

I yelled back, making sure my voice was loud enough for all the goons to hear, "You're an idiot! It's not like the shares are in an E-Trade account and I can just transfer them to you. That's not how this works. You planned this elaborate kidnapping, and for what? How are you going to pay these men?"

He shook me again, but this time one of the goons spoke up.

"Is that true? You said we'd get a cut of the shares."

Henrik whipped his head around. "Shut up and do what you're told."

I kept at it, hoping to widen the crack. "He has no way to pay you, just like I have no way to transfer the shares into his account. But he's a moron, so he doesn't know how basic finance works."

Henrik backhanded me again, and then, just for good measure, punched me just north of my stomach. The wind went out of me, hard, pain shooting through my chest and to my teeth, down my spine, to my fingertips and toes. I collapsed to the floor on Henrik's right side. *Good.* If I was going to get a shot at him, it had to be from the right.

While I wheezed, Henrik paced, waving his arms at the goons and yelling at them to "Fall back in line" and "Do as I say." The guys looked at each other, then at me, and I realized they were starting to get nervous.

Over the din, I heard Kaitlyn scream my name. "Sam!"

It was a primal scream and the sound gave me one last ounce of courage. I forced myself to breathe through the pain and keep my eyes open. Henrik had taken out a gun and was waving it around, brandishing it more as a prop than a weapon.

He aimed it at the two goons and barked, "Nobody moves unless I say so."

I locked eyes with Kaitlyn. She was staring at me, wild and panicked, but alert. I mouthed, *Turn away.*

She nodded, squeezed Joey so hard I thought he might pop, and turned both of their faces away from us.

Henrik's attention was still on the men, not me. I saw my chance, and I took it.

I kicked out both legs as hard as I could, catching Henrik behind the knee. He went down with a grunt, arms flailing for balance. The gun skittered across the floor. Before he could recover, I used the magic of my pointed-toe shoe to deliver a direct kick to his balls. The shoe wasn't a knife, but it would have to do. He roared in pain and I scrambled after the gun, getting my hands on the grip in three seconds flat.

My brain, fueled by every kickboxing and self-defense class I'd ever taken, immediately remembered to check the safety, which was on. I flicked it off, got to my feet, and pointed it at Henrik.

At this point, he was kneeling, breath coming in fast, shallow gasps. His face was red and shiny with sweat, and he looked up at me with a mix of fear and rage.

"If you move," I said, "I will shoot you."

He laughed, a hysterical, wheezing sound that made me wonder if he'd finally snapped.

"You won't do it," he said.

There was no arguing with someone who lacked both logic and intelligence, so I preemptively shot him in the knee. He crumpled to the ground, howling again.

I turned to the two men near Kaitlyn. "This man deceived you. He has money, he could've paid you already. So, if he hasn't paid you already and has promised you a cut of my shares, he's lying. He's not going to pay you at all."

The guys exchanged glances. One said, "Then we'll just kill you and ransom her. She's some big shot's wife, right?"

As if on cue, the sound of sirens flooded the air. Louder and louder, Dopplering toward us until even Henrik's laughter was drowned out. I raised my voice to cut through the wail.

"I have a camera on my body that has recorded everything and sent the footage to the police. It's also a tracker, and the police are on their way. If you leave now, you'll have a head start."

They exchanged another look.

I glanced over my shoulder at the other goon, adding, "Maybe you'll get away.

But if you kill me, the charge will be felony first-degree murder and not misdemeanor kidnapping."

A heightened pause followed, and then the guys bolted. They didn't even argue, just sprinted down the hallway toward whatever exit they thought would save them.

Henrik swore, tried to lunge for my leg. I didn't think, just pulled the trigger again.

The bullet caught him in the hand, exactly where he'd reached for me. He screamed, clutched the wound, blood spattering the floor.

He glared up at me, wild-eyed, furious, helpless.

"I know you killed my father," I said, raising the gun to bring the barrel even with his head, "and I know your father told you to do it."

He shook his head, the movement frantic. "You have no proof."

I kept the gun leveled at his face. "I found the medical examiner and he told me everything. He signed an affidavit saying your father paid him to change the cause of death."

Henrik's face went white, then red, then a weird, mottled shade in between. He howled, "It was me! It wasn't him, it was me! I did it and I would do it again!"

The sirens were so loud now I could barely hear my own voice.

A second later, the door exploded inward and a dozen police officers flooded the room. They shouted commands, weapons drawn, some running to Kaitlyn and Joey, some to Henrik, one barreling directly at me and snatching the gun from my hand before I even registered the motion.

And that's when I felt the pain, from my face and my ribs, so sharp and severe my knees gave out. I started to fall. But someone's arms were there, catching me and holding me up. Darkness edged into my vision, but I forced myself to look up. I saw his face.

Andreas.

I felt my mouth curve into a smile, but pain forced me to stop. He shouted something—my name, probably—but the sound was underwater, filtered through white noise and the pounding of my heart. His arms wrapped around me and I let myself lean in, just for a second, just long enough to remember what it felt like to be safe.

Everything else—the flashing lights, the screaming, the chaos—faded out. My vision tunneled, and the last thing I saw before blacking out was the look on his face. Not angry, not calculating, not even worried.

Just grateful.

Then the world went dark.

[24]

PHYLOGENETIC RECONSTRUCTION

Samantha

Waking up in the hospital is nothing like the movies. There is no dramatic beeping, no distant sirens, no heroic blur of action. It is just the dense, gluey awareness of a body that is not working the way you remember, and the certainty that you are being watched by an audience with at least three graduate degrees between them.

Also, there are more wires.

The first sensation was a weightless pressure on my right hand. Not the cold clinical clamp of a blood pressure cuff or a nurse's indifferent touch, but the clutch of a person who deeply cared if I woke up or not. I hovered there, in a swamp of anesthetic and somewhere between sleep and lucidity, and let my brain reconstruct the scene through the sticky filter of post-trauma. Plus whatever painkillers they'd given me.

There was the beeping, of course, my pulse monitor perhaps. There was the antiseptic tang that had been etched into my hippocampus by months of exposure to emergency rooms and a sick grandparent. There was the weight on my face, which registered as a dull ache first and then as a sharp, cartoonish throbbing the moment I thought about moving my head.

I tried to open both eyes. Only one complied. The other was fused shut with either swelling or the world's most aggressive adhesive tape. The sunlight that slithered through the blinds was both beautiful and toxic. I let the open eye close again.

Someone said, "I think she's waking up."

The voice belonged to Diya. Even with the cotton stuffing my skull, I'd know that voice anywhere. Warm, practical, and lightly laced with worry. I made a noise that could have meant "good morning" or "kill me," depending on your translation.

Diya said, "Sam, can you hear me?"

"Yes, I can hear you," I said. Or tried to. The sound came out as a low, sandpapered croak, but the effort was enough to send a wave of recognition through the hand holding mine.

"I'm so glad. You gave us a real scare. And you don't have to open your eyes if you don't want to. Your left eye is pretty swollen, but your right eye is okay. It might hurt to open either of them, however. And don't try to move your body. You have two broken ribs."

I attempted a nod, which was a mistake. A bolt of pain shot down the left side of my face and straight into my jaw. I winced and kept my head still. I could hear someone else in the room, breathing through their teeth, and then a string of foreign words that sounded like the cursing you save for when the toilet overflows while visiting an acquaintance's place. The curser was obviously Andreas.

I curled my fingers around the hand in mine and said, "Andreas?"

He answered instantly, "I'm here."

Relief hit me like oxygen after a long-held breath and tears pooled in my good eye. My chin wobbled with the effort of not crying, because crying would likely make everything more painful.

Andreas, apparently sensing my unsteadiness, said, "Do not cry. You are safe."

I felt the warmth of his lips, gentle and deliberate, pressing against the back of my hand. "You are safe. It is all over," he said. The words should have made me want to laugh at the finality, but all they did was make my vision blur.

I croaked, "Is Kaitlyn okay? How is Joey?"

A new voice answered, "Kaitlyn and Joey are perfect. Not a scratch."

I didn't have to open my eye to know it was Martin. The sound of him—so steady, so unbending—was its own anesthesia.

I said, "I am so sorry. I am so sorry they got dragged into this—"

Martin cut me off. "Stop apologizing. I just came in to check on you and make sure you're okay. Kaitlyn will be in again soon."

There was the soft squeeze of a hand near my ankle—Martin's, I guessed—and then, "Try to get some rest."

I heard his footsteps fade, then the hush of the door closing behind him.

Instinct wanted me to be clever, to say something that would erase the sadness and worry in everyone's voices, or at least make it seem like I could handle the pain.

Instead, I lay there, breathing, while Andreas's thumb rubbed mindless patterns on the back of my hand.

Diya's voice returned, soft but so clear. "I'll give you two some privacy, but I'll be back soon to check vitals again. If Sam wants to go back to sleep, she should. There is no sign of concussion."

Andreas said, "Thank you, Diya." His voice sounded rough.

I listened as Diya's sensible shoes squeaked out of the room. Silence, at last. Or almost. I could hear the faint sounds of the hospital and the tap of Andreas's heel on the tile.

He brought my hand up to his forehead and just held it there for a long moment.

When he finally spoke, the words tumbled out like pebbles over a cliff, nothing smooth about it. "I understand that you need to do things your way and make decisions for yourself, but you have to understand that I cannot lose you."

I tried to form a sentence, but my brain was a bowl of day-old oatmeal. It didn't matter. Andreas barreled on, his accent deepening with every syllable: "If you ever find yourself in a similar situation, you have to call me and talk to me. Just like you need to be consulted, I also need to be consulted. I have to matter to you, and factor into your decisions. I love you. And when I thought I would never see you again, I honestly did not know what to do. I mean it, I cannot lose you. I cannot." There was a break in his voice that made my own heart ache.

"I'm sorry," I said. And I was.

He sniffed hard, and I could feel the splash of hot tears on my fingers. "You have to apologize to me one hundred times for this."

My body wanted to laugh, but it came out as a short breath. "I love you," I said. "And I'm so sorry."

"Go to sleep," he said, sniffing again and pressing my palm to his cheek. "Sleep. And I will be here when you wake up."

* * *

ONCE YOU'RE past the initial shock of hospitalization, it's just boredom and a parade of well-wishers. Some bear food, some bear flowers, and other bear gossip. I'd spent exactly seventy-six hours under the fluorescent tyranny of the hospital lights, long enough to master the bed controls. My discharge instructions included a pamphlet on "gentle stretching," a full page on "managing emotional trauma," and a section on "when to return to sexual activity" that Diya had underlined in two colors and left, not anonymously, on my bedside table.

Andreas took the instructions literally. All of them. He briefed me on the correct positioning for sleeping, sitting, standing, and (in case I forgot) breathing. My only escape was the bathroom, which afforded me privacy for a few precious moments before he began to knock, ask if I was okay and if I needed help.

Back at his apartment, he installed me in his bed like a rare orchid. He went to the trouble of swapping out all the sheets for even softer, higher thread count ones. He suggested we buy a hospital-style trapeze bar to help me sit up without flexing my abs. But when I tried to point out all the ways the trapeze bar might be fun for other activities, he glared at me as though he found my flippancy toward the gravity of my medical condition both an affront and a disappointment.

Basically, Andreas hovered so aggressively that I actually grew a little sick of him.

But that's where I was, four weeks later, still propped up on a mound of pillows, one rib still sending out the occasional ping of protest, a thick book in my lap, and the residual feeling that I'd been both swaddled and imprisoned.

From the next room, I heard, "Are you hungry?"

I looked up, blinking out of my reading trance, and found Andreas in the doorway, arms crossed over his chest like he was auditioning for the role of Perpetually Concerned Boyfriend in a pharmaceutical ad.

Lifting my eyebrows, I said, "Didn't you just feed me a half hour ago?" My face was fully healed and I would never take my eyebrows or eyelids for granted ever again.

He ignored my question. "I want to ensure you do not require anything."

I grinned, half irritated and half smitten. "As I've said many times, I am fully recovered and fine. You do not need to keep waiting on me."

He frowned, as if this was a personal slight to his dignity. "I like waiting on you."

Before I could formulate a response, the doorbell rang.

Andreas glanced at his watch. "That should be Diya. Or Tara."

He vanished from the doorway, leaving only a faint smell of espresso and rosemary.

I put a finger in my book and let my head flop back against the pillows. For the record, I was fine. Diya had come by recently and pronounced my healing "well above baseline." Kaitlyn had delivered at least four casseroles—none of which Andreas let me eat, citing my body's need for a low-sodium diet to reduce inflammation—and Tara had dropped off enough sports drinks to hydrate an entire marathon.

Nakita hadn't come by, which was probably for the best since Andreas grew tense when she was mentioned. But she called often, sometimes twice a day, with live updates from the chess world and her patented blend of compliments and obscenity. Last week, she'd spent a full ten minutes recapping an influencer scandal involving a model, a side hustle, and three liters of coconut water. Her stories were, as always, better than television.

Because I was still technically housebound, Tara had volunteered herself as daytime distraction. She showed up with a sandwich most days, sat on the edge of the bed, and gave me play-by-plays of her most recent kickboxing classes. She seemed more relaxed now that Henrik had been locked up, and if she was bored during our visits, she didn't let it show.

The first thing Tara did when she entered the room today was raise a white paper bag and say, "It's a cheesesteak, since I know you'll only get rabbit food here."

Behind her, Andreas scowled and said, "I will be in the other room if you need me."

Tara called after him, "What if I need you?"

Without missing a beat, Andreas replied, "Do not bother me unless Samantha needs me."

Tara cackled, flopped down on the bed near my feet, and handed over the sandwich. "He loves you so much it makes my teeth hurt."

"Thank you for the sandwich, but I just ate," I said. "I'll save this for later."

She waved it off. "No problem. I'll bring you contraband anytime. How are you feeling?"

"I feel great."

She squinted at my face, then at my ribs, as if assessing whether to believe me. "Your face does look normal. How are the ribs?"

"Almost healed." I'd only needed real painkillers the first week, and the rest had been the slow ache of healing. Compared to grad school, it was a vacation.

Tara leaned back, bracing herself with her hands. "I heard you were discharged from the hospital in, like, record time."

I nodded. "I'm a model patient, apparently. But they wouldn't let me go unless I agreed to take time off work. I've spent this whole time reading novels. Why are fictional people so much more frustrating than real people?"

Tara grinned. "Dmitry sends his regards, along with several complaints about changes to the lab schedule. I guess you're not missing much at work."

"Yeah," I said, "but I actually miss the lab drama. And I miss my dissertation. And I miss being a real person and not a doll stuck on a bed of soft cotton."

She patted my leg, careful not to jostle anything. "Has your friend Kaitlyn been by today?"

I smiled. "Yes. She brought Joey this morning."

"Baby snuggles will fix you right up."

Kaitlyn was, as always, a bright spot. She'd come to see me every single day in the hospital, and now that I was home, she visited with Joey in tow, sometimes with Martin, sometimes not. Andreas always enjoyed both Joey and Kaitlyn. With Martin, however, Andreas had been frosty at best, and downright rude if the mood stuck him.

I suspected Andreas was still angry at Martin for sending me to Henrik alone, and the only thing keeping him from voicing that anger was my presence.

Tara glanced at the sandwich, then at me. "Any news on Henrik? How did the arraignment go? Wait, didn't he already have an arraignment? Or whatever his latest court date was—how did that go?"

I tried to sit with my legs crisscross and almost managed. "He was denied bail since he was determined to be a flight risk."

Henrik had been hit with a rapid-fire series of charges: assault and battery, multiple counts of kidnapping, one count of attempted murder, etcetera, etcetera. Due to the recording I'd handed over, his assets had been frozen and he was essentially broke. I'd been told he'd tried to call Tobias for help, but Tobias had gone radio silent.

"They say the legal situation with Henrik is all in limbo and may take several years to sort out."

"How do you feel about that?" Tara asked, sounding genuinely curious.

I shrugged. "As long as he's behind bars for the death of my father, and for framing him, I'm fine with it. It takes as long as it takes."

What I didn't say was that the situation with Henrik might never bring full closure. Henrik had already claimed sole responsibility for my father's death and, despite repeated interrogations, refused to implicate his father. He was stubborn, convinced that as long as he kept Oskar's hands clean, Henrik would one day somehow have access to my father's shares.

Again, there is no reasoning with someone who has no logic or intelligence.

I was working with my therapist to accept the possibility that the whole, true story of the past might never come out. I hated uncertainty, but I was trying to live with it.

"What about the other brother? Any news from that guy?" Tara asked, as if reading my mind.

I propped myself up straighter. "You mean Tobias? It looks like he didn't have anything to do with what happened to my father. He took the money Andreas paid him for the shares and has disappeared, more or less."

Tara grinned. "Is that good?"

"Very good. I hope I never see him again."

She cracked her knuckles. "Well, if I see him trying to approach you, I'll make sure he disappears."

I laughed, then winced. "Ouch."

She raised an eyebrow. "And you were just saying you feel great."

I made a face. "It aches only sometimes."

Tara stood, stretching. "You need more rest. Stop trying to rush back to work. Take the time off."

I eyed her. "Are you leaving already?"

"I have a class to teach tonight. When you're all healed up, I expect to see you there."

I smiled. "You got it."

Backing out of the room, she waved. "See you later."

"Bye, Tara," I said, then watched as she loped out of sight.

Andreas waited until the apartment was silent again before coming into the bedroom. He moved quietly, but there was nothing subtle about the way he crossed to the bed and sat near my knees.

Looking at me with a softness that still startled me, he plucked my fingers from the bed and began toying with them. "Do you want to watch a movie tonight?" Since the hospital, Andreas had developed an affinity for playing with my fingers.

"I have something else in mind," I said, and removed my fingers from his grip. Reaching forward, I drew a line down the front of his shirt. He caught my hand before I could get very far and I suppressed a groan of frustration. He was always turning me down these days. It wasn't like I was proposing a crazy position or anything. I just wanted to see a bit of skin. His skin. And by "a bit" I meant all of it.

Letting my chin drop to my chest, I sighed sadly. "Never mind. I guess, go turn on *Mister Rogers'* for me, *Dad*."

Andreas made a strangled laughing sound, but then simply outright laughed. "You are very bad," he said, his voice was full of affection.

Pouting, I lifted my head and stuck out my lower lip.

Eyes snagging on my bottom lip, Andreas suddenly leaned in and bit it softly, as though unable to help himself, which shocked the hell out of me. After a month of chaste hovering, censuring glares, this was something new. And welcomed.

When he pulled back, I said, "That's more like it."

He laughed quietly, his green eyes half lidded but bright. "Your grandfather should be calling soon. I am not going to start something we cannot finish before his call."

I sucked in a breath, not out of disappointment but out of hope. "After the call, then. Promise me we'll do something fun after the call."

He took my hand and kissed the back of it, his eyes never leaving mine. "After the call, I will do whatever you want me to do . . . wherever you want me to do it."

I didn't know what had suddenly gotten into Andreas, but I approved. Perhaps it was the conclusion of my hundred apologies. I would've said a hundred more if he'd let me.

Admittedly, I'd never been good at having good things. Sometimes, I found myself waiting for the other shoe to drop with Andreas. Every day it didn't, I felt a little less nervous and a little more certain.

I wanted to tell him this, but the words were clumsy in my mouth. Instead, I squeezed his hand, looked him in the eye, and said, "I'm so eternally grateful I have you."

He smiled, slow and real, his gaze lowering to my mouth and warming. "I am glad I have you, too."

The phone on the nightstand buzzed, interrupting our moment, and I exhaled at the imperfect timing. Nevertheless, I picked it up, saw the caller ID: "GRANDPA CARL."

Bracing myself, I answered, "Hi, Grandpa."

"Sammy! Just checking in. I hear from your boyfriend that you're feeling better." He sounded happy to hear my voice.

Andreas's smile grew infinitesimally bigger at the word *boyfriend* while he kept hold of my hand.

"I am," I said. "Thanks for calling."

We talked for a few minutes, mostly about the paperwork for the adoption, which was moving forward quickly. I couldn't wait to *not* be Andreas's adopted child. But I also couldn't wait to legally be part of my family again.

After we hung up, I set the phone aside and studied Andreas, wondering if he'd keep his word.

"All done."

"Does this mean I can have you now?" He grinned, glancing up at me, the heat behind his gaze making my heart flutter and my chest tight. *My, oh my, how I missed that heat.*

Using his hold on my hand as leverage, I pulled him closer, wanting at least a kiss. Just one kiss. But first, I pressed my face to his neck, inhaled the clean, warm scent of him, and let the future unspool in my head.

There were still things to finish and resolve. Whether Dr. Hauser would continue as the proxy for the shares once the civil suit was eventually overturned; how to hand the shares over to the Genetix employees when the time came; Henrik's trial; my dissertation and future at the university; whether I needed guards when I returned to work or not; my sleepwalking; Andreas's Genetix shares; the physical therapy; the endless, looming question of who I was supposed to be now that I was free of both the Kristiansen legacy and the burden of my parents' secrets.

But in this moment, all of that could wait.

I was exactly where I wanted to be, next to exactly the person I wanted to be with. Miraculously, I didn't feel fear or unease when I thought about a future with Andreas. He was the most loveable hovering boyfriend. And he was also the sneakiest partner I could ever conceive of, or wish for, or wake up next to.

Andreas wasn't just a good thing. He was the best thing. And I hoped our future was one of commitment, and expectations, and all sorts of strings.

EPILOGUE: HUMAN EVOLUTIONARY HISTORY
THREE MONTHS LATER

Samantha

I stood by the window in a brand-new negligee—black, lace, extremely transparent, skintight—and watched the setting sun flatten itself into the dusty mountains. The tournament, and therefore Andreas's hotel, was located in the heart of the Las Vegas Strip. Both the sun and the neon glow had sneaked through every crack in the blackout curtains earlier while I'd attempted to sleep after my red-eye from New York.

Technically, I wasn't supposed to be here.

Andreas thought I was still in New York City, working to finish my dissertation. But my dissertation was already finished. And I was a free woman who wanted to surprise her *boyfriend* with lit candles (battery powered, for fire safety), rose petals, big hair, red lipstick, and every possible surface of my skin waxed and exfoliated and moisturized to a glassy finish.

I'd never felt less like myself.

And yet, I'd also never felt more like the person I wanted to be: fun, spontaneous, exciting, sexy, and incredibly smooth—literally and figuratively.

Tonight would be the night. I was determined. Of course, as long as Andreas consented.

Initially, my injuries had thrown a wrench in our plans. Then, my physical therapy had caused additional delays. After that, I'd spent almost every waking hour and ounce of energy on my dissertation, wanting to hit the end-of-summer deadline set by Dr. Hauser all those months ago. But I'd done it. I'd finished ahead of schedule. Which was why tonight should be a total surprise for my unsuspecting, favorite strategic mastermind.

Perhaps it was merely my imagination, but the air in the room seemed to vibrate with possibility. Every few minutes, I paced from the bed to the bathroom to check the mirror. The black lace looked both explicit and demure. Covering my neck, arms to wrists, chest, stomach, hips, and down to mid-thigh, from a distance it might pass as a dress with a nude slip beneath instead of a nude body. I loved it and I'd wanted it the moment I'd spotted it, feeling certain it would be perfect for this occasion.

My phone sat on the nightstand, the screen currently dark. Andreas had texted me earlier, telling me he'd won all his matches, and that he'd missed me, and that he'd planned to go to bed early just in case I had time for a call.

Deceiving him in this instance didn't feel wrong. But standing here, waiting, did feel like I was counting down to the moment until the rest of my life would walk through the door.

Abruptly, a heavy thunk came from the outer door and I tensed, instantly aware of every nerve ending in my body. *It's time.* He was here.

Andreas's voice, muffled by the door, said something like, "This is a disaster. Elio is an idiot."

His accent sounded sharper than usual. I grinned, because I couldn't wait to see his face when he saw me.

A key card beeped. The handle turned. I could hear the scrape of shoes on tile and the rustle of plastic bags.

I thought about calling out, letting him know I was here and waiting for him. Instead, I tiptoed to the bed and sat on the mattress, deciding to wait for him to walk in and discover me.

See? Smooth. *Real smooth.*

A long, slow, beleaguered-sounding exhale met my ears from the entry, followed by Andreas's voice saying, "Elio was supposed to schedule all post-match press for tomorrow. Instead, he invited three separate interview teams and did not tell me. The final match has been delayed."

It sounded like he was speaking to someone on the phone. I bit my lip, wondering if I should call out after all. The last thing I needed was to startle him while he was on the phone, only half paying attention to his surroundings.

What to do, what to do . . .

There was nothing for it. I decided to alert him.

Inhaling deeply, I called, "Andreas! I'm here to surprise you." Wincing at the words, hoping they were the right ones, I tucked my hands under my chin and waited.

A pause, then, "Samantha?"

"Yes!"

Immediately, he spoke rapid fire, "SorryIwillcallyoubackbye." His words sounded slurred because he'd said them so fast.

I heard his footsteps move around the suite as he said loudly, "Where are you?"

"In the bedroom," I answered, and instantly regretted how much it sounded like a porn setup.

Another pause. "Which bedroom?"

My heart did a weird, uncoordinated dance. "The main one," I said, and instantly started second-guessing my entire seduction strategy. What if he'd had a terrible day? What if he was too tired, or too anxious, or just wanted to relax like the vegetables he loved so much? Maybe I should've waited, or at least worn something less "Seduction: Funeral Edition."

His footsteps echoed closer, deliberate and hurried. Then, he appeared in the doorway, and his gorgeousness took my breath away. He wore an impeccably tailored suit and, as usual, he was put together so precisely, I couldn't wait to get my hands on his body and mess it all up.

For a second I thought maybe he hadn't registered what I was wearing, or maybe he was so deep in chess brain that I'd have to wave my arms and shout, "Hey! Objectify me!"

But then the scowl melted off his face, and his eyes did that thing where they went from ice to wildfire in a nanosecond. He stood very still, looking me up and down, the rising and falling of his chest a perfect, escalating rhythm.

Then he said, "Holy shit."

I stood from the bed and held my arms out, wanting his inspection. "Like it?"

He closed the distance in three strides and, with zero warning, lifted me off the floor. He held me for a beat, as if weighing my entire body in his arms was a math problem he'd waited all his life to solve. Then he kissed me. Not the careful, practiced kisses he'd portioned out while I'd been injured, but the kind from before. The ones that left no doubt who I belonged to, and who he belonged to, or what was about to happen between us.

Between kisses, he sorta growled, "Is this to tease me? It better not be."

Leaning away, I moved my lips to his ear, my voice barely above a breath, and whispered, "No. To satisfy you."

He groaned, the sound low and seismic. Andreas set me gently on the bed, encouraging me to kneel on the mattress. His hands were already under the lace, fingers splayed on my back, skimming the edge of my ass, grabbing it, massaging it, giving it a tight, sudden smack.

I sucked in a pleasantly surprised breath and he groaned. "I need you," he said, seemingly already lost to the moment. "Fuck, I need you so badly."

I'd expected this part to be awkward, maybe a little rushed, but instead it almost felt choreographed. Perhaps he, too, had been planning and thinking about this moment for a long, long time. His mouth traced a line from my ear to my collarbone over the lace, then dipped lower, pausing just long enough to bite at my shoulder while his fingers moved to the front of my body. Administering a punishing pinch to my nipple, his mouth curved into a smile at my gasp.

Releasing my weight fully to the mattress, Andreas stepped back and began stripping off his suit, his eyes darkening as they moved over my body, and I shivered under his stare, the sweep of reverence but also possession I knew was echoed in my own gaze. He looked like he had *plans,* and I loved that for both of us.

Unable to help myself or hold still, I worked on the buttons of his shirt, tugging at the ends until he gave up and yanked it over his head, sending three tiny discs pinging off the floor and wall. When his body was bare, I wanted to stop and stare, because seeing him in sweatpants and T-shirts was great, but seeing him naked and hungry and absolutely mine was my favorite.

He noticed the staring and smiled, just a little, just enough.

"Are you sure you're ready?" I asked, because I wanted him to have an out. We could do so many other things tonight. I didn't want him to feel even a little bit pressured.

He didn't hesitate, reaching for me and speaking against my neck. "I have been ready since December of last year. I want you, I need you. Please. No more waiting. I need you. I love you."

It's easy to be cynical about declarations. But the way he'd said it—voice dark, eyes bright, body already trembling with anticipation—I believed every word. Not just that, but I knew Andreas. I trusted him. He always told me the truth, even when it made one or both of us uncomfortable.

He kissed me again, deeper this time, and when his hands slid under the hem of my negligee, I let him find what he was looking for. I was wet and so ready for his touch. He teased me through the lace, fingertips drawing lazy circles over my nipples, then down, then back up, until I was panting.

"I love this, but I want it off," he ground out, pushing up the negligee before I could utter a protest.

Not that I would.

Tossing it to the foot of the bed, Andreas stared at me like I was the world's rarest treasure, and I wrapped my arms around his neck, pulling him closer, skin to skin, my breasts pressing against his chest, our hips aligning in a way that felt both accidental and preordained.

His cock was hard and hot against my thigh, and I reached down, palming him, hungry for his reaction. He sucked in a sharp breath, then a shuddering laugh escaped him.

"If you do that, I will not last long."

"We can always do it more than once," I said, hoping my voice sounded casual, and nowhere near as desperate as I felt.

He shook his head, eyes narrowing. "You are so smart."

Holding his gaze, I turned us and guided him backward, using his shoulders as leverage, until he lay flat on the mattress. Then I climbed over him, straddling his chest, and looked down at his face. He gave me a small, crooked smile, his eyes half lidded, and for a second, I wanted to stay just like this forever.

But Andreas pulled my hips up, steady but gentle, guiding me with both hands on my ass so that I was perfectly positioned above his mouth. I was suddenly aware of how exposed I was and where his gaze met my body. Even in the haze of lust, I felt the hot knife-edge of excitement and fluttery nervousness. He made a show of looking at me—everywhere, all at once—with such open hunger that I felt my excitement melt into something else, something languid and hot and needy.

He hummed his approval, the sound deep and resonant, and then he started, at first with a single, exploratory lick, so light my breath hitched. Then with a firmer, more purposeful repetition. He found my clit immediately and lavished it with his soft tongue and sucking lips.

When I shivered, he doubled down. When I panted, he added teeth, just a feather's brush, then soothed the spot with his tongue again.

"Fuck," I said between clenched teeth. Nothing in my body felt real anymore except the heat building between my legs and the way his hands gripped my thighs, holding me steady, making me feel like the entire world might tilt if he let go.

I wasn't the only one unraveling. Beneath me, I could feel his body shift, the muscles in his arms flexing with every movement. He let go of my left thigh and slid his hand up to my waist, then higher, until his palm pressed flat against my lower back, drawing me closer, refusing to give me an inch of wiggle room. The certainty of his touch made my entire body clench. My hips began to rock, small movements at first, then full-on grinding, and he took it in stride, adapting to every motion.

The room felt too hot, the air too thin. Every sound became amplified—the slick, obscene noise of his mouth on me, my own whimpers, the soft give of the mattress beneath us. At some point, I looked down and caught his eyes, and the intensity of his stare nearly undid me. I realized he was watching me. Not just in the casual way, but like a man who'd waited very patiently, hoping for the chance to worship a woman he loved.

"God, Andreas," I gasped. "You're going to make me—"

He only groaned, pinching my nipples with just enough pressure to make my hips buck against his tongue. Every muscle in my legs went rigid. I clamped down on his head, holding him exactly where I needed him, and let my stomach twist tighter and tighter . . .

But in the very last moment, just before I toppled over, survival instinct (or maybe the desire to prolong the torture) kicked in. I released his head, tugged at his shoulders, and pulled myself away.

Andreas made a wounded noise, like I'd just canceled his birthday, but I could see the smile on his face, his lips and chin glossy. I slid down his body to straddle his hips, and lined him up with my entrance.

We locked eyes, a fossilized moment, even as I hovered above him, my thighs trembling with adrenaline and anticipation. He licked his lips, pupils blown wide. The head of his cock, slick and impossibly hot, kissed my folds.

He ran his hands up my thighs, gripping hard. "You are so fucking sexy," he said, voice ragged, an octave lower than I'd ever heard him.

I looked down at him—at the lines of his body, the flex of his stomach, the sweat highlighting every plane and hollow.

"So are you," I whispered.

His mouth tugged upward, a polite curve, but his eyes were almost feral.

Holding his gaze as I ground down against him, letting the friction draw both of us right to the edge of unbearable. The moment was so loud with possibility it was honestly painful. Then, holding him in place beneath me, I sank down slowly, every millimeter mapped against the deepest nerves in my body, and he arched his back and let out a sound I'd only ever heard from him right before he climaxed.

There was resistance, but also a perfect fit, and when I bottomed out, I was full in every sense of the word. Full of him, of the moment, of the knowledge that nothing about this could possibly be reversed or undone.

He let his head fall back, jaw sharp enough to cut glass, but his eyes didn't leave mine. I'd never in my life felt so wanted. It was as if all waiting had been burned off in the heat of this chemical reaction, and what was left was only the pure, undeniable truth of our love and desire for each other.

I rocked my hips, at first tentative, finding the angle and the rhythm that would make both of us see stars. His hands moved instinctively—one gripping my waist, the other skimming up my back, urging me forward until my breasts hovered just above his mouth. He sucked a nipple into his mouth, teeth grazing the edge, and then soothed the bite with his tongue. The dual sensation made my body clench around him, gripping so hard he groaned into my skin.

For a while, I lost myself in the friction and the heat, the rolling tension that made it impossible to tell where my body ended and his began. The room smelled like sweat and sex and something sweeter than either. My hair fell around us in a dark curtain, and I let it. I wanted to be lost in this cave with him, forever.

Soon, however, Andreas's body began thrusting up with a greedy rhythm, matching my pace and doubling it, his control slipping with every breath.

"You feel so good," he said, and his accent was thicker now, words pressed out between clenched teeth. "I cannot—Sam, you are—God."

I threw my head back and rode him harder, taking the compliment as fuel. My thighs were burning, my hands trembling as I braced myself on his chest. He was so beautiful. Lips parted, neck taut, eyes wide and awed.

His hands slid down to my ass, kneading and spreading me, guiding my hips just how he wanted them, as if he'd finally given himself permission to take what he needed. For a second, I thought I might come right then and there, the pressure between my legs a taut, electric line. I slowed my hips to keep the orgasm at bay, wanting to make this last at least a little longer. I knew he was close, too—the flush blooming across his chest, the wildness in his grip, the way his breath kept catching in his throat.

I leaned down so our faces were inches apart. His hands framed my jaw, pulling me in for a kiss that was all tongue and teeth and heat.

"Slow down," I told him, panting into his mouth. "We have all night."

He shook his head, refusing to listen. He was trembling, every muscle in his legs rigid, hips rolling up into me with urgency.

"You are so beautiful, I do not think I can—" But he never finished the thought, because suddenly he was saying something in a foreign language, a rush of syllables I couldn't parse, and all the while his hands dug into my hips, holding me how he wanted, chasing the sensation to its inevitable conclusion.

My climax hit me and my body locked up around him, inner muscles pulsing, and I came so hard, so fast, that I forgot my own name for a brief, brilliant second.

He followed half a beat later, hips bucking wildly, head thrown back, the cords in his neck standing out as he spilled into me. The sight of it, the pure abandon on his face, made my body clamp down again, a second orgasm rolling through just before I collapsed on his chest, both of us gasping, clutching at each other like castaways.

For a few seconds, there was nothing but our ragged breathing and the rapid thrum of his heart against my cheek.

But I soon discovered he wasn't done with me. Not even close. He grabbed me by the hair and pulled my mouth to his, kissing me deeply. I could taste myself on his tongue. He held me there, arms locked around my back, refusing to let go.

He rolled us with brute strength, switching our positions. Suddenly, I was on my back, pinned to the mattress, and he loomed over me, his body a furnace, his gaze still dark with need. Clearly, Andreas was already plotting the next move, the next game, and wanted to savor every second.

And a loud knock on the suite door ruined it.

I stiffened, blinking up at him, unsure if I'd imagined it, but then it came again. Insistent, louder.

Andreas's hands were still all over me. He didn't stop, just nuzzled my neck and started kissing me again, his mouth moving over my jaw, my ear, my shoulder. I could already feel him growing hard again against my thigh.

Elio's voice, unmistakably aggrieved, called out, "Mr. Kristiansen. You are five minutes late for the next match!"

A shocked laugh tumbled out of me. I covered my mouth with one hand, trying to push him off with the other. But Andreas lifted his head and smiled, a wicked flash of teeth, and tugged my hands away. He kissed me again, this time gentler, almost sweet.

Turning my head to the side, I whisper-shouted, "You have another match!?" Part outrage, part pure disbelief.

He sighed, then yelled in the direction of the door, "Elio, I will be there in fifteen minutes."

Elio's voice returned, muffled but dramatic. "That will only leave you ten minutes for the match!"

"Then I'll be there in twenty minutes," Andreas shot back, not missing a beat.

"Andreas!" I scolded.

"Shh. Do not worry, my love." Andreas gazed down at me, eyes sparkling, his rapidly recovering erection nudging against my entrance as he said, "For this guy, I only need five minutes."

Then he pushed inside me, filling me, his eyes glazing over just before he bent to my ear to whisper, "But for you, I think maybe a lifetime is not nearly enough."

Scan me to receive new book updates and news from Penny!

Scan me if you'd like a signed copy of this or any Penny Reid book!

OTHER BOOKS BY PENNY REID

<u>Knitting in the City Series</u>

(Interconnected Standalones, Adult Contemporary Romantic Comedy)

<u>Neanderthal Seeks Human: A Smart Romance (#1)</u>

<u>Neanderthal Marries Human: A Smarter Romance (#1.5)</u>

<u>Friends without Benefits: An Unrequited Romance (#2)</u>

<u>Love Hacked: A Reluctant Romance (#3)</u>

<u>Beauty and the Mustache: A Philosophical Romance (#4)</u>

<u>Ninja at First Sight (#4.75)</u>

<u>Happily Ever Ninja: A Married Romance (#5)</u>

<u>Dating-ish: A Humanoid Romance (#6)</u>

<u>Marriage of Inconvenience: (#7)</u>

<u>Neanderthal Seeks Extra Yarns (#8)</u>

<u>Knitting in the City Coloring Book (#9)</u>

<u>Winston Brothers Series</u>

(Interconnected Standalones, Adult Contemporary Romantic Comedy, spinoff of Beauty and the Mustache)

<u>Beauty and the Mustache (#0.5)</u>

<u>Truth or Beard (#1)</u>

<u>Grin and Beard It (#2)</u>

<u>Beard Science (#3)</u>

<u>Beard in Mind (#4)</u>

<u>Beard In Hiding (#4.5)</u>

<u>Dr. Strange Beard (#5)</u>

<u>Beard with Me (#6)</u>

<u>Beard Necessities (#7)</u>

<u>Winston Brothers Paper Doll Book (#8)</u>

<u>Hypothesis Series</u>

(New Adult Romantic Comedy Trilogies)

Elements of Chemistry

ATTRACTION (#1)

HEAT (#2)

CAPTURE (#3)

Laws of Physics

MOTION (#4)

SPACE (#5)

TIME (#6)

Fundamentals of Biology

INHERITANCE (#7)

REPRODUCTION (#8)

EVOLUTION (#9)

Irish Players (Rugby) Series – by L.H. Cosway and Penny Reid

(Interconnected Standalones, Adult Contemporary Sports Romance)

The Hooker and the Hermit (#1)

The Pixie and the Player (#2)

The Cad and the Co-ed (#3)

The Varlet and the Voyeur (#4)

Dear Professor Series

(New Adult Romantic Comedy)

Kissing Tolstoy (#1)

Kissing Galileo (#2)

Ideal Man Series

(Interconnected Standalones, Adult Contemporary Romance Series of Jane Austen Reimaginings)

Pride and Dad Jokes (#1, TBD)

Man Buns and Sensibility (#2, TBD)

Sense and Manscaping (#3, TBD)

Persuasion and Man Hands (#4, TBD)

Mantuary Abbey (#5, TBD)

Mancave Park (#6, TBD)

Emmanuel (#7, TBD)

Handcrafted Mysteries Series

(A Romantic Cozy Mystery Series, spinoff of *The Winston Brothers Series*)

Engagement and Espionage (#1)

Marriage and Murder (#2)

Home and Heist (TBD)

Baby and Ballistics (TBD)

Pie Crimes and Misdemeanors (TBD)

Good Folks Series

(Interconnected Standalones, Adult Contemporary Romantic Comedy, spinoff of *The Winston Brothers Series*)

Totally Folked (#1)

Folk Around and Find Out (#2)

All Folked Up (#3)

Three Kings Series

(Interconnected Standalones, Holiday-themed Adult Contemporary Romantic Comedies)

Homecoming King (#1)

Drama King (#2)

Prom King (#3)

Standalones

Ten Trends to Seduce Your Best Friend

Bananapants